"A masterpiece of high fanta[...]
Tolkien, Jordan, and Haydon[...]
pelling story of a land in cris[...]
Using wry humor and breakt[...]
fortlessly moves her complex, well-drawn characters through ever-escalating crises to an explosive (in every sense of the word) and deeply satisfying conclusion. I hope Resnick returns to Sileria again soon!"   —Mary Jo Putney,
        New York Times bestselling author of *The Bartered Bride*

Praise for *The Destroyer Goddess: Part Two* of *In Fire Forged*
"Strong storytelling and a sense of mythic overtones lend depth to a well-developed tale of personal courage and high adventure!"   —*Library Journal*

"Breathtaking scope and complexity. 4½ Stars."
                                            —*Romantic Times*

"The tale will certainly keep its series audience industriously turning pages and make them hope Resnick has more in store for them."   —*Booklist*

Praise for *The White Dragon: Part One* of *In Fire Forged*
"The long wait was well worth it. *The White Dragon: In Fire Forged, Part One* is a thrilling, brutal, take-no-prisoners tale of undeniable power. Fans of *In Legend Born* will be delighted to return to the fierce beauty of Sileria, its unique mythos and its complex, multifaceted people. A well-thought out, carefully crafted and thoroughly enjoyable read."
                                            —Elizabeth Haydon

"A suspenseful mix of vague prophecies, startling revelations, constantly shifting loyalties, and the occasional divine intervention, this stunning novel tantalizes right up to the last cliffhanger page."   —*Publishers Weekly* (starred review)

"Vivid descriptions, three-dimensional characters, and a story filled with echoes of a distant past make this a stand-out addition to a fantasy series that belongs in most libraries. Highly recommended."
—*Library Journal*

"Atmospheric world building, dry humor, and appealing characters make *The White Dragon* an epic fantasy not to be missed. New readers should check out the earlier book in the series, *In Legend Born*, for backstory, but this novel stands on its own as an enthralling fantasy adventure."
—*Romantic Times*

"Resnick has complete control of her craft. Not a word is wasted . . . The characters are complicated and real. There are plenty of twists and surprises, and the pace quickens as you go."
—*Cincinnati Enquirer*

THE

Destroyer
GODDESS

Books by Laura Resnick

In Legend Born

The White Dragon: In Fire Forged, Part One

The Destroyer Goddess: In Fire Forged, Part Two

available from Tor Books

THE
Destroyer
GODDESS

In Fire Forged, PART TWO

LAURA RESNICK

TOR®
fantasy

A TOM DOHERTY ASSOCIATES BOOK
NEW YORK

This is a work of fiction. All the characters and events portrayed in this book are fictitious or are used fictitiously.

THE DESTROYER GODDESS: IN FIRE FORGED, PART TWO

Copyright © 2003 by Laura Resnick

All rights reserved, including the right to reproduce this book, or portions thereof, in any form.

Edited by James Frenkel
Map by Ellisa Mitchell

A Tor Book
Published by Tom Doherty Associates, LLC
175 Fifth Avenue
New York, NY 10010

www.tor.com

Tor® is a registered trademark of Tom Doherty Associates, LLC.

ISBN 0-765-34796-2
EAN 978-0765-34796-1
Library of Congress Catalog Card Number: 2003054337

First edition: December 2003
First mass market edition: September 2004

Printed in the United States of America

0 9 8 7 6 5 4 3 2 1

VALDANIA
NORTH
KINTISH
KINGDOMS
Palace of Heaven
Shaljir
Cavasar
Zilar
Illan
Lake Kandahar
Belitar
Elelar's Estate
Zilar River
Emeldar
Mt Dalishar
Gamalan
Alizar
Mount Darshon
Britar
Adalian
N
Liron
SILERIA

Interregnum

DAR, THE DESTROYER GODDESS, CHOSE SILERIA
AS HER HOME . . . AND NO ONE LOVES DESTRUC-
TION THE WAY A SILERIAN DOES.
— Ambassador Kaynall, former
Imperial Advisor in Sileria

THE LAST OF the Valdani warships left Sileria
and set sail for the mainland, ending centuries of foreign rule
as Emperor Jarell's forces withdrew from the mountainous island nation which dominated the Middle Sea, once named
Sirkara—heart of the world—by an ancient people whose forgotten empire had been the first of many to rise in glory and
descend in flames.

The last of the Valdani ships left Sileria . . . but not the last
of the Valdani. During two hundred years of occupation, generations of Valdani had been born in Sileria, and this was the
only home they knew. Although some fled to the imperial city
of Valda or sought refuge somewhere in her sprawling empire,
many others remained, unwilling to abandon the land of their
birth. But after two centuries of harsh Valdani rule, many Silerians were eager to murder any Valdan who didn't leave the
newly freed nation which Josarian the Firebringer had died to
liberate from the heavy yoke of Valdani rule.

The last of the Valdani ships left Sileria . . . and finally
abandoned Silerians to their own private bloodfeuds, to enmity nurtured for centuries, to enduring hatred so fierce that
no outsider could truly understand it.

The Firebringer's loyalists declared war on the Honored
Society which had betrayed him. The waterlords and assassins

of the Society promised destruction to any Silerian who was not loyal to them, and they vowed to kill every last Guardian of the Otherworld. The *shallaheen,* Sileria's mountain peasants, chose one side or the other, then ferociously attacked anyone who chose differently. The *toreni,* Sileria's aristocrats, sought feverishly to protect their wealth in a land disintegrating into rampant chaos. The lowlanders and the city-dwellers were swept into the fiery whirlwind engulfing everyone in the country, while the sea-born folk tried to remain aloof from the quarrels of the landfolk. The *zanareen,* that religious sect of Dar-loving madmen, mourned the death of the Firebringer and wailed dark warnings about the suffering Dar would now inflict on Sileria for having murdered Her chosen one.

And as Sileria spiraled into the inferno of civil war, Dar demanded Her due. She Called people from all over the nation to come and worship Her, praise Her, comfort Her, and offer Her their lives. They came from the thirst-maddened cities, the war-torn mountains, the withered fields of the lowlands, and the villages devastated by earthquakes. They came to dwell upon Mount Darshon, the snow-capped volcanic mountain wherein the destroyer goddess dwelled. They came to die in explosive showers of burning rock, or to melt in the rivers of lava which streamed down the tormented slopes of the mountain. Vents opened in Darshon's ravaged skin to smother them with poisonous fumes, avalanches buried them alive, and the volcano threatened to consume them all in a massive eruption.

And still they came, drawn there by a summons they could not resist.

Strange colored clouds and dancing lights surrounded the summit of Darshon, visible from vantage points throughout much of Sileria. Meanwhile, in the night sky over Mount Dalishar, where perpetual fires burned without fuel in the sacred caves, pilgrims continued to see the now-famous visions there which warned of—or promised?—an imminent arrival.

No one could say what the visions meant, nor could anyone

bring solace to a nation so thirsty that it daily spilled and drank its own blood.

A child of fire, a child of water, a child of sorrow . . .

Sleeping in a mountain Sanctuary of the Sisterhood, where she awaited her fate, Mirabar the Guardian awoke with a pounding heart. Gasping for air, she sat up and pressed a hand to her sweat-dampened brow.

Fire and water, water and fire . . .

She heard the silent voice of the Beckoner, the mysterious Otherworldly being who brought her visions to her. He'd made her a prophetess and valued advisor to the Firebringer. Now she was a hunted enemy of the Honored Society.

Welcome him . . .

"Am I doing the right thing?" Mirabar asked aloud.

There was no answer.

"I failed Josarian," she said, her voice breaking, "and he's dead. Will I fail the new ruler I've foreseen in my visions? The Yahrdan? How can I protect him?"

Welcome him. . . . Welcome your fate.

39

ELELAR REALIZED WHAT Tansen had done
as soon as she saw the blood-soaked cloth wrapped around his
left hand. She had seen his protective affection for Zarien, the
sea-born orphan who traveled with him; so it didn't take a
shallah to guess that he'd recently cut his palm with a knife, in
a ritual typical of Sileria's mountain peasants, to make the
boy his bloodson.

"Are you sure that was wise?" she asked Tansen as soon as
they were alone together in Santorell Palace. They were in the
same room, in fact, where she had watched in horror as Searlon the assassin murdered Commander Cyrill to help Elelar
convince Advisor Kaynall that he must publicly announce that
the Valdani were surrendering Sileria to native rule.

"You're supposed to congratulate me," Tansen replied. "Becoming a father is—"

"Zarien is not like other boys. Surely you see that."

"Dying and being given new life by a goddess has a ten-
dency to set someone apart," he agreed dryly. "However,
since I saw my bloodbrother through a similar fate, who better than me—"

"This could be a very good thing for you," Elelar interrupted. "I see that. I understand that."

"Then why do you look like I've taken a fever instead of a
son?"

"Because men never think these things through practically."

"Don't start," he warned her.

"He was sea-bound for the first fourteen years of his life," she persisted. "How well do you really know him? How well could you *possibly*—"

"Much better," he pointed out, "than many people know each other before they get married." He lifted one brow but didn't bother to cite an obvious example. He didn't need to.

She sighed, recalling Tansen's insistence that she locate her husband. "I've had news from my estate. Ronall has been there recently."

"Is he still there?"

"No, he left again. Almost immediately. With no explanation about where he was going. And," she added with irritation, "he took my favorite horse with him again." She paused, then said in puzzlement, "He also brought my widowed cousin there for safety. Only . . ."

"Only?"

"I do not, as far as I know, *have* a widowed cousin."

"Perhaps she was widowed quite recently?"

"How would Ronall, of all people, know about it before I do?"

"Maybe he was visiting her and—"

"He wouldn't be welcome among any of my relations. *I* haven't been welcome among most of them ever since I married him."

Tansen shrugged off her family problems and said, "So you're no closer to locating him than you were before?"

"No. But I've been . . ." She couldn't help grimacing before she continued, "Talking about him here in Shaljir. In public. Saying . . . nice things about my . . . heroic husband." It made her want to kick someone.

As if sensing this, he edged away from her. "Good."

She turned to another topic. "We've received bad news."

"What?"

"Baran is siding with Kiloran."

His expression became focused and very serious as the

discussion turned to the Honored Society. "How do you know?"

"We've learned that they had a truce meeting."

"Ah. I knew there'd been one, but I didn't know if Baran attended."

"He did. And he and Kiloran made their peace there. Temporarily, of course."

"Of course."

"In front of quite a few witnesses from the Society, Baran agreed to oppose you and to help Kiloran bring the city of Shaljir under the Society's influence—by using the Idalar River, obviously." The river was the capital city's primary source of water, and Baran had spent recent years challenging Kiloran's sorcery for control of it.

Tansen's jaw worked for a moment as he considered the threat of those two powerful waterlords, usually at odds with each other, now unified to fight him. "Damn. That's discouraging." After a heavy pause, he added, "Still, maybe Mirabar can bring Baran around. He might still be—"

"Mirabar should stay away from him." When he looked sharply at her, she explained, "Before they parted, Baran and Kiloran divided up their tasks. Kiloran is coming after you . . . and Baran will take charge of killing Mirabar." A moment later she said to his retreating back, "Where are you going?"

"Home."

"What?" He had no home.

"I'm leaving Shaljir," he said, opening the door and pausing briefly. "I told Mirabar to do whatever she had to do to get Baran on our side. If she doesn't know about this truce meeting, she'll walk right into whatever trap he sets for her, especially if he baits it with promises of cooperation. I've got to stop her."

"Tan—" She closed her mouth. He was already gone.

A moment later, she heard him shouting for Zarien as he ascended the steps to gather his few belongings and set off for the mountains again.

* * *

NAJDAN LEFT MIRABAR in Sister Velikar's Sanctuary, where she would await Baran's return from Josarian's native village of Emeldar. Najdan had things to attend to while the *sirana* and his mistress, Haydar, were temporarily safe in the little Sanctuary on Mount Dalishar's slopes. Besides, he had no desire to be anywhere nearby while Haydar explained certain things about marriage and men to Mirabar. Many subjects were best left strictly between women, and that was one of them.

Just when Najdan believed the world could get no stranger or more bewildering—it did.

Mirabar, the most famous Guardian in all of Sileria, was going to marry Baran, a waterlord who was second only to Kiloran in power—and in the fear he had inspired for years. Perhaps Najdan, the Society assassin who now served Mirabar, shouldn't be shocked by the idea; but he was.

When Mirabar broke the news to him, he forbade her to marry Baran, or even speak to that demented sorcerer again. Had Mirabar lost all her wits? Did she really intend to accompany Baran to the moldy ruins of Belitar, where he could murder her at his leisure, in the comfort and privacy of his own home? When had any Guardian ever been able to trust a waterlord? And even if Mirabar *could* trust one, did she really want one as notoriously crazy as *Baran* for her husband? Najdan did not want to see so worthy a young woman bound to so repellent a man.

"Even if he *doesn't* kill you in some devious scheme or sudden fit of madness," Najdan had added furiously, "he's too old for you!" Though Mirabar didn't know her exact age, she was certainly no more than twenty, whereas Baran must be close to forty by now.

There was a lot of shouting, since Mirabar was being completely unreasonable. Haydar had ventured into the Sanctuary and tried to make them both calm down, and Najdan yelled at his warmhearted mistress for the first time in years. Seeing her stricken expression brought him to his senses, and that was when Mirabar also calmed down enough to explain herself.

And so it unfolded.

A child of water. A child of fire.

Things Najdan didn't understand and would really rather not think about too much. Baran's words to the *sirana* echoed the promises in Mirabar's visions; so now she was convinced the waterlord would somehow help her fulfill the prophecies of the Beckoner.

She was very confused, though. Well, that was understandable. Conversation with Baran would confuse *anyone*. Mirabar didn't know if she would be the mother of the new Yahrdan, but she seemed to think not. Somehow, though, the child she would bear would be integral to Sileria's future, and there were things at Belitar, Baran's home, which she must learn and understand.

If that was the way it had to be . . . Well, Najdan supposed he had already done stranger things in his life such as betraying his former master, Kiloran, to protect and serve a Guardian.

Baran had offered a home to Najdan and his woman at Belitar, too. Although the idea initially revolted Najdan, Haydar slowly made him see that if Mirabar was indeed going to marry Baran—and she was, Najdan had eventually agreed upon that point after being confronted with the will of Dar and the Beckoner in this matter—then the assassin must join her at Belitar or abandon her altogether. And no one, Haydar reminded him, should be abandoned alone with Baran.

Besides, Haydar was extremely tired of living in Sanctuary and of sleeping without Najdan at her side. They could be together at Belitar. And as long as Baran didn't kill them all, Haydar added, where would Najdan's women be safer from Kiloran, in all of Sileria, than in Baran's lair?

As long as Baran doesn't kill us all.

Yes, that could be the flaw in Haydar's plan—it relied on Baran being honorable enough *and* sane enough to keep his word and not harm any of them.

It had taken time, but Najdan had eventually agreed to Baran's plans, though not without some bargaining. The *sirana* was a great prize as a wife, and so Najdan deemed a high bride-price was required—particularly since Baran was a man of great means. After some thought, Mirabar herself had set the price: Baran must cure the poisoned water of Emeldar, so Josarian's people could one day go home to the village from which they had reluctantly set out to fight the greatest empire in the world and free Sileria. As the man responsible for her, in the absence of male relatives, Najdan presented this demand to Baran as the cost of winning the *sirana*.

According to Kiloran, Baran had originally come from a merchant family. Najdan believed it now, because the haggling over the bride-price had been energetic and skilled, and Baran had clearly enjoyed it. Until, that was, he suddenly seemed to grow tired. Then he agreed to Najdan's demands without further protest, and stayed behind in Sanctuary with Sister Velikar while the rest of them ascended to the sacred caves to observe the phenomenon everyone was talking about in these parts: the visions which sometimes appeared high over Dalishar, often accompanied by the promise, "He is coming."

Najdan had seen it before and had no interest in enduring that bloodcurdling Otherworldly experience again, but Velikar had insisted he leave, anyhow. She and Baran had private business of their own, she said, though she wouldn't reveal what business a Sister could possibly have with a waterlord.

There were huge numbers of pilgrims regularly crowding the camp at Dalishar these days. Even more were on the roads and rocky paths heading east, to distant Mount Darshon. The visions of glowing eyes or of a powerful fist in the night sky at Dalishar, the strange dances of colored smoke and flashing lights at the snow-capped summit of

Mount Darshon, the wild-eyed worshippers from all over Sileria streaming towards Dar's home in answer to some
strange summons from the volcano goddess . . . And
Mirabar, a Guardian of the Otherworld, preparing to share
the marriage knife with Baran.

Najdan supposed it was just as well that no one had ever
told him what his future held; he wouldn't have believed
them, anyhow.

Now he, after too long an absence, was returning home to
the miserable little village where he had been born. His
mother and his two sisters, both married, were still here—if
they were alive—and he had neglected them. He had ensured their safety and comfort throughout his years as an assassin, but he had not seen them or communicated with them
since betraying Kiloran. That change of allegiance was not
something he particularly looked forward to announcing to
these women whom he scarcely even knew anymore, and his
most urgent duties had kept him away from here recently,
anyhow.

He didn't think Kiloran would punish his betrayal by murdering his female relations, which would be a thoroughly dishonorable act; but he needed to make sure—and also to bring
them whatever money he could, as he had done for years. So
now that there was time for this task, before he accompanied
Mirabar and her new husband to Belitar, he came home again,
to the hungry and desperate place which had once given him,
in place of food, the passionate ambition to make something
of his life so that he would never be hungry again.

He no longer wore the clothes of an assassin, and he kept
his *shir* hidden inside one of his dusty boots. As Kiloran's enemy, rather than his servant, Najdan could no longer afford to
draw attention to himself with the red-and-black colors he had
worn for twenty years, or by openly displaying the beautifully
crafted water-born dagger he would never relinquish or surrender. So he looked like just another sojourner when he entered the village, just another tired and hungry traveler on a

hot Silerian day. Hardly anyone paid him any attention as he made his way to his mother's simple stone house.

The tattered *jashar* still hung in the doorway, blowing in the slight breeze. Its knotted, woven strands proclaimed his family's lineage and history, humble, even by the standards of *shallaheen*. He was the only man who had ever brought honor to the family, as well as food and security; the only man to make a name for himself, to improve his position, to gain even a little minor fame through his deeds.

Consequently, his mother and sisters thought he had hung the moons. Their fawning could be a little tiresome, but he looked forward to it today. After all, every man of worth enjoyed his share of it now and then.

He pushed aside the *jashar* and called out to his mother as he entered the low-ceilinged dwelling. She rose to her feet when she saw him. He was pleased to see her looking well— better than he expected, actually, considering the privations of the rebellion, the civil war, and the dry season.

He grinned at the shocked expression on his mother's wrinkled face. "Did you think I was dead?"

He glanced at the other woman in the room—his youngest sister, Neysar—and saw her swallow as she rose slowly to her feet, staring at him. Her wide-eyed gaze narrowed a moment later and she said, "We only hoped that you were."

He frowned. The instincts of a lifetime in the Society had him moving away from the door even before the attack came, even before his sister said, "And now you will be."

Someone *had* noticed him enter the village, he now realized, dodging the thrust of a *shir* from an assassin flying through the door of his mother's little home. Men too shrewd to show themselves, too experienced to let themselves be seen.

The second attacker came through the door as Najdan pulled his *shir* from his boot and started swinging his *yahr* in a circle over his head.

Clumsy, he noted absently. They should have killed him before he even knew they existed. They should never have given him a chance to fight back. Searlon would have advised an ambush, would have told them he couldn't be taken as easily as most men; but, no, these two were young and wanted to prove their honor, wanted to defeat him in combat rather than through stealth.

One dropped to the ground and went for his legs, a surprise ploy that worked against many opponents. Najdan broke his nose with the *yahr,* then trapped the *shir*-wielding hand beneath his boot heel. He came down hard on the assassin's spine with a knee and heard it snap. The screams told him his opponent wasn't dead, but Najdan knew he was no longer a threat, so he ignored him and went after the other one.

This one was impatient; Najdan saw it and guessed that he had been waiting for him to show up in this dull little village for quite some time. Najdan baited him, letting his impatience turn to recklessness. When the attacker overcommitted on a thrust, Najdan stunned him with the *yahr,* then drove the wavy-edged blade of the *shir* up under his ribs and into his heart.

The body dropped to the ground, the thud barely audible above the screams of the assassin with the broken back. Najdan walked through his victim's blood and tracked it across his mother's rush-covered floor, then slit the throat of the screaming man.

Only then did he look at the womenfolk who had betrayed him.

His mother was weeping, pleading for him to tell her it wasn't true, none of it was true, it was all a mistake. His sister was ordering her to be quiet, not even to speak to this filthy *sriliah.*

Najdan looked at his mother, at the woman who had loved and tended him until the day he left home to make his first kill and gain Kiloran's esteem, and he said something he didn't think he had ever said to anyone before: "Let me explain."

"No!" his sister shouted. "You betrayed Kiloran! You have betrayed us all!"

"There was a reason," he said calmly, already knowing it would do no good.

He knew these people. He knew their absolute loyalty to traditional ways, their overwhelming terror of the Society. Their awe of Kiloran. He knew, because he had been one of them.

"You are dead to us!" his sister hissed. "Dead! I have no brother!"

"Mirabar—"

"Has her own people! As you had yours!"

He heard someone approaching the door and he prepared for more combat. Then he saw his eldest sister and lowered his guard. "Nulimar . . ."

Her eyes were cool, where Neysar's were hot. She had always been the more intelligent one. "You made your choice, Najdan." She looked at the corpses polluting her mother's house. "And you will live with it for a while longer, I see."

"The world has changed," he began.

"Not that much," Nulimar said. "Not here. Some things are still unforgivable. Some things still make a man dead to his family, though he walks and talks even after they've finished mourning him."

"Kiloran takes care of us now," Neysar told him. "He mourns you, too, for he loved you like a son."

"And you betrayed him," Nulimar said.

Najdan said, "I did what I thought was right."

His mother wailed, and Neysar screeched, "You thought betraying your master was right? You thought humiliating us before the entire village—the entire clan—was right?"

"The Firebringer—"

"Is dead!" Neysar shrieked. "Now who is master of Sileria? Now who deserves all our loyalty and love?"

He said, "Kiloran will never deserve to—"

"*Get out!*" Neysar screamed. "Get out of this house! You are dead to us! Don't ever come back!"

Najdan looked at his mother, who was weeping uncontrollably in his sister's arms. He could think of nothing to say besides, "I've brought you some money t—"

"Don't bother," Neysar snapped. "Kiloran ensures that we have all we need."

He took the small purse he had brought and put it on the rickety wooden table. "I want you to have this, even so."

"We'll just put it on the funeral pyre along with the corpses you've given us today."

"That's your choice," he said quietly.

"Get out," Neysar repeated. She indicated their mother. "Can't you see how you're hurting her?"

He nodded. "I'll go." He took one last look at his mother. "Goodbye." He wasn't even sure she could hear him above the noise of her own sobs.

He walked past Nulimar, who followed him outside. Most of the village was gathered there now. Their expressions ranged from blank to openly hostile.

"You knew how it would be," Nulimar said quietly. "Surely you knew." When he didn't reply, she added, "Or did you even think about us at all?"

He had, but too late, much too late. Kiloran had thought of them first. And so Kiloran had won. They were his now.

TANSEN HAD TOLD Mirabar to go to Sister Velikar's Sanctuary to await news from Baran, so that seemed the best place to start looking for her. He had journeyed most of the way from Shaljir on horseback, despite Zarien's discomfort and occasional accidents, then simply abandoned their mounts when the way became too narrow, steep, and rocky for riding to be practical.

Now, as he approached Sanctuary, half-dragging the exhausted sea-born boy with him, he prayed silently to Dar to protect Mirabar, who had served Her so bravely and faithfully.

A sentry saw him, and before the *shallah* could even greet him, Tansen shouted, "Do you know where Mirabar is?"

"At Velikar's!" was the reply.

Relief flooded his heart.

"Gods be praised," Zarien murmured breathlessly, yanking his wrist out of Tansen's grip. The boy sank to the ground and urged him, between panting breaths, "Go. Leave me . . . here. I'll . . . catch up . . . later."

Mount Dalishar was safe enough, Tansen supposed—much of it well guarded ever since the ambush he had survived. "Don't be long."

Zarien fell back gratefully on the rocky soil, closed his eyes, and waved him away.

It didn't take Tansen long to reach the simple stone Sanctuary, especially now that he wasn't hauling an ever-growing and tender-footed boy behind him. He saw a number of people he knew gathered there, and he easily recognized Lann—by his size and his beard—from a distance.

Tansen ignored all greetings as he approached and demanded of Lann, "Where's Mirabar?"

"Around there." Lann gestured to the back of the building. "Tansen, there's something you should—"

"Later."

"Uh, Tan?" Yorin said, his one remaining eye blinking rather a lot. "Maybe you should—"

"Tansen!" Lann tried again.

Behind him, he vaguely heard Pyron saying to them, "Let it go."

"But—"

"You don't really want to be the one he hears it from, do you?"

Tansen ignored them all in pursuit of his woman. He found her standing in Velikar's garden, talking with Najdan. Her fiery hair was dressed with flowers today, a feminine whim he'd never seen her indulge before, and she wore unusually fine clothes—a simple confection of undyed wild gossamer. Her back was to him as she faced Najdan. Tansen stopped abruptly, willing the pounding of his heart to ease and let him behave rationally now that he knew she was safe.

"You're sure your family was well?" she asked the assassin probingly.

"Yes." Najdan's answer was quiet and without expression.

"Because you don't seem quite your—"

"They're well," was the terse reply. Najdan suddenly saw Tansen. "Uh . . ."

"Maybe you should bring them to Dalishar," Mira persisted.

"I already told you: Not with us, and not to Dalishar," Najdan replied, staring uncertainly at Tansen. "They're safe where they are."

"Then why are you . . ." Realizing he saw someone behind her, Mirabar looked over her shoulder. When her gaze met Tansen's, she gasped and flinched.

"I'm glad to see you, too," he said dryly.

"Tansen." Her intense tone surprised him.

It finally dawned on him that her unaccustomed finery must be for a special occasion. He frowned. "It's not a festival day, is it?"

The Guardian and the assassin just stared at him.

"Well?" he prodded.

Najdan and Mirabar exchanged a glance. Then they looked at him again.

"What?" Tansen asked.

Najdan suddenly moved. Mirabar put a hand on his arm. Her gaze, when the assassin looked down at her, was almost pleading.

Najdan said, in the sternest tone Tansen had ever heard him use with Mirabar, "I'm not staying for this. This is between the two of you."

Mira let out her breath in a puff of exasperation and released him. Her fire-bright eyes glowed almost yellow as she watched Najdan walk away. When she and Tansen were alone, she folded her hands and, after a long pause, asked, "What are you doing here?"

"What's going on?" he demanded.

"Aren't you supposed to be in Shaljir?"

"Mirabar."

"What happened at sea?"

"Oh, that. It's a long story, but nothing happened."

"So you're . . ." She looked a little upset. "You're not the one whom Zarien was sent ashore to find and bring back to Sharifar as her consort?"

"I don't know," he admitted, thinking of the price the sea goddess had demanded of Zarien in exchange for his life after a dragonfish killed him. Tansen had intended to go to sea with Zarien, who was convinced that Tansen must be the sea king he sought, but . . . "We had an unexpected change of plans."

"What happened?" Mirabar demanded.

"First, tell me what's—"

"Tansen!"

He made a vague gesture. Her eyes followed the movement—then widened. She came closer and took his left hand between both of hers. Her touch set his heart to pounding again.

"You've sworn another bloodvow," she observed.

"Oh. Yes . . ."

She looked so beautiful. As beautiful as the mountains of Sileria. How had he ever, even at first, failed to see her beauty? He couldn't even remember what idiocy had prompted him to flinch in superstitious fear the first time he had ever looked into those passionate flame-gold eyes.

She was a *shallah* and immediately understood the significance of the deep, slowly healing cut on his palm. "A blood-pact relation," she murmured.

"I've become a father," he told her.

She didn't have to ask whom he had taken for a son. "But doesn't he already have a fath—"

"When we got to Shaljir, we found out they were dead. His whole family and most of his clan."

"Dead?" Her face clouded with sorrow for Zarien.

"They died . . . well, not long after he did. Only no goddess brought them back to life."

"What happened?"

"They were killed at sea, when an earthquake on land swelled the waves and flung their boat against the rocks." He told her everything else that he knew about it. Except Zarien's secret, of course, which it was not his right to share without permission . . .

"My real father wasn't sea-bound. Not even sea-born. My father was a drylander." Zarien's words were choppy and harsh.

"Who was he?" Tansen asked.

"I don't know."

"I see. And your mother?"

Zarien shook his head. "I don't know."

"So Zarien threw Sharifar's gift to him, that oar—what did he call it, a *stahra*—into the sea?" Mirabar said, looking a little shocked. "To break the bargain she made with him the night she gave him back his life?"

The *stahra*—a traditional weapon of the sea-born folk—did indeed look like an oar. Tansen said, "He's very angry at her for letting his family die." Adopted in infancy, Zarien had believed they were his real family until the night, deep beneath the sea's surface, when Sharifar restored his life and told him the truth. And now the boy grieved for them as his real family. "He has turned his back on the sea."

Mirabar said with concern, "I understand. But even so . . . What if he changes his mind later? The *stahra*—"

"—was meant to lead him to me. It's not needed anymore."

"We don't know that," Mirabar objected. "Not really. Sharifar's will can be interpreted in a number of—"

"Well, it's gone, either way," Tansen said, "and there's nothing we can do about it now."

"A quarrel with a goddess is dangerous," Mirabar said pensively.

"I know."

Her gaze flashed up to his. "Yes. Of course."

Unable to resist, he reached up to touch one of the brilliant yellow flowers decorating her lush hair. "Now tell me: What's going on here?"

"Um . . ." She licked her lips. "Well, you're going to find this very strange. I didn't expect you back so soon. I hadn't yet really considered how I would tell you—"

"Tell me what?"

From behind him, a gruff female voice said, "Aren't you ready yet? Baran's getting bored."

Tansen whirled to face Sister Velikar.

"Oh. You're back. Hello," Velikar said, with about as much warmth as she ever showed.

"Where is Baran?" he demanded.

Velikar jerked her chin. "Inside."

"He's *here?*" His swords were in his hands before he realized he had unsheathed them. Halfway across the garden, he felt Mirabar's arms around him, her weight dragging against him to slow him down.

"Stop! No!" she cried.

"He's come to kill you!" Tansen said.

To his astonishment, Velikar laughed.

He stopped and glared at the Sister. "Sanctuary. I know. But whatever that madman is planning, Mirabar won't be safe the moment she leaves—"

"You haven't told him?" Velikar said to Mira.

"He just got here," Mirabar replied.

Still ready for combat, he snapped, "Told me what?"

Mirabar cleared her throat. "We're getting married."

"Who?"

"Me and Baran."

He was sure the sky tilted. "You're what?"

"Getting married. That's what I've agreed to, to convince him to side with—"

"You're *WHAT?*" he shouted.

Velikar said, "I'll leave you two alone."

He ignored the retreating old woman as he said to Mira, "What in the Fires are you talking about?"

"Baran set a price for his help," she said. "I've met it."

He stared at her in speechless confusion.

She continued, "There were things he said—"

"It's a trap," Tansen insisted. "He's promised Kiloran—"

"To kill me. I know."

"You *know?*"

"He's told me everything."

Tansen shook his head. "He's shrewd. He knew we'd eventually find out about the truce meeting, so he told you himself. To disarm you. To make you believe he was lying to Kiloran."

"I don't think he was lying to Kiloran."

"What do you—"

"Not at the time. I think he changed his mind afterwards."

"Then how do you know he's not going to change his mind about whatever he's promised *you?*" He was shouting again. He didn't care.

"Because this is our destiny. His and mine."

"Your destiny? To marry a waterlord? To trust that madman?"

Another voice came from behind him. "You say that like it's a bad thing."

"*Baran.*" Tansen turned his back on Mirabar and, swords poised for attack, faced the waterlord.

Baran frowned at Mirabar. "Did we invite him?"

"Go away," Mirabar said to her intended.

"You hot-headed *shallaheen,*" Baran said disapprovingly to Tansen. "Always drawing your weapons on Sanctuary grounds."

Through clenched teeth, Mirabar repeated, "Go away."

Baran smiled at Tansen. A tall, big-boned man with unruly hair and famously wild eyes, Baran looked surprisingly older and thinner than when they had last met, but still formidable. Tansen retrained himself from glancing at the well in the center of the garden, knowing full well how easily Baran could simply wrap its waters around his neck and strangle him.

"My condolences," Baran said to him, "on the death of your brother."

"Don't even speak of Josarian to me," Tansen growled. "You don't deserve to."

"On the contrary," Baran said, impervious to insult. "I know what it is to lose someone to Kiloran."

"And I'm not going to find out what it is to lose someone to *you*," Tansen vowed. He ignored the stifled sound Mirabar made and kept his eyes on Baran.

Baran's gaze sharpened with amused interest. What he said next, though, surprised Tan as much as the gentle tone in which he said it. "I swear I won't ever hurt her." He shrugged and added more prosaically, "Well, no more than men and women usually hurt each other."

"You're lying," Tansen said, wondering what would happen to him if he did violate Sanctuary and kill Baran right here and now.

"No," Baran said with quiet certainty. "If I'm lying, may my power forever desert me, and may I burn like the Fires for all eternity."

"I won't let her do this," Tansen warned him.

"How do you intend to stop her?" Baran asked curiously. "She's the most powerful sorceress in Sileria and, last I heard, you were still just a man."

Tansen drew in a sharp breath. "So *that's* why you want her." Maybe Baran really didn't intend murder, after all. Still, there was no way Tansen was letting this marriage take place.

"She knows why I want her," Baran replied. "I'll let her explain it to you."

"Thank you." Mirabar sounded exasperated.

As he turned to go, Baran added, "Try not to take too long. I'm getting bored."

Almost shaking with helpless anger, Tansen absently sheathed his swords and asked Mirabar, "So, why does he want to marry you?"

"Could your tone possibly be any less flattering?"

"*I* wanted to marry you," he snapped, "so I'm in no mood—"

"You?" She stared sadly at him. "You . . ." She made a helpless gesture. "You never said . . ."

"I didn't—I was going off to . . ."

"To Shaljir."

"To battle," he said defensively. "And then to—"

"To Shaljir. To her."

"No," he insisted. "To sea."

"Elelar's still alive, isn't she?" Mirabar asked wearily.

"And she's going to stay that way," he informed her. A moment later he wanted to bite his tongue until it bled. He did not want to talk about Elelar right now, and he certainly didn't want to get stuck in the mire of defending her to Mirabar. He said with strained emphasis, "I was going off to sea to meet Zarien's sea goddess, and I knew—"

She sighed. "Even if I had known . . ." Tears filled her eyes and she shook her head. "I don't know. I think . . . I think it really has to be this way, Tansen."

"No, it doesn't," he argued fiercely, feeling her slipping away from him.

The fire-fringed gold of her eyes revealed all the strength of her fervent belief in Dar, in destiny, in her decision. "This is what I must do."

"*No.*"

He seized her shoulders and drew her to him, desperate, scared, angry, bitterly jealous. Her lips were soft and warm. She was startled at first, and she struggled. But he wouldn't let go. Couldn't.

"No," he repeated against her mouth, willing her to understand him, accept him. To want what he wanted. To give him what he tried to give her, to take from him as he took from her when he kissed her again.

For a moment her body answered him, her will succumbed to his. For a moment, she was all living flame in his arms, all warm breath and soft skin and soul-deep longing. For a moment, they kissed as they were meant to, as they had always been meant to, and the wasted time and lost nights didn't matter anymore.

He felt heat, fire, the rich stream of lava-soaked desire which flowed between a man and a woman and made them forget everything but each other. He drowned in the hunger which led to delight, and the delight which led to more hunger. The craving which was pleasurable, the pleasure which hurt like pain. This was what only they could give each other, this and so much more. All the things he needed from her, all the things he longed to lay at her feet, welled up in him as his arms tightened around her and sought to keep her from another man.

For a moment, everything he wanted for them, together, seemed real, within reach. The fire and the warmth mingled in his blood, in his heart, in the breath they shared, in the frantic embrace they inflicted upon each other, in the hot union of their mouths . . . But only for a moment.

She was strong for her size, and so he stumbled when she pushed him away and staggered backwards. Driven by furious needs, he reached for her—but froze when he saw her scarred palm warding him off, begging him to stay away from her.

Blue-flecked flames danced across her skin for a moment, a glorious display he'd never seen on her flesh before. He smelled something burning and looked down. He absently patted the smoking sleeve of his tunic, vaguely noticing that it was singed now.

The hazards of making love to a Guardian, he supposed blankly. Or at least to an inexperienced one.

"Mira . . . Don't do it." He heard the pleading in his voice and didn't care.

Tears trickled down her face. Darfire, it hurt to see her cry. It hurt even more to be the one causing it. "I have to." Her voice was brokenhearted.

"Why?" He couldn't understand. "What in all the world could Baran—"

"A child of water. A child of fire."

He stared at her, stunned beyond words.

A child of water, a child of fire, a child of sorrow . . .

She saw by his expression that he remembered what she had told him about the Beckoner. "I don't know exactly what the Beckoner wants, but I've had more visions since the last time I saw you. I know that I have to go to Belitar. And that I have to bear Baran's child there."

"And this child," he said slowly, sure he was about to be sick, "is this the one . . ."

"I don't know," she admitted, increasingly distressed. "I don't know! I don't think so, but—"

He pounced, "Unless you're *sure,* why—"

"Because this child has to be born, whether or not it's the one I've been looking for. This is the child the gods want me to have, Dar wants me to have. A child born of fire and water, of a Guardian and a waterlord, of—"

"Of the woman I love and some insane murderer who—"

"Please," she begged, crying harder now. "Please don't make this even harder. Fires of Dar, do you think I *want* to marry him?"

He hated Dar. By all the gods above and below, he hated Her. She had let the Valdani slaughter his family, let Kiloran kill Josarian, let the sea make a shunned orphan of Zarien, and now She was doing this to Mirabar. As he watched Mira weep, Tansen felt as if all his blood was draining out of him.

Now he remembered what else she had told him. "A child of sorrow," he muttered. That much would be true.

"We need Baran." Mirabar started wiping tears away. "Sileria needs him. If he won't help us . . ."

He looked for some place to sit down, suddenly bereft of all strength. He damned himself for having urged Mirabar to do whatever she had to. He should have known that Baran, of all people, would demand what they had never foreseen.

"We'll find another way," he told her, already hearing how weak and hollow the promise sounded.

"We don't have time. And even if we did . . ."

"You and your visions," he said bitterly, unable to stop himself from lashing out at her.

She didn't fight back, which made him feel even worse.

After a long silence, during which Mirabar tried to compose herself, Tansen finally said, "You're really going to do this, aren't you?"

"Yes."

It felt like being stabbed, but only after already having received a mortal wound. The pain was almost a relief from the earlier pain. The loss of hope somehow eased his urgent desperation, the agonizing need to find a solution, to change her mind, to stop her.

He remained silent, all out of ideas, all out of things to say. After what seemed like a long time, she finally said, "They're waiting for me."

He nodded, but didn't move otherwise.

"Are you . . . coming?"

"I can't." He shook his head. "I can't watch this."

"I wish . . ." She didn't say any more.

He listened to her footsteps as she left the garden.

After a while, it occurred to him that he didn't want to see anyone, least of all the bride and groom, so he should probably leave before the ceremony was over and people started rambling around the Sanctuary's grounds.

Moving slowly, his mind blank while his heart bled, he set his foot on the path leading back the way he had come. So full of hope then, so empty of it now. So full of worry then . . . and, no, not free of it now.

If she's wrong, if I'm wrong . . . If Baran hurts her . . . If he kills her . . .

He tried to stop thinking, since it was futile right now. This wound wouldn't kill him, but precious few had ever hurt so much, and he couldn't think while this pain raged hot and fresh inside of him. Couldn't even consider the hundred other urgent things which would demand his attention the moment he reached the camp at the sacred caves of Dalishar.

"Tansen!"

He looked up, surprised to see Zarien approaching him. He'd been so absorbed in his sorrow he hadn't even heard the boy's boots grinding into the rocky soil just ahead of him.

Zarien said, "You didn't need to come look for me. I—"

"We're leaving," Tansen said.

"Already?"

"Yes."

Zarien frowned, studying him. His eyes widened slowly. "Is she dead?"

"No."

"Then what's wrong?" Zarien asked, falling into step beside him.

At least he had a son now. At least there was that.

"Tansen?" Zarien prodded, concerned, watching him closely.

Tansen stopped, looked at him, and said, "You know, you could . . ."

"What?"

"You could call me father." Tansen shrugged and added as casually as possible, "If you wanted to."

Zarien's frown cleared. He nodded. "Or . . . Papa?" He almost laughed, then shook his head. "Um, no. Father is probably better."

Tansen slapped him on the back and said, "Come on." He continued making his way along the path.

"Wait! Tan— Father." Zarien put a hand on his arm. "What's wrong? What did she say to you?"

"I'll explain as we walk." He would also omit all but the essential facts of the matter.

"What happened to your sleeve?" Zarien touched the singed spot. "Did you get too close to a fire?"

"Yes," he admitted on a sigh. "We should probably get up to the caves . . ."

Zarien groaned and looked up the steep, merciless slopes of Mount Dalishar. "I just knew you were going to say that."

40

NEITHER LOVE NOR MADNESS KNOWS A CURE.
                              —Silerian Proverb

THE FRESH CUT on Baran's right palm stung fiercely. He suspected that Mirabar had cut particularly deep on purpose with the marriage knife. Had he known how vindictive his bride could be, he wouldn't have agreed to marry her in *shallah* tradition.

Now, as they faced each other, alone in Sister Velikar's Sanctuary, Mirabar stared warily at him with those glowing eyes. Looking at her, he could almost believe some of the superstitions about her fire-colored kind . . .

He wondered if immolation in the marriage bed was grounds for divorce. Silerians were so strict about marriage that it actually might not be. He smiled, enjoying his thoughts as he shrugged out of his tunic—now grown loose on him—and tossed it aside.

The only place Baran and Mirabar could be safe from the Society, which he would completely alienate with this marriage, was Sanctuary or Belitar. Belitar was days away, and even the nearest Sanctuary was almost a full day's journey from here. So he and Mirabar had agreed to spend their wedding night here, in Sister Velikar's humble stone dwelling. Tomorrow they would commence the long journey to Baran's home.

Although he looked forward to returning home, Baran dreaded the trip, knowing how it would tax his diminishing strength. Making the journey to Emeldar and curing the water there had been too much for him. He had remained five days in Josarian's abandoned village, which was how long Mirabar and Najdan deemed their witnesses—Lann and Yorin—needed in order to be sure the slow poison which Josarian had ordered put in the water, during the early days of the rebellion, was now genuinely expelled from it. When the goats drinking the water were still hale and hearty five days after Baran cleansed it, the two men were satisfied and returned to Dalishar with him.

He had not enjoyed their company.

What a dull and ignorant lot the *shallaheen* were. How incurious about the world, how smug about the narrow boundaries of their own culture.

Baran sighed and looked again at his *shallah* wife. Oh, well. At least she wasn't as dreary as other *shallaheen*—or other Guardians. Her feral childhood had expanded the wisdom of her heart well beyond that of most other Silerians. Her extraordinary powers had made her intimate with things beyond the imagination of even most worldly and educated people. And her prophetic visions had forged in her a strength and determination that few people alive could match.

Now, as they shared a wary silence, Baran glanced at the simple bed where Velikar had recently spread fresh, sun-dried bedclothes for them, and thought more practically about his new wife. A virtuous young *shallah* woman, a sorceress gifted with enough power to scare away any man less brave than that poor sod Tansen, an endangered Guardian protected day and night by an assassin as strict and old-fashioned as Najdan . . .

"Do you know what's supposed to happen now?" Baran asked Mirabar abruptly, suddenly wondering if tonight would be even more awkward than he anticipated.

She blinked. "In general."

He lifted one brow. "*How* general?"

"Well, I, uh . . ." She licked her lips. "I understand the main, um, requirements." She folded her hands. Being a *shallah,* she didn't even seem to notice the cut he had made on the left one today. "No one who has lived long in the closeness of a Guardian camp could be unaware of . . . of . . ." She unfolded her hands. "And Haydar explained a few things to me." She nodded. "Things which were more specific than I had previously . . ." She met his gaze. "Some of them seemed reasonable."

Now he was amused. "And others?"

"Others . . . Well, I'm not sure I believe her. And even if I did . . ."

"Yes?"

"I don't think I *ever* want to know you that well, Baran," she admitted frankly.

"Ah. Well." He grinned. "Then I count on you to tell me when our acquaintance is crossing the boundaries of what you deem acceptable."

"Don't worry. I will." Her gaze dropped to his thin torso. "Have you been ill?" She caught herself a moment later. "I'm sorry. Perhaps that was rude."

"According to rumor, I've *always* been unwell." He tapped his forehead, distracting her from the subject of his physical health.

Her eyes narrowed, and she reminded him of a cat. "Are you as crazy as they say? Or saner than you want people to know?"

"It varies," he admitted.

He took a step towards her and, seeing her nearly jump out of her skin, decided that tonight might be a good time to work at ordinary sanity, if only for a few hours. He wanted this woman to ensure his immortality with a child, one strong enough to stand against Kiloran if need be; and that couldn't happen if she was too wary of him to let him touch her.

"I won't hurt you," he promised.

"You're damned right you won't," she growled.

He smiled, appreciating her spirit. He supposed that kind of fire and fury had kept her alive after her mother abandoned her as a small child and before the Guardians found her and raised her.

"I know it'll seem strange," he said, nodding towards the bed, "but shall we try acting like husband and wife for a little while?"

"It's what I agreed to," she said. But she didn't come closer.

Baran had once known love—passionate, hungry, joyful, uninhibited love. And, since those days, he had occasionally known the confident attentions of experienced women. But he had never before found himself in precisely this situation, and he was at something of a loss.

Mirabar evidently recognized this. Wearing an expression of such determination that he briefly wondered if she meant to attack him, she started undressing, her gaze fixed burningly on his.

"Ordinary people do this every day," she said. "So you and I should certainly be able to."

She dropped wild-gossamer garments at her feet until she was naked, and then she came closer, until the heat of her skin warmed his. She was young, smooth, lithe, softly curved, sun-kissed golden and lava-red. Warm and small and more womanly than he would have ever guessed before now.

"*Sirana,*" he said softly, lowering his face to hers, "we may even find it easy, after all."

"Perhaps you should just use my name," she murmured against his mouth.

"You wouldn't find it disrespectful?" he whispered teasingly.

She gave a faint gasp of surprise. "Considering where your hands are right now . . . no."

* * *

TRYING TO KEEP Tansen's mind off the *sirana*'s wedding night, now in progress further down the slopes of Dalishar, Zarien had asked his bloodfather to start teaching him to fight. It seemed a sensible precaution, if he was to live among the bloodthirsty landfolk with Tansen from now on. Besides, Tansen wasn't the only one trying to stay too busy for the intrusion of unhappy thoughts and futile memories.

By night, Zarien had bad dreams about his family's death, about Sharifar's betrayal, and about the vengeance she and Dar might take on him for refusing to bring Tansen to sea. By day, he grieved for the Lascari and nurtured a bitter hatred for the gods.

And now, by day and night, here upon the high peak of Mount Dalishar, Zarien could see the distant summit of Mount Darshon, and its colorful, violent tumult chilled him with awe and foreboding. What did Dar want? What was She planning? Even the Guardians didn't seem certain, though they babbled a lot of vague portents that sounded only slightly less bizarre than what the *zanareen* were saying. Did the unprecedented events at Darshon have anything to do with the sea king whom Zarien refused to bring to Sharifar now?

If so . . . Zarien was afraid, but his fear didn't diminish his anger. He would endure whatever he must, but he would never give in. Never. However, since Sharifar had not taken his life when he'd turned his back on her, he must now make a life for himself on the dryland; at least until *someone* took it.

Fortunately, the life he had found on land was not without value. Indeed, it was more extraordinary than any destiny he had ever imagined when he was sea-bound and never thought he would set foot on land even once in his life.

To have become the son of Tansen, the greatest warrior in Sileria . . . Zarien had trouble believing it, even now, when Tansen introduced him in this capacity to everyone they encountered at Dalishar. He would always mourn the loss of his sea-bound family, and he would always wonder what secret they had kept about his birth all these years. But if he had to start a new life, then he had found the only one worth having.

Tansen's son.

How many young men in Sileria might give up twenty years of their lives for such an honor? If his sea-bound parents, Sorin and Palomar, knew his fate, as they sailed in the seas of eternity, he hoped they were proud—knew they must be. Even they, usually dismissive of landfolk, had spoken Tansen's name with respect and admiration.

"Ow!" Zarien jumped as a wooden stick hit him.

"When you daydream," Tansen explained, "that's what happens."

They were each holding a single long stick; Zarien's first lesson in sword fighting. Once Zarien had learned the first eight basic attacks and blocks, they started practicing them back and forth with each other.

Zarien nodded in response to Tansen's comment and made himself concentrate. The stick lesson was easier than the *yahr* lesson they'd had earlier this evening. The *yahr,* after all, was a *shallah* weapon; so, of course, there was no way to learn it without lots and lots of pain. *Shallaheen.*

"Now," Tansen instructed, "come forward while you attack." He grinned when Zarien stumbled and clarified, "One step at a time, son."

Zarien tried it again. It wasn't much fun, this fighting business, and he didn't feel he had a knack for it. However, it kept him busy and . . . Well, Tansen was obviously pleased he had asked and seemed to enjoy teaching him.

He stumbled again, tried to right himself, lost track of where he was in his striking pattern, and stopped, confused.

"That's fine," Tansen said. "Don't go too fast. Take your time."

He tried again, moving forward slowly. "How long did you do this to become so good?"

"Five years."

"Five years?" He'd rather quit now and just hope no land-folk ever felt compelled to attack him.

"Well, not just this. I trained for armed and unarmed combat. Single sword, then double swords—"

"That must have taken a long— Argh!"

Tansen helped him off the ground. "That's all right. It happens. Don't let it bother you."

"Maybe I just shouldn't talk."

"No, it's often good to talk while you train. It's as if it frees your body to learn without the interference of your thoughts."

"My body is asking for something to eat."

"What a surprise," Tansen said dryly. To Zarien's relief, he set the sticks aside and declared the training over for the evening.

Now that they weren't occupied, Zarien again became aware of the Guardians chanting. Lots of people were chanting, in fact—Sisters, *shallaheen,* and those mad religious fanatics, the *zanareen.* There were even some city-dwellers who had come all the way from the southern coastal city of Adalian, having heard about the visions at Dalishar. The camp was very crowded compared to Zarien's previous visit here—before the events at Zilar, and before Shaljir.

It seems so long ago now.

"They're not going to do that all night, are they?" Zarien asked Tansen, indicating the chanting.

"Dar, I hope not," Tansen muttered.

Lann, who heard this exchange as he approached them, grinned, his teeth white against his black beard. "Don't worry. They usually stop when they get sleepy enough." The deep cut he had acquired while sleeping through an earthquake was now healing into a scar that started above one eyebrow and disappeared into his thick hair.

"Good."

Lann said loudly to Tansen, "I want to talk to you. I don't want to stay here. I should be fighting, not—"

"I know," Tansen said.

"I'm only waiting for you to put someone else in charge here," Lann continued.

"I've spoken to Yorin," Tansen said. "He'll do it. I want you to replace Emelen, who's in Zilar—"

"Still holding off the Society's attempt to regain the Shaljir River, at last report."

"—and tell him to meet me in Adalian. He'll be closer there to Jalilar, who's in Sanctuary."

"Josarian's sister?" Zarien asked.

"Yes. She's Emelen's wife."

"Adalian is in chaos," Lann said.

"We need to make sure it doesn't go the way of Cavasar and declare loyalty to Kiloran," Tansen said. "If we can keep Adalian, Shaljir, and Liron out of the Society's hands . . ."

"Then Cavasar will be the only major city loyal to them." After a moment, Lann said, "What about the mines of Alizar?"

Zarien knew that Kiloran had flooded the mines during the rebellion to help Josarian take them from the Valdani. The story of that battle was famous. Now Kiloran's watery power kept Josarian's loyalists from accessing Alizar's wealth.

A strange expression crossed Tansen's face. For a moment, Zarien wondered if he was going to throw up. Then he said, "We'll have to get Mirabar to ask . . . her husband about that. If anyone should know how to free the mines from Kiloran's sorcery, it's Baran."

"That's a good . . ."

The big man's voice trailed off as the chanting throng suddenly became frantic with excitement. He, Tansen, and Zarien all turned to look at them . . . and then looked up at the night sky, where everyone else's attention was focused.

Zarien heard praying, but didn't immediately realize it was his own voice. "May the winds carry me, may the waters be calm, may my sails remain strong and the skies clear above my head . . ."

By all the gods of wind and sea, even hearing about the visions had not prepared him for this. He wasn't sure if he was excited or afraid; if he wanted to see more or just go hide in one of the caves until this strange visitation was over.

He is coming!

Zarien jumped as the voice echoed inside his head.

Glowing eyes, so similar to Mirabar's, pierced his soul as they gazed down at him from the night sky. Until now, he had believed that the landfolk were being fanciful or were exaggerating when they spoke about this, but now he saw how true it all was. Those were *eyes*. This was real. No one who saw it could doubt it.

Zarien was shaking, overwhelmed by this strange presence, this intrusive power. If this was even a little bit like what Mirabar experienced in her visions, then he knew he ought to treat her with a great deal more respect. He couldn't imagine regularly facing this sort of thing alone.

It faded slowly, the eyes gradually dissolving in the sky, the echoing voice subtly dimming in his head, the unbearable, hot tension in the air finally dissipating.

Tansen continued staring at the sky, his breath coming fast and shallow. Zarien found a rock and sat down very suddenly. Lann folded his arms and said, "Now do you see why I want to leave?"

"Yes," Tansen said, his voice a little thin. "I just don't understand why Yorin's willing to stay."

"He closes his eye," Lann explained.

"I'm not hungry anymore," Zarien said.

Tansen let out his breath in a rush. "You wonder how Mira stands it . . ." He shook his head, staring off into the distant darkness.

"You wonder why everyone comes rushing up here to see it," Zarien added.

"So they'll know," Tansen said. "So they can be sure that the risk is worth the terrible price they'll pay."

"For what?"

"For defying the Society."

Lann nodded. "Every . . ." He stopped and looked around as a distant rumbling began.

Tansen's pensive mood turned to sharp alertness as the rumbling turned to a roar. "That's—"

Zarien felt shaking and realized it wasn't him this time.

"Earthquake!" Lann shouted, joining similar shouts amidst the now-deafening roar.

Zarien leaped up, then fell to his knees as the ground heaved beneath his feet. Tansen staggered over to him, pushed him facedown on the ground, then flopped down on top of him, shouting, "Stay down!"

Zarien squeezed his eyes shut and lay there, unable to breathe due to his bloodfather's weight on top of him. Lay there terrified as the land shook and groaned, screamed and undulated. He heard falling rocks, shouts of terror, a fierce crack as rockface split, the clattering of weapons and shattering of crockery . . .

Zarien screamed through clenched teeth, too scared to stay silent. Tansen didn't react, probably didn't even notice.

And then it stopped. Probably before Zarien actually realized it, because the pounding of his own heart was deafening once there was nothing to interfere with its thunder.

The whole camp waited in tense silence for a few moments. Finally, just when Zarien thought he would pass out, Tansen rolled off him and let him breathe again.

Tansen sat up. After another moment, he asked Zarien, "Are you all right?"

"No. Yes. I don't know. Yes."

Tansen actually snorted. "As long as that's clear."

Zarien smiled ruefully as he sat up. "I'm a little, um . . ."

"Me, too." Tansen looked at the big *shallah*. "Lann?"

"I don't like earthquakes," Lann said, sounding bad-tempered.

"I'll inform Dar," Tansen replied dryly.

"Why does She keep doing it?" Lann asked plaintively.

Tansen rose to his feet and dusted himself off. "Why do women do anything?" was his sour reply.

Zarien, so far from the sea he couldn't possibly smell it, wondered what tonight's earthquake had wrought for the sea-born folk.

"THE GROUND DOESN'T move for everyone on their wedding night," Baran said to Mirabar as morning brought heat and light to Sileria. "We should be honored."

"I could do with less honor and more peace."

She was tired. Their rest had been interrupted by the earthquake. After running outside to relative safety, they had waited until dawn, enduring several aftershocks, before coming back inside. Since then, they'd been putting Sister Velikar's Sanctuary back into some semblance of order.

Mirabar cast a critical eye on her husband. The wealthy life of a waterlord had evidently made him soft. A little honest work—cleaning up the mess left by the earthquake—had clearly exhausted him. Mirabar vowed silently that being a wealthy waterlord's wife would never make her that lazy.

"Are we still leaving today?" she wondered aloud. He didn't look like he could endure the journey.

"Yes." Meeting her doubtful gaze, he added, "I want to go home." He smiled beguilingly. "I want to bring *you* home."

She shrugged. "As you wish."

Their first night as man and wife had brought a few surprises, from the embarrassing to the unexpectedly pleasant. Baran himself was perhaps the greatest surprise of all. Mirabar had not told anyone, since everyone was already so uncomfortable with her marriage, but she had been genuinely afraid. What would a ruthless and half-mad waterlord do to her in the privacy of his bed? No matter whom she married, Mirabar would have been as nervous as any *shallah* bride on her wedding night, she supposed; but the peculiar nature of her groom had made it hard for her not to run screaming into the darkness to get away from him.

Until she realized that, contrary to her expectations, he

was nervous, too. Until she discovered that, despite everything she had ever seen or heard of Baran, he could be reasonable, courteous—even kind.

Yes, he had been kind. And mostly gentle—gentle until those strange, hot, dark moments between a man and a woman when gentleness became an obstacle to what they both blindly sought.

Now, knowing things about him she had never foreseen in her wildest imaginings, she wondered about her husband. Women gossiped enough for Mirabar to be aware, by now, that not all men knew how to please a woman. But Baran knew, and he used the knowledge well. It made Mirabar wonder: Who had taught him? Why did he care enough to learn? Had he, of all people, once loved?

Even now, with a frail rapport developing between them, she knew she couldn't ask him. Baran had claimed intimacies with her body which she could still feel lingering in her flesh, and he would do so again; they both wanted a child together. But their verbal relationship stopped well short of what they did together as man and woman, and her fear of him by day hadn't particularly decreased despite her acceptance of him by night.

So Mirabar wondered about him, yes; but she found it genuinely hard to believe that Baran—who had slaughtered hundreds in vengeance and greed, who hadn't bestowed a truly tender look upon her even in their most intimate moments, who seemed sardonic even in his sleep—had ever *loved*. Because love, Mirabar knew now, was the part of you that surrendered against your will, the part of your heart that bled willingly, the part of your nature that gave just for the sake of giving. And nothing about Baran suggested he was capable of love.

Mirabar thought of Tansen, up at the Dalishar caves right now, and wished things could have been different.

Love was the hunger that ate you alive a little every day.

"Damn it," Baran said restlessly, "where is Velikar? She said she'd be back in the morning."

Love was the fire even a Guardian couldn't control, and which even her tears couldn't extinguish.

"You're determined to bring Velikar to Belitar with us?" Mirabar asked, loathing the idea. "What about Sister Rahilar? She's up at the caves, and I like her. Well," she added more honestly, "I don't *dis*like her. I could ask—"

"Now, now, there's no reason for you to feel threatened by Velikar," Baran chided. "I swore vows of fidelity yesterday, and I will keep them, regardless of the temptation she presents."

Mirabar rolled her eyes. "I'd rather send for Sister Basimar."

"Who's that?"

"She was a personal friend of Josarian's. I've known her since . . ."

Baran's gaze wandered idly around the room, and Mirabar sighed and gave up, realizing she was wasting her breath. Baran was determined to bring Velikar with them, but he would enjoy teasing Mirabar with the futile hope of leaving the nasty old woman behind.

Baran took her arm as she turned away, and began, "Are y—"

He stopped when she gasped in pain as his fingers pressed against the cut made by the assassin she had killed during the nighttime battle on Mount Niran.

"Excuse me," he said, watching as she rolled up her sleeve to examine the cut. "I noticed that last night, but I forgot. It looks fresh."

"No," she said. "It's from a *shir*."

"You were attacked?" After she nodded, he said, "I can heal that for you."

She shook her head.

He seemed amused. "You don't trust me?"

"I can wait for it to heal."

"That takes a long time."

"I know." She rolled down her sleeve and said, "And until it stops hurting, it will remind me that I killed him."

He smiled. "You're more vicious than I guessed."

Mirabar didn't remember the incident with satisfaction. She wanted to remember the cost to herself of taking a life.

Baran persisted, "If you change your mind . . ."

"I don't want to talk about it." She poured them both some water to drink. "I'm hungry, aren't you?"

"No."

"You should eat." Darfire, she already sounded like a wife. "It'll be a long journey, and it was a busy night."

He snorted with amusement and cast her an impertinent look.

She ignored this and continued, "You don't want to eat now. You barely even nibbled at the wedding feast." She shook her head. "No wonder you've become so thin."

"This from the woman who loves Tansen, who's always been a bit on the skinny side." He blinked innocently as she choked in surprise, spewed some water, and started coughing. "I'm sorry. Is it something I said?"

She stared at him in wary confusion, her heart pounding hard.

He grinned, enjoying her discomfort. "My dear, it was written all over your face when I saw you with him yesterday. All over his, too, actually—which, I confess, surprised me. Tansen usually seems to be the ideal upon which the blank-faced *shallah* stare was originally based."

She cleared her aching throat and just kept staring at him, totally unprepared for this.

"Why are you looking at me like that?" he protested. "Am I some possessive, bloodthirsty *shallah?* I should say not! I'm hardly going to start a bloodfeud with the Gamalani—er, even if they still existed—just because one of them is in love with my wife." He leaned closer and murmured, "Not even because she returns his feelings."

"Waterlords kill for much less," she said tersely. "*You've* killed for less."

"True, but never my allies." He frowned. "Oops! I'm lying.

I've killed them, too, haven't I?" He shrugged. "But only when I was feeling particularly irritable."

Her stomach hurt. "Tansen has never, um . . . I will never . . ."

"I know." He smiled charmingly. "I wouldn't have married you if I questioned your commitment to the vows you made while taking a knife to my flesh." He looked down at his palm, where the long cut was red and angry. "Need you have made it quite so deep?"

"No wonder you're eager for Velikar's return," she murmured, realizing that she had perhaps been a bit too enthusiastic about slicing open Baran's hand.

Baran leaned back again and silently called to the water she had poured for him. It danced out of its cup drop by drop, and swirled towards his mouth. He parted his lips, and the quivering drops came to rest on his tongue. Baran closed his mouth, held her wide-eyed gaze, and smiled. "After all these years, that's still fun. Tell me, *sirana,* is fire magic ever just fun to you, just sheer delight? Or is it always wrapped up in duty, destiny, Dar-worship, and other dreary things?"

"It's, uh . . ." She frowned, trying to remember. Had it ever been "fun," even once? She didn't think so.

Baran glanced at the cup, indicating what he had just done, and said, "That was the first thing I learned to do upon apprenticing to water magic. Not the first thing I was *supposed* to learn," he added cheerfully, "but I was whimsical and lacked focus."

"Whimsical? You surprise me," she said dryly.

"I was, I fear, quite a trial to my teacher. He . . ." Baran sighed as he considered his past. "Ah, yes, he was perhaps the most focused individual I have ever met. Well, until *I* learned to focus, that is."

He was baiting her, of course. She knew it, but she was nonetheless curious enough to ask, "Who was he?"

His eyes danced and he clearly delighted in the shock he was about to deliver. "Kiloran."

Her breath came out in a rush, and she sat down abruptly. "Of course!"

He looked interested. "Why do you say that?"

She nodded, thinking hard. "The old proverb is true, isn't it, Baran?"

"Most of them are true, but which one——"

"The more intimate the friendship, the deadlier the enemy," she quoted.

"Oooh! Very good." He grinned, evidently pleased.

"No wonder the two of you hate each other so much. Whatever happened between you, whatever you did to each other . . ." She nodded again. "No one hates a stranger or an acquaintance nearly as much as he hates someone who was once a friend." She arched her brows. "You *were* friends?"

He considered this. "I don't think Kiloran has friends. He was, shall we say . . . more like a rich uncle to me." Guessing her next question, he added, "No, we're not related. He took an interest in my talent and tried to guide me." He paused and added, "For a while, that is. Mostly, of course—as you already know—he has spent the past fifteen years trying to kill me."

"So what happened between the two of you?"

"Well, I don't want to alarm you . . ." he replied coyly.

"Baran," she said in exasperation.

"If I tell you this, it's because I want you to understand, before we leave Sanctuary, just how serious I am about protecting you."

"You mean, not killing me as soon as you can?"

He touched her cheek. "I think I proved last night how serious I also am about getting a child with you."

She wondered how he knew what she knew, why a waterlord had been the one to echo her visions: *A child of water. A child of fire.* But she didn't want to be distracted from what he meant to tell her now, so she simply said, "Then tell me: What happened between you and Kiloran?"

"Come now, *sirana*," he challenged, "surely you must have

guessed by now that only one thing could make two men hate each other as much as Kiloran and I do?"

She was puzzled. "No, I don't . . ."

Then it came to her. She shook her head, sure she must be wrong—but she already saw it in his face. It seemed extraordinary that the years-long battle of these two giants had all begun over . . . "A woman?" she asked.

Baran nodded and raised a hand to idly stroke the silver-and-jade necklace he always wore. His face was more serious than she had ever seen it when he replied, "He killed my wife."

41

SILENCE IS ALSO SPEECH.

—Silerian Proverb

TANSEN LET SISTER Velikar precede him— by quite some distance—on the path to her Sanctuary. Part of him wanted to race ahead and make sure Mirabar hadn't been harmed in the earthquake. Mostly, though, he dreaded the possibility of finding her in Baran's arms—Dar have mercy, it was obscene! So he hung back with Najdan, who seemed equally reluctant to venture into a potentially embarrassing situation. Pyron and the rest of Mirabar's escort were trailing behind them.

Zarien, quite sensibly, had stayed up at the caves this morning. Tansen was currently fighting an impulse to turn around and run back to join him there.

"I have spoken with Baran several times since he proposed marriage to the *sirana*," Najdan said suddenly, speaking for the first time all morning, as far as Tansen could recall. "I believe his intentions are . . . serious."

"So do I," Tansen replied. "I just don't believe they're what he *says* they are."

Najdan looked at him. "You really think he's going to kill her?"

Tansen sighed. "*She* certainly doesn't seem to think so."

"If he tries—"

"I know, I know, you'll die to protect her." Tansen shrugged. "That's less comforting than it used to be."

"She believes—"

"I know. She told me."

There seemed to be little else to say. They hadn't stopped her from marrying Baran, and they couldn't stop her from going to Belitar. All they could do was pray that her instincts were right. . . . But since neither of them was on speaking terms with Dar, they weren't even praying.

Walking more slowly than they had ever before walked in their lives, they eventually came upon Vinn, Baran's surprisingly even-tempered assassin, who had been the waterlord's sole companion for his journey here.

"The earthquake?" Tansen said.

"They're fine," Vinn said.

Tansen and Najdan kept walking.

"I don't like him," Najdan said.

"Of course not," Tansen said.

They approached a bend and, knowing that Velikar's Sanctuary would be visible beyond it, they slowed down even more.

"Congratulations on taking a son," Najdan said.

"Thank you," Tansen said.

"Too bad about his family."

"Yes."

"But even if they were alive, being sea-bound, they would have shunned him—for having been on land."

"Probably."

"It's good he has you now."

"We have each other."

"Yes."

They stopped. Looked at each other. Looked doubtfully ahead. Decided to go on.

The Sanctuary was a bit of a shambles in the wake of the earthquake, but still standing. After a moment, Mirabar pushed aside the *jashar* covering the door and stepped out alone into the sunlight. Tansen's heart started thudding hard.

She saw him and Najdan and immediately said, "I cannot abide that woman!"

"Is she—"

"I suggested Sister Rahilar! I suggested Sister Basimar! But no," she said. "No, *he* has to have Sister Velikar with him. Only that sour-tongued, bad-tempered, nasty old woman will do for my half-mad husband. And I—*I* am cursed to live in the moldy ruins of Belitar with an insane waterlord and a Sister with the manners of a wounded mountain cat!"

Najdan wisely held his silence.

Tansen foolishly ventured, "Are you all right?"

"No, I'm not all right!" she snapped. "I am going to be stuck with *those* two from now on!"

"I, um . . ." Tansen looked at Najdan.

Najdan looked down at his worn boots.

Mirabar looked at them both. "What?" she demanded. *"What?"*

"Nothing," Tansen said.

"Nothing," Najdan agreed.

She collected herself. "I'm sorry. I didn't mean to shout at you."

"Sirana," Najdan said, "shall I help them prepare for the journey?"

"No. They want to be alone." She shook her head. "I could almost swear Baran wasn't joking when he said she tempts him to be unfaithful to me."

Tansen choked. Najdan said, "Why do they want to be alone?"

Mirabar shrugged. "She's tending his hand. He doesn't want me to watch. Or something." She waved a hand vaguely in the air. "I don't know."

"Well," Najdan said judiciously, "you did cut him rather—"

"I know, I know," she replied impatiently.

Najdan told Tansen, "It bled quite a lot, even for a—"

"I *know,*" Mirabar repeated.

"I'm almost sorry I missed that," Tansen murmured.

Mirabar looked at him. Their gazes locked. Within moments, the air was thick with tension.

"Will you excuse us?" Tansen said to Najdan.

"I will wait at the edge of Sanctuary grounds with the others," Najdan agreed, turning away.

When they were alone, Mirabar said, in a very different tone of voice, "I'm fine."

"I, uh, I guess I can see that." He looked away and added, "I was worried."

"So was I, to be honest, but, um, there was no reason to be."

He couldn't think of anything in the world more awkward than talking with the woman he loved about her recent wedding night with another man. It actually made his chest hurt.

"So . . ." Tansen cleared his throat and tried to think of the vaguest possible way of asking what he wanted to know. "He didn't hurt you?"

"He didn't hurt me. And, well, we talked some more this morning, and I believe he's not *going* to hurt me." She waited for him to look at her, then said, "I really believe that, Tansen."

He nodded. He hated this, but he would accept her judgment. The pain in his chest wasn't going away. Now he asked something else which had been bothering him since yesterday. "How did he know? 'A child of fire, a child of water.' Where did he—"

"I don't know. He won't tell me. At least, not yet." She folded her hands. "There are things at Belitar which I think he means to share with me. My visions tell me that many answers are there."

"Belitar," he said without enthusiasm. You'd have to be as crazy as Baran to like that gloomy, damp place. Tansen's peasant blood assured him it was haunted, as legend said.

"I'll be safer there than . . ." Now her face clouded. "Than you will be."

"I'll be careful," he promised, feeling hollow as he looked at her. "I . . . Pyron told me about Tashinar. I'm so sorry." Mirabar's mentor had been captured and taken to Kiloran's underwater lair at Lake Kandahar.

Her face clouded with grief. "I make a fire every day to pray for her, pray that she's already dead, pray that Kiloran isn't . . . I pray that she's already dead."

"You can't tell?" he asked uncertainly.

She shook her head. "No. But that's not unusual."

"Oh."

She shrugged and added pensively, "It feels strange, when I look for her. Even when I went up to the sacred caves and sought her in the ancient fires there, while waiting for Baran to return from Emeldar. It's as if . . ." She shook her head. "As if she's not in either world. Not this one or the Other one, but not lost or gone, either. Almost as if she's . . . I don't know . . . hovering somewhere."

He had no idea what she was talking about, but he tried to be comforting. "I'm sure she's dead by now." He wasn't at all sure, but didn't know what else to say. "If I find out anything, I'll send word to Belitar."

She nodded. After a quiet moment, she changed the subject. "What will you do now?"

"I need to establish our influence across the central portion of the country, spreading through the mountains from Shaljir to Adalian."

"Separate Kiloran's foundation of power in the west from the Idalar River and the mines of Alizar?" she guessed.

"Yes. And separate the eastern and western waterlords from each other." He asked her to speak to Baran about the mines of Alizar, and also to find out whatever she could about the rest of the Society, particularly the individual weaknesses of the waterlords whom Baran knew.

"I will," she promised, "but I don't know how cooperative he'll be. All he cares about is destroying Kiloran. I don't think he cares who wins the war, or what happens to the Honored Society, the Guardians, or anyone else."

"Now that," Tansen said, "I believe." It was even comforting in a way. If Baran's priorities remained unchanged, and he saw Mirabar as essential in his fight against Kiloran, then he really would protect and care for her.

Still thinking, he flexed his hand, where the *shir* wound acquired in the ambush on Dalishar still troubled him from time to time.

Mirabar noticed. "Surely whatever force healed the wound in your side, which was much worse, should be able to heal that, too?"

Tansen shrugged. "It's getting better by itself."

"Maybe if you tried—"

"I don't remember how it happened the first time," he reminded her. He'd been unconscious in a cave, tended only by a frightened sea-born boy, when the deadly wound in his torso suddenly healed, leaving only a silvery scar.

"Maybe if Zarien tried," Mirabar suggested.

"I've been wondering . . ."

"What?"

"Do you think *he* might be the sea king?"

"I don't know." She frowned. "Why do you think so? Because of the way the wound healed?"

"It could be the answer, couldn't it?"

"I don't know," she repeated. "I don't know what the sea-born say about the sea king. Anyhow, if that wasn't it, then why—"

"Something the Olvar said when Zarien and I visited the Beyah-Olvari in the tunnels beneath Shaljir."

"This boy will be," the Olvar said to Tansen, *"more than you imagine. Perhaps more than you can accept."*

"He said . . ." Tansen stopped, remembering other things the wizened Olvar, the gentle leader of his ancient tribe of small blue-skinned beings living in great secrecy, had said.

"There are other Beyah-Olvari," he said slowly, crying with joy. *"Others like us. Alive. Somewhere in Sileria."*

Tansen almost told Mirabar this extraordinary news, but then he recalled the Olvar's prophecy which had made his blood run cold while he was in Shaljir.

"He told me," Elelar said, *"that Mirabar's going to kill me."*

Staring stupidly at Mirabar now, Tansen suddenly realized that she had married someone who could help her kill Elelar, or even do it for her. Easily and—knowing Baran—cheerfully.

He had no idea what to say to her about Elelar now. Besides, Mirabar was about to leave for Belitar. Tansen didn't know when he'd see her again—if they both even lived to meet again—and he didn't want his last memory of her to be soiled with yet another fight about the *torena.*

"Tansen?" Mirabar prodded.

"Huh? Sorry."

"What did the Olvar say?"

"Oh. It's not . . . It doesn't matter."

"Tansen." She sounded exasperated.

"You know how vague the Olvar is."

"Not from experience, no."

He smiled. "Well, you'd probably find him irritating."

"Speaking of irritating . . ." She sighed. "It's a long journey to the next Sanctuary. I suppose I should go convince . . . *them* that it's time to leave."

If they never met again, he wanted her to know. "I'll think of you often."

Her mouth trembled. "So will I."

"If you're ever afraid—if you ever feel he has lied to you, I want you to promise me you'll leave him." When she didn't reply, he urged, "Send for me. I'll come get you."

She looked uncomfortable. She compromised by saying, "If I think it's necessary, I will."

"And I, uh . . ."

She waited.

He said, "I'll miss you."

Her golden eyes glimmered with tears and she pressed her lips together. He filled his heart with the sight of her, then turned away, unwilling to stay and watch her leave with her husband.

IN THE GOLDEN glow of the setting sun, *Toren* Ronall crawled half-dead onto Sanctuary grounds and called for help. When no one came, he tried, with the last strength he had left, to think of the *shallah* word for "help."

He couldn't. Didn't even know if it was indeed different from the common Silerian word for it.

So he just kept rasping, "Help! Someone, help!"

Maybe the Sisters weren't coming because they just didn't hear him. His swollen tongue and aching throat, he now realized, barely produced any sound.

He lay facedown on the rocky soil. Something sharp poked him in the belly. His swollen face, his abused ribs, his back, his legs . . . everything hurt abominably. His left arm was broken. His bare feet were cut, bleeding, and desperately sore.

Oh, Three have mercy, just let me die. Let me die now.

He started retching again. Dry heaves. The pain had made him black out before. He hoped it would make him black out again, because enduring it was *awful*.

He was swimming darkly towards oblivion when he suddenly heard a woman's warm voice: "By all the Fires!"

He groaned when she touched him, her hands running over

him to check for injuries. His loud gasps of pain let her know every time she found another one.

"Can you stand up?" she asked at last.

"No," he insisted.

"I can't carry you," she advised him.

"Get help," he muttered, eyes still closed, head throbbing violently.

"There is no one here but me."

"Then leave . . . me here," he mumbled.

"I can't do that."

He gasped a moment later when her strong hands seized him by the shoulders and started trying to haul him upright.

"Ow! Ow! Ouch! Stop!"

"Then help me," she insisted.

He opened his eyes and squinted at her. His first comment was probably beside the point: "You're not a Sister."

"No," said the voluptuous *shallah* woman whose humble clothes didn't resemble the austere gown of a Sister. "The Sister who lives here abandoned me. She's gone east."

She spoke *shallah*, but clearly and slowly enough that he understood most of it.

"She's gone . . . to Darshon," he guessed hazily.

"Yes. Dar Called her."

He closed his eyes again and summoned what little will he possessed. "All right. I'll try to get up."

"I'll help." She slung his arm around her shoulders and, demonstrating more physical strength than he expected in a woman, hauled him to his bloody, aching feet.

He swayed dizzily. "Give me a moment."

"How did you make it here?"

Good question. "I don't really know. I just . . . kept moving." Even after being reduced to crawling, or just dragging himself along.

"Take a step," she instructed. "Lean on me."

The pain was nauseating, but he was too exhausted to protest, so he did what he could to assist her as she dragged him into the stone Sanctuary, bearing most of his weight herself. She was tall for a woman, particularly for a *shallah* woman.

Once they were inside, she hauled him over to a simple bed and helped him lie down upon it. He must have passed out after that, because when he opened his eyes again, he was mostly unclothed and she was dressing his now-clean, though still throbbing, feet.

She started speaking to him. When he didn't understand, she made an obvious effort to switch to common Silerian, though it was still liberally sprinkled with *shallah* words.

"A Sister could heal you more quickly, *toren,*" she explained, evidently having guessed his rank, "but I can't leave Sanctuary to find one for you elsewhere. Besides, you shouldn't be left alone. Don't worry, though. I have enough experience to help you. I'm just not . . ." She shrugged. "I don't know the arts of the Sisterhood. Just practical things."

He nodded his understanding.

"Your arm is broken, and your ribs are damaged—but not badly, I think."

"They feel bad," he said, his voice weak and cracked.

She shook her head. "No. It's nothing."

Shallaheen. Yes, he had no doubt that to *them* his injuries seemed like nothing. He, however, was trying hard not to cry like a baby in front of this woman.

Not that he had any tears to spare. "Water," he croaked, nearly maddened by now with thirst.

"Of course." She lifted his head and gave him a little at a time, showing more patience than he would have had in her position.

The water finally revived him enough to answer her questions about what had happened to him. "I was attacked last night," he said. "By bandits. While on my way here to seek shelter for the night." He sighed, drank a little more water, then continued, almost shuddering at the horrifying memories, "One pretended to be a pilgrim, and when I stopped to speak to him, two others jumped me. They were armed with *yahr* and Valdani swords."

He had never before been hit with a *yahr,* and he had never guessed how much it *hurt.* Darfire, it was painful!

"They took everything," he continued. "My money, my boots, the horse, my few possessions . . . Then they beat me unconscious."

"Why?" she wondered. "They had no need t—"

"Because I was rude."

"Rude?" she repeated.

"I said, er, vulgar things to them."

"That was . . . not wise, *toren.*"

"I was very drunk," he admitted. "As usual. And good judgment is always the first thing to desert me."

He had awoken at dawn—badly injured, terribly hungover, and already dying of thirst—and decided his only hope was to try to reach the Sanctuary he had been seeking. His pampered feet suffered terribly, and the merciless heat of the dry season came close to killing him.

"But you're safe now," she assured him. "You'll be well again in no time."

"I've never been well," he muttered.

"Toren?"

"Never mind."

He looked at her with clearer vision now. She was a lovely woman, in the harsh way of Sileria's mountain peasants. Earthy, strong, her modest clothing somehow emphasizing rather than concealing her sexuality. Her black hair gleamed cleanly, and she smelled . . . good. She looked about Ronall's age, but he knew that *shallaheen* often aged fast, so he figured she was probably a few years younger. And he, he knew, looked a little older than he was, thanks to years of self-indulgence.

"Thank you," he said. "I think you've saved my life."

She smiled. "I am glad I was here to help, *toren.*" She sighed. "It's the first time I've ever been glad I was here."

"You don't like it here?" he asked, watching the way the sunlight, shifting through the windows, played across her high cheekbones and dark skin.

"It's very dull here. And I'm not used to being alone like this. I miss my husband. I miss my friends and family. I miss . . ." She suddenly looked terribly sad. "I miss the way it used to be."

"How did it used to be?" he asked idly, hoping but doubting that her conversation could keep his mind off his throbbing feet, aching ribs, painful face, and agonizing arm.

She shook her head. "It can never be that way again, *toren,* so why dwell on it now? So many are dead. So much is lost."

"Is your husband dead then?"

"No," she said quietly. "Not yet." Something bitter passed across her expression. "But he is trying hard."

He wished the poor bastard luck. Dying just wasn't turning out to be as easy as Ronall had always assumed. "Don't you have any family you can go to?"

"I must stay in Sanctuary." She clearly wasn't pleased about it.

"Why?"

Instead of answering him, she gestured to his arm. "I must splint that."

Fear made his belly roil in protest. "Uh, I think I'd like something strong to drink before you do that."

"Oh. Yes. I'll get you something."

When he opened his eyes again, she was lifting his head to help him drink some . . . "Kintish fire brandy!" He choked and his eyes watered.

"Is it too strong?" she asked.

"Absolutely not," he said, afraid she'd take it away. "Give me some more. Lots more."

"As you wish, *toren.*"

"Bless you . . . Uh, what's your name?"

She hesitated briefly, then replied, "Jalilar."

"Jalilar," he murmured. "A lovely name."

42

BY THE TIME they reached Baran's home at
Lake Belitar, five days after their marriage, Mirabar knew that
something was wrong.

Although Baran had married her to get a child, he hadn't
touched her since their wedding night. Mirabar might be inexperienced, but she wasn't naive; men did not normally neglect
their new brides this way. Moreover, the journey back to Belitar clearly taxed Baran more than it should. He looked gray-
faced and exhausted. In addition, she knew by now that he
rarely ate—and then only nibbled disinterestedly at his food
when he did. Mirabar also realized a few days ago that Sister
Velikar was treating him for something. However bizarrely
fond of Velikar Baran might actually be, he hadn't brought her
along to keep him company or even to vex Mirabar; he needed
her to keep him functioning.

Mirabar didn't discuss this with Najdan or anyone else.
Whether she liked it or not, Baran was her husband, and she
must treat her marriage with respect. She would not gossip
about him with others. She would, however, immolate him in his
own bed if he didn't treat *her* with enough respect to tell her the
truth now that they had finally reached the safety of his home.

"Some say this place is haunted," Najdan told her, with a
failed attempt to sound casual, as the two of them now gazed
upon Baran's notorious abode.

Mirabar shivered, well able to believe that the many people

who had died violently here over the centuries still wandered Belitar, lost and helpless, unable to find their way to the Otherworld. Mist rose from the chilly, ensorcelled mountain lake, making this a damp place even in the dry season. Lush greenery thrived in the moist air, keeping the lake hidden and eerily remote. Now that she stood at the water's edge, Mirabar's vision was so obscured by the ever-shifting enchanted fog that it was easy, even by day, to imagine she saw fleeting shapes and shadows that were neither living people nor mere vapor.

Now, at Baran's silent command, the mist parted as smoothly as curtains, revealing the large, dank, gloomy, crumbling castle which squatted on the island in the center of the lake.

Baran turned to her and smiled sardonically. "Welcome home."

Far in the distance there was a crack of thunder from the volcano wherein dwelled Dar. Everyone in their party froze, looking at the sky to the southeast, waiting to see if the noise heralded an eruption. They were still too far from Darshon to be immediately affected, but they would certainly see it. Now black smoke billowed out of the snow-capped caldera to mingle with the brightly colored whirling clouds still surrounding the summit.

Baran laughed, evidently delighted. "And the same back at you, you old bitch!" he called.

Mirabar gasped. Her escort of *shallaheen* muttered nervously. Velikar snorted. Haydar crept closer to Najdan.

"Can we leave now?" Pyron asked faintly.

"Not yet," Najdan replied.

The column of black, angry smoke rose higher and higher in the distant sky, filling Mirabar with mingled awe and fear.

Pyron said in a breathless voice, "I'd really rather be in battle. Or . . . or almost anywhere else than here with this madman."

Mirabar heard Najdan reply, "When you report back to Tansen, do you really want *these* to be the circumstances in which you last saw the *sirana?*"

Pyron groaned. "You just had to think of something that would be even worse than being *here* right now, didn't you?"

"You can leave in a few days," Najdan said tersely.

Mirabar didn't take her gaze off Darshon, but nothing else seemed to be happening there. If this was a tantrum of Dar's, it evidently wasn't going to be a severe one. She shuddered, waiting for guidance, waiting for a sign. Had she been wrong about Baran, about Belitar, about her destiny? Had she misunderstood?

Someone touched her sleeve. Mirabar jumped and turned to find Haydar looking at her with sympathy.

"Who knows the ways of Dar, *sirana?*" Haydar said. "Perhaps She is . . . congratulating you on your marriage?"

Mirabar gave the woman a shaky smile. "Thank you. I hope so."

She glanced up at Darshon's tumultuous peak again and prayed that such was the case, because she wasn't turning back now.

"Nyahhh!" Pyron's incoherent protest attracted her attention now. "I hate water magic! I just *hate* it."

She followed his gaze and saw the evidence of Baran's formidable power as water gathered itself together from the lake and rose to form a shimmering bridge across its surface. Mirabar met her husband's gaze.

"After you," he said with silky courtesy.

She was the most powerful sorceress in all of Sileria and would not be intimidated by the *second* most powerful waterlord. She nodded graciously and proceeded across the distinctly slippery bridge without hesitation.

The others followed more cautiously, but everyone eventually made it across the long, slightly wavering bridge and into the ancient castle. Four assassins, alerted in advance by Vinn, awaited them in front of the massive door of crystallized water. One of them pushed it open and escorted them all inside.

After entering the castle's gloomy interior, Mirabar said, "It's a little dark in here, don't you think?"

She summoned the fire which lived in her veins, in her breath, in her soul. Feeling the heat rush to her palms, as commanded, she waved her arm and flung a ball of fire at the wall, where it settled itself and remained as a glowing torch. Not waiting for Baran to approve or object, she did this seven more times, until the shadowy great hall of Belitar was blazing with enchanted Guardian light. The *shir* of Baran's assassins were shivering wildly, she noticed with satisfaction.

She smiled at Baran. "I won't make *many* changes, but a new wife has certain rights, doesn't she?"

He looked amused. "My home is now *our* home, my dear. Do whatever you wish." He glanced at his uneasy assassins and said cheerfully, "I'm sure my men will be stimulated by the changes."

Vinn looked startled for a moment, then suddenly laughed. "Only you would do this, *siran*. Only you."

The rest of the men gradually relaxed and seemed to adopt Vinn's wryly resigned attitude. Well, Mirabar supposed that it took a certain kind of personality to serve Baran for years.

Baran now started issuing instructions to his people on the housing and care of his bride and her various guests. Mirabar listened as he did so, but wandered away looking around her new home, wondering what mysteries would be revealed to her here.

She knew already—knew the moment she crossed the threshold—that she had been right to come here, Dar's ill-timed explosion notwithstanding. Already, she could feel something here. Something . . . strong.

Mirabar assumed that Baran wouldn't help her secure her position as mistress of his household, and that his servants and assassins would try to walk all over her if she didn't take immediate steps to establish herself. She knew nothing about running a home, let alone the strange domain of a waterlord, but she had learned by now how to take charge of people. It also helped, of course, that these people were rather afraid of her.

After examining her own bedchamber—separate from

Baran's, she noticed with mingled relief and surprise—she found some minor faults with Najdan and Haydar's chamber and so instructed a servant to make improvements. Baran had disappeared by now, so it was Mirabar who insisted that one of the assassins make Najdan familiar with the grounds of Belitar, and also make plans to show him around the surrounding countryside and nearby villages in the days to come. She wanted Najdan to be no less informed and able than Baran's most favored assassin, Vinn.

Haydar was scandalized by the condition of Baran's kitchen, tended by an ex-Sister who had been ejected from the Sisterhood for lewd public behavior. Mirabar agreed to let Haydar take over the cooking duties at Belitar, and she assigned the ex-Sister some menial cleaning tasks which she suspected the woman probably wouldn't bother to do.

Mirabar was satisfied and tired by the end of her first day at Belitar. Now, she decided, it was time to seek out her husband.

She found him, as she expected, in his bedchamber, attended by Vinn and Sister Velikar. Mirabar entered without invitation, met Baran's gaze, and said, "I want to speak with you. Alone."

Baran nodded briefly at Vinn, who crossed his fists, bowed his head, and departed. Sister Velikar hesitated, saying to Baran, "Don't you want—"

"Come back later," he instructed her.

"Much later," Mirabar said to Velikar.

Baran lifted one brow, but he didn't contradict her. Velikar scowled at Mirabar, but left without further protest.

Mirabar turned and thoughtfully examined her husband, who was reclining on his bed.

It was hard to get used to sharing a bed with someone, particularly someone she didn't trust, so during their nights together on the road, she was well aware of every movement he made as he lay beside her, every shift, every sigh. So she knew he didn't sleep well, in addition to not eating and to needing treatment from Velikar.

"What's wrong with you?" she asked bluntly.

"Wrong with me?" he repeated.

She nodded.

"Hmmm, let's see . . . I was raised badly?" he tried. "I have no shame? My morals were corrupted by a wasted youth?"

She came forward and sat beside him on the bed. "I'm sure all of those things are true, but that's not what I'm talking about."

He took her hand and raised it to his lips. "Ah, have I been neglecting you, my dear?" he purred.

"Well, you're certainly acting strangely for a man who wants an heir," she pointed out, "but I haven't taken offense."

"I'm glad."

"Because you're very ill, aren't you?"

He looked away. After a long, tense moment, he said, "Yes."

"How ill?"

"As you just noted," he replied, "*very* ill."

"What's the matter with you?"

He still didn't look at her. "Velikar says it's a wasting disease in my stomach."

She tried to find a tactful way to ask. "You mean . . . you won't get better?"

"No."

She stared in silence, considering this. She hadn't truly expected it, not even after realizing he was ill. "You're dying?"

"Yes." His voice was pleasant and calm.

She lowered her head as it all became clear to her now. "That's why you want a child. An heir. Immortality of a kind."

"When I knew, when I realized . . ." He nodded. "Yes, that's when I started thinking about an heir."

"Someone to carry on your bloodfeud against Kiloran after you're dead." After another pause, she asked, "Soon?"

"Yes." He smiled a moment later. "Tansen will be pleased, won't he?" He touched her chin as he added, "And you're probably not terribly sorry."

She couldn't pretend that she felt sorrow, but she did feel enough pity for him—even for him—that she didn't admit that relief was her primary emotion after sheer confusion.

She tried to sort out her chaotic thoughts. "Fire and water, water and fire . . ." Perhaps she was beginning to understand. "I will be the one left in charge of Belitar and your legacy."

"Yes. In trust for our child."

"But if you barely have energy to sire a child, and very little time left in which to do it, what makes you so sure—"

"I've been promised."

She glanced sharply at him. "By whom?"

He smiled. "I still have enough time left to tell you that. And more." He shook his head. "But not tonight, *sirana.* Tonight, I'm tired."

"Do you have visions?" she prodded.

He stared at the cracked ceiling over his head as he said quietly, "Visions? My dear Mirabar, I don't even have dreams anymore. Now leave me in peace, won't you?"

"No. There's something else," she began.

"Of course there is," he said wearily. "Do you know, you've already learned to nag like a wife?"

"I didn't realize it was missing at first . . ." When he gave her a brief, questioning glance, she said, "Your power."

He looked insulted. "I assure you—"

"Oh, I know you've still got it. I can feel it when we're in the same room like this." She shook her head. "But I used to feel it even before I saw you. Not anymore, though. You're getting weak."

He stared at the ceiling again.

She asked, "Does Kiloran know?"

"I'm not sure," he admitted. "I've tried to keep him from finding out. But he . . ." He sighed. "No one knows better than me how hard he is to fool, to trick, to defeat."

"Tansen knows," she murmured absently, since Tansen was among the few who had ever succeeded. He had killed his bloodfather, Armian, and thereby taken away from Kiloran all that Armian promised—unchallenged rule of Sileria. And then he had escaped the old waterlord's wrath. Mirabar wondered what Kiloran's next move would be if he knew about Baran's illness.

"Ah, yes. Tansen." Baran perked up a bit as he asked, "Why does Kiloran hate him so much? Possibly even more than he hates me—which, I confess, makes me feel rather jealous and left out."

"It's not for me to say." She decided to change the subject. And she had learned from Baran himself that shock tactics were usually effective in this respect. "Why did Kiloran murder your wife?"

He drew in a sharp breath through his nostrils. "Does it matter now? I've promised you—"

"Yes, yes, you'll protect me. But since I'm your wife now, I am more than a little curious about it."

He had refused to say more about it that day in Velikar's Sanctuary. After making his startling announcement about the original source of enmity between him and Kiloran, he suddenly fell into a morose bout of brooding, rudely rebuffing any further attempts at conversation. Then Velikar had arrived and started an argument with Mirabar.

Now Mirabar meant to know more. "Did you love her?"

"I don't want to talk about this."

With a sudden surge of impatience and a sharp gesture, she set his bed on fire. A violent enchanted inferno nearly destroyed it within moments.

Baran shouted in surprise and leapt up, moving faster than he had in days. At his bidding, water came pouring through the open window from the lake outside, to douse the flames, filling the chamber with smoke.

The door to the chamber flew open. Two assassins came running into the room, their shuddering *shir* drawn and ready for combat. *"Siran! Siran!"* They started coughing, looking around for the source of danger as Baran and Mirabar stared at each other in consternation.

Baran, who was patting his singed clothing, held up a hand. "It's nothing," he assured them. "Just a little argument with my bride."

They looked warily at Mirabar.

"He annoyed me," she informed them. "And that's never wise."

One assassin bowed his head and backed out of the room without another word. The other looked questioningly at Baran.

"I can handle my own wife," Baran said dryly. "You may go."

When they were alone again, Baran suggested, "In the future, if you could perhaps call me nasty names prior to actually attempting to kill me, I would appreciate—"

"I wasn't trying to kill you. I was just trying to get your attention."

He laughed. "I'd have remarried years ago if I knew it would be so entertaining."

"Why did you marry the first time?" she pounced.

His face went suddenly serious and wistful. "Believe it or not, *sirana,* I was in love." He smiled when he saw her doubtful expression. "Even I was once young and full of hope, Mirabar. And, well, I used to be very different. I was even . . ." He considered his words and nodded. "Yes, I think most people would say I was a good man. Or at least a decent one. But that was a long time ago." He sat down on the edge of the charred, wet, smoking bed. "Her name was Alcinar," he said. "I met her on my travels."

"What travels?"

"Trading. Mostly with the Kintish Kingdoms. I was born to a merchant family. In a moderately prosperous village north of Adalian." He absently brushed cinders from the ruined bed. "The village is abandoned now, of course."

"Valdani?"

"Kiloran. He was trying to make me let go of the Idalar River, which I had frozen all the way from Illan to Shaljir. He flooded my entire native village. Right up to the edge of a cliff, where the water just stopped, as if it had run into a solid wall. It stayed there for a whole season." Baran smiled. "He really is very good."

"What did you do?"

"Oh, I retaliated. Then he retaliated. And so on."

"And your village?"

He shrugged. "Some lives were lost in the flood, and most dwellings were ruined. The village has been abandoned ever since."

It sickened her that he was so indifferent to the suffering he had helped cause. She couldn't imagine that he had ever been, as he claimed, a decent man. "Did love make you so hard?" she asked in bewilderment.

"Love? No." He closed his eyes, evidently remembering. "Love made me happy. Made me whole and content. Love gave my existence the real meaning it had lacked, the joy without which life isn't worth living." He opened his eyes and surprised her by saying, "You can't imagine how much I loved her."

"Did she love you?"

He blinked. "Yes." Then he seemed to understand the question, and he grinned. "I know. You find that hard to believe, to understand. But I've told you—I was a different man then. So different, I doubt you can imagine who I was. Just as I know Alcinar would never believe who I have become."

"So she married you, and then . . . What happened?"

"My family's business had always required me to travel a great deal, and I didn't want to be away from her."

"And she couldn't travel?"

"Alcinar had . . . made certain choices in order to marry me, and it seemed best for her peace that we, er, settle down somewhere. So we went to live in the hills near Lake Kandahar."

"Why? Didn't you know it was Kiloran's lair?"

He nodded. "That's why we went there. Kiloran, who had taken an interest in me several years earlier, had always been frustrated by me. I loved water and wanted to explore my gift, my talent; but I had no interest in becoming a waterlord. I came and went, never staying at Kandahar for long. And he always said that if the time ever came that I was prepared to settle down, live nearby, and devote myself seriously to my apprenticeship, then he would welcome me."

"So you changed your mind? You were ready to become a waterlord?"

"No. I've told you, I lacked focus. I also lacked ambition. I just knew I didn't want to be a traveling trader anymore." He sighed. "We were so young, Alcinar and I. Even foolish. We thought we could live simply in the mountains, far from her past, and find a new future together. I knew from Kiloran that my talent was special, extraordinary, even for a waterlord. I could develop it, hone it, and eventually use it to be . . . I don't know. Something new, different. Something besides a waterlord." He shook his head, his expression sad. "I was dreamy-eyed, impractical, naive."

"Well, naive to think Kiloran wouldn't pull you into his web," she agreed, "but these were . . . worthy ideas, Baran." She thought briefly of the Beyah-Olvari. "Water magic itself isn't inherently evil; it's just the Honored Society which is."

"That's what I thought," he said softly, looking away. "But you have no idea how seductive water magic is, Mirabar."

"Then it seduced you?" she guessed.

"Not then. Not while I had such love in my life. Only later, after she was dead. Only after I . . . went mad with grief and hatred."

"Why did he kill her?"

"I don't actually know," Baran admitted, surprising her. "I suspect it was an accident."

She frowned. "An accident?"

He glanced at her, his dark eyes tormented now. "Kiloran fell in love with her. Well . . . not *love*," he amended. "He became obsessed with her. He wanted her for himself. Wanted her so badly that—I've come to realize—it was a desire which overruled his usual cold rationality."

"And you didn't get her away from him?" she asked in astonishment. "Away from Kandahar?"

"I didn't know. He concealed it from me. Even from her. She'd have told me if she knew." His face seemed to age moment by moment as he continued. "One day he sent me to Lake Ursan for a training exercise. I was away for ten days. When I returned home, Alcinar was gone. Missing. I was terrified beyond coherent thought. I knew she hadn't left me." He glanced briefly at her. "We were so happy, Mirabar. The two of us . . . What a place the world would be if everyone was as happy as we were."

"Did you suspect anyone?"

"I thought it must be Outlookers, or bandits, or some savage *shallah* who thought abduction was the way to get a woman." He absently touched the necklace he always wore, that sturdily beautiful ornament of Kintish silver and jade. It had never before occurred to Mirabar, but now she knew it had once belonged to a woman. She felt sure it had once been Alcinar's. "I imagined horrible things," Baran continued, "things which drove me straight to Kiloran to beg for his help. I knew if anyone could get her back for me, it was the greatest waterlord in the Society."

Already realizing what he had discovered next, Mirabar sank down onto the ruined bed beside him. "But Kiloran was the one who had taken her."

"He knew I would come. His assassins ambushed me. I survived, but then I knew. I *knew*." He lowered his head. "*He* had her. She was his prisoner. His victim." His face contorted terribly. "And I was the one who had brought her to Kandahar in the first place."

Now Mirabar knew. Now she understood what had driven Baran mad. Now she recognized how the demon inside him had been born and taken control of his soul. "And Kandahar is impregnable."

"I tried." He covered his tormented face with his hands as he spoke. "I was very talented, and I already had some skill. But nothing worked. I couldn't breach Kandahar. Couldn't get to Alcinar or help her. Couldn't kill Kiloran or stop what he was assuredly doing to her night after night . . . after night . . ."

Horrified, Mirabar was starting to wish she had never asked, had never pursued this subject.

"I offered him anything," Baran continued. "Everything. My life. My family's wealth. The lives of other people. I'd have gone to Valda itself and brought back Emperor Jarell's head if it would have saved Alcinar."

"But Kiloran didn't want anything except her."

"Oh, he wanted one thing," Baran said. "My life. And I'd have given it up gladly. I *wanted* to die. But not before saving her from him. I wasn't going to let him kill me so he could go on raping her in peace and safety for the rest of his life."

"How did you find out she was dead?"

"He told me. In a letter. Of course, I didn't believe him at first. For months, I . . . I believed she was still alive and he just wanted me to give up trying to get her back." He took a few shaky breaths. "Finally, though, I knew it was true. Kiloran chose another mistress and brought her to Kandahar."

He paused for a moment before continuing, more calmly, "I had already killed more than twenty of his men, including all the most trusted ones. Of those left alive after that, none whom I captured or interrogated even knew Alcinar's name when I asked about her."

Mirabar briefly wondered where Najdan had been during all this; he would have told her if he knew about Baran's brief apprenticeship under Kiloran, or Kiloran's capture of Baran's wife. She supposed that, whatever Najdan had been doing during those months, he had been nowhere near Kandahar. She knew that, throughout his twenty years in Kiloran's service, he was capable enough and trusted enough to work far from Kiloran's supervision for long periods of time. And given how things had turned out at Kandahar, she supposed that after Alcinar died, anyone left alive who even knew about these events was too afraid of Kiloran's wrath to gossip about them.

Baran added, "Even assassins who betrayed Kiloran for generous bribes, now and then, assured me that his new mistress was the only woman at Kandahar. Yes, there had briefly been another woman before her, one assassin told me, but no one knew what had happened to her."

"Alcinar."

"I later realized that she had probably died well before Kiloran told me about it. And I think he only told me because he hoped it would make me reckless, impetuous, even crazier with rage and bloodlust."

"So that you'd do something careless or stupid," she said, "and be easier to kill."

"I surprised him, though, just as I've been surprising him ever since."

Baran might be educated and worldly, but he was still a Silerian. "Vengeance gave you something to live for," Mirabar surmised.

"Exactly so." He lifted his head, clearly trying to shake off the horrifying memories. "So I disappeared. He undoubtedly began to hope I had killed myself."

"And you eventually came to Belitar."

"Yes. Where my destiny unfolded, as yours will, too."

"There's something here," she murmured. She would have simply taken it for Baran's strength, his power, had she not already discovered how quickly that was fading.

"Ahhh . . ." He nodded. "I wondered if you'd feel it."

"What is it?" she asked.

"Are you afraid?"

"I'm not sure," she admitted.

"Well, I was," he confessed, surprising her. "But I had nothing left to lose, and I was desperate. Desperate enough to come to this gloomy, haunted ruin."

"Why?" she asked. "Why did you come in the first place?"

"This was the seat of Harlon's power, who was once almost as great as Kiloran, and who fought the Valdani to a standstill for years." He hesitated, then added, "And long before that, this was Marjan's home."

"Marjan," she breathed. "The first waterlord, who betrayed and murdered Daurion, the last Yahrdan."

"So they do teach Guardians history?"

"Then Marjan really did live here, that's not just a tale?"

"He really lived here. A thousand years ago."

"And you wanted whatever it was that Marjan and Harlon had found here, whatever had bolstered their strength."

"Yes. I wanted that. I came here looking for it, believing in it. I braved the ghosts and the fog and the damp. I remained even after, like you, I realized there was something here. Something very strong. Maybe stronger than me." He met her gaze. "I'd have done things which frightened me far more than that, in order to avenge Alcinar."

And he had *become* far worse things, she now knew, than he had ever imagined.

She thought of Elelar, thought of the vengeance she wanted against the *torena* for betraying Josarian. She looked at Baran . . . and saw where the lust for revenge could lead a person. Especially someone as gifted and powerful as Baran. Someone like herself.

Baran studied her expression. "I've upset you," he said apologetically.

She wanted to get away from him. "It's late." She rose to her feet, as eager to escape as if his bloodlust, his insanity, were contagious.

His gaze sharpened, assessing her mood. "You're not going to invite me to share your bed tonight, are you?" He glanced down and added, "Even though you've destroyed mine."

"There must be other beds in this vast place. Besides," she pointed out, "you said you were tired."

"I was, but now I don't think I'll sleep anytime soon. Not

after this conversation. So perhaps you and I could . . . comfort each other for a while."

Their gazes locked.

She was afraid of him again. More so, perhaps, because now his eyes urged her to remember he could be kind, could even give her pleasure. She suddenly didn't want to be that close to him again, lest his sickened soul somehow infect her own struggling one.

Mirabar shook her head slowly. "Not tonight. I'm . . ."

"You've made sure I don't want to be alone tonight," he murmured, his eyes taking on a dark glow. "And you are my wife."

She didn't want to be alone tonight, either; but her husband wasn't the man whose company she wanted now. Torn between fear and duty, tormented by what she wanted and couldn't have, she felt herself starting to tremble.

"Come, *sirana*," Baran coaxed, his voice almost affectionate. "Why not share a little human warmth on a night when we both suddenly find ourselves in need of it?"

"I don't—"

"Don't you?" he challenged.

She stared at him in tumultuous silence, no longer entirely sure she wanted to say no, yet also afraid of what he might do if she tried to leave now.

There was a knock at the door, dissolving the moment.

Baran sighed and called, "Come in."

Velikar entered the room, holding a cup of some smelly brew. She froze when she saw the bed, then whirled on Mirabar. "What have you done to the *siran?*" she demanded.

"Our first marital spat," Mirabar said.

Velikar began, "You mustn't—"

"It's all right, Sister," Baran interrupted. "I knew I was marrying a spirited . . ." He glanced at some floating cinders and amended, "Er, *fiery* woman."

Velikar insisted, "It's a disgrace, *siran!*"

Baran took the tisane from her. "Velikar, would you be so

kind as to find me a fresh bed for the night while I . . ." He peered into the cup and grimaced. "While I attempt to choke this down without dying on the spot."

"I don't want to leave you alone with this wild arsonist!" Velikar protested.

Mirabar rolled her eyes. "Don't worry. I'm leaving."

Velikar shook her head, "How the two of *you* ever thought you could make marriage work . . ."

"Now Velikar," Baran said soothingly, "any half-wit can get a child, and I'm sure the *sirana* and I will work that out before long. As to the marriage itself . . . Well, I trust I've given my wife rather welcome news tonight."

"That all depends, Baran," Mirabar said from the doorway. "If you die before we can defeat Kiloran . . ." She shook her head, depressed and worried. "Tansen was counting on you. We're not sure anyone but a strong waterlord can stop him."

"Well then," he said. "We'd better get serious about that child, hadn't we?"

She met his gaze. A wary acceptance unfurled within her; a need, like his, for comfort in the dark. The kind of comfort he had already shown her he knew how to give.

"Oh, very well," she said with ill grace, though she was now more nervous than reluctant or afraid. "I suppose you had better stay with me tonight."

Yes, he had changed her mind. Water magic was not his only gift.

"My dear!" He grinned. "Far be it from me to reject my eager bride." He raised his cup and added, "I'll be there shortly."

ALTHOUGH IT WAS broad daylight, Sister Rahilar shrieked in startled fear when Cheylan came upon her suddenly in Velikar's Sanctuary.

"I'm sorry, excuse me," she babbled, "I didn't mean to, um, you know. But you—you surprised me."

"So I gathered," he said, letting the glowing eyes which so distressed her now dismiss her with a brief glance.

"Are you just returning now from . . ."

He looked around. There was no sign of anyone else. "From the east. Yes. Where is—"

"I, uh, I just came here to get some of Velikar's supplies," she said. "She wouldn't mind. I've run out at Dalishar. There are so many people there these days that I can't kee—"

"Where *is* Velikar?" he asked, knowing Rahilar could just keep talking until someone stopped her.

"Belitar."

"Belitar?" He asked a more important question. "Has Mirabar returned?"

She frowned. "You mean from Belitar?"

"No," he said irritably, "I don't mean fr . . ." He stopped and stared at her. "What do you mean by that?"

She shrugged. "Well, that's where she's gone."

He didn't think he had heard right. "Mirabar has gone to Belitar?"

Rahilar jumped at the sharpness of his tone. "Yes."

"With Velikar?" he demanded.

"And Baran."

"And Baran?" he repeated, astonished.

"And Najdan, Haydar, Pyron, and that assassin, Vinn . . ." She shrugged again. "And an escort of five or six other men. I don't remember who they all were, what with so many people coming and going at Dalishar these da—"

"Why did she go to Belitar?" It seemed too risky, no matter what Baran had promised. "Does Tansen know?"

"Yes," the Sister replied, gathering some of Velikar's herbs and ointments as she spoke. "He was here—well, not *here*, but up at the caves when they . . . you know."

"No, I don't know." He tried to keep the impatience out of his voice.

"Oh. That's right," she said absently, now starting to pack

some of the supplies she was gathering. "You've been away." She suddenly stopped and her eyes flew wide open. "You don't know!"

"Know what?"

"You'll never believe it!" A love of juicy gossip flooded her voice. "You'll probably make half a dozen people tell you the same thing before you'll really believe it. *I* wouldn't believe—"

"Believe what?" he asked wearily. He had forgotten how tedious he found Rahilar.

He forgot everything else a moment later, when she told him what Mirabar had done.

43

WHAT TREE IS NOT TORMENTED BY THE WIND?
—Kintish Proverb

"HE'S DONE *WHAT?*" Kiloran demanded of Dyshon the assassin, whose green eyes looked weary from having made the long journey from Kandahar to Cavasar at top speed so he could deliver this news in person.

"He has married Mirabar," Dyshon repeated.

"How do you know this?"

Hot air drifted through the windows of the fortress from which Commander Koroll, and later Commander Cyrill, once governed this city. Now Cavasar belonged to Kiloran; and, like a good master, he had abandoned the serenity and delightful coolness of Kandahar in the dry season to attend to various pressing concerns in the city which was now one of his most important possessions.

However, this startling news obliterated all thoughts of his business in Cavasar. He listened while Dyshon recited a fairly typical trail of common gossip.

"In other words," Kiloran concluded, his thoughts veering from one speculation to another, "neither Baran nor Mirabar made any attempt to keep this a secret."

"No, *siran*." Dyshon went on to report that word was spreading about the marriage, as was the news that Baran had joined Tansen's bloodfeud against Kiloran. "What do you think it all means, *siran?*"

It was a fair question. Even Searlon would have asked it. And Kiloran couldn't answer it.

"With that madman," he replied, "who can say for sure?" After all these years, Baran was still surprising him. And it was still as unpleasant as ever.

Kiloran wondered aloud, "Has Baran set an elaborate trap for Mirabar? It's possible. Indeed, I expected something of the kind—though *this* never occurred to me. And Baran certainly wouldn't explain his plans to me. He would even enjoy my uncertainty. Is that his game? Or . . ." He sighed, feeling old mistakes return once again to haunt him. *Alcinar.* A wild lust, a seething obsession unlike anything he'd ever known, even as a young man. In the years since her death, he had come to regard his uncharacteristic, ungovernable passion for her as a panicked protest against the loss of his youth and the approach of old age.

"Or," Dyshon finished for him, calling him back to the present, "has Baran betrayed you?"

"Yes," Kiloran said, "it's a possibility we must consider." A very real possibility, if Mirabar wasn't already dead at Belitar. *Damn Baran.*

Dyshon said, "But he made a vow, swore a binding oath with you at the truce meeting."

Kiloran thought back to that day. "At the time," he mused, "I think he meant it."

For a moment that day, despite all the hatred and bloodshed over the years, he and Baran had been mentor and apprentice again. But only for a brief moment; and then a world of vengeance came between them again, as it would always do until Baran was finally dead, his golden gift for water magic perishing with him. What a pity. What a waste.

Who else taught him, I wonder? Who else had the shaping of that diamond-bright talent?

Kiloran almost felt jealous at the thought. Baran's talent had been a joy to see, a thing of beauty, a rich pleasure to guide. There had never been anyone else whose gifts rewarded Kiloran's teaching as Baran's once had.

Baran could have been his heir; would have been, if not for Alcinar.

"Impetuous acts and ungoverned passions always cost too much and should never be indulged," he murmured to himself.

"Siran?"

"Nothing."

Armian, Srijan, Baran . . .

The disappointments of life were hard to bear. Only the ruthless survived. Only a heart of stone triumphed in the end.

"But to betray the vows of a truce meeting!" Dyshon protested, warming to his theme. "Without fulfilling the promises sworn that day! To end the truce without a warning or an honorable declaration! No, surely Baran—even *Baran*—surely he wouldn't . . . wouldn't . . ." He trailed off, evidently realizing that if anyone would do such a thing, it was indeed Baran. "Would he?" Dyshon sighed. "He would, wouldn't he?" He rubbed his forehead. "I humbly suggest, *siran,* that we have been betrayed." He nodded and concluded, "And we must take vengeance, if that is so."

"If that is so," Kiloran agreed, "then we certainly must. But it will be very inconvenient."

"Damn Baran," Dyshon muttered.

"Yes," Kiloran said.

"What shall we do?"

Kiloran thought it over. "In the interests of saving time, I think a direct approach would be best."

"An attack?"

"Not that direct," Kiloran said dryly. "A letter."

"Oh." Dyshon looked disappointed. "I will arrange for a courier."

"Make it a Sister. Just in case."

"Ah. You're thinking of the courier Wyldon killed," Dyshon guessed.

"Yes," Kiloran agreed, thinking of the hot-headed water-lord who was at odds with him. "That was when Wyldon finally made me truly angry."

Dyshon grinned. "The bracelet you sent to him worked, *siran*. Wyldon thinks Baran is the one who has invited him to meet." He asked hesitantly, "The bracelet was Baran's once, wasn't it?"

"Not exactly," Kiloran said, his tone and expression discouraging further questions on the subject.

The bracelet had belonged to Alcinar. So had the necklace which it matched. She always wore them. But the necklace had broken in the struggle when two of his men—long since killed by Baran—removed her from Baran's simple mountain home near Kandahar that day so long ago. Alcinar was wearing only the bracelet when they brought her to him. When he took possession of the woman he must have. The woman he would kill for. Yes, he would even kill the most promising apprentice in Sileria for her.

Kiloran supposed Baran had found the necklace somewhere in his empty home. He had worn it ever since, and he always made his *shir* hilts in its image, despite the extravagant cost of Kintish silver and jade under Valdani rule. A sentimental indulgence? Or a constant reminder of the vengeance he lived for?

Knowing Baran, both.

It was strange that two men so different from each other should love the same woman. Baran was at least twenty years younger than Kiloran, and in those days he had been a whimsical dreamer, more prone to laughter than to anger. A widely traveled, well-educated young man whose worldliness warred with an inherent idealism, he naively believed he could practice water magic without bowing to the dictates of the Society, without becoming one of them. Without belonging to the only kind who could ever truly understand him.

Baran had never been greedy, despite what most others thought. His ruthless seizure of wealth and power over the years had all been in pursuit of one sole aim: destroying Kiloran. He had never been interested in wealth for its own sake. More than fifteen years ago, in fact, Baran had abandoned his family's immensely profitable business to take his new wife far into the mountains. Far from the sea, because she wished to be far from it after choosing him over the sea-bound life of a Lascari. Baran wanted no serious profit from his wizardry, either, and the young couple lived simply in the hills near Kandahar.

Kiloran had never known a more devoted couple. In retrospect, he recognized with a clear head that many newlyweds were besotted, at least if they married for love as Baran and Alcinar had; but, at the time, Kiloran had secretly envied Baran his wild happiness with his wife. There was something between those two which . . . Well, it seemed to surpass the ordinary in a soaring way which eventually stirred Kiloran to dark jealousy.

Kiloran's obsession with Alcinar began subtly. It was a while before he himself was truly aware of it, though he knew he thought about her—and asked about her—more often than was his normal habit. He seldom saw her, since Baran usually kept her well away from any place frequented by assassins; but he found his eyes straying to her often on those rare occasions when he was in her presence. Well, why not? She was young and lovely, and a sea-born woman was an unusual sight in the mountains.

Her behavior was always discreet, as was Baran's, yet Kiloran was intensely aware of the earthy sexuality which constantly flowed between them, as rich and lush as the waters of the Idalar River itself. Their secret smiles, the way their fingers touched when they thought no one was looking, the warmth in Baran's eyes when he gazed upon Alcinar, the glow in her own eyes when she watched him . . . Kiloran went from being amused by it, as a man well past the age for such things, to being annoyed by it, to eventually being hotly angry about it.

When he finally recognized his grinding jealousy and realized what he felt for Baran's wife, he thought he could control it. And he knew he must. A strong waterlord could usually take an assassin's woman, even an ordinary apprentice's woman. But Baran's woman? No, Baran would die before he'd let another man, even Kiloran, touch his wife.

Yes, I knew that from the first.

Kiloran also knew that Baran was worth too much to sacrifice over this inconvenient obsession with a woman. Water magic was a gift, a mystery, a glorious birthright beyond the rigors of ordinary life and above the needs of lesser men. No, Kiloran would not murder his brilliant student to satisfy the passion which any aging man might feel for a desirable young woman.

Or so he thought.

He could still remember the moment he lost all control, all reason, all sense of proportion. It was during a celebration to mark the start of the dry season, traditionally a time of power and profit for the Honored Society. Kiloran provided music, singing, dancing, wine and ale, plenty of food . . .

It was a good day, settling into the golden glow of evening. While watching some performance staged in his honor, Kiloran glanced at Baran and Alcinar, who were nearby. He always glanced at Alcinar, far more than anyone knew. As he watched, Baran held a fig up to her mouth, stroking her black hair with his other hand. She bit into the smooth purple flesh with those straight, white teeth of hers and then, her eyes glowing with promises, fed her husband that dripping piece of fruit from between her own lips.

Kiloran was suddenly consumed with lust: blinding, deafening, overpowering desire. He would kill to have her. He would commit murder, break vows, sacrifice the future, betray his sorcery and even his destiny . . . As he watched Baran whisper to her and then draw her away into the softening twilight, towards the path which led to the humble home where they lived so quietly, and to the bed which they shared with such heedless pleasure . . . Yes, Kiloran knew then that he would do every terrible thing within his power to have this woman.

And the price was even higher than I anticipated.

Baran had never stopped making him pay.

Now, fifteen years later, Kiloran found it strange to remember—and hard to believe—that those feelings had ever lived within him, let alone ruled him to the exclusion of reason, sense, and cold wisdom. He knew Alcinar had been lovely, but now he had trouble recalling her exact features. He knew that her exotic tattoos had seemed burningly erotic to him . . . but now he couldn't remember why.

He . . . yes, he even regretted having destroyed her. He was certain that hadn't been his intention, though he must have known—surely, even in his fevered state, he must have realized?—that she would never accept any man other than Baran.

No, he acknowledged honestly. *No.* He hadn't even considered that before capturing her, and wouldn't have cared if he had. It was only after she was gone that he began to suspect, appalled at his own weaknesses, that he hadn't wanted Alcinar so much as he had wanted the untamed joy that Baran knew with her.

How strangely foolish of me.

That whole brief episode of Kiloran's life was one he had ensured remained secret. Of course, Baran had unwittingly helped, in a sense, by killing almost everyone who knew; even as Kiloran mourned their loss, he felt a private relief that his secrets died with them. Najdan, who had been busy making war on Gulstan's assassins at the time, never knew about those days at Kandahar; and a few months later, he brought Haydar, a very forgettable woman, back to his home near Kandahar. Searlon entered Kiloran's service the following year, and prying curiosity was not among his faults. There were few left alive who had even the vaguest knowledge of those strange months at Kandahar when Kiloran had behaved so irrationally, and Kiloran had made sure they knew better than to ever speak of that time to anyone.

Such passions, Kiloran knew—had probably known even then—were for younger men. And for weaker, lesser men. He had been too greedy, he saw that now; saw it soon after losing Alcinar. A man could not be what Kiloran was and also be what Baran was in those days; he could be a great waterlord of immense power and influence *or* a dreamily contented lover. He could never be both at once.

And the choice was so clear. Had Kiloran ever doubted it (which he hadn't), he need only consider how warped and wildly grieving Baran had been ever since then, insane with rage and sorrow for all these years. No, Baran had never recovered from the loss of his wife—a loss which would never crush a stronger, wiser man.

A loss which did not crush me.

But what an expensive lesson that period of folly had become. Kiloran was well aware that living without ever having tasted Alcinar would be much easier than living with fifteen years of Baran's enmity had been.

And now there was this unexpected marriage to Mirabar. Kiloran sighed, acknowledging that he might once again have erred in his dealings with Baran.

"*Siran.*" Dyshon's voice again captured his attention.

"Hmmm?"

"Will you entrust the kill to me?"

Kiloran was startled, suddenly realizing he hadn't been listening to Dyshon. "The kill?"

"Wyldon."

"Oh, Wyldon," he murmured, gradually pulling his thoughts back to the subject at hand.

Dyshon's face was intent, his ambition overriding his fear of Wyldon's sorcery. "May I be the one to kill him?"

"Ah."

Forcing his attention away from fruitless memories and back to current business, Kiloran considered the request for a moment. He had proposed a meeting place to Wyldon which was bone dry at this time of year. For a meet between wary waterlords such as Wyldon and (as Wyldon thought) Baran, it was almost as good as Sanctuary; their power was useless so far from a water source, a situation which would help secure a temporary truce between them.

Stripped of his sorcery, Wyldon would be defended only by his assassins. So Dyshon wasn't asking to match power with Wyldon, only combat strategy.

"Very well," Kiloran agreed.

He was tempted to remind Dyshon to take Wyldon by surprise, not to waste time gloating about the trap they had set. However, he resisted. If Dyshon knew this already, then the reminder would be an insult, a sign that Kiloran doubted his shrewdness. And if Dyshon didn't know it . . . then Kiloran hoped he would learn from his mistakes, though dying from them was also a possibility.

"And when I'm done, *siran* . . ."

"Ah." Kiloran nodded, guessing the rest. "You would like his territory." Still only an apprentice, Dyshon hoped to become a waterlord.

"Only when you deem me ready, *siran*." Dyshon bowed his head and crossed his fists, evincing his respect as he made his bold request.

Kiloran liked ambition, at least when it was no real threat to him. So he was pleased to see it growing within Dyshon.

"I'm sure you will be ready soon," he lied, not at all sure Dyshon would ever be able to hold Wyldon's territory. However, men worked harder when they desired something passionately, and people had surprised him before. So Kiloran would dangle the promise of Wyldon's territory before Dyshon, hoping—without expecting it—that the assassin's ambition would someday prove great enough to compensate for his modest talent.

In any event, the need to kill Wyldon was entirely Tansen's fault. Tansen had won six of Kiloran's *shir* by surviving the ambush on Mount Dalishar shortly after Josarian's death. Undoubtedly knowing how notoriously rash and suspicious Wyldon was by nature, Tansen had then disguised some of his men as assassins, led an abortive attack on Wyldon's stronghold, and left behind one of the *shir* to cast suspicion on Kiloran. The plan had worked; Wyldon not only blamed Kiloran, he was also asking other waterlords to side with him in a feud against Kiloran—at a time when they should unite in crushing Tansen, the Guardians, and the Firebringer's loyalists.

"Have you had news," Dyshon now asked, "about how Meriten is faring?"

"Not well," Kiloran admitted, thinking of the loyal but modestly powerful waterlord trying to reclaim territory which the Society had recently lost. "The Guardians are holding fast to the Shaljir River." He silently cursed Abidan and Liadon, who had been twin brothers and waterlords; they had jointly ruled the Shaljir River, which they had lost when they both died fighting Tansen's attack on their territory. Their homes were now burned-out ruins, and sheep were reputedly being stabled in what little was left of them.

"And Verlon?"

"I've sent a letter assuring him I have no designs on his territory." But he knew Verlon, the most powerful—and the most hot-tempered—waterlord in eastern Sileria. "I doubt he'll believe me." Not with Wyldon's behavior stirring up suspicion and ill-feeling.

"And Tansen?"

"Tansen . . ." This made Kiloran think of Baran again.

What had one of them promised the other—if anything—in order for that bizarre marriage to take place? Could Tansen possibly trust Baran?

"Why are you laughing, *siran?*"

"I've had a laughable thought."

No, not Tansen. He would never make that mistake. And Baran? Kiloran wondered if Baran could be foolish enough to trust Tansen. It was a pleasing thought, but probably a futile one. Yes, Tansen would presumably show Baran what he wanted to see; that was Tansen's way. But Baran knew—surely he must know—that Tansen wanted all the waterlords dead.

All of us, Baran. No mercy for an ally.

By all the gods above and below, Tansen had killed his own bloodfather! He would spare no one if he was the victor now.

Then again, would Baran care? He was presumably dying. Besides, he had killed his own allies before, and might believe he could kill these, too, when the time came.

Or . . .

A new possibility occurred to Kiloran, one which chilled him. Did Baran know something he didn't? Something which had convinced him to side openly with Tansen and the Guardians? Could that be what this marriage was about?

Yes, Kiloran needed to know what Baran was up to. He would write that letter to Baran today and make sure it left Cavasar for Belitar by tomorrow.

"Tansen's influence is growing," Dyshon warned him, "every day. Whole villages are defying us now, refusing to pay tribute. Refusing to obey. He is . . ." The assassin hesitated. "He is not the Firebringer, *siran,* but he is a very dangerous man."

"I know," Kiloran said. "I know better than anyone how dangerous Tansen is."

"How will we stop him?"

"We won't," Kiloran replied. "In the end, we won't need to."

"Siran?"

"Tansen wants all-out war with us. Nothing less will satisfy him." Kiloran suspected it was what that murderous *sriliah* had always wanted.

"Will we oblige, *siran?*"

"Oh, yes," Kiloran said. "We will. And when Sileria bleeds hard enough, she will finally turn on him."

Kiloran looked forward to it with relish.

ELELAR WAS RELIEVED to abandon Shaljir as the city sank deep into the deprivations of the dry season. The city-dwellers were hoarding water and rationing their supplies, nervously watching the Idalar River fall lower and lower between its broad banks as the season progressed. If Kiloran meant to act, meant to cripple the city and bring it under the Society's influence, there would never be a better time.

It would happen soon. Everyone believed it.

Then we will find out just how strong or weak we really are.

Elelar, however, would not be in Shaljir for the coming struggle against life-stealing thirst and the fierce power of the Society. The Alliance believed that, due to Elelar's public betrayal of Kiloran the night that Advisor Kaynall declared Valdani surrender in Santorell Square, when she had announced the waterlord's murder of Josarian to the crowd, Shaljir would be too unsafe for her if the city fell to Kiloran.

Torena Elelar shah Hasnari was "only a woman," but she was currently the most important, most popular woman in Sileria after Mirabar—an irony which Elelar knew the fire-eyed Guardian would not appreciate. Elelar was deemed not only a great heroine of the rebellion who had risked and sacrificed much for Sileria's freedom, but also the legal and moral heir of her grandfather Gaborian's great legacy, since he had founded the Alliance and left his secrets and duties in her care when he died.

Chaos, bickering, war, and religious fervor currently threatened the newly freed, war-torn nation, but it was predicted that Elelar, though "only a woman," would play an important (or at least highly visible) role in her country's future, though that role was currently undecided.

Elelar didn't care.

Unlike *Toren* Varian and the other leaders of the Alliance eagerly hoping—expecting—that their years of service and sacrifice would now reap them power and influence, Elelar expected to die soon. And she was ready.

The Olvar's prophecy had frightened her at first, but she had grown used to the idea. Even welcomed it now. Yes, *welcomed* it.

To surrender to Mirabar's vengeance for the sake of Sileria; to yield to fate and relinquish her transgressions in the hot flow of Dar's retribution; to be purified by this final sacrifice.

Yes.

If that was her destiny, then she was ready for it. If that was the way it must be, then she didn't want to wait any longer. Indeed, she now longed for it the way other women longed for love.

So she hadn't resisted the Alliance's exhortations that she flee to the safety of a comfortable lowland Sanctuary until Shaljir's ultimate fate was determined. The city was in chaos, the city-dwellers needed their leaders to set a strong example for them, and the problem of the Silerian-born Valdani was far from resolved. Normally, Elelar would have insisted upon staying and doing her duty; she knew that her closest associates were surprised when she didn't.

Her servants were even more surprised when she abandoned Sanctuary only a few days after being left there by her escort from the Alliance. Her personal maid, Faradar, was the only one to whom she explained her actions.

"You know the reports I received yesterday?" she said to Faradar as they rode their well-rested mounts deeper inland, heading towards the country estate which Elelar had inherited from Gaborian. They traveled slowly, since the four *shalla-heen* whom Elelar employed as bodyguards were all on foot.

"Yes, *torena?*"

"They advised me that Baran has married Mirabar—"

"What?" the maid exclaimed.

"—and joined Josarian's loyalists."

Elelar wondered how Tansen had reacted to the match. With violent opposition, she suspected. Yet Mirabar had done it anyhow. Elelar also wondered—sometimes speculated with wild curiosity—about what Baran had said when he proposed to Mirabar. As for the marriage itself . . . Even Elelar, who had used sex as a weapon for years, nearly shuddered with cold fear when she considered embracing that half-mad and wholly dangerous waterlord.

So Mirabar is braver than ever. And Tansen will be more enthralled than ever, no matter how this marriage wounds him.

"Baran on our side," Faradar murmured. She was intelligent and quickly guessed the most obvious ramifications for Elelar. "So you will rely on Baran's protection against Kiloran?"

"Something like that," she replied.

She felt a little guilty about not telling her loyal companion her real plan, but she knew Faradar would never understand. Faradar knew nothing of Elelar's betrayal of Josarian. So she would object to Elelar's destiny even more strongly than Tansen had, though for simpler reasons.

Elelar would let Mirabar know where she was. Baran could keep Kiloran from interfering. And Elelar would wait for Mirabar to come kill her.

It was a simple enough plan. It was also the reason she had left Derlen the Guardian behind in Shaljir. She knew he wasn't strong enough to stop Mirabar, and she saw no point in letting him sacrifice his life trying, as he probably would if he were with her when the time came.

Anticipating her own death, Elelar had resolved her affairs as best she could in Shaljir, and she would do so now at her estate, too. Ronall's two estates—which he had inherited from his parents upon their violent deaths in Shaljir—were undoubtedly in utter disarray, but that was no longer her concern. Even if Elelar cared, she couldn't visit those lands now; they were in territory under Kiloran's control. She idly wondered if that's where her husband was now. Perhaps his fear of the mob had conquered his fear of the Society and drove him to seek shelter there?

She briefly considered Tansen's orders to her about Ronall. . . .

"Find him and make him a hero, Elelar," Tansen ordered. *"Make the people love him the way they love you."*

She was aghast. *"I can't—"*

"You have to," he said inflexibly. *"If you don't, every man, woman, and child in Sileria with any Valdani blood will be slaughtered within the year. That's not what Josarian wanted, despite how many Valdani he killed."*

Now Elelar was abandoning her duty in that respect. She didn't really care about that, either. She felt the call of destiny, the way she imagined Josarian had once felt Dar summoning him to the Fires; the way the pilgrims streaming east under the blazing sun claimed they felt Dar Calling to them now.

Someone else would have to determine how to prevent more massacres, how to save Valdani women and children from murderous Silerian mobs. If Tansen wanted to exalt Ronall—assuming he was still alive—more power to him. Her husband wasn't her problem anymore. She was shedding her burdens with every step she took towards her fate.

Her mind rested briefly on her final conversation with the Olvar before her departure from Shaljir. He had lost all interest in what happened to her. Now he and the Beyah-Olvari were deeply absorbed in their sudden conviction that they were not, after all, the last of their kind. The Olvar was convinced that there were other survivors somewhere in Sileria.

It was, to be sure, extraordinary news. She felt more than a little curiosity about it, but the Olvar knew nothing more specific, and Elelar doubted she would live to know the answer to the riddle which now stimulated his followers with hope. So she wished him well when she spoke with him for the last time, and then she put his concerns, like so many other things, behind her.

Growing thirsty now, Elelar reached for her waterskin. It was nearly empty, so she drank sparingly. They'd need to find more water soon.

The country was now locked in the cruel grip of the dry season. The brassy sunshine was brutally hot, the air tormentingly still. The fertile soil of the lowlands gradually baked into hard clay, greedily hiding the water it had absorbed during the long rains. Elelar knew from the reports she received that the *shallaheen* were becoming bitterly divided throughout Sileria, some siding with the waterlords and the promise of survival—and others ruthlessly slaughtering them for betraying the Firebringer's legacy.

Tansen had begun an intense campaign of resistance to the Society throughout the mountains of central Sileria, trying to bring all the land between the Shaljir River and Idalar River under his influence. It was a bold strike at the heart of Kiloran's power, attacking the Society in territory which included the mines of Alizar, the Zilar River where Josarian had died, and additional territories controlled by waterlords loyal to Kiloran. It was a huge risk, but a necessary one. And if anyone could make it succeed, it was Tansen. Unfortunately, if anyone could stop him, it was Kiloran.

Adalian remained free of the Society's influence, but not without sacrifice, as Elelar knew from the reports she received. The city was suffering the privations of drought and growing desperate for the relief which only the waterlords could grant at this time of year. Meanwhile, fighting in the east was so furious that there was less and less reliable news to be had. Elelar did know, however, that an entire Guardian circle had been brutally slaughtered by Verlon; the news particularly caught her attention because it had happened, of all places, in Tansen's long-abandoned native village of Gamalan. Now, as

then, there were no survivors. Only the ashes of their mass funeral pyre were left behind.

From the city of Liron itself, there had been little news for
quite some time now, cut off as it was by the intense fighting
in the surrounding mountains. Meanwhile, in a boldly ruthess
move, Jagodan—leader of the Lironi, the biggest, most powerful *shallah* clan in the east—had executed the heads of three
rural *toreni* families who wouldn't declare their loyalty to his
cause. Now other aristocrats in the east were practically el-
bowing each other aside to declare their allegiance to the
Lironi and, by extension, to Tansen and the Guardians—except for a handful of *toreni* who believed Verlon and the other
eastern waterlords would protect them from annihilation.

It was certainly possible, of course, but any *toren* must realize just how expensive the friendship of the Society would become. In a nation which had never provided easy answers,
Elelar felt only contempt for those of her class who were still
trying to find them.

And Cavasar . . . Elelar sighed, feeling unwelcome regret
stir within her again. Cavasar was still firmly in Kiloran's
grasp and, by all reports, willingly paying heavy tribute for
the water which he kept flowing in the city's fountains and
canals. Cavasar obeyed the dictates of the Society and willfully ignored the ominous warnings from distant Mount
Darshon, where colored clouds which seemed almost alive
danced amidst flickering lights and rumbling thunder. The
smoky tantrums of the volcano were growing more frequent,
casting ashen clouds over the land by day and making the
moons glow increasingly red at night.

Blood moons, people called them. Another portent, Silerians claimed. Another warning that Dar was angry and screaming for vengeance.

*I am surrendering, Dar. I will not resist. I am penitent and
filled with humility.*

Elelar's mare suddenly started dancing nervously. In the
distance, she heard a dog bark. Then another, then another.

Something in the mountains let out a fierce howl. Foreboding filled Elelar even as Faradar's gelding started snorting and trembling, shaking its head and refusing to take another step.

One of the *shallaheen* started panting.

Another warned, *"Torena . . . Torena!"*

"Oh, nooo . . ." She was sliding off her mount, already aware of the danger, already hearing the distant rumble which turned to a scream, echoing Faradar's startled scream as her horse reared and threw her.

"Faradar!" Elelar dodged the gelding's kicking hooves and tried to reach the maid, but the shaking ground made her stagger and fall.

"Ow!" Elelar cried out in mingled fear and pain when one of the horses—she didn't know which one—kicked her in the stomach. The animals were crazed with fear, squealing with alarm.

"Stay down!" Elelar shouted at the protective *shallaheen* trying to reach her, falling and careening on the unstable ground. *"Faradar!"*

The maid held up a hand to indicate she was conscious, but her arm shook as wildly as everything all around them.

Elelar put her head down. With her face buried in the dust and her hands covering her skull, she prayed for mercy, prayed for an end to the earthquake. She prayed that she wouldn't be trampled by her own horses, crushed by falling rocks, or swallowed by a sudden rent in the earth's skin.

She heard her gasping breath and feverishly muttered prayers before she heard the eerie silence. Then she heard her servants.

"Torena! Torena!"

"Faradar!"

"Get the horses!"

"You get them!"

"I'll help the *torena,* you get the horses!"

"No, I'll help the women, you get the—"

"Quiet!" Elelar snapped. *Shallaheen.* Any one of these men would face down six assassins; but they were all afraid of horses.

She lifted her head out of the dust, saw them all looking at her, and sighed. "I," she said, "will get the horses."

"*Torena!*"

"No! You will wait in the shade, *torena!*"

Now their honor was offended.

"I will get the horses," she repeated impatiently. "You will find water and replenish our waterskins."

Since any water they found was likely to be ensorcelled, this was a dangerous enough task to appeal to them.

Men.

Shaking violently, Faradar climbed awkwardly to her feet. "Would it be all right if *I* wait in the shade, *torena?*"

"An excellent idea," Elelar agreed, pleased to see that Faradar was uninjured. "I'll join you as soon as I've got the horses."

The animals were not far away, and their nerves were so agitated that Elelar was glad she hadn't sent jumpy men after them. She soothed them, made sure they weren't injured, and then led them back to where Faradar was waiting in the shade of a large fig tree.

"They'll need water, too," Faradar murmured.

Elelar nodded, now realizing she was very thirsty. It was a long time before the *shallaheen* returned, water having proven difficult to find. Tired as she was in the aftermath of her terror, she nonetheless insisted on leading the horses to the water source herself, letting two of the men guide her while two more stayed with Faradar.

The whole incident, which was becoming increasingly typical in Sileria these days, wound up eating their time and prevented them from reaching Elelar's estate until late the following day. By the time she finally got there, she was so sweaty, dirty, and unkempt, she was almost surprised her servants there recognized her.

She was even more surprised by the plump and vacuously pretty woman she found inhabiting her house. Her steward was under the cheerful delusion that this *torena,* whom Ronall had brought here, was a cousin of hers. Choosing to keep her problems as private as possible, Elelar didn't correct this impression, though she was annoyed at being greeted as "my dear cousin" by a total stranger.

Elelar dismissed Faradar, who looked ready to collapse, dealt with a few pressing matters, and then asked the woman—*Torena* Chasimar—to speak with her privately in the coolest salon in the house.

Torena Chasimar, who seemed slightly less intelligent than the horse which had kicked Elelar in the stomach yesterday— Darfire, it hurt now!—immediately burst into tears and commenced a long, incoherent, and bizarre explanation of how she had come to inhabit Elelar's private home. Along with her maid, Yenibar, who—it did not take much insight to figure out—had bedded Ronall. Probably more than once.

Probably in this very house, Elelar thought irritably.

Tansen's plans be damned. Elelar sincerely hoped her revolting husband was already dead and his carcass rotting somewhere in Sileria's driest hinterlands.

So this was *Toren* Porsall's half-Valdani wife. Elelar had heard of her. Indeed, Faradar had pretended to *be* her, with Zimran's help, when entering Shaljir last year to help Tansen free Elelar from the old Kintish fortress where she was being held prisoner. Elelar knew that Chasimar had once pretended to be an abduction victim so that her husband would pay Josarian a small fortune in much-needed gold to get her back. Elelar also remembered Tansen telling her that Chasimar was so enamored of Zimran that the rebels had trouble convincing her to return to her husband once the ransom was paid.

Now, as Elelar found another handkerchief for the sobbing and astonishingly silly half-Valdani *torena,* she reflected sourly that Zimran had really had no discrimination and would, it was clear, sleep with just about anyone. Had Elelar ever been flattered by his devotion to her, she might be rather disappointed now. Fortunately, she had never cherished any illusions about her lusty and self-centered *shallah* lover.

Torena Chasimar continued pouring out her tale, increasingly agitated as she explained how Ronall had found her and Porsall at the mercy of vengeful *shallaheen* in the middle of the night.

"Wait," Elelar said. "Stop. Go back."

Chasimar sobbed and just kept babbling.

"No," Elelar said, "I don't think I heard you right. You're saying that Ronall—*Toren* Ronall . . . my husband . . . *Ronall* rescued you from a bloodthirsty mob of *shallaheen?*"

"Yes!" Chasimar wailed. Then she kept babbling, the facts of her near death and her husband's murder pouring from her lips in a mind-numbing torrent of unconnected details which were, to say the least, a trifle hard to follow.

"No," Elelar said again, "that doesn't make sense. Ronall, all by himself—"

"On a horse!" Chasimar sobbed.

"Yes, yes, on a horse . . . Stormed into a murderous mob of *shallaheen* and . . . rescued you?"

"Yes!"

"There must be some mistake," Elelar said with certainty. She described Ronall in detail. "Surely that wasn't the man who—"

"Yes!"

"Alone? By himself? *Voluntarily?*"

"Yes!" Chasimar howled.

"Just how drunk was he?" Elelar demanded.

"He wasn't drunk!"

"You needn't shout," Elelar assured her wearily.

"Well, I don't think he was drunk. Well, maybe a little drunk." Chasimar wailed even louder now. "I don't know! Does it matter? *I don't know!*"

"Calm down," Elelar insisted irritably. If anyone had a right to hysterics here, surely it was her.

"I'm sorry, *torena!*" Chasimar cried loudly enough to disturb the Otherworld. "I'm just so emotional these days! It's no doubt due to my condition!"

"Your condition?" Elelar's gaze suddenly dropped to the woman's round belly. "Fires of Dar. You're not plump. You're . . ."

"Expecting!" Chasimar bleated.

"Whose is it?"

"Porsall's!" Chasimar shrieked, looking a little offended.

"Just asking," Elelar replied, knowing full well that this woman had been no pillar of faithful devotion to her late husband.

Her late Valdani husband. Father of this mostly Valdani child.

"Oh, damn Ronall," Elelar hissed.

"Please don't throw us out of your home, *torena!*" Chasimar wept.

"He did this to me on purpose!"

She would kill him. She would find him herself and gut him like a Valdani tribute goat. She would haul his worthless carcass up to the rim of the volcano and throw him into the Fires, laughing while he burned. She would—

"Please, Elelar," Chasimar sobbed. "Where can I go? Where can my child go?"

A child, a child . . .

"Oh, no." Elelar felt sick with rage. Horrified at the implications. Even if she could eject this noisy, vapid woman from her house with a clear conscience—and, no, she probably couldn't—she knew she couldn't abandon Chasimar's unborn child to whatever fate awaited it without her protection.

Ronall had counted on that, knowing her better than she'd ever realized.

"I am a Silerian!" Chasimar's watery voice carried conviction. "I know no other land. No other people. I have no one and nothing on the mainland!"

Elelar sighed. Yes, Ronall finally had his revenge.

Oh, that filthy swine.

Who would have thought Ronall, of all people, capable of devising such a perfect punishment for her? Then again, who would have ever believed *Ronall* capable of the heroism which Chasimar described?

People just never stopped surprising you, and Elelar really hated that.

Chasimar sniffed noisily. "There is nothing for me in Valdania. I would be a stranger there, without family or property . . . I barely even speak Valdan!"

Knowing she had no choice, and bitterly hating Ronall for this, Elelar said, "Of course you can stay here, Chasimar. I invite you to stay until . . ."

Chasimar's stupid face looked forlorn and hopeful all at once. "Yes?"

"Until I can think of something better," Elelar promised. "Until we can find a permanent place for you."

"If Tansen could free the western districts from the Society and I could return to my mother's people . . ."

Elelar nodded vaguely, her head pounding by now. "Uh, yes, something like that." As Chasimar started babbling again, Elelar realized that she had never wanted Tansen's victory as dearly as she did at this very moment.

Damn Ronall.

She hoped he burned like the Fires for all eternity, wherever he was right now.

44

THE BEST WAY TO KILL TIME IS TO WORK IT TO
DEATH.

— Armian

Western Sileria,
The Year of Late Rains

"WHY ARE WE here, father?" Tansen asked Armian as they entered an impoverished mountain village suffering under the harsh yoke of Valdani rule. The dry season beat down with merciless heat on this bleak community.

"These people haven't paid their tribute to the Society," Armian replied. "To Kiloran."

Tansen knew what that meant. "But why are *we* here, father?"

They were accompanying three of Kiloran's assassins: bold young men who surely didn't need Armian's help to make thirsty *shallaheen* relinquish whatever they had that the Society wanted.

"Because I'm bored," Armian said with a shrug. "Sitting around Kiloran's camp just waiting for the rains to come. I'll get as fat as he is if I don't find something to amuse me." He added with a grin, "Even *you* might stop being so skinny if we don't get some exercise."

Tansen tried to control the unpleasant thing coiling inside him. "If you're bored, we could train more."

Armian looked pleased and clapped him on the back. "You never get tired of training, do you? Well, you're a natural. You'll be a great fighter, son."

"Then—"

"But training's pointless if you don't ever put it to good use in a real fight."

Tansen hedged, "I don't think I'm ready for a real f—"

"Not with another assassin," Armian agreed. "Not yet. But you can certainly take on a few scared *shallaheen*."

Tansen felt increasingly uneasy as he looked at the frightened faces peering at them as they walked through the humble village and approached its main square. The villagers knew why they had come. They knew what would happen now. There was only one way of doing things in Sileria. Tansen knew that. He had always known that.

Perhaps if someone talked to these people, explained . . .

No. That would be wasted breath, Tansen realized. They didn't need warnings. They had understood, from the moment they failed to pay tribute to the Society, what it would lead to. Whether their failure was due to defiance or merely terrible poverty didn't matter; they had disobeyed, and they were being punished. Kiloran had already made their wells as hard as crystal and their fountains as dry as dust. Now his assassins would ignore their pleas and excuses, and make them bleed. This was how it had always been here, and it would never change.

Now everyone in this village just waited to learn who in particular would suffer the most, and just how much it would hurt. A death, or merely a beating? One man, or more? The village headman, or his grown sons?

Tansen's stomach hurt. Shame crept through him. He willingly trained long hours in Kiloran's camp, alone as well as with Armian, but not so he could beat unarmed men pleading for mercy.

He had once dreamed of becoming an assassin and thereby escaping the helplessness and poverty which was a *shallah*'s birthright and destiny in Valdani-ruled Sileria; but he had been a naive child, he knew that now. He had not really understood what it meant to become one of them. Now that he was living among them and did understand, he found that he was sickened by them—yet also ashamed of being sickened by them. After all, the waterlords were the only great men among Silerians, and their assassins were the only warriors. Everyone admired them.

No . . . Everyone *feared* them. The way everyone feared Outlookers. The real difference was that everyone also despised Outlookers, whereas everyone respected the Society. It was . . . not Silerian to despise the waterlords and their assassins. It was not the way Tansen was supposed to feel. Not the way he had always felt until now.

Worst of all, his confused feelings were disloyal. Armian was an assassin, after all, and he intended to become Kiloran's heir. And Armian was not only a great man, a legendary figure, and the Firebringer, but also Tansen's own father.

Help me, Dar. What is wrong with me?

Tansen prayed often to Dar lately, seeking Her wisdom, begging for Her guidance. She didn't answer, though, and he had no one else in whom to confide; so he was too alone with his own thoughts. Somewhere deep inside, he felt that the way they all lived in Sileria, the only way any of them knew, was wrong. Within his soul, a voice he couldn't seem to share coherently with his bloodfather told him that a real hero would stop what was about to happen here today, rather than participate in it.

This village—so poor, so bereft of hope—reminded him of Gamalan, and of all he had lost there. What would his grandfather think of him now, he wondered? Was there a woman in this village whose life was as hard and grief-burdened as his mother's? Had any of these women's sons run off to join the mad *zanareen* at the fiery peak of Mount Darshon, only to die in agony there as Tan's brother had? Was there a girl here who would one day die the way his sister had? The memory of that still made him shudder with horror and hatred.

Had the Gamalani, on that terrible day, watched the Outlookers enter the village the way these people here now watched him?

"Tansen?"

Startled, he glanced up at Armian, suddenly realizing he'd made a strange sound as these ugly thoughts flowed through him.

Armian frowned at him. "Are you all right?"

"I . . . I was thinking about Gamalan," he admitted.

Armian stopped walking and looked around them, aware of the scrutiny they were under from hundreds of eyes. "This is not the moment to remember that."

Tansen stopped, too. "I can't help it."

Armian took him by the shoulders. "Concentrate," he said quietly. "This is work, and there is no time for grief or sorrow when you're working."

Something inside Tansen rebelled. "This is not work, father. This is Kiloran's bidding."

Armian's gaze went hard and cold. "I don't do anyone's bid—"

"Hurting and frightening some helpless peasants because Kiloran wants it done and you're bored," Tansen said through tight lips. His heart pounded so loudly he could scarcely hear his own voice. To speak to Armian this way! He couldn't even imagine where he found the audacity—and the sudden flare of fury in his father's expression made him deeply *regret* finding it.

"That's enough." Armian's voice could have frozen water.

"Let's leave," Tansen urged suddenly. "You're the Fire-bringer, you should not be part of—"

"Shut up," his father snapped.

The other assassins, who were now ahead of them, stopped and turned back to look at them. One of them prodded, *"Siran?"* They didn't know Armian's real identity, but they knew he held a position of great favor with their master.

Armian replied tersely, "Get on with it. We'll be with you in a moment."

"No," Tansen said, willing himself not to give in, despite his father's furious expression. "This isn't right."

"Come with me," Armian commanded in a hard tone which forbade further dissent. *"Now."*

Tansen glanced uneasily at the other assassins, who were watching the two of them with undisguised interest. "Father, why must you—"

"Keep your mouth shut," Armian ordered, "and just do as I tell—"

"No," Tansen repeated. "Let them do it without you, father. Don't be part of this."

Armian's face was dark with frustrated anger. "This is the last time I'm telling you," he warned.

So scared that he was surprised he wasn't shaking, Tansen stood his ground and held his father's gaze.

"Are you coming?" Armian ground out the words.

Tansen's throat was so tight he couldn't speak, so he just shook his head.

For a moment, he thought Armian would strike him. He knew he deserved it. He had never even defied his grandfather to this extent, and his grandfather was neither an assassin nor the Firebringer.

Instead, Armian turned and stormed away in silence, shoving past the other assassins, his violence barely controlled. As Tansen watched them hurry to follow his father, his breath started coming in hard little pants, and he felt a humiliating impulse to weep. He stood there alone, ignoring the curious stares of the villagers, and tried to compose himself.

He didn't want to be a bad son. He felt an urge to run after his father and tell him so. He wanted Armian to understand that he would never defy him like this if it weren't so important to him; if there were any other way.

Confused and heartsick, he wished Armian would turn back, but he knew he wouldn't. What was about to happen in the village square wasn't just work to Armian; he enjoyed it. Tansen knew that by now. Armian truly relished threatening, beating, and even killing strangers, acquaintances, and enemies. Armian's blood sang most ecstatically when he inspired fear and exacted revenge. He was so gifted and generous in some ways, yet so terrifying in others. Not that Tansen feared for himself. No, Armian was a tolerant father, even an indulgent one. And Tansen wanted to make him proud; but not by doing things that felt shameful.

Father, father . . .

In the end, Tansen couldn't stay away from the main square, even though he had refused to accompany Armian there. He had to know what was happening. So he crept towards the square and, keeping to the shadows, watched Armian and the three assassins brutalize the village headman, his two grown sons, and an old man who got in the way. One of the assassins killed one of the sons. When the mother screamed and wailed in mourning, Tansen blinked away the appalled tears that came to his eyes.

Still unsatisfied, Armian suddenly began beating someone else in the crowd. Even after the villagers started bringing forth everything of value that they owned, including the only food they had, Armian would not be appeased. As he condemned a stranger to the deadly violence he had chosen not to inflict upon his defiant son, he seemed to exult in the blood and the screams and the fear.

Tansen felt sick with guilt, aware that the villagers were paying for his disobedience as well as their own. He wished Armian would have just beaten *him*. This was so much worse. It was not even intended as a lesson, he realized; Armian didn't know he was watching. Armian thought so little of *shallah* lives that he probably wouldn't ever mention to Tansen that today, even after the villagers offered him everything they had, he nonetheless beat a man to death because of the violent rage his own son's defiance had provoked in him.

There *was* a lesson here today, however, though it was not one of Armian's choosing: Now Tansen knew that he must treat his father very carefully indeed, lest others again suffer and die for his mistakes.

Help me, Dar, he begged. *He is Your Chosen One, the Firebringer. Help me, and I promise I will bring him to You.*

But the destroyer goddess did not answer his prayers. Not then, not later. Not at all.

"WELL, WELL," THE young *torena* said to Tansen that evening in Kiloran's tented camp. "I heard about what happened."

Tansen, who was brooding in solitary silence well away from the rest of Kiloran's entourage, spoke words he had never imagined uttering to the beautiful young woman who held his heart captive: "Go away."

"You have the manners of a peasant," *Torena* Elelar informed him. "But I suppose that's to be expected."

He turned his back on her and muttered, "Leave me alone."

"I brought you something to eat," she said enticingly. When he ignored her, she added, "Tansen, are you completely unaware of how utterly extraordinary it is for a *torena* to serve a *shallah?* This is a unique moment."

He finally looked at her. Now his shame was complete, he acknowledged. "Did you come to ridicule me?"

She blinked. "For standing up to Armian? For refusing to help him beat to death a few unarmed *shallaheen?*"

His face felt hot. "He told you?"

"No." She put down the food tray she carried, and sat down on an immense fallen log. Under her elegantly booted feet, the withered foliage of the land crinkled noisily in the moisture-stealing air of the dry season. "But people talk. Even assassins talk. And I'm very good at listening. Well," she amended, "at eavesdropping, in this case."

He couldn't meet her gaze. "They're talking about me?"

"Of course they're talking about you!" She sounded amused. "What did you expect? They don't know who he is—your bloodfather, I mean—but I doubt one of *them* would defy him and stand their ground. He's not the sort of man that other men are willing to annoy."

"He must be very ashamed of me," Tansen said heavily.

"So what?"

His gaze now flashed up to her lovely face. "He's my father! He's a great warrior! He's . . ." He lowered his voice and continued, "He's the Firebringer. How can you say 'so wh—' "

"You really believe that?"

"What?"

"That he's . . ." She looked around first, then whispered, "The Firebringer."

"Of course!" He blinked, stunned at her implication. "Don't you?"

"No. But I suppose many of the *shallaheen* believe it?"

"Yes!"

"I see."

He said incredulously, "You don't believe—"

"In any event," she interrupted, shrugging off his enormous conviction with careless ease, "I certainly didn't come over here to ridicule you for not participating in yet another Society bloodbath in some starving mountain village."

Surprised, he stared at her in wary silence.

She saw his expression and said, "You surely didn't suppose I approved of that kind of thing?"

"You are Kiloran's ally," he said bluntly. "You and your grandfather, *Toren* Gaborian."

"Of course," she replied. "After all, they're the strongest faction in Sileria. We can't defeat the Valdani without them. And defeating the Valdani is the most important thing. They are the only enemies that matter."

He repeated her words in his mind, then said, "Are you saying the Society are enemies that *don't* matter?" It made no sense to him.

"Well, I suppose I wouldn't go so far as to say they don't matter," she admitted, "but they are part of Sileria, whereas the Valdani are foreign invaders who must be forced to leave Sileria. No matter what the cost. No matter whom we must ally ourselves with to accomplish that."

"But enemies? How can you say that? The Society—"

"—are certainly enemies of the *toreni*," she said. "The abductions, the ransom demands, the murders."

He was confused again. Something sly and traitorous inside him welcomed the implication in her words, but he protested, "The Society are not *our* enemies. The *shallaheen*, I mean. They give us justice and exact vengeance for us wh—"

"Oh, for the love of Dar," she said, "you can't really be that stupid, Tansen. At least, I didn't think so. If you really believe that Armian's brawl in that village today was about justice, then why did you refuse to participate? Why did you—if the assassins' gossip is accurate—even try to convince him to turn back?"

"It was . . . If the villagers couldn't . . ." Feelings welled up inside him for which he had no words. He was too inarticulate to organize and explain his feelings the way she and Armian did with such evident ease. And he felt too guilty about his most secret thoughts—vague ideas that no one should have—to even search hard for the right words for them. "There was . . . I'm not a good . . . I don't know," he finished lamely, his face burning and his stomach churning.

Her expression was serious and intense as she leaned forward and said, "Because you know—you must surely know—that the Society, in their way, are as bad as the Valdani. The assassins are as bad as the Outlookers."

"No!" He rose to leave, sure he shouldn't listen to this.

"Who starves the cities of water when tribute doesn't arrive on time or isn't deemed generous enough? Who rules the mountains through terror and violence? Who controls the *toreni* with abduction and robbery?"

"No, these are . . . You're . . ." He should walk away. He was sure he should. But he was listening. And she knew it.

"Who destroyed Sileria's last Yahrdan and subjected us to centuries of slavery?"

"The last . . ." He looked at the ground, searching for a response, almost deafened by the roaring of his blood. He couldn't read the histories of his people, but he knew songs and stories of his nation's past. Everyone did. Marjan, the first waterlord and founder of the Honored Society, had quarreled with Daurion, the last Yahrdan, and destroyed him. "It happened because the Society was stronger and . . . and should rule . . . They have always been stronger."

"It happened because a water wizard murdered the rightful ruler of this land, started a chaotic civil war, and made us vulnerable to the Conquest a thousand years ago." She studied his confused expression. "Does *any* of this sound familiar?"

He scowled silently and endured the insult about his ignorance. He wouldn't walk away now. He knew it, and so did she. She was making him hungry in a new way now. His hopeless longing for her touch, her regard, was almost smothered by his sudden craving to understand what she was talking about. To know the things she knew.

"Tansen." She shook her head, and her expression was a mixture of pity and exasperation. "Who has already killed more *shallaheen* than the Valdani ever will?"

"You're wrong," he said. "You must be wrong. If you're not wrong . . ." If she wasn't wrong, if he believed her . . . then his most secret thoughts might break free and consume him.

"They're not warrior kings or outlaw heroes, Tansen, and you seem smart enough to understand that. Isn't that why you stood up to Armian today?"

He looked away. "I don't know why I did that."

"They're thieves and killers. Opportunists. They prey on the rest of us. Make us victims. Slaves." She sighed. "Has any waterlord ever once used his power to help Sileria instead of hurt it? To shield us rather than brutalize us? Has there been even one waterlord in all of history who has given rather than taken, and made us stronger rather than weaker?"

"I don't know," he admitted. He knew nothing.

"Not one, Tan," she said. "Not even one."

"Yet here you are, for the Alliance. In Kiloran's camp. Plotting with the Society."

"Can you think of any way to defeat the Valdani without them?"

"The Firebringer," he said hopefully.

Elelar rolled her eyes. *"Shallaheen."* She sighed and shook her head.

"Where are you going?" he asked as she rose to her feet. He suddenly had so many questions he wanted to ask her.

"Here comes your demigod."

"What?" He saw her looking past him. Realizing what she meant, he whirled to face his father, who was leaving Kiloran's tent and now coming towards him.

"You did the right thing today, Tansen," Elelar said quickly. "Don't back down now." With that unsettling comment, she retreated.

A chaotic tumble of guilt, shame, defiance, and distracted curiosity filled Tansen as he met his father's gaze and stood waiting for the harsh reprimand he knew he had earned today.

It was only when Armian got close that Tansen realized his father no longer looked angry. He just looked tired. And perhaps even a bit wary.

They stared at each other for a long, awkward moment.

Finally Armian said, far more calmly than Tansen expected, "You were thinking like them today. You must learn not to do that."

Tansen found himself nodding to please Armian. Silent protests rose in his mind, but he chose not to voice them. Not now. Another time, perhaps, when his thoughts were clearer. For now, he let Armian see the contrite son he wanted to see.

"If you want to be one of us," Armian said, "then you cannot be one of them."

Rather than agreeing, Tansen said politely, "You've told me that before."

"You and I have given a lot of attention to your physical training, and you've done very well. Not one in a thousand young men would progress as fast as you've been progressing."

"I have a great warrior for a teacher," Tansen said.

Armian smiled briefly. "But now I realize that I have not given enough thought to training your mind, too."

"So that I will stop thinking like them," Tansen said, beginning to understand what Armian intended. What Armian wanted.

"Yes." Armian shrugged. "I hadn't realized it would be necessary. But now I see that it is."

Tansen kept his glance from flickering towards Kiloran's tent, but he could guess who had suggested this idea to his father. He began to realize that Kiloran's attention could be a dangerous thing, so he silently vowed that he would not give the old waterlord any more reasons to think about him after today.

Aware that a response was now needed, he said what Armian wanted to hear. "I'm sorry, father."

"I'm sure it's just your youth." Armian paused before continuing, "It's rare that someone who isn't raised to be an assassin comes to this life when he's as young as you are, Tansen. And you've come here so unexpectedly. You didn't set out to make a first kill and seek a waterlord's attention. You've simply . . . wound up here. With me."

Now Tansen saw Armian's hesitation, his uncertainty. So he said, "This is my life now, father."

Evidently relieved by this answer, Armian said, "Yes. And you must embrace it. I'm here to help you. I will always be here for you. But you must leave your old ways of thinking behind. You're not some peasant boy, anymore, Tan. Your destiny is now a great one, and you must prepare for it."

Tansen didn't want anyone else to suffer for his mistakes again. So he made sure he said exactly the right thing, despite the burgeoning truth in his heart which increasingly demanded he listen to its dictates. "I'll try harder, father."

Now Armian smiled. All worries put to rest, all wrongs forgiven. "I know you will, son. And I know you'll do well."

As THEY WAITED for the dry season to end, for the rains to come, for the moment to arrive when Armian could make contact with the Moorlanders, Tansen continued his training, tried to be a dutiful son, and did his best to evade Kiloran's shrewd scrutiny.

His primary interest, however, became learning things which *Torena* Elelar seemed only too willing to teach him. There was a strange, awkward pleasure in the time he spent with her, since his hopeless passion for her remained undiminished. Guilt, however, was probably his most overwhelming emotion during these unchaperoned discussions, as he listened to her castigate the assassins, condemn the practices of the waterlords, and blame the Society for many of Sileria's woes.

Yes, he felt guilty that he listened. He felt even more guilty because he agreed. Soon, new beliefs sprouted and took root in his heart as a result of the silent questioning and reasoning he continued in his head after these conversations were over.

"Kiloran has decided he likes Armian's plan," Elelar informed him one day as he walked beside her horse, still traveling as part of Kiloran's entourage through the mountains which the old waterlord, even more than the Valdani, ruled with such ruthless strength.

"I thought he liked the plan all along," Tan replied.

"He's a cautious man. Shrewd. Suspicious. He had many questions, many concerns. But finally . . . Finally he has become very enthusiastic."

"So . . . We will rebel. With the help of the Moorlanders."

"We'll fight the Valdani." Though she spoke softly, her voice was exultant. "At last, we will fight them."

"And the Society?" he asked.

She frowned at him from atop her horse. "They'll fight, too, obviously."

"I mean . . ." Actually, he wasn't sure what he meant. So he looked away and said nothing.

She scarcely seemed to notice. She was wrapped up in dreams of glory. Dreams of killing Valdani.

How she hated them, he thought absently. He sometimes wondered how she restrained herself from spitting on them in the streets, so much did she hate anyone with even a drop of Valdani blood.

TANSEN WAS PICKING at his food one evening in Kiloran's tent, his stomach roiling as he listened to the old wizard's conversation with Armian. According to Armian, Kiloran meant to honor Tansen by including him in this private meal. Kiloran was treating him as an adult, as a loyal servant.

Armian had not taken Tansen on any more disciplinary excursions into *shallah* villages, and Tan didn't suppose for a moment that either of the men had forgotten about his behavior that day. But he had been obedient, hard-working, and respectful ever since then, and he knew they were pleased with him. He just hoped they weren't pleased enough to suggest it was finally time for him to go murder some helpless peasant.

"Aren't you hungry?" Kiloran asked him.

"I'm sorry to waste such fine food, *siran*. I think the almond milk I drank this morning was starting to spoil," Tansen lied, forcing warmth into his voice lest either man guess how much he disliked even being in the old wizard's presence. "My stomach doesn't feel right."

"You're just like Srijan." Kiloran smiled indulgently. "Ah, boys. Always so greedy!" He shook a forefinger at Tansen. "You should have stopped drinking if you thought it tasted a little off."

Tansen sincerely hoped he wasn't remotely like Kiloran's revolting son. Srijan was spoiled, rude, stupid, and thoroughly obnoxious. Now Armian, who had privately agreed with Tansen about Srijan, flashed Tansen a brief, amused glance, probably guessing what it cost him not to blurt out a protest at being compared to Kiloran's son in any way.

Tansen meekly accepted Kiloran's friendly rebuke and pushed his plate away, relieved he didn't have to keep pretending to eat. Food lodged in his throat tonight as he listened to his father make plans with Kiloran.

"The Moorlanders' support must be for us," Kiloran advised Armian. "Not the Alliance. Not the *toreni*."

"And certainly," Armian added with a knowing grin, "not the Guardians."

"The Guardians are our problem, as they have always been, and we will deal with them," Kiloran replied. "After we deal with the Valdani."

Armian caught Tansen's gaze and said, by way of instruction, "One enemy at a time. That's the way to win."

"Indeed." Kiloran said to Tansen, "Listen to your father."

"Always, *siran*," Tansen responded instantly.

Kiloran smiled at Armian. "He's a good boy."

Armian glanced at Tansen, his expression fond. "Yes, he is, *siran*."

"Mistakes are so easily made," Kiloran said to Tansen.

"Yes, *siran*," Tansen said, knowing that the old man was referring to the day he had defied Armian.

"Learn from your mistakes, correct yourself, and move on. Can you do that?"

His stomach churning with dread, Tansen replied, "Yes, I can, *siran*."

Kiloran nodded, satisfied. Then, after a servant took away the empty plates and the remaining food, he said to Armian, "If the Moorlanders are right, if we can indeed force the Valdani to withdraw from Sileria by working together, then our primary concern is to be in a position of strength when that happens, rather than finding ourselves depleted by the effort."

Armian nodded. "So we want the *toreni* and merchants to bear the cost—"

"And the *shallaheen* and lowlanders," Kiloran added, "to bear the loss of life."

"So the Society," Tansen said slowly, "will be strong when this is all over."

Armian looked pleased he had been bold enough to contribute to the conversation. "The strongest."

"In power," Tansen said.

Armian smiled. "Completely."

"And you, *siran* . . . ," Tansen said to Kiloran.

Kiloran looked exhilarated. "I will rule Sileria." They all considered this in silence for a moment. Then Kiloran placed a hand on Armian's shoulder and added, "And now I have an heir."

"I would not dream," Armian said politely, "of usurping your son's place."

"Sadly, the boy has shown no talent for water magic. And only a waterlord can rule Sileria. Srijan could not survive if he tried to command the waterlords. But you . . . You show real promise."

Armian crossed his fists over his chest and bowed his head. "Then, *siran,* I am deeply honored."

Tansen knew he had to try again. "But, father, what about Mount Darshon?"

Armian laughed. Kiloran regarded father and son with interest.

"Tansen," Armian said, "if you want me to jump into that damned volcano, then you're going to have to drag me up to the rim and *push* me off."

TANSEN TRIED TO talk to Elelar about all this, but it was hard to find enough time alone with her, especially since Armian wanted more of his company lately. And when Tansen did get her alone, she couldn't seem to understand anything except the imagined victory she craved with obsessive passion. Sileria would drive out the Valdani conquerors, and Elelar was so excited she scarcely heard anything Tansen tried to say to her in his awkward, stumbling way.

This war, Tansen became convinced, wouldn't free Sileria for Silerian rule once the Valdani were defeated—if such a thing was even possible. No, if the Moorlanders' plan worked, then the Society would dominate Sileria when this was all over. And would that be any different from being ruled by the Valdani?

Who starves the cities of water?

Yes, he realized. It would be different—because it would be even worse. Who could overthrow the waterlords? No one. Who would ever drive *them* out of Sileria? Who would ever unite against them?

Sileria's fate would be hopeless.

Who rules the mountains through terror and violence?

The Society, led by Kiloran and Armian, would rule Sileria more harshly than the Valdani or any other conqueror ever had. Silerians would endure another thousand years of slavery, this time under the heaviest yoke of all.

Who has already killed more shallaheen *than the Valdani ever will?*

Why didn't Elelar see that there would be no freedom in Sileria if they went ahead with this plan?

As Tansen wrestled with his confusion and dread, the cruel heat of the dry season finally began to relent. The days grew softer, and cool winds from the north sweetened the nights. Distant thunder teased Sileria with the promise of relief, and Kiloran prepared to retreat to his hidden stronghold—wherever that was—as the season of his greatest power and influence drew to a close.

Then one evening, as darkness descended upon Kiloran's camp, something cold fell on Tansen's cheek. He brushed it away, and it happened again. He heard a sound, like softly rattling pebbles, and smelled a fulfilled promise perfuming the air . . . *Rain,* he realized, as it started coming down: the longed-for feel of the first drops of the long rains. This was a gentle beginning, a thick drizzle which would help prepare the thirst-hardened soil for the torrents that would follow as the season ripened and matured.

Rain, Tansen thought, letting it soak him as he stood under the open sky.

Rain. Sileria had run out of time.

"Tansen!"

He turned and saw Armian coming towards him, big and dark and powerful as he strode through the rich shower of life-giving water which fell upon them. Armian's black hair was wetly plastered to his head as he came forward with a pleased grin on his face.

"This is it," he said to Tansen.

Tansen nodded.

"We can leave for the coast tomorrow!"

"The Moorlanders will be expecting you," Tansen said.

Armian's grin broadened and he slapped Tansen on the back. "We can finally do something besides just talk!"

Yes, you and Kiloran can make all of Sileria do your bidding if we don't want to die of thirst. We will all be slaves forever now.

He thought he would be sick.

He had saved Armian's life that fateful night on the eastern shore. He had helped Armian make his way through Sileria so that he could find the Alliance, evade the Outlookers, and meet Kiloran.

If he succeeds now, it will be my fault. My responsibility.

"Not the coast, father," Tansen pleaded. "Darshon."

Too happy to be irritable, Armian laughed as if it was a joke, shook him hard, and tousled his wet hair.

Tansen tried to say it again, but his voice failed him.

Why bother? He already knew the truth. Armian would never go to Darshon. The Firebringer would never embrace Dar. He would, instead, fulfill his destiny without Her, driving out the Valdani with the Society's help rather than the goddess's. And then . . .

No. I have to stop them. I have to stop him.

"I have something for you," Armian announced. He reached into the top of his right boot and pulled out a beautifully made *yahr*. "Careful how you swing it," he warned. "It's made of petrified Kintish wood."

Tansen stared at it. "Like an assassin's *yahr*."

"It's from Kiloran. He thought I might like you to have it."

He willed his hand not to shake as he accepted it. "Thank you."

Tansen closed his fingers around the smooth, rock-hard wood of the weapon. He felt its power, felt the weight of what it could do.

· "Use it in good health," Armian said.

Tansen looked up at his bloodfather's rain-soaked countenance. "I will." .

Only one person in all of Sileria was completely trusted by both Kiloran and the Moorlanders. Only one person could unite them.

"Tan?"

Father, father . . .

"I, uh . . ." His heart pounded. He couldn't think of anything to say, so he repeated, "Thank you."

"You might want to thank Kiloran," Armian suggested. "He's honoring you."

"Well, I'm your son." His mind was whirling, his blood thundering wildly. He couldn't even believe what he was thinking.

"No, he's honoring *you*," Armian said gently. "He sees great potential in you, despite . . ." Armian shrugged. "You're still young, with much to learn, but he is interested in you."

He wanted to cry. He wanted to run away and pretend he knew nothing about any of this.

"Father, please, can't we . . ."

Don't do this, Armian. Don't make me do this.

"Tan . . ." Armian took him by the shoulders and studied his face. Mistaking the anguish he saw there, he said, "The old man was right: Learn from your mistakes and move on. Don't torment yourself about what happened that day. I'm not still angry at you. Neither is he."

"I'm sorry, father," said Tansen, not talking about that day. "I want you to know I'm so sorry."

"Don't worry about it," Armian replied. "The first kill is always the hardest. But you'll do it. I know you will."

Tansen nodded, sick at heart. "Yes. I will."

Dar help me. Dar shield me. Dar show me the way.

Dar did not answer, but it really didn't matter anymore. Tansen already knew what he must do. What he *would* do.

He was planning his first kill. And when it was done, he knew he could never pray to Dar again. So he prayed tonight, as he stared at his father in the life-giving rain, for the only thing he still wanted from the destroyer goddess: *Dar have mercy on Armian's soul.*

45

WHEN SOMEONE MAKES YOU PAY IN TEARS, YOU
MUST MAKE HIM PAY IN BLOOD.
— Silerian Proverb

"FATHER! DID YOU hear me?"

Tansen blinked in surprise, then swiftly focused his attention. "What?" he said to Zarien.

"You didn't hear me," Zarien concluded.

The sea-born boy frowned, studying him for a moment. Tansen suspected Zarien thought he was brooding about Mirabar. He chose not to correct the impression by explaining that, actually, he was remembering the father he had slaughtered in cold blood years ago.

Indeed, it was unsettling how often he thought of Armian lately, even while wide awake. Memories of his bloodfather came to him unbidden, unsought, unwanted . . . Maybe because, as he now tried to be a good father in his turn, he finally understood the enormity of the responsibility Armian had undertaken.

And so, after all these years of doing his best not to think about it, Tansen now let himself wonder what those final moments of Armian's life had been like, when he realized his own son meant to kill him.

. . . *Armian froze, like a statue, when he saw his son stand-*

ing above him on that windswept cliff, swinging his yahr *with deadly intent.*

If Tansen lived for all eternity, he would never forget the sound of Armian's voice as he said, "Tansen?"

Tansen felt a sudden, soul-deep pain so immense it blocked out everything else.

Father . . .

"Father!"

"Hmmm?"

"I *said* . . ." Zarien's voice, calling Tansen back to the present again, revealed the immense patience the boy felt he was exercising. "Give me your waterskin."

"Why?" Tansen asked absently.

"So I can use it to play a little tune."

Emelen, who was walking ahead of them, snorted with amusement. Tansen gave Zarien a bland glance.

"There's water over there," Zarien explained, nodding to some vague spot beyond a heat-cracked ridge in the mountain.

Emelen—who had recently come from Zilar, as ordered, to join them here in the mountains north of Adalian—glanced over his shoulder at Zarien. "How do you always know that?"

"Can't you smell it?" the boy replied.

Emelen sniffed the air. "No."

Zarien rolled his eyes. "Landfolk."

Tansen unslung his waterskin and handed it to the boy. "Be careful. That water you smell might be ensorcel—"

"I know, I know." Zarien was already turning away, youthfully heedless of the danger.

Tansen willed himself not to say more. Emelen, who had only been with them for a few days, had already mentioned that Zarien wasn't entirely wrong when he claimed Tansen could occasionally nag like an overbearing mother.

Emelen thrust his own waterskin under Zarien's nose and said, "You were, of course, about to offer to fill mine, too."

Zarien blinked innocently. "Of course."

Tansen turned and called out to the men and the Guardians

that they were stopping for a water break. He traveled with nearly fifty people today, which was more than Tansen usually liked to bring on raids against the Society. Too many people were too noticeable—hard to hide or to travel with stealthily. The Society were not the Valdani; someone in Sileria would always tell the Society about what they saw, what they knew, or what they heard. Today, however, it was worth the risk of being seen in such numbers; they planned to attack Ferolen's stronghold, north of Adalian, and he was too powerful a waterlord for them to defeat with smaller numbers. Fifty more people would meet them at a prearranged location tomorrow, and then they would all attack at nightfall.

Now, as Tansen watched Zarien disappear over the ridge, followed by others, Emelen said, "He's a good boy, Tansen."

"Yes, he is."

"But there's something about him . . ." When Tansen glanced at him, Emelen shrugged. "I don't know. He's different."

"There's no denying that," Tansen agreed reasonably.

After a moment, Emelen said, "He's too young for battle, Tan. In fact, he seems far from ready for any kind of fight."

"I know."

Zarien wasn't a natural; he didn't catch on quickly when they trained. Despite the boy's desire to please him, Tansen had also begun to realize that Zarien had no heart for combat. His mind often wandered when they trained. He certainly wasn't lazy, but he was always ready to quit training well before they really should.

"What'll you do with him when it's time to fight?" Emelen asked.

"What I usually do. Put him in a safe place during the battle." He added, "Ealian has agreed to protect him this time." The elderly Guardian, whom Tansen had first met in Zilar and who was here with them now, lacked the stamina needed for battle against waterlords; but he was still a skilled fire sorcerer, and Tansen trusted him to safeguard Zarien.

Emelen prodded, "Why drag Zarien all over Sileria with

you in such dangerous times? Wouldn't it be better to leave him somewhere?"

"Where would I leave him? With whom?" When Emelen didn't answer, Tansen said, "He likes to be with me."

"And you like him to be with you."

"He belongs with me."

"You seem very sure of that."

Tansen glanced at his friend in surprise. "You think otherwise?"

Emelen looked up at the ridge where Zarien had disappeared. "I don't know. Our way of life doesn't really seem to suit him well."

"He can't return to his clan. He doesn't—"

"I know. I don't mean to . . . Never mind." Emelen shrugged. "I'm probably just worrying about your family so I don't have to worry about mine."

"You'll see Jalilar soon," Tansen promised.

"And you may have to replace me then, since she's bound to kill me for tricking her and leaving her behind in Sanctuary the way I did."

"Yes, well, that's why I thought I'd come along," Tansen said dryly. "Say hello. Tell her about Josarian's final hours. Introduce her to my son. Prevent her from castrating you."

"Good idea," Emelen agreed faintly.

"Ah, here they come." Tansen saw a few men appearing on the rise, their now-bulging waterskins in hand. Zarien—walking more slowly than anyone else, of course—brought up the rear.

Watching the boy approach in the distance, Emelen asked, "Do you really mean to let this question of the sea king go unresolved?"

Tansen squinted in the harsh sunlight as he gazed at his remarkable son. "Oh, I don't think it will go unresolved."

Emelen glanced sharply at him. "You think you're the one?"

"Hmm? Oh. No." Tansen turned his back on the approach-

ing men and boy, and looked eastwards, towards the tumultuous whirl of colored clouds at the peak of Mount Darshon.
The magically healed *shir* wound which had nearly killed him
now seemed to throb momentarily with a cool fire as he
thought of what the Olvar had said about Zarien. "No, not me."

Tansen would rather his son always walk the dryland with
him, but if Zarien's fate was to be the sea king . . . Yes, if that
was indeed his future, then Tansen would do his best to prepare the boy for such an important destiny.

"WHERE HAVE YOU been?" Mirabar demanded of her husband, upon finding him conferring with an assassin in the
main hall of Belitar's gloomy castle. "I've been looking
everywhere for you."

He glanced at her, dismissed the assassin with a nod, and
turned away without acknowledging her, his attention captured by a letter he started reading.

"Baran," she persisted, following him into the shadowy
study where he kept books, papers, and a magically whirling
fountain of stunning beauty.

"Hmmm?" He took a seat without ever lifting his gaze from
the letter.

Mirabar didn't bother looking over his shoulder, since she
couldn't read. "Who is it from?"

He didn't seem to hear her, or maybe he was just ignoring
her. Either way, he was clearly very absorbed in the letter, and
his expression was increasingly intense as he continued reading it. She decided to wait until he was done before explaining
why she had been looking for him today.

Watching his face now, Mirabar couldn't tell whether he
was upset or amused. Both, perhaps. She still found Baran's
conflicting and volatile emotions bewildering and difficult to
discern. His sharp intelligence sometimes made her forget
that his madness was not just legend or pretense, and his wild
mood swings and bizarre behavior sometimes made her forget

that he was dangerously shrewd and seldom missed anything.

As a husband, he was exhausting. As an ally, he was unnerving. As a lover, he was . . .

"Not a father yet," she muttered.

He finished reading the letter and stared blankly at her. "Hmmm?"

"I'm not with child," she clarified, glad to have his attention at last for this news.

He glanced down at her lap, as if expecting to see proof of her claim staining the fine clothes he had insisted she acquire. She pressed her legs together, suddenly embarrassed.

"Oh." He turned away and stared out a window, his thoughts apparently still captured by the contents of the letter.

"You're taking my news well," she noted. There was no response, no acknowledgement that she had spoken. "Baran!"

He didn't look at her. "So we'll keep trying," he said without much interest.

She supposed it was a reasonable response, but she still felt annoyed. She was as ignorant of Belitar's secrets as she had been the day she first arrived here, and now the child Baran said he had been promised—*by whom?*—was not even on its way to soothe Mirabar's irritated nerves. Why was it that women who didn't want a baby became pregnant the moment they strayed from chastity, whereas Mirabar, who was completely committed to conceiving a child, had lain with her husband more than a dozen times with no results?

Looking to inflict her ill humor on someone, she said, "Let's hope we have *time* to keep trying."

"I'm not dead yet," he replied absently.

No, but he had awoken her two nights ago when he doubled up in bed with a sudden attack of excruciating pain which eventually led to him bringing up blood. The sight had terrified Mirabar, who now truly understood how imminent Baran's death was. She could not afford to be patient with him, lest he die with his secrets intact and her womb still empty.

She watched him as he now fingered the costly parchment of the missive which occupied his mind. "Who is it from?"

"Kiloran." He finally looked at her. "He knows."

Ah. "Well, we knew he'd find out fairly soon," she said, wondering at Baran's strange expression.

"Hmmm."

Realizing there was more, she prodded, "And?"

Baran's sudden smile was both bitter and amused. "He's impatient. He's trying to force my hand now, rather than waiting to see what I intend."

"What does he say?"

"He says we will commence holding back the Idalar River from Shaljir the day after tomorrow, at sundown, and he counts on my strength to help him swiftly bring the city under the Society's influence."

"What does he say about our marriage?"

"He congratulates me on such a shrewd plan for destroying you." Baran studied her with dark, brooding eyes. "He also says that others in the Society doubt my loyalty, now that Tansen has proclaimed my alliance with him."

"And?" she prodded.

"And if I will send your body to Kandahar, it would assuage any fears among the other waterlords that I have betrayed them all." His expression was unreadable as he added, "He concludes with a sort of peace offering."

Belitar seemed suddenly chillier to Mirabar. "What?"

"In exchange for requesting the corpse of my second wife as a trophy," Baran said slowly, "Kiloran has offered me the truth about what happened to my first wife."

Mirabar held his gaze, hoping that today was one of his saner days. "You already know the truth, don't you? He killed her."

Baran's eyes started to take on a wild glitter. "He says he didn't."

She kept her voice steady and reasonable. "So she killed herself, then."

"No."

Mirabar frowned. "Now, after all these years, he's claiming she's still alive?"

"Not exactly."

"What then?"

He looked down at the letter. "Kiloran says Alcinar escaped him, escaped Kandahar one day, all those years ago."

"He's lying. Surely she would have come to you?"

"He told her I was dead. She believed him."

Yes, Mirabar realized, Alcinar probably would have believed him. It must have shocked even Kiloran that he couldn't, in fact, manage to kill Baran. Besides, with their home abandoned, where would Alcinar even have looked for Baran after she escaped Kiloran?

"Do you believe he's telling the truth?" Mirabar asked.

His face took on the tormented expression it bore whenever he thought of his wife's tragedy. "I don't know."

Mirabar saw the struggle going on inside him. Oh, Kiloran was very shrewd. He knew that if Baran had decided to betray the Society, then the enmity of the waterlords wouldn't frighten him or change his mind. But the faint possibility of finding Alcinar after all these years? Oh, yes, that was a promise which might sway Baran, bring him under control . . . and even convince him to sacrifice his unloved new wife.

Mirabar would not show fear. "Does Kiloran offer any proof?"

"Only if I give him your dead body."

She would *not* show fear. "He's lying," she repeated.

Their gazes locked. She saw the relentless obsession which had made Baran what he was. Saw the ruthlessness which had led him to become one of the most powerful and feared waterlords who had ever lived.

"After all these years," Mirabar said, keeping her voice even, "will you let him make a fool of you now?"

Baran laughed, a disturbingly cold sound. "After all these years, I finally have something else he wants so much it has driven him to desperation once again."

"Me." She felt Belitar's damp chill all the way through her vitals.

"I wonder if it's true," he murmured.

"He's not desperate, he's clever," Mirabar snapped.

"Alcinar had seen enough of my sorcery to have at least some knowledge of how water magic worked. If an ordinary person could spot a weakness at Kandahar and escape that place . . . yes, it would have been her."

"Or perhaps Kiloran killed her the very first time he raped her," Mirabar said harshly, "and is just smart enough to know how to get you to do exactly as he wants, despite having murdered your wife."

"At moments like this," Baran said, "I absolutely cannot fathom what Tansen sees in you."

"At moments like this," she replied, "I am certain your wife didn't love you for your mind."

"You're *afraid*," he guessed, clearly enjoying the realization.

"Oh, for the love of Dar, will you pull yourself together and *think?* What proof could Kiloran possibly offer? Alcinar's footprints leading away from Kandahar, miraculously preserved in the mud for fifteen years? A witness to her fate, someone whom Kiloran can convince you he didn't threaten or bribe? A letter from Alcinar saying, 'Please tell Baran I escaped and am—' "

"She couldn't write."

"What proof?" Mirabar persisted. "If she's been alive all these years, she would surely have heard of you and let you know *she* was alive. Everyone in Sileria has heard of you!"

He rose to his feet and went to stand by the window, looking out across his enchanted moat. "Who knows what she would have done?" His voice was bleak. "Kiloran captured her, told her I was dead, and did Dar-only-knows-what to her. Maybe she died after she left Kandahar—"

"*If* she left. If he's not lying."

"Or maybe she's still alive," he continued, "but her mind was so disordered by what happened to her that she wasn't even capable of hearing my name, let alone recognizing it, as my reputation grew over the years."

"You can't trust Kiloran," Mirabar said.

"Considering his request, your views on this may be somewhat biased," Baran pointed out dryly.

"And yours aren't?" she demanded. "You, who destroyed your whole life—and so many other lives—because of one sole tragedy in your past?"

He glared at her, his dark eyes coldly angry. "It was not just any tragedy."

"Oh, yes it was!" She rose to her feet and crossed the room to confront him face-to-face. "You were betrayed by someone you trusted. So what? Could Dar Herself count how many people in Sileria, including the Firebringer himself, could say the same thing? And *you* were fool enough to trust Kiloran, a waterlord who had killed hundreds even before you ever met him!"

The water in the room's elegant fountain started hissing angrily as Mirabar recklessly tried her husband's temper.

She ignored this warning and continued, "So your wife died horribly. Well, the tears of men whose wives have died horribly in this country could fill every river and lake to a surfeit and still keep coming." Mirabar blocked Baran's path as he tried to escape her torrent of angry words. "You were widowed young and grieved hard for a love you could never replace. Well, that was Josarian's fate, too! And Basimar's! And who knows how many others?"

"They did not love—"

"The way you did?" she demanded scathingly. "You will never convince me that you loved more than Josarian did, Baran. Only that you lacked the strength to go on, as he did, after your wife died. Only that you are nowhere near the man that Josarian was, the man that thousands of others have had to be after losing a loved one!"

"Josarian's wife died in childbirth," he growled. "Mine was taken—"

"I know. I realize that. Alcinar's fate was dreadful." She shook her head. "But Tansen's whole family was slaughtered by Outlookers. Their deaths were so hideous they still haunt his dreams. Yet he did not let such a tragedy make him demented and weak, as you did."

"It will be a *pleasure* to give your corpse to Kiloran," Baran snarled, his expression dark with rage.

"Even Tansen's son, just a boy, bears his grief better than you ever h—"

"Tansen doesn't have a . . ." He blinked and suddenly laughed, his mood going through one of those unnervingly fast shifts. "Well, well, Mirabar. Who bore a son to the man you want for yourself?"

"Zarien is his bloodson," she ground out.

"Ah . . . A recent addition to Tansen's bloodline, I gather? I haven't heard about this happy event."

"Your informants must be failing you."

"Well, to be truthful, I haven't been following Tansen's activities for some time," he confided. "It did not, after all, take any great insight to realize what he would do after Josarian died."

"You have extraordinary gifts, Baran," Mirabar said coldly, detesting him at this moment. "You're also intelligent and educated. You could have been anything, made anything of your life." She let her disgust show plainly in her expression as she concluded, "And you became *this*."

"I became what I had to in order to defeat Kiloran."

"No, you—"

"Even you need me to defeat him," he reminded her. "You can't do it without me, so your self-righteousness does not shame me as you'd like, my dear."

She knew she was wasting her breath on him. She suddenly felt very weary. "You didn't have to become the way you are, Baran. You had other choices."

"Did I?" He smiled whimsically. "Perhaps I did. But I swear to you, I don't remember them."

She glanced at the letter, recalling what had started this argument. "What are you going to do?"

He put his hand under her chin and tilted her face up, smiling nastily as he studied her expression. "Am I going to kill you, do you mean?"

"You can certainly die trying," she replied, tempted to immolate him on the spot . . . if she could. She wasn't sure. He was still very powerful, despite his illness.

"I admit it's tempting," he said, "especially when you're at your least charming." His mood changed again and he turned away from her. "But Kiloran has, once again, misjudged me." Baran glanced over his shoulder at her, his expression more malevolent than she had ever seen it. "Might I have found my wife, all those years ago, if he hadn't convinced me she was dead beneath the surface of Lake Kandahar? Would I have grieved myself insane if I'd had hope, if I'd been able to search for her?"

"You do believe him," Mirabar breathed, surprised by the way it refreshed his hatred for Kiloran.

"Actually, I don't know if I do," he admitted, sounding momentarily stable. "And his attempt to manipulate and distract me this way would amuse me if he had chosen any tool other than Alcinar to use against me now."

She was relieved to realize that, however much Kiloran's letter had overset him, Baran's shrewd intelligence was now taking over. He understood Kiloran's ploy and wouldn't succumb, no matter how tempted he might be in his darker moments.

"Even if he's telling the truth," Mirabar said, attempting to bridge the rift of today's quarrel, "he can't give her back to you. You know that."

Now he looked sad. "No. And even if he could, he wouldn't. Kiloran does not give back what he has taken away."

"Do you think she might still be alive?"

"Now there's a vicious question," he said wearily. "Would I rather she have died years ago, as I've always believed? Or do I want her to be alive now, but so changed that she's never tried to reach me . . . or so damaged that she's never been able to?"

Mirabar approached him and placed her hand on his necklace. "Let me Call her."

He flinched with surprise. Then he considered the idea with wary interest. "But don't you have to Call the dead at the right time of year?"

"Yes," she admitted. "The Otherworld revolves in harmony with this one."

"If she is dead," he said, "then I have no idea when she died."

"I'll try often, then," she offered.

"Here?" he asked doubtfully. "At Belitar? Can you?"

"I have been looking for my teacher in the flames while I've been here," she admitted.

"The one Kiloran took?"

"Yes. Tashinar is—was—very powerful, and if she makes her way to the Otherworld, I think . . . I believe I will feel it in the fire when I look for her there." She held out her hand. "I can look for Alcinar, too. Someday, she may be there, and then we'll know."

He touched the necklace. His mouth quivered briefly, and then he reached behind his neck to unclasp it. Handling the thing more tenderly than he had ever touched Mirabar, he gave it to her, unable to take his eyes off it even as she turned away.

"Wait," he said as she headed for the door.

"What?"

"In two days, Kiloran will wait for me to help him stop the Idalar River from flowing to Shaljir. When I don't—"

"He'll know you have indeed betrayed him."

"And he may put a great deal of effort into trying to do it without me."

"So? You've prevented him for years from completely controlling the Idalar."

"Still, it won't be easy. Especially not if he chooses someone to help him."

"Who would he trust?"

"He has an assassin, Dyshon, whom he's been teaching."

"How do you know?"

He smiled. "I *do* still spy on Kiloran, my dear."

"Oh." She frowned. "Is Dyshon strong enough to help him?"

"Quite possibly." He shrugged. "It would probably be sensible of me to kill Dyshon before he adds to my problems. Even after I do, though, and whether or not Kiloran decides to trust someone else . . ." Baran sighed and admitted, "I'm getting weaker now. Almost every day." He nodded. "I'll need help."

"Who can help you?" she asked worriedly. "Who can *you* trust?"

He grinned at her expression. "My teacher."

"You said Kiloran was your teacher."

"He was only my first teacher."

"Who was the next one?"

"Ah, *sirana*." His expression was impossible to interpret. "I think it may be time to introduce you."

She suddenly realized. A dark flash of instinctive fear swept through her. "Your teacher is *here*. Somewhere in Belitar. That's what I've been feeling ever since I arrived!"

"You have proven—sometimes with pleasing enthusiasm—your sincere commitment to getting this child with me."

She ignored his suggestive smile and asked, "What does that have to do with . . ." Her eyes widened. "Are you telling me that your teacher is the one who told you . . ."

"A child of water. A child of fire." His expression was dreamy. "A woman with eyes of fire who would be . . . Well, not my final love," he admitted dryly. "Shall we say, my final mate."

She studied him suspiciously. "I've never heard of a waterlord uttering prophecy."

His dark eyes danced with delight at her surprise when he said, "My teacher is not a waterlord."

"Then what is your teacher?" she demanded.

"Have you ever heard, *sirana,*" he asked silkily, "of the Beyah-Olvari?"

THEY KNEW MIRABAR was at Belitar. Baran had warned them. He had promised them, as they desired, that he would eventually share the secrets of Belitar's ancient subterranean caverns with her, and bring her down here to meet them.

Even so, they chanted and gibbered with nervous fear upon meeting her, being timid creatures who were easily unsettled. Accustomed to them after all these years, Baran watched impassively as the Beyah-Olvari got acquainted with his wife.

No one could deny Mirabar's courage, though Baran thought her intense curiosity was probably a little unwise. She was so eager to discover and understand Belitar's secrets that she had readily come down here with him today, even though he suspected she half-feared he was bringing her to these dark, damp, underground caves beneath the ancient foundations of his castle to kill her.

True, there was a rather surprising affinity between them in their marriage bed; Baran wasn't dead yet, nor completely lost to the simple pleasures of life, and Mirabar had turned out to be a woman of healthy human appetites, despite her Otherworldly visions and spiritual vocation. Nonetheless, Baran knew that Mirabar feared him—and that was just sensible of her, he acknowledged. After all, today he had indeed contemplated sending her corpse to Kiloran in exchange for the truth about Alcinar. Yes, he was that ruthless, that utterly lacking in honor. He would break every promise and betray every ally, if it was what he had to do to get what he wanted. That was who he was; that was what he had made of himself. She'd be a fool to ever doubt it or forget it; and Mirabar was no fool.

Tansen wouldn't love a fool.

Oh, yes, the day Baran married Mirabar, he had seen the unruly passion and heartsick longing in the *shatai*'s eyes. Even Baran, who scarcely knew him, could see that giving up this woman was one of the hardest things Tansen had ever done, so hard it made him briefly rash and heedless, like lesser men. He had even come within a hairsbreadth of attacking Baran, something he must surely know he would never survive. And right there, on Sanctuary grounds, too! Unthinkable. No one did that. *No one.* Least of all a smart, coolheaded, focused man like Tansen.

But thwarted love, as Baran well knew, was a wild madness that robbed even the shrewdest men of their reason. And for a moment, Tansen's famously unreadable face had been hot with hatred, possessive jealousy, and bloodlust.

If Baran were anything less than what he was, he'd never have married Mirabar once he realized that Tansen wanted her. However, Baran could protect himself even from Tansen, and he certainly wasn't going to let the *shatai*'s wishes interfere with his plans. He only wondered how Mirabar had managed to convince Tansen to go along with the marriage. He even felt a brief moment of pity for her; it must have been hard for her, since she clearly wanted what Tansen wanted.

Whatever secret sorrow might eat Mirabar's heart when she thought of Tansen, though, she did her best to keep it hidden from Baran. She was an admirable woman in many ways, and Baran might even have felt a little sorry about slaughtering her at Kiloran's behest. He'd have done it, though, to get what he wanted.

But what Baran wanted most was vengeance. Destroying Kiloran or, if he failed, giving Mirabar the child which would fulfill their mutual destiny . . . After a brief struggle today, Baran had reaffirmed what he most wanted. And Mirabar, the child, even Tansen—they could help him achieve his goal.

Whereas Kiloran could only dangle empty promises in the

twisted maze of his deadly schemes. Baran knew that. Whatever had happened to Alcinar—the pain in his heart caught fire again as he thought of her—nothing would bring her back now. Oh, Kiloran was clever. It was true that Baran had been tempted, so tempted for a moment. But he was not a weak-minded acolyte like Meriten, or a sulking fool like Dulien, or a hot-headed idiot like Abidan and Liadon had both been. Baran had never let Kiloran manipulate him like all the others, no matter how skillful the attempt, and he wasn't going to start now.

His insides burning with the pain which was now rarely absent, Baran smiled faintly as he imagined what Kiloran's face would look like if he ever found out about the Beyah-Olvari. Sometimes the image was so amusing, Baran was tempted to reveal what might well be the best-kept secret in all of Sileria. However, that would be a betrayal which was beneath even his undeniably low nature.

Baran's teacher, the Olvara, was a wizened female who had been old even when Harlon, Baran's predecessor, had come here as a young man more than sixty years ago. Her pale blue skin was mottled like a lizard's, and it was as dark as indigo dye in the deepest wrinkles and crevices of her heavily lined face. Her tiny, almost-translucent fingers constantly wove in and out of a gentle flow of water which spilled down the rockface, flowing from Belitar's moat in a shimmering sheet which crossed the floor of the cave and then climbed the opposite wall, where—transported by Beyah-Olvari magic—it returned once again to Baran's moat.

The Olvara stroked and stirred the wall of flowing water which she faced, her gaze returning again and again to the questions and answers which she and she alone could read there. That was her special gift, the power by which a new leader among the Beyah-Olvari was recognized each time the old one died—which didn't happen often. The Beyah-Olvari,

Baran had learned, lived far longer than the New Race did.

Now, as the Beyah-Olvari chanted and wailed all around her, the Olvara told Mirabar, the first servant of fire in many centuries to venture into these subterranean caverns, about the riddles she saw in her enchanted water.

"A child of water," the tiny old female said. "A child of fire."

Mirabar said something in reply, her glowing gaze fixed on the Olvara; but Baran couldn't hear her above the chanting of the Beyah-Olvari all around them.

The Olvara took one dripping hand away from the water and placed it over Mirabar's belly. The Guardian's bright red curls hid her face from Baran's view as she looked down at the tiny blue hand. The two of them were very still for a while, then the Olvara returned her attention—and both of her hands—to the water again. Baran saw Mirabar brushing absently at the small wet palm print left on her clothes.

Now the Olvara turned and, to Baran's surprise, left the chamber. Interested, Baran came forward and stood beside Mirabar.

"I've never seen her leave this cavern," he said. "Never. What did you say to her?"

Mirabar shook her head. "Nothing. I mean—she said that something has been waiting here for me, and she's gone to get it."

"Ah. What did I tell you?"

She turned a fiery glare upon him. "You didn't tell me *anything*. You let me wander aimlessly around your damp, gloomy ruins ever since I came here, without an—"

"And here I had hoped you were becoming fond of my home."

Mirabar studied him. "Did the Olvara make you so powerful?"

"No, I was powerful when I came here. She taught me how to direct my power. Focus it. Use it."

"Why?"

"Why not?" he countered.

"Because it takes only a few words with her to realize that she hates violence and killing."

"Ah, but she and her followers hate the thought of extinction even more."

Mirabar's eyes narrowed. "You threatened to destroy them?"

"No, I promised to protect them."

She understood immediately. "From the other waterlords."

"Yes."

"Who would kill them all . . . or enslave them all."

"One or the other," he agreed.

"So protection in exchange for teaching, knowledge, support. . . . That was the agreement you made with them."

"Yes."

"And before you, Harlon? And before him . . . every waterlord who ever lived at Belitar?"

"It's one of the reasons I don't encourage visitors. Well, not powerful ones."

She nodded. "Visitors like me. Like Kiloran."

"Or your friend Cheylan."

She looked startled, as if she'd forgotten about the existence of that other fire-eyed Guardian. "Cheylan," she repeatedly pensively.

He nodded. "People who might feel what I felt when I first came here. Who might guess that it's not *my* power they're sensing, but something else that lives here."

"So Kiloran's never been here?"

"Certainly not while it's been my home. He may have come here long ago, for all I know, when Harlon lived here—though I doubt Harlon encouraged visitors, either. But Kiloran has no idea what's here, I'm sure of that. If he was ever here and felt anything, then he mistook it—"

"—for Harlon's power."

"Undoubtedly."

"You said Marjan lived here." She blinked at the way the chanting around them immediately changed to wailing.

"The Beyah-Olvari don't tell fond tales of Marjan. He was, I gather, not very kind to their ancestors." He smiled and added, "He was a Guardian, you know."

"Once upon a time," she admitted. "Before he gave it up. . . ." She looked around, her face changing as she realized the weight of what Baran was revealing to her here today. "For this."

"Yes. For this." Even now, so full of bitterness, so near to death, he felt the seduction of water magic all around him. Baran wouldn't have given up love, not even for this. But fire? Absolutely. From the moment Marjan had found *this*, Baran doubted there'd been any question in his mind about which magic to consecrate his life to. Not if he felt what Baran always felt here. Not if he had the gift.

"So he didn't learn water magic by himself," Mirabar mused aloud, "by studying the paintings which the Beyah-Olvari left all over Sileria."

Baran grinned. "Of course not. I'm a very skilled waterlord, my dear, and *I* can't begin to decipher those things."

"He found *them* here," she looked around at the Beyah-Olvari, "when everyone thought they were already extinct, and he made them his slaves."

"He did, indeed. Then he built Belitar around them, to protect his secret from others, and to imprison the Beyah-Olvari here."

"And it's never occurred to you to let them go?" she asked, with obvious distaste for his character flaws.

"That was all a long time ago, Mirabar. They don't want to leave now. They don't know what's out there—apart from almost certain death, that is."

Her face took on a strange, thoughtful expression. "They don't know . . ."

He wondered what she was thinking. "Mirabar?" When she didn't respond, he prodded, *"Mirabar."*

She gathered her drifting thoughts. "What?"

"You're not to tell anyone about this." She didn't reply, so he prodded impatiently, "Do I have your word?"

"You forgot to threaten me," she pointed out.

He placed his hand over her belly, right where the Olvara had left a wet patch. "Do I need to?" Mirabar drew in a sharp breath, and he asked, "What did she tell you?"

"We're going to have a daughter," she said bluntly.

"But you just told me you're not—"

"I'm not. But we're going to have a daughter. And please," she added, "don't tell me you were praying for a son."

"I don't pray," he said. "Not anymore. Besides, no, I'm delighted. I much prefer girls. Boys are violent little war-mongering monsters."

"Are you quoting your own mother?" she asked dryly.

"Believe it or not, my mother doted on me." He paused, then asked, "Our daughter—is she this ruler you're supposed to find?"

Mirabar shook her head. "No. But he will need her. She will be born to shield him, as I was supposed to shield Josarian." She looked down, troubled and sad.

He toyed with the lava-rich curls which fell across her shoulder. "Josarian did what he was meant to do. You helped him achieve his destiny."

Her expression was bemused. "Baran, are you actually . . . trying to *comfort* me?"

He snorted, then realized that was indeed the case. "Old habits surface when you least expect them." He sighed. "I was, once upon a time, a good husband."

He glanced away from her uncertain expression when the chanting around them grew suddenly louder. The Olvara was returning to the cavern. She was dragging something behind her. It was a long, slim, and narrow object wrapped up in a darkly moldy cloth, and it was heavy enough to cause her to struggle.

Baran moved towards her, making a gesture to help her, but the Olvara stopped him. "No. You may not touch this. It is not for you. It has never been for you."

He blinked, then smiled wryly. Even in his illness, he was more powerful than the Olvara; but she was still his respected teacher, and he had done extraordinary things—such as marrying Mirabar—based on her guidance. So he shrugged and made no attempt to touch the object as she dragged it past him.

The Olvara was panting with exertion, her breath as fast as an excited puppy's, by the time she reached Mirabar's side with her mysterious burden.

"I have waited all my life," the Olvara told the Guardian, "for you to come and claim this. And before me, others guarded it. It has been here a long time, waiting for you."

Baran grinned when he saw Mirabar steel her expression as she accepted the moldily wrapped offering.

"What is it?" his wife asked, looking as if even she found it a bit heavy.

"You'll understand when you unwrap it. No," the Olvara added, when Mirabar started to fiddle with the wrapping. "Not now."

"When?"

"Only you can know when."

Baran sighed, well accustomed to his teacher's vague and portentous comments. "How about giving us a hint, *sirana?*"

"When you are ready," the Olvara said to Mirabar.

Baran prodded, "A slightly more specific hint?"

The Olvara gazed up into Mirabar's face and said, "You will be ready to appreciate this gift when you are ready to protect what you most long to destroy."

Baran guessed from the way Mirabar flinched that this pronouncement meant something to her.

"*Sirana,*" Mirabar said hesitantly. "Do you know who the Beckoner is?"

The Olvara only repeated, "A child of water, a child of fire."

"What about . . ." Mirabar looked down at the long, slender bundle in her arms. "A child of sorrow?"

"Yes!" The Olvara seemed exultant. "All of these things. They are the future, because they are the past."

"She's always this cryptic," Baran said apologetically to Mirabar. "I honestly wasn't sure if I was supposed to marry you or become a *zanar*."

Mirabar favored him with an irritable glance before saying, "*Sirana,* how will I—"

"When you are ready to protect what you most long to destroy," the Olvara repeated, "your path will unfold."

46

DO NOT LAUGH AT THE FALLEN; THERE MAY BE
SLIPPERY PLACES AHEAD.

— Moorlander Proverb

"WYLDON IS DEAD," Dyshon reported to Kiloran. "It is done, *siran*."

"Good work," Kiloran said absently, staring out over the city of Cavasar from the tower window where he stood.

"His territory is now ours, *siran*."

"Yes, of course." Kiloran frowned, thinking.

"*Siran?*"

"Hmmm?"

"I have carried out our plan and lost no men." When Kiloran didn't reply, Dyshon prodded, "You don't seem pleased, *siran*."

Kiloran finally gave his full attention to the green-eyed assassin who was still covered with dust from the road, having come straight to Kiloran upon returning to Cavasar. "You've done very well," Kiloran assured him, "and I am pleased. But disturbing news has preceded you." Kiloran turned away again and informed him, "Ferolen is dead. Tansen attacked a few nights ago, destroyed his stronghold, killed everyone, torched everything . . ." He shrugged and added, "Well, one assumes it was the Guardians who did the actual torching. Ordinary fire could never have overcome Ferolen's power."

"That is . . ." Dyshon shuffled his feet. "Yes. That is distressing news, *siran*."

"And Baran has indeed betrayed us."

"The Idalar River?"

"I can't get control of it. Not completely. So I can't get control of Shaljir."

"Baran must die."

"Yes," Kiloran agreed. "Baran must die."

It was very disappointing. Kiloran had cherished high hopes when he sent that letter to Baran. Playing on Baran's wild emotionalism had worked occasionally in the past. Then again, Baran had always been, above all, unpredictable.

"Do you have new orders for me, *siran?*" Dyshon asked.

"Yes. In view of—"

Kiloran was interrupted by a knock at the door. An assassin came in, carrying a folded, sealed parchment. He was even dustier than Dyshon, and he looked even more tired and disheveled.

"A letter from Searlon, *siran*," he said.

"Ah." Kiloran took it from him, hoping for encouraging news.

The first few lines of the letter explained why Searlon had been out of touch longer than anticipated. The sea-bound Lascari had suffered severe losses to their numbers and were not easy to track down. Moreover, like so many sea-born folk these days, they were now bound for the waters off Sileria's eastern coast, right where the summit of Darshon was most visible from the sea, due east of the deserted *shallah* village of Gamalan. Like the rest of the east-bound sea-born folk, they couldn't say why they were going, they only knew they must go—and go so fast that Searlon had had trouble catching up with them.

However, he had indeed finally found them. And what they said about the boy Zarien was very surprising: He had died at sea during the *bharata,* the bloody dragonfish hunt which was an annual ritual of the sea-born folk. His clan seemed utterly and completely convinced of this. One of them had seen the jaws of a dragonfish close around the boy's torso, crush it, and pull his corpse into the depths of the blood-dark sea. Even if the beast had later let him go, the clan members all assured Searlon, there was no way he could have survived the attack. Whatever sea-born boy was now wandering the dryland, he was definitely not *their* Zarien, they said; it simply wasn't possible. There were presumably other sea-born boys named Zarien, ones who were not of the sea-bound Lascari, let alone dead; Searlon had merely come to the wrong clan. It was, after all, the sort of mistake a drylander would make.

Nonetheless, mindful of Kiloran's orders and slightly skeptical about any death which he himself did not witness, Searlon questioned Linyan—Zarien's grandfather and leader of the surviving clan members—very rigorously about the boy. The old man's initial story was that Zarien was the child of a now-dead Lascari couple, Sorin and Palomar. Searlon found this interesting, since he had already learned that was exactly who Tansen's young companion claimed *his* parents were. However, the old man's tale soon gave way, under the influence of stern persuasion, to a much more intriguing version of the boy's origins.

Kiloran sank slowly into a chair as he read Searlon's explanation, extracted from Linyan, about the presumed-dead sea-bound boy who was not only Tansen's constant companion but even, Searlon had recently learned . . .

"Tansen's bloodson," Kiloran read aloud, his heart pounding.

"Tansen doesn't have . . ." Dyshon drew in a swift breath. "He's taken a son?"

But Kiloran scarcely heard him. His thoughts were whirling in a chaos of shocked realization.

She didn't die in the mountains.

Alcinar had survived. She had lived to reach the sea. He had never believed it, had always thought she must have died on land. But, no, she had returned to her kind, even though they'd have shunned her, despised her, rejected her. . . . She had returned to them because she knew she could convince them, in the end, to shelter the child she bore. And they had. Kiloran had never known, never suspected . . . Nor, it seemed, had Baran.

A child . . .

A child who would eventually come ashore—without his family's knowledge, it seemed, since they thought he was dead. A sea-bound boy who would desert the Lascari to walk the dryland, as his mother once had. . . .

Why?

Did Baran know now, after all these years? Was that why he had betrayed Kiloran and violated the truce agreement?

If so, then why was the boy with Tansen, not Baran? And why not keep the boy at Belitar, which was virtually impregnable? Why let him wander war-torn Sileria with the *shatai?*

Why let him swear a bloodvow with Tansen?

Would Tansen want the boy, if he knew? Would Baran let Tansen keep him, if he knew? Was it possible . . .

By all the gods above and below . . .

Yes, Kiloran realized. It was possible. Even likely.

They don't know.

After all, who would have told them? According to Searlon's letter, the elderly Lascari clan leader said the boy himself had never known. Sorin and Palomar, who adopted him as their own after Alcinar died, had decided not to tell him until he was an adult.

The boy doesn't know.

He might suspect something, it might be why he had disappeared, but he didn't know the truth.

"Siran . . ." Dyshon ventured. "Have you had good news?"

He realized he was chuckling aloud. "Ah, Dyshon. To think, only a few moments ago, I thought that learning of Wyldon's death would be the high point of my day."

"What does Searlon say, *siran?*"

Kiloran smiled broadly. "Searlon has discovered the most worthwhile thing of all."

"Siran?"

"A secret."

"Ah." Dyshon nodded. Everyone in Sileria understood the inherent value of a secret. "What will we do with it?"

"Searlon will pursue it. You will remain here in Cavasar, to rule the city in my absence."

Dyshon bowed his head and crossed his fists. "You honor me, *siran.*"

"You," Kiloran advised the assassin who had brought Searlon's letter to him, "will return here tonight for my reply to Searlon, and you will leave Cavasar with it at first light."

"Of course, *siran.*"

"And I . . ." Kiloran nodded. "Yes, I will leave Cavasar tomorrow."

There was a great deal to do. And the first task, of course, was to write detailed instructions to Searlon regarding Zarien.

Tansen must cherish the boy, to have made him his bloodson. If Tansen died protecting him, so much the better. And if not . . . Kiloran wondered which course of action would profit him more after capturing Zarien: Telling Baran who the boy really was? Or making sure that Tansen never guessed?

A bloodson . . .

Oh, yes, the *shatai* would even *help* Kiloran get control of the boy. Tansen had already given him the weapon he needed, long ago. And who could say for certain—perhaps it had always been meant to be this way?

Ah, it was wonderful when fate suddenly showed a man that he would indeed have everything he sought.

STANDING IN BARAN's depressingly damp library at Belitar, Najdan watched Mirabar with dark concern. Ever since receiving this strange gift from Baran, wrapped in a moldy blanket that looked almost as old as Belitar itself, the *sirana* had seemed haunted, distracted, even tormented.

Mirabar didn't know what the gift was; and Baran, for reasons which remained unclear, was evidently incapable of telling her. Prophecy had warned Mirabar not to unwrap the gift until she was ready. Mirabar seemed convinced that Sileria's fate relied on her being ready soon, yet she evidently had no idea how to *become* ready.

Najdan found it all very annoying.

Now, as Mirabar sat staring at the gift with such intensity that Najdan thought she might accidentally immolate it, the assassin silently cursed Baran again. The *sirana* had been under a terrible strain ever since marrying that madman and coming to this damp, gloomy, haunted place. Now Baran had abandoned her alone here at Belitar, having gone off on some mysterious task of his own. He had taken Sister Velikar and Vinn the assassin with him, as well as half a dozen others, effectively leaving Najdan in charge. Which was a strange position to be in, considering that Najdan had served Baran's worst enemy most of his life.

"*Sirana*," Najdan said. When she just continued to stare at Baran's gift with a fierce frown, he repeated, "*Sirana*."

Those glowing golden eyes shifted their gaze to him. "Hmmm?"

"We've had news. A courier."

"From Baran?"

"No. From Wyldon's people."

That got her attention. "Well?"

"Wyldon is dead."

"Dead? Is this Kiloran's doing?"

"That's what Wyldon's assassins believe, though it was supposedly a message from Baran which lured him to the meeting where he was ambushed."

She finally turned completely away from the moldy wrappings to focus on their conversation. "A message from Baran?"

Najdan unwrapped the small package which the courier had given him. Mirabar drew in a sharp breath when she saw the bracelet which so clearly matched the necklace Baran always wore.

She murmured, "That was from Kiloran, wasn't it?"

Najdan nodded. "I've seen it at Kandahar." He looked down at it now and shook his head. "But until it was brought here today, I never recognized the resemblance. Now it's so obvious that I . . ." He searched her gaze, wondering how much more she now knew about the secrets of these two giants than he did. "What exactly is between Kiloran and Baran?"

She folded her hands. "I'm sorry. I can only tell you if he gives me permission."

He nodded, respecting that. She had a husband now. Mirabar often seemed to both fear and despise Baran, but many people married without affection, and husbands and wives must honor each other's confidences.

"So," Mirabar guessed, "Wyldon's people want our assurances that Baran didn't kill him?"

"And then they want Baran to take over his territory before Kiloran can do it."

"I don't know if he can," she admitted.

Their eyes met. One secret Najdan did know, though they

hadn't discussed it openly, was that Baran was dying. He had deteriorated enough, just since the marriage, that he couldn't hide this fact from anyone inhabiting Belitar.

"Even if he can," Mirabar added, "it might not be the wisest use of his remaining strength."

Najdan nodded. "Then perhaps you," he suggested, "could use your own power to keep Wyldon's territory from another waterlord?"

Her eyes brightened with interest for a moment, but then her face clouded. She looked again at the moldy gift which captured so much of her attention these days, and she ran a hand absently over her stomach. "Not me," she said at last. "I can't go there. We'll need to find someone else."

He glanced down at her stomach. "How are you feeling?" he asked tactfully.

"I'm not pregnant yet," she replied bluntly. "And with my husband gone from home now . . ."

"So we should ask other Guardians—" He stopped speaking when he heard a familiar footstep behind him. He glanced over his shoulder to see Haydar approaching them. He almost smiled, pleased as always by how content her face was these days. He and she were together after such a long time apart, and she had work to keep her busy. Unlike almost everyone else, she even liked living at Belitar; she enjoyed the challenge of making Baran's ruins moderately inhabitable for the *sirana*—and perhaps for a baby.

"What is it?" he asked her.

"The sentries say a Guardian is approaching." Haydar glanced at Mirabar and added, "They say it's Cheylan, *sirana*."

"Cheylan! Dar be thanked! That's who we can send to try to prevent Kiloran from taking over Wyldon's territory." Mirabar started for the door, then suddenly stopped and turned to Najdan again. "He . . . He can't cross the moat, can he?"

"No, *sirana*. No one else can enter Belitar until Baran returns and permits it." Najdan added, "I used the boat to go meet Wyldon's courier."

"So we'll row across and meet Cheylan on the other side of the moat?"

"Yes." And there, in full view of Baran's many sentries, there would be no opportunity for Cheylan to exchange tender words, let alone improper embraces, with Mirabar.

There were ways in which Baran was shrewder than Tansen was, Najdan reflected.

"CAN'T YOU GO hunt something?" Jalilar asked Ronall.

"Hmmm?" He lay naked on his back, wishing the Sanctuary's bed were more comfortable. And bigger. The two of them were always uncomfortably squashed together when they made love in it.

Well . . . *love* might be an exaggerated word for what they shared in this bed, or in the other places where they had mated as carelessly as wild animals ever since Ronall's ribs started healing.

Jalilar was a voluptuous and sensual woman, and Ronall's brief flirtation with celibacy had ended within a few days of arriving here. Her body brought him endless and varied delight, as did her frank, earthy passion. No wonder so many *shallah* men had that swaggering, smug air about them; if their famously modest wives were all this uninhibitedly sexual in private, they had plenty to be pleased about.

Unfortunately, Jalilar's delightfully energetic nature as a lover had many annoying corollaries. She expected him to do *work* around the Sanctuary, as she did, and she didn't seem to understand that he had never worked in his entire life and didn't know how—or have any interest in learning. Jalilar had a *shallah*'s traditional contempt for pain and weakness, so she disapproved of the way Ronall coddled his healing injuries rather than manfully ignoring them. And although she wouldn't leave Sanctuary grounds—for reasons which she refused to specify—she had no compunction against constantly nagging him to do so.

Very soon, he acknowledged privately, she would nag him right into leaving for good. This had been a delightful idyll, but he could now feel it turning into a mistake—and the Three knew what a familiar feeling *that* was for him.

"Go hunt something," Jalilar repeated, rising from the bed and reaching for her simple homespun clothes. "We're out of fresh meat, and the Sister's supplies are dwindling."

She frowned suddenly, looking both sad and worried. He suspected she was again thinking about her husband, who had abandoned her here. Jalilar wouldn't say much about that, but Ronall gathered that she hadn't wanted to be left here and she blamed her husband very sorely for her current situation. Ronall fully suspected she was sleeping with him now for revenge as much as out of sheer loneliness.

He watched her pull the humble fabric over her firm, golden flesh, then start to tie back her coarse, gleaming black hair.

"I don't have a horse," Ronall pointed out, not at all eager to stalk these mountains in search of food.

"So?"

"I've only ever hunted on horseback."

She snorted in disdain, as she often did when the subject of his privileged existence came up. "It cannot be so hard on foot. Everyone does it."

He sighed. "I know. Your brother regularly killed mountain deer on foot, and then carried them home on his shoulders without ever drawing a deep breath." Jalilar's brother, some paragon of every manly virtue ever defined, had died during the rebellion, though she wouldn't say how. "And your husband can catch wildfowl with his bare hands."

"He usually sets a snare," she prodded, lifting one dark brow.

"I don't know how."

She sighed. "What *can* you do?"

"Very little." He rose to his feet, reached for a bottle of fire brandy, and admitted, "Almost nothing."

She looked exasperated. "We need meat."

"If you make some snares and tell me how to set them," he said, relenting, "I'll go do it."

Jalilar rolled her eyes. "Very well."

She turned away from him, her whole attitude remote now that passion had been sated. Ronall watched her finish dressing, admiring her grace . . . and thinking again about leaving her.

If only he still had a horse, he mused regretfully, he could leave here tomorrow. But without one, the thought of *walking* to his next destination . . . Actually, no, he didn't have a destination. He couldn't return to Elelar's estate, since she might be there now, and he never wanted to face her again (no matter how much he amused himself by picturing her finding Chasimar there).

Where would he go? He didn't know. The empty ache which lived inside him was deeper, more hollow than ever. His vague and nameless hunger for . . . for *something* was eating him alive. He swallowed more fire brandy, knowing by now that it couldn't drown the beast consuming him, and yet still willing to try. What else was there to do?

Jalilar turned her head, and he saw her dark eyes flash as she watched him drink. She said nothing. She never said anything about his drinking, actually, but he knew it disgusted her. She thought his hunger for alcohol and oblivion was a weakness. And she was right. So he shrugged off her dark, quiet gaze and drank again, suspecting that she knew he was thinking of leaving soon and wouldn't be very sorry to see him go.

She suddenly drew a sharp breath. "Someone's coming," she warned, her glance taking in his nakedness.

He crossed the Sanctuary and reached for his clothes without asking how she knew. Her mountain-born ears always heard approaching pilgrims well before he did. This Sanctuary was isolated, but they still had visitors once every few days. He had learned by now that Jalilar preferred to remain hidden and let him make sure their visitors weren't assassins. He wondered if her fear of the Society was mere prudence, or if it had something to do with why she wouldn't leave Sanctuary grounds. She didn't tell him and, since there were so many questions he would rather not answer either, he didn't demand an explanation.

It was after midday now, but still early enough that Ronall figured he could reasonably hope their guests were just stopping for food and water rather than planning to spend the night. Ronall had to sleep outside, rather than in Jalilar's bed, whenever visitors spent the night here.

He finished pulling on his clothing, now in tatters thanks to the bandits who had attacked him, briefly met Jalilar's eyes, and then went outside. Another recent explosion from the volcano had filled the sky with ash, streaking it with fantastic colors even at this time of day.

To his relief, the new arrivals were *shallaheen,* not assassins. Two grown men and a . . . a sea-born boy, Ronall realized in surprise. As incongruous as the sea-born lad was in these surroundings, though, it was the taller of the two *shallaheen* who captured Ronall's attention. He had rarely seen a more intense-looking man. The *shallah* was lean, with a serious, hawklike face, hotly dark eyes, and long coarse hair which was even blacker than Jalilar's. His tattered clothes were liberally stained . . . with blood, Ronall suspected, which someone had unsuccessfully tried to wash out.

Ronall took a step back, suddenly wondering if he was wrong, if this *was* an assassin. The shreds of the man's clothes revealed enough skin to display a wealth of combat scars, and he was armed . . . "With two swords," Ronall murmured, realizing. Finely crafted hilts stuck out of long, slender sheathes in an engraved leather harness which fit the warrior as if he'd been born wearing it. Even Ronall knew that one man in all of

Sileria was famous for such an appearance. "Tansen?" he blurted doubtfully.

The warrior stopped and gazed at him, assessing Ronall. Evidently realizing they'd never met, he replied, "Yes." His quiet voice was deep, as if it belonged to a larger man.

Ronall just stared. So this was Tansen, the most famous warrior in Sileria after the dead Firebringer. He glanced down at the torn neckline of the man's homespun tunic and saw— yes, there it was—the start of that famous scar of his, the one some Kintish *shatai-kai* had carved into his chest with a red-hot poker, Dar have mercy, to mark the successful completion of his training as a swordmaster.

"Tansen," Ronall repeated, sure now.

The man who killed my wife's lover, he thought with a faint grimace, remembering what he had learned when dallying with *Torena* Chasimar's chatty maid.

The man who was now leading Sileria in a bloodfeud against the Society. Interesting—Tansen didn't *look* that crazy. Then again, *shallaheen* loved a bloodbath, even the best of them.

Tansen's gaze remained impassive. "We're looking for Jalilar."

"You know Jalilar?" Ronall said in surprise. In all the time they had been together, she had given no hint of such an illustrious acquaintance.

The other *shallah* now came forward and said, a little tersely, "She's my wife. Where is she?"

Your wife?

Sudden panic spread through Ronall like wildfire. The *shallah* looked strong, violent, and less than friendly. The glance he now exchanged with Tansen showed Ronall that these two were friends.

I'm a dead man.

A faint frown now creased Tansen's brow. "Where is she?"

"In . . . Inside." Ronall choked out the word.

There was an uneasy pause as the two *shallaheen* watched him in puzzlement.

Then Jalilar's voice came from inside. "Emelen?"

The *shallah*'s face cleared, a smile transforming it. He was a good-looking fellow, and a little younger than Ronall had thought at first.

"Jalilar!" he called.

Ronall heard Jalilar's footsteps behind him. He quickly stepped out of her way. Tansen's expression lightened into one of indulgence as Emelen shoved past them both to rush forward and embrace his wife as she emerged into the sunshine.

While Emelen kissed Jalilar, Tansen discreetly turned his back, silently directing the sea-born boy to do so, too. Then he caught Ronall's eye and lifted one brow slightly—which Ronall took to be a sign of amusement in this famously stoic man.

"I'm thirsty," the sea-born boy said.

"There's a well around back," Ronall said absently, listening to the terrified pounding of his heart.

"Yes," the boy replied with an intent expression, taking a step in that direction even before Ronall was done speaking.

"Wait." Tansen removed the waterskin slung over his own shoulder and tossed it to the boy. "While you're there, fill the waterskins," he instructed.

The boy paused to ask Ronall, "Is there any food here?"

"Yes," Ronall replied weakly. They were all speaking *shallah,* but after so much time spent wandering the mountains he could follow most of it, though he still replied in common Silerian.

"It's been at least two hours since he ate," Tansen told Ronall dryly. "He may perish of hunger if I don't feed him soon."

"It was a very long walk here," the boy insisted, in what sounded like an ongoing but good-natured argument between them.

I'm a dead man, Ronall kept thinking.

"Shall we go inside?" Tansen suggested to Ronall.

"No!"

The *shatai* eyed him inquisitively. Even the sea-born boy paused again to look at him.

"Uh . . ." Ronall gestured to the still-embracing couple in the doorway. "Perhaps we should give them some time alone." And the bed inside the Sanctuary was still rumpled and ripe with sex.

Dar and the Three pity me.

"They'll get time alone after I leave," Tansen said reasonably. "Let's—"

"Emelen . . ." Jalilar finally found an opportunity to speak between her husband's hungry embraces. "What are you doing here?"

She sounded so nervous that Ronall thought she might just as well *say* she'd been bedding another man only moments ago. He was tempted to run, so tempted . . . but, cursing the gods, he knew that he couldn't leave Jalilar alone here to endure whatever her husband might do to her when he found out she'd been unfaithful. Cuckold was the second worst thing one Silerian could call another, and Emelen looked like a man who took a traditional view of such matters. Not that Ronall was in a position to criticize; he had once beaten Elelar for her infidelity.

He tried not to think about it now. Actually, he always tried not to think about it.

Please, Dar, let this Emelen be a complete idiot who'll never guess the truth.

But a moment later, Emelen stopped happily babbling something about being camped only half a day's walk from here and having missed Jalilar so much, and he stumbled to an awkward halt, evidently realizing that something was wrong. "Jalilar . . ."

Don't look, Ronall ordered himself, *don't look at her.*

But Tansen was looking, and the sea-born boy was looking . . . and it was somehow irresistible, so Ronall found himself looking, too.

It was a mistake. Jalilar looked right back at him, her face betraying everything.

Tansen saw it immediately. He stiffened, subtly but perceptibly.

"Kadriah?" Emelen said, the *shallah* endearment sounding worried. "What is it? I know you're angry about the way I left, the way I made the Sister . . ." Emelen paused again, then said, in a different tone of voice, "Where is the Sister?"

"Gone," Jalilar replied, her voice low and harsh. "She left not long after you did. I've been alone here ever since."

Now Emelen looked at Ronall, but so far there was only confusion in his dark eyes. "Alone?" he repeated blankly.

"All alone!" Jalilar replied, her expression fierce. "There has been no one for me! No word from you or Tansen! My brother dead, my clan scattered, my village abandoned! And I am left here with no one and nothing! Where have you *been?* Why could I not be with you? I told you I would not stay here and—"

"You smell . . ." Emelen's expression underwent a fairly hideous transformation. "You smell of . . ."

"Zarien," Tansen said suddenly, "go fill those waterskins."

Ronall glanced at the boy, who ignored Tansen. The tattooed young face showed the dawning of understanding, and his gaze shot to Ronall—who was fervently hoping to be swallowed in a sudden, ground-splitting earthquake.

Jalilar yanked herself out of Emelen's embrace, glaring at him with the fury which only a spouse could feel. "What did you think I would do?" she shouted. "What did you think would happen if you abandoned me here alone, with no one to—"

"I left a Sister with you!" Emelen shouted back.

"She went off to Darshon!"

Emelen's anger dissolved into regret. *"Kadriah,* I'm sorry. I didn't know. How could I . . ." He suddenly seemed to remember what she smelled of. He turned very slowly and confronted Ronall now. "Where is the rest of your party?"

"There's just me," Ronall said faintly.

Tansen said, "Zarien. The well."

The boy didn't move

"Zarien."

Emelen's face darkened with growing rage as he glared at Ronall. "How long have you been here?"

Jalilar spat, "A *long* time."

I'm a dead man.

Emelen whirled on Jalilar, searching her face for the truth. She gave it to him. He backed away from her, shaking his head. "Oh . . . *no*. No! How could you do that?"

"How could you leave me?" she screamed.

"You've been with another man?" he screamed back.

"Every day since he came here!" she shouted.

"Not *every* day . . ." Ronall closed his mouth again, realizing that the details hardly mattered now.

While the couple hurled angry accusations at each other, the sea-born boy—Zarien—crept up to Tansen and murmured, "What should we do?"

"We should stay out of it," Tansen replied firmly.

Emelen pulled his *yahr* out of his *jashar*. Ronall flinched.

Zarien gasped and asked Tansen, "Is he going to beat her?"

Tansen shook his head. "Not her."

Ronall felt sick with fear.

Zarien gasped again. "We must stop him!" Incredibly, he leapt in front of Ronall. "No, Emelen!"

Emelen shoved him aside, swinging that *yahr* with deadly menace.

Ronall backed away. "Please, I'm unarmed!"

"Not in my wife's bed, you weren't, you stinking *sriliah!*" Emelen snarled.

"No, Emelen!" Jalilar shouted.

Zarien cried, "Father! Stop him!"

Tansen tugged at the sea-born boy, who was trying to interfere. "It's not our affair, Zarien!"

Jalilar shrieked, "Emelen, don't kill him!"

Zarien bleated, "*Kill* him? Father, he's going to kill him!"

"I'll take care of it," Tansen snapped. "Get away from them."

"Take care of it *now!*" the boy insisted.

"Wait!" Ronall pleaded.

"Say your prayers," Emelen advised.

"No!" Zarien evaded Tansen's grasp and succeeded in getting in the way—just in time to be struck by Emelen's *yahr*. "*Ow!*"

"Zarien!" Tansen's voice was harsh with alarm.

There was a bewildering flurry of movement, and then Emelen was on the ground, Tansen had the *yahr*, and Zarien was clutching his bleeding nose.

"Ow!" Zarien repeated. He looked at Emelen, who lay sprawled on the ground. "You hit me!"

Still shouting, Jalilar ran to Emelen and knelt beside him, trying to keep him from rising.

Tansen was saying to Zarien, "You just *had* to get in the way, didn't you?"

"It really hurts," Zarien informed him.

"Let me see," Tansen muttered.

"Is it broken?" Zarien asked.

"Does it feel broken?" Tansen replied, examining the bleeding appendage.

"Get away from me!" Emelen snapped at his wife.

"Stop it!" she cried. "You can't kill him! Emelen, you can't!"

"Oh, yes I can," he replied grimly, shoving her away as he rose to his feet.

"Father," Zarien prodded.

Emelen shouted at Tansen, "You tell him to stay out of this!"

"I've *been* telling him!" Tansen snapped back. "And if you ever hit him again—"

"He got in my way!"

"Don't ever hit him again," was all Tansen said.

Emelen evidently knew when it was wise to appease Tansen. Sounding far more exasperated than apologetic, he said, "I'm sorry I hit you, Zarien."

"I don't think it's broken," Zarien offered. Then he winced, "Hurts like all the Fires, though."

"Let that be a lesson to you," Tansen said.

Zarien demanded of him, "Are you really going to let this happen, father? This poor, scared, unarmed man, and Emelen angry enough to kill him before he has time to beg for mercy!"

Ronall felt humiliation wash over him at the boy's description of him. As if it even mattered, he realized that Tansen looked too young to be Zarien's father.

"No!" Jalilar screamed, flinging herself in front of Emelen as he moved towards Ronall again. "Don't! No!"

Emelen stopped, his expression growing even more awful as he said to her, "Are you telling me you're in love with him?"

"Him?" Her tone could not have been any less flattering. "No!"

Emelen seized her by the shoulders and said between gritted teeth, "You are, aren't you? That's why you're so—"

"Fires of Dar, of course I'm not in love with him!" she shouted. "He's a weakling, a drunk, a lazy fool!"

"Then why—"

"Do you think I'd have let this useless coward touch me if I hadn't missed you so much?" Jalilar demanded of her husband. "If I hadn't wanted you so much, been so sure you were dead or about to die without me?"

"Jalilar . . ." Emelen sounded pained.

Ronall burned with shame as Jalilar continued, "Ronall means nothing to me! Less than nothing! Can't you understand how unhappy I was, to turn to *him?*"

Tansen, who was dabbing at the boy's gushing nose, suddenly jerked sharply, causing Zarien to grunt in pain.

"Dar have mercy," Ronall muttered, covering his face with his hands. "I really, truly, sincerely hate my life."

Tansen said, "Jalilar, did you say *Ronall?*"

"I love *you*," Jalilar said fiercely to her husband. "Only you. I want to be with you. Only you."

"Did she say Ronall?" Tansen asked Ronall.

"Yes," Ronall admitted wearily. "I'm half-Valdan. Just kill me now and get it over with."

"No!" Jalilar shrieked again, rushing at Tansen now that she evidently had Emelen under control.

"Calm down," Tansen ordered her. "No one's going to kill anyone."

"Oh, good," Zarien said, pressing a messy sleeve to his nose.

"Who is this?" Jalilar asked suddenly, staring at Zarien.

"My son," Tansen said. "He doesn't like killing."

"Travels in strange company, doesn't he?" Emelen said to no one in particular.

"You've taken a son," Jalilar murmured, momentarily distracted. Then she added in amazement, "A sea-born boy?"

"It's a long story," Tansen said absently, "and we have other things to discuss now."

"I'm Jalilar," she said to Zarien, extending her hands to him, "and now you and I are family, because Tansen was Josarian's bloodbrother."

Ronall stared stupidly while the boy, still bleeding profusely, took Jalilar's hands and murmured polite things.

"Josarian's blood . . ." Ronall's head started pounding. No, it wasn't possible. If Tansen was related to her through Josarian, then . . . "You're . . . Jalilar, are you saying Josarian was your . . ."

She flung a reply over her shoulder, not even bothering to look at him. "My brother."

"The Firebringer was your brother?" Ronall demanded.

"Yes," Tansen answered for Jalilar, who was busy embracing Zarien as a new relation.

"The Firebringer?" Ronall repeated in horrified shock. "I've been sleeping with the Firebringer's sister?"

Emelen punched him, knocking him down. "You been sleeping with *my wife,* you bastard!"

"No!" Tansen shouted, jumping between them. "Emelen, stop!"

"Stay out of this!" Emelen shouted back.

"No!" Jalilar screamed, abandoning Zarien to fling herself at Emelen again.

Ronall lay in the dirt and just wished they would all go away. No *wonder* Jalilar was so afraid of assassins, considering who her male relations were. And Ronall supposed the Society would be only too happy to kill anyone she cared about—including the drunken coward who'd been sleeping with her lately.

Damn her. Damn them all.

"No, Emelen," Tansen repeated, "you can't!"

"By the eight winds!" Zarien said, his voice muffled by his sleeve. "This is *Torena* Elelar's husband!"

Emelen froze and stared at Ronall, clearly stunned.

Tansen nodded to Zarien and said, "Exactly."

Emelen blurted, *"Him?"*

"Him," Tansen replied. He turned to look at Ronall. "Yes?"

Ronall returned his gaze uncertainly. "Yes."

"I know *Torena* Elelar," Jalilar said, staring at Ronall, too. *"You're* her husband?"

"Yes," Ronall repeated wearily.

Tansen expelled his breath in a rush. "We've had people looking everywhere for you. Or your body."

"Me? Why?" he asked, baffled.

"This is *Toren* Ronall." Emelen shook his head. "Wonderful." The *shallah* gave his wife a disgusted look.

"What does it matter who he is?" Jalilar asked Emelen. "You had to pick *him.*"

"Please, Emelen," Jalilar pleaded. "Try to understand."

"Let's not keep talking about this in front of Tansen and

Zarien and . . . *him,*" Emelen added, with a dark glare at Ronall.

Getting teary, Jalilar said, "I . . . I can't let you hurt him or . . ."

"I won't," Emelen promised, sounding depressed. "Tansen will make sure of that. Now let's go inside."

"No, there's something else," Jalilar insisted.

"What?" Emelen asked warily.

"And . . . and he should know, too," Jalilar said, glancing at Ronall. "It's his right."

"What?" Emelen repeated with a frown.

"Oh, no," Tansen muttered.

"*No,*" Ronall said, already guessing what Jalilar would say next.

"I'm going to have his child," she told her husband sadly.

47

A MAN'S FRIENDS ARE ALWAYS MORE DANGEROUS THAN HIS ENEMIES.

— Najdan

By NOW, TRAVEL was sheer agony for Baran. Even Sister Velikar's noxious tisanes and chanting couldn't control the debilitating pain which consumed him, and he became exhausted so easily now that his pace was affected—his judgment, however, was not.

So he viewed Dulien's awkward overtures of friendship with amused skepticism. The tedious waterlord, having requested this private and secret truce meeting at a Sanctuary deep in the mountains, now sulked and scowled, as was his unattractive habit, while he spoke with Baran—who airily claimed that his own rather grim appearance these days was due to a recent illness from which he was now recovering.

Struggling with pain, fatigue, *and* the tedium of Dulien's conversation, Baran was relieved when the waterlord finally got to the point by saying, "Kiloran has killed Wyldon."

"Ah. Art lovers everywhere will be relieved to hear that." Baran added with a dramatic shudder, "Did you ever *see* any of Wyldon's water sculptures?"

Dulien scowled. "Kiloran tried to make it look like you did it."

"How enterprising of him."

"He thought you would be blamed."

"Well, yes," Baran conceded affably, "that would be the point of trying to make it look like I did it, wouldn't it?"

"But Wyldon's assassins say it was Kiloran, not you."

"Then they're smarter than I gave them credit for."

"It really wasn't you, was it?"

"No."

"Kiloran wanted to discredit you within the Society."

"Perhaps, but I imagine he mostly just wanted Wyldon dead." Baran smiled. "Besides, I thought that my marrying Mirabar had already discredited me within the Society."

Dulien leaned forward, his beady eyes alight with speculation. "You married her because you thought if you allied yourself with the Guardians, Tansen would let you live."

Baran leaned forward, too, and confided honestly, "I don't really think it's up to Tansen whether or not I live."

Dulien asked with ghoulish curiosity, "Can *she* kill you?"

"Mirabar?" Baran shook his head. "She's not going to try." He didn't usually tell so many truths in a row, but it amused him today.

"You're not claiming she *loves* you?" Dulien's incredulity made Baran laugh.

"Are you implying that I'm not lovable?"

"Does she know you vowed to kill her?"

"Yes. It made the wedding night a little awkward."

Dulien's eyes bulged. "So you've actually . . . You two have . . . You and she . . ."

"Was avid curiosity about my married life the reason you asked me to come here?" Baran asked.

The waterlord blinked. "No. Where was I?"

"I really couldn't say."

Dulien scowled again. "Did you know that as soon as the Valdani abandoned Cavasar, he killed the two waterlords who used to control the city's water?"

"He?"

"Kiloran!"

"Oh, yes. Do forgive me. Go on."

"Now he's got that sycophant, Meriten, trying to wrest Abidan's and Liadon's territory from the Guardians."

"I gather that *shallaheen* are stabling sheep in the ruins of the twins' houses." Baran sighed and shook his head. "Does no one have any respect anymore?"

Dulien continued sulkily, "Kiloran also had Searlon openly helping Meriten."

"So I heard."

"And now . . ." Dulien paused dramatically. "Searlon has disappeared."

"Dead?" Baran asked with hopeful interest. Kiloran's favorite assassin had always been a shrewd and dangerous enemy.

Dulien shook his head. "No. Surely someone would boast of Searlon's death, if that were so. And Kiloran would certainly mourn him."

"True. So . . . Searlon's on some delicate mission for his master," Baran surmised, "and no one knows where or can guess what."

"It makes me nervous," Dulien admitted.

"I imagine it makes everyone nervous."

"It means there's something even more important to Kiloran than just the things we already know about," Dulien explained, as if Baran might somehow have failed to grasp this implication. "You know: helping Meriten reclaim the brothers' territory, destroying you, killing Tansen, accessing the mines of Alizar, get—"

"Yes, yes, you needn't go through the whole list, Dulien."

"Meriten is practically Kiloran's servant. So if Meriten gets that territory, it will be the same as Kiloran having it." Dulien waited for Baran to agree with him. Baran merely gazed at him with a pretense of polite interest. Dulien continued angrily, "Kiloran's already got Cavasar, Kandahar and its territory, the Zilar River, the mines of Alizar, the Idalar River . . . Well, the Idalar River if you can't hold onto it. And having the Idalar will give him Shaljir. And now he's after Verlon's territory!"

"Verlon's territory? Really?"

"Attacks on Verlon's assassins. Many dead."

"Jagodan shah Lironi is making war on Verlon," Baran pointed out, "so surely that's why many are d—"

"Yes, yes, but Kiloran is attacking, too."

"How do you know?" He could already guess, but he wanted to be sure.

"A *shir* of Kiloran's was found at one of the massacres."

Oh, yes.

"Ah," Baran said, encouraging Dulien, "just like the initial attack on Wyldon's stronghold?"

"Precisely!"

"Very, very disturbing," Baran agreed gravely.

"And now a *shir* of Kiloran's has been found among Gulstan's slain men, too."

"My, my. Who's next?" Baran mused.

"Exactly!" Dulien pounced. "Kiloran wants it all!"

Oh, yes. This strategy had Tansen's name written all over it. Not that Tansen could write his name, of course. But this sort of calculated misdirection which was wasting the waterlords' energy and scattering their focus was precisely the sort of tactic at which Tansen excelled—and the sort of thing he had taught the Firebringer himself to do. Such tactics had enabled those two, with no help, to victoriously attack a hundred Outlookers in a fortress near Britar and free twenty *shallah* prisoners. Really, it was surprising that the other waterlords couldn't see that now.

Then again, considering what a fool Dulien was, and what a bloodthirsty hothead Verlon was, perhaps it wasn't so surprising, after all. Gulstan, who was smarter than many waterlords, might have his doubts about the whole thing. However, Gulstan suspected Kiloran's ambition more than anyone else, so perhaps he believed exactly what Tansen wanted him to believe.

The most delightful aspect of all this, Baran thought, was that Kiloran surely knew what was going on, and it undoubtedly made him ache with impotent rage. Even if Kiloran suppressed his pride enough to admit to the other waterlords that Tansen had killed enough of his assassins to plant their *shir* all over Sileria, the damage was already done: suspicions were raised, accusations circulating, counterplots being hatched.

"So what do you want from me?" Baran asked Dulien. "Apart from the pleasure of my company today, I mean."

"Why did you marry Mirabar?"

"Her girlish laughter enchanted me."

Dulien scowled. "What promises did Tansen make you?"

"Actually, Tansen opposed the marriage. He lost his head and nearly tried to kill me. Right there on Sanctuary grounds."

Dulien looked shocked. *"Tansen?"*

"I don't think he likes me," Baran confided.

"No one likes you."

"That's not true. Sister Velikar adores me. And Vinn admits he has become very attached to me."

Dulien made an impatient gesture. "Why are you with Josarian's loyalists? Why did you betray the Society?" He leaned forward again, his voice intense as he demanded, "What do you know that we don't?"

"Ahhh . . ." Baran leaned back in his chair, fighting a wave of dizziness. He needed Sister Velikar's attentions, but he decided he'd better finish this business first. "You think that Searlon's secret task may be to bring down other waterlords."

"Possibly."

Baran studied him with growing amusement. "You're afraid of what will happen if Kiloran has his way in this war."

Dulien nodded. "In all things."

"Kiloran ruling Sileria?"

"Yes!"

"Would that be so bad?" Baran asked curiously. "He's ruled the Society, after all, since before you and I became waterlords."

"But there were always the Valdani to keep him in check! He always . . . *needed* the Society. Needed the rest of us."

"And now?" Baran prodded.

"Now, if he can destroy Josarian's loyalists, what will Kiloran need with the rest of us once the fighting is over?"

"When Tansen and Mirabar are dead, I'm dead, the Guardians are all dead, and Josarian's cause is just a memory."

Dulien nodded. "Kiloran's already killing other waterlords and taking over their territories."

"First, Cavasar," Baran mused. "Then, Wyldon." Smiling maliciously, he added, "And, of course, there's the Zilar River . . . which *you've* always wanted, if memory serves."

His expression dark with envious fury, Dulien said, "And those are just the things we're certain about! What about Verlon's accusations? What about the *shir* found among Gulstan's men? What about the Shaljir River, which Meriten will get for him? What happens when you're dead and nothing stands between Kiloran and the Idalar River, nothing between Kiloran and the city of Shaljir?" Dulien pounded his fist on the table and shouted, "He will get rid of us all, I tell you! We will be nothing but a threat to him after you and Tansen and Mirabar are dead!"

"Yes, yes, I see your point."

"Why are you with them?" Dulien demanded.

"Do *you* want to be with them?" Baran asked with interest. He enjoyed imagining Tansen's reaction when he heard that a waterlord wanted his friendship. Surely even Tansen's face would be vivid with surprise at such news. When Dulien didn't reply, Baran prodded, "Do you?"

Dulien shrugged sulkily. "I want to know what the circumstances of our friendship would be."

"In other words, can the waterlords rule their territories without interference after Kiloran is dead?"

"Yes."

Just when you think you've seen everything . . .

Dulien was an even bigger fool than he had realized. Baran asked, "What about Verlon? Does he want new friends, too?"

"Verlon says he has already reached out to someone."

"Who?" *Who is there besides me?*

"He won't say who," Dulien grumbled. "But he believes that, with this ally, he can protect himself from Kiloran." He frowned a moment later and added, "And from Tansen and the Guardians, too."

"Well, well." Baran wondered who Verlon believed had that kind of power. "What about Gulstan?"

"Gulstan says that you are an unpredictable madman and I'm a fool to approach you."

"He's right." Gulstan might be obscenely fat, but he was no fool.

"Even so," Dulien added, "Gulstan wants to know what you say today."

"Tell him I miss his keen wit and handsome figure."

"You hate Kiloran."

"Who told you?"

"You've done what you've done because of that."

"True."

"You believe that if he wins now, you will never have a chance to destroy him. So you're trying to help them defeat him now. That's why you're with them, isn't it?"

. Terribly pleased, despite the pain which was now making him sweat like a nervous bridegroom, Baran replied, "Yes, I think you'll all be extra waterlords if the Society wins. Fire and water may be enemies, but they can probably share the future in Sileria, if they really want to. Whereas Kiloran will certainly wipe out all the weaker waterlords once he no longer needs them."

He didn't believe it for a moment. Tansen and the Guardians would let no waterlords survive this war. And Kiloran wasn't reckless enough to kill the other waterlords—not unless they became the sort of intense nuisance that Wyldon had become.

Yes, Dulien, Verlon, Gulstan, and whoever else was experiencing misgivings had it all wrong. They were making a huge mistake, because Kiloran was still their friend, and Tansen and the Guardians would always be their enemies. If any waterlords betrayed Kiloran now, they would destroy themselves.

Even better, they would damage Kiloran. He couldn't fight Josarian's loyalists all by himself. He needed the Society.

"Dulien," Baran said kindly, reveling in the sweet taste of ripening vengeance, "would you like me to speak to Tansen for you?"

Dulien hesitated only a moment before condemning himself to certain death. "Yes."

"WHAT'LL WE DO with him?" Zarien asked Tansen while wrapping a fresh wound on his bloodfather's arm.

"Not too tight," Tansen instructed, his long hair gleaming blackly under the ash-streaked light of the setting sun.

"It's still bleeding a lot."

"Let me see." Tansen frowned at the messy gash. "Put pressure on it for a bit, then wrap it when the bleeding has slowed."

Zarien put pressure on the wound, then repeated, "What'll

we do with him?" He looked across the encampment at *Toren* Ronall, who sat drinking a rather large quantity of volcano ale and gazing blankly into an enchanted Guardian fire, where someone cooked the evening meal.

"I'm not sure," Tansen admitted.

"He says he won't go back to Shaljir. Won't go back to the *torena.*"

"I know. I was going to send him there with the next courier, but I don't think we can trust him not to run away."

"It seems strange, since you're trying to save his life."

Tansen shook his head slowly. "I'm not sure he *wants* to live."

"Also the lives of other Valdani," Zarien added.

"That seems to be the only way we'll influence him." Tansen gazed at the drunken *toren* for another moment. "But I think he's past listening to sensible conversation today. We'll have to try again tomorrow, before he starts drinking . . . Which, I've noticed, means we'll have to catch him very early in the day."

"It's the right thing to do, father." Zarien still felt sick when he remembered those heads decorating the gates of Shaljir.

"Saving Valdani lives." Tansen sighed. "Josarian would enjoy the irony. His sense of humor was easily tickled."

After a long moment of silence, during which Tansen was undoubtedly brooding about the Firebringer's death, Zarien asked, "Do you think the *toren* loves Jalilar?"

"No."

"But he's upset about the baby?"

"Not as upset as Emelen is," Tansen admitted.

"But . . . but you think they'll . . ."

Tansen shrugged. "Emelen and Jalilar love each other. They could work this out, I'm sure, if . . ."

"If she weren't carrying the *toren's* child."

"Emelen is struggling hard with the idea that he'll be father to another man's child." His gaze caught Zarien's as he added, "It's nothing like a bloodvow, Zarien. Emelen didn't choose this. When I look at you, I see my son. But that baby . . . Emelen's afraid he'll always see Ronall's child when he looks at it."

"Yes. I suppose choosing a child is different from . . ."

"From your wife announcing that she's having one that isn't yours," Tansen concluded.

"Or from another woman announcing she's marrying a man to have *his?*" Zarien guessed, thinking of the *sirana.*

"I knew you would say that," Tansen said wearily. "Let's leave her out of this, shall we?"

"Of course, father," Zarien said politely.

He ignored the suspicious glance Tansen sent him. His bloodfather didn't show it, not to anyone, not even to him, but losing Mirabar to Baran had wounded him badly. And Zarien found it hard to see Tansen bear a wound he couldn't bind for him. So he poked and prodded, thinking that maybe they'd both feel better if Tansen would at least talk to him about it . . .

Zarien sighed and shrugged off the thought, knowing it was pretty futile. Tansen did not have a confiding nature. There was so much, Zarien was coming to realize, that his father might never tell him. Including what haunted his dreams at night. Yes, Tansen's nightmares came to him even more often than did Zarien's nightmares about his dead sea-bound family.

"Will Jalilar and Emelen really be safe there?" Zarien asked now, turning his thoughts away from those painful memories, away from the consuming hatred he felt for the goddess Sharifar.

"In Sanctuary?" Tansen replied. "Of course."

Tansen had instructed Jalilar and Emelen to remain together in that remote little Sanctuary of the Sisterhood. It was more imperative than ever, he insisted, that the Firebringer's sister remain in a secure place every moment of every day and night. Emelen would stay there to provide for her . . . and to try to repair their damaged marriage. Tansen would give them some time alone together, and then he would send men to guard the Sanctuary and watch over Jalilar, as well someone named Sister Basimar to tend her in her pregnancy while Emelen returned to the fighting—as he would have to do. He was needed.

Meanwhile, Tansen and Zarien returned to their encampment with Ronall in tow. Zarien had never met anyone quite like the *toren* and wasn't sure what to make of him. Tansen seemed to alternately pity and despise the man.

"It seems strange that *Torena* Elelar married him," Zarien mused.

"Strange beyond words," Tansen agreed, his tone unusually dry.

Somewhere between the Sanctuary and camp, the three of them had stumbled upon a battle. Ronall seemed scared and confused. Tansen had left Zarien with him and joined in the fighting. *Shallaheen* loyal to the waterlord Kariman were attacking a village loyal to the Firebringer. Zarien, hiding on a ledge overlooking the village, had watched his father in fascinated horror. Tansen was like a different man when he fought, almost like some sort of sorcerer: faster, stronger, sharper than all other men; deadlier, more ruthless; far less susceptible to pain.

Zarien didn't understand how Tansen could view all that killing, all that violence, as his "work."

Zarien was learning that there were things about being a great warrior which he had never considered before coming ashore to find the father chosen for him by destiny and the gods.

"There," Zarien said to Tansen now, "the bleeding has slowed." Living with Tansen, he was becoming adept at binding battle wounds, and this one presented no challenge to him.

"How's your nose?" Tansen asked.

It still hurt, but he knew Tansen disapproved of the way he had interfered between Emelen and Ronall, so he said, "Fine."

Suddenly Tansen stiffened. "There She goes again."

Zarien looked up at the dramatically streaked sky, painted

in the colors and shadows of Dar's frequent fury. In the distance, where the strange, never-ending display of violent lightning and whirling, colored clouds continued to dance around the peak of Mount Darshon, a shower of fiery sparks now flew out of the caldera. He knew they must be enormous boulders of fire, up close. "All those pilgrims at Darshon . . ."

"No one seems to understand why they go there. All the stories of people dying in showers of burning rock, sudden explosions of deadly gases, avalanches during the earthquakes . . . And still people keep going." Tansen's voice was pensive. "What does She want from us? Why does She call them to Her?"

"And why them and not us?"

"Oh, She knows I wouldn't listen." Tansen paused, then added more seriously, "And She knows I wouldn't let you go."

Zarien nodded, knowing that was true. At his repeated urging, Tansen had finally related to him the tale of how he had ascended Mount Darshon to try to stop Josarian from leaping into the volcano to become the Firebringer—or rather, as Tansen believed at the time, to certain death.

Yes, father, you would fight Dar Herself again for what you wanted.

Zarien took extra care with the bandage he was tying off, as if his attentions could protect his reckless bloodfather from the goddess's wrath. Then, when his task was done, he asked the question which had been on his mind for some time now: "This baby of Jalilar's . . . You think it's the one, don't you?"

Tansen didn't seem surprised. "The Firebringer's sister bearing a child, Mirabar in search of a child foretold in her visions . . ."

"But a Valdan's child?" Zarien asked doubtfully.

In the volcano-tinted light of the setting sun, Zarien could see his father's repugnance, but Tansen shrugged and said, "What if it was meant to be this way? If the new Yahrdan is part Valdani, then maybe the Valdani won't attack us when their wars on the mainland are over."

"*Their* wars will never be over," Zarien said with certainty. "That's just how they are."

"We can't count on that, son. And fighting them again . . . It would be so costly, even if we won again." He looked across the encampment at Ronall and said, "If we could satisfy them by recognizing a Yahrdan with some of their blood in his veins, maybe we could have peace with them for the rest of our lives."

"He seems a very peculiar choice for . . ."

Tansen's mouth quirked. "I know," he admitted wryly.

"So how can you determine if Jalilar's child is the one?"

"Luckily, that's not my problem. I've sent word to Mirabar."

"Ah. It's *her* problem."

"She gets the visions. I just do the fighting."

"Tansen!"

They both turned as Pyron, who had been with them ever since seeing Mirabar safely to Belitar after her marriage, came forward. "Sentries have spotted a runner."

"Ah! Good."

Tansen had been expecting a runner from Shaljir for several days now and had been worrying that the man might have been ambushed. It was happening more and more frequently.

As the runner approached, Zarien smiled, recognizing him. "Teyaban!" It was Elelar's servant, whom he had met in Shaljir.

The young man grinned. "Zarien! Still tattooed, I see."

Zarien rolled his eyes. "They don't wash off, you know."

Teyaban's gaze swept the camp. His eyes widened when he spotted Ronall. "*Toren!*" He crossed his fists and bowed his head, showing more respect to Ronall than anyone else here had thought of doing. "I'm relieved to see you. We have long wondered what happened to you."

Ronall gazed up at him blearily. "Do I know you?"

Tansen rubbed his forehead and said to Teyaban, "We have managed to find the *toren,* but we're having some difficulty convincing him to return to the *torena*. Perhaps if you could advise her—"

"But I can't, *siran*," Teyaban said.

Tansen went still. "Why not?"

"I don't know where the *torena* is."

"What?"

"No one does."

"*What?*"

Teyaban explained why Elelar had left Shaljir. "Anyhow, your friend Radyan was able to find out which Sanctuary the *torena* was sent to . . . To be honest, he's got more than a passing interest in her maid. You remember Faradar, don't you? After Radyan first arrived in Shaljir on your orders, he saw her, and the two of them just—"

"Get to the point," Tansen ordered.

"Oh. Yes. Well, Radyan found out that the *torena* left Sanctuary. Without telling anyone where she went."

"Let me make sure I understand you. Elelar has disappeared?"

"Yes."

"There's been no word from her?"

"None."

"And no word of a Society abduction?"

"No, *siran*. She left Sanctuary with her servants—including Faradar, which really disappointed Radyan—of her own free will, traveling at a sedate pace. The Sisters there had no idea she wasn't supposed to leave, so they didn't think anything of it."

Tansen's face darkened, but his expression revealed little. "Did she say anything or leave any message?"

"Only that no one was to worry about her, she knew what she was doing."

Tansen folded his arms across his chest and looked over at *Toren* Ronall. "I don't suppose *you* have any idea where she might have gone?"

Ronall shrugged indifferently and took another drink.

"No," Tansen said, "of course not."

Zarien realized what this meant. "We, uh, we can't send him back to her if we don't know where she is, can we?"

"We'll find out," Tansen said grimly.

"And until we do?"

"I suppose we'll have to keep him with us." And even Tansen couldn't hide his distress over this situation.

"Where might she have gone, father?"

"Almost anywhere," Tansen acknowledged. "But I'm very much afraid . . ."

"Yes?"

"That she's gone to court destiny."

MIRABAR HEARD CHANTING. Trilling. Ululating. A bewildering mixture of voices filled with passion and fervor, the ghostly praise-singing of exultant worshippers . . .

Lava moved through the veins of the earth, flowing somewhere beneath Mirabar's feet, making the ground tremble with Dar's blood, Dar's breath, Dar's life . . .

She was burning up in the heat. Calling on all her power to protect herself from immolation as Dar's will forged the future of Her people . . .

Mirabar inhaled deadly fumes as sudden flames erupted out of the glowing ooze of the lava spilling forth from the world's womb to flow over her . . .

A woman was screaming. Screaming for help. For mercy. Screaming in pain, in terror. Mirabar waded through the lava. Oh, how it burned! The agony was unbearable, but the screams pulled her on, beckoning her to help whoever was crying out to her.

Mirabar heard the wailing before she actually saw the baby . . .

My baby?

No . . . Mirabar's baby was an enchanted chill in her womb,

trying to help shield her from this all-consuming heat.

Who was the woman screaming in such agony and terror? It must be *her* baby, her birthing screams, her destiny come to pass . . .

Then Mirabar saw him, cloaked in his mother's blood. The infant's orange eyes and red hair glowed like all the Fires of Dar. He seemed at home in the liquid flame which engulfed him in the hot flow of Dar's birth throes . . .

He is coming. . . . Welcome him, welcome him . . .

The passionate trilling and chanting filled Mirabar's head as the rumbling roar echoed all around her . . .

Now she heard heavy groaning. Felt something cold and hard against her cheek. Against her shoulder. Her palm . . .

"Sirana?"

"How long has she been like this?"

The damp stone floors of Belitar. *Her* groans of pain.

"Stay away from her!"

"She *is* my wife, you know."

Najdan's and Baran's voices. Najdan's sharp with worry. Baran's detached and reasonable.

"Really," Baran said, "it's amazing that no superstitious *shallaheen* ever killed her during one of these fits." After a brief pause, he added, "Or bloodthirsty assassins."

"I told you not to touch her."

"Put your *shir* away," Baran said wearily, "and help me get her off the floor and into her bed."

"Don't—"

"Can't you see she's coming around?"

She tried to speak, but only wordless grunts came out of her mouth. She heard Velikar's voice, and possibly Haydar's. Then Baran ordered someone to bring her some wine.

She tried again. "When . . ." *When did you get back?*

He evidently understood what she wanted to ask. "Just now. Yes, I came home to find you writhing and screaming on the floor. Does this mean you've missed me?"

She didn't bother trying to answer.

There was a lot of fussing for a while, during which time she gradually pulled her senses together and became capable of sensible speech. It took some urging, but once she was alert and self-possessed, the others finally agreed to leave her alone in her bedchamber with her newly arrived husband. While she drank her wine and composed herself, Baran told her a little about his recent travels. She already knew about Wyldon's death, as she told him, but the rest of Dulien's comments were very interesting.

"You can get a message to Tansen right away about Dulien," Mirabar said, when he had concluded his account of his meeting with the other waterlord. "A runner has recently arrived from Tansen, so we can send him straight back."

"What news did he bring?" When she hesitated, he prodded, "Mirabar?"

"The Firebringer's sister is pregnant."

His brows rose. "Oh?"

"And the father . . ."

"Yes?"

"A Valdan."

"Rape?"

She shook her head. "Um. *Torena* Elelar's husband."

Baran burst out laughing.

She sighed, having expected that.

"Please," he said, "oh, *please,* tell me that a Valdan's bastard is the prophesied Yahrdan. Don't disappoint me by saying it's only—"

"I don't know. It's . . . it's certainly possible." The Firebringer's sister—yes, very possible.

"So, are the Valdani the thing you most long to destroy?"

The question made her feel ill. "I don't . . ." She started wringing her hands . . . then looked down at them and immediately stopped, wondering when she had developed such a silly habit. "I scarcely even think about them since they surrendered."

"Oh. Well, how do you get along with the Firebringer's sister?"

"Jalilar? Fine. I hardly know her."

He glanced at the moldily wrapped gift from the Olvara, which was sitting on a small table near the bed upon which Mirabar lay. "Don't you feel tempted to just cheat and look at it now?"

"Not really." Seeing his skeptical expression, she explained, "If I'm not ready, and I misuse it or misunderstand it, whatever it is . . ."

He shrugged. "As you wish."

Since his own men would tell him anyhow, she admitted, "We had a visitor while you were away."

"Cheylan."

"Oh." So they already *had* told him.

"I assume he didn't come here just to congratulate you on marrying so well?"

"He brought news from Dalishar." The visions in the night sky continued to help the Guardians convince people to oppose the Society. "And from the east." Verlon had found Semeon, the fire-eyed Guardian child, before Cheylan had—and Verlon had slaughtered him, along with his entire Guardian circle.

So Semeon wasn't the one. He couldn't have been the one. Mirabar prayed hard that he wasn't the one . . . And reminded herself often that surely her visions wouldn't be full of fire and promise, of warning and portent, if the young Yahrdan was already dead at the behest of a waterlord.

Cheylan seemed weighed down by the burden of the boy's death, by his failure to protect him. The two of them had talked a long time. He had seemed particularly taken aback by what she told him about her reasons for marrying Baran—and so disappointed by her married status that she'd found his protestations . . . well, a little embarrassing. She hadn't realized the extent of Cheylan's hopes for the two of them together, and she found herself obliged to make him understand that she could never give him what he wanted. Mirabar would have guarded the secret of Baran's illness in any case, since it was among the things her husband didn't want her discussing with anyone; but she was particularly careful to ensure that Cheylan had no idea that she expected to be a young widow. She didn't want to give him any reason to hope for a future with her.

She cared about Cheylan, but that was all. And she already knew she would never marry a second time without love. It was more than her heart could bear again.

"*What* news from the east did Cheylan bring?" Baran prodded, reclaiming her attention.

"Oh! Mostly about Jagodan shah Lironi's triumphs and defeats. Verlon's suspicions about Kiloran. The pilgrims going to Darshon from every part of Sileria."

Cheylan had also, she told Baran, agreed to gather Guardian forces and attempt to seize Wyldon's territory before Kiloran—or some other waterlord—could establish control over it. With little energy to spare for new conquests, Baran agreed with the decision she and Najdan had reached about this in his absence.

Now Baran shifted and moved towards the door of the chamber as if he meant to exit. Flooded with purpose in the wake of her vision, Mirabar forestalled his departure by asking, "What did you do besides meet with Dulien?"

"Ah. Well, I haven't killed Dyshon," he said regretfully. Looking tired, he came closer and sat down on the bed. "He's now in Cavasar, I gather, which is farther than I felt able to go. Anyhow, safely escaping that region once Kiloran realized I was there . . ." He shook his head. "If I want to kill Dyshon, I suppose I'll need to think up some way to lure him closer to Belitar."

"What about Alizar?"

"Yes, I made it to Alizar." The Olvara, when asked for help against Kiloran, had said she would need some of the enchanted water flooding the mines of Alizar. Since she couldn't go there to collect it herself, Baran had done it for her. "I'll take it to her later, after most of the household is asleep."

Mirabar nodded, wondering if the Olvara would confide in him. During Baran's absence, she had told the Olvara the extraordinary secret which was her right to know—that there were other Beyah-Olvari alive in Sileria. Baran's teacher had been so moved that she was virtually incoherent for days, and the exultant chanting and celebration in the subterranean caverns was so loud, Mirabar initially feared that the rest of Belitar's inhabitants might hear it. However, the sound didn't carry that far, through that much rock, and so no one else learned the secret which Mirabar now helped Baran guard here.

The secret which, Mirabar now understood, would help their child become immensely powerful even though Baran wouldn't be alive to teach her anything. Or to corrupt her with his tormented, amoral, embittered soul.

"Baran . . ." she murmured, ignoring how ill and exhausted he looked.

"Hmmm?" He glanced towards the closed door, evidently anxious to retreat to his own bedchamber—or maybe to seek the relief of one of Velikar's potions.

Mirabar traced the finely embroidered collar of his tunic, which was now too big for him. "I want this child," she whispered.

His mouth quirked. "I'm a little . . . tired."

This child would be what Baran could have been. Should have been. Would have been, had fate and a wildly grieving heart not twisted him into what he was.

She moved closer to him, sliding her hands down his thin torso and under his tunic, seeking his skin. "I'll do all the work," she promised. "Stay."

His eyelids lowered and his breathing started to change. "I won't die in the next few hours," he assured her softly. "We could wait until I'm feeling . . ."

"Don't make me wait," she murmured against his mouth.

"Uh . . ."

She shrugged out of her tunic, then pulled her undergarment over her head and tossed it aside. "I'm your wife," she whispered, kissing his neck. "Don't deny me."

"What did you see in that vision?" he asked with a frown, letting her draw him down into the pillows with her.

"I'm not entirely sure," she admitted. "But this child can save me."

"From what?" His eyes closed as she kissed his chest and slid her palms along his ribs.

"From what I must do." She framed his hollow-eyed face with her hands. "She can even, in a way, save you."

"From Kiloran?" he asked vaguely, his hands starting to tug at her pantaloons.

"From yourself."

His hands went still. He turned his head to evade her next kiss. "I don't need—"

"She can make a new future, and your power in her will be part of that, healing the very wounds that you have inflicted."

Baran shook his head. "There is no such thing as redemption," he said, "in the land of the destroyer goddess."

"You're wrong," she replied. "You could have changed Sileria, Baran, but your heart broke you. So now you will leave behind a daughter to do your work."

"I'm leaving her behind to kill Kiloran in case we fail," he reminded her. "Don't confuse—"

"Yes," she agreed, "but that's not the work you were born for."

"It doesn't matter why I was born," he said stonily, pushing her hands away. "Not now."

Exasperated with him, she said, "You probably could have killed him years ago—but you couldn't bear to, could you?"

"Kiloran?" He scowled at her. "I have tried with all my—"

"No, you haven't," she said. "You've become a living legend over the years. You're one of the strongest waterlords who's ever lived. Yet Kiloran's still alive."

"Because he's even str—"

"Not that much stronger," she persisted. "Not enough. Not if killing him really meant everything to you."

"It does! It always has."

She shook her head, no longer believing this. "You waited until you were dying, until you knew your life was over. Because before that, you didn't want to live without him."

"Even I'm not that crazy," he snapped.

"Yes, you are," she said sadly. "And now you may have waited too long. You may already be too weak."

"Waited?" His tone was vicious. His grip on her arms hurt. "Why, pray tell, would I ever have waited, *sirana?"*

"Because you couldn't bear it if Kiloran died and left you alone in the world," she replied with certainty, finally understanding the wildly grieving madman she had married. Baran had ultimately grown demented mourning the loss of his own soul as much as the loss of his wife. "You would have to face yourself if you couldn't spend all your energy hating Kiloran anymore."

"I *have* faced my—"

"No. You've always told yourself that this is the way you must be, that you have no choice. That he gave you no choice."

He sat up suddenly and pushed her away. "I did . . . I *do* have to be this w—"

"No."

"He *didn't* give me a choice," Baran insisted, his voice suddenly despairing. "Dar didn't give me a choice. And you cannot imagine how I hate Her for it."

"They had nothing to do with it, Baran. It was always *your* choice. And when you have lived for nothing but vengeance, what's left after you get it?"

"Stop it," he ordered her, rising from the bed.

She clung to his arm and gazed up into his tormented face. "You needed Kiloran too much to kill him. Until you finally knew you'd soon be dead."

"No!" He tried to tug away from her. "I won't listen . . . Stop. *No*." He shook his head. "Don't."

"Baran . . ."

"I could not . . ." He was breathing hard, his expression stricken, his eyes glittering with reckless emotion. "I could not have been anything else. Don't convince me, when it's much too late, that I could have been something else."

She found herself pitying him despite the many people he had killed and terrorized during his reign as a waterlord. "I promise you," she vowed, "your daughter *will* be something else."

"My daughter . . ." His face crumpled and he sank slowly onto the bed again, sitting with his back to her. "My daughter."

"She will be something new," Mirabar told him gently. "A woman with the power which has belonged only to men in Sileria. A water wizard raised by a Guardian and the Beyah-Olvari. Baran . . ." He flinched when she touched him. "She will be the future. The Olvara sees it, and so do I."

"And I . . ." Baran sagged in defeat. He buried his face in his hands and sat there like that for a long moment, shutting her out. Finally, his voice muffled, he said, "If you're right, then it's a good thing I'll be dead. It's too late for me. I can't . . . It's too late for me to become something else, Mirabar."

She said nothing, knowing he was right.

"I chose things . . ." He nodded slowly. "Yes, I suppose I did *choose* . . . things which can never be undone. I left parts of myself behind to die, and they can never be resurrected."

She touched him again. He didn't flinch away this time.

"Give me this daughter, Baran," she urged. "Give her to me before your time runs out."

He finally lifted his head. "We must succeed. Kill him. Destroy Kiloran," he said harshly. "So that she won't have to. So that she . . ." He took a few gusting breaths before concluding, "So that you can keep your promise. So that our daughter never becomes what I've become."

She sighed and pressed her cheek against his shoulder, relieved that he understood. Glad that he *could* understand.

"And when Kiloran's dead," Baran concluded, "I'll be ready to die." After a moment, he added, "You're right—I'll *want* to die. And then I can finally . . ."

She heard what he didn't say: *Finally go to her, to my wife, to Alcinar.*

She leaned against him, pressing her breasts against his back, reminding him of what he owed her before he could seek out his love in the Otherworld—if Alcinar were indeed dead, and if Dar granted him such a fate.

Baran sighed and sagged back against her, understanding her silent demand. Accepting it. Clinging to life to fulfill their mutual destiny. He turned to her, his eyes wild with madness and sorrow, and sought her kiss. His arms came around her with a strength she hadn't suspected he still possessed, and his mouth was urgent upon hers.

A child of fire . . .

His skin was hot, and she didn't know if it was anger, excitement, or the start of a fever which would further weaken him. His kisses were hungry, as if he sought her life force to keep him alive just a little longer, just long enough to destroy his enemy and sire his heir.

A child of water . . .

They touched each other with a familiarity which seemed unthinkable, even bizarre, whenever they weren't actually together, alone, like this. She clung to him because she must, because it was a destiny more imperative than any dictates of her heart. And there were thoughts, needs, longings she would never bring to her marriage bed, because they had no place here.

A child of sorrow . . .

His bitter heart engulfed her, and for once she did not shy away from his torment, not even from his madness. She let his terrible sadness consume her, let his heart wail inside her chest, let his hopeless yearning and insane bloodlust pour into her even as his seed did. The seductive cold of his power washed through her, flooding her senses, filling the vessel which Dar had chosen for his immortality. And Mirabar, who finally understood why Baran, of all men, must father her child, welcomed him.

Fire and water, water and fire . . .

Flame and ice mingled in her veins, in her blood, in her womb. She moaned and writhed beneath him, burning and boiling as the gift was given and taken, crystal-bright and lava-rich. The waters of eternity and the fires of the Otherworld, the ebb and flow of man and woman, the mingled heat and chill of passion and sorrow, of trust and enmity coursed between them and found a new beginning in her, a new caldera in which to grow and ripen.

After he rolled away from her, she lay still for a long time, staring at the damp-marred ceiling overhead, knowing that Belitar would forever be her home now.

She thought he had fallen asleep, so she was surprised when he finally spoke. "There will always be water magic in Sileria." She could hear in his voice that he already knew they had finally succeeded, had finally conceived their child. "Always," he repeated. "Tansen can't change that. No one can."

"I know," she replied, feeling the cool glow in her womb. "I know that now."

48

TO RULE WATER IS TO RULE SILERIA.

— Marjan

THE SUN BLAZED hotly down upon the stark mountains, dry lowlands, and thirsty cities. Volcanic ash streaked and clouded the sky, and the nights were on fire with Dar's fury. She shook the ground with rage, Her tantrums coming ever more frequently and more violently as the season advanced. And while withering heat sucked life from the land, Sileria daily shed rivers of blood.

Josarian's loyalists swept through the mountains like the enchanted fire they bore with them, torching the holdings of the waterlords, destroying their influence wherever they could, and urging people to pledge their lives to the Firebringer's cause. The visions at Dalishar, like the visions which blessed Mirabar, promised a proud future if Sileria had the courage to fight for it. Josarian's dream of freedom from the Valdani was meant to be a new beginning, not a new enslavement to the Society. Thousands had died in the rebellion, but not so that those they left behind could serve the waterlords the way they had once served the Valdani.

The Society splintered and quarreled, some blaming Baran for Wyldon's death, others blaming Kiloran. If weaker sorcerers like Geriden and Meriten were too afraid of the old man to speak up, then stronger ones like Gulstan and Verlon were willing to do it for them. Having foreseen this, having recognized what Tansen was trying to do, Kiloran sent emissaries, peace offerings, and even assistance to embattled waterlords. After some of Kiloran's own valued men died helping Gulstan repel an attack led by Tansen himself, Gulstan relented and reaffirmed his friendship with Kiloran.

Other waterlords were harder to manage, though. Kiloran soon learned that Dulien had betrayed him and secretly sided with Tansen, foolishly believing that Tansen would let him maintain his territory after Kiloran was dead and the war was over. Kiloran knew he must remind the rest of the Society how costly betrayal was, so he killed Dulien himself. Unfortunately, Baran had foreseen this and was waiting to spring a trap of his own; that demented *sriliah* drowned every man Kiloran had left behind to guard Dulien's territory after he'd killed him.

Searlon sought Tansen and the sea-born boy, but Tansen's camps were too well guarded for Searlon to approach Zarien there; and those loyal to Tansen died under interrogation rather than give away his plans, if they even knew them, so Searlon was unable to anticipate his movements. Meanwhile, Kiloran received word that some of Verlon's assassins had somehow managed to locate and ambush Tansen. They failed to kill him, and Kiloran couldn't find out who had betrayed the *shatai* to Verlon, though he remained curious about this.

The great waterlord Kariman went on the attack, trying to reclaim the territory which Tansen had seized from the now-dead Ferolen. Kariman lost many men and his strength was depleted by the time he succeeded. It was estimated that dozens of Guardians died trying to stop him. Once in control, though, Kariman consolidated his power and struck out from his vast combined territory. It was now only a matter of time before Kariman brought Adalian to its knees. Although fanatically loyal to the Firebringer's memory, the city was suffering terribly. It was said that one out of every ten people there had died of thirst since the start of the dry season.

Cavasar remained mostly loyal to Kiloran, though its people were reluctant to leave their region and fight for him elsewhere. He convinced many of them to do so, though, by promising them a lifetime of lushly flowing water, and even a fair share in the mines of Alizar, if they helped him secure his power across Sileria. Sometimes though . . . Yes, sometimes it was necessary to inspire fear rather than love. The Cavasari had not forgotten Josarian, and a few of them were even brave enough to demand that others honor his legacy, too. Every so often, Kiloran ensured that a few of these upstarts' bodies decorated the city's main square, usually encased in a block of crystal-clear solidified water. An effective means of public execution; and an equally effective means of reminding the people that disobedience was not tolerated.

"THE *TOREN* WILL stay with me," Zarien offered, as Tansen fretted about whom to leave behind with Zarien while the rest of their group attacked yet another waterlord's stronghold.

"Yes, but while you're looking after Ronall," Tansen replied dryly, "who will look after you?"

"We'll be fine," Zarien assured him.

"We have *got* to get rid of him," Tansen said with an uncharacteristic flash of desperation.

"He seems very unhappy."

"That's a very generous interpretation of his character, son." Tansen shook his head. "For possibly the first time ever, I think I genuinely pity Elelar. Living with that man for years . . ." After a moment, he added, "Of course, I pity him, too. Living with Elelar . . . I wonder if he always drank this much, or if marriage to her was what got him started?"

"Well, *toreni* are . . . different, aren't they?" Zarien said tactfully.

"We can't keep dragging him around Sileria with us." Tansen sighed and added, "I'm very tempted to let him just run away and get himself killed, but . . . it's not convenient now."

"Jalilar's baby," Zarien murmured.

"Yes. Jalilar's baby. And showing Ronall off in Britar," Tansen admitted, "did serve to stop the massacres there."

"Until all the fighting started, anyhow."

Tansen's face clouded. Many had died, on all sides, during his battle against Gulstan, who ruled the waters all around Britar—and Tansen had failed there. He rarely failed at anything, and the defeat took him hard. Zarien could tell, and he was sorry he had brought it up.

He tried to change the subject, "If only we knew where *Torena* Elelar was."

"I think I may know."

"You do?"

"But let's focus on the problem at hand," Tansen suggested.

"You don't need to leave anyone with me wh—"

"Yes, I do."

"I can stay behind by myself."

"No." Tansen hesitated, then slowly said, "In fact, it's very important that you never go anywhere alone anymore. Not for any reason."

"There are some things I prefer to do alone," Zarien said with a pointed look. Seeing how strangely distressed his bloodfather now seemed, he prodded, "What's bothering you?"

Tansen started pacing. Zarien watched with interest, wondering what could actually make Tansen, of all people . . . yes, *fidget*.

"All right," Tansen said at last, evidently coming to a decision. "It's better if you know this. You're old enough to know this." He looked at Zarien and added, as if trying to convince himself, "It's dangerous for you *not* to know this."

"Are you going to get to the point?" Zarien inquired.

Tansen took a deep breath. "I've learned that Kiloran is looking for you."

"Me?"

Tansen's face darkened. "Because you're my son."

"Oh." Zarien's heart started pounding.

Kiloran is looking for you.

He thought he felt a little sick suddenly.

Tansen's expression twisted into something truly awful.

"He wants you because . . . because he knows nothing would hurt me as much as his hurting *you*."

In truth, the news frightened Zarien terribly. But he could tell it frightened Tansen even more, so he said, "I'm always with you, so you can stop whoever comes for—"

"But you're *not* always with me. And since *Toren* Ronall is not an adequate protector—"

"Maybe I should come to your battles with you."

"No. That would be too dangerous—for both of us. And with Ealian gone now . . ." Tansen looked down, studying his dusty, worn boots. He had sent the elderly Guardian away to perform other duties. "I'll need to leave another Guardian with you from now on. Maybe two. Or three."

Zarien tried to think like a man, ashamed that Tansen found him such a liability. "They're needed more in battle."

"It's only temporary. Until . . ."

"Until what?" Zarien demanded, full of foreboding now.

"Maybe . . . we should separate," Tansen said slowly.

Zarien felt his stomach drop. "You want me to go?"

"I want to find someplace safe for you."

"I don't want to—"

"Just for a while."

"No." Being on the dryland—now and forever—was difficult enough to adjust to. Being all alone, without Tansen . . . "*No.*"

"We need to think about it," Tansen insisted.

"What makes you think I'd be harder to find just because I wouldn't be with you?" Zarien protested, his panic overwhelming his desire to stop being a burden to Tansen. "Kiloran can find me anywhere if he—"

"I've been considering Belitar," Tansen admitted. "Kiloran would probably find out where you were, but he couldn't reach you there."

"Belitar?" A haunted ruin inhabited by the *sirana,* her pet assassin, and her notoriously crazy husband. "No!"

"Sanctuary, then."

"I don't want to go to Sanctuary." He heard how querulous he sounded, but he was past caring.

"Then maybe if you went back to sea for a wh—"

"No!" Zarien hadn't meant to shout. He made an awkward gesture. "I'm never going to sea again."

"Zarien—"

"I want to stay with you," he said stubbornly.

Tansen took him by the shoulders. His lean face looked dark and restless as he said, "I'm afraid he'll find you and kill you if you stay with me."

"You can protect—"

"I couldn't protect Josarian from him." Tansen's voice was rough and full of self-loathing.

Zarien would not show tears. He would *not*. "Don't make me go," he said, trying to control his voice. "Please, don't."

Attempting to appease him without promising anything, Tansen said, "We'll think of something."

"I won't go back to sea," Zarien warned him. "I *won't*."

"Someday," Tansen said gently, "you will."

"No!" Bitterness and a burning sense of betrayal flooded him with rage all over again. "*No*. I am done with the sea! With Sharifar!"

"Zarien." Tansen brought the rare sternness into his tone which was a sign that he was insisting Zarien heed him. "Listen to me. I know what it is to be hunted by Kiloran. When I was your age . . ." Tansen's face changed and he stopped speaking.

"What?" Zarien prodded.

"Nothing."

"When you were my a—"

"Never mind."

Zarien wondered what the strange expression on Tansen's face meant, but he was more interested in his own problem. "Are you going to make me go away?" he demanded.

"I don't . . ." Tansen rubbed a hand across his face and admitted, "I don't know."

"You won't . . . trick me? Just leave me behind somewhere and not come back?"

Tansen's expression changed again, and this time Zarien understood what he saw there. "No."

To his surprise, Tansen suddenly embraced him. Holding him in a grip so fierce it hurt, his bloodfather promised, "No, I won't just leave you. Not ever."

Zarien closed his eyes and let himself be hugged.

THE ZANAREEN GAINED new recruits faster than they ever had before, as religious fervor swept across the land. The rages of the destroyer goddess, the frequency of the violent earthquakes, the inexplicable displays of color and fury at the summit of Darshon . . . These were all portents which drove men as mad as their raging thirst. They abandoned their homes, their families, their livelihoods. They turned their backs on everything they owned, everyone they knew, everything they had once been. Some threw themselves into battle against the Society under such suicidal circumstances that they became legends upon their deaths. Others went to Darshon, like so many people these days, to praise Dar, seek Her favor, beg for Her mercy, and endure whatever She chose to inflict upon Her people.

Many of Sileria's abandoned women joined the Sisterhood and began tending the wounded, the thirsty, the dying. Sanctuary was safe for them in these chaotic times, and many Sanctuaries needed fresh recruits, having been drained of their women by Dar, who continued Calling Her worshippers to Darshon in a frenzy of divine hunger for praise, for worship, for sacrifice.

Whole villages were destroyed in the earthquakes, and many lives were lost. The waterlords began claiming they could protect the people from Dar, as they had protected themselves from Her for a thousand years. But Sileria must turn to them, and away from the Guardians, away from the

Firebringer's memory, to earn the protection of the Society and reap the benefits of its mercy.

The Guardians, meanwhile, promised a golden age for anyone who served Dar now, and eternal punishment for anyone who sided with the Society.

"Look how Dar rages against Kiloran's murder of the Firebringer! The waterlords are lying when they say they can protect you from Her, and you'd be fools to think She won't cherish and reward you as they never could." Ealian, the elderly Guardian from Zilar, honed his gift for oration, inspiring loyalists and gaining converts wherever he went, obeying Tansen's orders to spread courage throughout Sileria. "The volcano will rest when every waterlord is dead or has fled Sileria, and not before! Loyalty to the Society now will mean *centuries* of earthquakes and eruptions as Dar fights to reclaim Her nation from it!"

Villages and clans which had been aggressively attacking their enemies now lost their convictions and started descending into internal chaos and bitter family disputes as all of Sileria confronted the darkest questions of their destiny.

Could the Honored Society protect people from the destroyer goddess?

Could Dar protect them from Kiloran and the waterlords?

Individuals once loyal to the Society began to fear the goddess even more than they feared the waterlords, and so they switched their allegiance to the Firebringer's loyalists. Other people now turned their backs on the Guardians in search of an end to their terrible thirst, seeking the cold comfort of the waterlords who promised protection from the raging volcano and the ash-darkened skies.

If Kariman would water their fields, if Gulstan would let their streams flow so their sheep could drink, if Kiloran would open the mines of Alizar so that they could work honorably to earn money in place of the drought-withered crops which would not feed them this year, then they would defy Dar for the waterlords.

If Dar would fulfill the promises of the visions at Dalishar, if Mirabar would proclaim the identity of the ruler she had foretold in fiery prophecy, if *someone* could explain why Dar had let the Firebringer die, then Her people would defy the waterlords for Her.

Shallaheen began abandoning the most severely drought-stricken villages. Lann, who was still fighting Meriten's attempts to gain control of the Shaljir River and the territory all around Zilar, was surprised when his wife simply arrived in Zilar one day without warning. She had walked all the way from Islanar, where no one would now return until the rains finally came. The wells were dry, the livestock bloated and dead, the crops brown and stunted, the larders empty. There was nothing in Islanar's central fountain now except volcanic dust. Many people had died there—including, Lann's wife informed him with haunted eyes, their youngest daughter. Lann, always volatile and unashamed of it, broke down and wept like a child in front of his men. His wife and surviving daughters chose to remain in Zilar with him, despite the state of siege which existed throughout the whole district.

When Tansen defeated yet another waterlord and freed the water in his territory, more people rallied to his cause . . . And more were slaughtered for this very reason when the Society struck out to demonstrate the price for betrayal and the terrible penalty for disobedience.

Iyadar, the pretty young Guardian whom Tansen had first met in Zilar, was captured by Kariman and tortured to death. Her maimed, headless body was hung upside down at the gates of Adalian to warn the city of how much more they would suffer if they continued resisting Kariman's influence.

Tansen never knew who did it, but some loyalist then cut open Iyadar's belly, pulled out the young woman's entrails, and used them to make a gruesome *jashar* which hung over her body thereafter: *Free water for all*.

No, there would be no compromise, no peace in Sileria until one side or the other was completely vanquished forever.

* * *

MIRABAR RETCHED VIOLENTLY while Haydar held her head over a basin. When Mirabar's stomach was finally as empty as it could get, Haydar said to her, "You should eat something now."

Mirabar glared speechlessly at her.

Sister Velikar, who watched the proceedings with ghoulish interest, said, "I'll make her a tisane."

Mirabar shuddered. "Oh, no, you won't."

Now Baran entered what passed for the sunroom at Belitar. He looked even worse than Mirabar felt, his cheekbones starkly sharp in his thin, pain-lined face. Taking in the scene, he frowned. "What's going on?"

"You did this to me, you bastard!" Mirabar said viciously, feeling too weak to set him on fire as he deserved.

Baran's eyebrows rose. "I beg your—"

"Women in her condition," Haydar explained, "have these little moods."

"My *condition* is that I'm dying because of what you did to me," Mirabar snarled at Baran, pleased to have someone upon whom to vent her temper.

"That remark," he pointed out, his red-rimmed eyes looking smudged and sunken, "is in rather bad taste, under the circumstances."

Mirabar groaned and sank into a chair. "Why didn't anyone warn me I would feel this way?"

Baran looked at the other two women. "Is she going to be in this mood right up until she delivers the brat?"

"No, no," Haydar assured him.

"Probably," Velikar replied.

Haydar frowned at the Sister. "The *sirana* is just adjusting to her condition. She will soon improve."

"Will I?" Mirabar whimpered.

Haydar returned to her original theme: "You should eat a little something."

Mirabar's hand covered her mouth and she murmured feebly, "Dar have mercy." She glared at Baran when he laughed. "Did you come in here for any reason other than to make my life even more miserable than it already is?"

He held up a parchment he was carrying. "I have a message for you."

Her heart pounded hard for a moment, but then she realized Tansen wouldn't have *written* to her. He couldn't. "Who is it from?"

Baran's gaze swept the other two women as he said, "Would you excuse us?"

Haydar nodded and left the room. Velikar needed some nudging, but she finally went, too.

"Who," Mirabar repeated, "is it from?"

"*Torena* Elelar."

Her eyes flew wide open. She sat bolt upright, forgetting about her nausea, her headache, and the mood swings which had plagued her since the night Baran had given her the child which now bathed her womb in cool enchantment.

"Elelar?" she repeated incredulously.

"Yes." He watched her with interest.

"Elelar." The chilly magic of a waterlord was nothing compared to the cold hatred which suddenly flooded her. *Elelar.* "What does *she* want?"

"I'm not sure." He glanced down at the letter. "Knowing that I'm now your husband, and that I can read, she writes asking me to tell you where she is—"

"I don't care where she is," she said querulously.

"—and that she is ready."

"Ready for what?" Mirabar snapped.

He shrugged and read directly from the letter. " 'Tell Mirabar that I have made my peace with Dar and am ready.' "

"Ready for *what?*" Mirabar repeated irritably.

"She also asks me to keep Kiloran from interfering."

"Interfering with *what?*"

"Apparently the *torena*'s habitual obliqueness is wasted on you in this instance." Baran lifted one brow and added, "As I suspect it usually is, my dear."

Mirabar scowled. "What's it to me if she's made her peace with . . ." She trailed off, feeling strange as memories flooded her.

"You really hate her, don't you?" he observed with interest.

"I . . ." The chill was fading, being replaced by a wave of crippling heat.

"Is it just because she convinced Zimran to betray Josarian and lead him into a Valdani ambush? Or is there more?"

"With her, there is *always* more," Mirabar choked out, barely able to hear her husband above the roaring in her ears.

Protect what you most long to destroy.

"Mirabar?"

"No." she gasped, shaking her head. "Oh, no."

"Made her peace with Dar and is ready . . ." Baran mused. "Did you two ever discuss some sort of plan?"

"No," she repeated, but not in answer to him.

There was no death she had ever longed for more than Elelar's, and no one she had ever hated as much. Elelar was the one person in the world whom she had personally longed to murder, so much so that she saw a terrifying reflection of her own potential in Baran's vengeful madness, his wasted life, and his corrupted use of his great power.

She held her hands up to her reeling head as the fiery heat of visionary knowledge poured through her. "I tried to make . . . make Tansen do it . . ."

"Do what?"

Kill her. Kill Elelar. "I thought it would make him stop . . ." *Stop loving Elelar. Stop caring for her.* "Maybe prove . . ." *Prove that he didn't?* "After Josarian died, all I wanted was . . ."

"Vengeance," Baran guessed.

"Yes. Even for things Elelar . . ." She shook her head. "Wasn't really responsible for." Such as Tansen's feelings,

Mirabar's sense of failure, and Dar's betrayal of the Fire-bringer.

Why did You let him die, Dar? Why?

"I wanted to save Josarian," she muttered. "I wanted to understand Dar. And to be the only woman Tansen . . . cared for."

"Ah."

She met Baran's dark gaze and, for just a moment, saw the decent man he used to be, long ago. The man who understood—even sympathized with—things like love and human frailty.

"So it's Elelar," Baran murmured.

She glared at him. *"What's* Elelar?"

" 'Protect what you most long to destroy.' "

Mirabar shook her head. "No."

He started to look amused. "Oh, yes. It's so obvious, I'd have realized it the moment the Olvara said it, if you and I were, er, better acquainted."

"No," Mirabar repeated.

"What I don't understand is why *you* didn't realize it." He sighed, clearly enjoying himself now. "No, actually, I suppose I do understand. No one knows better than me how bloodlust clouds the mind. But now that you know what you must do—"

"No!" she shouted.

His voice oozed with commiseration as he said, "Vengeance isn't any easier to give up just because your spouse thinks it's unworthy of you, is it?"

"I really detest you," she hissed.

"It's part of what keeps our marriage lively," he assured her cheerfully.

"I'm going to be sick again," Mirabar threatened.

"Very likely," he agreed.

She wrapped her arms around herself, constantly aware of the cool glow in her belly, and said, "I can't . . . I can't do it. . . ."

"Protect Elelar?"

"Dar can't ask that of me," she moaned, fully indulging in her emotionalism.

"While you're moaning and whining—"

"Go away," she snapped.

"—perhaps you could find time to consider the relevant question here."

"The relevant question?" She rolled her eyes. "Oh, please, share it with me, *siran*."

"Protect her from *what?*"

She stared at the empty space he left behind after he departed the chamber, his amused chuckles floating through the damp air as he abandoned her to her turmoil.

He was right, she knew. Nonetheless, a different question flooded her thoughts and consumed her energy.

Why Elelar? Dar have mercy on me, why her?

PILGRIMS STREAMED INTO the permanent encampment atop Mount Dalishar. They came in search of visions, of courage, of inspiration and leadership—and of Dalishar's unensorcelled water supply, as their villages withered and died beneath the burning sun and ash-clouded sky.

Yorin, still in charge at Dalishar, had grown so used to the visions which appeared in the night sky there that he sometimes slept through them now. Then, one night, an assassin who had come to Dalishar in disguise murdered Yorin in his sleep.

Tansen sent Pyron to take over Yorin's post—after giving him strict instructions to improve security at the sacred site. According to Pyron's somewhat hysterical first report after that, the battle for Alizar had been a more peaceful experience than dealing with the thirsty, frightened, and confused throng which daily flooded Mount Dalishar.

The city of Adalian became increasingly desperate for relief. Funeral pyres of the dead burned every day and, with too little water left to keep all the city-dwellers alive, many of them began escaping into the war-torn countryside. Tansen's attack on Gulstan had failed, and his victory against Ferolen had been short-lived, since Kariman soon thereafter assumed control of the dead waterlord's territory; if Tansen couldn't find a way to break the Society's power in the south soon, Adalian was doomed.

"If only Kiloran hadn't managed to regain Gulstan's friendship," Tansen said pensively one day as Zarien bandaged another minor battle wound for him. "If only he'd found it necessary to kill Gulstan the way he killed Dulien."

"I don't understand how Kiloran found out Dulien was betraying him," Zarien said absently as he expertly dressed the wound. "No one knew about Dulien besides you, Baran, and—"

"I told Kiloran."

"You *what?*"

Tansen made a dismissive gesture. "I mean, I made sure Kiloran found out. He doesn't know the information came from me, of course."

Zarien froze. "Why did you do that?"

"So Kiloran would kill him for us, of course." When the boy remained motionless, Tansen prodded, "Finish the job, would you? I have work to do."

"But Dulien . . . sought your friendship. And you agreed."

Tansen replied, "Dulien sought the best way to keep everything he had, and to get whatever else he could with no risk to himself—or so he thought."

Staring in dark wonder, Zarien said, "You betrayed him?"

Tansen looked at him in surprise. "He was a *waterlord,* Zarien."

"But don't you . . . Doesn't . . ."

"They all have to die," Tansen said. "Or be driven out of Sileria. We can't leave *part* of the Society alive and functioning after the war, son. Nothing would change. Within a few years, things would be just as bad as if we had fought no war at all. And thousands of lives would have been lost for no reason."

Moving slowly, his face dark with thought, Zarien returned to bandaging the wound. "Will you betray Baran, too?"

"No."

"Because he has served your cause?"

"Because betraying him would endanger Mirabar."

"And if it wouldn't?" the boy prodded.

"Baran may be demented, but he's much smarter than the rest of them. As smart as Kiloran, I think, but hotheaded and sometimes reckless." He shook his head. "Anyhow, I doubt Baran would ever put himself in a position where he needed to trust me, as Dulien did. He's certainly too smart for that."

There was a long, deafening silence between them. Realizing he had shattered some of Zarien's ideals—particularly the ones the boy cherished about *him*—he said, "What are you thinking?"

"Nothing," Zarien replied.

"If there's some—"

"I'm done." The boy finished dressing the wound, then turned away, vanishing into the general bustle of the encampment.

Tansen repressed a sigh and decided to let the subject rest for now. He had too many other things to accomplish today.

Kiloran's grip on his own territories was so strong and secure that nothing had so far succeeded in disturbing it; and Tansen knew he could only vanquish the old waterlord by first eliminating Kiloran's additional support—the rest of the Society.

The ultimate fate of Zilar and the Shaljir River was still uncertain. Kiloran and Meriten both understood how destructive it would be to the Society if the Firebringer's loyalists finally achieved all-out victory there, so they still fought bitterly for it. In the east, Verlon and a few of the lesser waterlords still defended their territories more desperately, shrewdly, and ruthlessly than the Valdani themselves had during the rebellion.

This deep into the dry season, there was no relief for the

water-starved nation. The long rains were still some time away . . . if they came. If this was one of the occasional years in which the rains were late, sparse, or simply never arrived, then Tansen knew Sileria could not hold out against what the waterlords were doing to the land and its people.

He needed victory. Sileria needed it. Tansen knew this, and the knowledge had led him to attack Gulstan . . . which he now saw, with bitter regret and self-condemnation, had been a mistake. What did Kiloran always say? Mistakes were so easily made.

Too easily. Much too easily.

Tansen knew he couldn't afford any more.

He had been thinking like a *shallah* when he led the Firebringer's loyalists into battle against Gulstan, one of the Society's most powerful and ruthless waterlords—and certainly the fattest. Tansen's plan to sow dissension between Gulstan and Kiloran had failed, and he had fallen back on the simple Silerian solution of all-out violence.

Mistake.

It was time to think like a *shatai*. It was time to remember the training and education drilled into him by his *kaj*: the teachings of great Kintish swordmasters and philosophers which had been distilled, over the centuries, into pure, poetic, simple lessons taught to the finest warrior caste in the three corners of the world, that they might always be the best, wherever they went, whatever challenges they faced.

It was time—past time—to be the best, as he had been taught to be.

Tansen's *kaj* had always said he was too quick to choose violence, too ready to fight. That trait, Kaja said, was the Silerian in him, the bloodthirsty *shallah*.

"A *shatai* should always win a fight," Tansen murmured, remembering what Kaja had tried again and again to make him understand and accept, even after putting two deadly swords into his hands, "but to win *without* fighting is the pinnacle of skill."

To this wisdom, Tansen now mentally added the gift which had rarely failed him over the years: *Make them see what you want them to see.*

He needed a plan.

And he thought he had one.

If it didn't work . . .

Focus on the task at hand.

But if it didn't work . . .

I am prepared to die today. Are you?

Zarien would be orphaned again.

Tansen sighed heavily, filled with a tremendous guilt he had never before known upon risking his own life. A terrible, devouring fear crept through his blood when he thought of Zarien alone in the world, without him.

He wondered now if Armian, who had seemed so powerful, so reckless and invincible, had felt this way, too.

He wondered now, with a sudden shaft of piercing sorrow, if Armian had loved him even as Tansen murdered him.

"I can't get near Tansen, so I can't get access to the boy," Searlon reported to Kiloran as they met in Kiloran's underwater palace at Lake Kandahar. "So I'm working on a plan."

"To separate him from the boy?" Kiloran asked.

"I've come to believe that, under current circumstances, he will not leave the boy somewhere—at least, not long enough for me to locate him. Tansen is, based on what I can learn, very protective of Zarien and much attached to him."

Kiloran's blood felt cold with memory. "Is he indeed?" It wouldn't matter. Not in the end. Not with Tansen.

"However," Searlon continued, "if I can distract Tansen with an unexpected problem, perhaps I'll have a better chance of getting close to the boy."

"No matter what," Kiloran began, "the boy is very valuable and—"

"Must not be harmed. I understand, *siran*." Searlon added,

"Baran still shows no interest in Zarien. He has made no effort to communicate with the boy, let alone to get him away from Tansen."

Kiloran murmured, "So Baran really doesn't know."

"As far as I can ascertain, *siran*, no one else—not even Zarien himself—knows what you, I, and a few of the surviving Lascari know about him."

"Even so, secrets are like children," Kiloran said. "No one can guard them day and night forever, and no one can predict what they will become."

"I'll find the boy," Searlon promised.

"Tell me about your plan."

"Ah!" Searlon smiled. "It comes as part of a bundle of good news I bring today, and it's a plan which should also solve certain problems in the east."

"Verlon?" The old waterlord, although still part of the Society, was quite clear by now about his uncompromising enmity for Kiloran.

Searlon shook his head. "The Lironi and their allies."

"The Lironi?" Kiloran considered this with interest. Despite his problems with Verlon, destroying the Firebringer's loyalists everywhere was indeed still his primary concern. "So your plan will leave Verlon unchallenged in the east?"

Searlon shook his head. "Not quite, *siran*. I have discovered that Verlon has a burden we didn't even know about, one which I wouldn't wish on anyone." When Kiloran gave him a quizzical look, Searlon grinned, the scar on his cheek flowing into a dimple. "Verlon," he said, "has an ambitious heir."

Kiloran laughed and realized how much he had missed Searlon.

"The news gets even better, *siran*."

"Oh?"

The assassin helped himself to a modest quantity of Kintish fire brandy as he continued, "I've finally found someone who's willing—even eager—to betray Mirabar. Someone ready to offer us friendship."

Kiloran accepted the brandy which Searlon offered him, too, and said, "In truth, it's probably worth almost any price at this point, but I feel obliged to ask, nonetheless: What will this friendship cost us?"

"Nothing we can't afford, *siran*," Searlon assured him. "And our investment in it should reap many profits."

EMPEROR JARELL SENT warnings to the temporary government in Shaljir: The killing of Silerian-born Valdani must cease, or there would be reprisals from the mainland.

The imperial warnings inspired horrified alarm in the leaders of the Alliance, who sent appeasing replies back to the mainland. However, no one really knew how to protect the Valdani, in particular, while an inferno of murderous violence and centuries-old enmity now consumed Sileria in all its explosive fury. There was no longer any such thing as order—let alone safety—anywhere in the mountains, and the lowlands were awash with fighting, refugees, pilgrims, ambushes, deadly water magic, and raging wildfires. While Adalian grew weaker and more desperate under Kariman's onslaught, the food shortages in Shaljir led to riots and violent factionalism even though the Idalar River—now very low and sluggish— still flowed into the city.

Everyone knew that Baran had sided with Tansen by marrying Mirabar—but what if that madman changed his mind? Or what if Kiloran killed him and gained full control of the Idalar? What would happen if Tansen died? If the Lironi lost their war in the east? If more earthquakes destroyed Shaljir beyond repair? If Mirabar's visions were false and never came to pass? Or if Kiloran killed her prophesied Yahrdan the way he had killed the Firebringer?

Others insisted that now was the time to be strong. Baran

and Mirabar working together could certainly keep the capital city from falling completely under Kiloran's influence. The Society, despite months of trying, had yet to regain control of the Shaljir River or the town of Zilar. Now was the time to support the Firebringer's dream of freedom for Sileria, not turn away from it in spineless terror of what *might* happen.

Now was the time for fire or water to gain ascendancy forever in Sileria, and there could be no turning back.

A CHILD OF *fire* . . .

It was a dark place full of light, a bright place shadowed by darkness. A vast cavern, heavy yet airy, immense yet encroaching.

A child of water . . .

Fire and water were all around her. The churning lava of the volcano dripped into water which flowed through strange tunnels lit by unfamiliar glowing shapes. Angry hissing filled the air wherever fire and water met, and steam rose to obscure Mirabar's vision.

A child of sorrow . . .

Tonight the past and the future came together in the present. The tragedy of wasted lives, the waste of squandered talents, the enmity which ran stronger in their blood than love, the love which they had twisted into something so destructive that the future could only survive if they perished . . .

Fire and water, water and fire . . .

The bloodlust of a people which they must learn to stop quenching. The vengeance which could no longer be their whole way of life. The passion for betrayal which they must stop indulging . . .

Mirabar noticed little glowing shapes moving now, in this strange sunless place of lava and crystal, this domain of mingled fire and water. Some slithered leglessly, and others seemed to have a thousand legs. Mirabar shuddered, praying that, despite the power of this vision, she was still, in reality, safely at Belitar.

She saw the Beckoner now, distant, evasive, and she asked him, "What is this place?"

Protect what you most long to destroy.

"Where is this place?"

Are you ready?

"To protect her?"

She didn't need to ask if she was right; she knew Elelar was somehow the answer. She knew by her own revulsion, her repugnance, her screaming reluctance to relinquish her craving for vengeance, for Elelar's blood. She wanted Elelar to suffer the way Baran wanted Kiloran to suffer . . . And daily exposure to her husband's hate-driven madness was why she knew she must surrender her bloodlust and protect Elelar. Mirabar must not squander her gifts in hatred as Baran had. She must not sacrifice Sileria and its well-being to personal vengeance as her husband had.

She had to be more than Baran was, better than he was. Dar had sent her into that madman's arms so that she would know and accept her duty: for the good of Sileria, the good of the powerful child she would bear Baran, and the good of her own soul.

"I'm ready," she vowed.

And she knew she spoke the truth.

"Sirana?"

She frowned, startled by the intrusion of Najdan's voice.

"Sirana?"

She whirled to face him as her vision melted away.

His *shir* shuddered wildly, and he took a sudden step backwards, bouncing away from her as if he had walked into a solid wall. His expression hardened as he realized what he had just wandered into—the midst of one of her visions—and he studied her with narrowed, assessing eyes.

Breathing hard and shivering a little from the sudden transition, Mirabar assured him faintly, "It's over now."

He watched her warily for a moment, then nodded. "We have a visitor."

"Right now?" She was in no mood for a visitor.

"It's Cheylan," Najdan said without enthusiasm.

"*Cheylan,*" she repeated with relief.

Najdan gave her a disapproving look. "The sentries have spotted him approaching the lake."

"We need him," she said. "I need his help." She smiled and assured Najdan, "He was meant to come here now."

He inclined his head and said, with a noticeable lack of conviction, "If you say so, *sirana.*"

"Where's Baran?" she suddenly wondered.

"Occupied. He says Kiloran has enlisted help in trying to gain full control of the Idalar River. He can feel it."

"Help?" she repeated. "Is it Dyshon?"

"Almost certainly. I can't think of anyone else Kiloran would trust enough to admit into his struggle for the Idalar."

"Do you think Baran can withstand this?" she asked worriedly, well aware of how fast he was losing strength.

"Attend to Cheylan," Najdan advised. "You and I can discuss this later."

She nodded, knowing he was right. "Row me across the lake, Najdan. I have many things to tell Cheylan."

"Oh?"

"Yes," she said. "We're . . ." She placed a hand over her belly, resisting the nausea which she felt threatening as she mentally committed to her appalling destiny. "We're going to become allies again with *Torena* Elelar."

Najdan looked startled, then a strangely resigned expression settled into his hard features. "I believe your husband," he said wearily, "will find that very . . . amusing, *sirana.*"

"Yes," Mirabar agreed sourly. "I believe you're right."

49

I CAN TAKE CARE OF MY ENEMIES, BUT DAR
SHIELD ME FROM MY FRIENDS.

— Josarian

"WHAT IS THAT?" Cheylan asked, studying the rather revolting bundle which Mirabar carried in her arms as she approached him. It was long, slender, and completely wrapped in a moldy old blanket.

"It's something Baran gave me. Something which has been hidden in Belitar for a very long time."

"How thoughtful of him," Cheylan said dryly. He lifted his gaze to where Najdan stood glowering at him. "Hello."

Najdan didn't even blink or nod.

Mirabar seemed untroubled by the assassin's bad manners, and suggested to Cheylan, "Let's walk a little."

"All right," Cheylan agreed. "May I carry that for you?"

She hesitated for a moment, then nodded. She let him take the disgusting bundle from her, and he wondered at the expression in her glowing eyes as she stared at it in silence.

"It's solid," Cheylan remarked.

"And heavier than it looks," she murmured.

"Yes. What is it?"

She raised her gaze to his. "It's time for me to find out."

"Oh?"

She took a shaky breath. "I'm glad you're here. I'm, well, a little frightened."

He supposed a mysterious gift from the madman she had married might reasonably cause that reaction, so he nodded. He turned and, letting her set the pace, started walking.

The ensorcelled chill of Belitar permeated the air all around the gloomy, enchanted lake. Even now, as the rest of Sileria sweltered under the killing skies of the dry season, Belitar was cool . . . and as damp as ever. If the assassins' *shir* weren't made of water, Cheylan suspected they'd be rusting.

"Have you been well?" he asked.

She smiled. "Not really."

He saw her place a hand over her belly, and he guessed immediately. "So it's happened, then. You're expecting his child."

"Yes."

The shock he had felt upon learning of her marriage, like the rage he had felt upon hearing from her own lips the reasons she had done it, had driven him to extraordinary measures. He tried to believe it had always been meant to be this way, because the alternative was unthinkable; but at this particular moment, having faith in Dar and in his destiny was a bit difficult. He felt a surge of dark envy and mild revulsion as he contemplated the still-flat belly hidden by Mirabar's modest clothing.

Baran's child resting inside this powerful woman. Baran's seed growing where Cheylan's own should have grown. Baran with yet one more claim on the loyalty of the woman whom Cheylan himself had hoped to rule.

However, he had come here knowing she might have such news for him, and so he mastered his envy and disgust by calling upon the clear, cold hatred which, ever since he'd learned of Mirabar's pact with Baran, had kept Cheylan sharp, focused, and committed to his own path.

His voice sounded quite normal as he asked, "When is the baby due?"

He was surprised to see something like happiness bring a soft glow to her fiery features. "In the spring."

"And you're still sure about this?" he prodded.

"Yes."

No doubt. No hesitation. And certainly no apology.

He felt another surge of fury, but he knew that it was wasted energy now. Mirabar had made her choice when she married Baran, who was even more powerful than he was crazy. And so Cheylan had made his choice, too. He was determined to have everything he wanted; now he'd have it despite her rather than because of her.

"Is he treating you properly?"

She looked surprised. "Baran? No, of course not."

He thought he saw an opportunity, so he suggested, "Then, now that you've got what you wanted from him, perhaps it's time to leave Belitar. I could escort—"

"I haven't got what *Tansen* wants from him," she pointed out.

"Victory over Kiloran." He frowned. "Does Tansen really expect you to remain here with this—"

"No, but it's what I'm going to do." She held his gaze for a moment. "This is my home now, Cheylan. Forever."

So there was clearly no chance, today or any time soon, of getting her away from Belitar.

"Forever? With *him?*" he tried, hoping she'd confide in him.

She didn't. Instead she smiled wryly and agreed, "With him."

"It seems . . . a very big sacrifice."

"I've gotten used to him. Besides . . ." She suddenly gave a strange puff of laughter. "Well, the truth is, Baran sort of grows on you."

"Baran?" He didn't have to pretend his astonishment.

For a moment, her amusement almost reminded him of Baran. "I loathe him and I'm afraid of him . . . but I've also become, as absurd as this sounds, rather fond of him."

"Fond? of *Baran?*"

"I know, I know." She shrugged, gazing absently into the distance as they walked side by side. "In fact, although I'm sure Najdan would rather die than admit it, I think he's becoming a little attached to Baran, too."

"That's . . . hard to believe."

"Yes, it is," she agreed. "But Baran has a strange effect on people. Once upon a time, he must have been . . ."

"Yes?" he prodded.

She shook off her pensive expression and concluded, "A very likeable man. I mean, before he became a murderous and insane waterlord."

He was genuinely curious when he asked, "So you're happy with him?"

She almost laughed again. "Oh, no. Not a bit. Which is just as well. I don't think Baran would tolerate happiness in his midst." Her pensive look returned as she murmured, "No, I'm not happy with him."

A dark stab of wounded pride pierced him, because he was suddenly sure she was thinking of Tansen now.

Time to change the subject, he decided.

"Rumor has it that Baran's not well," he essayed, watching her reaction closely.

"He was very sick for a while," she admitted. "But Sister Velikar is a talented healer and . . ." She smiled wryly. "Believe it or not, Baran seems to find the air here invigorating."

"So he's better?"

"Yes," she replied absently.

If she was lying, she had become skilled at it.

Knowing that Kiloran and Searlon would want something more definite than that, Cheylan said, "I need to speak with him. I have some concerns about keeping the waterlords out of Wyldon's territory. Maybe Baran can advise me."

"I'm afraid he's heavily occupied at the moment."

"I can stay until he's got time."

"I'm not certain when he'll have time."

"Surely, at some point within the next few days, he could spare me a few moments?" he persisted.

"A few days? No, I'm sorry, Cheylan. Baran really hates visitors, and he can be very difficult about it." Seeing his expression, she added, "Perhaps if you told me what you wanted to know . . ."

Ahhh . . .

She continued, "If you annoyed him, he might simply refuse to help you. But I've learned how to deal with him, so it might be best if I spoke to him for you."

"Yes, I see," Cheylan said, satisfied now. "As you wish."

She didn't want him to see Baran.

She *was* lying about Baran's health. And to *him*. Yes, it made him furious all over again.

It almost made him want to kill her.

But not yet.

Baran's sentries were everywhere, and even if they weren't, Cheylan knew Najdan would never let Mirabar out of his sight on this side of the water, where Baran's protection could (if an attacker were reckless enough) be breached. No, Cheylan would have no real privacy with Mirabar, even though Najdan and the others had already given the two of them enough space for confidential conversation.

Indeed, Cheylan knew that, apart from Baran or Najdan, it was unlikely that any man would ever be alone with Mirabar again. A waterlord's wife lived under even stricter prohibitions than a respectable *shallah* woman. Any of her male relatives—a description which, according to the traditions of the Society, now included all of Baran's bloodthirsty assassins—would almost certainly kill an unattached male like himself who sought private moments, let alone private acts, with her.

That poor fool Tansen.

Cheylan again wondered what strength of will it had taken for Tansen to permit the marriage that day at Velikar's Sanctuary. And he really couldn't imagine what sheer idiocy had prompted Tansen to trust Baran, of all people, with such a valuable prize as Mirabar.

Now Baran and Mirabar would be the parents of an immensely powerful child who would benefit from both their legacies. The child, like its parents, would theoretically serve Tansen and the Firebringer's memory.

And no one, when making these plans, gave any thought to Cheylan and his place in Sileria's future.

On the day Mirabar told him why she married Baran, he

knew that she would now never be his, and that she would willfully pursue her own destiny without him, leaving him behind with scarcely a regret. Even what Searlon had revealed to him—the likelihood that Baran was dying—didn't change that. Cheylan could feel the truth just as plainly today as he had felt it upon his last meeting with Mirabar: He had lost her. She would not let him take Baran's place after her husband was dead.

Cheylan also knew that without Mirabar at his side, he was ultimately in danger from Tansen. The Firebringer's brother wanted all the waterlords dead, and he was capable, if anyone in Sileria was, of achieving this goal.

So Cheylan had betrayed Tansen to Verlon, helping his grandfather plan an ambush against the *shatai*. Unfortunately, Tansen had survived; but there would be other opportunities, and Cheylan hadn't expected him to be easy to kill.

As for Kiloran . . . Yes, an alliance with Kiloran had been the obvious solution, for the time being, if Cheylan wanted to prosper. Kiloran was old and had no heir. If Cheylan outlived both him and Verlon, all their combined territory could be his, especially if this war ensured that most of the other waterlords were already dead.

Especially if Baran were already dead. Baran, whose illness was evidently so severe that he didn't even want to risk being seen by anyone outside of his family anymore.

Yes, Kiloran would find that very interesting.

Cheylan didn't plan to tell him about Mirabar's baby, though. At least, not yet. Not until he knew more. Cheylan had so far pretended complete ignorance of the reasons behind the marriage, apart from the obvious ones: Baran's obsessive hatred of Kiloran and Tansen's need for an ally from the Society. Cheylan didn't want Kiloran to know about Mirabar's baby until *he* knew for certain whether the child would be a threat or a boon to himself. The less the old waterlord knew, all round, the better.

In any event, Cheylan knew that handling Kiloran would be

much more difficult than managing Verlon was. Verlon's volatile temper could make him unpredictable, but Kiloran's cold, shrewd intelligence was much more dangerous.

So the best thing, of course, would be if this alliance with Kiloran revealed the old man's weaknesses to Cheylan, so that he could eventually kill the waterlord if need be. It would take patience, though. Kiloran didn't have many weaknesses, and he certainly concealed them well.

In the meantime, it was essential to be useful to Kiloran, so the old man would find him too valuable to kill, betray, or neglect. Hence, his intention of getting whatever information he could out of Mirabar today. Including the very interesting news she imparted to him now, as they walked through the damp forest, about the Firebringer's sister bearing the child of *Torena* Elelar's half-Valdani husband.

"So if the child you bear is meant to . . ." He shrugged. "Shield the child you're looking for, and it wasn't Semeon—"

"It wasn't," she assured him, having no idea how disappointing he now found the wasted effort involved in plotting the boy's murder.

"Then is it Jalilar's baby?"

"I don't know."

"But she's the Firebringer's sister, so . . ."

"I just don't know yet."

"Where is she hiding?"

She told him the location of the Sanctuary, as relayed to her by Tansen's messenger. "No one knows but us," she added. "For her own safety."

"Of course," he agreed. "Does Tansen intend to move her?"

"No. It's remote and quiet there. He's sending for Sister Basimar to take care of her, and he's posting sentries all around the place."

"As long as Jalilar knows never to set foot off Sanctuary grounds."

"She knows," Mirabar assured him. "Of course she knows. She's Josarian's sister."

"Now how can you determine if her unborn child is indeed the one you've foreseen?"

She nodded to the bundle he carried for her. "Maybe this will tell me."

"*Baran's* gift?" he asked in surprise.

"Yes." She made no attempt to explain. Instead she walked ahead of him, led the way into a small clearing, and told him, "I think this will be a good place."

He nodded and gave Mirabar the bundle when she reached for it. Moving with easy grace, she knelt upon the wet ground with it, careless of the fine garments her husband's blood-stained fortune had paid for, and began unwrapping the thing.

When she was done, Cheylan frowned at the long, rusty, ancient, damaged object before finally recognizing it as . . . "A sword?"

He heard her draw in a swift breath. "I know this sword . . ." she said slowly. "I've seen it before."

"Where?"

"In my visions," she answered breathlessly, her whole body stiff with tension as she stared at the pitiful weapon.

"What does it—"

"Make a fire," she said. "I'm going to Call him."

Cheylan ignored the seductive beckoning of the water magic emanating from Baran's eerie lake and focused on the gift of fire so improbably born in his chilly veins. Drawing heat from the Dar-blessed core of his gift, he blew an enchanted blaze into life before Mirabar.

She didn't acknowledge him, didn't even look at him. Her glowing gaze remained fixed on the sword, which seemed too frail even for her gentle touch as she picked it up. Parts of it crumbled and flaked off. As she dropped it into the fire, Cheylan saw that her scarred palms were now smeared with its rust.

"He is coming," she said, her voice filled with exultation.

Cheylan mentally reached into the fire and also felt the shade there, awaiting him, awaiting them both. Reaching out to them both. Opening the void between this world and the Other one.

A wave of heat assaulted him, washing through him with such power that he knew instantly they were Calling a Guardian. A very formidable one.

"And his name," Mirabar said, "is Daurion."

MIRABAR WATCHED AS he formed himself from the enchanted flames, reaching across the centuries to communicate with her.

She had seen his face before. In the night sky over Dalishar. In the chaos of her visions. In the heavy promise of her dreams.

Yes, she had seen this face, just as she had seen the sword which now danced in the fire with him. This was the sword which, in her visions, had once swept across the sky to smash the Sign of Three, the symbol of Valdani supremacy in Sileria for more than two hundred years.

"Daurion," she murmured. The last Yahrdan of a free and prosperous Sileria, dead for a thousand years. Daurion, the Guardian who had held this island with a fist of iron in a velvet glove, driving back wave after wave of Moorlander invasions . . . Until Marjan, whom he trusted like a brother, betrayed and murdered him.

"Marjan brought your sword here after he killed you," she realized.

Where it has remained, Daurion said, his voice shuddering through her—and through Cheylan, whom she saw react on the other side of the fire. *Where it has awaited you.*

"Why me?" she asked, staring into the glowing eyes of the dead ruler.

Only you can protect her.

She knew whom he meant. "But why must I?"

She will bear my heir.

"*She's* the mother of the child I'm meant to shield?" Tears filled her eyes and a terrible weight settled into her chest. "Is she . . . descended from you?"

No, but her child will be.

"Then his father . . ."

Has my blood. Mine and Marjan's.

"Marjan's?" she repeated, shocked. Through the flames, she saw Cheylan make a reflexive, jerky movement, evincing equal surprise. "Both of you?"

His power and strength are unique.

And he would pass on that power and strength to Sileria's new ruler. "Who is he?"

A man who has murdered the innocent, lied to his allies, and betrayed everyone in his quest for influence . . .

"As did Marjan." Fear flooded her as she realized Daurion was, in fact, describing a waterlord. "We can't let such a man have influence over the child!" Mirabar said with certainty. "Over Sileria."

Then you will have to be stronger than he.

"Is it . . . Kiloran?" Indeed, whose power and strength could better be described as unique? Who was truly Marjan's most likely heir? "Is this why I was chosen? To face him? *Can* I defeat him?" Could she even survive the attempt?

Past and present, present and future, all united . . .

"By a child of fire," Mirabar said slowly, "a child of water . . ." And a child of sorrow? Born of Elelar and Kiloran?

The next ruler was meant to carry on the bloodline of the last one, dead for a thousand years, as well as the bloodline of the *sriliah* who'd been strong enough to destroy him. "To end the enmity," Mirabar murmured. "At last."

Fire and water, water and fire . . .

Could the elements which ruled Sileria finally make peace? *Unite them,* Daurion exhorted.

"So Sileria can survive," she murmured.

Baran was right. There would always be water magic in Sileria. No one could change that. No one was *meant* to change that.

Help her unite them.

Confusion, fear, and loathing clouded her thoughts. "Why *her?*" Kiloran was bad enough, but of all the women in Sileria . . .

Dar has chosen her.

"She betrayed the Firebringer!"

Dar's will be done.

"Why did Dar let him die?" she cried.

To fulfill his destiny.

Yes, the Valdani had surrendered Sileria.

"Did he really need to die?" she asked despairingly.

But Daurion knew her real question: *You didn't fail him.*

"I did!" she insisted.

Dar chose him. Dar knows what he can bear.

"Why must he bear such a death? Why?"

Because Dar is the destroyer goddess, and She will not be forsaken in Her own land.

"He didn't forsake her! He gave everything—"

And he will give more, because Dar demands it.

"What more can he give now?" she asked, bewildered.

You must give more, too.

She thought of Kiloran. "I am ready," she vowed, fighting her dread.

Not yet, you aren't, Daurion said chillingly.

"What must I do to be ready?"

You must, he told her, *accept the unbelievable and do the unthinkable.*

"I'm ready!" she insisted.

Not yet, he assured her. *Not yet.*

"YOU LOOK EVEN more bad-tempered than usual," Baran remarked when Mirabar entered his study.

"It burned up. Crumpled. Melted. I don't know." She flung herself into a chair, looking positively haggard.

"Dare I hope you're going to explain that statement?" His head felt pleasantly light as his dying body absorbed the effects of a rather remarkable brew which Velikar had just prepared for him.

Mirabar gazed up at the cracked ceiling. "I was ready. I opened the gift from the Olvara. I did a Calling."

"With Cheylan, I gather?" Fortunately, she had known better than to invite the Guardian into Belitar.

She nodded. "Yes, with Cheylan."

"And, if I understand your rambling despair correctly, whatever the Olvara gave you burned up in your holy fire?"

She gave him a look of sheer loathing. "Yes."

He frowned. "So you don't even know why the Beyah-Olvari guarded that moldy thing for centuries?"

She sighed. "Actually, I do. It was . . . a very successful Calling. Bewildering. Baffling. Disturbing."

"Guardians," he muttered. Always so serious and so vague. Baran found it very tedious of them.

"But," Mirabar said crisply, "a very successful Calling."

"Then you're done with the Olvara's gift," he said, "and it doesn't matter that it's gone. Er, burned up. Whatever."

"I hope not." She sighed. "I just wish . . ."

"So do you know what to do now?" he asked.

She nodded. "Cheylan has gone to Elelar's estate to bring her here . . . so that I can . . ." It amused him to see how hard she found it to conclude, "Protect her."

"Are you sure you're ready for this?"

"I'm ready!" she shouted, delighting him.

"Just asking," he murmured soothingly.

As he had hoped, it annoyed her.

Now he asked, "Did you send some of my men with him?"

"No. Cheylan thought it would be best not to attract that much attention. He said he'd travel quietly with her, trying to keep out of sight."

"What a bold fellow," Baran murmured sardonically.

"He can probably protect her better than your men can," she pointed out. "Especially from a waterlord."

"If you say so, my dear."

"And if Cheylan succeeds, Baran, nothing and no one must harm the *torena* once she's here."

"Why?" Upon seeing her hesitation, he reminded her, "I can lose my head and kill her just as easily if I *don't* know why she's suddenly under my—"

"*Our.*"

"—protection. In fact," he added silkily, "I'm so irrational, I might be *more* likely to hurt her if I don't know why she's—"

"Because she's to be the mother of the new Yahrdan!" Mirabar snapped.

"Ahhh." He considered this. "What about the child carried by the Firebringer's sister?"

"Jalilar's baby," she murmured absently, frowning.

"The bastard sired by a Valdani *toren*," Baran added unnecessarily, still entertained by the prospect.

Mirabar rubbed her hands over her tired face. "I think . . . it may just be what Tansen would call . . . bad luck." She glared when Baran laughed. Then she said, "There's more."

"Oh?"

"It's . . . *possible* . . . not certain, I can't be sure, but it does seem very . . . I mean, there's a good chance . . ."

"Could you possibly finish this thought before I die?"

She met his gaze. "I think Kiloran may be destined to father the new Yahrdan."

That felt like the thrust of a *shir*. "Kiloran?"

"It's possible. I don't know."

"*Kiloran?*" he repeated.

"Yes. Of course, it was very vague, and it's not necessarily . . ."

It hurt like a mortal wound to think of that old man's greatest desire finally being fulfilled: Kiloran having an heir who would rule Sileria. It hurt so much, Baran started laughing with wild, bitter amusement.

Mirabar gave him an exasperated look, which made him

laugh all the harder. "However," she said acidly, "the powerful, murdering, lying *sriliah* prophesied in the Calling could just as easily be *you*."

"In that case," he said, gasping for air, "how trusting of you to bring the lovely *torena* into our home."

She shrugged. "Well, I don't really believe it."

"Apart from the fact that I'm already expecting a child from my virtuous wife . . ." He caught his breath before continuing. "No one knows better than you, my dear, that Elelar would have to be able to coax life out of a corpse to get a child from me, at this point."

Their eyes met, and her mood slowly changed from exasperation to a subtle tension he was now too ill to find alluring. "There are things I've missed," she admitted quietly.

Careening immediately into despair, he asked, "If you think Kiloran may be destined to sire a child on Elelar, why have Cheylan bring her here? If this child is so necessary to Sileria's future, then—"

"Because I could be wrong about who the father is! What if it's not Kiloran, and I do nothing and let him just *kill* her? What then?"

"Prophecy," Baran said gloomily, "is very inconvenient."

"All I know is that I'm supposed to protect Elelar and, if I can, keep the father from dominating the child."

"You mean, kill the father?"

"I don't know," she said faintly.

"As the prospective father of a powerful child myself," Baran said, "I can assure you that only death will keep me from our daughter, Mirabar. So unless the Yahrdan's father is a weakling or a fool, I think it very likely that only the most extreme measures will keep him from his child. And if it's Kiloran—"

"Even if it's not . . ." She nodded. "The man prophesied in this Calling is neither a weakling nor a fool."

"And so you were chosen to protect Elelar and this child."

She made a frustrated gesture. "I wanted to go for her myself, but Cheylan argued against it. He said if Kiloran has already taken Elelar and set an ambush, I might die pointlessly and fail my duty."

"How thoughtful of Cheylan to have such concern for my wife and unborn child." Baran asked, "Do you think Elelar knows?"

"About Kiloran?" she asked blankly. "Since even *I'm* not sure that's wh—"

"I mean," he said, in the tone he would use to instruct a slow child, "do you think she knows that she herself is to give birth to your prophesied hero?"

"Oh!" She blinked. "You're thinking of that letter she sent you?"

" 'Tell Mirabar I have made my peace with Dar and am ready.' "

"How would she know? *I* didn't know. Who could have told . . ." Her eyes flew wide open with startled realization.

"Who?" he prodded, already suspecting.

"No one," she said quickly, lowering her gaze.

"Hmmm. Now who, I wonder," he mused, enjoying her discomfort, "might *Torena* Elelar know who has a gift of prophecy? Besides you, that is."

"I don't know."

"Ah, you're not going to tell me, are you?"

"Tell you what?"

"You actually think I'd hurt them?"

Her gaze flashed up to collide with his. "Them?" she repeated warily.

He smiled, enjoying the fact that, for all her power and courage, she was still afraid of him. Really, he'd had no idea he was that formidable, even half-dead as he was.

"My dear Mirabar," he said, "I have protected the Beyah-Olvari here for years, and treated them far better than any of my predecessors did. I am even, in my own unique way, rather fond of the Olvara."

"She told you," Mirabar realized.

"Yes."

Mirabar nodded slowly and admitted, "I wondered if she would."

"She trusts me."

"She's very naive."

He grinned, rather fond of Mirabar in his own unique way. "Agreed."

"What are you going to do?"

"Me?" he replied innocently. "I'm only going to make a suggestion."

"Go on."

"Is there someone you trust who can safely contact the Beyah-Olvari in Shaljir?"

She continued to regard him warily. "There's Derlen. A Guardian in the *torena*'s household in Shaljir. If he's still there. He knows about them."

"Then I suggest we tell your friend Derlen to have them help me resist Kiloran's pull on the Idalar River."

She let her breath out in a rush. "Can they do that?"

"They should be able to. They're very close to it there. They may even have direct access to it through underground tunnels." He studied her for a moment. "Did this *never* occur to anyone who knows about them?"

"I don't . . . I suppose not. Hardly anyone does know, and the few who do . . ."

"Aren't waterlords," he concluded. "And so don't know anything about water magic."

"And were mostly concerned with concealing their existence from everyone," she added.

He nodded. "Of course."

"Will the Beyah-Olvari in Shaljir need . . . instructions from you? Advice or . . ." She shrugged.

"Yes." He asked, "I don't suppose Derlen reads?"

Her face brightened. "He does!"

"That's a relief." He'd write a letter and simply have one of his men take it to Derlen.

She rose to leave, so that he could write his letter in peace, but she paused when there was a knock at the study door.

Najdan entered a moment later. "Ah, you're both here," he observed.

Baran said, "I admire the way *nothing* slips past you."

Najdan scowled. "We need to talk."

IT WAS A simple dwelling by the standards of waterlords, though extremely grand compared to the way *shallaheen* lived. The blood moons were full and ripe tonight, shedding an eerie orange glow upon Geriden's stronghold as Tansen approached it stealthily, creeping silently through the lush growth which always surrounded a waterlord's lair, even in the dry season.

His black hair, like the black clothes he wore tonight, would absorb the moonlight, and he had streaked his face and hands with dirt, ensuring that no one was likely to see him unless he wanted them to—and guaranteeing that no one here could possibly identify him.

Armian had taught him to feint and confuse an opponent. His *kaj* had taught him that skillful warfare was based on deception. He had taught himself that doing the unexpected always worked best.

And the waterlords had taught him to be ruthless.

Crawling on his belly, he moved silently past Geriden's sentries until he was very close to the house. It was a square, stone structure built across the top of a waterfall, so that the cascades seemed to fall from its foundations.

There was some artistry to it, Tansen admitted. The late and unlamented Wyldon should have taken a lesson or two from Geriden; Tansen still shuddered when he recalled Wyldon's water sculptures.

Elsewhere tonight, Tansen had separate forces making attacks—which would be aborted before incurring serious losses—on both Gulstan and Kariman. The attacks were simultaneous, and each one was reputedly led by Tansen. Although real targets had been chosen, the primary purpose of the attacks was to gain the waterlords' attention tonight—and to create confusion by tomorrow. If things went well, the confusion would be swiftly followed by hostility, accusations, and enmity.

Excite the enemy's ambitions, his *kaj* had taught him, *and play upon his fears.*

Tansen had no idea whether Gulstan or Kariman wanted Geriden's territory; but he had learned by now that Geriden *feared* they did. So Geriden worked hard at maintaining his friendship with Kiloran, believing he might one day need it. Tansen knew that Geriden had, for instance, supplied the assassins who'd attacked the Guardian encampment on Mount Niran, abducted Mirabar's mentor Tashinar, and taken her to Kandahar—where Tansen could only hope the old woman had died quickly.

Now that Tansen was close enough to Geriden's house, he studied it with disappointment but without surprise. It was far from the riverbanks on either side of it, and it sat at the very precipice of the steep gorge into which the water fell. The river around it—sluggish, this far into the dry season—was unquestionably ensorcelled to protect the inhabitants of the house.

No way in, unless Geriden permits it.

Oh, well. He had known it would probably be this way. Even minor waterlords like Geriden were far from easy to kill.

He waited patiently in the shadows on the banks of the river until another sentry passed him. Knowing that mortality made quite an impression, even on assassins, Tansen simply attacked this one in silence, grabbing his forehead from behind and then driving the blade of a *shir* into the vulnerable soft spot just below the base of the skull, killing the man instantly.

He let the body sink to the ground, then withdrew the *shir* made by Kiloran, flicked the blood off the wavy blade, and tucked it back into the assassin-red *jashar* he wore tonight.

Geriden's stronghold was better guarded than Wyldon's had been, and it wasn't very long before another sentry came along. Tansen waited until the man was bending over the corpse before he ambushed him.

The assassin gasped in pain when the *shir* pressed against his throat.

"No noise," Tansen warned him in a whisper.

The assassin's gaze sought the handle of Tansen's *shir*. Recognizing the workmanship, as anyone in the Society would, he blurted, "Kiloran sent you? No! We are loyal! You can't—"

"Get me inside the house," Tansen ordered.

The assassin spat on him. Tansen slashed his cheek open, then immediately clapped a hand over his mouth to stifle the man's scream.

"I want to go inside," Tansen murmured into his ear, "and you have only a moment left to be smart."

The assassin snarled something unintelligible and struggled—with both strength and skill. Realizing this wasn't the man he needed, Tansen killed him, then dumped his body next to the first one. He collected their *shir*, tucked them inside his tunic, then retreated once again to the shadows.

It was a rather long wait for the next sentry, but as soon as Tansen saw him, he believed he had found the key to this particular lock. This sentry was younger than the other two, and he looked jumpy even before coming upon the bodies of two of his fellow assassins.

He gasped when he saw them, panicked immediately, started to run, then froze in his tracks, apparently afraid he might fall into whatever trap had taken them.

Tansen stepped into the moonlight and, before the man could call for help, he instructed in an urgent whisper, "Don't cry out! I think he's nearby."

The assassin drew his *shir* and backed away from Tansen,

radiating hot suspicion in the eerie volcano-red moonlight. "Who are you?"

"Kiloran sent me to help protect your master." He held up his *shir* so the assassin could see the proof of his allegiance. "Geriden is in danger." Tansen gestured to the two bodies and shook his head. "It looks like he got here before me."

"He?"

"Keep your voice down. He's probably nearby."

"He?" the assassin repeated, evincing a habit of obedience as he lowered his voice to a whisper.

"Tansen."

"Tan . . ." The young assassin suddenly looked around with wild energy. "*Tansen* is here?"

His horrified tone was flattering. Even a disciplined *shatai* enjoyed being so feared by his enemies.

"Yes, Tansen," Tansen replied. "Haven't you been warned?"

"Warned?" the assassin repeated, still looking around.

"That he's vowed to kill Geriden next."

"What? No! Are you sure?"

"Pull yourself together," Tansen ordered in a whisper, coming closer. "You're under attack."

"We can't be under . . ." The assassin finally focused on Tansen. "We're under attack?"

"Unless," Tansen gestured to the two corpses, "you think they're just taking a little nap."

"But . . . but the alarm hasn't been sounded."

"The alarm," Tansen said slowly. He looked towards the house. "You think Geriden's already dead?"

"What? No!" A pause. "Geriden? Dead?"

"Tansen's gotten into the house," Tansen said with certainty.

"No, he couldn't possibly."

"Who knows what those Guardians of his can do?"

"They can't . . ." Ragged breathing. "You think they could—"

"Abidan and Liadon are dead. Ferolen. So many others."

"No," the assassin protested, "it's too quiet. If Tansen got into the house, Geriden would sound the . . . the alarm . . . Unless . . ."

"Unless Tansen killed him in his sleep," Tansen suggested convincingly.

"Geriden? No! He can't be dead!"

"If he's not dead, then we'd better wake him up." He glanced at the corpses and added, "Tansen is here, even if he hasn't killed Geriden yet."

"Yes." The assassin nodded. "Yes, we've got to wake Geriden." He was about to bellow his master's name.

Tansen reminded him, "Quietly. No need to let Tansen know that we know he's here."

No need to brings dozens of assassins down on my head.

The assassin nodded and, to Tansen's surprise, picked up some pebbles and threw them at a shuttered window in the house which squatted on the falls. He did this twice more before someone opened the shutters and peered out at them. It was a young woman, and her face was alight with expectation as she gazed out, across the ensorcelled water, at the assassin.

Ah, Tansen thought, *he's done this before. Often, I'll bet.*

While the girl softly greeted the assassin, her voice rich with promise, Tansen tucked Kiloran's *shir* into his boot, not wanting her to see it.

"Wake your father," the young assassin said urgently to the girl. "Tell him it's very important. I've got to speak to him."

She nodded and disappeared. As Tansen and the assassin waited in the shadows, Tansen made a few more remarks designed to keep the young man in a state of confused panic. Finally, in a display which made Tansen feel a little queasy, the water in the river started churning, crystallizing, and then solidifying until it was a smooth, hard surface which he and the assassin could walk across.

Tansen had already guessed that Geriden wouldn't let any

assassins sleep inside his modest house, not with a marriage-able daughter in residence, so he acted immediately. The moment he was across the threshold, he seized his young companion and broke his neck. To murder a girl's sweetheart right in front of her was a cruel and grisly thing, but this was war, and Tansen knew that even one mistake now would ensure his death.

He heard the girl scream as the young man's body hit the floor, but he was already reaching inside his tunic for one of the *shir* he had taken from Geriden's slain men. He threw it across the room, aiming for the middle-aged man who had recognized the trap and was now attempting to bring water through the window to defend himself.

Geriden screamed in agony when the *shir* pierced his thigh. He lost control of his magic, and the roaring river water fell away from the window, no longer a threat to Tansen. Relieved he wouldn't have to use the girl as a hostage, Tansen ignored her, crossed the room, and pressed the second *shir* of Geriden's to the waterlord's throat.

"Tell her to look away," Tansen advised him.

"Who are you?" Geriden cried.

"My master got tired of waiting for Tansen to kill you."

"Help!" the girl screamed.

"Tell her," Tansen warned.

"I'll give you anything," Geriden promised.

"It's too late for that."

The girl's screams were attracting attention. Tansen doubted anyone else could cross the river right now, but he still needed to finish this fast and disappear.

"You can't do this!" Geriden shouted, tears streaming down his face from the pain of the *shir* in his leg.

"It has to be this way."

Tansen slit his throat. Geriden clawed at him in panic for a moment, then shuddered and sagged, his eyes closing as he died.

The girl ran forward now, flinging herself on her father's body as shrieks of wild grief and terror tore through her.

But the waterlords had taught Tansen to be ruthless. So he grabbed her hair and hauled her to her feet.

"Listen to me," he ordered.

Her eyes full of hot hatred, she snarled, "His men will kill you for this, *sriliah!*"

"Tell his men," Tansen said sternly, "that they may serve my master loyally when he takes over this territory, or they may die. There is no third option."

"Your master?" she hissed.

He moved away from her and opened the shutters of a window overlooking the gorge. He looked down at the raging river far below and wished he had asked his son for a few swimming lessons.

"*Your* master?" the girl shrieked. "There is no master here but Geriden! Geriden is master here, you *sriliah!* You filthy, stinking, dung-kissing bastard! You master will die terribly for this! Your master will pay! He will *pay,* I tell you!"

Tansen climbed out onto the ledge, half-hoping the girl would push him so he wouldn't have to steel himself for the jump. But she seemed to have forgotten him now in favor of keening over her father's body, so it was up to him. He looked down at the gorge, so sinister and violent in the darkly orange light of the moons, in the wildly churning fury of the water he had just freed forever from Geriden. Tansen wondered if Josarian had been this terrified upon looking into the caldera at Darshon before he jumped.

No, Josarian had had all those mind-clouding potions of the zanareen to keep him calm and the passionate beckoning of the goddess to distract him.

And here am I, without even a little fire brandy to get me through this.

He briefly considered praying to Dar, but then decided that might be tempting Her too much.

Instead, he recalled a Kintish proverb and muttered to himself, "Whatever doesn't kill us sets us free."

Then he jumped into the roaring river gorge, hoping that he would survive the fall well enough to worry about drowning.

50

ANYONE CAN DO WRONG, BUT TO BE LOVED FOR
IT TAKES ART.

— Baran

"WHAT DID YOU *do?*" Zarien asked in horrified wonder.

"I jumped into a very deep river gorge," Tansen replied.

"Why?"

"It seemed like a good idea at the time." Tansen lowered himself gingerly onto a bench in the Sanctuary where he had left Zarien days ago.

"Next time," Zarien suggested, "you might just consider fighting a dragonfish."

"Are they easier to kill than waterlords?"

"Well, I didn't live through my only battle with one," Zarien admitted, hovering over him, "so perhaps not."

Tansen smiled up at the boy, having missed him.

He hadn't seen his own face since the jump into the gorge, but he knew that the rest of him looked pretty grim. His many large bruises were already a rainbow of colors so vivid they rivaled the never-ending display of dancing lights at the summit of Darshon. Several enormous gashes and deep lacerations added to the impression that he was more dead than alive, and a few of his bones, though not broken, were still protesting his dramatic escape from Geriden's lair.

"You should probably help me improve my swimming," Tansen said, "in case I ever have to do that again. Not," he added, "that it's an experience I'm ever going to repeat, if there's any possible way to avoid it."

Stunned from the fall, he had immediately been swept into a terrifying torrent which introduced him to the blunt edges of many rocks. Most of Sileria was dying of thirst, and he had nearly drowned in the newly freed rapids below Geriden's home.

"So now another waterlord is dead," Zarien said.

"A very minor one. And, if things go well, his death will now cause two great ones to turn on each other."

"Do you think they will?"

"I don't know," Tansen admitted, "but I'm certainly going to give them all the help I can."

SEARLON ARRIVED AT Kandahar as summoned, politely greeted Kiloran, and said, "I understood from your message that the matter was urgent, *siran*."

"I'm aware that you have plans you're eager to pursue—"

"Yes."

"—but there is something of utmost importance which I need you to do first."

"Then, of course, I shall give it all my attention."

"You were right about Cheylan."

"Ah." Searlon smiled. "His intimate knowledge of our enemies is indeed proving to be useful, isn't it?"

"Very. Of course, Cheylan is . . . somewhat less trustworthy than a venomous serpent." Kiloran sighed. "I find I almost pity Verlon."

Searlon shrugged. "Certainly Cheylan has proven, in Wyldon's territory, that he is strong and can resist waterlords. But he cannot rule water like one. So whatever Cheylan's ambitions are, surely he needs Verlon alive, at least for the time being?"

"I think Cheylan's ambition," Kiloran said, "is to rule Sileria."

"On what basis?" Searlon asked, his expression both contemptuous and dismissive.

"Who knows? It doesn't matter. What matters is that the rash ambition which has led him to betray Mirabar for having the bad taste to align her power with other men will now lead *us* to what we want."

Searlon drew in a swift, sharp breath. "He got Mirabar to tell him who she has foreseen in her visions."

"Yes. I know who the new Yahrdan is," Kiloran said with immense satisfaction, "and *where* he is."

"So all that remains is for us to kill him."

"And, by all accounts, it's going to be considerably easier than killing the Firebringer was. Especially," Kiloran added, needing Searlon to understand what Cheylan himself had so clearly understood upon relating the information to Kiloran, "if we're willing to be ruthless."

"Of course."

"This is a situation," Kiloran said, preparing the assassin, "a challenge, which calls for new solutions. Old rules and old ways can no longer apply to us if we are to prevail."

Searlon studied him for a moment before saying, "You and I have come too far to turn back now, *siran*. We have no choice but to prevail."

"You may find what I'm about to ask you to do . . . distasteful," Kiloran warned him.

"If you can assure me, *siran*," Searlon said slowly, "that our deeds will ultimately ensure our dominance of all Sileria, I think I can manage a distasteful task or two."

Yes, Kiloran realized, pleased. Searlon would be with him all the way. Searlon understood that terrible times called for terrible measures.

In the end, only a heart of stone triumphed.

GERIDEN'S DAUGHTER AND his assassins were lusting with violent rage against a waterlord . . . only they weren't quite sure which one. The girl knew she had seen an assassin murder her father and one of his men right there in her own home. There was no doubt he had also murdered the other two men later found dead beside the river. And he had told her that his own master intended to take over Geriden's territory now.

She also distinctly and wrathfully remembered what she had heard the assassin say directly to her father before murdering him: *"My master got tired of waiting for Tansen to kill you."*

However, what with all the violence and terror of the few brief murderous moments the assassin had been in her presence, she hadn't studied his red *jashar,* so she couldn't begin to identify him, apart from attributing to him a general aura of deadly, ugly, vicious, goat-molesting evil—and a slightly (but only slightly) more helpful description of him as a man of average size who was probably a *shallah* by birth. It was a description which fit most of the assassins in Sileria, including those who served Kariman and Gulstan—the two great waterlords whose important territories bordered Geriden's negligible one.

The girl didn't know who had sent the assassin. She only knew, as did her father's men, that either Kariman or Gulstan, both of whom had surely always coveted Geriden's territory, finally got tired of waiting for him to die—and whichever one of them it was, he must pay dearly for what he had done.

Upon hearing this, Kariman insisted he was not only innocent, but had, in fact, been under attack by Tansen on the night of Geriden's murder. This immediately aroused Gulstan's worst suspicions about Kariman—the greedy waterlord who had, after all, already taken over the dead Ferolen's territory—since Gulstan happened to know that he himself had been the one under attack by Tansen at the time of the murder. Kariman's response to this information was to ridicule Gulstan's claim; that further convinced Gulstan that Kariman was indeed the backstabbing *sriliah* who had ordered Geriden's death. Kariman, in his turn, knew that Gulstan was bitterly jealous of Kariman's ascendancy since Ferolen's death; it was obvious that Gulstan, who—oh, yes!—had always coveted Geriden's territory, had finally decided it was time to increase his own influence by killing Geriden.

Tansen, pleased that his plan was going so well, quietly provided plenty of fuel to turn the dispute into a raging inferno. He made sure that Kariman's assassins picked up some gossip about Gulstan's designs on Geriden's territory as merely the first step in a larger plan to increase his holdings. It was common knowledge that Kariman (who was no Kiloran, after all) was stretched to his limit trying to control Ferolen's lands as well as his own; so Tansen made sure that Kariman soon believed that Gulstan planned to take away some of that territory.

Meanwhile, Tansen also made sure that Gulstan heard that Kariman was urging Kiloran to help him eliminate Gulstan (for all Tansen knew, it might even be true). Although Gulstan had made peace with Kiloran for the sake of unity and strength in the Society, he was still highly suspicious about that *shir* of Kiloran's once found among his slain men, so he immediately became reckless with rage and fear over the possibility of Kariman and Kiloran uniting against him. After all, the deaths of Geriden, Wyldon, and Dulien proved that those two were not only capable of killing other waterlords, but positively eager to do it!

Tansen also ensured that Geriden's vengeful assassins remained confused enough to feel convinced that no one could be trusted and everyone must be punished for their master's death. Wild with a hunger for revenge, they began launching attacks against both Gulstan and Kariman, who blamed each other, as well as the actual perpetrators, for these attacks.

When Kariman decided to seize Geriden's territory so that Gulstan wouldn't reap the profits of his treacherous murder of Geriden, Gulstan was waiting for him, already trying to lay claim to the territory himself. Most of Geriden's assassins died in the first few days of the raging struggle as the two waterlords used the power of their sorcery and the strength of their assassins against each other. By the time Kiloran tried to intervene, it was too late for a truce meeting, too late to reason with any of them. And much too late to convince them of his own suspicions—that Tansen himself might have plotted this entire disaster.

Gulstan and Kariman were already committed to something which Kiloran couldn't stop, something which even Tansen hadn't foreseen, and nothing in their lives had ever been so satisfying.

Fighting Tansen had been work, duty, a rational agreement among men with something in common, something to lose. But this? Two great waterlords—two true equals—engaged in the fiercest, most vengeful, most ruthless fight of their lives, with no restraint from a truce agreement and no interference from the Valdani ... Ah, *this* was a passion which consumed them. This was better than love, better than hate, better than whatever Josarian had felt when Dar embraced him in the volcano! Gulstan and Kariman were two true kings of the seductive sorcery which so few men could even understand, let alone master. No war, no woman, no *shatai* could give these two waterlords the rich, raw satisfaction they now found, after all the years of restraint and subterfuge, in summoning all their strength, all their cunning and skill, all the crystal, cold beauty of their magic in all-out war against each other.

Even Tansen, who watched with satisfaction as his enemies destroyed each other, had to admit that there was something a little glorious about it.

BARAN QUARRELED WITH Najdan, who fled Belitar hotly pursued by Vinn and a contingent of assassins. News of the quarrel quickly spread, especially among those who always had a keen interest in Baran's activities and Mirabar's vulnerability.

"What do you suppose happened at Belitar?" Dyshon asked Kiloran in the cool security of Kandahar.

"With Baran?" Kiloran made a dismissive gesture. "Anything is possible."

"True," Dyshon agreed. "With that madman, anything at all is possible." Dyshon then excused himself to go greet a messenger.

Unfortunately, Kiloran reflected once he was alone, it seemed that throughout all of Sileria these days, anything was indeed possible. In fact, there were moments when Baran almost seemed sane in comparison to some of his former associates.

Gulstan and Kariman were so busy warring against each other that their territories—as well as Geriden's—were in total chaos. If they even saw how their wild bloodfeud was helping Tansen, then they didn't care. Kiloran wondered with bitter fury how they could be so reckless, so short-sighted . . . but he had only to remember Alcinar to realize that an overwhelming passion, of one kind or another, was probably every real man's destiny and curse at least once in his life. And if Gulstan and Kariman's ungovernable passion was now for power, or even for the rich satisfaction of fully engaging a true equal in a world where such a thing was so rare for a great waterlord, Kiloran could at least understand that.

He was annoyed, though, that they were too foolish to wait for Tansen to fail and die before they indulged in tearing each other apart this way.

Kiloran wondered once again, aware that he'd probably never know, if Tansen was behind their quarrel.

Meanwhile, there was some new, inexplicable influence on the Idalar River. It wasn't Baran regaining strength, Kiloran was sure of that. This was a wholly unfamiliar power, something altogether different from the edgy, glittering brilliance of Baran's sorcery. This power was so different that Kiloran couldn't even imagine who was its source; but it was working in harmony with Baran.

Even worse, something was now reaching out for the mines of Alizar, too. Something very similar to the new power now flowing through the Idalar River.

Baran has found an ally.

A very strange one, that much Kiloran could ascertain with senses attuned day and night to the waters he ruled; but an ally with enough power to be annoying.

Still, Kiloran didn't fear defeat. Baran was dying—and quickly, if Cheylan was right. Searlon would kill the prophesied Yahrdan, destroy the power of Mirabar's visions, and remind all Silerians that not even the Firebringer had been able to withstand Kiloran. If no one was left alive at the end of Kariman and Gulstan's bloodfeud (as seemed increasingly likely), then Kiloran would eventually acquire their territories. Yes, these were terrible times, and each day brought new challenges—some of them really quite discouraging, if truth be known. Nonetheless, Kiloran remained ascendant, and he still foresaw no problems which he couldn't master and overcome.

As for Cheylan . . . Yes, he was an immensely useful young man. Kiloran would eventually be obliged to kill him, of course, because it was too dangerous to rely on someone so treacherous for long. But he'd certainly like to keep Cheylan alive until after the war. Until after Tansen and Mirabar were both dead and forgotten.

Kiloran also knew it was possible that Cheylan, whom Tansen mistook for an ally, had met Zarien, perhaps even knew a little about him. But to ask Cheylan about Zarien would be to betray his interest in the boy, and he doubted that Cheylan knew anything which was worth taking such a chance—because if he did, he probably would have offered it already. Cheylan was greedy for Kiloran's support, and also eager to prove he was valuable enough to keep alive.

Besides, there was no real need to ask Cheylan about Zarien. Kiloran already knew what mattered most, and sooner or later, Searlon would bring the boy to Kandahar.

It was a shame that Kiloran couldn't trust Cheylan, though, because there was certainly one thing he would ask him about if he weren't so determined to reveal no weaknesses at all to the traitorous Guardian: *Fire.*

The vague and disturbing comments of the old Guardian woman who had turned into a human volcano before Kiloran's very eyes here at Kandahar did, he admitted only to himself, still bother him from time to time. Was it the mindless babbling of a sick old woman dying in agony after prolonged torture? Or was there something here which only a Guardian could sense and understand? Something which eluded Kiloran in all his talent and power?

Was there some slight possibility that Josarian, being the Firebringer, was not as thoroughly dead as any other man would be after being devoured by the White Dragon?

Had Kiloran, in killing him that way, brought something dangerous into Kandahar?

"Siran?"

He nearly jumped at the sound of Dyshon's voice.

Realizing that his thoughts were becoming unproductively morbid, Kiloran was relieved to see the assassin had returned from greeting the messenger. And judging by the light of bloodlust in Dyshon's eyes, the news was interesting. "Yes?"

"I have received a message from Najdan."

Fire. Ah, yes. It suddenly flooded his heart.

"Najdan."

Two of Kiloran's assassins had died attacking Najdan in his native village, their attempt to exact vengeance a complete failure. Searlon had accepted the blame, and Kiloran had been free about assigning it to him. Searlon claimed he had underestimated Najdan. Two men had not been enough to take him. At least not two young men. It would require someone experienced to kill Najdan. Someone much better than average.

In other words, Searlon dearly wanted to do it, and he probably wouldn't try terribly hard to have Najdan killed until he had the opportunity to do it himself.

Dyshon said, "Najdan knows he can never come home, but now that he's enemies with Baran, he asks me to meet with him. He wants a truce with us."

"Does he really?" Kiloran replied cynically.

"He says that, although he will never betray Mirabar, not even now that she has forsaken him—"

"Well, what did he expect?" Kiloran snapped.

"—he will, in exchange for our letting him leave Sileria alive with Haydar, give me information about Baran."

"We already have information about Baran."

"But you don't trust Cheylan," Dyshon pointed out.

"True, but that's no reason to trust Najdan again," Kiloran replied irritably.

"Surely someone who has been living within Belitar," Dyshon persisted, "will have information that Cheylan couldn't possibly have. I suggest, *siran*, that it would benefit us to know as much as possible. Baran is too dangerous for us to neglect the opportunity which Najdan offers to us."

"Hmmm." Kiloran considered this. "Najdan really has no honor left, does he?"

How the changing times have changed us all.

"What are your instructions, *siran?*"

It would require someone experienced to kill Najdan. Someone much better than average.

Someone, for example, who had successfully killed Wyldon.

Kiloran smiled, feeling better again. "Oh, meet with him, Dyshon. By all means. See if he knows anything interesting. Then kill him." Searlon would just have to bear the disappointment like a man.

Dyshon shook his head and reminded him, "It's to be a truce meeting, *siran*."

"Najdan is likely to be wary, even so." Najdan had survived twenty years in the Society, betrayal of Kiloran, and a quarrel with Baran; Najdan wasn't a waterlord, but he was smarter than Wyldon, and—as Tansen had certainly proved time after time—smart men were more dangerous than powerful ones.

"So don't be careless or overconfident. Go to the meeting place a day early. Set your trap well, and eliminate any possible escape route for him."

Dyshon seemed to have trouble understanding. "Trap? But I can't kill him at . . . a *truce* meeting."

Kiloran snorted. "Of course you can. He's not one of us anymore, Dyshon. He made his choice, and he is no longer protected by the honor of the Society. So find out everything he knows about Baran, and then kill him."

"I . . ." Dyshon looked queasy. "*I* am still of the Society, *siran,* and I . . . I don't want—don't like—"

"Neither do I, Dyshon, but these are difficult times and we must be strong. Najdan betrayed us, and now he's betraying Baran. Do you really think *anyone* will care when or where we kill him?"

Kiloran gave him a hard look, hoping he wouldn't have to remind him of the inestimable honor he was doing Dyshon by allowing him to assist in the struggle for the Idalar River.

After an awkward moment, Dyshon crossed his fists, bowed his head, and said, "It will be my honor to kill that *sriliah* as he deserves, *siran.*"

"I thought so," Kiloran said dryly.

Yes, Searlon would feel cheated. But Searlon was a practical man who would understand that his master was obliged to use the very trap which Najdan had so thoughtfully proposed for his own demise.

A truce meeting. As if I could ever overlook what that sriliah *did to me.*

Really, it was amazing, the things some people thought they could get away with.

ELELAR'S TENANTS WERE engaged in wild celebration, every bit as exultant as the day they had received word of the Valdani surrender in Shaljir. The power of the Honored Society was far older and more enduring in this district than a mere two hundred years of Valdani rule. And now, for the first time in a thousand years, the waterlords had lost all control of the water here.

True, these were still terribly dangerous times. Bands of murderous assassins roamed the district at will, not necessarily caring whether they were killing genuine enemies or just helpless innocents. Refugees now poured into the area from regions still crippled by the waterlords; disputes—even terrible fights—broke out when there wasn't enough free water here to slake their terrible thirst. Fierce earthquakes shook the land, destroyed homes and villages, created avalanches and landslides. Wild-eyed *zanareen* and passionate Guardians wandered everywhere, their proclamations and promises alternately terrifying and inspiring. Bandits took advantage of the utter chaos throughout Sileria, and they were especially bold wherever the disciplined protection of the Honored Society no longer existed.

Yet Elelar's people now celebrated with reckless jubilation, because Kariman had lost his grip on their water, and—for the first time since the Conquest—no other waterlord flowed into the void to demand tribute and obedience from them, or to punish them with thirst and drought if they refused to comply.

Tired from all the celebrations of recent days, and having endured all the general goodwill she could really stand, Elelar now sat examining accounts in her grandfather's study; but she could still hear the songs, the cheers, the wild cacophony of her ebullient tenants, and she knew the villages and estates all over this district were equally noisy these days.

"Free water for all! Free water for all!"

Elelar raised her head and listened for a moment. She heard some commotion coming from the kitchens next to the house, but it was a familiar occurrence by now. The hoards of hungry pilgrims, mystics, and refugees roaming the district were welcome to stop for a meal at the *torena*'s kitchens as they passed. Lately, these mealtimes inevitably turned into still more buoyant celebrations, and Elelar had given up reprimanding the cook for being too generous with her wine and ale.

"Dar bless *Torena* Elelar!" someone shouted outside her house.

"Dar save the *torena!*"

She had long since given up going to the windows in acknowledgment of these revelers. She'd never get anything else done if she waved to them all.

"Free water! No more tribute! Free water!"

There wasn't an abundance of water, of course, since it was late in the dry season, and the very nature of the climate had always ensured the waterlords' supremacy at this time of year. But what water now was here was free. No one ensorcelled it. No one could keep it from them anymore because of disobedience or terrible poverty.

"Free water for all!"

Tansen's promise had come true here, as it was coming true elsewhere. Not in the west, of course, where Kiloran, powerful beyond the dreams even of other waterlords, still ruled with unassailable dominance; but here and elsewhere, the waterlords—those seemingly invincible kings of life's most precious element—were now melting and dissolving. Dulien, Abidan, Liadon, Ferolen, Wyldon, Geriden, and so many others were already dead. Gulstan and Kariman were absorbed in a wrathful bloodfeud, destroying each other with a passionate fury unlike anything they had ever brought to their war against the Valdani or their battles against Tansen. Meriten had yet to claim the Shaljir River from the loyalists, and now rumors suggested that he was weakening, losing strength; now he would *never* take the Shaljir River, some said. His time was past, as was the time of so many of his friends.

Neither Kariman nor any other waterlord could reclaim the territory which the Society had lost and was still losing. The Guardians saw to that. Every liberated water source in Sileria was protected by Guardian fire, and Dar's servants would never yield what they had fought so hard to win.

And Verlon? Oh, yes, he was powerful, but everyone knew how recklessly hot-blooded the Lironi were; and their many allies had swelled their numbers to a force which, in the end, even Verlon and his friends could never defeat or destroy. No, the Lironi would never give up. Once fired, their bloodlust could never be cooled. Everyone knew that about them.

Under different circumstances, Elelar would be as celebratory as everyone else. Under different circumstances, though, she would not be waiting for the most famous Guardian in Sileria to come execute her as punishment for betraying the Firebringer.

As Tansen's influence spread, as the Society spiraled into confusion and defeat, and as all of Sileria struggled with destiny and Dar's rages, Elelar grew to believe that her own death might even be the key to defeating Kiloran, the one waterlord who still seemed truly invincible; the waterlord whom even Tansen, surely, couldn't destroy.

As Elelar waited, she often wondered *how* her death would save Sileria. She hoped she would understand her destiny in the final moments of her life. She also wondered—sometimes with genuine dread—exactly how her life would end. Would Mirabar choose to publicly humiliate her? Drag her through the dusty roads of Sileria, proclaiming her infamy and exposing her treacherous schemes? Would there be a painful, fiery sacrifice to Dar? A traditional execution for a traitor, something even worse than Valdani death by slow torture?

Elelar willfully mastered her fears, as she had to do almost daily now, and took a deep breath, reaffirming her resolve.

If this is the way it must be, then I am ready.

She only wished Mirabar would come, because the waiting was becoming intolerable. Almost as intolerable as the praise, admiration, and sheer adulation Elelar encountered every time she left the safety of her home.

A great heroine of the rebellion, she thought, torn between ironic amusement and bitter self-loathing.

"Dar be praised for giving us *Torena* Elelar!"

"Elelar! Elelar! Elelar!"

Elelar sighed. Mirabar would probably immolate the crowd in a fit of righteous fury if she arrived during one of these emotional gatherings outside of Elelar's house.

Elelar was also worried that something might happen to spoil her plans. Tansen had somehow guessed where she was now; she had recently received a message from him. She suspected that he might even know what she intended. If he was still determined to protect Mirabar from herself, and Elelar from almost everyone, then he might try to interfere. He had already, Dar curse him, tried to convince her to take responsibility for Ronall again.

I really would *rather jump into the volcano*.

She'd had to keep her reply moderately civil, since Tansen couldn't read and always had to communicate with her through trusted messengers. Had she been able to respond to him in the privacy of a letter, her language might have shocked him.

Tansen had found Ronall, so Tansen could worry about him hereafter. Elelar was not going to have that lazy drunkard clinging to her now as she advanced to meet her destiny.

If only Mirabar would come, she fretted. Or send a message. Or do *something*. If only Baran would write from Belitar. Elelar fell into a useless bout of worrying that that unpredictable madman had never even bothered to share her letter with his wife.

"Elelar! Elelar! Elelar!"

"May Dar always favor *Torena* Elelar shah Hasnari!"

It was a relief when something finally disrupted all the cheering and shouting outside. Elelar was starting to get a headache. When she heard footsteps in the hallway, she gladly pushed aside the estate accounts, aware that she wasn't really seeing the figures anyhow, so absorbed was she in her thoughts and anxieties.

"Yes, Faradar?" she said when the door opened and her maid entered the study.

"You have a visitor, *torena*."

"I don't want to see any . . ." A strange feeling came over her as she noticed Faradar's serious expression. "Is it . . . Mirabar?"

Faradar looked surprised by the question. "No, not the *sir-ana*."

Elelar sagged with momentary disappointment.

"Another Guardian." Faradar paused. "Cheylan."

No wonder Faradar looked strange. And no wonder the crowd outside had grown suddenly quiet. The locals had surely never before seen the fire-eyed Guardian whose looks were almost as arresting as Mirabar's.

The fire-eyed . . .

Suddenly tense, Elelar rose. "Cheylan?"

Faradar nodded.

"Show him in."

"Unfortunately . . ."

"What?"

"*Torena* Chasimar has already, um . . ."

"Pounced on him?" Elelar suggested. Chasimar required a great deal more stimulation and entertainment than Elelar chose to provide, and tended to eagerly accost any respectable visitor here—particularly, Elelar had noticed, if he was a man.

Faradar agreed, "As you say, *torena*."

Elelar had only met Cheylan briefly a few times, but she knew that he was a *toren* by birth and had the manners of one. So he probably had little chance of escaping *Torena* Chasimar's attentions anytime before he died of old age, not unless someone rescued him.

Elelar followed Faradar out of the room and went down the hall towards the front of the house, where she came upon Cheylan and Chasimar in the largest reception room.

The Guardian's lava-rich eyes sparkled with strange intensity as he greeted Elelar with all the polished courtesy of their class. *Torena* Chasimar was fluttering and chattering even more than usual, and Elelar realized the half-Valdani woman was unnerved by Cheylan's looks. Not enough to be rude; just enough to be extremely irritating.

Suddenly impatient with everything but the burning question inside of her, Elelar interrupted Chasimar's nervous chatter and said to Cheylan, "You've come for me, haven't you?"

Even his well-governed features betrayed a reaction to her bluntness. "Yes."

When the one with eyes of fire finally comes for you, the Olvar had told her, *you must not resist.*

"Are you the one, then?" Elelar asked, gazing intently into those eyes of fire. "The one I've awaited?"

Now his face went blank with surprise. He nodded slowly and said, "Yes. I'm the one."

Torena Chasimar giggled a little and said, "What are you two talking about?"

"What about Mirabar?" Had Elelar been wrong all along about her?

"She sent me."

"She knows, then?"

His gaze was sharp. "Knows what?"

"What my destiny is?"

He suddenly smiled, looking very pleased. "I know what your destiny is, and only I can lead you to it."

Her head started spinning as if she had drunk too much wine. After all the waiting, all the fear, all the patience and secrecy and strangely dark hope, the moment had arrived. The Olvar had been right. Elelar had been right. Only now, as Cheylan confirmed it, did she realize what a relief that was.

If this is the way it must be . . .

"Then I am ready," she said.

Cheylan nodded. "We should leave immediately."

"Leave?" Chasimar blurted.

"Will I . . . need anything?" Elelar asked.

"All your courage," he said. "All your resolve."

Elelar nodded and allowed Cheylan to lead her to the door.

"Wait!" Chasimar bleated. "Where are you going?"

Cheylan said over his shoulder to her, "It was a pleasure to meet you, *torena*."

"Elelar!" Chasimar protested.

Elelar paused. Without looking back at Chasimar, she said, "Tell Faradar I have written down my instructions. She'll know where to look. And, uh . . . Tell Tansen . . ." She felt Cheylan stiffen slightly when she mentioned that name, but he didn't interrupt. "Tell him if everything had been different . . ." She gave a little puff of laughter and admitted wryly, "No, it probably would have always been this way between us."

"But Elelar!"

"Stay here, Chasimar," Elelar ordered.

The *torena* continued protesting as Elelar and Cheylan left the house together.

"What is she doing here?" Cheylan asked.

Elelar shook her head. "It's a long story. But she's like all Valdani. Once they make themselves at home, it takes an act of Dar to get rid of them."

As they emerged into the dying sunlight, she murmured, surprised, "It's getting late."

"We should travel by night," he explained, leading her to where he had two horses tethered. "We're too easy to recognize."

She supposed he meant *he* was, since, without the elaborate headdress she usually wore when traveling, which identified her, nothing about her appearance was distinguished enough to reveal her name. And with no servants or entourage, the only thing about the two of them particularly likely to attract attention was the color of Cheylan's eyes.

"What about bandits?" Perhaps a pointless question, since she was riding to her death, but she didn't particularly want to be raped by bandits on the way.

Also a *silly* question, she realized, when Cheylan replied, "I'll take care of them."

Yes, the Guardian who, as everyone knew, had been keeping waterlords out of Wyldon's territory could certainly get rid of a few bandits.

"*Torena* Elelar!"

"*Torena! Torena! Torena!*"

They were spotted by the crowd which peopled her grounds today. Elelar waved briefly, hoping they'd leave her alone. Instead, they came rushing forward in an aggressive wave of adulation, shouting her name, praising her for her courage and generosity—and frightening the horse she was trying to mount. Someone clumsily but kindly pushed her up into the saddle—and was then a little too familiar about helping her foot find the stirrup.

"Cheylan!" someone cried.

The crowd had evidently figured out who he was. Only one man in Sileria fit his description, after all.

"Thank Tansen for us!" a lowlander urged Cheylan.

"Tell Tansen we love him!" an old *shallah* woman cried.

"Tell the *sirana* we believe in her!"

"Yes, tell Mirabar we love her!"

"*Siran*," a *zanar* exhorted Cheylan, "do you not hear Dar Calling to you?"

"I do indeed," Cheylan replied.

The crowd cheered, even though Elelar suspected they'd all rather go without water again than go to Darshon themselves. The tales about the mystical ecstasy of the pilgrims and the many deaths at Mount Darshon these days were as terrifying as they were inexplicable.

"Dar is also Calling the *torena*," Cheylan announced, "so you'll have to let us pass, now."

This made quite an impression, and Elelar could hear them screaming and chanting her name in a fever of holy praise for far too long after she followed Cheylan off her grounds and into the arms of whatever fate Dar had chosen for her.

51

REFUSE TO DO EVIL; THAT IS THE BEGINNING OF DOING GOOD.

— Creed of the Sisterhood

WHEN TANSEN CAME back to camp one day, Ronall finally summoned all his liquor-soaked courage and spoke to him.

"I think," he said to the *shatai*, "I should go . . . Darfire! Doesn't that hurt?"

"Hmm?" Tansen followed Ronall's gaze to where a singed hole in his leggings revealed a patch of burned skin. "Oh. Yes," Tansen replied absently, "it does."

"What happened?"

"I stumbled into some Guardian fire."

Since he was returning from a skirmish, Ronall assumed that he had "stumbled" while fighting several men simultaneously. Tansen didn't talk about his feats, but everyone else did, all of the time.

Now Tansen's tattooed bloodson peered at the burn and said critically, "You would never survive at sea. You're much too clumsy."

"Then it's just as well we're not going to sea, isn't it?"

The boy's gaze flew up to his young father's face. There

was a strange tension between them for a moment, then Zarien said, "I'm *not*." It sounded like a warning, or maybe a vow.

"Did I say you were?" Tansen replied innocently.

Zarien rolled his eyes, then he gestured to the burn. "That needs to be cleaned."

Tansen nodded and sat down so the boy could start tending the burn. Then Tansen looked up at Ronall. "You were saying, *toren?*"

Ronall noticed, as he often did, that Tansen addressed him coolly. Tansen was never—well, rarely—rude to him, but the *shatai* didn't like him and couldn't hide the fact. Ronall, who would certainly never have expected such a man to like him, mostly avoided him.

"I've heard," Ronall said, "that—"

Tansen drew in a sudden, sharp breath.

"Does it hurt?" Zarien asked.

"Of course it hurts," Tansen replied. "Don't interrupt the *toren.*"

Ronall tried again. "That there've been—"

"Ouch!" Tansen scowled at his son. "Now *that* hurt."

"Sorry," Zarien said.

"Why don't you get the Sister for me?" Tansen suggested to Zarien. "You're not used to treating burns."

"I won't get better without practice," Zarien pointed out. "Now hold still."

"I don't want to hold still. I want the Sister," Tansen insisted.

"This won't hurt less if *she* does it."

Ronall felt sadly envious as he listened to them bicker mildly, Tansen obviously tired and in discomfort, Zarien asserting his abilities and—as always—testing the boundaries of his father's authority. They were such an unlikely pair, the sea-born orphan and the *shallah* rebel who was much too young to be his real father. Ronall knew by now that they hadn't even known each other all that long, and yet they were already so much closer than he had ever been to his own father. Nothing like their easy bickering—as affectionate as it was irritable—had ever existed between Ronall and his parents. Or Ronall and his wife.

Get out, get out, get out!

"I want to go east," Ronall suddenly blurted, trying to smother the memory of Elelar's open loathing the last time he'd seen her.

They both looked at him in surprise.

"Are you being Called by Dar, too?" Zarien asked. "Does She even speak to Valdani?"

"Uh, no," Ronall replied. "I mean, I don't know. I mean, not to me. But I—"

"Even the sea-born are going east," Zarien murmured, his gaze pensive as he stared at Ronall. "Even, it's said, the sea-bound . . ." The boy's voice trailed off and he looked down. "I didn't mean to interrupt, *toren*."

Tansen, without even glancing at Zarien, put a hand on the boy's neck. An absent gesture of comfort. Ronall couldn't remember when anyone had last tried to comfort *him,* let alone done it as a mere reflex, a bone-deep habit.

"Why do you want to go east?" Tansen asked.

"I heard some of your men talking, after the last runner came."

"The last runner never came," Tansen said wearily. "His body was found—"

"Yes, I mean the one before that." He wished Tansen wouldn't mention things like ambushes and corpses. It weakened Ronall's resolve, which it had taken a lot of really bad wine to make strong in the first place. "They were talking about the massacres in the east. The Lironi and their allies hate the Valdani just as much as Verlon and his friends do, and no one there is . . . is speaking for the Valdani. Um, the ones like me. The ones who . . . are Silerians," he finished lamely.

Tansen looked like he was having trouble understanding. "You're saying you want to go east to try to save the Valdani there?"

"It worked in Adalian," Ronall reminded him. "When the city-dwellers wanted to celebrate freedom there by killing Valdani *toreni,* and you . . . introduced me to the city as Elelar's . . . um, brave husband who had . . ."

"Supported the rebellion," Tansen finished crisply.

Tansen had made a sudden surprise appearance in the city, accompanied by Ronall, a few days ago, after Kariman completely lost his grip on it. Adalian had suffered terribly, but the city had kept faith with the Firebringer and had believed in Tansen. It had endured and survived, and now it had water. If Kariman even cared about this tremendous loss, he was too busy trying to kill Gulstan to do anything about it—especially now that Guardians were protecting the city's water sources.

"Yes," Ronall said. "Supported the rebellion . . ." He was thirsty again. Thirsty—and hungry, as always, for *more,* for something he couldn't name, something he couldn't even really imagine. But when he saw the silent glance of understanding which passed easily between Tansen and his son, he had a feeling that what he wanted was nearby, even if it wasn't his and he couldn't have it.

"I'm not going east," Tansen said, "and so I can't protect—"

"I'll go alone," Ronall replied, having anticipated this.

"And probably get yourself killed," Tansen pointed out, clearly trying not to sound unkind.

"I'm not going back to my wife," Ronall insisted, "and you don't nee—"

"I've found out where she is," Tansen said, surprising him.

Ronall nodded in resignation. "Her estate."

"You knew?" Zarien blurted.

"No, but it was the likeliest place," Ronall said, "if she wasn't in Shaljir."

"That's what I decided after thinking about it," Tansen said. "Property and people require attention, and Elelar is very conscientious about such things."

"Yes," Ronall agreed faintly, feeling queasy as someone

who knew Elelar now spoke of her, bringing her to life among them.

"So I sent a messenger to her estate."

"You did?" Ronall bleated.

"Her reply was . . ." Tansen frowned down at the burn Zarien was again tending. "Well, it wasn't very useful."

Ronall watched him warily, waiting for him to continue.

"She tells me," Tansen said, "that she wants to thank you for *Torena* Chasimar's delightful company." When Ronall snorted, Tansen asked, "That means something to you?"

"It's a . . . husband and wife joke."

"I see."

Ronall doubted it. "Does she also tell you that I am not welcome there?"

Tansen rubbed his forehead. "Something like that. So I suppose there's not much chance of you talking her into leaving her estate now?"

"Why would you want me to?"

Tansen's gaze was dark and hard. "You evidently don't realize how dangerous it is for her to be there."

"You mean because of the chaos there?" Kariman had taken control of that district upon Ferolen's death, and so it was now part of the extremely messy bloodfeud going on between him and Gulstan.

"Partially," Tansen acknowledged. "But mostly because Kiloran—or any of his assassins—can probably still reach her there, despite the chaos. She's not their primary concern these days, but they do want her dead; so they'll see to it if they realize she's there."

Ronall frowned. "But she betrayed Josarian to Kiloran, so why would Kiloran now—" He stopped speaking when Zarien gasped and made a jerky movement which caused Tansen to flinch and pull his burned leg away from the boy.

Zarien said slowly, "*Torena* Elelar helped the White Dragon kill—"

"No," Tansen replied. "She didn't know about the White Dragon."

Ronall's heart was pounding as he stared at the *shatai*. "You know what she did, don't you?" He almost laughed as he realized, "Of course, you do! After all, you killed Zimran, who was sleeping with Elelar. And if you know my wife, then you know that she can convince a man to do almost anything."

Tansen's expression had gone quite blank—which probably meant that he did indeed know what Ronall knew, and probably much more. "How do you know this?" he asked evenly.

"I know *her*." Ronall sighed.

Tansen's face changed, and Ronall thought that he almost looked . . . guilty. "Yes, I suppose so."

"If you know," Ronall asked, suddenly curious, "why haven't you killed her?"

A *sharp* look of guilt now. Unmistakable. Ah, yes. That was the *shallah* in him. He hadn't avenged his bloodbrother's murder, and the stain on his honor was dark and heavy.

Tansen replied quietly, "I don't kill women."

Ronall nodded, understanding that, at least. Silerian women, though their lives were hard, held a rather exalted status in the eyes of Silerian men. And Elelar . . . Ronall suddenly wondered with almost wild curiosity if she had the effect on Tansen—even on this ruthlessly disciplined *shatai*— that she'd had on so many other men.

"*Torena* Elelar betrayed Josarian," Zarien murmured, looking strangely at Tansen. "She, not the Valdani, convinced Zimran to lead Josarian into the trap you saved him from."

Before Tansen could reply, Ronall said, "Yes."

"And you," Zarien said, his voice dark as he addressed Tansen, "knew that, but you kept it a secret. You let Josarian's loyalists blame Zimran alone, while the *torena* was admired. You told *me* she was a great heroine of the rebellion."

"She was," Tansen said, meeting his son's gaze. "She sacrificed—"

"She sacrificed the Firebringer!" Zarien sounded hurt. "Maybe even the sea king!"

"The who?" Ronall asked.

Tansen shook his head. "She didn't sacrifice the sea king, Zarien."

The boy's eyes were wide with dismay. Perhaps even disillusionment. "You don't know that. Maybe it's not you. Maybe I was wrong."

Tansen made an obvious attempt to get control of the conversation. "I'll never forgive what Elelar did, Zarien, but she was still needed. I couldn't kill her for—"

"*Kill* her?" Zarien's voice was suddenly harsh and angry, making Tansen blink. "Why is *that* always the only answer for you? I asked you not to kill her in Shaljir, and I'd ask you again if she walked into camp right now!"

"Then—"

"Don't you *ever* think there's a way of punishing someone besides killing them?" Zarien cried, his voice now attracting the attention of others in the camp.

Tansen rose to his feet. Zarien leapt back as if afraid Tansen would strike him. Tansen saw this and froze.

Ronall wondered how Elelar managed to do this to men even when she was nowhere in the vicinity.

"Calm down," Tansen said to Zarien.

"*Me?*" Zarien's voice was rich with a scathing contempt which Elelar herself might have envied. "*I* am not the one who unsheathes my swords every time something goes wrong." He turned his back and stormed away from his father.

"Zarien!" Tansen called, his voice filled with the authority which had commenced a rebellion and led a civil war. "*Zarien!*"

The boy ignored him and disappeared into the woods.

"I told him not to go anywhere alone," Tansen muttered, starting to pursue him.

"There are sentries everywhere," Ronall pointed out, "and, if I might suggest—he needs some time alone now."

Tansen stopped in his tracks. The expression of uncertainty on his face was so unfamiliar that it almost made him look like a stranger. He clearly wrestled with the decision for a moment before admitting, "You're right."

It was hard to remember the last time someone had said that to Ronall; and that it should now be Tansen, of all men . . . However, all the time Ronall had lately spent with Tansen and Zarien had certainly revealed to him just how humbling fatherhood was.

Ever since meeting Tansen, Ronall had seen how he—even *he*—struggled with raising a son, albeit under very unusual circumstances. Watching Tansen now, Ronall was again filled with fear and dread—the two primary emotions which clouded his mind every time he thought about Jalilar's pregnancy. Not that he supposed Emelen would ever let him near Jalilar's baby. Not that Tansen, Mirabar, and the Guardians were likely to let a drunken Valdan influence the childhood of their prophesied Yahrdan.

Ronall didn't believe for one moment that *his* child, gotten so carelessly on a woman whose face he was already forgetting, was the one chosen by Dar Herself to rule Sileria in the Firebringer's wake.

Trying to distract his thoughts, yet again, from that whole bizarre, frightening, and bewildering situation, he now said to Tansen, "I guess fatherhood is a challenge even to the most capable of men."

"Dar knows it challenged *my* father," Tansen muttered.

"They say he died when you were very young."

Tansen went very still. "Yes. Yes, he did."

"So when you were Zarien's age, did you—"

Tansen snapped, "I don't want to talk about when I was Zarien's age."

Ronall nearly flinched. "I didn't mean to intrude."

"I'm sorry, *toren*," Tansen said, recovering his self-control. "I didn't mean to be rude."

Relieved, Ronall replied, "I think you can call me Ronall."

"Yes," Tansen agreed dryly. "Considering that you've more or less been my hostage ever since we met, perhaps I needn't be so formal."

"I would probably be dead if I weren't your hostage," Ronall admitted.

"Which is why I don't think I can agree to let you go east on your own."

"I'm a burden to you here," Ronall said, "and I—"

"You've done some good here," Tansen argued. The mildness of his tone made the comment seem sincere.

But Ronall knew better. "*You've* done the good. For the Silerian-born Valdani, I mean. The people in Britar, in Adalian, elsewhere—they listened to you, not to me. You didn't need me. People do what you want them to do because of who you are, not because you display me to them."

Tansen studied him with a serious, considering expression. "Do you think that, on your own, you can make people listen? Can you stop the killing?" He seemed as if he genuinely wanted to know, even sincerely hoped it was a possibility.

"It worked once before." Ronall thought of *Torena* Chasimar. Then he thought of Porsall, whose dying scream still haunted him. "Well, partly, anyhow," he amended. "I don't know. I just know that I need to try." He smiled wryly. "Perhaps being forced to live among a bunch of self-sacrificing warriors and fire-eating mystics has destroyed the last of my reason. Or maybe you just don't have enough liquor here to keep me calm. I just know that . . . I have no home but Sileria, and neither do the rest of my kind. If I'm going to die violently, and soon, it might as well be because I was trying to help my people, instead of just because I finally ran out of places to hide." When Tansen didn't say anything, Ronall added, "I want to help. I want to . . ." Oh, how Elelar would laugh right now. "Do the right thing." He took a breath. "I want to die doing something worthy, instead of knowing, when they finally kill me, that I wasted everything I was born with, everything that was given to me, and every chance I ever had of becoming a man."

Tansen stared at him in silence for a long moment. Ronall wondered what he was thinking, since his face was again living up to its reputation for inscrutability.

What the *shatai* finally said stunned him: "You would have liked Josarian."

"The same Josarian who killed so many Valdani?" Ronall asked doubtfully.

"He had a very generous heart and ... would probably have been moved to embrace you for such a brave decision."

"Brave?" Ronall repeated faintly.

Tansen lifted one brow. "Surely even the Valdani teach their children that courage isn't the absence of fear, but the ability to carry on despite it?"

"I'll need a lot of fire brandy to do this," Ronall warned him, not wanting Tansen to expect more of him than he could give.

"Sometimes even Josarian needed it," Tansen assured him with the hint of a smile. "And I ... I have been very, very thirsty for it on occasion, Ronall."

"So you'll let me go?" Ronall asked, confused and pleased and afraid.

"Tansen!"

They both turned quickly as a runner came stumbling into camp. Ronall recognized him as someone Tansen trusted, though he didn't know the *shallah*'s name.

"Tansen!" the man shouted, looking so wild-eyed, sweat-drenched, and exhausted that Ronall's belly immediately roiled with fear.

"Here!" Tansen stalked towards him, his posture tense.

Ronall followed, already knowing that this runner was bringing bad news.

"Tansen!" The man's face crumpled horribly when he saw Tansen, and he fell to his knees.

Tansen crouched beside him, heedless of the burned leg which must make that painful. "What is it?" he demanded.

"Something terrible has happened!" the *shallah* reported between heaving breaths. "So terrible!"

Ronall watched with dread as the man—a tough, battle-hardened mountain peasant—started to weep like a child.

"Dar have mercy on us all!" the *shallah* cried. "It's over. We're finished. Kiloran has won."

Tansen took him by the shoulders. "What are you talking about?"

"Jalilar is dead!"

"What?" Tansen shot to his feet, dragging the *shallah* with him. *"What?"*

"Jalilar is dead," the runner repeated.

"How?"

"Kiloran has had her assassinated. Her, her unborn child, Emelen, all the sentries . . ."

Ronall stared in blank-minded shock, unable to form words.

"How did Kiloran lure them out of Sanctuary?" Tansen demanded.

The *shallah*'s tear-streaked eyes were dazed with horror. "He didn't."

Tansen shook his head, frowning. "No, they were in Sanctuary. Jalilar knew not to . . . not to . . ." A look of shocked disbelief washed across that hawklike face. He shook his head. *"No."*

"Yes," the *shallah* wept.

Tansen took a step back. "No. Not even Kiloran would . . ."

"He violated Sanctuary!" the *shallah* screamed. "He violated Sanctuary and murdered Jalilar and her unborn child!"

Tansen just stood there, his face twisted by grief and shock. "Even Kil . . . Even . . ." He lowered his head. *"Jalilar."*

"Dead with a single thrust of Searlon's *shir,*" the *shallah* reported, his weeping starting to fade into hollow grief.

"How do you know that?" Tansen asked without looking up.

"Sister Basimar saw the whole thing. She came to our encampment for help after it happened. She was done crying by then, and she was very clear about what happened."

"They spared her?" Tansen asked dully.

"No. Searlon . . . maybe he didn't know she was already in residence to tend Jalilar, because he didn't even look for her. Basimar was returning from gathering herbs in the woods when she . . . heard the screams."

Many Guardians and *shallaheen* were now gathered around Tansen and the runner, all listening in horrified, wide-eyed silence.

"The sentries were all dead by the time Basimar got close enough to see anything. Some of their bodies were lying inside Sanctuary grounds, where the assassins had killed them. Basimar thinks there were six assassins, but she's not sure about that. Everything happened so fast."

The Sister living in this camp now came forward and silently offered water to the runner. He shook his head and continued, "The sentries were dead, and then Emelen . . ." His voice broke again. No one said anything, no one moved, while he composed himself enough to go on. "Emelen was shouting that this was Sanctuary, they couldn't do this. When they tried to get past him, to go inside and . . . and kill Jalilar, he fought them. He shouted for her to run, and he fought them, trying to give her time. Trying to stop them . . . to . . ." He gasped, and tears started streaming down his face again.

"*Emelen.*" It was Tansen's voice, raw with grief.

"They killed him. Searlon caught Jalilar while she was trying to escape." More harsh, panting breaths. Then he concluded, "And he killed her."

No one said anything. Ronall had never heard such a silence. Then again, probably no one in all of Sileria had ever heard anything as shocking as this tale.

The Sister finally said what everyone else was surely thinking. "I've never heard of anyone violating Sanctuary. Not any Silerian. Not ever. Not even . . ." She shook her head. "Not ever."

"Kiloran did." Tansen's voice was low and deadly. "Once before. He used Outlookers to ambush Josarian in Sanctuary after inviting him to a truce meeting there." His chest was heaving. "I should have . . . I should have remembered and known . . . Known that if Kiloran found out about Jalilar . . ."

"Those were Outlookers, Tansen," another *shallah* said, his voice soft with lingering shock. "Kiloran was slippery, but he didn't actually violate . . . Not like this. And Searlon was too fastidious to be there himself the day they attacked Josarian in Sanctuary."

"How could they do this?" the Sister wondered, anger starting to give strength to her voice. "How could anyone do this? The murder of a woman is disgusting enough—but to violate Sanctuary? How could a Silerian do that, even a waterlord?" She started crying.

"And Jalilar's baby was . . . Is this the end, then?" someone asked Tansen. "Is it over?"

"Over?" Tansen repeated, his face darkening. "It won't be over until I gut Kiloran like a fish and roast him in the Fires for all eternity. And Searlon . . ." He made a terrible sound. "I should have killed him before this, should have cut off Kiloran's right arm a long time ago."

Another *shallah* unsheathed his sword—the sword he had undoubtedly taken from an Outlooker's body. "What do we do now? Give us our orders, *siran!*"

"No." Tansen shook his head. "I need to think. We can't afford to act rashly now. And . . ." He glanced at some of the Guardians. "You should go to the Sanctuary and burn their bodies."

"Dar have mercy on Jalilar's soul!" someone shouted. "Dar have mercy on her child!"

"Jalilar." It suddenly hit Ronall. His legs buckled and he found himself sitting awkwardly in the dust.

The Firebringer's sister. Jalilar. The woman Ronall had made love to with such abandoned frenzy, the two of them bound together by their terrible loneliness. Jalilar, who was the mother of . . .

"My child," Ronall murmured. "My child is dead."

Tansen flinched. "Someone get my son," he ordered. *"Now."*

"I was . . . going to be a father," Ronall said, his voice sounding far away. "I was . . . There was a . . . would have been a child." It was as if he only really understood that now, when it was too late.

Amidst the shouting for Zarien, the sudden rage-inspired bustle of the camp, and the vows of vengeance all around him, Ronall couldn't seem to rise to his feet or to think about anything but the part of him which Kiloran's assassins had murdered. Inside of the woman who had given him such pleasure. Along with the husband who had loved her enough to forgive her for that in the end.

He didn't know when he had started crying, he only knew that he was doing so now. And, for the first time in his life, his tears were all entirely for someone else. Jalilar, their baby; even Emelen.

Why ask Dar for mercy? She would never give it. Not here. Not in Sileria. Not the destroyer goddess.

An expensive pair of dusty, worn boots ran straight past Ronall. Then he heard Zarien's voice, high with shock and panic.

"Father! Is it true?"

Ronall looked up and saw Tansen embrace the boy fiercely, a terrible fear written all over that brave man's face.

"I won't let him have you, too," Tansen muttered. "I won't."

"Jalilar . . ." The boy's voice was now dark and breathy with sorrow.

Still holding his son, Tansen closed his eyes. "He won't get you. I promise you he won't."

And Ronall knew that Tansen was making the promise to himself rather than to the boy.

"What'll we do?" Zarien asked. "What does this mean?"

Tansen released the boy and, still keeping him close, answered, "It means that even I didn't realize how dangerous Kiloran is. How desperate. Even I didn't understand how far he would go. It means . . ." He sighed and straightened

Zarien's tunic. "It means we have to be stronger than he is, no matter what it costs us."

Zarien looked away, his young face as troubled as everyone else's. When he saw Ronall, he said, "I'm very sorry about your child, *toren*."

Still sitting in the dust, Ronall looked up at the two of them and wondered, "Do you think . . . her child . . . our child . . . was really the one? Or do you think Kiloran just . . . murdered some poor peasant girl bearing a drunken *toren*'s bastard?" He felt tears slide down his cheeks.

"How did Kiloran know?" Zarien asked.

Tansen gave him a sharp look. Then he drew in a swift, sharp breath. "How *did* he know?"

Even Ronall immediately understood the implications of the boy's question. Very few people had known about Jalilar's condition, and even fewer knew where she was hiding. "Someone betrayed her."

Zarien gasped. "Baran?"

Tansen frowned, but he shook his head after a moment. "He would die before he would give Kiloran that kind of advantage." His shoulders sagged. "I've got to get word to Mirabar about this. Right away."

Ronall watched Tansen turn away to find someone to take this terrible news to Belitar. Zarien followed him.

And Ronall sat in the dust, desperately trying to remember what Jalilar's face had looked like.

52

THE MORE INTIMATE THE FRIENDSHIP, THE DEAD-
LIER THE ENEMY.

—Silerian Proverb

NAJDAN HAD PROPOSED a place for the truce
meeting which was in the chaotic, war-torn district where
Meriten and the loyalists still fought hard for ultimate victory.
It was a reasonable place for him to suggest, since neither side
of the conflict was in control of the area, and since neither
Kiloran nor Baran currently had any real advantage over an
enemy like Najdan there.

There was also only one convenient way to get there from
Kandahar, where Najdan's message had reached Dyshon. So
Najdan set his trap on the ancient road well east of his proposed meeting place, and waited. As he expected, Dyshon
came early to the meeting, and came in force, planning to trap
and kill the assassin who had betrayed Kiloran for Mirabar.

Dyshon had no advantage here, either, so the ambush which
Najdan led against him was successful. It was a messy battle,
due to the heavily armed skill of both sides, but the element of
surprise was as effective as Najdan had hoped.

"You proposed a truce!" Dyshon screamed when Najdan
overcame and disarmed him.

"And you agreed to one," Najdan pointed out, then gutted
him with his *shir*.

"No!" Dyshon gasped, falling to his knees.

"It had to be this way," Najdan said, watching him die.
"Kiloran knew it when he sent you to murder me at a truce
meeting."

Dyshon gazed at him with astonished, pain-glazed green eyes.

"He just," Najdan added, "didn't realize that I knew it, too."

Najdan looked around after Dyshon's body hit the ground and shuddered in its death throes. All nine of Kiloran's men lay dead now. The *sirana* wasn't here to order it, so no one even considered burning the bodies. The men who had come here with Najdan were all assassins, and their ways were different from hers.

Now Vinn wiped his *shir* on the tunic of one of Kiloran's dead assassins, then joined Najdan as he gazed down at Dyshon's corpse.

"Did you know him well?" Vinn asked.

"Not really," Najdan said, slipping his own *shir* into his boot.

"Disgraceful," Vinn said. "Planning to violate a truce meeting with an assassination."

Najdan gave him a skeptical look.

Vinn returned his gaze innocently, then gestured to the slain. "You think *this* work was disgraceful, too?" He smiled and pointed out, "You are no longer of the Society, and *I* didn't invite him to a truce meeting." He thought it over for a moment and added, "Actually, since Baran betrayed the waterlords, I suppose I'm no longer of the Society, either."

Najdan said nothing, since there was no going back on the choices he had made once and would willingly make again. Besides, dishonorable or not, this work was now done, and nothing could be gained by dwelling on it.

Vinn, however, cheerfully continued, "Besides, I am a long-time enemy who just happened to be here when Dyshon so carelessly entered a district which everyone knows is wild with violence and treachery." When Najdan still didn't respond, Vinn concluded, "Your plan worked. Baran will be very pleased."

Najdan nodded. "He will also be very pleased that it didn't get you killed. He warned me he would be very cross with me if that happened."

"I'm glad he let me help you. It's been a while since I've had a good battle," Vinn said. "I enjoyed it."

"I'm sure Tansen could use fresh fighters," Najdan suggested dryly.

As he expected, Vinn shook his head. "Tempting, I admit. But then who would protect the *siran?*"

"From Kiloran?"

"Ah, Najdan. Have you learned nothing in all your time at Belitar?" Vinn tilted his head to one side. "More than anything, Baran has always needed protection from himself."

Since it struck Najdan as true, he asked, "Why do you do it?"

Vinn smiled. "Because he grows on you." After a moment, the assassin slanted a shrewd glance at Najdan and added, "Haven't you noticed?"

Najdan only replied, "Let's go home."

KILORAN KNEW THE moment Dyshon died. He felt the sudden shift of power in the Idalar River as it sank more deeply into Baran's embrace.

Rage flooded him as powerfully and coldly as he himself had once flooded the mines of Alizar—the mines which also now resisted his control, trying to elude his mastery, trying to ebb and flow away from his will.

Trap, he realized.

Najdan had lured him with the sweetest bait of all: the promise of vengeance. The assassin had known it would cloud his judgment and make him vulnerable. Najdan was not the most imaginative of men, but he hadn't served Kiloran well for twenty years without coming to thoroughly understand his master. Yes, the best assassins always grew to know their masters almost as well as a wife would, with a mutual trust which ran that deep in a partnership which was that secure. When Najdan violated all of that with betrayal, he didn't forget anything he had learned about Kiloran over the years; and so he knew exactly how to convince his former master to send

Dyshon, someone whom Kiloran needed and valued, right into his trap.

Waves of cold self-recrimination washed over Kiloran. He had treated Najdan's offer of a truce meeting as if it had come from just anyone, rather than from someone who knew him so well for so long. With Kiloran's judgment swayed by the temptation Najdan had provided, perhaps Searlon might have seen the danger and suggested caution. But Dyshon? No. He'd never been that shrewd.

Losing the assassin at this particular time was a terrible blow. There was no denying that.

But at least Searlon's letter this morning confirmed that the Firebringer's sister and the child she bore were dead. At least there was that.

And Mirabar's fiery prophecies were now all ashes.

Now THAT THEY were so close to Mount Darshon that it entirely blocked the sky in front of her, Elelar finally began to suspect she had made a grave mistake.

She rode quietly beside Cheylan, physically and emotionally drained from the journey. They had come through days and nights of heat and dust, the perils of their trip augmented by occasional earthquakes. The treacherous paths they followed were sometimes blocked by avalanches. Elelar was wary of prowling assassins, and Cheylan had been obliged to protect her from a group of particularly persistent bandits. Elelar had brought nothing with her—not even a change of undergarments—and she wasn't used to traveling like this: no servants, no money of her own, no authority, and no comforts. She hadn't bathed since leaving home, and she was *definitely* not used to smelling like this. By now, she was rather relieved that Cheylan avoided people as much as possible, since she felt embarrassed by the image she presented.

So much for dying with dignity.

If she didn't wash and change her clothing soon, she'd be mistaken for a goat when she finally met her destiny.

She was also beginning to fully understand why hardly anyone liked Cheylan. She had had very little contact with him before now and was previously inclined to attribute people's dislike of him (including Tansen's) to superstitious fear, even to jealousy of his power. Now, however, she fully understood that any distaste for Cheylan was almost certainly inspired by his personality, rather than by his fiery eyes.

Mirabar had certain things in common with Cheylan which had forged a bond between them, evidently making it easier for her to overlook Cheylan's cool, sour, smug nature than it was for others, including Elelar.

It might be petty and querulous of Elelar, but if she had to give her life as payment for what she had done to the Firebringer, then she didn't want Cheylan to be the one to kill her. She wanted, she now acknowledged with weary futility, Mirabar to do it. Elelar didn't like Mirabar, but she trusted and respected her—and she knew by now that she'd never be able to say that about Cheylan. Being with him felt increasingly wrong; and the more she tried to understand him and put these feelings to rest, the worse she felt.

Elelar believed in her destiny, in the Olvar's vision, in her duty to surrender to "the one with eyes of fire . . ." She had been so sick of passively waiting for her fate, so relieved to see Cheylan and commit to decisive action, that she had readily and recklessly assumed he was the one to whom the Olvar had advised her to surrender.

She now wished, with mingled irritation and fear, that the Olvar had been more specific. What if she *was* supposed to wait for Mirabar? What if she was supposed to wait for someone whose identity she didn't even know? What if meekly following Cheylan to wherever he was leading her was actually interfering with her destiny, rather than fulfilling it?

What if Cheylan, with his vague answers and unexplained actions, was not telling her the truth?

After Elelar's initial holy fervor had worn off, in the dreary reality of uncomfortable travel with a strange companion, she had started questioning Cheylan. Where was Mirabar? Back at Belitar. Why hadn't she come? She couldn't. Why not? She was not meant to. Where was Cheylan taking her? East. Where in the east? She would see. Why were they going east? Because Mirabar had insisted. Why? She would see.

And so on.

He was polite, and even soothing—but Elelar was increasingly dissatisfied with his answers, and increasingly worried that whatever he intended was not what *she* intended . . . which was a difficult distinction to make, since she didn't really know what she intended, and Cheylan wouldn't clarify what *he* intended.

Elelar sighed, feeling glum, scared, and frustrated.

"Torena?" Cheylan said in polite inquiry, having heard the sigh.

"Where are we going?" she asked.

"We'll be there soon."

"Where?"

"It's difficult to explain," he replied kindly.

Elelar sighed again.

The farther they traveled from Mirabar and Belitar, the more Elelar began to suspect that Mirabar might not, in fact, have ordered this journey. Might not even know that Elelar was following Cheylan towards some mysterious destination.

Elelar's stomach churned as she tormented herself with these fears. Now, conversely, she wondered if she was just trying, as she approached her death, to find an escape, a rationalization, a justification for fleeing the unknown punishment she had thought herself so willing to endure.

Why would Cheylan have come to her estate and taken her away, full of his vague and portentous comments, unless he was indeed the one she had awaited? He certainly alluded, however vaguely, to a more thorough knowledge of Elelar's future than she herself possessed; and he was, after all, a Guardian of phenomenal power.

Of course he's the one I've awaited. I'm just frightened. I'm just trying to talk myself out of this.

Which was wrong of her. It was too late, anyhow. She had come this far. There was no turning back.

But where was Mirabar? Why didn't Cheylan tell Elelar more, prepare her for what was to come? Why wouldn't he specify where they were going and what would happen when they got there? Why didn't he want her even speaking to the Sisters or *zanareen* they came across during their journey?

And were the two of them actively avoiding Guardians, or was Elelar merely imagining that?

She clenched her jaw, suddenly aware that her lips were trembling. She was making herself crazy with these wild speculations.

She could, of course, simply balk and refuse to let her horse take another step until Cheylan told her everything she wanted to know and eliminated every one of her worries. But she suspected that would be foolhardy, even dangerous. The time for such behavior had been back at her estate, where she was surrounded by her own servants and able to challenge Cheylan from a position of strength. Unfortunately, she had not done so. She had been a fool. And now she regretted it.

Now she was all alone, far from home, in a strange and dangerous place with a man she hardly knew; a man whom, she now realized, she didn't trust. He was a very powerful man, too. She had seen him incinerate two bandits and send their companions fleeing in terror only last night. He needn't humor her demands here, where she was so far from help or protection. He needn't even keep up a pretense of courtesy or respect, if she pushed him.

Elelar shivered, chilled by her own dark imaginings.

We're approaching Darshon, she reminded herself as her horse plodded towards the slopes of Dar's imposing domain.

Cheylan was taking her to the goddess. Whatever his intentions, they must surely be directed by Dar Herself.

But when she looked at him . . . she felt afraid.

Enough of this.

She was tired of enduring this uncharacteristic indecision and mind-tangling fear.

Cheylan was a man, she reminded herself in exasperation. His Otherworldly insights and fiery power notwithstanding, he was just a man, like any other. Elelar knew better than any woman in Sileria how to get what she wanted from a man, and how to convince him to tell her what she wanted to know.

It was time—past time—to take control of the situation, using the same skills she had always used to take charge of men. The two things which made a man easiest to manipulate, she knew, were letting him believe he was in control, and letting him believe he was desired. Men who were convinced of those two things were usually as easy to dominate, thereafter, as hungry puppies.

Cheylan already believed he was in control of her. And Elelar could tell by the arrogance of his manner that he would be very easy to convince of the second thing, too.

"I'm so tired," Elelar murmured. "Can we stop to rest soon?"

"Of course, *torena.*"

"And," she asked with genuine longing, "is there any chance of a bath and a bed?"

"A bath, no. But a bed . . ."

"Yes?"

"We're not very far from my father's hunting lodge. It's a simple place, with no servants, but it will serve our needs."

Certainly it sounded far better than sleeping on the ground outside yet again.

"Oh, good!" Elelar added wistfully, "I feel so dowdy and unkempt."

"You always," Cheylan assured her, "look lovely, *torena.*"

"You could . . ." She lowered her eyes.

"Yes?" he prodded.

"You could call me Elelar," she said softly.

In the long silence that followed, she finally raised her gaze to his. She was puzzled by what she saw there, but after a moment he smiled slightly, then murmured, "Elelar."

Their eyes held for a long moment. Then he turned his horse and again led the way.

Oh, yes. Cheylan could be convinced to lower his guard. And when he did, Elelar would learn whatever she wanted to know.

"I'M SORRY, FATHER," *said Tansen. They stood together in Kiloran's encampment, where Armian had just given him the* yahr *which Tansen would soon use to murder him. "I want you to know I'm so sorry."*

"Don't worry about it," Armian replied. "The first kill is always the hardest. But you'll do it. I know you will."

Tansen nodded, sick at heart. "Yes. I will."

Josarian asked, "Does he know what you're going to do?"

"Don't tell him!" Tansen insisted.

"Are you afraid?"

"I don't want him to know. He should never know what I've done!"

"You can't keep this from him," Josarian said.

"I have to. He could never understand."

"You know it's wrong," Josarian warned.

Tansen squinted through the rain at his brother. "He's only a boy," he protested.

"So were you," *Josarian pointed out gently.*

They were on the cliffs east of Adalian. A dark-moon night, a treacherous landscape. The long rains had finally come.

"But what if the rains don't come this year?" Tansen asked Josarian. "What'll I do? I'm not the Firebringer."

Elelar said, "He is not like other boys. Surely you see that."

"You shouldn't be here," Tansen told her.

"How well do you really know him?" she persisted.

"Go away," Tansen said.

"You're making a mistake," Elelar warned.

"I've made many," he reminded her.

Armian stood boldly at the cliff's edge, searching the cove below for some sign of the Moorlanders he awaited.

"I should do it now," Tansen said, unsheathing his swords and stalking Armian.

Josarian urged, "Tell him now."

"I curse Dar every day for letting you die," Tansen told his brother.

"What about the day She let *him die?*" Josarian asked.

Tansen shook his head. "No. That was my choice, and mine alone. I don't blame Her for that."

"Don't you?" Josarian murmured.

Fast, please Dar, let it be fast. Let him not suffer. I can't bear to make him suffer . . .

"This silence . . ." Josarian said. "It's like killing him twice."

"I have *killed* him twice. I've killed him a thousand times."

"He won't stay dead," Josarian said. "You know that."

"Yes, I know. But what else can I do?"

He struck out. The blow connected, reverberating through Tansen's soul. Armian fell to his knees.

Josarian said, "Tell him."

"Get away," Tansen warned. "He might hurt you."

"No, you're the only one he can still hurt," Josarian replied. "Be careful."

Armian rolled away from the next blow, moving so fast he escaped it entirely, while simultaneously reaching for his shir . . . But Armian froze, like a statue, when he saw

his son standing above him on that windswept cliff . . .
"Tansen?"

"I never forget the way you said that," Tansen told him. *"I never stop hearing it."*

"Father . . ."

"Tell him," Josarian repeated.

"It's too late," Tansen insisted.

"Father?"

"Tell him."

"I can't!"

"It's not too late."

"No, I can't!"

Armian said, just as he had said a thousand times, "Tansen?"

"Armian . . ."

Forgive me, father.

"Father, wake up. Father!"

Tansen sucked in air on a huge, painful gasp as he sat bolt upright, fleeing his dreams, his father, his brother, his past. Running from what he had done. From what he knew.

"You were dreaming," Zarien said, his voice sleepy and irritable.

Breathing hard, Tansen rubbed his hands over his face, feeling sweat there. Feeling the fear and guilt which oozed out of him in the night, when he couldn't control them.

With his head still down, he heard Zarien return to his own bedroll. He wondered if he had woken anyone else. He hoped not. Zarien slept closer to him than anyone else, and was usually the only one he disturbed. Usually, but not always.

He cautiously looked up—and immediately saw Ronall staring at him. The *toren* was always wakeful when the camp ran out of liquor, and tonight was no exception. Tansen casually glanced around, decided that no one else was awake, and lowered his head again, ignoring Ronall. As soon as he judged the *toren* recovered enough from the news of Jalilar's murder to be trusted, he would send him east, as they had discussed. Ronall, however, seemed as if he might take a while to pull himself together.

Tansen started measuring his breath, controlling it, physically calming himself so that his heart would stop racing and his mind would stop leaping wildly.

He thought Zarien had gone back to sleep, as he usually did, so he flinched when the boy said the very last thing he ever wanted to hear on his son's lips: "Who's Armian?"

Darfire, was he actually *shaking* now?

"Go back to sleep," Tansen murmured, trying to make his voice soothing.

Zarien, of course, ignored his instructions and repeated, "Who's Armian?"

Don't answer without thinking. Don't tell a lie he'll catch you in later.

"Armian?" Tansen repeated vaguely, glad that the sea-bound boy didn't recognize the name which any *shallah* child probably would.

"Did he die with Josarian?"

"No."

"Oh."

"Why do you ask?"

"Sometimes you say his name. Sometimes Josarian's. Sometimes . . ."

"Yes?" he prodded, hearing his blood roaring in his ears.

"Sometimes you, um, cry for your father."

"Oh." His chest hurt.

"What was he like?"

Tell him.

No.

"It's late," Tansen said.

"No, it's nearly dawn," Zarien replied. "Not much point in going back to sleep."

"Oh."

There was a long silence.

"Did your father die terribly?" Zarien finally asked.

Dar have mercy.

"Outlookers killed him," he said, since it was true of the man who had sired him.

"How old were you?"

Tansen looked up and met Ronall's silent gaze. "Too young to remember him."

"But you . . ." Zarien's voice was puzzled. "You have nightmares about him."

"Yes," Tansen admitted.

"Him and Armian. Josarian and the White Dragon," Zarien continued, naming more of Tansen's demons, "Gamalan and the Valdani."

"They're all jumbled up in my head," Tansen replied, which was true enough. "And it's hard to lose a father."

"Yes. I know."

He heard the quaver in Zarien's voice and cursed himself for wounding the boy so carelessly while trying to dodge his questions. Now he asked, concerned, "Do you still have nightmares?"

"Yes," Zarien admitted. "Not so much as before, though."

Hearing the silence between them, and shying away from his duty to fill it with the truth, Tansen said, "Tell me about Sorin. Tell me what he was like."

"He was . . . very traditional," Zarien said, hugging his knees. "Not strict like my grandfather, who didn't like us even talking to drylanders, but Papa did everything the old-fashioned way."

Tansen listened to him talk about his life on the sea, and the parents who had raised him. About the past, which both he and Zarien revisited too often in their dreams. About the good things, which were part of what made each of them strangely reluctant to banish the nightmares that tormented them. In the boy's voice, he heard the guilt which was another reason neither of them could let go; Zarien had been spared his family's fate, and he didn't really understand why.

Tansen also heard Zarien's tone rich with the love that stayed with you long after the loved one was dead. And Tansen knew they had been good parents to Zarien, that couple who had raised him as their own, and who had hidden the truth—whatever it really was—about his birth, throughout his childhood.

Had Armian been a good father?

To this day, Tansen wasn't really sure. He only knew that Armian had tried very hard. He only fully realized just *how* hard now that he was a father, too.

Am I a good father?

Tansen listened to Zarien, and he knew with certainty that his own dream was wrong. He could not tell this innocent boy, this youngster who so loathed killing, what he had done.

Tell him.

I can't. I just can't. Don't ask again.

"Tansen?"

He heard the soft voice of one of the sentries. Zarien stopped speaking as Tansen reached for his harness and rose to his feet, ready for trouble, ready to draw his swords.

"A messenger," the sentry said.

"Now?" It wasn't even dawn yet. "He must have traveled all night." Which was damned dangerous in the mountains.

"It must be important," Zarien murmured.

It was. When the messenger arrived, he didn't want water or food or rest. He just wanted to unload his burden onto the leader of the Firebringer's loyalists, because it was too heavy to carry alone any longer.

"The Lironi alliance has collapsed," he said. "Jagodan shah Lironi found Kiman shah Moynari with his wife, Viramar, and killed them both."

"What?" Tansen said, shocked.

"Found him with his wife?" Zarien repeated, clearly confused. "But why did he kill . . ." The boy's eyes flew wide open as he realized what Kiman and Viramar had been doing that would have driven Jagodan to murder. *"Oh!"*

The messenger continued, "The Moynari and the Lironi have declared a bloodfeud against each other, and Viramar's clan has declared one against them both."

"Oh, no," Tansen said, feeling cold dread wash through him.

"It's over in the east, Tansen. No one has time to destroy the Society now. They're too busy destroying each other."

"Oh, no, they don't," Tansen said, already knowing what he had to do. "I won't let them. No bloodfeuds. No clan wars. They finish Verlon, and they do it *soon*. Those are their orders, and that's damn well what they're going to do."

"Tansen," the demoralized messenger protested, "it's too late."

"No, it's not," he snapped, pulling on his tunic. "Get dressed," he told Zarien.

"What? Why?"

"We're going east, that's why." He glanced at Ronall. "You might as well come with us."

To his surprise, Ronall merely nodded and started dressing.

"Zarien," Tansen said tersely to the astonished boy, *"dress."*

"Huh? Oh!" Zarien started struggling into his shirt and searching for his boots. "But how can—"

"I assume you ride?" Tansen said to Ronall.

"Yes."

"Horses?" Zarien exclaimed with unconcealed horror. "We're not going by horseback?"

"Only to the coast," Tansen said. "And then you're getting us onto an east-bound boat."

"The sea? No!"

"Zarien." Tansen put his hands on the boy's shoulders and forced him to hold still and pay attention. "Everything depends on speed now. There's heavy fighting everywhere. Loyalists against the Society, and Society factions against each other. We don't have time to fight our way overland. We have to go by sea."

Zarien was pale. His eyes were bright and watery, and he suddenly seemed shaky and fragile. "I don't want to see the sea again. Smell it."

"We can't—"

"I don't want *you* to go to sea!"

"Zarien—"

"Sharifar took my whole family!" Zarien's voice was rich with panic now. "Please, *please,* father—"

"It'll be all right."

"There are earthquakes all the time now!"

"Put on your boots," Tansen ordered.

"You're not a good swimmer," Zarien babbled. "And that won't even matter if you're smashed against the rocks. My parents and my brothers were good swimmers, and they're all dead! You won't survive!"

"Your family was unlucky. The wrong place at the wrong time. Most of the sea-born are living through most of the earthquakes."

"Don't do this," Zarien begged.

"I'll be fine as long as I'm with you," Tansen insisted, believing it. "Sharifar won't let you die."

Zarien frowned. "I won't let her have what she wants. Don't go to her."

"I won't," Tansen promised, knowing he wasn't the one the goddess wanted—and hoping she understood that Zarien wasn't ready for her yet.

"Not the sea, father," Zarien pleaded.

"Zarien, I'm going." He made his tone hard, because there was no time for anything else. "Now are you coming with me or not?"

Glaring at him, the boy held out for a moment longer, then nodded sulkily.

"Then put on your boots and pack food for all three of us."

Zarien nodded and did as ordered while Tansen started issuing instructions to his men. He needed messengers sent to Pyron at Dalishar, to Radyan in Shaljir, and to Lann in Zilar.

He also gave orders about how the war here was to proceed in his absence. "Keep pressure on Gulstan and Kariman's territories. We can't afford to lose our advantage now, and we can't risk other waterlords taking over their leavings. Proceed with the assaults we talked about." He sighed. "We'll have to forget about Searlon until I return."

He'd been developing a plan to lure Searlon into a trap by making him think he was closing in on Zarien. However, getting rid of Searlon would now have to be postponed.

Only when the preparations for their hasty departure were nearly complete did Ronall, looking hollow-eyed and haggard, ask Tansen, "What was all that about?"

He frowned. "What?"

Ronall nodded to Zarien, who was approaching them with their food and water all packed and ready to go. "Shar . . . Shari . . ."

"Sharifar," Tansen supplied. "A sea goddess."

"Oh. And?"

"She's . . . hurt Zarien."

"Of course," Ronall said sourly. "She's a woman, isn't she?"

53

HE WHO BETRAYS YOU IS NEVER ONE FROM AFAR.
                                    —Silerian Proverb

"SO KILORAN VIOLATED Sanctuary," Baran mused, slumped in his chair, light-headed with weakness and pain as he considered the news from the courier who had come to Belitar.

Mirabar nodded, still weeping. This morning she had been

fretting ceaselessly (yet again) about there still being no sign of Cheylan and Elelar. Now she was sobbing her heart out about Jalilar's murder.

He regarded her with some impatience. "You told me that Jalilar's baby was just bad luck. Not the one you've prophesied. Not the one meant to save Sileria. And so on and so forth."

She nodded and sobbed harder.

Baran sighed. "So why all the tears?"

"Oh, you really are a monster," she snarled, "aren't you?"

"Your moods," he observed, "are becoming quite intolerable. It makes me positively glad that I won't be around for your second pregnancy, whenever that happy event may occur."

She cried even harder, and it was really no fun tormenting her when she wouldn't fight back. At a loss, he sipped some more of the brew Velikar had prepared for him. It was disgusting and mind-clouding, but he could no longer function at all without large doses of such things all day and half the night.

Fortunately, Najdan and Vinn chose that moment to return to Belitar. They entered the study only moments after being announced. Both well trained, they crossed their fists and bowed their heads, murmuring polite greetings.

"Dyshon is dead," Najdan said.

"Ahhh." Baran smiled, pleased. He had felt the sudden dissolving of the novice's grasp on the Idalar River, of course, but he never liked to assume victory without definite confirmation. "I thought so, but this is nonetheless worth celebrating. And, naturally," he added, still a great waterlord, "you will be rewarded."

Vinn grinned, but Najdan's frowning gaze was already fixed on Mirabar's swollen, tear-streaked face. He moved protectively towards her and glared at Baran. "What have you done to the *sirana?*"

"I've been as well as can be expected, thank you," Baran said mildly. "And you?"

Najdan, a stern man, made no move to embrace Mirabar, but his very presence seemed to calm her a bit, and her sobbing started drifting into broken little sighs.

Vinn ventured, "Is the *sirana* still suffering from, er, difficult moods?"

"Yes, and the *sirana* is still making sure the rest of us suffer along with her." Baran ignored the scowl this comment produced on Najdan's forbidding face. "Haydar assures me this period will pass and my wife will become more agreeable as she gets, er, riper. But I am increasingly skeptical about being around to enjoy the fruits of my labors in her bed."

"Oh, do shut up," Mirabar said, which was certainly an improvement over her earlier behavior.

Vinn protested, "You have cheated death too often to succumb now, *siran*."

"It's very touching that you can't face facts, Vinn," Baran said, "but not very useful."

The assassin's face fell and he said nothing more. Baran sighed. It was so frustrating to be in the mood for a fight and surrounded by people who wouldn't let him pick one.

"Tell them," Mirabar said to Baran.

He shrugged and did as ordered, while his wife composed herself. And even these two assassins, who had just circumvented—if not precisely violated—the age-old rules governing a truce meeting, were shocked by the news of Kiloran's treachery. Well, it *was* shocking, after all. Even Baran, half-mad and wholly without scruples, had never once considered violating Sanctuary. Not ever.

"Kiloran had to be desperate to do such a thing," Najdan murmured, staring contemplatively down at Mirabar's fiery, bowed head. "I, who have known him for so long, would never have imagined him doing this."

"Oh, he's done all sorts of things you probably haven't imagined, Najdan," Baran said. "In fact, I was there for one or two of them."

The assassin's gaze flashed to his face with sharp curiosity for a moment, and Baran was pleased to realize that Mirabar hadn't violated his confidences, not even with Najdan. She was, in her own way, a good wife.

Najdan nodded in acknowledgment of whatever secret existed between Baran and Kiloran, then said, "Still, I think he must be afraid, though he would not acknowledge it even to himself, to do such a thing."

Baran made a dismissive gesture. "He must be a *fool* to do such a thing." He shook his head. "It very rarely happens. But, oh, yes, once every so often he wants something so badly that it makes him act rashly: What he did to me, long ago; what he's done now . . ." Baran shook his head. "No. Even I would never have anticipated such an error."

Mirabar stared at him in puzzlement. "Because he killed the wrong woman?"

"No," Baran said impatiently, "because he's finally done something so appalling that surely no normal, decent, bloodthirsty Silerian can ever forgive him for it."

"But," Vinn ventured, "if the *sirana* says he's killed the wrong woman—"

"Give me strength!" Baran prayed to no one in particular. He waved his cup of painkilling brew at them all, careless of how it sloshed onto the floor, and reminded them, "I'm the one whose mind is fogged with pain and Sisterly potions. What excuse do the rest of you have?" They all looked at each other, then looked back at him, their gazes blankly confused. "If you would all look past Mirabar's Dar-cursed babbling about prophecy and the next Yahrdan, you would see that Kiloran has finally done the unthinkable!" When this statement produced no dawning understanding on their faces, he continued more calmly, "Murdering the Firebringer, while terrible enough to start a civil war, was nonetheless the deed of a bold and powerful waterlord. It was, dare I point out to Josarian's personal prophetess, a respectable act of vengeance against the man who killed Kiloran's only son, and a shrewd act of war against an enemy."

Najdan made a sudden sound of surprise and slowly said, "But killing a helpless woman . . ."

Vinn added, "A helpless *pregnant* woman . . ."

Baran nodded. "A helpless pregnant woman *in Sanctuary*."

Mirabar's expression now sharpened with understanding. "A woman who posed no threat to him."

"Ahhh . . ." Baran grinned. "Because Sileria knows only that she was the Firebringer's mourning sister."

"Sileria knows only . . ." Mirabar's face got pensive again.

"Whatever Kiloran may have imagined," Baran said, "Jalilar was, in fact, just a *shallah* woman awaiting her first child."

Vinn folded his arms across his chest, looking bright and energetic now as he pursued this view of the slaughter. "Kiloran wasn't content with triumphing over Josarian, so he murdered Josarian's only surviving female family member. And he violated Sanctuary." Vinn shook his head and said, "Filthy. Disgusting. Cowardly."

"Gives waterlords a bad name," Baran agreed.

Vinn nodded, following his master's premise easily due to years of practice. "He'd probably kill Josarian's wife, too, if she were still alive."

"Even if she were in Sanctuary," Baran added, "because that's the kind of man he has now shown us he is."

"None of his enemies' women or children are safe," said Vinn.

"Even his *friends*' women aren't safe," Baran said. "All of Sileria will perhaps understand just how true that statement is when we reveal that, years ago, while I was his apprentice, Kiloran raped and murdered my wife."

The effect of this announcement was so stunning, it would have satisfied Baran immensely had the subject been anything besides Alcinar.

"*Siran* . . ." Vinn's face was almost innocent with mingled sympathy, shock, and outrage.

"The bracelet," Najdan said suddenly, his voice breathless with surprise. "The necklace."

"Yes," Baran acknowledged.

Najdan nodded. "Now I understand."

Baran glanced at Mirabar, the object of so much deadly paternal devotion, and murmured, "I thought you might."

Kiloran's great weakness was that he could not understand, and therefore always underestimated, the power of love.

Vinn's complexion was dark when he vowed, "All of Sileria will now know what kind of man he is, *siran*. And all of Sileria will hate him for it."

"Killing Jalilar," Baran mused. "Violating Sanctuary." Vengeance was sweet. "I never dreamed he would be so reckless."

"It doesn't make sense," Mirabar said, finally coming out of her pensive silence.

"I believe that's my very point," Baran replied.

"No, I mean . . ." She spread her hands. "Why did he do it?"

"Because he was so sure that . . ." His heart thudded with sudden surprise as he realized what she was saying. She was right. Kiloran wouldn't have done something this rash based on just a hunch. "You mean, why was he so sure Jalilar's child was a threat to him?"

"Someone had to convince him," Najdan said with certainty. "And Searlon, who actually killed her, is extremely shrewd and patient. Without a very good reason to do this, Searlon would have insisted on a better plan, and Kiloran would have listened to him." Najdan nodded. "They had to be very sure—completely convinced—that Jalilar's unborn child was a terrible danger to them."

Vinn asked, "Then what convinced them?"

"Or who?" Baran added.

"Who knew that Jalilar was pregnant?" Najdan asked.

"And also where she was?" Vinn pondered.

"There was Tansen," Baran said, "and whoever he told."

"And me," Mirabar said, "and I only told . . ."

Her glowing eyes widened into round circles in her sun-kissed face as she drew in a stifled gasp.

"Oh, dear," Baran said, somewhat amused by the sight. "Were you indiscreet?"

Najdan's voice could have frozen water when he said to Mirabar, "You told Cheylan about Jalilar, didn't you?"

Baran was startled, not only by the cold dislike in Najdan's voice, but also by the implications of the comment.

"Cheylan?" Baran said. "A Guardian? Do you really think he would—"

"No!" Mirabar said. *"No."*

But Baran could see by her expression that she was suddenly full of uncertainty.

"He knew where she was hiding, didn't he?" Najdan prodded.

"Yes, but—"

"Did you tell anyone else where?"

"No, but—"

"So, if anyone betrayed you," Najdan persisted, "it had to be him."

"He also knew that child wasn't the one!" Mirabar jumped to her feet. "But no one around Tansen knew what I—"

"Tansen would have been very careful about whom he told. Only men he trusted completely would have known where Jalilar was."

"*I* was careful about whom I told!"

"Evidently not careful enough," Najdan snapped.

"Cheylan knew Jalilar's baby wasn't the one!"

"Then," Baran said, "perhaps we should consider what Cheylan could possibly have to gain by convincing Kiloran to kill Jalilar."

"Nothing," Mirabar said firmly.

"Don't you think he has taken a very long time about returning to Belitar with *Torena* Elelar?" Najdan said nastily.

"He might be dead!" Mirabar's lips trembled as she looked up at Najdan. "Who knows what difficulties—"

"Where are they?" Najdan persisted. "Why aren't they here yet? Why don't we even have word of Cheylan's death, if he's dead?"

"You were saying only this morning, my dear," Baran pointed out, "that they should have been here by now. You've been saying it, with wearying repetition, for several days, in fact."

"Cheylan is like me," Mirabar insisted. "He wouldn't—"

"He's nothing like you," Najdan snapped, "but he's gained your trust by letting you think he is."

"All Guardians have my trust!" she shouted.

"That might not be wise," Baran murmured.

"Him more than others," Najdan reminded her. "Whereas Tansen has never trusted him. And I—"

"Tansen has never liked 'demons!' And neither have you!"

Najdan looked as if he wanted to strike her. Baran and Vinn exchanged a glance, then continued to watch the two of them with riveted fascination.

Unfortunately, they came to their senses then. Mirabar waved a hand, as if to brush aside her words. Najdan said something gruff about pointless bickering.

Vinn sighed with momentary disappointment, then suggested, "Perhaps we can determine the truth if we return to the *siran's* question. What possible reason could Cheylan have for betraying Jalilar to Kiloran?"

"And then," Baran added, "abducting *Torena* Elelar?"

"He hasn't abducted her," Mirabar insisted.

"The future mother of a ruler foretold in prophecy," Baran murmured. "*I* would certainly abduct her."

"Yes, I know," Mirabar said testily, "but you're a . . ."

He met her gaze after her voice trailed off, but he had the distinct feeling she was no longer seeing him.

"Marjan's blood," she murmured, so softly he thought he had heard wrong.

"What?"

"Daurion's and Marjan's blood," she said, her voice growing stronger.

Baran prodded, "What does that mean?"

"In my vision. The Calling I did with the, uh, gift you gave me . . ."

"Yes?"

"Daurion told me that the prophesied Yahrdan was his heir, and would have both his and Marjan's blood in his veins."

"And is there some reason you're telling us this *now?*"

"Because . . . this inheritance will come from his father."

"Whom you thought might be Kiloran."

Her face was very still with certainty when she said, "But Cheylan thinks it means *him*."

Baran considered this. "I can understand why Cheylan might think he is descended from Daurion, a *toren* who reputedly had those Guardian eyes. But why—"

"Because Cheylan also has the blood of waterlords in his veins."

"What?"

"Verlon is his grandfather." Her voice was absent, her eyes clouded as she looked inwards, remembering things which she was suddenly viewing in a new light.

"Verlon?" Baran loved surprises.

"Yes. So . . . it's at least possible that Cheylan is descended from Marjan."

"Verlon," Baran repeated, "whose men nearly succeeded in killing Tansen in an ambush not very long ago?"

She blinked vaguely. "Many waterlords send their assassins after Tan—"

"Verlon's assassins had inside knowledge of his activities."

Her voice was too soft and uncertain when she said, "Many people know how to find him."

"Did Cheylan?"

"I . . ." A tear escaped one golden eye. "I don't know."

"He certainly could have," Najdan said with certainty.

"And if Cheylan does think he's going to father *Torena* Elelar's child . . ." Baran snorted briefly with amusement, then continued, "Why didn't he tell *you* so, Mirabar?"

"Perhaps he will," she replied. But he could see in her face that she already didn't believe it. "Maybe he was too astonished at the time . . ."

"Or maybe he thought," Baran suggested, "his best chance of fathering Elelar's child without interference was to convince Kiloran that Jalilar was going to bear the child you have prophesied."

"Oh, I like that, *siran,*" Vinn said. "It's a good theory."

"Why, thank you."

Mirabar argued, "You have no proo—"

"What you believe is, of course, entirely your own affair," Baran said. "But if I were in your position, I think I would assume, for my own safety, that Cheylan is betraying . . ." He laughed and said, "Well, *everyone*. All so he can sire Elelar's child and become the single most influential person in Sileria."

"No! He doesn't have such ambitions!"

"What in the Fires makes you so sure of that?" Baran asked curiously.

"Because . . . because . . ." She put a hand to her head and murmured, "Oh, no."

"Now what?"

"Daurion described him . . . the man . . . as someone who has murdered the innocent, lied to his allies, and betrayed everyone."

"No wonder you thought it might be me or Kiloran," Baran said in amusement. "And no wonder Cheylan didn't immediately turn to you and say, 'That's me.' It would have called for explanations which one can only imagine would have been extremely awkward for him."

"And he knew . . . He realized I would oppose him, once I knew."

"He's neither a weakling nor a fool," Baran said, recalling their previous conversation. "And he doesn't want you interfering any more than he wants Kiloran in his way."

"We should consider ourselves lucky," Najdan said heavily, "that he didn't kill you then and there, *sirana*."

"He may not be sure he can kill her," Baran mused. "Or he may have feared it would take long enough that he couldn't easily escape the rest of us. So," he said to Mirabar, "he convinced you to let him go after Elelar alone."

"He has certainly abducted her," Najdan said.

"Daurion also said I . . ." Mirabar licked her lips. "I wouldn't be able to protect Elelar until I . . . I was ready to accept the unbelievable and do the unthinkable."

Baran rolled his eyes. "Don't these shades ever think to warn you in more specific terms?"

"Then," Najdan said, ignoring Baran, "are you ready to accept that Cheylan has betrayed you?"

Baran laughed again. "Not to mention betraying Kiloran. Cheylan must be much braver than I th—"

"Oh, do shut up," Mirabar said.

"And far more clever than I would have supposed," Baran continued airily. "Convincing you to confide everything to him. Using Jalilar to distract Kiloran while Cheylan makes off with Elelar, free of pursuit. Even convincing Kiloran to make a mistake—in murdering Jalilar—so disastrous that Kiloran's enemies will now take advantage of it. Making Tansen think Cheylan is his ally, and then making Verlon think he's *his* ally."

"You don't know—"

"Oh, yes I do," he interrupted Mirabar, remembering. "Dulien, before he died, told me that Verlon had reached out to someone he thought could help him against Kiloran."

Vinn breathed, "His grandson the Guardian, in other words."

Baran nodded. "Judging by everything else, Cheylan's probably betraying Verlon, too. Or planning to." Baran paused for a moment of admiration. "I must say, I'm terribly glad Cheylan never befriended *me*. Such men are extremely dangerous."

Mirabar tried, "But perhaps we're overlooking—"

"Accept the unbelievable," Baran cheerfully quoted back at her.

"I've failed." Mirabar looked sick as she added pensively, "And now I must do the unthinkable."

"What does that mean?" Vinn asked.

She took a breath and then let it out in a rush. "It means I'm going after Elelar."

"What?" Vinn blurted.

"No!" Najdan said. "You can't."

"I would suggest a disguise," Baran advised.

Najdan glared at him. "Surely you, the father of her child, aren't agreeing—"

"She would go whether I agreed or not," Baran pointed out, "and I'm far too ill to waste energy trying to stop her. Besides," he added, "if Cheylan is indeed the man described in that Calling, then it's evidently Mirabar's destiny to confront him. And you know how stubborn my wife is about destiny."

Najdan argued, "There's still plenty of time to—"

"Is there?" Baran asked. "If I wanted what Cheylan wants, then I would conceive that child as quickly as possible and keep Elelar prisoner somewhere until the baby was born."

"Then murder the mother?" Mirabar guessed.

"A woman like Elelar? Yes," Baran agreed. "She would be impossible to control. If I wanted unchallenged influence over the child, in order to secure dominance of Sileria, I'd kill Elelar soon after she delivers the baby. It would be easy enough to explain. Women die in childbirth all of the time."

"Protect what you most long to destroy," Mirabar said, a terrible understanding dawning on her features. "I must stop him. He'll destroy our future . . . I have to go after Elelar. I have to protect her and . . . if there *is* to be a child . . ."

"You still think the father might be someone else?" Baran asked skeptically.

"I don't know what I think anymore." She turned to Najdan. "We must leave immediately. Tell Haydar to pack a few things for me."

Najdan nodded and left, followed by Vinn, who volunteered to have two horses saddled for them.

Baran rose and went to her. "Where will you go first?"

"Elelar's estate."

"She won't be there anymore," he said with certainty.

"I pray that you're wrong." She sighed. "But if you're right about Cheylan, then that's where I'll have to start hunting him." Her jaw trembled. "If you're right . . . I'm the one who caused all this. I told him about Jalilar, about Elelar. I let him—"

"Do you have any idea where he might have taken Elelar?" he interrupted.

She stopped the pointless self-recrimination. She was strong and understood. Regrets would only cripple her now, and she couldn't afford any weakness. "In a way. I think I've seen the place in visions. The first time I ever saw it, it somehow seemed like . . . like a prison to me. If he means to hold Elelar against her will, I believe it will be there. I just don't know where it is."

"No idea at all?"

"I think . . ." She nodded. "I think it must be in the east, where Cheylan grew up. Close to the volcano."

"It'll be a difficult journey now."

"I know."

He placed a hand over her womb, delighting in the cool power he could sense there. "Take good care of her."

She covered his hand with her own. "We will take care of each other, as Dar intended."

"This child," he whispered to her, "is very powerful already. I can feel her when I'm this close to you. Trust her."

She nodded.

He was surprised by the sudden impulse to be, if only for a moment, a good husband again . . . as he sent his wife off to perhaps the most dangerous task in Sileria, short of storming Kiloran's lair at Kandahar. So he thought of the most tender thing he could say. "May the wind be at your back."

Mirabar gave him a puzzled look.

He shrugged as he realized, "That may have been an unwise blessing. It was the last thing my wife ever said to me. The day I left our home at Kandahar, thinking I'd soon see her again."

She frowned slightly. "It sounds like something Zarien would say."

"Who?"

"Tansen's son. He's sea-born."

"Really?" That surprised him. A *shallah* and a sea-born boy. "So was my wife."

"Then . . ." Mirabar held his gaze for a moment. "Then I hope I take her blessing with me."

ELELAR HEARD TRILLING, chanting, feverish ululating in the distance. The night was aglow with the fiery light of the restless volcano. The exalted praise-singing of Dar's worshippers, who populated the slopes of Darshon, filled the air all around Elelar.

She smelled sulfur and brimstone, the powerful odors of the angry goddess. It was both heady and nauseating, somehow seductive and menacing all at once. The belly of the mountain rumbled so loudly Elelar could hardly hear herself think.

Cheylan had insisted they abandon their mounts before dark, and Elelar hadn't objected. The animals were jumpy and unpredictable by then, at the foot of Darshon, where the ground seemed to move with Dar's poisonous breathing and hot bleeding, where the sky was on fire with Otherworldly smoke and steam, where the destroyer goddess groaned and screamed at will.

Cheylan had been receptive to Elelar's subtle overtures since yesterday, but he was still not noticeably more communicative. Now that she was so afraid she could hardly speak, Elelar accepted the hand he offered her as he helped her over a bed of crumbling pumice. She asked him, "Are we climbing to the summit. Are we . . . going up there?"

Up there. Where half-mad mystically summoned pilgrims ascended when Dar Called them. Where some were dying in calamitous eruptions of smoke, boiling mud, and deadly fumes. Where others survived to sing wildly, day and night, in praise of Dar.

"No," Cheylan promised, "we're not going up there."

"I don't have to . . . jump into the volcano?" she asked, hearing her voice falter.

The ground suddenly shook again, and Elelar flinched as the volcano roared overhead. The trilling of Dar's faithful swelled to an ear-shattering pitch as the rumbling slowly faded.

"No," Cheylan said.

Elelar looked at him blankly. "No . . ."

"No, you don't have to jump," he explained, his expression kind and sympathetic.

"What do I have to do?" she demanded.

He gazed at her with longing. Even with tenderness. "Please, Elelar. Just come with me."

"Where are we going?"

This was all so strange, and she was afraid. So afraid now.

"We're nearly there," he promised.

"Where?"

"You'll see."

"But—"

Elelar gasped as the ground started trembling again. She stumbled and fell away from Cheylan.

A volcanic vent suddenly opened and started spewing yellow smoke at her.

"Cheylan!" She was completely separated from him by the glowing, billowing smoke. *"Chey . . ."* Elelar starting coughing violently, then fell back, realizing that she mustn't inhale this deadly vapor.

"Chey . . ."

Elelar fell to her knees, choking harder as the smoke wrapped itself around her. Her eyes watered. The ground shook more. She couldn't see Cheylan. Couldn't hear his voice. She felt dizzy and sick, confused and weak. The violent praise-singing filled her ears.

Why didn't Cheylan help her? Where were all those mad praise singers when she needed them? Why didn't anyone try to . . .

This is it, she realized, clutching her throat as she fell facedown onto the pumice and ash, her head swimming with bright lights and black oblivion.

I thought there would be more to it than this . . .

But no. Dar wanted her dead carcass to rot on the slopes of Darshon, forgotten and ignored.

There would be no glory for the woman who had betrayed the Firebringer.

Wondering how Cheylan knew, and whether Mirabar had really foreseen this, Elelar surrendered.

I am coming, Dar. I am coming at last.

Josarian was finally avenged.

MIRABAR PASSED THROUGH so many stages of self-condemnation, despair, disbelief, and dread that she felt numb by the time she reached Elelar's estate. Even the bandits which had attacked her the night before, mistaking her for a *torena* due to the disguise she wore, had been unable to stir a healthy level of terror in her. She felt almost detached as she frightened them away with spears of fire. Even the sight of Najdan killing one of them failed to affect her the way such violence usually did.

Not even Mirabar's numb, exhausted condition, however, could mitigate the jarring shock she got upon being welcomed into Elelar's home to discover *Torena* Chasimar in residence there.

"A Valdan?" Mirabar blurted rudely to Elelar's maid, Faradar, who escorted her into a grand reception room. *"Here?"*

Torena Chasimar twisted her hands, her eyes bulging like melons as she gazed at Mirabar and murmured, "Half-Valdan."

"Here?" Mirabar repeated to Faradar. "In *Elelar's* home?"

She knew that Elelar, who had married one Valdan and slept with numerous others, hated them with an obsessive passion.

"It's a long story, *sirana*," Faradar said, looking positively haggard.

"And probably a very interesting one," Mirabar replied, tempted. "But, unfortunately, I haven't got time to hear it." She tore off the hot black wig she wore, along with the headdress Haydar had woven for her. Faradar took the wig and headdress from her, absently murmuring something about having them brushed before Mirabar left again. *Torena* Chasimar gasped and fell back a step as Mirabar's lava-red hair tumbled down around her shoulders.

"It's true!" Chasimar blurted, gawking at her undisguised appearance.

Mirabar's gaze dropped to the woman's bulging belly. "Darfire, is *everyone* in Sileria breeding?"

Chasimar covered her womb with her hands, as if fearing Mirabar's fiery gaze could penetrate her flesh to disturb the child she carried.

Too tired to think before she spoke, Mirabar frowned and asked, "Is it Zimran's?"

Chasimar made a strange gurgling sound. Faradar snorted, brought a hand up to her mouth, and started coughing.

"It's my late husband's!" Chasimar's tone was outraged.

Mirabar eyed her skeptically. "It was a reasonable qu—"

"*Sirana*," Najdan prodded from behind Mirabar.

Mirabar cleared her throat. "Yes. Excuse me. I apologize. Never mind." She looked at Faradar, "Where is *Torena* Elelar?"

Faradar's uneasy expression shifted into dark dread. "You don't know?"

Najdan came forward as he said, "Cheylan has taken her, hasn't he?"

Torena Chasimar edged backwards, her frankly stupid face alarmed as she stared at the assassin. "She left with him."

"Where did they go?" Najdan asked tersely.

"Well . . ." Chasimar looked at Faradar.

Najdan looked at Faradar, too. "Well?"

The maid shook her head. "He and the *torena* spoke alone and then left without telling me."

"They weren't alone," Chasimar protested. "I was with them."

Mirabar guessed from Faradar's expression that she considered that roughly the same thing as being alone, only much noisier.

Najdan turned back to *Torena* Chasimar. "What did Cheylan say?"

"Um . . ."

"Speak up," he snapped.

Chasimar flinched and backed up again. Tears welled up in her cowlike eyes. Mirabar sighed in exasperation.

Faradar stepped forward and said, "The *torena* left me instructions which indicate that . . . she did not expect to return."

"What?" Chasimar said, clearly surprised.

Mirabar, who wouldn't have confided in Chasimar either, asked Faradar, "What else?"

"I did not initiate any pursuit, because her letter to me indicated that her death—"

"Her *death?*" Chasimar cried.

"—was necessary for the good of Sileria."

Mirabar frowned. "She thought she was going to die?"

Faradar nodded. "She wrote that someday you or Tansen might explain it to me, and she . . ." The maid glanced at *Torena* Chasimar, then continued, "She hoped I, who knew her so well, would understand."

"Understand what?" Chasimar whined. "*I* don't understand!"

"Unfortunately," Mirabar said, "neither do I."

Faradar asked faintly, "You didn't send Cheylan?"

"Actually," Mirabar admitted, "I did."

"Then—"

"I told him to bring her to Belitar," Mirabar continued. "He has not done so. We must assume that Cheylan is now . . . acting in his own interest, not ours. Not hers."

Faradar's expression reflected suppressed panic. "So you don't know where he has taken her?"

"No."

"Or why?"

"Oh, I know why," Mirabar said. "And we've got to get her back."

Chasimar ventured, "But Elelar seemed to know . . ."

They all turned to look at her.

The silly woman stopped speaking and simply stared back at them.

"Know *what?*" Najdan prodded.

"Know why Cheylan had come," the *torena* said shrilly.

"Go on," Najdan ordered.

"She had been expecting him—"

"She had?" Mirabar blurted.

"And was not surprised when he said you had sent him."

" 'Tell Mirabar I have made my peace with Dar and am ready . . . ' " Mirabar turned to Najdan. "That's why she went with him. She thought . . ."

"That it was Dar's will that you kill her?" Faradar asked in bewilderment. "Why?"

"It doesn't matter," Mirabar said, surprised that Elelar, of all people, evidently felt guilty about betraying Josarian—guilty enough that she was, it seemed, willing to be executed for her sins.

She knew Tansen wouldn't do it, but she thought I would.

Was it only because she knew how Mirabar hated her and wanted her dead? Or was it because she had misinterpreted something the Olvar, who had the gift of prophecy, had said to her? No one knew better than Mirabar how hard prophecy was to understand.

"*Sirana,*" Faradar began, "what did the *torena* believe—"

"It is Dar's will that I protect her, not kill her," Mirabar said tersely. "We've got to find her."

"What else did Cheylan say?" Najdan asked Chasimar. When she just looked blank-faced, he added, "Did he say where he was taking her?"

Chasimar's face cleared. "Oh, yes!"

"*Where?*" Najdan's voice was getting brusque with impatience.

"To her destiny," Chasimar supplied helpfully.

"That's all?" Mirabar asked.

"Um . . ."

"Is he going to kill her?" Faradar asked.

"He seemed so nice!" Chasimar protested.

"He won't kill her right away," Mirabar said. "Not . . . for at least nine months, I suppose."

"*Sirana,* are you saying . . ." Faradar looked stunned.

"Nine months?" Chasimar looked bewildered.

Mirabar sank wearily into a chair, finally convinced beyond all doubt that Cheylan had betrayed her. It was a deep wound, but she had no time to nurse it.

"We'll keep heading east," she said to Najdan. "That's all I can think of. That's where this place in my visions must be."

Najdan noted her wilting condition and told Faradar, "The *sirana* requires refreshment and a place to rest."

Mirabar protested, "No, we should—"

"Yes," Najdan interrupted. "You must think of the child."

Mirabar absently spread one hand over the cool glow in her belly, feeling confused and tired.

"Oh, are you expecting, too?" Chasimar asked with girlish interest.

"Yes, but we don't have time—"

"In that case, *sirana*," Faradar said, "Najdan is right. You will only weaken yourself if you do not attend to your needs now, and the *torena* needs you too much for you to do that."

Mirabar rubbed her throbbing temples.

Protect what you most long to destroy.

She nodded. "Yes," she decided. "You're right. I need to rest a bit."

"We'll leave after you've eaten and rested," Faradar said.

"We?" Mirabar blinked at her.

"The *torena* will need me, too, if she's . . ." Faradar smoothed the dusty headdress in her hands and concluded, "If she's alive."

Mirabar met Najdan's gaze for a moment. Then she said to Faradar, "Yes. It would be best if we had someone with us who can tend the *torena* when we find her." Dar only knew what condition Elelar would be in if Cheylan . . . was this determined to father the child she was destined to bear.

Mirabar shuddered, suddenly very grateful that fate had put her in Baran's bed rather than Cheylan's.

"I'll show you to a bedchamber, *sirana*," Faradar said, "and then prepare for our departure."

"And while you eat and rest, *sirana* . . ." Najdan eyed *Torena* Chasimar with cold determination, "I will make this woman repeat to me every single word Cheylan said while he was here."

Chasimar looked as if she might swoon.

54

DAR IS MY GODDESS AND THE QUEEN OF SACRED
DARKNESS AND LIGHT.

—*Zanar* Prayer

"WHAT IN THE Fires is happening here?"
Ronall asked as their two-masted vessel approached a vast
cluster of bobbing boats moored just off Sileria's eastern
coast.

Due east of Gamalan, Tansen thought, looking up at the
looming cliffs beyond which lay the mountains where he
had been born and the humble village where he had been a
child.

He wanted to tell Zarien. He wanted to point out to his son
the summits which he recognized, and take him to explore the
coves where he had once smuggled Kintish contraband with
his grandfather. He'd like to show him the abandoned ruins of
Gamalan and tell him stories of the clan which had lived and
died there.

However, there was no time for such indulgences now. And
even if there were . . . relations were currently, oh, a little
strained between Tansen and his son.

Zarien had been apprehensive ever since boarding this
boat. He had watched Tansen with relentless suspicion, day
and night, as if expecting Tan to transform into the sea king
and sneak off with Sharifar the moment he looked away.
Tansen tried very hard to be patient and reassuring, but after
almost two straight days and nights of the boy's dark, unwa-
vering, vaguely hostile stare . . . Tansen simply lost his tem-

per in a flare of exasperation which made the boat they were on seem even smaller than it really was.

Oh, yes. Much, much smaller.

After that, Tansen suspected Zarien's obsessive fear that Sharifar would claim him was replaced by a heartfelt desire to push him overboard.

Meanwhile, the sea-born family giving them transport stared as hard at Zarien as Zarien had been staring at Tansen. Or, rather, they stared at the tattoos which identified Zarien as sea-bound. Zarien was distressed by it, which in turn distressed Tansen; so he suggested to the family that they stop it. And since he was already feeling rather irritable from the quarrel with his son, the advice came out sharply enough to ensure that the family now also probably wanted to throw him overboard. In addition, far from being grateful, Zarien was deeply embarrassed by Tansen's interference, and so they fought about that, too.

The boy had been sulking ever since, which got on Tansen's nerves; and his irritability, in turn, only made Zarien sulk more. All the tension inspired Ronall to drink even more than usual; then the *toren* spent a lot of time with his head hanging over the side of the boat while his stomach rejected almost every drop of liquor he put into it.

If this journey didn't end momentarily, Tansen wouldn't really *mind* being pushed overboard.

He was also in no mood to humor Zarien's moods now that the fate of eastern Sileria—and probably the outcome of the entire war—depended on whatever Tansen did next. He knew that being snappish with his son wasn't helping either of them, but he couldn't seem to help himself.

Darfire, I wish Josarian were here.

Now Ronall, who was very nearly sober despite his persistent efforts to get drunk, looked at the vast cluster of bobbing boats they were sailing towards. "This must be what everyone has been talking about. All those east-bound sea-born folk.

Just . . . sitting here now, waiting around for something." The *toren* shuddered and added, "Such as an eruption, perhaps?"

"Always the optimist," Tansen said sourly.

Ronall took a long swig of fire brandy, closed his eyes, and immediately looked queasy. "I can't decide if I'm more afraid to go ashore or to stay on this damn boat."

"You're not coming ashore," Tansen informed him.

Ronall eyed him with suspicion.

"Not yet," Tansen added.

"You're worried about what's happening . . ." Ronall waved vaguely at the looming Lironi cliffs. "There."

Tansen nodded. "It's possible the eastern clans will blame me for what's happened."

"Why?"

"I'm the one who ordered Kiman shah Moynari to unite with the Lironi. With Jagodan."

"So, with the smooth logic for which *shallaheen* are famous," Ronall surmised, sober enough for irony, "the Lironi may decide it's your fault that Kiman seduced Jagodan's wife."

"It's possible," Tansen admitted gloomily.

"And even if they don't, Kiman's own clan may decide that it's your fault he got involved with Jagodan, his murderer, in the first place?"

"Yes, that's possible, too. Or the Marendari—the clan of Jagodan's wife—may decide it's my fault that Kiman ever met and then seduced Viramar." He thought back to the day he and Kiman had spoken in the Kintish temple at Zilar, and now he supposed he knew what it was about Kiman which had vaguely reminded him of Zimran: the inability to keep his hands off another man's woman. And, like Zimran, Kiman had evidently appealed to women—enough to make them override good judgment and marital vows.

"Yes, I see," Ronall mused. "The possibilities for blaming you for this mess seem quite fruitful, don't they?"

"Quite." No one knew better than Tansen, born to a clan which had destroyed itself with bloodfeuds, just how unreasonable *shallaheen* could be when their bloodlust was aroused.

Ronall shrugged. "Still, why shouldn't *I* go ashore? All of that has nothing to do with me. I'm . . ." His expression sharpened, and then he glanced over his shoulder. Zarien was sitting on the deck, busy tying knots in something. "Ah. If any of these clans want to wage a bloodfeud against you . . ."

"My son may well be too old for them to spare." At fourteen, Zarien was at a difficult age in more ways than one.

"What about you?" Ronall prodded. "Surely you're not just going to let them kill you over this?"

"No, of course not. But my work will be easier if I don't also have to worry about protecting Zarien from them."

"Yes, of course. But you couldn't leave him behind when you came east, because Kiloran is still looking for him . . ." Ronall's face clouded as he concluded, "And Zarien wouldn't be safe from Kiloran even in Sanctuary. Not anymore. Not since . . . Jalilar."

Tansen nodded. "Until I've made sure Zarien's in no danger from the clans here, the sea seems the safest place for him. So I'm leaving him here for now."

"He won't like that," Ronall warned.

"I don't like it either," Tansen admitted, "but this is the way it has to be."

"And I . . ." Ronall squinted uncertainly at him. "I get the honor of guarding your son?"

"For the time being."

Ronall absorbed this, then asked, "What are you planning to do when you go ashore?"

"Whatever it takes to stop the bloodfeuds and resurrect the Lironi alliance." No matter how strong their bloodlust, his determination had to be even stronger.

"What *specifically* are you planning to do?" Ronall prodded, then drank some more fire brandy.

"Why do you bother doing that?" Tansen asked, eyeing the *toren* with misgivings.

"Force of habit."

"It's just going to come right back up."

"As you said, I'm an optimist. I'm convinced that if I keep trying hard enough, I can get drunk. Or at least less sober."

Tansen shrugged, well aware there was no point in trying to come between Ronall and a bottle. Of all the strange caretakers he had chosen for Zarien, the *toren* was the strangest yet. However, the only alternative was to leave Zarien here with no one he knew, which would be even worse. And at least the boy got along with Ronall.

Fortunately for Tansen's already morose mood, Ronall didn't pursue the subject of the brilliant plan which Tansen didn't have for restoring the Lironi alliance. Instead, the *toren* hung his head over the side of the boat and vomited.

Feeling a little seasick himself, Tansen moved away from him.

Let me off this boat soon, Dar, and I may even be moved to make an offering to You after all these years.

Maybe it was fate. Maybe this journey was destined to be one of the worst experiences of Tansen's entire life so that he'd be positively eager to go ashore now, despite his fear of what he would find—and how he might fail—when he got there.

Now Zarien came to stand beside Tansen at the railing. He tensed as they approached the vast cluster of bobbing boats, then suddenly turned and—rather rudely, Tansen thought—issued navigational instructions to their boat's pilot.

"Zarien," Tansen began, annoyed, "don't tell these people how to sail their own b—"

"The Lascari are here." Zarien's voice was choked.

Tansen tensed, too, momentarily forgetting about the Lironi and their bloodfeuds as he realized what this meant. His son's clan was here. What was left of them. "Shall we go talk to them?"

"No!" Zarien's expression was horrified, even afraid—as if he expected Tansen to *force* him to speak to his clan.

Tansen put a hand on his shoulder, worried, concerned—and already forgiving the strain and irritation of the past few days. "Calm down. We don't have to." Then, even as the boat they were on shifted, he realized what Zarien's instructions must have meant. He lowered his voice and guessed, "You're trying to make sure we don't drop anchor anywhere near the Lascari, aren't you?"

Nearly shaking with tension, Zarien nodded.

Tansen gazed at his son and wondered exactly what was going on in the boy's head. Fear of being shunned by his own clan, as he had been shunned by a distant relative in the Bay of Shaljir? Fear of being shamed in the midst of so many sea-born? Perhaps Zarien was even afraid that, when his clan learned about his death and rebirth, they would insist that, despite his family's fate, he was obliged to obey Sharifar's dictates.

"Siran," the head of this sea-born family now said, interrupting Tansen's thoughts, "do you want to go ashore right away?"

"Yes." And he would kiss the ground when he got there.

Me, the sea king? I think I'd rather crawl all the way back to Dalishar than get on another boat after this.

He had never liked the sea to begin with, and this trip had ensured he would never think of it again without getting profoundly depressed.

The sea-born man asked, "All three of you are going ashore?"

"No. Just me."

"What?" Zarien blurted.

"Oh." The tattooed man didn't bother to hide how disappointing he found this news.

"What do you mean, 'no'?" Zarien demanded.

"The *toren* and the boy will stay here until I send for them," Tansen advised the sea-born man.

"*What?*" Zarien repeated.

"And when will that be, *siran?*" the man asked warily.

"I'm not sure. Until then, you will stay far from shore—"

"But, father—"

"And let no one board this boat except for my emissary—who will carry my *jashar* as proof that he comes from me."

"I understand, *siran.*" The sea-born man looked dour with resignation. Tansen couldn't really blame him for having wanted to get rid of them all. They had not been pleasant passengers. "I'll have my eldest take you ashore in the oarboat, *siran.*"

"Thank you," Tansen replied as the man turned away.

"You're leaving me here?" Zarien demanded incredulously.

Tansen gave all his attention to his son now, trying to keep his voice soothing and reasonable as he explained the situation.

Zarien had no interest in being soothed—let alone reasonable—and his protests eventually grew loud enough to attract the attention of people on another boat. There were hundreds of vessels all around them now, anchored so closely together that Tansen suspected he could probably get to shore just by going from deck to deck until he reached land.

"Keep your voice down," Tansen ordered Zarien.

The boy lowered his voice to a burning growl of bitter resentment. "You said you would never just go off and leave me. You lied."

Tansen forgot that he had intended to be patient. "Start acting your age," he snapped, "and use your head. Do you really want a dozen *shallaheen* to beat you to death with their *yahr?*"

Zarien made frustrated, inarticulate noises.

"You and your problems," Tansen continued, knowing he'd hate himself for this later, "are not the most important things in Sileria right now."

"Or even to you!" Zarien accused.

"Or even to me," Tansen agreed. "I have a war—"

"Fine," Zarien snapped. "Fine! Then go. Just go. Go without me. *Fine.*"

Seething with frustration, Tansen tried again: "It's for your own safe—"

"*Don't* say it again."

"Don't use that tone with me."

Darfire, I sound like my mother.

"You don't have to hear 'that tone' if you'd just go ahead and *leave.*"

Trying to remember that he was the adult here and really needed to keep sight of that fact, Tansen forced himself to take a breath, pause, and take another one before he spoke again. "I'll send for you as soon as I know it's—"

"I don't care," Zarien said sulkily.

Tansen tried to keep in mind how alone Zarien must feel without him. He tried to see how hurt Zarien was, and how much the boy struggled with feeling like a burden.

He's a child, Tansen reminded himself. No matter how brave or smart, no matter how extraordinary his circumstances, Zarien was still a child, and so he was responding like one.

Tansen didn't want to part like this, in anger and harsh words, but he didn't know how to put a stop to it. What in the Fires did other fathers do when their children behaved this way? Had he ever made Armian as crazy as Zarien was making him right now?

Oh, yes, he recalled. *Yes, I did.*

"I . . ." Tansen watched as Zarien folded his arms and looked out at the horizon. "I'm leaving the *toren* in your care."

No response.

"He'll keep you company."

Nothing.

He wanted to shake the boy. Instead, he tried, "When this is over, if the Lascari are still here, I could talk to—"

"Stay out of it." Zarien's voice was sullen. He shifted his gaze to the deck.

"You wouldn't even have to see them, if you don't want to. I could—"

"It's *my* problem." There was a bitter satisfaction in Zarien's tone as he added, without looking up, "And not the most important thing in Sileria, after all."

Tansen was about to remonstrate when the sea-born man interrupted, from the other side of the boat, "*Siran,* the oarboat is ready."

"What a shame," Tansen said. "We've run out of time for quarreling."

One corner of Zarien's mouth twitched downwards. He shrugged and looked out at the horizon again.

"When you come ashore," Tansen said, filled with sudden inspiration, "I'll show you Gamalan."

Finally! Zarien was startled into meeting his gaze. "Gamalan?"

Tansen nodded.

"Where you were born?"

Four words in a row, none of them hostile. This was progress.

Tansen risked a quick smile. "And where, like other *shallah* boys, I learned to lie, fight, and tell tall tales."

Now Zarien made a genuine effort to be pleasant. "And smuggle?"

"Yes, and smuggle. If we have time, I'll show you where."

Zarien nodded. Still sulky, but evidently agreeing to a truce for now.

"*Siran?*"

Tansen acknowledged the prodding of their sea-born host and said to Zarien, whose face looked so young and unhappy beneath its tattoos, "I have to go."

Zarien nodded again and turned away.

Clearly dismissed, Tansen crossed the deck, eased himself over the railing, and climbed down into the oarboat. Restless and edgy, he offered to help row. They had only gone a few strokes when he heard Zarien calling to him. He turned and saw the boy hanging precariously far over the railing as the boat bobbed gently on the water.

Zarien called, "It won't be a long time?"

"No." Tansen hoped he wasn't lying. "It won't be long."

"You'll send for me? You promise?"

"Of course I'll send for you." He didn't understand how Zarien could think otherwise, but he saw it wasn't enough, so he added, "I promise. As soon as I know it's safe."

Still looking unhappy, Zarien watched him float away.

In the distance, where the ever-tumultuous summit of Mount Darshon rose high in the cloudless sky, Dar rumbled with angry menace, reminding Tansen that the fate of Sileria was not, after all, entirely up to him.

IT WAS A dark place full of light, a bright place shadowed by darkness. A vast cavern, heavy yet airy, immense yet encroaching.

Fire and water were all around her. The churning lava of the restless volcano extended its reach to this forgotten place, dripping into the water which flowed through strange tunnels lit by unfamiliar glowing shapes. Each time lava touched water, angry hissing filled the air and steam rose to obscure her vision.

Elelar's lungs ached as she inhaled the hot, damp air. Her head throbbed as she rolled it sideways, trying to get her bearings. She was lying on rock, solid and black, glassy in its smoothness. There was a muted roaring all around her.

Where am I?

She had thought the glowing lumps on the cave walls were candles, but now one moved. Elelar gasped and opened her eyes wider, focusing with more serious intent.

Now she recognized the phosphorescent shapes which helped the lava illuminate this strange, skyless place. She had seen such glowing plant and animal life in the ancient tunnels underneath her home in Shaljir, whenever she went there to meet with the Beyah-Olvari. Some of these little glowing things had a thousand legs, others had no legs at all.

Elelar's grandfather, Gaborian, had always told her that such creatures were even more frightened of her than she was of them. Now, as then, she hoped that was true. And just in case it wasn't, she made the monumental effort of sitting upright and tucking her feet underneath her.

Am I dead?

"How are you feeling?"

Elelar whirled to face . . . "Cheylan?"

He wore only his dark green leggings, no shirt or tunic. It was hot in here, and *toreni* were not as fanatically modest as *shallaheen,* but Elelar nonetheless found his state of undress disconcerting as he came close to her.

He smiled. "You were unconscious for a long time. I was worried."

"What's happened? Where are we?"

"A safe place," he replied.

"Safe from what?"

"Mirabar wants to kill you," he said.

"I know." When he looked momentarily perplexed, she asked in confusion, "Where is she?"

"She can't hurt you here," he assured her.

Her mind was still befogged from the volcano's sudden tantrum on the mountainside. "Why are you hiding me from her?"

Cheylan came even closer. "I couldn't let her kill you." He stretched out a hand to stroke her hair—and froze when she jerked away from him.

"Are you afraid?" he asked.

"No . . ."

"Do you think I'm a demon?"

"I think," she said, "that you owe me a thorough explanation."

He lowered those glowing golden eyes and nodded. "All right."

"Well?" she prodded impatiently, starting to feel a little more like herself.

"I knew what Mirabar intended. Baran's madness has infected her. I had to take you out of her reach, get you to safety." He gestured to the strange cavern of fire and water which surrounded them. "There is no safer place in all of Sileria. I have always come here when I needed a refuge."

"Why didn't you tell me any of this before?" she asked suspiciously.

"I was afraid you wouldn't come with me if I told you the truth."

She frowned. "Why?"

"I was right, wasn't I?"

"But how—"

"All that matters is that you're safe now. Don't worry about the rest."

Just like a man.

She looked around her in frustration. "How did we get here? The last thing I remember—"

"I brought you here after you passed out."

So that I don't know where we are, or how to get back out. How convenient.

"Cheylan," she said carefully, "I appreciate your trying to protect me—"

"Mirabar has become even more powerful since marrying Baran," he said. "No one else can protect you from her."

"Even so, I don't—"

"She's not who she was," he insisted. "You can't trust her. No one can. Not anymore."

"Tansen trusts her," Elelar argued.

"Tansen's in love with her. She can convince him of anything."

"He wouldn't . . ." Elelar stopped and stared at Cheylan.

"Wouldn't he?" Cheylan prodded. "Is he so incapable of

making a foolish mistake? Especially where a woman is concerned?"

What's really going on here?

Had the Olvar's prophecy referred to Cheylan or to Mirabar? *The one with eyes of fire . . .*

The Olvar *had* clearly said that it was Mirabar's actions upon which the fate of Sileria—the fate of the awaited child—depended.

"*But her heart is so set on vengeance,*" he had said, "*that she may not shield the child. She may fail her duty.*"

Had Cheylan cleared the way for Mirabar's destiny by removing Elelar from her path at this moment in time?

Or was Cheylan lying to her? Certainly the way he had lured her here suggested a deliberate attempt to isolate her and gain control of her. But why?

Aware that Cheylan was still waiting for her response, Elelar finally admitted, with perfect sincerity, "Tansen sometimes makes mistakes."

"He can't protect you from Mirabar, not even if he's still willing to try."

"What I don't understand," Elelar said slowly, "is why *you* want to protect me from her."

"Don't you?" he murmured.

When he tried to touch her this time, she didn't shy away.

"Elelar," he whispered, leaning closer as his gaze drifted down to her mouth.

"You hardly know me," she pointed out, trying to determine his true motives.

"You only think I don't know you." He stroked her hair. "I have watched you a thousand times when you didn't know it."

She doubted that. Elelar noticed such things. Especially when the eyes watching her were as unusual as Cheylan's.

Why has he brought me here?

"And," Cheylan added, "I have thought of you a thousand times a day when we were far apart."

What does he really want?

When he touched her cheek and lowered his head to kiss her, she knew what he wanted right *now* . . . but Cheylan was a complicated man, and Elelar didn't really believe he had betrayed Mirabar's trust, spirited her away from her estate, and brought her to this bizarre place out of a desperate love which he, an articulate *toren* and powerful Guardian, had never before found the courage to express to her.

While he kissed her, demonstrating more skill at the art than she had expected, Elelar wondered what to do. Spurn him . . . and possibly make him angry enough to abandon her alone here—wherever this was? Could she even find her way out? No one in the world knew where she was. He could even kill her here; no one would ever know. And he was surely aware of that . . .

Since she didn't resist, Cheylan kissed her again, and this time he let his hands wander down her back, pulling her closer.

She could pretend to be flattered by his declaration but uncertain what to do about it. Stall him. But to what end? He would still want her to surrender to him before he would trust her enough to reveal his true intentions. And as for letting her escape . . .

Surrender.

Yes, she realized. That was what she had to do to learn why Cheylan had brought her here and what he intended.

"What you do will change everything," the Olvar had said.

No one knew better than Elelar how to manipulate a man through his desire and control him through sex. She had made Advisor Borell betray Valdani plans to her again and again; she had made Zimran betray Josarian. She could certainly make Cheylan reveal his secrets to her. Borell and Zimran had trusted her after conquering her body; Cheylan was no different, no better. He, too, would do what she wanted after he won the prize from her which men so absurdly valued. The prize which she had already, during their journey here, encouraged him to believe could be his.

"You must surrender," the Olvar had warned her.

Once Cheylan thought he had mastered her, she could master him. As soon as he believed he ruled, he could be ruled.

"Elelar," Cheylan whispered, bearing her down to the smooth, hard surface of the lava stone.

His eyes glowed hotly, and there was something cold beneath his skin when she touched him, something strange which she had never felt before and didn't understand. She shied away, startled and uneasy.

"Don't," he murmured. "Don't."

Fire and water surrounded them, hot and cold, freezing and burning. Lava streamed into the underground river, oozing slowly down glassy black cave walls to plunge hotly into the water, shuddering ecstatically in the brief, destructive union of liquid and flame.

Surrender.

Elelar ignored her nerves and willfully banished her flash of anxiety. She lay back and forced herself to relax, inhaling the strange steam of this secret abode while Cheylan's hot lips explored the hollows of her throat and the rising curve of her breast.

Glowing shapes slithered past her hazy vision, as if fleeing the sight of two people mating in a domain which had, until now, always belonged wholly to something else.

Dar . . .

The muted roar filling Elelar's ears was, she now realized, the sound of exploding air and flowing lava, of melting rock and burning mud, moving through the volcano. They were under Dar's skin here, inside the goddess's sacred kingdom of darkness and light, intruding on such dangerous ground that even the mad *zanareen* and exultant praise singers didn't dare come here.

No . . . I can't stay here!

She surged against Cheylan in sudden panic. Whether or not he knew she was trying to escape, he chose to treat her desperate writhing as an expression of passion, and his hands were quick and ruthless on the silken ties of her tunic. Then he pulled apart the garment to expose her bare skin to the chilly heat and fevered coolness of this forbidden world where he held her prisoner.

When their eyes met again, Elelar was panting, undeniably afraid now. Cheylan didn't reassure her, nor was he gentle as he finished undressing her. She quivered in nervous indecision when he rose to shed his own clothes. She could see by his expression, as well as the tension in his body, that it would be very, very dangerous to thwart him now.

Surrender . . .

She had done this more times than she could count, with more men than she could easily remember. It was her weapon, her power, her means of conquest. This man was strange and unpredictable, and this place was as frightening as it was eerily beautiful, but the act was the same as it had always been. Surely, she could make Cheylan weak and helpless now, make him grateful that she gave what he wanted. Make him subject to her will and desperate to serve her.

I have always won this game. Surely I can win now.

The arms which came around her were hard, and much stronger than she had ever supposed. His weight pressed heavily down upon her, crushing her against the smooth rock beneath her back, smothering her, making it hard to breathe.

She found herself pushing him away, struggling against him, even though she knew it was a mistake. Cheylan seized her arms and pinned them beneath her, impatient and fierce. She fought him mindlessly for a few moments, and then their eyes met. Elelar froze, truly captive now. He held her gaze, his expression determined, his fire-rich eyes demanding that she accept him. Neither of them moved, or even breathed. Elelar sank into his gaze, losing herself in an enchantment she had never expected to experience, least of all with him. Feeling dizzy, she tried to draw breath, barely able to move beneath the hard weight of the man crushing her will with his own. Her senses swam wildly as he kissed her, dragging her deep into the volcanic fury of his desire. She was so confused. If only she had time to think, to clear her head . . .

Cheylan's body was hot and urgent against hers. His gleaming hair tickled her as it slid over her shoulder, her belly, her thighs. His muscles bunched and flowed smoothly as he moved, and his knowing hands were ruthless on her flesh. The misty air around the two of them filled Elelar's throat and chest, clouding her mind as it sang to her blood.

You must surrender.

"No," she murmured weakly, but the word was drowned in the rasp of her frantic breath.

Surrender . . .

It would be the first time, in a way.

"Surrender," he whispered.

She shuddered, full of longing and fear, revulsion and desire. "I can't . . ."

"Yes, you can."

She closed her eyes, hearing his voice echo around the cavern as the Olvar's words echoed inside her head.

"You must surrender."

His eyes were like the heart of a fire, like she imagined the caldera of Darshon to be. His breath burned her skin wherever his lips touched, even as something deep inside of him chilled her with a cold flame as exotic and forbidden as the touch of a *shir*.

He arched against her, eager and bold as he sought to claim what he wanted, introducing their bodies to a dark intimacy while they themselves remained strangers. The heat she sensed, as he eased insistently past her defenses, was unbearable, unbelievable, unlike anything she'd ever felt emanating from a man's body.

Naked and vulnerable, pinned between her demon lover and the unforgiving surface of glossy rock, she still sought power over him. "Do you love me?" she asked, probing.

"Of course," he lied.

"No," she whispered suddenly, finally understanding. Now she realized the truth, and she panicked. She had lost this game the moment she'd decided to play. He had tricked her, from the very start. This was his dance, not hers. "Wait!"

"For what?"

Elelar's head banged briefly against hard stone as Cheylan claimed his victory. He filled her with such fiery power that she couldn't breathe or cry or even plead for mercy—and she *wanted* mercy, would have begged for it if she could. She wanted him to free her, to release her, to spare her . . . until she didn't want any of that anymore, until all she wanted was more of *him,* more of whatever he offered, even more of this darkly sinister defeat. By the time he flooded her womb with bitter cold and cruel heat, she was weeping with passion, with fear, with relief. By the time he was finally done, she wanted mercy the way she had once wanted to live, the way she had once wanted to die.

By the time he abandoned her to lie alone in the glowing darkness, her body throbbing with pleasure and pain, she felt scalded down to her very soul, and the hot glow of life in her womb warned her that he had gotten what he wanted.

55

THE SMALLER THE MINNOW, THE GREATER THE
HOPE OF BECOMING A DRAGONFISH.
                    — Proverb of the Sea-Born Folk

THERE WERE DISTINCT advantages to being famous and feared, and Tansen made full use of his reputation as he confronted various clan leaders in the eastern mountains.

The Marendari, who were Viramar's clan, were inflamed by the murder of a woman of their own blood, but also ashamed enough of her behavior—caught by her husband in bed with Kiman shah Moynari!—to agree to a temporary truce so that Tansen could attempt to repair the collapsed Lironi alliance. However, their price for once again cooperating with the Lironi, they warned Tansen, would be very high. Honor demanded it.

Kiman's clan, the Moynari, were more stubborn. As Tansen had feared, they blamed him, in part, for the current disaster. Knowing there was no way to avoid it without causing even worse problems, Tansen agreed to settle his own differences with the clan in formal combat. He really didn't want to kill the swaggering young man whom the Moynari chose as their champion, but if Tansen refused to accept their challenge, he knew they'd simply attack him at random, and he'd wind up killing a lot more of them that way. Besides, there was Zarien to consider. Tansen didn't want his son facing a bloodfeud with the Moynari.

He also didn't want the clan deciding they had chosen the wrong champion and demanding that Tansen fight yet another one, so he didn't kill his opponent nearly as quickly as he could have. Only when he judged that the Moynari had seen enough sweat and blood to feel satisfied by the outcome did Tansen finally execute the young man.

Even after they accepted Tansen's victory and reaffirmed their friendship with him, however, the Moynari still clung to their bloodlust with hot passion. They had lost their clan leader with Kiman's death, after all. Tansen's discussions with them were long and frustrating, and only came to a successful conclusion when he promised the clan a satisfactory peace offering from the Lironi . . . and a bloodfeud with Josarian's own clan, the Emeldari, if they wouldn't honor Tansen's status as the Firebringer's brother and attend the truce meeting to which he invited them.

Yes, it was hard work, but the Moynari and the Marendari,

along with several other clans engaging in this destructive feud, could be convinced to make peace and return to devoting all their energies to defeating the Society. But only, Tansen knew with weary certainty, if the Lironi agreed on the price which the rest of the clans had set.

Thanks to the internal feuding of Verlon's enemies, the old waterlord had recently regained some territory which he had previously lost. And that was just the beginning, Tansen knew, if he couldn't quickly reverse the situation here.

But the waterlords had taught him to be ruthless. So Tansen invited Jagodan shah Lironi to meet him in Gamalan.

NAJDAN STOOD AS far away from Mirabar's enchanted fire as possible while still remaining close enough to guard her. The logistics were tricky, but he was accustomed to it after all this time.

When Mirabar finally slumped in weariness and turned away from the woodless flames she had blown into life, he asked, "Anything?"

Mirabar shook her head. Ever since they'd left Elelar's estate, she had Called shades several times a day in hopes of learning where to find Cheylan and the *torena*.

"Nothing." Now the *sirana*'s voice was dark with fatigue and frustration.

"And the Beckoner?" he prodded.

Mirabar shook her head. "He does not answer."

Feeling rather irritable, Najdan clapped a hand tightly over the *shir* tucked into his *jashar*. He was used to the way it quivered in Mirabar's presence and shook so wildly near her fire magic, but the shivering was getting on his nerves today. He supposed he was a little tired.

"We can't protect Elelar if we can't even find her," Najdan said.

"I know," she snapped.

"We'll never—"

"I *know*."

He fell into a moody silence which matched hers.

"I wish Faradar would return," Mirabar grumbled after a while. "I'm hungry."

They had sent Elelar's pretty maid into a nearby village for supplies. Mirabar's disguise wouldn't protect her identity upon close scrutiny, so she and Najdan remained camped far from the village awaiting Faradar's return.

"I'm hungry, too," he admitted. He was also relieved that Mirabar had apparently passed the phase of her pregnancy which made her vomit every day. Not that her temperament seemed to be improving all that much. However, he acknowledged, these were unusually trying circumstances.

Aware that she was looking a little pale, Najdan picked up the waterskin and suggested she have something to drink.

She shook her head wearily, gazing into her fire with a distracted stare. A moment later, a peculiar expression crossed her face. She made a soft sound and pressed a hand over her womb, looking a little dizzy.

Najdan suddenly felt the sides of the waterskin sag as water floated abundantly out of its mouth. Startled, he dropped it. The water kept flowing—through the air, across the clearing, and straight towards Mirabar.

Water magic.

Mirabar gasped when she saw it and leaped to her feet.

"Sirana!"

Najdan seized his *shir* and lunged towards her.

The water stopped flowing when it reached her face, then just hovered in the air right in front of her. Najdan sliced at it with his *shir*—which was pretty foolish. He circled Mirabar, his back to her as he looked for the imminent attack.

"Najdan," she said softly.

He glanced over his shoulder.

Mirabar hesitantly touched the hovering stream of airborne water. A moment later, she opened her mouth and stuck out her tongue. A few quivering drops separated themselves from the stream and danced onto her tongue.

Mirabar closed her mouth and swallowed.

Their gazes met.

"My daughter," Mirabar finally said, her voice a little shaky, "thinks I should drink something."

Najdan grunted, too stunned to say anything. His heart was still pounding hard as he crossed the clearing and picked up the fallen waterskin. He dropped it again when he heard a footstep behind him. With his *shir* ready for the kill, he leapt upon the intruder—

"Don't *do* that!" Faradar shrieked.

Najdan sighed and turned away without apologizing. "I think I'm getting too old for my work."

Mirabar said to Faradar, "He's a little tense just now."

"So I see." Faradar lowered herself shakily onto a fallen log. "I feel ill."

"Did you bring food?" Mirabar asked.

"Yes," Faradar replied. "Also news."

"What?"

"Good news." Faradar took a calming breath, then announced, "Tansen is here in the east."

"What?"

"He has summoned the leaders of some feuding clans to a truce meeting," Faradar said. "In Gamalan."

Mirabar looked at Najdan. "Maybe we should find Tansen—"

"Before we find Cheylan." Najdan nodded, feeling a little better.

CHEYLAN STUDIED ELELAR in the dim light of the cavern. She looked different already. It was as if she glowed from within. "Prophecy is indeed an amazing thing," he murmured, pleased. Nothing had ever confirmed his destiny as thoroughly as the woman standing before him now did.

I will have it all.

Mirabar would take it from him if she could. He had seen

that in her reaction to the Calling at Belitar. Once Elelar was pregnant, Mirabar would oppose the sire.

You will have to be stronger than he, Daurion had said to her.

Well, Daurion, reaching across the centuries through that rusted sword Baron had given Mirabar, might want Mirabar to oppose Cheylan; but he knew that Dar, at least, cherished him. Dar and the mysterious Beckoner had shown Cheylan, through Mirabar's visions, that he was chosen for something special. It all became clear to him after that Calling. His secret lair, seen but never understood in Mirabar's visions, sheltered all his ambitions now. He had known, upon going after Elelar, that he was meant to create his future here with her; and he had been right. He'd sensed it the moment it happened, a mystical act of procreation which left him burning with Dar's searing favor.

Cheylan would deal with Mirabar in time. When it was too late for her to come between him and his child. Between him and undisputed rule of Sileria through his son.

Now he gazed at the woman who bore his future in her womb.

Her dark, long-lashed eyes studied him suspiciously. She kept her distance, as if afraid he would attempt a repetition of their previous encounter here. Memorable though the experience had been, Cheylan had no interest in repeating it.

"How can I make you more comfortable here, *torena?*" he now asked politely.

"Let me go," she snapped.

Amused, he came closer. "I'm afraid that's not among your choices."

"If you ever touch me again," she warned him, backing away, "I'll kill you."

"I thought you enjoyed it," he said silkily.

"Men always think that."

"I'm wounded." He smiled. "And you are being less than entirely truthful."

"Then we have that in common."

"In any event, *torena,* I confess that your pleasure, while well worth the effort I invested, was not my primary goal."

She went very still. "You know, don't you?"

"Of course."

"That's why you brought me here. Why you told all those lies, confused me . . . trapped me here." She looked around. "Wherever this is."

"I assure you, you'll never find your way out. Not without me."

"In other words," she said coldly, "don't try to escape, and don't try to hurt you."

He casually ignited an explosion of fire practically under her feet. Elelar screamed and flung herself away from it. He winced as she landed hard on a jagged volcanic boulder.

"My mistake," he acknowledged. "I had no idea you'd be so careless in your current condition."

"You've made your point," she said. "I can't hurt you."

"Only my tender feelings," he assured her dryly, knowing full well that that was precisely the sort of battle *Torena* Elelar would try to wage, if she intended to fight.

"What I don't understand is: Why?" When he didn't reply, she placed a hand over her smooth, silk-covered stomach and looked down at it. "Or *how.* I thought I was barren."

"Dar did not intend your womb for the offspring of the drunken Valdan you married," he informed her. "Or the many other men who've shared your bed."

She had evidently expected insults from him, since she didn't even look embarrassed, let alone angry. "You're claiming Dar willed this?"

"How else do you explain it?"

She snorted. "A fertile man kidnapped and raped me, and I ran out of luck. People don't talk about it publicly, but this sort of thing is hardly unknown, Cheylan. Under normal circumstances, I'd go home now and pretend it's my husband's child."

"I didn't rape you." Annoyed, he added, "Has *anyone* ever needed to rape you?"

"I now fully understand why no one likes you." Her voice dripped with distaste.

"Our child," he replied, "will love me."

"Not if I have anything to say about it."

"You won't."

The comment startled her and, for a moment, he glimpsed her fear. "Which brings me back to my earlier question: Why?"

"My reasons don't matter," he said, though he assumed she'd keep guessing until she figured it out. He did not underestimate her intelligence, no matter how much she had underestimated *him*. "What matters is that you should be comfortable and—"

"Then let me go."

"No."

"You surely don't intend to keep me *here* for nine months, do you?"

"I haven't decided yet. But it's convenient for now."

"It's *uncomfortable*."

"My apologies."

"Why *my* child, Cheylan? Why am *I* the woman you wanted to do this to?" Elelar persisted. "Surely if there were one woman in all of Sileria whom you . . ." The realization flashed across her face a moment later. "Ah, but she loves one man and married another. There's no place in her bed for you, is there? Not a woman like Mirabar, who'll be faithful to Baran with her body and to Tansen with her heart for the rest of her life." She shook her head. "So I suppose it doesn't matter how powerful she is, how powerful a child of hers is likely to be. Not if you can't have her."

"Actually, Baran's dying."

That surprised her. "How do you know?"

"I see no one trusted you enough to tell you."

She smiled unpleasantly. "So . . . even widowed, Mirabar still wouldn't have you, would she?"

"And Tansen's heart," he countered, "would always be Mirabar's, wouldn't it, even if you finally let him into your bed." He paused and asked innocently, "Or have you already? I'm surely not the only person who's wondered. You've never been discreet, of course, which is why I assumed—"

"Yes, given my notoriously loose morals, why did you go to such elaborate lengths to seduce me?" Her eyes narrowed as she speculated, "Because this has to remain secret?"

"Well, that would certainly be more convenient," he admitted. "For the time being. Eventually, of course, it may make things much easier if you are known to have been the child's mother. Despite what you did to Josarian, you're very popular with the people."

" 'Known to have been . . .' " she repeated.

He didn't reply.

"It's not me you want at all, is it? It's this child."

"I will take very good care of you until he's born," he assured her.

Her jaw dropped and she stared hard at him. "Fires of Dar," she finally murmured. "An *unborn* child. One not even conceived yet. That's it, isn't it? That's why Mirabar didn't know whom she envisioned. And you . . . You think your child— yours and mine, for some reason—is the one she has foreseen."

"You've been blessed," he told her.

"You have an exaggerated notion of your virility."

"I was referring," he said, "to the importance of the child you've been chosen to bear."

"And, as his father, you expect to be the one who rules the ruler?" She shook her head. "I never realized what a fool you are, Cheylan."

"Under the circumstances," he warned her, "you should be more polite."

"Why? If you want this child to be born, you'll have to treat me well while I'm carrying it, no matter how rude I am. And even if I'm polite, you'll still kill me when you no longer need me." She made a disgusted sound. "This is pathetic, Cheylan. You lack the qualities to be a leader, and instead of accepting that, you've deluded yourself into believing you'll rule Sileria through a bastard child whose mother you're already planning to murder."

"Phrase it how you choose, this is my destiny, *torena*."

"Hasn't it occurred to you that our child might dislike you as much as everyone else does?"

"I may have to keep you healthy, but I don't have to make you *comfortable* for the next nine months," he warned.

"You're as crazy as Baran, aren't you? But at least he doesn't have grand delusions about a destiny he can't possibly live up to. Do you *really* think that this child you've planted in me is going to be——"

"I *know* it is. After all," he pointed out, "Mirabar is a gifted prophetess." Seeing that this made Elelar pause and look uncertain, he added, "And whereas she despises you, she trusts me. Well . . . *trusted* me," he amended. "I have a feeling that may have changed by now."

"You mean you didn't give her some elaborate story to——"

"There wasn't time," he admitted. "Things happened very quickly. You may find it heartwarming to know that as soon as she realized you were destined to bear the new ruler, she became desperate to protect you."

"That had to be an interesting moment," Elelar murmured dryly. "And so she sent you to me?"

"I convinced her to let me go to you."

She sighed. "Well, a woman who would marry Baran and maintain such a peculiarly devoted relationship with Najdan . . . I should have realized her judgment in men was unreliable."

"You're in no position to criticize anyone's judgment, *torena*. You were practically inviting Kiloran to kill you by then. It was a relief to arrive at your estate and discover he had not yet realized you were there."

"He'll kill us both now," she predicted.

Cheylan shook his head. "I distracted him. By now, he's probably already killed the woman he believes is bearing the child he so wants to eliminate."

She looked puzzled, and he realized that her friends hadn't trusted her enough to tell her about Jalilar, either.

Elelar ignored his comment, though, in favor of her point. "Sooner or later, Kiloran will realize you betrayed him, and then he'll—"

"Undoubtedly. But he won't find us."

"You're very sure of that, are you?"

"And he'll have tremendous problems of his own to face."

"Tansen?"

"Among other things." If Kiloran had indeed taken the bait and had Jalilar murdered . . . in *Sanctuary,* too . . . "Really," Cheylan murmured, "it's amazing, the things some people think they can get away with."

"WHAT DO YOU *mean,* 'the wrong child?' " Kiloran demanded.

Meriten, who had come to see him at Kandahar after yet another failure to take control of the Shaljir River, spread his hands and looked disgustingly helpless. "That's what people are saying, *siran.*"

"What people?" Kiloran snapped.

"The rumors apparently come from Baran—"

"Who is lying, of course!"

"He is given credence because he's Mirabar's husband."

"It doesn't matter what lies Mirabar wants to tell; Jalilar was the mother of the unborn ruler whom that demon-girl foresaw, and now Jalilar is dead. It's finished," Kiloran insisted coldly.

He already knew that, unfortunately, there'd been a witness to the massacre at the Sanctuary. Mirabar and Tansen would certainly have suspected, regardless, that Kiloran was behind the killings; but they never could have proved it, and he could have denied it. However, Searlon—*damn him!*—had failed to kill everyone, not realizing that there was a Sister hiding in the woods; and she had recognized him. Searlon so rarely made mistakes, and this one was proving to be costly; word was already spreading across Sileria that Kiloran had ordered Jalilar's murder in Sanctuary.

However, what was done was done. As with Josarian's murder, Kiloran fully intended to turn these events to his advantage. Fear and respect would instill obedience in the people of Sileria, who would understand—even if Tansen and Mirabar had briefly made them doubt it—that Kiloran was destined to rule the nation. He had destroyed the Firebringer, he had shattered Mirabar's prophecy about the new Yahrdan, and he would emerge victorious. He acknowledged no other possibility.

"*Siran . . .*" Meriten hesitated. "I don't wish to intrude, but was Cheylan the Guardian the source of your information about Jalilar?"

"Why do you ask?"

"The Emeldari want vengeance for the murder of Jalilar and her husband, Emelen. They're already at war with you, of course, but now they have declared a bloodvow against Cheylan. They believe Baran, who says that Cheylan betrayed Jalilar to you."

Kiloran narrowed his eyes. "Go on."

"They say that killing Josarian wasn't enough for you, you wanted his nearest kin's blood, too. Even though she was a harmless woman hiding from you in Sanctuary." Meriten paused and then repeated, "In Sanctuary."

Kiloran heard the distaste in the other waterlord's voice and pointed out, "She was pregnant with a child who threatened all of us, Meriten."

"That's not what people say."

"What they say doesn't ma—"

"They say Cheylan was angry about losing Mirabar to

Baran and so betrayed her and everything she stood for. He told you where to find Josarian's sister, and then he fled."

"Fled? Are you saying Cheylan has disappeared?"

"Yes. And rumor has it that Mirabar is hunting him now."

"She's left the safety of Belitar?" That surprised him.

"So they say. And, no, no one has any idea where she is."

"What a pity." And his own men, he reflected with frustration, were currently stretched too thin to try to track her for him.

"Now that Baran has told the Emeldari about Cheylan, though," Meriten continued, "it's probably just a question of who finds him first, them or Mirabar. Either way, Cheylan is finished."

"He was careless," Kiloran concluded dismissively.

"I don't understand, *siran*. Cheylan's a Guardian. Why did he help you?"

Kiloran shrugged. "As people say. He was angry about losing Mirabar to—"

"Even so, *siran*, why would Cheylan help you eliminate the prophesied ruler of Sileria and destroy his own life in doing so? It doesn't make sense. He is a Guardian, an educated man, and rumored to be quite clever. Wouldn't he have tried to align himself with Jalilar and her child rather than expose himself and help the Society prevail?"

Kiloran shrugged. "Cheylan's a very twisted . . ." There was a sudden chill in his blood. ". . . complicated . . . cunning . . ." *Why, indeed?* "Yes," Kiloran said slowly, "what did he have to gain by helping *me*?"

I thought it was just my favor. What if it was something else? Was I so arrogant in my dealings with him that I failed to perceive the real reasons for his actions?

The cold spreading through him almost made him tremble as he ordered, "Tell me what else people are saying."

"It's . . . disrespectful, *siran*."

"Yes, I've heard some of it already," Kiloran replied.

He had realized from the start that violating Sanctuary was

extremely risky. Knowing what he knew about Jalilar, though, it had seemed worth the gamble, worth whatever it might cost him in the long run.

He felt his stomach roil, though, as he now considered that all he really knew about Jalilar was what Cheylan had chosen to tell him.

If that child wasn't the one, what did Cheylan have to gain by telling me it was?

"I'm sorry to report, *siran,*" Meriten said, "that I have been losing allies since the news of Jalilar's death reached the region around Zilar. Many people are . . . appalled by the violation of Sanctuary." Meriten's eyes shifted nervously. "And now people tell another story . . ."

Losing allies . . .

"Go on," Kiloran prodded.

"Baran says that the cause of the bitter hatred he has always borne for you . . ."

Kiloran drew in a sharp breath. He knew, even before Meriten spoke again, that after all these years Baran had finally sacrificed his privacy and admitted his terrible shame.

"Baran says that you abducted and murdered his wife," Meriten said. "That you are the kind of man who treats the women of his enemies and his rivals that way. That you have no honor. He says that no woman is safe while you live. He has offered formal apology to your enemies for not having told them earlier what he knew, for not having warned them that you might well kill their women."

"And their unborn children?" Kiloran muttered.

Meriten nodded. "Many people are listening to this talk, *siran.* And repeating it to others."

Kiloran closed his eyes and felt the watery domain of Kandahar quiver all around him as he absorbed this.

Baran saw my mistake and recognized his opportunity.

People would believe Baran because anyone would understand what such a terrible admission—that he'd been unable to protect his own wife—cost such a great waterlord. They would understand why he had kept silent all these years; and they would cherish his revelation now.

Had Cheylan known about Alcinar?

Perhaps, perhaps not. It didn't matter. Cheylan had planted the seed, and Baran was now reaping the harvest, shrewd enough to use the incident to weaken Kiloran's influence. And if that madman was actually telling the truth for once, if Jalilar's child wasn't the one, if Cheylan had lied, if Kiloran had ordered Searlon to kill a thoroughly harmless *shallah* woman in Sanctuary . . .

"You say other . . ." Kiloran cleared his throat. "Other people are echoing Baran's sentiments about me?"

"Yes, *siran*," Meriten admitted.

He would have to send new instructions to Cavasar to keep the city under control. The Cavasari had mostly remained loyal to him throughout the war; but this, Kiloran realized, sick at heart as he contemplated the trap into which he had stumbled . . . Yes, this could change things for him, even there.

If only he could prove to the *shallaheen* that, in killing Jalilar, he had defeated an enemy as great as Josarian had been . . . But how could he prove it if Mirabar wouldn't acknowledge it, if she insisted on claiming that Jalilar's unborn child wasn't the one? He would have to think about this and find a solution.

If this turn of events was what Cheylan wanted, *why* had he wanted it? Not for Mirabar's sake, certainly; not if she and the Emeldari all wanted Cheylan dead now. Kiloran briefly considered that this might be another trick, like the time Najdan had pretended to quarrel with Baran. Then he dismissed the notion. The Emeldari were a large and violent clan with many allies who might well fulfill a bloodvow on their behalf. Although Cheylan could protect himself extremely well, he was nonetheless in real danger now that the Emeldari had publicly sworn a bloodvow against him.

"Do you think this is what Cheylan intended all along, *siran?*" Meriten asked hesitantly.

Kiloran felt nauseated with rage. "If your information is accurate, then he betrayed both sides. Me and Mirabar. The Guardians and the Society."

"Yes, but why?"

"I underestimated him," Kiloran suddenly realized. "Or, at least, his ambition."

"How can being marked for death by all of us fulfill his ambitions?"

"It doesn't. He simply thought . . ." Kiloran recalled his own decision to violate Sanctuary. "He thought it was worth the risk." He nodded slowly, thinking aloud. "Gulstan and Kariman are tearing each other apart. Their fortunes are destroyed, their lands lost, their homes under constant siege, their men dead or exhausted and doomed to die soon. I can't prove it, but I believe Tansen caused their bloodfeud; and he did it to free those territories for his own people. To weaken— even destroy—Gulstan and Kariman with as little cost to himself as possible."

"What does that have to do with—"

"Cheylan probably hoped the same sort of chaos would ensue here once Jalilar was dead. And even if it didn't, everyone's attention was diverted long enough for him to follow his own plan in relative safety."

"But what was his own plan?"

"Isn't it obvious to you yet?" A frigid fury boiled inside the old waterlord. "That goat-molesting demon-eyed *sriliah* wants to control Sileria himself. So he's hoping we'll all eliminate each other and save him the trouble."

"But how can he—"

"Don't you see? Mirabar *did* confide the identity of the prophesied ruler to him. She's not hunting him to avenge Jalilar; she means to stop him from getting to the child before she does. Because now, just as you surmised, Cheylan does indeed intend to align himself with the ruler she has foretold.

He doesn't want me to kill the child—nor does he want Mirabar to find him."

"Then, *siran,* I respectfully submit that murdering Jalilar was a very grave mistake in the light of tremendous ill feeling it's causing."

Kiloran fixed Meriten with a glare that reminded the other waterlord he had not asked for an opinion. "Mistakes are so easily made."

"What will we do now?"

Kiloran thought it over. "We'll forget about Cheylan."

"How can we?" Meriten demanded. "He betrayed you. He—"

"We have far too much to do to waste time doing what Cheylan's former friends are so eager to do for us. It doesn't really matter who kills him now, as long as he dies; and Mirabar probably knows better than we do where to look for him."

In truth, the murder of Jalilar, especially followed by Baran's emotional manipulation of the masses, might now create problems for Kiloran that would make pursuing Cheylan a foolish waste of energy.

Meriten nodded. "Yes, I understand. As always, *siran,* you know best." After a moment, he added, "What about the child Mirabar has foreseen? That threat still remains, it seems."

"It does," Kiloran agreed heavily, "and we know as little as we did before. All we can do is watch for an opportunity to learn more and to strike when we see our chance. In the meantime, our primary concern is to win this war. The season is advancing. The long rains are approaching, and we'll lose some of our advantage when they come."

"Perhaps they'll be late this year," Meriten said optimistically, "or not even come at all."

"We can only hope. But we would be fools to count on that. It would be best to prevail soon, Meriten."

"In that case, *siran,* the business I originally came here to discuss is of paramount importance."

"You need help to reclaim the Shaljir River," Kiloran guessed.

"There are too many Guardians protecting it. I'm sorry, *siran*. I can't do this alone. I have tried and tried. I am not strong enough." He paused, then added, "And I have lost too many men fighting their men, who are commanded by a relation of Josarian's—a huge, hairy, loud *shallah* who wields a Moorlander sword and is, unfortunately, a strong fighter and a leader who learns from his mistakes."

"Lann. I know of him." Kiloran scowled. "Tansen no doubt taught that illiterate peasant how to make war on us."

"Lann's not Tansen, but he is more capable than I expected."

"It would have been a blessing if the entire Emeldari clan had perished in an earthquake many years ago."

"They are hard to kill," Meriten said grumpily.

Kiloran rubbed his temples and tried to come up with a better solution than offering to help Meriten himself. Gulstan and Kariman, he already knew, wouldn't even reply anymore to a summons for help. The other waterlords were all deeply embroiled in defending their own territories from the Firebringer's loyalists—or else dead. Yes, so many were now dead.

Kiloran didn't admit it aloud to anyone, but since Dyshon's death, his own strength was undergoing the most severe test of his life. Whatever strange force was joining Baran in his claim on the Idalar River and the mines of Alizar, it was growing stronger, taxing Kiloran as he resisted it. Meanwhile, the vast territory under his control needed his constant vigilance, as did the city of Cavasar. It was all more than any one waterlord had ever before ruled, as far as he knew, and now he knew why; it was exhausting.

Still, the Shaljir River must be reclaimed, and soon. So he said to Meriten, "Very well. I will lend my strength to yours."

And when Searlon found Zarien, as his last message indicated he expected to do soon, Kiloran would have a truly effective weapon to use against both Tansen and Baran. Indeed, he would have a great deal more than that when the boy finally came under his influence.

"We will prevail, Meriten," Kiloran said reassuringly. "Never doubt that. Victory is all the sweeter when it requires such effort, that's all."

ZARIEN SIGHED IN restless boredom, wondering how long he'd have to wait before Tansen would let him go ashore.

Nothing was right anymore. He had never felt confined or imprisoned on his family's boat, which was smaller than this one, even though he had spent virtually his whole life aboard it before the night he died. However, now that he found himself restricted to this boat for the time being, he felt practically crazy with the desire to get *off* of it. The monotony of long days at anchor made him anxious and irritable now. He was dying for some open space and solitude. He would even, Dar help him, like to go for a walk.

Being back at sea . . . well, nothing was the same anymore. Nothing was the way it was supposed to be; the way it used to be.

Zarien gazed at the vast cluster of moored boats all around him, peering through the gently bobbing masts in search of a few familiar vessels. The few remaining boats of the sea-bound Lascari . . .

He didn't want to talk to them. He just wanted to know where they were.

Zarien sighed and tried not to think about what he would say or do if he saw them, if they found out he was here. He tried not to . . . but he nonetheless *kept* thinking about it, because there seemed to be little else to think about at the moment. Besides, he was tired of the curiosity of this tedious sea-born family with whom Tansen had left him. He was sure they were gossiping about him with the families moored all around them, and he found it embarrassing.

Zarien sighed again.

However, at least Tansen was no longer on board. He was once again out of Sharifar's reach. At least there was that.

The voyage here had been nerve-wracking for Zarien, expecting something to happen every single moment they were at sea. And Tansen . . . Tansen just didn't understand. He still really didn't believe. He had no idea how dangerous it was for them to be here, where Sharifar might demand her due at any time. Tansen was sure he knew better than Zarien.

Tansen could be amazingly stupid sometimes.

Zarien was startled out of his private thoughts when *Toren* Ronall, always a late riser, stumbled over to the railing, still groggy—and still, Zarien saw, reluctantly sober.

"I keep asking them all," Ronall said after a while, "and no one really knows."

"Asking them what?"

"Why they're all here. What they're all waiting for."

Zarien looked up to the peak of Mount Darshon, where colored clouds and flashing lights whirled passionately above the goddess's domain. "Maybe it's the same thing the pilgrims at Darshon are seeking?"

"But why here?" Ronall wondered. "And how do they know? I mean . . ." He shrugged. "What? One day you hear a little voice in your head that says, 'Sail to the east coast and wait for further instructions?' "

Zarien thought of the *stahra* which had helped him follow Tansen once upon a time. "Maybe it's more as if . . . as if their boats know where to go."

Ronall looked up at the sky-piercing volcano. "We're all going to die in a massive eruption. I'm sure of it."

Zarien rather wished the *toren* could get drunk. Being sober made him depressing company. He looked away . . . and sucked in his breath when he caught sight of a familiar foresail.

"Is something wrong?" Ronall asked as Zarien fell back a step.

Linyan's boat.

He would know his grandfather's boat anywhere.

"Zarien?" Ronall prodded.

It was moving slowly, careful not to bump the closely moored boats between which it passed. Zarien's eyes were fixed on it in mute horror. He knew he should hide, lest a stray glance expose him. . . . But he felt frozen, unable to move a muscle.

Ronall finally said, "They're coming towards us, aren't they?"

Panic filled Zarien. "No! They can't! *No*."

"Well, they are," Ronall pointed out.

Breathing hard as he watched the approaching vessel, Zarien knew it was true. "Someone's told them I'm here."

Ronall straightened up, looking worried and even a little alert. "Who would have done that?"

"Anyone might have told them," Zarien realized with sick dread. This family had indeed been gossiping. A *lot,* it seemed.

"Why?"

"My tattoos," Zarien said absently, still staring at Linyan's approaching boat. "Anyone can see that I'm a sea-bound Lascari and shouldn't be with you. With Tansen."

Ronall digested this. "So who's on that boat?" When Zarien didn't reply, he guessed darkly, "Your relatives?"

Zarien nodded, hurt and angry that Tansen had abandoned him here to deal with this alone.

"Ah." Ronall sighed. "Not fond of your relations?"

"No, it's . . . They think I'm . . . I can't . . ."

"Just tell me," Ronall suggested as Linyan's boat pulled so close that Zarien could leap onto its deck if he chose, "are you in danger from them?"

Zarien shook his head. His heart seemed to stop as familiar faces now swam before his eyes. Linyan stood at the railing, a fresh, angry scar running diagonally across his face, from forehead to chin. There was Zarien's grandmother at the helm, and one of Zarien's uncles was brailing the foresail up to the yard . . .

Linyan's voice was hoarse. *"Zarien."*

Zarien met Linyan's gaze. Had his grandfather been this old the last time he'd seen him?

"Zarien?" Linyan prodded, his expression dark with confusion.

"Yes," Zarien choked out, ashamed and relieved and scared and glad, all at once.

Tears welled up in Linyan's eyes and streamed down his wrinkled brown cheeks. "We thought you were dead."

"I was."

Ronall's head jerked sharply in surprise. *"What?"*

"We told that assassin . . . the one who did this to me . . ." Linyan touched the fresh scar on his face. "We said you were dead. We *saw* you die. We said he was looking for another Zarien, not ours. Ours couldn't possibly be alive."

"An assassin looking for me?" Zarien felt his chest heaving. "Who was he?"

Linyan shook his head. "I don't know his name. He was a big man. Younger than your father was. A handsome man. Well dressed. Very cruel."

"Did Kiloran send him?" Zarien asked.

"Well spoken," Linyan continued in a daze.

"Did he have a scar on his cheek?" Zarien persisted. "And short hair?"

"Yes." Linyan frowned. "You know him?"

"No. But that's what Tansen told me Searlon looks like." And Searlon was looking for him. "I'm sorry, grandfather."

"He seemed so polite until . . ."

Ronall blurted, "Until he did *that* to you?"

Linyan touched the awful scar on his face again. "He wanted to know everything about Zarien. Everything there was to know." Now Linyan was weeping again. "He made me tell him . . . I told him the secrets we had kept. The things no one but you ever had a right to hear from me, Zarien!"

"What secrets?" Zarien demanded.

"Then the Kurvari sailed east, like everyone else these days."

"Who?" Ronall interrupted.

Zarien said briefly, "The Kurvari are sea-bound relations of the Lascari."

"When they finally found us," Linyan babbled, "they said they had seen you, in the Bay of Shaljir. That you were still alive."

"So you didn't die, I take it?" Ronall sounded relieved.

"Oh, yes," Zarien replied. "I died."

"They also said . . ." Linyan hiccoughed and stared sadly at him. "Zarien, did you really . . ."

"Go ashore?" There was a heavy silence. "Yes. I was dead for three days and nights. And then I set my foot upon land."

"Um, Zarien . . . ," Ronall said.

"I've been on the dryland ever since. Looking for the sea king. Looking for Sharifar's mate."

Shaking with a mixture of emotions he couldn't contain, Zarien pulled his tunic over his head. His grandmother gasped loudly as he revealed the dragonfish scars. Linyan cried harder. The sea-born family on whose boat Zarien sailed made a lot of noise, too.

Ronall rubbed his eyes a few times, then finally murmured, "Dar and the Three have mercy." He reached out a trembling hand to touch one of the enormous scars which covered Zarien's torso. "You're telling the truth, aren't you?" Then the *toren* hung his head over the railing and was sick again.

56

A POWERFUL FRIEND IS WORTH   ALL THE DIA-
MONDS OF ALIZAR.

—Silerian Proverb

"NAJDAN!" TANSEN THOUGHT he had never been so glad to see anyone in his life, not even Mirabar, who looked like a real *torena* in the elaborate headdress and wig she wore, mounted on a fine mare which trailed behind Najdan's gelding. Tansen wondered briefly about her expensive clothing and the elaborate quality of the horse's bridle and saddle . . . and then remembered that Mirabar was now a waterlord's wife, supported by more wealth than most *toreni* possessed.

He fed his heart with the sight of her as she road into Gamalan be-hind Najdan, but only for a moment. His mind was too filled with panic, caused by what he'd recently learned, to let him feel all the things he had expected to feel upon seeing her again. For now, he just thanked all the gods above and below that Najdan was here. Then he saw another woman behind Mirabar—whom he quickly recognized as Faradar, Elelar's pretty maid.

Tansen frowned suspiciously at Mirabar. "What's going on?"

"We're looking for Elelar," she said as Najdan dismounted and moved to help Mirabar dismount, too.

"Now?" Tansen added in confusion, "*Here?* In Gamalan?" He glanced at Faradar. "With *her?*"

Faradar crossed her wrists and bowed her head. "It's a pleasure to see you, too, *siran.*"

"What's going on?" Tansen repeated. He couldn't believe that anything would have convinced Faradar to turn aguinst Elelar and help Mirabar kill her.

Apparently realizing her disguise was no longer necessary, Mirabar pulled off the wig and headdress, which she tossed carelessly on the ground. Her brilliant red hair was flat and dark at the temples with sweat. Her glowing eyes were anxious and exhausted as they met his. And her brief, blunt explanation stunned him.

Elelar . . . favored by prophecy and destiny, then abducted by Cheylan and now in terrible danger.

Elelar . . . No, he supposed he would never stop caring what happened to her, even if that made him a fool.

"You have no idea where to look for them?" he asked, leading Mirabar towards one of the few buildings still standing in this abandoned village.

Faradar, who had also dismounted, bent to retrieve the fallen headdress and wig, then followed them. Najdan told one of the many men milling around to take care of the horses, then followed them, too.

Mirabar rambled vague descriptions of a cavern of fire and water as Tansen led her inside and found a stool for her. She slumped into a sitting position and kept talking, pausing only long enough to let Faradar make her drink some water. Both the maid and the assassin studied her with obvious concern. Her face looked drawn and her cheekbones more prominent.

"Have you been unwell?" Tansen interrupted.

There was a stunning silence as the three people with him exchanged uncertain glances. The awkward moment dragged on, as if there was something they needed to tell him but which none of them was willing to be the one to say.

Then it hit him like a blow from behind. "Fires of Dar, it's happened, hasn't it? You're pregnant."

"Yes."

"With *Baran's* child?"

She frowned. "Yes, *Baran's* child. Whose child *would* I be carrying?"

"I didn't mean . . . Um . . ." He lost track of his words and decided to stop speaking before he said something even stupider.

He should have expected it—it was why she had married Baran, after all—but Tansen nonetheless felt as if someone had kicked him in the chest. Then fury flooded him as he thought of her, in her condition, traveling across war-torn Sileria, where every living waterlord and assassin would leap upon the chance to murder her while she pursued the ruthless Guardian who had already betrayed her and abducted another woman. "How could Baran let you make a dangerous journey like this?" Tansen demanded. "What in the Fires was that madman thinking?" He turned on Najdan, pleased to have a convenient target for his anger. "How could *you* do this?"

Najdan scowled back at him. "This isn't my doing."

"You're supposed to protect her!"

Najdan unleashed some temper of his own. "Don't try to blame me. You should know by now——"

"Stop it!" Mirabar snapped at both of them.

"You shouldn't be here," Tansen said to her, nonetheless wondering how he had lasted so long without seeing her. Even now, weary, bad-tempered, and carrying another man's child, her presence filled him after such a long, empty season without her.

"There's no one else who can do this, Tansen," she said quietly. "There is only me. Baran understands that." Their eyes met. "I need you to understand it, too."

Now he felt it, that horrible mixture of emotions—desire, jealousy, impotent anger, love, loyalty, loss, sorrow. He felt it all. He wanted to curse Dar, but he supposed that would only upset Mirabar. So instead he said, "You heard I was in Gamalan and came for my help."

"Yes."

He nodded. "I'm glad." Their eyes met again, and he knew he would lay the world at her feet if it was what she asked of him. As it was, now that he had agreed to help her, he had no idea what to do. "How will we find Cheylan and Elelar?"

Her golden eyes clouded with tears of frustration. "I don't know. I've tried so hard, and I just don't . . ."

"Shhh, *sirana*." Faradar put a hand on Mirabar's shoulder then said to Tansen, "She needs to rest."

"No," Mirabar protested, "I need to——"

"Rest," Najdan said firmly. "Even if Cheylan came to *us* right now, how could you defeat him?"

"You're going to fight him?" Tansen asked worriedly.

"I don't know what I'm going to do," Mirabar admitted. "I just know that I have been chosen to protect Elelar and the child she'll bear, and that's what I have to do."

She was still the same in every way that mattered. And

therefore no easier than she had ever been; but he hadn't been made for an easier woman. "Then I'll do whatever I have to do, too," he promised. "But for now, they're right, you need to rest. You look terrible."

Mirabar gave a trembling puff of laughter. "Thank you."

Najdan shook his head. "You have never known the things to say to a woman, have you?"

"Both of you," Faradar said, "please go outside while I make a comfortable place in here for the *sirana*."

"Don't *wait* on me," Mirabar snapped. "I don't like it."

"I'll get her bedroll," Najdan said to Faradar, who nodded.

The assassin left the humble dwelling. Tansen started to follow, then paused at the door. "Faradar."

"Siran?"

"I believe Radyan will be very pleased to learn you're alive and well."

She lowered her eyes. "You will tell him?"

"Next time I send a message to Shaljir." It was too dark in here to be sure, but he thought she was blushing.

"And will you tell him that I . . ."

"Yes?"

"Um . . . Nothing, *siran,*" she mumbled, turning away.

He smiled. "Yes, I'll tell him that, too."

"Thank you," she said faintly over her shoulder.

He glanced at Mirabar again. "Do you want something to eat?"

She made a face, which he assumed meant *no*. Najdan returned then with her bedroll, which he handed to Faradar. Then the two men left the two women alone together.

Out in the arid sunshine, under a sky streaked with smoke and ash, Tansen remarked, "The *sirana* seems a little temperamental."

"You'd be surprised at how much she's improved, actually," Najdan muttered. The assassin gazed around the ruins of Gamalan, his eyes taking in the dozens of men gathered here, tending their weapons, mending their shoes, chatting quietly in the shade. Most of them politely ignored Najdan now that they knew he was a friend of Tansen's. "So this is your truce meeting."

"Not yet," Tansen said. "The Marendari and the Moynari, as well as some other clans, are here; but the Lironi haven't arrived yet and I'm not quite sure when they will. And I have to be here when Jagodan comes."

"Naturally."

"Yet I was about to leave," Tansen added. "So I'm very glad you're here, Najdan. More than you can imagine."

Najdan studied his face. "What's wrong?"

"Gossip among these men. I've just learned that Searlon was responsible for the destruction of the Lironi alliance."

Najdan looked surprised. "How?"

"Kiman received a request to protect Marendar, Jagodan's village, while Jagodan was supposed to be off raiding in Verlon's territory. Meanwhile, Jagodan received an offer from an assassin willing to betray Verlon, and offering to prove his good faith by meeting Jagodan in—"

"—in Marendar."

"Yes. But, of course, the assassin never showed up."

"And Jagodan caught Kiman and Viramar together." Najdan nodded. "So that's how it happened."

"That's how it happened."

"What makes you think it was Searlon?"

"Because people around here have also gossiped about a tall, well-spoken, short-haired assassin whose good looks are marred only by—"

"—a scar on his cheek," Najdan said slowly.

"Yes. I didn't fully understand it until you arrived." Tansen glanced over his shoulder to the humble dwelling where Mirabar was now housed. "But after what she's told me, I do now. If Cheylan told Kiloran about Jalilar . . ."

Jalilar, Emelen, and now Elelar . . .

Darfire, Tansen wanted to kill Cheylan himself, regardless of the sorcery which only Mirabar could confront with equal power.

"Cheylan was in the east throughout the spring," Najdan said suddenly.

"So he might have known about Viramar and Kiman," Tansen said. "He seems to have a way of finding out things he shouldn't."

"He told Searlon about them, and Searlon saw it as a way to destroy the Lironi alliance."

"And perhaps more than that," Tansen added, his stomach clenching as he tried to keep his terror under control. "Searlon has been looking for my son."

Najdan lifted a brow. "Where is Zarien?"

"He's at sea. It seemed the safest place. It never occurred to me that Searlon was here. I would have brought Zarien ashore with me if I'd known. I thought I had left Searlon a cold trail when I came east. How was I to know he'd be here?" Tansen realized he was babbling and clenched his teeth together for a moment. "By now, he probably knows that *I'm* here. In fact, I suspect he expected the crumbling of the Lironi alliance to bring me here. If so, he probably also knew that I wouldn't leave Zarien behind. Not with Searlon looking for him."

"And not with Searlon willing to violate Sanctuary to kill," Najdan added gloomily.

"For Zarien's protection, I've told no one how I came here or where he is; but I thought I only needed to protect him from the eastern clans."

Najdan nodded, understanding. "So whatever measures you took will not protect him from Searlon."

"I left him at sea, in the care of a sea-born family and of . . . of *Toren* Ronall."

"A Valdan?"

"Elelar's husband."

Najdan frowned. "Isn't he supposed to be a drunkard and a fool?"

"Yes."

"Have you lost all your wits?"

Tansen ignored that. "I need you to go protect Zarien for me. You're the only person I would trust to keep him safe from Searlon." Najdan was not only a skilled and shrewd fighter, but he also knew Searlon and his methods very well.

"Why can't you—" Najdan stopped as he realized, "You're waiting for Jagodan."

"If he arrives and I'm not here to keep them under control," Tansen said, indicating the hardened *shallaheen* who were gathered there, "it'll be a bloodbath and the end of any hope of saving the Lironi alliance or winning the war in the east."

Najdan said, "I don't want to leave the *sirana* alone to face Cheylan."

"She won't be alone," Tansen assured him.

"If anything happens to her—"

"I have trusted you with her life for a long time," Tansen said. "You know you can trust me with it."

Their eyes locked for a long moment, then Najdan nodded. "I accept the honor of protecting your son, and I promise you that I will let no harm come to him."

"You need to leave immediately."

"I will go tell the *sirana*."

When Najdan returned from his brief farewell to Mirabar, Tansen already had a fresh horse waiting for him. He removed his *jashar* and handed it to Najdan. "Zarien knows you, but this will identify you to *Toren* Ronall and the sea-born family as my messenger. My orders are that you're to keep your distance from other boats and refuse all approaches until I myself come to you."

"I hate the sea," Najdan muttered.

"Don't we all?" Tansen replied.

He gave Najdan the best instructions he could about finding the right boat in the crowded bay where he had left Zarien.

"Najdan," he added as the assassin mounted and prepared

to ride away, "this is about my son's life, not your honor. If it will keep Zarien safe, then running and hiding are perfectly good options."

Najdan paused for a moment, then nodded briefly. "I understand. I have given my word. The boy will stay safe."

Then Tansen, who had been raised very traditionally, bowed his head and crossed his fists. "Thank you."

He watched Najdan ride out of the crumbled ruins of Gamalan, fighting the urge to change his mind and go to Zarien himself. But it didn't take a gift of prophecy to foresee the disaster that would ensue here if Tansen abandoned his duty to Sileria in favor of his duty to his son. Najdan's arrival had been the answer to an unspoken prayer, ensuring that neither Tansen's son nor his nation's future need be sacrificed today.

If anything happens to that boy, Dar, he warned silently, *I will never forgive You, and never stop trying to punish You for it.*

Since he had never forgiven Her for taking Josarian, though, he supposed his threats wouldn't bother the goddess, who rumbled and roared beneath the skin of the soaring mountain which was so nearby that it filled the smoky sky over Gamalan.

BARAN LAY ON the damp floor of his study at Belitar, shaking with shock and weakness as Sister Velikar bathed his forehead and wiped blood and spittle off his face.

"*Siran!*"

He recognized Vinn's panicked shout and was vaguely aware of the scuffle which then ensued between the assassin and the Sister. Baran was too weak to intervene and in too much pain to be as amused as he ought to be.

"What have you done to him, you ugly sow?" Vinn demanded.

"I found him collapsed here," Velikar snarled in reply, "unconscious and facedown in the blood he had vomited. Would you prefer me to leave him like that?"

The two of them had never learned to play nicely together, Baran reflected. No one was more devoted to him than Vinn and Velikar, not even his own wife (especially not his own wife!), but their mutual dislike ensured that each of them pretended the other was a danger to him. Well, mutual dislike laced with a heavy dose of mutual jealousy; each wanted to be his favorite, of course.

It might be nice, Baran thought wearily, if they would at least declare a truce long enough to tend him now, rather than leave him lying here shaking, barely conscious, and covered in his own disgusting excretions.

Really, it was rather a relief that his wife was off chasing some demented fire wizard halfway across Sileria rather than staying home to witness moments like this. A man who had made love to a woman—and rather skillfully, if he did say so himself—didn't really want her to see him like this even while the fruit of his efforts ripened in her womb.

Finally, to Baran's relief, Vinn muttered something sensible about how they should help the *siran* now and quarrel later. Then Baran felt them lifting him off the floor to haul him over to some cushioned surface (which, alas, smelled of the damp which permeated everything at Belitar). One of them started undressing him while the other commenced washing the parts of him that now needed it. He supposed he must have slipped into unconsciousness again after that, since the next thing he knew he was wrapped in a clean blanket and Velikar was forcing one of her tisanes down his throat.

"Perhaps," Baran mumbled, "you would consider poisoning the next cup of brew you give me? I find I'm getting a trifle tired of all this."

"Would you give up before Kiloran is dead?" Velikar snapped.

He opened his eyes. "Oh, damn. You had to remind me."

"*Siran,* your plan is working well." Baran recognized Vinn's voice again and turned his head to focus his gaze on the assassin as he hovered behind Velikar. "Meriten's allies are turning on him, and I think it likely he'll be dead before long. Two more waterlords have been defeated, their bodies displayed in public, their lands overrun by Guardians."

"Who ever would have thought," Baran murmured, "*you* would be so pleased about Guardians killing waterlords and *shallaheen* killing assassins?"

"He just likes all the killing," Velikar growled, "regardless of who winds up dead."

"We have chosen our side, woman," Vinn responded, "and Kiloran's friends are our enemies, as his enemies are now our friends."

"What news of Kiloran?" Baran asked, his mind starting to clear as Velikar's brew slightly soothed the fiery pain consuming his body.

Vinn grinned. "Ah, you were right, *siran*."

"I love those words."

"Even Kiloran has his limits. He is spreading his power too thin, trying to control too much. He has tried but has been unable to claim the territories of dead waterlords. There are riots in Cavasar now that the news of Jalilar's murder in Sanctuary has spread among them, as has the story of your own sad loss at Kiloran's hands. The Cavasari accepted everything until now; but they will not accept a ruler who murders helpless pregnant women and who violates Sanctuary."

"Oh, very well," Baran conceded, "I suppose I do want to live a little longer."

"The chaos in Cavasar is leading to turmoil in the rest of the district, keeping Kiloran's assassins there very busy. I've heard rumors that Guardians are already sneaking into the district, preparing to come between Kiloran and the city."

"Oh, that's very heartening. Perhaps I'll even sit up now."

"No," said Velikar.

"If the *siran* wants to sit up, woman, then you will assist him or I will gut you with my—"

"Now, now," Baran admonished. "We're all friends here."

"No, we're not," they said in unison.

Baran sighed. "Velikar, please, I would very much like to sit up."

"You'll just start puking your guts up again."

"Oh. Well. In that case, perhaps lying here for a little while longer would be prudent," Baran opined.

"When the tisane has had time to move through your body," she said, softening as she sometimes did only for him, "you can get up. Not before then."

"I would never dispute such a learned woman," Baran assured her.

"You dispute me all the time," she muttered. "Luckily, I am not weak-willed."

"I assume," Baran said to Vinn, "that Kiloran is denying all accusations?"

"Yes."

"And?"

"No one seems to believe him."

"How gratifying."

"People don't believe you would, er—"

"Shame myself with such a terrible story if it weren't true."

"Yes. And they remember that he killed Josarian."

"The Firebringer," Baran said. "Dar's Chosen One. The man responsible for driving the Valdani out of Sileria." Baran sighed with pleasure. "I always thought that killing him might turn out to be a mistake."

"I liked Josarian," Velikar said grumpily.

"He was a likeable fellow," Baran admitted. "Even I was in danger of liking him, but I controlled myself."

"So of course the loyalists believe Kiloran murdered Jalilar out of . . ." Vinn shrugged. "A fear of Josarian's bloodline. Or perhaps simple malice. Or maybe Kiloran has become too much like the Valdani, who slaughter women and children, too. And even Kiloran's *allies* are disillusioned. Whole clans are turning against him. Even *toreni* are speaking out against him."

"*Toreni?*" Baran smiled slightly. "Well, better late than never, I suppose."

"They say if we no longer respect womanhood, then we are not Silerian. And if we no longer respect Sanctuary, then we are worse than any barbarians who have ever invaded our nation."

"Goodness, I feel positively rejuvenated," Baran announced, aware that his voice was nonetheless thin and weak.

"With events proceeding so well, *siran,* what shall we do now?"

"Now?" Baran closed his eyes and inhaled, feeling the great Idalar River flowing through him, feeling the flooded mines of Alizar quiver in his embrace . . . feeling Kiloran's strength and power in them both, resisting him with a brilliant, masterful clarity. Baran inhaled again and felt himself weakening, losing command of his own power. Dying. "Now," he said slowly, "I think we must pray for rain."

"Yes," Velikar said, "if only the rains would come. The suffering everywhere is appalling."

"Hmm? Suffering? Oh, yes. I suppose it is bad." He was a waterlord, and the curse he would carry throughout eternity was that he himself had often caused such suffering. It didn't matter, though. It *couldn't* matter to him. Cultivating a conscience at this late date would destroy everything he had lived for—as well as everything he had promised to his wife and his unborn child. "No, I was thinking of the Idalar River, Sister. If the rains would come soon, if the river would swell, even flood . . . It would help me." When the river rampaged in a good rainy season, even Kiloran couldn't control it; so then Baran could relax a little rather than daily spending so much of his waning strength on keeping it from Kiloran's domination.

"However . . ." Baran sighed. "Neither Dar nor anyone else has ever listened to my prayers, so I suppose I must pursue practical measures."

"Don't!" Velikar protested as he started to rise.

"Help me," he ordered now, in the tone with which he had

commanded dozens of assassins over the years. It still worked—even with Sister Velikar.

He needed to send a message to the Beyah-Olvari in Shaljir, which meant writing a letter to Derlen, the Guardian who still dwelled in *Torena* Elelar's house.

He also needed to speak here with the Olvara. But even if he could find the strength to descend into the ancient underground caverns alone, he knew he'd never make it back out without help. With Mirabar gone, he had no choice about what he was going to do now; besides, if neither he nor she survived, he supposed *someone* he trusted ought to know what lay beneath Belitar. He now regarded Vinn and Velikar with some amusement, picturing the two of them bound together for the rest of their lives by the secret he was about to impart to them both.

"I need more help from my teacher," he told them, "and I'll need you to help me get to her."

"Her?" Velikar repeated.

"Your teacher?" Vinn looked puzzled.

If Baran weren't quite so ill, he would have delighted in the slack-jawed astonishment which his revelations inspired in both of his companions that day.

ELELAR FORCED HERSELF to eat some of the meal which Cheylan had brought to her. It was rather unappetizing fare, and her own shock and fear made it difficult to swallow or keep down; but she supposed that letting herself grow weak from lack of food would be foolish right now, so she consumed what she could.

How long had she been here? It was impossible to be sure. She had no idea how long she'd been unconscious after inhaling those terrible fumes on the slopes of Mount Darshon. Since then, she'd been so agitated and anxious that the time seemed to pass very slowly, so she might not have been here nearly as long as it seemed. The lack of day or night in this strange cavern of fire and water further disoriented her.

It was a very effective prison. She had already explored this murky world for an escape route and felt quite discouraged. There were dozens of passages down here, and she knew she would quickly become lost and never find her way out. Nor could she trace Cheylan's route; he left by a different passage each time he was here, and he always left an enchanted fire blocking the way to prevent her from following him. If she was going to escape this place on her own, she'd need a good plan—and so far, she didn't have one.

The river which flowed through the cavern was clear and cold, so at least she didn't fear dying of thirst while she was imprisoned here. However, she was terrified of what would happen if the volcano acted up. There were trickles of lava everywhere here, making the whole place unbearably hot and steamy—as well as hazardous to roam around. It seemed likely that the many lava leaks in this cavern were from a tributary to the main caldera of Darshon.

Which meant it was undoubtedly a very holy place; and perhaps the Beyah-Olvari had known this—in the dim orange glow of the lava streams and puddles, Elelar saw their strange, ancient paintings decorating the cave walls all around her. However, being sacred didn't make the cavern *safe*. The volcano had been agitated and active ever since Josarian's death, and there was no reason to suppose that the frequent earthquakes which had plagued Sileria since then, too, were now over. All of which made this cavern very dangerous—particularly if Dar was, as Elelar believed, terribly angry with her for betraying the Firebringer.

Is this my punishment? she asked the goddess.

If so, it was a confusing one. Abducted and raped—well, all right, *seduced*—by a Guardian claiming Elelar was destined to bear a new ruler foretold in prophetic visions . . . Though it was an intriguing idea, Elelar didn't want to sink into Cheylan's delusions of grandeur. She'd been exaggerating, of course, when she compared him to Baran; he didn't have the waterlord's mercurial madness. No, he was just conniving, bitter, and wholly unprincipled.

Moreover, Cheylan wasn't as clever as he thought he was. Elelar's verbal sparring had irritated him enough to make comments which gave her hope. He admitted he hadn't laid a false trail for Mirabar, and so Mirabar surely knew by now that he had betrayed her and abducted Elelar.

Please Dar, let it be so.

Elelar wanted to believe that Mirabar would realize what had happened and, as was her nature, would therefore take action. If Cheylan's extraordinary revelations were true, then Mirabar believed Elelar was destined to bear the ruler of Sileria and would be desperate to find her.

It takes nine months to bear a child, Cheylan, so time is on my side.

If, that was, Mirabar had not already suspected Cheylan's perfidy and therefore lied to him when she told him Elelar would bear the child she saw in her visions.

Oh, wouldn't that be just perfect?

Perhaps Mirabar had seen a way to get rid of Elelar *and* to protect the true ruler from Cheylan at the same time.

Elelar felt a little depressed as she considered this.

Maybe this was her punishment, after all. Perhaps she was meant to suffer long and die horribly here, buried beneath rock and lava after months of despair, loneliness, and discomfort.

If this is my punishment, Dar, then I will endure it . . . Only, do I have to endure Cheylan, too? That seems too much to inflict on anyone.

In any event, whatever Mirabar believed, *Cheylan* quite clearly believed he had just sired the next Yahrdan of Sileria, so he wouldn't kill Elelar until the child was born. And anything could happen before then. Surely someone would start to look for her; if not Mirabar, then Faradar, Tansen, or *Toren* Varian and the Alliance. Even some of her relatives—Elelar was the wealthiest of the Hasnari, thanks to her marriage to a

Valdan, and sooner or later one of the family would want money from her, especially in these hard times.

Of course, she'd have a better chance of being rescued, or of escaping on her own, if she could get Cheylan to move her to a more accessible place. Which was precisely why he wouldn't want to do it. She'd have to think of a way to sway him. The obvious one would be to convince him she was in danger of miscarrying—or of dying in a massive eruption or earthquake—if she stayed here.

She looked around her and knew that she wouldn't even have to pretend when she broached the subject with him.

Then she put a hand over her stomach, still amazed at how strongly she could feel new life glowing there. Did all women feel this way after conceiving? If so, none had ever mentioned it. This was, she suspected, an extraordinary child.

She smiled wryly, supposing that many expectant mothers thought the very same thing.

Expectant mother . . . Me!

It seemed so strange. She had believed herself barren and, given the life she had led—as well as her recent expectations of dying soon—she had never regretted it as another woman might. After all, she had never lain with a man whose child she *wanted* to conceive, least of all her husband's.

Ronall . . .

She wondered briefly if he was still alive. Now, for the first time, she genuinely hoped so. If she escaped Cheylan and survived, then bearing this child would be less complicated if she could claim it was her husband's. Ronall would acknowledge it as his own; Elelar would insist.

A child . . .

She let herself wonder if it was true; if she really was chosen to be the mother of a child foretold in prophecy and destined to become the first Yahrdan in a thousand years. The first ruler of the newly freed nation of Sileria.

Why would You choose me for that, Dar?

If it was true, then, for the sake of Sileria, Elelar had to survive. Cheylan must not become the most powerful person in Sileria when his son took his rightful place.

Elelar smoothed her dirty silk tunic over her stomach as a new thought occurred to her. Even if she was destined to bear the Yahrdan, could Dar really intend Cheylan, of all men, to be his father?

Ahhh . . .

What if Cheylan was only *half* right?

Elelar looked down at her abdomen. Maybe this glow she felt was just an indication that the child would be a Guardian, like its father. The more she thought about it, the more possible that seemed. People as different from the norm as Mirabar and Cheylan were must also have been very different in the womb.

In which case, if Cheylan was right about the prophecy, maybe Elelar's true destiny was to survive this incident, defeat him, and go on to bear another child.

I have to get out of here.

She forced some more food into her mouth, trying to cultivate whatever strength she could, and set her mind to planning.

Maybe none of it was true, but if it was . . . if Dar needed her to complete Sileria's destiny as a free and powerful nation, then Elelar knew she must defeat Cheylan and survive.

57

LET YOUR LOVE BE LIKE MISTY RAIN, GENTLE IN COMING BUT FLOODING THE RIVER.

—Kintish Proverb

CLEAN, GROOMED, AND looking more rested, Mirabar joined Tansen that night around a small fire he had made in the shadows at the edge of the ruined village. The heavy reddish glow of the moons blazed through the smoke and ash which filled the sky, but it had been a while since anyone in Sileria had seen the stars. Meanwhile, those colored lights and dancing clouds continued to illuminate the snow-capped summit of Mount Darshon, reminding everyone who could see it that their fate was always, ultimately, up to Dar. Here in Gamalan, so close to Darshon, the nights weren't really dark anymore, so bright was the light from Dar's eerie display.

"Hungry?" Tansen asked Mirabar as she came to his side.

"I've just eaten. Faradar brought me something." Mirabar paused and added, "Elelar's maid is very efficient."

He smiled. "You sound annoyed."

"I'm not accustomed to being waited on. It makes me feel . . ." She shrugged. "Spied upon. How does she know exactly when I wake up? When I'm hungry? When I want to rest? When I want to, er, dismount and find a bush?"

"Don't servants behave that way at Belitar?"

She snorted. "No, servants at Belitar talk back, quarrel, and usually disappear when there's work to be done."

"Ah. Well, if that's what you're used to, I suppose Faradar would be a little unnerving." Tansen brushed off a smooth rock and offered her a seat on it, then knelt on the ground next to her.

"The *torena*," Mirabar said, "must be far more helpless than I ever realized if she needs someone like that to be with her all of the time."

"*Toreni* are raised to expect such service."

"I doubt she's getting it now," Mirabar said gloomily.

"No," he agreed. "But it seems likely she's at least still alive, if not happy or comfortable."

"Yes. Cheylan can't kill her. Not for quite some time."

"We'll find her before then." He fed some more wood to the fire, though there was no real reason to do so now that Mirabar was here; with a single breath, she could make it twice the size it was now. Still, tending the flames gave him something to do with the hands that wanted so much to reach for her.

"While you were resting, I sent some men off to gather whatever information they could about Cheylan. If he's anywhere in the district, chances are he hasn't traveled completely unnoticed. Not him."

"That's a better plan than anything I've been able to come up with so far."

"I think you're right. The place you're describing must be here in the east. Close to Darshon."

"Lava flowing," she murmured.

"We'll find them." He hoped it was true.

They were both silent for a while, lost in their thoughts.

Mirabar finally said. "Najdan can protect Zarien. He has protected me from terrible dangers, you know."

They both knew that Mirabar was not as helpless as Zarien was. Still, the sea was Zarien's native ground, so to speak, so perhaps he would be less helpless there than he always seemed on land, if danger found him.

"I know," he said slowly, "that you would rather have had Najdan with you when you face Cheylan."

She shrugged. "Perhaps this is the way it's meant to be."

Their gazes locked. "The two of us?"

"Sword and shield." Her expression crumpled a moment later, and he knew that she was thinking of how they had failed Josarian.

Though it was a subject which wouldn't cheer her up, he nonetheless said, "I'm sorry, I've never been able to learn what happened to your teacher, Tashinar."

"Neither have I," she said quietly. "It's almost as if she's neither alive nor dead."

"Like Josarian," he muttered. Caught in the agony of the White Dragon as long as Kiloran lived.

"Perhaps very much like Josarian." She shook her head, her expression terribly sad. "I don't know. I can't tell."

They were silent again. And, as if sensing the tension which surrounded and grew between them, no one else camping in these sad ruins attempted to approach them.

Finally she said, "So this is Gamalan."

"A long time ago it was," he replied. "Now it's just . . . the past which clings to us all in Sileria."

In the shifting glow created by the dancing lights around Darshon's summit, Tansen's gaze traveled to where, so long ago, he had seen Armian fight and kill the Outlookers who had ambushed them here.

He knew from the gossip among the Moynari and Marendari here that some people feared Gamalan was haunted. Tansen *knew* it was; but he said nothing.

And over there, he thought, looking elsewhere, *is where Armian urged me to kill for the first time, and I couldn't do it.*

"Nothing good has ever happened here," he said quietly. "Nothing."

Gamalan was a bitter place. It always had been. It was the worst of Sileria.

"You're wrong," she said. "*You* were born here."

He heard the warmth and affection in her voice, heard the things he longed to hear from her. He couldn't look at her, because he knew that if he did, he wouldn't be able to bear not touching her. And she was another man's wife.

He just stared into the fire and said, "It's neutral territory. No one left alive can call it their home. Not even me. Not anymore." There was nothing left for him here, not since the day he had found his family dead and then followed Armian away from here and towards his fate. "So it's the only place I could think of where everyone would agree to come for a truce meeting."

"Yes, that makes sense." Then she asked, "Whose house am I sleeping in?"

"I don't remember," he admitted.

"Where was your house?"

He nodded to a hillside full of rocky ruins. "Up there. But they've all fallen down and tumbled together. I can't tell which one was ours anymore."

After a long moment, she sighed and said, "There's a lot of sadness here."

Recovered from his moment of uncontrollable craving for her, he glanced her way. She turned her head, and he was briefly chilled to see how unerringly her gaze went to the spot where the victims of the Valdani massacre had lain ten years ago. Her posture was rigid, and she was as still as an animal scenting danger. He wondered what she sensed there, but didn't want to ask, didn't want to call up more of the memories which haunted his nightmares. Not now. Not tonight.

Then her attention shifted to another spot which was scorched from a relatively recent funeral pyre. "That must be where Semeon's body was burned, along with his entire Guardian circle." She made a soft, grieving sound and covered her face with a hand. "I sent Cheylan to protect him."

"The Guardian boy with red hair?" When she nodded without looking up, he said, "You think Cheylan killed him?"

"Of course he did!" Her voice was harsh with self-condemnation.

"The boy was killed in a Society ambush." He suddenly realized what that meant, and added heavily, "Ah. And Cheylan has been plotting with Verlon."

"Yes. Verlon may have killed Semeon, but I'm sure Cheylan's the one who's responsible. The one who told Verlon where the boy was and when he was vulnerable." She dragged her hand down her face now and let him see the tears in her glowing eyes. "And I'm the one who told Cheylan—"

"Mira, he'd have killed the boy anyhow."

"You don't know that. Maybe he—"

"Of course he would. What Baran said to you is right." Her husband's name slithered between them like a poisonous snake. "Cheylan has betrayed everyone and done so with as little risk to himself as possible, right up until he abducted Elelar. Just knowing what anyone in Sileria knows about your prophecy, he would have decided to kill the boy. He wouldn't have taken the chance of Semeon's being the one you foresaw.

Maybe he wouldn't even have taken the risk of letting the boy grow up to be as powerful as you."

Tansen thought it would be tactless to mention right now how profoundly relieved he was that Mirabar had long ago decided—and had convinced Cheylan—that Zarien was not this child of fire and water and sorrow whom she sought. Tansen had always disliked Cheylan, but even he had never suspected the Guardian was capable of killing a child. Now that he knew better, he gave silent thanks that at least it hadn't been *his* child.

He studied the way Mirabar's fire-red hair glowed in the golden light of the ordinary fire he had built and realized how much else he was thankful for, too. "Cheylan might well have killed you, too, except that he has no gift of prophecy himself."

"Maybe he does but just doesn't tell—"

"No, I don't think he'd have tried so hard to win your trust if he hadn't needed you and your visions so much."

"I should never have trusted him," she moaned.

"No, but, as Kiloran says, mistakes are so easily made. Cheylan was very good at winning trust where he wanted it. You, Kiloran, Searlon, Verlon, Semeon, other Guardians. Even Elelar, who is not prone to trust, apparently trusted him when she left her estate with him. He's a shrewd deceiver." He paused and added, "He and Elelar might have found a lot in common had he tried courting her instead of abducting her."

Despite her tears, she choked on a laugh. "He probably would have preferred that, but he knew he had very little time." After a moment she asked, "Why her, do you suppose?"

"Don't your visions tell you why she was chosen?"

She shook her head.

He thought it over and admitted, "In many ways, there could be no better choice." Her appalled gaze made him continue, "She's an educated aristocrat who understands political scheming, balancing power, playing factions against each other, and mixing lies with truth to achieve a goal. These are all things even a ruler chosen by Dar and foretold in prophecy will have to learn and understand to rule Sileria effectively."

"She's also . . ." Mirabar rubbed her face and grimaced. "A great heroine of the rebellion, loved by the people. And I suppose the *toreni* might not accept a *shallah* as Sileria's ruler, even if the Guardians insisted."

"It would be difficult," he agreed. "Elelar also has respect and influence in the Alliance. Although no one can claim ultimate power in Sileria without our support, it's also true that it probably can't be done without their support, either."

"And if the father is descended from both Daurion and Marjan . . ." She frowned and didn't finish the thought.

Probably descended from Marjan through Verlon, Mirabar had told Tansen. He hadn't found the revelation about Cheylan's relationship with Verlon that astonishing, having seen the mingled familiarity and enmity between those two during the rebellion. Though it never would have occurred to him, it immediately answered the vague question which had previously existed in his mind about those two.

Then he remembered Ronall. "I wonder how Elelar's husband will take this news when Najdan finds him." Tansen had been so worried about Zarien that he hadn't even thought of this until now.

"Elelar's Valdani husband . . . ," Mirabar gasped. "Surely Dar wouldn't choose a Valdan to be involved in this?"

"You know much better than I what Dar might or might not do," he reminded her, "but Ronall could well be another reason Elelar was chosen."

"A *Valdan?*"

"He's half-Silerian," Tansen pointed out, "and he looks and sounds Silerian. But having a Valdan connected to this child could help improve our relationship with the Valdani—and, after all, we really don't want them trying to invade us again."

"You mean they'll view him as an ally?"

"It would be very convenient for Sileria if they did."

"But if he's not really the child's father—"

"But if the Valdani *thought* he was—"

"Ah. Then they'd be more likely to leave us in peace."

"Especially since Ronall has begun trying to save the remaining Valdani in Sileria from being massacred. The Imperial Council will like that." He thought it over and added, "Silerians might even obey Ronall if they thought he was father to the Yahrdan."

"No more killings," she murmured. "But I thought *Toren* Ronall was a drunkard and a fool?"

"Everyone seems to know that," Tansen muttered. "And, in truth, he is. Well, a drunkard, anyhow. But a fool? I don't know. He often seems that way, but now I think Zarien was right all along. Ronall is mostly just very unhappy." He shrugged and added, "And loving Elelar hasn't helped."

"He loves her?" Mirabar sounded surprised, which was understandable, considering how often and openly Elelar had cuckolded her husband.

"Oh, yes. He loves her, all right. Anyone can see that in him." Tansen sighed. "Meanwhile, she doesn't even want to be in the same country with him and probably wishes he was dead."

Suddenly the air hummed with renewed tension, and Tansen felt the unasked questions hovering between them. Knowing he was inviting another pointless argument, he nonetheless ventured, "So, in light of your visions, it's evidently a good thing I didn't kill Elelar after Josarian died."

"Yes." She evidently didn't want to argue about the past, because she then said, "If only Cheylan hadn't convinced me to let him go after Elelar alone. If only I'd gone. Or if only I'd sent assassins with him, as Baran suggested."

"Cheylan would have just tricked you or killed them," he pointed out.

"I had finally accepted my duty . . . even though it meant having that woman in the same home with me." She gave a watery sigh. "But if I hadn't been so stubborn, resisted for so long . . . If I had accepted my duty sooner, before Cheylan appeared at Belitar, maybe everything would be different now, and Elelar would be safe at Belitar where Baran and I could protect her."

He couldn't help asking: "*Would* Baran have protected her?"

"Well, not *her,* I suppose. But Baran protects Belitar, and I certainly wouldn't have let her leave Belitar while the Society survives in Sileria. Elelar would have been safe there until I knew what to do."

Of course. Kiloran would kill Elelar if he knew the truth. Still, Tansen couldn't resist asking, "But doesn't the Society survive at Belitar, too?"

"Not really." She shrugged. "Baran chose our side in this war, and his men follow him loyally."

"Who's to say Baran won't choose something else once Kiloran is dead?"

"He won't."

This appearance of loyalty to her husband annoyed him. "How can you be so sure?"

"Because I know him very well now."

"Are you saying he's not insane and treacherous, that he just pretends?"

"No, he's even more dangerous than I realized when I married him. All the same, I trust him in this."

"Why?"

"I understand him, and I know what he wants."

He stared at her profile, noticing how she avoided looking at him. A terrible trembling started deep inside of him, making it a strain to keep his voice even as he said, "It's more than that, isn't it? You've become . . . fond of him." He would not—could not—use a word like *love.* Not for her and another man.

" 'Fond' might be an exaggeration." When he made no effort to fill the tense silence, she continued awkwardly, "I have feelings which . . . I mean, he's a man who . . ." She sighed and concluded, "I couldn't turn on him, Tansen."

"I'm not asking you to." He heard how cold his voice sounded, but he couldn't help it.

"The ironic thing is that, given the right incentive, he could turn on *me*. Even kill me." She made a little sound and placed a hand over her belly, looking down to contemplate the child which rested therein. Baran's child.

Her child, too, Tansen reminded himself, trying to keep his wits. *It will be hers, too.*

"No," she amended, "he wouldn't really kill me. Not anymore. He wants this child, and he wants me to raise her."

"And before you were pregnant? You lived with him believing he might kill you, and you stayed there?" His voice was far from cold now. Anger, fear, and desperate jealousy heated it. "You stayed with that madman, slept in his bed, let him frighten and threaten you? And you never sent for me?"

His attack didn't make her angry, which was what he expected. She just shook her head, her expression contemplative. "It's so complicated at Belitar. You can't imagine how . . . different things seem when you're there."

"I've been there. I can imagine."

"No, Baran is far more . . . And then there are . . ." She seemed to reach a sudden decision. "There are things you need to know. If he and I don't live, you've got to protect them."

"Who?"

"The Beyah-Olvari."

"Fires of Dar! You didn't tell him about—"

"No! He told me."

Tansen frowned. "How does he know about them?"

As she explained, her warm voice soft and melodious in the volcano-glowing night, so many things became clear to him, from the origin of Marjan's power over water a thousand years ago to the Olvar's insistence in Shaljir that, somewhere else in Sileria, other Beyah-Olvari had survived.

"They want to meet the others," she finally concluded.

"Yes," he said, feeling dazed. "I mean, so does the clan in Shaljir."

"We can't arrange it without exposing them, can we?"

"No," he agreed. "And we can't risk exposing them . . ." He made a vague gesture. "Until all our own problems are resolved."

"But someday . . ."

He nodded. "If we kill all the waterlords—"

"No."

"What do you mean, *no?*"

"I mean, we have to break the Society, now and forever. That's really what this war is about. But Baran is right—"

"Do we have to keep talking about him?" He didn't care that he sounded petulant, he really couldn't stand the other man's constant presence between them.

"There will always be water magic in Sileria. No one can change that. Not you, not anyone. No one *should* change that."

"It's harmless among the Beyah-Olvari, Mira, but—"

"Tansen, *I* can't let you change that."

"You're asking me not to kill Baran."

"No, I'm telling you I will never let you kill my daughter."

He was stunned. "I would *never* hurt your child! Any child! I would never hurt you or anything you love. I couldn't. How could you even—" He stopped abruptly. "How do you know it's a girl?"

"The Olvara told me."

"And what makes you think that I would ever . . ." He drew in a breath so sharp it almost hurt. "Dar have mercy. *Baran's* daughter." He wondered stupidly why this had never occurred to him before. "A child of water . . . Sired by one of the greatest waterlords who's ever lived . . . A child Baran wanted enough to betray the Society . . . Of *course.*"

"My daughter—"

"Will be one of *them.*"

"No!" Her fierceness forced his galloping thoughts to focus on her words. "She will have the power they do, but she'll be better than they are. Better than you, or me, or any of us. She'll help Elelar's child make a new Sileria where no one will ever again starve us for water or kill us for failing to pay tribute for it. She'll respect Dar, as they never have, and she'll learn from the Beyah-Olvari, and from me."

"And from her father, too?" he prodded. "Dar alone knows how many people that demented husband of yours has killed—"

"How many have *you* killed?"

"You know what I mean!"

"Baran will not be there!" she snapped.

He waited in fuming silence for an explanation for this statement, but didn't expect the one which he got.

"Baran is ill and very near death."

"What?"

"I'm not even sure he can last until our child is born."

He didn't know what to say for a moment. "You've kept that secret very successfully."

"Outside of Belitar, you may be the only person who knows."

"May be?"

"We believe Kiloran suspects."

"Dar give me patience! You didn't think this news was worth sharing with me?"

"Baran wouldn't let me. It was his secret, and he wanted it kept. I've told no one until now."

"Not even Cheylan?"

"No."

"What about the Beyah-Olvari?"

"No, Cheylan doesn't know about them, either. That, too, is Baran's secret, not mine." Her eyes asked him to appreciate that for him, and him alone, she was violating her husband's confidences.

He didn't even know what to think, with these eruptions she had suddenly set off inside of him one after another tonight. She was carrying a child who would be a water sorceress, and she was urging him to accept that there would always be such power in Sileria, that they mustn't try to eliminate it completely from their land. She would be a widow within the year, free of that madman she had married . . . and to whom she had become . . . Attached? Devoted? Darfire, it was obscene! Meanwhile, Kiloran might know that Baran, their most important ally against him, was dying, and all the old waterlord had to do was wait for that happy event.

"Can we win the war without Baran?" Mirabar asked softly.

"It doesn't matter, does it?" Tansen said sourly. "If the answer's no, it's not as if we can force him to live longer." He eyed her suspiciously, wondering what other strange surprises she might have in store for him. "Or is it?"

"Sister Velikar does her best, and Baran's will to live is strong. He doesn't want to die without destroying Kiloran. He doesn't want our daughter to face Kiloran someday."

The words *our daughter* cut through Tansen fiercely, linking Mirabar to Baran in a way which excluded him.

"In that case, why hasn't Baran done it yet?" Tansen snapped. "Why is Kiloran's power still secure?"

"Because it's far from easy."

"You're defending him!"

"You're being unreasonable."

"I'm not . . ." Actually, yes, he supposed he was. "There's no . . ." Oh, why bother? "It's hard for me," he admitted, "to listen to you talk about him as you do while you sit there with his child in your body."

"Then perhaps you can finally understand," she said quietly, "how hard it is for me to know that you still care for Elelar. That you always will."

"I always understood, Mirabar," he said wearily. "It wasn't what I wanted, but it was something I could never change. I still can't, not even now. Anymore than I can change . . . how I feel about you."

"Yes." Her voice was scarcely more than a whisper. "That's what I finally understand."

He watched the faint shifting light play over her sculpted cheekbones and waited for her fire-blessed eyes to meet his. When they did, she said, "I didn't want to care for a half-mad waterlord who has already hurt far more people than Elelar will hurt in the whole of her life. I don't love him. I often despise him. I sometimes fear him. But I care for him; and whether that's right or wrong, I can't change it."

Tansen thought she might as well cut out his heart with one of his swords, because it would hurt less than hearing her express such feelings for the man whose bed she shared. "I'm sorry," he said at last, his throat a little raw. "I don't think I really understood, after all, how it's always made you feel that I can't just . . . kill her, or hate her, or even be indifferent to her."

"No, I really didn't think you did." A moment later she added softly, "Until now."

"And since neither of us knows what will happen now, or who'll live and who'll die, I want you to know . . ." He reached out and took her hand. "You're the one I love."

Her mouth trembled in the flickering light. "I know." She reached out to touch his face, and he closed his eyes, letting himself pretend it was only the beginning. "And loving a man who isn't my husband isn't something I can stop or change, either."

"Does he know?" Tansen whispered.

"Ever since the moment he found you trying to talk me out of marrying him."

His eyes flew open. "What did he— Has he ever—"

She shook her head. "Depending on his mood, he either thinks it's funny or else pities me."

"I have never," Tansen said, "understood him."

"But learning to understand him saved me from becoming like him. Knowing Baran has taught me that someone gifted with as much power as he has—as I have—can't afford such bitter, obsessive hatred."

He kissed her hand. "If he's dying, then you'll be free t—"

"It doesn't seem right to talk about it," she said. "I mean . . ."

"To talk about what we'll do when he's dead."

"It feels . . . disloyal."

Part of him was appalled by this sentiment, but the rest of him was still *shallah* enough to understand that he shouldn't dishonor her by forcing his point. So he nodded, stood up, and helped her rise, too.

"In that case," he said, "I think it's time for me to return you to Faradar."

She nodded, accepting that they had moved too far forward to retreat easily back into safe territory tonight. "When will your men start returning to report on whether or not Cheylan has been seen?"

"A few days, I would think." He turned and let his gaze survey the many men camped in these ruins. "Hopefully Jagodan will have arrived by then, we'll have ended the bloodfeud, and we can devote our full attention to hunting Cheylan as soon as we get the first news of him."

"May Dar make it so," she prayed, because she was still on speaking terms with the destroyer goddess.

58

WINE IS SWEET, BUT THE BLOOD OF MEN IS SWEETER.

— Jagodan shah Lironi

THE NORMALLY BRASSY sunshine of the late dry season was heavily dimmed by the smoke and ash filling the sky. The volcano had been menacingly active throughout the past two days and nights, with showering explosions of lava spewing straight up out of the caldera to mingle with the dancing lights and colored clouds which surrounded the mountain's peak. Loud explosions coming from Darshon woke

Mirabar on those rare occasions when her nerves even allowed her to fall asleep. Towering columns of dark smoke billowed out of the caldera more and more frequently. Shimmering ash had fallen on Gamalan throughout most of the day, and it was now ankle-deep in some places. Mirabar tried to shake some of it off her expensive boots as she crossed what had once been the village's main square and looked for Tansen.

She knew he wasn't entirely happy about her choice to leave certain things unsaid between them, but he respected her wishes. She suspected Baran would be amused if he knew about her scruples, but it nonetheless felt wrong to plot with the man she loved about what they'd do once her dying husband was safely on the funeral pyre. Meanwhile, there was real understanding between her and Tansen, perhaps for the first time, and that was not a gift either of them took for granted. However, the feelings between them were stronger than ever now, so they had avoided speaking privately again after her first night here, three days ago; the temptation to violate her wedding vows was unbearable, and she could tell that Tansen knew it and didn't enjoy the struggle any more than she did.

The tension among everyone gathered in Gamalan was also unbearable. Jagodan's continued absence inspired some of the men here to claim that he didn't intend to come, and to insist they were wasting their time here; they should go hunt down all the Lironi and slaughter them like the beasts they were. In addition, the persistent thunder and roar of the volcano scared them all; and since *shallaheen* didn't like to admit fear, they let it come out as quarrelsome bad temper. And even if they didn't all die here in an eruption, an earthquake, or an avalanche, they foresaw a terrible harvest if the volcano didn't stop these rages soon. Everyone here knew what would happen when the sky became too perpetually dark for the remaining drought-withered crops to survive.

"Not that it will matter," one of them said, "what happens to the sky if the rains don't come—and *soon*."

"They will come. They must come."

"But if they *don't* come this year, we're all as good as dead."

"Why worry? The volcano will kill us before we can leave this miserable, haunted place to starve to death somewhere else."

Feeling depressed by such comments, Mirabar finally found Tansen talking with an extremely dusty-looking man. When Tansen saw her, he dismissed the other man and said, "It's good news, Mira. Cheylan and a woman were seen riding away from a *toren*'s hunting lodge a few days after Elelar left her estate with him."

"Then they are here!" It was the first real confirmation she'd had that she wasn't looking in the wrong part of Sileria.

"And they were heading towards Darshon."

"Can we go after them?" When he started to shake his head, she said, "I know *you* have to wait for Jagodan, but I can—"

"I don't want you going after Cheylan alone."

"Then send men with me."

"I meant, alone without *me*. And I definitely don't want you wandering the countryside without me. Verlon's assassins are everywhere, and he may have already heard that you're in the district."

"But I can't just—"

"Mirabar, all we've done so far is confirm that you're right, Cheylan's in the district and probably close to Darshon. You believed that already, and this information doesn't give us a better idea of where to look for him."

"But—"

"Give the men a few more days to find something else, something more specific. Cheylan was seen once, so it's likely he'll have been seen again."

She bit her lip, folded her hands tightly together, and nodded her head. He was thinking more clearly than she was, and he was right.

"How are you feeling?" he asked, changing the subject.

She unfolded her hands and smoothed them over her stomach. "Not bad. Just tired."

"Yes. I don't think anyone here has gotten much sleep these past two nights."

She sighed. "And it's making them . . ."

Mirabar stopped speaking as a terrible rumbling swept through her and filled the air around her. There was a fierce explosion, followed by the sound of crashing rock. The ground started shaking—subtly at first, and then with sudden, violent heaves that knocked her off her feet. Somehow Tansen's arms were around her and he cushioned her fall. Then he rolled on top of her, shielding her with his body as he pressed her face into his shoulder.

Mirabar clutched at him and ground her teeth together, praying for the earthquake to stop. She heard an ear-splitting crack, then a horrifying shower of rocks thundering down the mountainside. Pebbles rattled against the ground all around them, and a sharp one struck her calf, making her grunt. She heard men screaming, then there was an inhuman spine-chilling screech that sounded as if the mountains themselves were screaming.

Then, gradually, she heard something else in the midst of the terrible cacophony . . . She finally recognized it as the frantic pounding of her own heart . . . or maybe Tansen's heart. His chest was pressed so hard against hers that she could scarcely breathe. But she must be breathing, because she could hear herself panting. Or was that him?

Both of us . . .

Heartbeat. Breathing. Yes, she could hear these things now, and she realized that the thundering of the ground was already drifting into a dying rumble.

Mirabar was shaking hard when Tansen finally helped her to her feet. His hands held her shoulders as he looked her over, his dark gaze intent. "Are you hurt?" he asked.

She shook her head, still not ready to speak, then raised a

hand to the gash on his cheek and showed him her bloody fingertips so he'd realize that *he* was hurt.

He barely acknowledged the sight before pressing his palm over the slight bulge of her belly. "You're not . . . I mean, *nothing's* hurt? You're sure?"

She placed her hand over his. "I . . ." She coughed. "I feel fine. Just . . . you know."

He nodded and wrapped his arms around her, hugging her fiercely. She hugged him back.

His heartbeat, his warmth, the strength of his arms, the brush of his lips on her hair . . .

Then he made a strangled sound, pushed her away, and whirled around, gazing east. It took her only a moment to realize why he seemed to be staring into thin air.

"You're thinking of Zarien," she said. "At sea." Due east of here.

"Yes. I didn't think this would happen here. Not while he was at sea."

"What?" She didn't understand. "Why?"

He glanced at her, then his attention was caught by something behind her. "I'll explain later," he said, already brushing past her.

She turned to look at what had captured his attention and saw that one of the Moynari had been hurt. It occurred to her then that she'd better go find Faradar.

RONALL LEANED OVER the railing of the boat and stared down at the water. He held his breath . . . watching . . . watching . . . staring hard at the shifting surface of the sea, peering into its mysterious depths . . .

There!

Or no, maybe not.

He'd never seen a dragonfish, and he was pretty sure he didn't want to. He wondered if he really *was* seeing something preying on this boat far beneath the water's undulating surface, or if that was just his imagination.

Imagination, probably.

He'd imagined seeing things before. Plenty of times. When he was drunk, of course; but especially when he couldn't get *enough* to drink. He shuddered. Yes, that was the worst. When the Valdani had imprisoned him in Shaljir after Elelar's violent escape, they had deprived him of all soothing drink, and he'd seen horrible, terrifying things even worse than these shadowy glimpses of what he now feared was a dragonfish. So he knew his own eyes were not always reliable.

Especially now. His seasickness ensured he was appallingly sober, and his body didn't like it. He was also bored, lonesome, melancholy, and ever more hungry for . . . *something* . . . anything. A life that meant something; a death that would free him from one that didn't; a reason to live; the courage to die. Above all, he longed to escape his own company, which had never been more oppressive than it was here, now, confined aboard this boat with a sulky boy and a seaborn family who were about as interesting as rocks.

So, no, it wouldn't be surprising at all if he were merely seeing things that weren't there. Especially considering the horrors he'd been imagining ever since seeing those incredible dragonfish scars on Zarien's torso.

But if a dragonfish *was* now circling these closely clustered boats . . .

He might mention it to the sea-born, but he was afraid they'd believe it and scare him with their speculations. He'd already discovered how much they hated and feared the dragonfish even while they also—with an irrational streak which the *shallaheen* would doubtless appreciate—longed obsessively to confront them in combat.

In the damn water, no less.

Now Ronall begged Dar and the Three not to let a dragonfish get him. He wanted to cry with fear every time he thought of those terrible scars on Zarien's body.

Ronall believed Zarien's story about Sharifar saving him. After all, who but a goddess could have saved the boy from such terrible wounds?

No one and nothing.

Ronall had never seen anything like it. Clearly no one else around here had, either. Everyone else's reaction, when Zarien bared his torso, had been just as shocked and dazed as a mere drylander's. Ronall shuddered now, trying not to think about what a dragonfish could do to a boy—or a man.

Or a toren.

As for the coming of the sea king . . . Well, why not? Dar had found the Firebringer, so why couldn't some sea goddess get what she wanted, too?

As long as a dragonfish doesn't get me, *Sharifar. That's all I ask.*

He leaned over the railing and peered hard at the water, watching for the shadowy shape of a voracious monster in its depths.

"Are you going to be sick again?" Zarien asked him.

Ronall flinched. "Don't sneak up on me like that!"

"I didn't."

"I . . . I suppose I'm a little jumpy," Ronall conceded, peering over the railing again. What in the Fires was down there? "Anyhow, no, I'm not going to be sick. I was already sick, just a little while ago. I don't suppose you noticed, though."

Zarien had been so introspective, Ronall wasn't even sure the boy had noticed the increasing activity at Mount Darshon. Ronall had noticed it, and he alternated between wanting to go ashore and then pessimistically deciding he wouldn't be any safer there.

At least if I die at sea, no one will try to burn my corpse.

There was enough Valdan in him to be repulsed by the way Silerians disposed of their dead. A watery grave seemed better than a funeral pyre. Besides, he'd always had a morbid fear that someone would mistake him for dead when he was really just dead drunk, and burn him alive.

Three help me, where is my life going?

Far from "saving" the Silerian-born Valdani here in the east, he was stuck on this boat with a brooding boy who'd scarcely said a word to him in days. And unless Tansen stopped the *shallaheen* from feuding with each other, Ronall would be afraid to go ashore here, anyhow, because the Society would certainly prevail; if they found out he was a *toren*, they'd hold him for ransom, and if they found out he was a Valdan, they'd kill him.

Suddenly Zarien lifted his head and stared landward with more interest than he'd shown in anything but his own thoughts all day. Ronall followed his gaze and saw a boat approaching them.

"More of your relatives?" Ronall asked.

Zarien shook his head.

"Who, then?"

Zarien shrugged.

Ronall was rather relieved that it wasn't more of those Lascari people. After the astonishing story Zarien had told about dying and being reborn, his grandfather had taken him aboard his own boat to talk. Ronall was not invited. He was "landfolk," which evidently put him roughly on the social level of dragonfish excrement, and the Lascari had private and important things to discuss with Zarien which Ronall had no right to hear. Indeed, just the fact that Zarien was on friendly terms with a "drylander" like Ronall seemed to appall his grandfather.

"Old-fashioned," the sea-born folk aboard this boat had said.

"Rigid and narrow-minded," Ronall had opined.

Zarien had stayed with his family until very late, and he'd returned to this boat wide-eyed, shaken, uncommunicative, and profoundly affected by whatever his relatives had said.

His visit with them the next day had been equally private and much briefer. After that, the boy brooded on this boat, refusing to tell Ronall anything and rejecting most of the food offered to him. Sometimes he helped with the chores on the boat, clearly trying to lose himself in hard labor; other times he sat alone and gazed into the distance, lost in thought and rebuffing any attempts to find out what was bothering him.

Ronall was starting to feel very, very sorry for Tansen. Marriage to Elelar was beginning to look easy compared to being a father to the sea-bound boy.

When Ronall asked Zarien why he didn't visit with his family again, the reply was, "I don't belong with them. I never did."

Whatever they had said to him, it must have been pretty harsh. Surely dying and being forced to look for this sea king should have excused the boy from the usual strictures of sea-bound life, but apparently he was being shunned. At least, this was the best guess of the sea-born family on this boat.

So it didn't surprise Ronall that this wasn't another Lascari boat sailing towards them now.

The next thing Ronall knew, sheer chaos broke loose. The little girl on lookout aboard this boat screamed, "It's an assassin! An assassin! I see his *shir!*"

Someone on the approaching boat shouted, "Zarien? We're looking for Zarien!"

The father on this boat started shouting, the eldest son seized an oar, the mother started screeching in dialect, and Ronall felt terrified.

A moment later, the other boat was close enough that Ronall could see someone who, though not dressed like an assassin, must surely *be* one. No normal person looked that mean. "Darfire, what's going on?" Ronall choked out. He grabbed Zarien. "How did an assassin find you here? What's he *doing* here?"

He had never thought he would really have to protect Zarien—and he'd certainly never thought he'd have to protect him from an assassin!

"What's *he* doing here?" Zarien said, clearly stunned.

"That's what *I* just said."

This is it. My time has come. I'm going to die.

He would die defending Zarien from the assassin, because that would at least be better than facing Tansen and admitting he'd let Zarien be killed.

"No," Zarien said, "I mean—"

"Get behind me. Go below. Um . . ." Ronall glanced at the boy. "Maybe get in the water?"

"The water?" Zarien repeated.

"No! Don't!" Ronall said, remembering. "The dragonfish!"

"What dragonfish?"

"He's coming aboard!" someone shouted.

Zarien muttered, "He should ask for permission."

"Killers don't need to be polite!" Ronall tried to push Zarien down onto the deck.

"What are you doing?" the boy demanded, easily evading his grasp.

"You're right." Ronall realized. Not the deck. "Up the mast?"

"What?"

"Go!"

"*Toren,* stop pushing me—"

"*Now!*" Ronall insisted.

The assassin jumped from that boat to this one and raised one arm, holding something in his hand.

Ronall flinched, then knocked Zarien down, leapt in front of him . . . and saw . . . "A *jashar?*" he said blankly, staring at the object in the man's hand.

"Tansen's *jashar.*" The man eyed Zarien sprawled on the deck. "Have I come at a bad time?"

Zarien sighed. "Hello, Najdan."

"You *know* him?" Ronall demanded.

"Hello, Zarien."

"You *know* each other?"

There was a lot of shouting and it was all very confusing for a few moments. Then Zarien, speaking in sea-born dialect, calmed everyone else. Finally, Najdan, so stern and terse it was hard to believe he'd really come here to protect rather than slay Zarien, briefly explained his purpose. He spoke common Silerian, rather than *shallah* dialect, so that everyone could understand him.

"Searlon?" Zarien said in response to Najdan's horrifying explanation. Now the boy looked scared. "I saw what he did to my grandfather."

"Searlon has been here already?" Najdan asked sharply.

"Not recently," Zarien replied. "He found my family a while ago and questioned them about me."

"Ah." Najdan shrugged. "Well, he has always been very thorough."

"Thorough?" Ronall repeated, appalled.

Najdan looked around, as if surveying the chosen battleground. "By now, Searlon knows that Tansen is here in the east."

"How can you be sure?" Ronall asked.

"Because he's Searlon," Najdan replied.

"Oh. Yes. And he's thorough."

"Exactly. He'll also have determined that no one has seen the boy with Tansen and realize that Tansen has left him somewhere safe. Although there will be a number of possibilities to eliminate, he'll know that Tansen will no longer trust the safety of Sanctuary. It will soon occur to him that the best place to hide a sea-born boy is among thousands of sea-born people." Najdan paused before adding, "He will find, as I did, that the sea-born folk gossip more readily than *shallaheen* do, particularly when the subject is as interesting as a boy bearing seabound tattoos who came here in the company of drylanders."

"You have a gift for making things very clear," Ronall said sourly.

"Thank you."

"Why couldn't Tansen come himself?" Zarien demanded. "Why did he have to send *you?*"

Najdan started to explain about the problems among the *shallaheen* which Tansen must solve, but the boy interrupted him rudely, then turned away and started sulking. Najdan looked at Ronall, as if expecting him to do something about it. Ronall shrugged.

I think I'm glad that Elelar and I never had children.

"Our orders," Najdan began, "are—"

"Orders?" Zarien repeated in a surly tone.

Najdan gave him a hard look. "When I reached Gamalan, your father was about to abandon everything to come here and protect you." He paused before adding, "I really cannot understand why."

Zarien's tattooed face flushed with strong emotion and his mouth worked silently for a moment. Then, as if remembering he'd been raised better than his recent behavior suggested, he lowered his eyes and stiffly murmured, "I'm sorry. What are our orders?"

"We're to go further out to sea and . . ." Najdan's voice trailed off, his eyes widened, and he went very still.

"What?" Ronall asked.

Zarien looked around, as if hearing something. "What is that?"

There was a distant rumbling.

Najdan said, "It sounds like . . ."

It got louder.

"No," Zarien said.

There was a terrible crash, as if rock and sky and air all collided in sudden fury.

Oh, no.

People started screaming as they realized what was happening.

"I'm going to be sick," Ronall said.

"What happens at sea during an earthquake?" Najdan shouted above the growing roar from the coast.

Zarien shook his head, his young face contorted with emotion. "This is my first time!" he shouted back.

The sea-born family was frantically trying to do something. Zarien apparently understood, because he moved to try to help them. Ronall looked at Najdan, who shrugged, as ignorant as he.

"Didn't Zarien's family die this way?" Ronall asked.

No one heard him above the screaming and shouting of the sea-born and the terrible roar coming from land.

Suddenly the sea exploded and the world fell away. It was as if the water upon which the boat floated instantly disappeared, and they dropped fast, falling through thin air.

Ronall screamed and fell down. Najdan grabbed his hand and caught him. His whole body jerked to a painful halt—which was when he realized he'd been sliding across the deck, which was suddenly vertical instead of horizontal.

We're capsizing!

Water everywhere. Covering them all. Filling Ronall's mouth and nose. And falling, they were still falling.

Then a horrible heave threw them skyward. Dangling from Najdan's grasp, Ronall had no breath left to scream in mindless terror. There was a hard thud, then a terrible crash. He heard a spine-chilling splintering sound, as if the boat were coming apart.

Something's hit us, he realized.

Another boat?

There was another hard thud, and the whole boat shuddered while being tossed about like a feather on the wind. Ronall's body kept flailing against the hard deck, and it felt as if Najdan's grip would tear his arm from his body.

Only when he heard himself moaning in terror did he realize that the wild tumult was now settling into a series of big, irregular swells in the sea which the little boat rode with buoyant surety.

He was promptly sick.

He felt Najdan release his grip, then heard the assassin rise to his feet.

"Zarien!" Najdan shouted. "Zarien!"

There was a frantic babble in sea-born dialect.

"What are they saying?" Najdan asked.

Ronall lay on the deck groaning.

Cruel hands hauled him to his feet and shook him. "What are they saying?"

"I don't speak sea-born," Ronall muttered, wiping his mouth.

Najdan looked at the shouting sea-born again . . . and drew his *shir*.

Ronall staggered backwards. "What are you *doing?*"

"I can't let Tansen's son die." He bent over and tugged off his boots. "I gave my word."

"Zarien?" Ronall said vaguely. "Where is—*wait!*"

He stumbled after Najdan, who evaded his grasp and, *shir* in hand, jumped overboard.

"No!" Ronall cried. "There's a dragonfish down there!"

The sea-born family turned as one to stare at him.

"A dragonfish?" the father croaked in common Silerian.

"Didn't anyone but *me* see it?" Ronall demanded. "Where's Zarien?"

"In the water."

"Zarien!" he shouted in panic.

Tansen will kill me. It's not my fault, but he'll kill me, anyhow.

IT DIDN'T TAKE Mirabar long to find Faradar, despite the confusion which reigned in Gamalan immediately after the earthquake. There were only about one hundred people here, after all, and Faradar was the only other woman.

Fortunately, the maid had not been hurt. So the two of them started helping those who hadn't been quite as lucky. A few people had been injured, though none of them very badly. Still, everyone was shaken and even jumpier than they'd been before. Mirabar herself flinched when she heard the sudden piercing cry of a sentry.

Her eyes met Faradar's, who asked, "Could it finally be Jagodan?"

"It had better be," Mirabar replied. "Even Tansen can't keep these men here much longer."

Like everyone else around them, she and Faradar rushed to the remains of the main square. Tansen was already there, tense and waiting. Mirabar went to his side and followed the direction of his gaze. The parched, ash-caked land looked grim, and the heat-baked, earthquake-cracked cliffs were both beautiful and forbidding.

Tansen shifted suddenly and looked up at a sentry perched on one of the cliffs above them. A moment later, he waved to acknowledge a signal which meant nothing to Mirabar, and he murmured to her, "It's him. Finally." She could hear the relief in his voice.

More than thirty men appeared over the rise of the main trail leading into Gamalan. They came on foot, moving fast, as indifferent to the heat as they were to their own thirst. Their long strides kicked up volcanic ash which rose to cloud the air around them, so that they seemed to approach in a whirl of smoke and mist. Battle-hardened *shallaheen,* they were lean and scarred, with sun-darkened skin and long hair as black as polished lava stone. These were the Lironi, the biggest, fiercest, and most powerful *shallah* clan in the east, notorious for their hot-headed violence, their love of fighting, and their reckless courage.

"That's him, isn't it?" Mirabar whispered to Tansen. "The big gray-haired one walking ahead of them all."

"That's Jagodan," he confirmed.

As Jagodan approached, Mirabar could see that he had the face of a tough, proud, and shrewd man, but not of a forgiving one. She supposed that Viramar had either loved Kiman shah Moynari more than life itself, or else she had been an utter fool; one only had to look at Jagodan shah Lironi to guess what he'd do to a faithless wife and her lover.

And now that he'd done it, it was also hard to imagine him apologizing for it, let alone offering reparations to the other clans.

"What do these clans want?" Mirabar asked suddenly, keeping her voice low.

Tansen kept his gaze fixed on the approaching clan leader as he quietly replied, "They want me to kill him."

"SHOULDN'T SOMEONE GO in after him?" Ronall prodded, gazing out across the tossing waves, his mind reeling with fear for Zarien.

"The assassin just did," the sea-born father pointed out. "It's not wise to send more than one rescuer into the water unless it's necessary."

"Then let's get into the oarboat and go after—"

"We just lost it in the earthquake, *toren*."

Ronall considered jumping in after Najdan, because drowning in those big waves—which he would surely do if the dragonfish out there didn't get him first—would be preferable to facing Tansen if Zarien died.

"*Toren,* the dragonfish can't kill him, even if it attacks," the sea-born man said soothingly. "You saw the scars."

"Josarian only jumped into the volcano once," Ronall pointed out. "Even the Firebringer didn't count on living through something like that twice. Zarien shouldn't, either."

"Look!"

Amidst the heaving waves, Najdan's arm stuck up, *shir* in hand, signaling to them.

"Is Zarien alive?" Ronall asked weakly.

No one answered. Najdan started swimming back to the boat, towing Zarien with one arm. The boy looked dead.

Oh, Dar, just take me now.

Ronall stared stupidly, feeling numb and useless, as the family sprang into action, throwing a line to Najdan to haul him in, then bringing Zarien's limp form aboard the boat.

"He's bleeding," Ronall mumbled, watching the sea-born mother and her two daughters work on Zarien's prone body.

The sea-born man pointed to the foremast, which was now destroyed, as if broken in half by the hand of a goddess.

"When the other boat hit us, it smashed our mast. It hit Zarien, and he was tossed from the boat."

Ronall heard Najdan climbing on board behind him, breathing hard, but he didn't take his eyes off Zarien.

"I don't think there can be a dragonfish stalking us, *toren*," the sea-born man opined.

"I saw one. I'm sure I saw one," Ronall murmured.

"No. The boy was in the sea, bleeding, for too long. If a dragonfish were so close, it would have attacked before we brought him aboard."

"Maybe it was frightened away or hurt in the earthquake." The man shrugged.

Suddenly Zarien gasped, choked, spewed sea water, and then started coughing violently.

"Is he all right?" Ronall asked.

"Yes," the mother assured him. "He will be fine."

"That boy," Najdan said wearily, "is a lot of trouble."

"We should go ashore," Ronall suggested.

"Or farther out to sea," Najdan countered.

"No one's going anywhere today," the sea-born man informed them. When they both looked at him, he explained, "One mast is destroyed, the other badly cracked, and our oar-boat has been lost. Until we can repair the cracked mast, we're anchored here, whether we like it or not."

"There are hundreds of boats here," Ronall said. "Maybe one of them will take us ashore."

"That will depend," Najdan pointed out, "on finding someone who doesn't have similar problems right now."

"THE OTHER CLANS want your life," Tansen said to Jagodan. "Yours for the ones you took. That will cancel the debt and end the bloodfeud."

They sat alone together in the little stone dwelling where Mirabar and Faradar slept each night. The two women, as well as more than a hundred men, waited outside, beneath the smoke-filled sky, while Tansen presented the terms of truce to the clan leader whose impetuous slaughter of his wife and her lover had destroyed the eastern *shallah* alliance and put all of Sileria in jeopardy.

Jagodan nodded, his expression stoic and weary.

Tansen studied him. "You expected this, didn't you?"

"Wouldn't *you* have expected it?"

Relief, dark and sad, unfurled inside of Tansen's chest. "It's why you were so late in coming here, isn't it? You had to . . . make plans. Prepare your clan to carry on without you."

"I've chosen my eldest daughter's husband to lead the clan after my death. You will like dealing with him. He's honorable and more . . . cool-headed than my brothers or my sons."

"Good." Tansen couldn't take his eyes away from the dark, haunted, intelligent ones which gazed into his. "We're facing—*making*—a new world here."

Jagodan nodded. "Yes. I understand that now." His voice was raw and exhausted. "One act of vengeance . . . so typical, even so honorable . . . my faithless wife and the *sriliah* who dishonored me by bedding her . . . To kill them for their betrayal, and to kill others in order to defend my right to kill them . . ."

It was their way. It had always been their way in Sileria.

"But then I saw it destroy the alliance I had built," Jagodan continued. "I saw Verlon regain territory we had taken away from him, and I saw people go thirsty because of it. I saw clans who had fought together against the Valdani and against the Society now turn on each other . . ." Jagodan's eyes misted with tears as he whispered, "I saw what I was destroying. Not just the alliance, but the whole future. I have dishonored all the sacrifices which my clan has made, and forsaken all the people who've died to free Sileria. Forsaking my slain loved ones, and even the Firebringer himself . . ." He sighed heavily. "All for one act of vengeance, so typical . . . even so honorable."

"I'm so sorry I sent Kiman—"

"No, Tansen," Jagodan said. "He was a good fighter, a shrewd warrior. We brought the Society to its knees. We were nearly free. You couldn't have known what he would do, what my wife would want. I don't blame . . ." Jagodan shrugged. "It was just . . . Honor. Vengeance."

Tansen nodded. "I understand."

"Yes. If anyone would understand that, it would be the last of the Gamalani." After a moment, he added, "And if anyone would understand why I'm willing to die for it now, it would be the *roshah* who has led all of Sileria against the Society."

Roshah. Stranger. Outsider. Foreigner.

"No one here has called me that for a long time."

"It's what made you who you are," Jagodan told him. "I don't mean a great warrior. You would always have been that. Oh, you wouldn't have those two swords and all of those . . ." He made a vague gesture. ". . . fancy Kintish fighting skills. But you would always have been a great fighter. You were born to be one. Anyone can see that."

"I will always remember a compliment like that coming from a warrior like you," Tansen said sincerely.

"But if you had not traveled in other lands and learned to think like a *roshah*, not just like a *shallah*, where would Sileria be now? Who would have taught Josarian how to fulfill his destiny? Who would have led us after the Firebringer died? Who would have challenged Kiloran himself?"

"Sometimes," Tansen admitted quietly, "I wonder if I've done the right things."

"What man does not, unless he's an unthinking fool?"

Tansen nodded. "We can no longer be who we have always been here."

"I know that now. I understand that there is something beyond the battle, beyond the bloodlust, beyond the pleasure of killing assassins and waterlords." Jagodan sighed. "The Lironi have sworn a bloodvow." He opened his fist and showed

Tansen the recent cut on his palm. "We are done killing other *shallaheen*. Forever. The Lironi have sworn to shun any member of the clan who kills any Silerian except those who support the Society. My son-in-law will ensure that the clan honors this vow, after I die."

Tansen closed his eyes. "I wish there was another way."

"But there isn't, and you know it. I have to die. My clan can only lead the others again and our vow can only have meaning for them if I pay for the two lives I took in vengeance." After a pause, he asked, "You will do it?"

Tansen nodded. "The other clans agreed. I have no clan of my own anymore. No feud with any of you. I seemed the best choice for an . . . executioner."

"You are. They knew I would recognize that they're offering me an honorable death." Jagodan nodded and stood up. "I'm ready. Shall we go do it now?"

Tansen rose. "You are a great man, and Sileria will be poorer for your death."

"Perhaps not," Jagodan said. "Perhaps my time is passing even as we speak, and the time for cooler heads is arriving as I die. If the days of vengeance and bloodfeuds must come to an end, then those of us who lived by them must come to an end, too."

"That's . . . too many people."

"Then may my death teach them to embrace a new way." Jagodan placed a hand on Tansen's shoulder. "I understand you have a son now?"

"Yes." He smiled. "I do."

"That's good." Jagodan nodded. "I wish I could have met him."

"So do I." He was being polite; he didn't think Zarien and Jagodan would have liked each other. There was so much about a man like this that Zarien could never understand, just as the boy could probably never understand Tansen's genuine admiration for him—or how Tansen could now kill him.

This was their way. This had always been their way in Sileria.

"You must teach your children," Jagodan said, "differently than our fathers taught us."

"Yes," he promised, the sorrow of his memories sweeping through him.

"So that they will be better than we are."

He heard Mirabar's voice in his heart: *She will have the power they do, but she'll better than they are. Better than you, or me, or any of us.*

"Because," Jagodan said, "Sileria needs them to be better than we are."

"Yes," Tansen vowed, "they will be better. They must be, or we will dishonor every sacrifice we have made and every death we have mourned."

"I won't ask you to swear a bloodvow," Jagodan said. "I know you'll give your life to make it so."

"I will," Tansen said—wishing, after all, that Zarien could be here to meet the man he was about to kill.

59

WIFE AND WEAPON ARE NOT TO BE LENT.
— Silerian Proverb

ELELAR PLACED HER hands over her belly, where the hot glow felt like it would soon immolate her. She clenched her teeth as fiery pain seized her body, and when that wasn't enough, she screamed.

What was happening? Was she miscarrying?

The mountain roared, making the cavern tremble. There

was a sudden flurry of hissing and steam as lava dribbled into the watery domain from a thousand different sources. The volcano was becoming more restless, the tributaries more active.

I'm not going to live long enough to miscarry.

Where in the Fires was Cheylan? With no sense of day or night, Elelar found it impossible to measure time; but it seemed like a long while since he had last been here.

Please, Dar, don't tell me he died in the earthquake.

Elelar closed her eyes, fighting panic. She doubted anyone but Cheylan knew where she was. If he was dead . . .

No. He's coming. I know he's coming again.

Everything Elelar had feared was coming true. She'd been hit by falling rock during the recent earthquake, and she believed the cavern could well collapse if a more severe one occurred. The flow of lava was also increasing here, and she could hear the rocks groaning under its onslaught. How soon before it broke through and flooded the cavern?

Her heart pounding with fear, Elelar lay on the hot, damp floor, tired, sweating, and filthy. Something incendiary churned inside her womb. She doubled over with a renewed wave of pain and screamed again.

This pregnancy is killing me.

She wouldn't survive much longer here, that much was clear. However, since she didn't particularly relish the idea of wandering through these tunnels until she died, she would give Cheylan a little more time.

He had agreed with her persistent demands to be moved to a more comfortable location. She suspected it was her deteriorating physical condition which convinced him to do so; she'd seen something like shock at her appearance cross his face the last time he'd been here. He had said, in his detached and unpleasant way, that he'd make other arrangements and then take her to her new prison the next time he came. She suspected it was inconvenient for him to keep bringing her food here, since his alacrity suggested he'd always intended to remove her from here—perhaps just not so soon. However, he hadn't seemed to accept Elelar's assertions that this cavern was deadly as well as uncomfortable.

As the mountain rumbled again and the rock groaned eerily under the strain of the lava pushing against it, Elelar shivered and hugged her knees, praying for the hot pain in her belly to fade. Cheylan was an idiot. If he were here right now, he'd realize just how much he was risking by keeping Elelar in this cavern any longer. What good were all his grand plans if she died here within a day—perhaps within moments?

Damn you, Cheylan, where are *you?*

MIRABAR WATCHED JAGODAN, more impressive than most of the waterlords she had ever seen, address the crowd gathered in the tumbled ruins of what had once been Gamalan's main square. She and Faradar stood quietly together as he accepted the eastern clans' price for a renewed alliance, and as the other clan leaders acknowledged his decision, made peace with the Lironi, and recognized Jagodan's chosen successor—not only to lead the Lironi but also to lead the rest of them, as Jagodan had done.

She felt her mouth tremble when Jagodan announced he was willing to die, because she knew what that meant.

Why does it always have to be him?

Tansen stood beneath the ash-dulled sky, his coarse black hair flying in the dusty wind which whistled through Gamalan, the village where he had once found the mutilated corpses of everyone he loved.

I can't watch this.

But she couldn't turn away, either. She couldn't leave Tansen alone with this.

Jagodan exhorted them to free Sileria from the Society and to follow the example of the Lironi, who had sworn a blood-vow to end the centuries of bloodfeuds and vengeance which had been their whole way of life.

Mirabar placed a hand over the cool glow in her womb.
Things will be different. I swear they will.

As the sole Guardian present, Mirabar came forward, prayed for Jagodan, and asked for his *yahr*. This she gave to his son-in-law, who could give it to another Guardian someday if he wanted to Call Jagodan from the Otherworld.

The westering sun streaked the tormented sky as red as blood, casting grim shadows across this mournful place as Jagodan spoke his last words and knelt in the dust and ash. He fixed his gaze on the tumultuous peak of Mount Darshon, offered whatever silent prayer he wished to share with the destroyer goddess, and then said to Tansen, without taking his eyes off of Dar's mountain, "I am ready."

"Stand back," Tansen muttered to Mirabar without looking at her.

She felt Faradar's firm grasp on her hand pulling her away. "Perhaps you shouldn't watch."

Mirabar let Faradar pull her far enough away so that blood wouldn't splatter on her. "If he must do it, the least I can do is watch."

Tansen spoke, his voice so subdued she could hardly hear it. "May Dar honor you as I have always honored you."

He raised his sword, paused as a gust of wind blew his hair across his face, and then brought the blade down on Jagodan's neck. It was over instantly.

Faradar gasped and turned her head away. Mirabar never saw the blood, or the head separate from the body, or the corpse fall to the ground. She never took her eyes off Tansen's face. And he never revealed any emotion at all.

"YOU'VE GOT *WHO?*" Verlon exclaimed, pushing himself to his feet with the aid of his cane as he gaped at Cheylan.

"I've got the Yahrdan," Cheylan repeated to his grandfather. Verlon's momentary excitement now shifted to hostile skepticism. "You told me the Guardian boy Semeon was the Yahrdan, and you were lying."

"I wasn't lying, I was wrong. I've explained before," Cheylan said. "Mirabar thought her visions indicated Semeon, but when her visions persisted even after the boy was dead . . ." He shrugged. "Since then, she has learned much more. Meaning *I* have learned much more. Everything I need to know, in fact."

"Then where is the child?" Verlon demanded darkly.

"I've got the woman whose womb carries him."

"So kill her!"

"Actually, grandfather, I was hoping to convince you to shelter her here." Verlon's home wasn't completely impregnable, but it was warded and very well defended, and far more comfortable than the cave where Elelar, who was deteriorating at an alarming rate, now huddled. Cheylan didn't believe Dar would destroy the ancient and sacred cave where Sileria's future now ripened, but he did believe that Elelar's terror might lead her to do something foolish.

Verlon's face contorted with suspicion. "Why would I shelter her here?"

"Because it's my child whom she carries," Cheylan said.

The old waterlord's jaw dropped. A moment later, he guessed, "You're lying."

Cheylan smiled. "No, I'm not. Ask her, if you don't believe me."

"What makes you so sure this child is the—"

"Prophecy. I know what Mirabar knows. And perhaps slightly more." Cheylan added, "My child. Just think of it, grandfather. Your bloodline ruling Sileria. Isn't that what we both wanted?"

Verlon studied him with cold, dark eyes. "You seem very sure about this."

"There can be no doubt."

"Who's the mother?"

"*Torena* Elelar shah Hasnari."

"She's married," Verlon pointed out. "You'll have no claim—"

"No one, including Elelar, seems to know if her husband is even still alive. Besides, he's a Valdan."

"You're saying she will acknowledge you as the father?"

"Oh, I don't think she'll survive the birth," Cheylan said gravely. "At least not for long."

"Ah. You're abducting her," Verlon guessed.

"I've already abducted her. Now I need a safe place to keep her until the child is born."

"What about Tansen and Mirabar?"

"Let's be optimistic and hope Kiloran kills them both. If not, of course, then we'll have t—"

Verlon gave an ugly cackle. "You don't know, then."

Cheylan went still. "Know what?"

"They're both here."

"Here?"

"Here in the east, I mean."

"Where?" he snapped.

"The ruins of Gamalan. Tansen is trying to end the bloodfeud of the eastern clans. Mirabar . . ." Verlon smiled unpleasantly. "No one knew why she was suddenly here, too. Until now, that is." When Cheylan didn't reply, Verlon added, "She's come here looking for you, hasn't she?"

"Dar curse that woman," Cheylan muttered.

"Maybe you are telling the truth this time," Verlon muttered. "If she's come all this way in pursuit of the *torena* . . ."

Gamalan.

It was much too close to where he'd hidden Elelar.

"The *torena's* current prison is inconvenient. I need to move her as soon as possible," Cheylan told his grandfather.

"And bring her here? To live the remaining months of her life under my protection?" Verlon nodded slowly. "By all means."

Their gazes locked. Verlon tried to look reasonable and guileless. Cheylan smiled pleasantly. He knew this old man well, knew what he was thinking right now. Once Verlon had the unborn child under his control, he would be eager to get rid of the child's uncontrollable sire. Standing there with a bland expression as he leaned on his cane, the old man was now plotting Cheylan's death.

However, Cheylan knew there was no better place to keep Elelar—*especially* if Mirabar was now this close to her—and certainly no hope that Verlon wouldn't find out what Elelar knew, as soon as she was under his roof. It was essential to give the old man a good reason to open his home immediately to the *torena* and make every provision for her confinement here; and this could best be accomplished, ironically, by telling him the truth. Once Elelar was safely imprisoned here, Cheylan would finally be obliged to kill Verlon, since he knew full well that Verlon would thereafter look for a chance to kill *him*.

So he was doing a little plotting, too. Of course, it would be extremely convenient if someone *else* killed the old man. So perhaps Tansen's arrival here in the east was a good thing, after all, even if Mirabar's presence in Gamalan was alarming.

"It was I who destroyed the Lironi alliance," Cheylan reminded Verlon, having always neglected to mention that Searlon was the one who did the actual work of making sure that Jagodan found his wife in bed with another clan leader. "So now, what are *you* going to do to stop Tansen from resurrecting it?"

"He and Mirabar should never have come to *my* territory," Verlon said grandly.

"Well?"

"Don't worry," Verlon said. "I've made plans. They won't live through the night."

TANSEN SAT IN the tumbled ruins as a murky, shifting twilight descended upon him. This house still had walls, though the roof was gone. Had this once been his house? He wasn't sure.

After killing Jagodan, he'd ascended to the cliff where his childhood home had once stood. Long abandoned and turned to rubble, this whole part of the village looked nothing like what he remembered, and try as he might, he couldn't tell which one of these heaps of tumbled rock had been his birthplace.

At least this one had a few walls still standing, though, so he chose to think it had been his home.

He heard a footstep close behind him, but he didn't flinch or move. He recognized her stealthy step, as he recognized the feel of her presence. He should have known she would come. He supposed he was only surprised she hadn't come sooner.

"They're not here," he said quietly.

He heard her come close to stand directly behind him. When she placed a hand on his shoulder, he closed his eyes and focused his senses on her.

"No," she said after a moment. "They're not."

"I'm not even sure this is the house we lived in."

"You had a grandfather . . ."

"And a mother and a sister." He put his hand over hers. "A brother, too, but he went off to join the zanareen and died in the volcano . . . a long time before the massacre here." After a moment, he added, "I hardly remember him. Don't remember my father at all."

"Well," she said, "me, neither."

"Do you ever wonder? About him or your mother?"

"I used to. But now I don't think they can be alive. Or if they are, they don't want me to know."

"Ah. You're the most famous woman in Sileria."

"Well, famous enough, anyhow, that whoever they were . . ."

"If they were alive . . ."

"Or if they wanted me to know them . . ."

"They'd have come forward by now."

"Yes. I really think so."

He said, "Your mother must have loved you."

"I know."

Children like Mirabar were usually killed at birth.

"Tashinar used to tell me," she said, "that someone must have cared for me. I don't remember anyone, but . . . I suppose it feels true."

"Maybe your mother died."

"Maybe so. Maybe that's how I wound up alone as I did."

"Before Tashinar found you."

"Living like an animal. Barely able to speak. Terrified. Hunted. Lonely." She put her arms around him and whispered, "I was so lonely."

He didn't move or say anything. He couldn't. Just breathing took all his conscious effort. His heart started pounding, his mind swamped by her scent, her heat; her embrace.

Finally she said, "There was no other way. You know that."

"I liked him, Mirabar." He heard his voice break. "I always liked him."

"He liked you, too," she whispered against his hair. "I could see it. He wanted you to be the one."

"I didn't."

"I know."

Her hand moved across his chest and into the neckline of his worn tunic. He felt his head swim and his vision fade before he remembered to keep breathing. Her breath was warm on his neck, her cheek rubbing softly against his hair. He was trembling with waves of instinct and emotion that howled to be unleashed.

"Are you sure about this?" he whispered.

"Yes," she murmured, smoothing her hands down his sides to find the hem of his tunic.

He stopped her from pulling it up. "What about—"

"Don't," she said, tugging the frayed garment out of his grasp and sliding it up his back. "Don't bring anyone else in here with us."

"No," he agreed, feeling the hot rush of need flow through him unguarded now. "No one else. No one but us."

Her palms were warm against his skin as she pushed his tunic up. He ducked his chin and raised his arms, letting her pull it over his head. The night air on his naked back had never felt so soft before, so full of promise. Mirabar tossed his tunic aside as he turned to her, still seated, and drew her to stand between his legs.

Her eyes glowed like the heart of Darshon's caldera, and he would never look into another woman's eyes again without finding them dull and lacking. Her fiery hair was soft in his hands, tangled from the winds which had swept Gamalan all day. Her touch was firm, cherishing him, inviting him to be bold.

There was so much to discover, so much to learn. All the wonders hidden beneath a *shallah* woman's modest clothes. All the secrets hidden beneath a lover's skin. The whispers they had never exchanged before, the looks they had veiled, the desires they had kept secret and fiercely imprisoned. All this was theirs now, without reserve or thought or caution. It seemed incredible they had waited so long, and unthinkable that they should wait even a moment longer.

He kissed her hungrily, feeding on her, devouring her, letting her passion sweep him away from the sorrow and regrets of the day, from the burdens of his duty, from the memories which haunted him and the doubts which consumed him. He inhaled her scent, floated on the music of her sighs, drank the sweetness of her love, and gave everything he had in return.

"More," she murmured, sinking to the dust-and-rock-strewn ground with him as they struggled with the last of their garments and discovered each other's bodies with fevered longing.

The damp heat of her kisses, the quivering warmth of her flesh, her once-small waist now thickening ripely with new promise . . . Her body was so firm from the hard life she had led, so lush with youth, so feminine and giving. Tansen ventured into this womanly land like a dry branch tumbling into the fire. He found the hollows of her neck, the soft skin behind her knees, the flowing wonder of her naked back . . . Unlocking secrets he hadn't even dared let himself dream about, exploring every curve and crevice which he had always forbidden himself even to imagine. In return, her lips sought every scar on his war-weary body, soothing the wounds on his spirit as she tasted the ones on his flesh. Her hands made him feel treasured, whole, healed. Her passion made him feel worthy, strong, triumphant . . . and also weak, helpless, and willingly vulnerable.

Love was a fire between them, sizzling where they touched, incendiary on their skin. It glowed in the breath they exchanged, their mouths clinging together, their arms fierce and possessive, their bodies straining to absorb each other. All the mysterious wonder of a woman's welcome had never before seemed so explosive, so tender, so rich and humbling and overpowering. He no longer remembered his sorrows or his fears, no longer even remembered his own name . . . But he remembered hers, and he said it over and over as they surrendered to a shower of darkness and light which eclipsed even the tempestuous passions of the volcano goddess.

"REALLY, VINN, CAN'T you be more thoughtful?" Baran chided. "That blood will ruin the carpet."

"With respect, *siran*," Vinn replied, "damp ruined it years ago."

Baran pursed his lips and assessed the bloody assassin whom Vinn had hauled into his study at Belitar. "You were very zealous, Vinn," he observed. "He looks half dead."

"I wanted to be sure it wasn't a trick before I brought him to you, *siran*."

"Very wise." Baran looked down at the battered, splattered assassin and prodded, "Well?"

"Meriten is dead," the man said.

"You sound as if your nose is broken."

The man gave Vinn a cold glance. "It is."

Baran smiled. "Sister Velikar, a gifted healer, lives here. If I should happen to decide not to kill you, I may let her tend you."

The man was no newcomer to the Society. Though undoubtedly in considerable pain, he didn't show a flicker of fear. Or hope. He was well trained, this one; but slightly stupid and a tad impetuous, to seek Baran out as he had.

"So Meriten is dead?" Baran mused, more pleased than surprised.

"The loyalists," the assassin said through bloody lips, "have beaten him."

"So the Emeldari have prevailed. Led by that noisy fellow with the beard," Baran murmured. "Some relative of the Firebringer's, as I recall. What was his name?"

"Lann," Vinn supplied.

"Ah, yes. Lann. Such a talker," Baran said. "Did I mention how much he *talked* the whole time I was journeying to Emeldar and back with him, when Mirabar sent me there before our wedding? Without ever saying a single thing worth listening to. Really, it's a wonder no one killed him years ago out of sheer boredom."

Their visitor looked a little perplexed by this digression, but gamely continued, "The Society has lost the Shaljir River and all the territory around it. For good."

"It almost makes one feel like celebrating," Baran said.

Vinn replied gloomily, "Well, it would if the volcano weren't threatening to kill us all now."

"Yes, the destroyer goddess does seem determined to ruin everyone's plans."

Could his pregnant wife, now somewhere in the east, even still be alive? Or had Dar decided to amuse Herself once again at Baran's expense?

"So," Baran said, returning his attention to the assassin who was bleeding all over the carpet. "Meriten was your master?"

"No. Kiloran."

"Really?" Baran lifted his brows. "Whatever are you doing here?"

"I want to live."

Baran laughed. "I repeat, what are you doing here?"

"You are allied with the loyalists."

" 'Allied' might be a slight exaggeration," Baran confessed.

"They think of you as their ally. So if there's one water-lord in all of Sileria who might survive the war now, it's you."

His insides on fire with mortal illness, Baran laughed again. "You're not very well informed, are you?"

The assassin's pain-glazed eyes focused more sharply. "Are you saying they'll kill you, too?"

"No." Baran sighed. "Well, admittedly, I think Tansen would seriously consider it if the circumstances were a little different; but, no, they won't kill me."

"So they probably won't kill your men, either."

"No," he agreed, "they probably won't kill my men." His assassins would transfer their loyalty to his wife and daughter after his death. Mirabar had already shown a tremendous fondness for her own loyal assassin, so Baran counted on her to protect all of his, too. "And so, having guessed they'll survive, *you* want to become one of my men?"

"I want to live," the assassin repeated. "I believe my best chance is if I offer you my service."

"And why in the Fires would I—"

"I can tell you many things about Kiloran."

"I already know many things about Kiloran."

"I know more."

"Probably true. But what makes you think I'd ever trust a *sriliah* who—"

"You are one," the assassin pointed out. "Argh!"

"Now, now, Vinn," Baran admonished. "No need to kick him like that."

"He *dares*—"

"Well, it *is* true," Baran admitted. "I swore a truce with Kiloran, then betrayed him."

"And you have befriended Najdan, who betrayed Kiloran

for Mirabar," the captive assassin added, his face contorted with fresh pain.

"*Befriended?* No, I don't think you can reasonably accuse me of that," Baran protested, "I really don't."

"You are like no other waterlord. I served Kiloran because he was the greatest. But now he is doomed—"

"That seems a little rash. He's still got—"

"He is weakening."

"Is he really?" Baran asked with interest. He thought he'd felt it—in the Idalar River, in the mines of Alizar—but he himself was weakening so much that he couldn't be sure. "Do tell."

"He will lose Cavasar. He may even have lost it already."

Baran sat down and sipped some of Velikar's latest pain-numbing brew. "What makes you say Kiloran is about to lose Cavasar?"

"Guardians have been sneaking into the city—"

Vinn said, "We knew that, *sriliah*."

"And did you *also* know they've now managed to take control of some of the secondary water supplies?" When they didn't respond, the assassin continued, "It's only a matter of time before they control it all. And the Cavasari, though once loyal to Kiloran, have turned on him because he murdered Josarian's sister in Sanctuary. It's just a matter of days—if that long—before Kiloran's rule is over in Cavasar."

"You have my undivided attention," Baran assured him.

"Kariman is dead, too."

"Vinn," Baran said irritably, "have all our informants fled to the mainland? Why are we the last to hear about—"

"Not the last," the battered assassin assured him. "I fled Kandahar right after we learned this. And the moment Tansen finds out, Gulstan is finished, too. Gulstan lost so many men and so much territory during his bloodfeud with Kariman, the loyalists can finish him if they strike right away."

"Which they will," Baran surmised. "They've been waiting

for this. For one feuding waterlord to eliminate the other and leave the survivor weakened and depleted."

"You see," said the assassin, still kneeling on the floor—and still, Baran noted, getting blood on the carpet. "The Society is surely doomed."

"Things certainly look very bad," Baran agreed.

"And Kiloran is finished."

"Oh, I am desolated to be rude to a guest, but I find your conclusion specious. You must know him far less well than you claim."

The assassin straightened his sagging shoulders. "You're wrong. He is finish— Oof!"

Vinn ordered, "Don't contradict the *siran*."

"Kiloran is in a very bad position," Baran said, "but do you honestly suppose he's never been in one before? That he has no contingency plan? No new alternative? No nasty shock to offer his enemies?" Baran smiled bitterly and shook his head. "He is *Kiloran*, you slack-jawed idiot. Not just the most powerful. Not just the most skilled and experienced. Not just the most ruthless. He is also the smartest. The one who always has another plan ready. Do you honestly think he survived the chaos following Harlon's death, Valdani persecution, the Firebringer's enmity, Tansen's opposition, and my hatred all these years without always having another plan ready?"

"Not this time. He cannot—"

"You gave up on him too easily. You abandoned your master before he was dead, or even beaten." Baran regarded the bloody assassin with contempt. "Do you really imagine I'd want someone like you in my service? Well, I'm sorry to disappoint you, but my standards are much higher than that."

The assassin's hard gaze met his. "If that is your view, then I request an honorable death, Baran. Since I have brought you valuable information, it is the least—"

"Can I kill him now, *siran?*" Vinn asked.

"I'm tempted to say 'yes' just because of the mess he's

making of the carpet," Baran said, "but the *sirana* has had a bad influence on me. So let's just throw him out into the fray to fend for himself."

"Mercy?" Vinn muttered with distaste. "If you insist, *siran*."

"I'm afraid I do, Vinn. And I find your tolerance of my little eccentricities to be your most endearing quality."

Only after Vinn had called for men to roughly escort Kiloran's former assassin away from Belitar did he return to the study. "A very interesting visitor, was he not, *siran?*"

"Indeed."

"You let him go because you're hoping he'll talk," Vinn surmised, considerably smarter than their guest had been.

Baran smiled. "It's heartwarming, isn't it, to think of him fleeing as far from Kandahar as he can get, all the while telling everyone he meets that Kiloran is doomed? Gossip is a very effective weapon."

"Yes, *siran*." Vinn added, "So you don't think Kiloran sent him to disarm you?"

"No," Baran said, "I really don't. I'm not disarmed by any of this news, and Kiloran wouldn't have expected me to be."

"What do we do now?"

"Now I think we should ask Haydar to see if that blood can be removed from the carpet." Baran sighed. "Perhaps having a challenge will keep her from moping so much about Najdan's absence. I find her long face very depressing."

"I meant," Vinn said patiently, "what do we do now about—"

"Oh, that." Baran felt his vision go dark as a fresh wave of mortal pain assaulted him. "That may well depend on what Kiloran's contingency plan turns out to be."

NAJDAN DREW HIS *shir* and ordered everyone on board to prepare for attack as another boat approached this one.

"Wait," said *Toren* Ronall, coming to his side. "Put that thing away. Those are Zarien's relatives."

"The Lascari?" Najdan kept his *shir* ready but said, "Their boat seems undamaged."

The *toren* caught his eye and evidently realized his plan. "Zarien won't like this. There's something . . . not right between him and his family."

"He would like being dead even less than he will like being aboard their boat," Najdan replied.

As the other vessel pulled alongside them, an old man bearing a fresh facial scar stared at him, then noticed his *shir* and fell back a step, his expression contorted with horror. The old man said something in a harsh voice, though Najdan only caught one word amidst the dialect: *Kiloran*.

Ah. Searlon had come to them, so they had seen a *shir* like this before. Najdan bent slightly to slip his *shir* into his boot, then said to the old man in common Silerian, "Zarien needs your help."

"Who are you?" the old man demanded.

"Najdan. I have been sent by Tansen to protect Zarien from Kiloran. Who are you?"

"My name is Linyan. I am—was Zarien's grandfather. But you carry Kiloran's *shir*. Why—"

"This boat is crippled," Najdan interrupted. "Zarien will be in danger if he stays aboard, whether from another earthquake or from the people looking for him. One mast is gone, the other—"

"Yes, we heard," Linyan said. "We also heard that Zarien fell overboard. Is he hurt?"

"Not badly. He's resting now, a little stunned, but he'll be fine."

"Let me see him."

"Have you come to help him?" Najdan would simply force them to do so if he had to, but it would be easier if they helped the boy of their own free will.

"He is no longer one of us—"

"Do you want him to die?" Najdan prodded.

"He is no longer one of us," Linyan repeated, "but we still care about him. We will help him."

"I'll wake him." Najdan turned to Ronall. "Get your things. We're changing boats."

The old man looked appalled. "I didn't say—"

"The *toren* and I have sworn to protect the boy with our lives. We will try not to disturb your family, but we will not be separated from Zarien until his father comes for him."

Linyan looked wary. "His father?"

"His bloodfather," *Toren* Ronall clarified, evidently aware that Zarien's sea-bound father was dead.

"Oh. Tansen," the old man muttered. "That . . . *shallah* blood ritual." Linyan sighed. "Still, if Zarien must walk among the landfolk now, it's good that he has someone to care for him. And if Tansen is devoted to the boy—"

"He is," the *toren* said.

"Such a great man, by all accounts. He cannot possibly be the sea king, of course, but—"

"I don't care who the sea king is," Najdan said. "I just care about keeping the boy alive."

"Zarien won't like this," Ronall repeated.

"I don't care about that, either," replied Najdan.

"YOU HAVEN'T TOLD him?" Mirabar asked.

Lying together atop a messy pile of their clothes, they held each other, unable to stop touching, and talked in quiet voices.

"I can't," Tansen said. "I've tried, but I . . . No, I'm lying. I don't think I've even been able to try."

She knew how Tansen hated the memory, and she could imagine how it tormented him to look at Zarien and remember himself as Armian's son. To keep the most important secret of his life from someone who had a right to know it, to be so ashamed of it that he couldn't bring himself to share it.

"Don't you think he could forgive you?" she murmured, brushing her hand across the hard muscles of his shoulder. She closed her eyes as he caressed her back and considered her question.

"Sometimes I do, but . . . Not always. Sometimes . . ."

"Yes?" she prodded, brushing his ear with her lips, reaching up to touch his hair, his face, the line of his jaw.

He looked at her, his gaze troubled in the shifting volcanic light pouring through the roofless ruin in which they lay. "Sometimes . . . he almost seems like a stranger."

"He is a stranger," she said reasonably. "He came from another life than ours, and he hasn't been with you very long."

"I can't tell him," Tansen insisted. "I can't tell my son I killed my father. Not Zarien. He wouldn't understand. I can't."

"You can't let it go unsaid forever," she said gently.

"His family is gone. He looks to me for guidance."

"And you give it to him."

"I try, but . . ."

"But what?"

Tansen sighed unhappily. "Sometimes I feel he wants to see someone else when he looks at me."

"His real father?"

"No. He doesn't even know who that is."

"What do you mean?"

"The sea-bound couple who raised him adopted him in infancy. He doesn't know who his real parents were."

"Now *you're* his real father. That's all that matters."

"Yes." He sounded dissatisfied.

"Then who do you think he wants to see when he looks at you?"

He shrugged. "A different man."

"Different?"

"Different from me. Perhaps . . . perhaps the man he expected me to be."

"Ah. Yes. Being a legend can be inconvenient," she said dryly.

"Very inconvenient for a father, anyhow," Tansen agreed.

"Well . . ." She rubbed her cheek against a scar on his arm. "Perhaps this isn't the right time to tell him. We're in the middle of war, he's still new to life on land and still quite young."

"When I did it," Tansen said bleakly, "I wasn't much older than he is now."

She tightened her arms around him and thought of the brave boy he had been, with the weight of Sileria on his shoulders, and no one to support him except Elelar—who, instead, betrayed him. "I love you," she whispered.

He kissed her hair. After a while, he asked darkly, "Would Baran hurt you for this?"

"I don't intend for him to find out, but, no, I don't think he'd do anything about it," she said. "He's not a jealous man, and he's never loved me. His heart has been ashes for fifteen years."

"Why?"

She propped herself up on his chest and said, "It's why they hate each other. Kiloran became obsessed with Baran's wife—who was sea-born, like Zarien—so he abducted her and eventually killed her. Baran was his apprentice, perhaps even destined to be Kiloran's heir; but then he became the old man's worst enemy."

Tansen toyed with her hair. "So that's what made Baran the way he is?"

"No, his flaws made him the way he is. I came to understand that, and then I knew . . . I could become that twisted—"

"No, not you."

"—if I kept hating Elelar so obsessively. A wasted life is bad enough, but when someone has the kind of power Baran does—or I do—then such hatred can make too many people suffer."

"You really think you needed him to teach you that?"

"I do. Who else could have taught me? Certainly not you. I was too jealous of how you felt about her."

He snorted. "Mirabar, even *I* don't know how I feel about her."

"As long as you know how you feel about me."

He kissed her, then said wryly, "Another man's wife. Another man's *pregnant* wife." He shook his head. "My grandfather would have beaten me for this. *Armian* would have beaten . . . Well, no. Probably not. He was always indulgent with me."

"He loved you." She knew that. She had once Called Armian and therefore knew everything that mattered now that he was dead.

"I loved him," Tansen admitted, "even the night I killed him. And, now, sometimes . . ."

"What?"

He looked away and took a long moment before saying, "Sometimes I wonder if I should have done it. If there was another way. Was killing him the only answer? Zarien says . . . Zarien says that I too often think it is."

"You think Zarien would say you made the wrong choice, that you should have done something else," she realized.

"Something better. Stopped Armian without . . ." She felt a faint tremor pass through him. "Without beating him to death in the dark."

"Oh, Tansen." She pressed her face against the Kintish brand on his chest. "I don't know what—" She went silent, hearing an intrusive noise even as his body tensed and his hands tightened warningly on her. Mirabar lifted her head and their eyes met. Yes, they'd both heard it.

She silently pushed herself away from him. He rose and started to reach for something. She frowned questioningly as she came to her feet, too, then realized what he had reached for and didn't find.

"Your swords," she whispered.

He jerked his head, indicating he'd left them down in the main village. He looked disgusted with himself as he silently pulled on his clothes.

She started dressing, too, hoping they'd only heard an animal, but knowing better already. She'd *been* an animal as a child in the mountains, and so she already knew the soft movements she'd just heard were human and deliberately stealthy.

"Keep talking," he whispered, then moved away from her.

Realizing Tansen didn't want the intruders warned by their silence, Mirabar began an inane stream of soft chatter as she finished dressing, then she crouched down amidst the tumbled rocks and watched while Tansen quietly slipped over a ruined wall in search of whoever had joined them here.

After she lost sight of him, her heart started pounding with sharp fear. She tried to hear what was happening, letting her chatter trail off into silence, but she heard nothing. Not knowing what else to do, she started talking again, praying to Dar not to let Tansen get killed now.

No, of course, he wouldn't. He had survived much more challenging things than an ambush in . . .

She heard a footstep behind her, the way she had originally come in here, and turned to see—

Assassin!

His *shir* was drawn for combat, and he rushed at her so fast she didn't have time to scream. Mirabar leapt away in terror and fell awkwardly over a tumbled stone wall.

She felt his hand on her pantaloons, struggling to capture her.

No!

She called fire into her flesh, becoming a human torch. He cursed and snatched his hand away from her. She flung a ball of flame at him, searing and wild with her startled fear.

"*Arrrrgggh!*"

He fell back screaming, and she pressed her advantage, engulfing him in her deadly fire as he tried to escape it.

"*Mira!*" Tansen shouted.

She heard Tansen grunt loudly nearby, then she heard thudding, scuffling, sounds of a fight. Then he shouted, *"Attack! Get ready!"* very loudly. Mirabar didn't look, though, didn't take her eyes off the assassin as he fell to the ground and rolled frantically. Even after he stopped moving, stopped screaming, she didn't look away, didn't douse the fire.

"*Mirabar*. It's all right. Stop now."

She recognized Tansen's voice and realized her whole body was still aflame. She commanded the fire to die. It did, slowly, until only she remained.

Then Tansen touched her. "Did he hurt you?"

She shook her head, then sank against him as he embraced her. "I've done it before," she babbled brokenly. "Killed a man like that. When we were attacked on Mount Niran. Oh, Dar have mercy, it's awful. You were right. It's not a thing to be done lightly. You were right."

"Shhh," he soothed. "It's done now. No, don't look. Don't look, *kadriah*."

She heard shouting now and felt afraid again. "What's happening?"

"Those were advance scouts. We're coming under attack."

"Who?" She realized where she was. "Verlon?"

He looked down at the ground. "Yes. Verlon."

She followed his gaze and saw the dead assassin's *shir* on the ground. She bent to pick it up.

"Mira . . ."

"I may need it," she said, forcing calm into her voice.

"Come on." He scooped his shirt off the floor and pulled it over his head. "We have very little time now. Let's get down to the main village and find someplace safe for you."

They emerged from behind the tumbled walls which had sheltered them for too short a time. In the eerie glow of the volcano's restless peak, Mirabar looked down at the village and saw the *shallaheen* of the eastern clans frantically readying for the attack which Tansen had just warned them was imminent.

He was right once again: They didn't have much time. The two of them had only just reached the main square when the attack on Gamalan began, and the Society made its bold move to kill every last one of them.

60

IF YOU WANT TO BE ONE OF US, YOU CANNOT BE ONE OF THEM. IT IS THE FIRST RULE.

—Armian

CHEYLAN TRAVELED OVER the tumbled rocks and thick ash which covered the ground. His horse had broken a leg earlier, leaving him on foot. He'd been stunned in the fall and was bleeding from a cut on his face, but he didn't slow his pace, let alone consider turning back for another mount. Riding a horse had been foolhardy over this terrain, and he'd known it. Speed was imperative, though, so he'd taken the risk. Speed was still imperative, so he pushed himself hard now.

He hoped Mirabar would die in the attack on Gamalan, but he knew he couldn't count on it. She was at least as hard to kill as Tansen was, perhaps more so. Two lesser waterlords, allies of Verlon's, were participating in the attack, Verlon himself being too old and physically weak to make the demanding trek up to Gamalan. Cheylan hoped they would prevail; but Tansen and Mirabar had defeated waterlords before, as Cheylan had pointed out to Verlon before leaving to retrieve Elelar from the sacred cavern which was too close to Gamalan for Cheylan's peace of mind.

He wouldn't underestimate Mirabar. Despite Verlon's smug confidence, she might live through the surprise attack. So he must get the *torena* safely away before any survivors of the battle had time to regroup and go in search of her.

"NO!" TANSEN SHOUTED at Mirabar as the fighting grew furious around them. He tried to drag her to shelter. "I'm putting you somewhere safe! No discussion!"

"Verlon or another waterlord will be with them!" she shouted back, resisting his rough tugging. "Let me put fire around the water supply! You *know* I have to do it!"

She saw his jaw work as he ground his teeth. "Do it fast," he snapped. "And then you stay where I put you."

She nodded, then felt her heart collapse in her chest as an assassin appeared behind him. Tansen had yet to retrieve his swords and was still unarmed! Her horrified expression must have warned him, since he turned to confront the attacker before she'd even drawn breath to scream. Tansen broke the arm thrusting a *shir* at him, knocked the pain-stunned assassin to his knees, and twisted his head hard enough to break his neck. The body had barely hit the ground when Tansen seized the *shir,* which was now his.

"Do it now!" Tansen ordered her, moving to fight two more men who were coming straight for them.

She turned her back, having no doubt that he could protect it, and started calling forth fire to surround the well in the the main square. Her senses immediately touched something cold and intrusive, dark and resistant.

There *was* a waterlord here. Already reaching out to this well, trying to coax it to his will.

But Mirabar's will was stronger, and so was her power. She struggled fiercely against the unseen sorcerer for long moments, all the while aware of the fighting around her. Then there was a sudden crumbling of opposition, a shuddering collapse in that chilly magic as she overpowered it—and Mirabar set the well on fire, protecting it from other sorcery.

"All right, inside!" Tansen shouted, shoving her towards an old hovel. "Make a fire around this house, and stay here until I come for you."

"Sirana!"

Mirabar turned and shouted, "Faradar!" The disheveled maid was running across the square. Mirabar caught her hand. "You're safe!"

"Neither of you is safe!" Tansen gave Mirabar a very hard push. *"Get inside!"*

Mirabar tumbled into the abandoned stone house, dragging Faradar with her. Then, as ordered, she called enchanted fire to encircle the whole thing, protecting them from further attacks for the time being.

"Thank Dar you're all right!" Faradar said, panting. "I looked everywhere for you."

"I was . . . Never mind where I was."

"Are these Verlon's men?"

"Yes."

Terrified, Mirabar tried to peer out a window and see what was happening. The fire she had made was dense and bright, though, obscuring her view of the battle. Even the noise was dimmed by the roar of her Guardian flames.

She turned away, frustrated, scared, anxious—and fell back with a gasp of startled fear as someone came through the flame-veiled doorway.

"What is it, *sirana*?" Faradar demanded. "What's wrong?"

He stood golden and burning before her, neither screaming nor reeling in blazing agony. And, as the flames melted away, she finally recognized him and understood.

"You!"

Faradar asked, "Who? What?"

Her time is at hand, the Beckoner said, his skin shimmering with Otherworldly light.

"Where have you been?" Mirabar snarled. "I've *begged* you for help! For guidance!"

Faradar gasped. "You're having a vision, aren't you?"

You must go to her.

"Now?" Mirabar asked incredulously

Time has run out. . . .

"I'm surrounded! How can I go to her now?"

"Is it a vision about the *torena*?" Faradar asked hopefully.

Come to me. . . .

"Where is she?" Mirabar asked the Beckoner. "Tell me, and as soon as the battle—"

You must come to me. . . . .

There was a terrible crash from the volcano, so violent it shook the house . . . and then Mirabar realized it wasn't just the volcano.

"Earthquake!" Faradar shouted.

"No," she muttered, horrified. "Not now. Not *again*."

They crouched down, huddling together and covering their heads as the ground shook insistently and the fire-shielded house began collapsing all around them.

"No!" ELELAR SCREAMED as the cavern shook wildly and rocks fell all around her. "Not again!"

The walls of the cavern groaned hideously, terrifying her. She scrambled to her hands and knees and stared in horrified fascination as a deafening, indescribable sound intensified along the far wall of the cavern . . . and then a river of lava broke through the wall, which began collapsing with chaotic violence.

Screaming in mindless panic, Elelar begged Dar to help her as she tried to save herself from certain death.

TANSEN HAULED HIMSELF to his feet the moment the ground stopped heaving, then launched himself in the general direction of several stunned assassins.

Then a sound that terrified every *shallah* in Sileria made him freeze in his tracks as his blood ran cold.

"Avalanche!"

* * *

MIRABAR SLOWLY ROSE to her feet, with Faradar's help, and surveyed the wreckage around her.

"*Sirana,* are you hurt? Is the baby all right?"

"I think so," Mirabar panted. "I mean, I think the baby's fine. I think . . . Are *you* hurt?"

"No, I'm fine. But this house isn't safe, *sirana.* What should we . . ." Faradar went still. "What's that noise?"

Mirabar wanted to weep as she heard a terrible, ear-shattering rumble which she'd feared her whole life, accompanied by the warning shout, *"Avalanche!"*

"Tansen!" She ran to the door, but it had collapsed during the earthquake and was now impassable.

Come to me . . .

"Is he alive?" she begged, pushing futilely at the tumbled stone and crumbled mortar blocking her escape.

Only you can protect her . . .

"Tansen!" she screamed.

"*Sirana*, this house will collapse if there's another tremor."

You must come . . .

"Dar have mercy," Mirabar wept.

This is your destiny. Your duty. This is what you were chosen for.

"He's alive," she promised herself. "He's alive, I know he's alive."

"Of course he is," Faradar said firmly.

Mirabar closed her eyes. Tansen was too hard to kill for a mere battle, earthquake, and avalanche combined to finish him off. "Oh, Dar, please let him live. If You don't, I will kill the Yahrdan myself as vengeance for his death, do You hear me?"

Now . . . the Beckoner prodded.

She looked towards the window, their only possible escape now. "If assassins kill me the moment I leave this house," she warned the Beckoner, "my destiny won't matter, will it?"

The ground started shaking again, and the roof overhead—or what remained of it—groaned alarmingly.

"All I know, *sirana*," said Faradar, "is that we'll die if we stay in here."

"I WANT TO go ashore!" Ronall said insistently. "I want to go ashore *now!*"

The Lascari boat heaved and rolled on the wildly rocking sea.

"We don't know where Searlon is, and we don't know if Tansen's plans are succeeding." The grim assassin at his side frowned in thought as he clung to a rope tied to the mast. "At least here, on a good boat, no one can approach without our knowledge."

"After we've drowned, that will be a great comfort to me!" Ronall shouted above the roar of the angry sea.

A huge wave washed across the deck, silencing them for a moment. When he was able to breathe and see again, Ronall glanced over to where Zarien, still a little disoriented from his accident, sat huddled on deck, also clinging to a rope. His relatives tended him conscientiously and were clearly concerned about him, yet they made no effort to bring the boy out of his increasingly dark, withdrawn mood. They might not be shunning him in the usual sense of the word, but Ronall could easily understand why Zarien had protested hotly when Najdan had presented (and then harshly insisted upon) this plan. The family's attitude towards the boy suggested he had some hideous, contagious disease which revolted them all.

Ronall had felt like the diseased, revolting one among his own family often enough to have tremendous sympathy for the boy; particularly since Zarien was wholly blameless for the circumstances which had made him violate his people's rigid sea-bound traditions.

The boy's awkward misery now strengthened Ronall's determination. "Linyan!" he shouted. "Don't you think we'd be safer ashore?"

Najdan gave him an impatient look. "They don't ever go ashore."

" 'We,' " Ronall clarified to Linyan, "meaning me, Zarien, and the assassin."

Linyan pointed landward, where burning boulders were now flying out of the volcano, visible even at this distance. "With the destroyer goddess determined to kill every drylander in Sileria, what makes you think you'd be spared once you were ashore?"

"She seems likely to kill everyone at sea, too!" Ronall argued. "At least on shore, we might be able to run away!"

"And straight into the arms of the assassin hunting my grandson?"

"I thought he wasn't your grandson anymore?" Ronall snapped.

Linyan looked sad. "No, he's not. He can't be. He made his choice—"

"*Choice?* What choice? He was killed by a dragonfish, you bigoted old—"

"We are protecting him now!" Linyan's sea-drenched face blazed with defensive anger. "We have *always* protected our own when they are threatened by you people! When Zarien's mother—"

"Do you want *praise* for helping an innocent boy from your own family? Do you think that makes you—"

"This is our way!" Linyan shouted. "This has always been the way of the sea-bound!"

"Since the world seems to be coming to an end," Ronall shouted back, "maybe tonight would be a good time to *change* your ways!"

"This bickering is pointless!" Najdan barked at them both.

"I agree," Ronall said. "Let's take the boy ashore!"

"No!" Linyan shook his head. "We'll go farther out to sea."

"How much farther?" Ronall asked suspiciously.

"We can probably ride out more earthquakes safely if we're well away from the shore," Linyan said.

"Probably?" Ronall repeated, far from satisfied. *"Probably?"*

"Survival on shore isn't a certainty right now, either," Najdan said, gazing at the distant volcano.

"If another earthquake came while we were trying to navigate through all those crippled boats and sailing so close to the rocks . . ." Linyan shook his head. "No, it's not safe, *toren*. Not right now. Not with the sea so violent tonight."

Ronall looked out across the black, roiling water. Many other boats were doing what Linyan advised. Beneath the impenetrable black of the ash-dark night sky, torches blazed brightly on hundreds of boats as far as the eye could see, and virtually all the vessels which were still seaworthy were sailing away from shore, bobbing erratically on the tormented waves.

"Why are they all here?" Ronall wondered. He turned to Linyan, "Why are *you* here?"

"We felt we must come," was the answer.

"Like the pilgrims at Darshon," Ronall said wearily. "Did Dar bring everyone here just to watch Her tear Herself apart?"

Najdan announced, "We'll go farther out to sea for now."

As the boat rose dramatically and then dropped sickeningly, Ronall wanted to vomit again, but his stomach was empty. He gave Najdan a pained look.

To his surprise, Najdan added, "I hate the sea, *toren*. I assure you I'll reconsider as soon as I deem it wise."

"TANSEN! YOU'RE ALIVE!"

"So are you," Tansen replied to the *shallaheen* who cheered this discovery. "Find out who's confirmed dead and who's missing, then organize two search parties to find the missing. Post new sentries. Then I'll need runners who can go round up reinforcements before we make our move against Verlon."

Tired, bloody, and relieved to *be* alive, Tansen automatically reeled off post-battle orders as he passed through the exhausted but exhilarated men with long, fast strides. He was heading back to the house where he'd left Mirabar before the battle had become wild with confusion from the earthquake, the aftershocks, and the avalanche. Mercifully, the deadly assault of rock and debris had swept down a north-facing slope and fallen well away from the village. Even better, he'd just been informed that it had killed two waterlords who had been participating in the attack from a safe distance. That knowledge made Tansen feel tolerant about the dust which the event added to the ash-thick air.

It had been a long, difficult, chaotic battle, and it was very late now. Perhaps even close to dawn. He looked up as he approached the main square of Gamalan. If not for the lights from Darshon's summit, he suspected this would be the darkest night which had ever fallen upon Sileria. After a brief respite, ash once again fluttered thickly upon them now, drastically reducing visibility, clogging the air, powdering everyone's hair, and dirtying their clothes.

Tansen passed the ancient village well and saw that Mirabar's fire was still blazing there. She'd need to douse it so the men could draw water. He approached the house where he'd left her, peering through the falling ash . . .

His heart stopped. The house was a collapsed heap of burning rubble now. *"Mirabar!"*

"Tansen, no!"

He fought the hands pulling at him as he tried to go to her, to the tumbled stone and mortar which hid her body. *"No!"*

"She's alive!" someone screamed at him. "Stop it! She's not in there!"

Panting hard and almost dizzy from the roaring of his own blood, Tansen tried to focus.

Faradar shouted right into his face, "She's not in there!"

He seized the maid's shoulders. "Where is she?"

"I don't know, but—"

He shook her. *"Where is she?"*

Someone hit him. "Stop it, Tansen!"

He removed his hands from Faradar and tried to pull himself together. "Where is she?" he asked more rationally.

"She escaped and went into the woods." Faradar pointed. "There." When he moved to follow, she said, "No! Wait!"

"What?" he snapped.

"Her vision—"

"She had a vision?"

Faradar nodded. "She told me to tell you the Beckoner was leading her to *Torena* Elelar."

"Now?"

"That's what she said." Faradar impatiently brushed dusty hair away from her smudged face. "I wanted to go with her, but she said the attackers wouldn't kill me—an unarmed woman— and so I had to stay behind to tell you where she'd gone."

"Where?"

Faradar again pointed. "Into the woods. In search of the *torena.*"

"That's it?" Tansen demanded. "That's all you know?"

"It's all *she* knew." Faradar sounded upset and defensive. "And she was in quite a hurry."

Tansen again looked in the direction Faradar had pointed. Then he lifted his gaze higher, to where Darshon loomed in its fiery fury. "I'll have to track her."

"I'm coming with you," Faradar said.

"You won't be able to keep up."

"I'll keep up or die trying."

Tansen supposed he understood what Radyan saw in her, but he warned, "I'll leave you behind rather than slow down for you."

"Of course," she agreed. "But the *torena* will need me if she . . . if she . . ."

"Pack some supplies for us," Tansen said. "We may be going all the way to Darshon." He glanced at the burning well and added, "No wonder Mirabar forgot about that."

"We'll need torches," Faradar murmured.

"Yes. We'll leave as soon as I've given everyone their orders." With the Lironi alliance reestablished, the dreary remains of the village in shattered ruins, and the well now inaccessible, there was no reason for anyone to stay here. He'd order the clans to abandon Gamalan immediately and rally with reinforcements elsewhere in the eastern mountains.

He accomplished his tasks quickly, his mind distracted with fear for Mirabar pursuing Cheylan alone in this dark war-torn terrain, and with dread for Zarien, probably still at sea during these earthquakes.

Tansen reminded himself that Najdan would give his life to keep Zarien safe. Besides, Zarien had a destiny which both Dar and Sharifar wanted fulfilled. Surely they wouldn't let the boy die now?

"I'm ready to leave, *siran*," Faradar said, rejoining him after she'd gathered supplies and prepared herself for a hard trek.

Tansen nodded, soon finished giving the men instructions, then took a torch and said to Faradar, "Show me *exactly* where she went into the woods."

What she showed him, in the flickering light of their torches, was not encouraging. Alone in the night, without food or water, Mirabar had headed up a steep, rocky path going west. His heart flooded with renewed fear as he thought of her now and wondered how far ahead of them she was.

Focus on the task at hand.

Once people moved into his heart, even a *shatai* had trouble keeping a cool head.

ZARIEN SAT HUDDLED on deck, soaking wet, miserable, and wishing he had never come back to sea. He wished Sharifar had simply let the dragonfish have him the night he died.

The secret his family had kept from him all his life was bad enough. The thought of telling it to Tansen, though . . .

I can't. I just can't.

He remembered the night he learned Tansen had betrayed Dulien.

"He was a waterlord, Zarien."

"But don't you . . . Doesn't . . ."

"They all have to die," Tansen said. *"Or be driven out of Sileria."*

Yes, Tansen wanted to kill all the waterlords. He didn't want any to remain alive in Sileria. Everyone knew that about him.

What'll I do?

He couldn't tell Tansen.

But how could he keep this a secret?

He couldn't. Not for long. He already knew that.

At first, he'd just been shocked. Stunned. Even convinced it was a mistake. A lie. A dream.

And now . . . Now he could think only about what Tansen would say, what Tansen would do.

Nobody hated waterlords the way Tansen did.

Zarien ignored Ronall, who tried to speak to him, and looked out across the violent sea where hundreds of torches blazed, tiny dots of glowing gold under the dark menace of the ash-filled sky.

He suddenly wished the sea would simply swallow him before he had to face Tansen again.

MIRABAR WAS THIRSTY and exhausted, in no condition for this kind of trek by day, let alone by night.

The dark was clinging to the sky for such a long time. Would morning never come?

She stopped walking and sat on a fallen, drought-withered tree trunk.

Come.

"I need to rest," she insisted.

Fiery pain shot through her, an Otherworldly punishment for her weakness, her disobedience.

Only you can protect her.

"How much farther?" she asked wearily, rising to her feet.

You must come . . .

Hating Dar and the Beckoner with all her heart, Mirabar began plodding forward again. Her tormentor was little more than an elusive glowing figure far ahead of her, relentlessly leading her over ancient, rocky, quake-damaged goat paths, taking her west through the dark, treacherous mountains. Darshon loomed directly overhead; they were now very close to the sacred mountain's slopes. The dancing lights and colored clouds at its peak—even the noisy explosions of flaming rock and showering lava from the caldera—looked dim in the dirty air, though huge and terrifying from this perspective.

Surely the sky shouldn't still be dark? Mirabar had a good sense of the passage of time and felt disoriented by the never-ending night. It wasn't right. A faint, eerie glow in the thickly black sky east of here seemed to promise dawn—had seemed to promise it for some time now—but it still didn't come.

Ash flew into her eyes, stinging for a moment. Then she realized. "Morning won't come, will it?" she muttered. "That's not night covering the sky. That's ash and smoke and volcano dust."

The Beckoner didn't answer. Of course.

An eerie, obscure grayness finally spread slowly across the land as she continued her journey, but it was nothing like sunlight. Nothing like any day she had ever seen in her life. Visibility improved slightly, but not enough to make this trek notably less hazardous. Since starting out, she'd left occasional signs for Tansen to follow, hoping he would try to track her. But now that she knew he wouldn't have sunlight to help him, she was afraid he might not see her markers if he tried to find her.

She grew weak and light-headed, and the ever-present cool glow in her belly turned into an insistent throb.

"I have to have water," she told the Beckoner. "*Now.* I can't go on like this."

There is water.

"Where?"

Here . . .

"Where?" she demanded.

Glowing more faintly now, he led her off the path and over an enormous pile of jagged, tumbled rocks. She followed him into a narrow crevice with sheer stone walls so close together it was as if someone had sliced open a cliff but forgotten to push the two halves apart.

That was when she heard it: the faint, sweet music of running water. Her womb responded convulsively, startling her.

She entered a tiny clearing, now covered in ash, which ended in a cliff face concealed by the crevice she had just come through.

The Beckoner floated over to a low, shadowed hole in this hidden wall, then disappeared, as if melting into the rock. Mirabar hesitated briefly, then followed him by going through the hole in the rockface.

She entered a cave, of course. A tunnel, really. Probably carved by old lava flows from Mount Darshon.

Mirabar stumbled on the uneven floor, unable to see anything in here except the Beckoner himself. She grew nervous as he drew her deeper and deeper into the oppressively dark, dank tunnel.

"This isn't safe," she said, thinking of the earthquakes. But he ignored her, and the distant sound of running water lured her onwards, a temptation she couldn't resist, a necessity which was close to breaking her.

The tunnel split and divided into several other tunnels, which also split and divided. Mirabar blew torchlight into life at the entrance to every tunnel the Beckoner chose, knowing she'd never find her way back out without them if he, as was his custom, suddenly abandoned her.

Finally, when she was hopelessly disoriented but fairly sure she was very far inside the belly of a mountain, the frustratingly faint and alluring trickle she'd been hearing turned into the promising babble of a stream flowing over rocks. Even as she heard it, the powerful life inside her womb reacted violently.

Something was wrong. This wasn't a craving for water she felt coming from her unborn child ... This was something else.

Mirabar hesitated, unnerved.

Then the Beckoner proceeded down the next twisting lava-carved tunnel and left her alone in the dark. Mirabar decided that staying here felt no safer than going forward would, so she followed him.

As soon as she entered the chamber into which he led her, Mirabar caught her breath and felt her heart start to pound with stunned recognition.

A child of fire ...

It was a dark place full of light, a bright place shadowed by darkness. A vast cavern, heavy yet airy, immense yet encroaching.

"It could almost be ... a big prison," she whispered, dazed as she looked around her.

A child of water ...

Fire and water were all around her. The churning lava of the volcano dripped into water which flowed through a cavern lit by unfamiliar glowing shapes. Angry hissing filled the air wherever fire and water met, and steam rose to obscure Mirabar's vision.

A child of sorrow ...

"This is the place," she murmured in wonder. "The place I've seen so many times ..."

The place where Cheylan must have brought Elelar.

Sileria's future depended upon what happened here. On what Mirabar did next.

"What do I do?" she whispered.

Fire and water, water and fire ...

Mirabar was distracted by little glowing shapes moving around in this strange sunless place of lava and crystal, this domain of mingled fire and water. Some slithered leglessly, others seemed to have a thousand legs.

"Ugh!" Mirabar backed up a step.

Her gaze sought the Beckoner again, and she noticed with fear that he seemed to be fading, spreading himself thinly on the hot, damp air and gradually disappearing now that he had brought her here.

Are you ready?

"I don't know," she admitted. "What do I do? What am I looking for?"

The Beckoner floated above the underground stream flowing through this cavern. As he sank into the water, he set the river briefly ashimmer before disappearing altogether.

You are looking for me.

"For you? I'm *always* looking for you," Mirabar protested.

There was no answer, of course.

She sighed and looked around her. There were several passages leading out of this cavern; so it would be very easy to make the wrong choice and get lost. She was briefly tempted to turn around and follow her trail of torches back out into the sunless day; but she knew she couldn't. Great forces had conspired to lure her here to protect Elelar, and her life was consecrated to this purpose.

Her womb quivered disconcertingly as she approached the stream, desperate in her thirst.

"It's enchanted, isn't it?" she murmured. Warded. She could sense it now that she tried to, now that she was this close. It was the awareness of hostile water magic which had alarmed her daughter, so richly imbued with Baran's talent.

What had Baran said?

"This child is very powerful already. I can feel her when I'm this close to you. Trust her."

Mirabar placed a hand over her stomach, where the glow now felt both agitated and eager. "And I said, 'We will take care of each other, as Dar intended.' " Knowing she had reached the end of her endurance and couldn't go on without water, Mirabar took a deep breath and made her decision. *Trust her*.

"Protect me," she whispered, crouching beside the flowing stream and reaching into it to obtain some water in her cupped hands.

"Agh!"

She fell back in fear, instinctively calling forth fire in a shielding circle as the water responded to her presence, her touch. It hissed angrily and rose off the streambed into a towering wall which surged forward to kill her.

Mirabar met it with a wall of fire as she scrambled backwards, her skin engulfed in her own protective flames; but whoever had set this trap was incredibly powerful, his magic terribly strong. The water came straight through the fire, scarcely affected by it at all.

Mirabar screamed in mingled terror and pain as her belly exploded in a shower of cold fury, flooding her with watery belligerence, with an icy rage so startling and powerful she lost control of her own fire and saw it doused by the attacking water.

"No!"

The towering river suddenly froze, turning to solid crystal before her very eyes.

Shivering with terrible cold, Mirabar stared dumbly at it, blank-minded with shock.

Her belly throbbed with chilly exuberance, the unborn sorceress in her womb evidently sensing the triumphant test of her power.

"B . . . Bar . . ." Mirabar placed a shaking hand over her stomach and murmured. "Baran's daughter . . ."

She'd be dead right now if she hadn't made this child with him.

Shaking in reaction to the attack and the unfamiliar power

which had saved her from it, Mirabar started picking herself off the damp floor of the cave . . . which wasn't cool, as caves usually were, but warm—even hot. She looked around at the blindingly bright drizzles of lava here and there and realized they were leaks from bigger lava flows—whole rivers of lava which were close enough to these caverns and tunnels to make the rocks uncomfortably warm and the air hot and steamy.

Sweating now, Mirabar rapped her knuckles against the crystal wall which had been her watery attacker and decided it really was no longer a threat to her.

"Can I drink now?" she wondered aloud, cautiously approaching the stream again.

The water now flowed around the hardened, distorted portion of it which had tried to kill her; indeed, the stream didn't even touch that section now, as if revolted by its failure or repelled by the rival magic which had conquered its power.

Steeling herself to try again, Mirabar reached into the flowing water. Nothing happened. The power guarding it—or at least this portion of it—was broken. Now it was just water.

"Thank you," Mirabar muttered, indulging herself with abandon now. She had never been so thirsty in her life! She brought her cupped hands to her mouth again and again, then rested, then drank still more. She probably consumed enough to fill two waterskins by the time she felt satisfied and ready to proceed.

But proceed where? Which direction? Even the water offered no useful ideas, since the river seemed to split into three separate streams as it left this cavern and . . .

The river. The stream. The water.

Mirabar stared at it, thunderstruck. She'd been too frightened and too thirsty to recognize the ramifications until this moment.

Water magic.

"Fires of Dar . . ."

Yes, perhaps Verlon could have enchanted the stream. If

Cheylan, who betrayed everyone and trusted no one, actually trusted the old man enough to reveal this well-hidden lair to him. If Cheylan . . .

No, of course he wouldn't trust him that much.

Verlon had sworn a bloodvow against Cheylan years ago. He had rescinded it in support of the rebellion, true; but even Kiloran had rescinded his bloodvow against Tansen, whom he hated with an obsessive passion that no truce could ever mitigate. Kiloran had never given up his intention of someday killing Tansen in vengeance for murdering Armian, so it seemed unlikely that Verlon—notoriously hotheaded and malicious—had ever abandoned all hope of someday killing Cheylan, either. Even if Cheylan was cooperating with Verlon for the time being, to strengthen his position, would he trust him enough to invite Verlon's magic into this secret, remote place?

Never. Mirabar was certain.

So the sorcerer who had taught this river to kill an intruder was . . .

"Cheylan." Mirabar shivered as the full force of this realization struck her.

Dar wanted fire and water united in Sileria—by uniting them in the person of Sileria's new ruler.

A child of fire, a child of water . . .

"Of course," she murmured.

The sire was a man from both Marjan and Daurion's bloodlines—but also, Daurion had told her, a man of *unique* power. Cheylan's fire magic wasn't unique; it was the power which he had *in addition to* his fire magic that made him unique.

She was exasperated with herself for not having thought of it before.

Then again, how could she have guessed before now? No one had ever heard of such a thing. Even now, it was difficult to accept. No one in Sileria had ever commanded both fire and water. They were mutually exclusive, incompatible, forever apart. According to legend, Marjan had had to *give up* fire magic to attain mastery over water, because it was impossible to master both elements. This was the world as they had known always know it. This was what they had always all believed.

Now Mirabar wondered distractedly if legend was fanciful. Or just plain wrong. Perhaps when Marjan became so enthralled by water magic he didn't have to *sacrifice* fire magic, he just lost interest in it. And why wouldn't he, after all? A thousand years ago he forced the Beyah-Olvari to teach him a power unknown to anyone else in Sileria, a sorcery against which no one had ever developed any defense. He conquered and murdered Daurion, devastated Shaljir, and was the most powerful man in war-ravaged Sileria until his death, whereupon he became a legend every bit as enduring as the ruler whom he had betrayed.

Yes, what interest would fire magic have held for him once he learned to command water? None, probably. Even if he still used fire magic in minor ways thereafter, it wasn't surprising that it was not part of his legend. Silerians loved a well-told tale too much to spoil it with facts. And given how unusual it was for someone even to be *capable* of power over both elements, Mirabar supposed it was natural that Silerians had believed for centuries that it was, in fact, impossible.

She studied the glowing, crystallized wall of water, curled in the menacing shape it had assumed as it tried to murder her.

"Accept the unbelievable," she murmured.

Oh, yes, if anyone could have—would have—kept such astonishing sorcery a secret, it was Cheylan, who had murdered the innocent, lied to his allies, and betrayed everyone in his quest for personal power. He'd killed the boy Semeon, even if he'd used Verlon's people as his instrument. He had lied repeatedly to Mirabar, since the night they first met, back when Josarian had yet to be revealed as the Firebringer and the Valdani thought they would always hold Sileria. He had convinced Kiloran to murder Jalilar and her unborn child. . .

Jalilar . . .

Guilt still consumed her as she thought of her part in that. If she had not trusted Cheylan, had not told him . . .

Stop it. There's no time for this now.

He had done it all hoping for . . . What? Had he himself hoped to be the prophesied and undisputed new ruler of Sileria? Yes, it seemed likely his ambitions had flown that high. But when he'd looked into the fire with her at Belitar and heard his destiny written on the flames along with Elelar's . . .

"Then he really is destined to be the father," she whispered to herself. She gazed uneasily at the cavern's ceiling as it groaned slightly. A new trickle of lava fell through to start forming a glowing puddle nearby, which gradually burned a deep hole in the rock as Mirabar watched it, her thoughts churning madly. "Cheylan's not deluded or crazy. It's not a mistake."

And the unthinkable thing which Mirabar had to do was murder the sire of the future ruler of Sileria.

Baran was right. Only death would keep Cheylan from this child. And Daurion had made Mirabar's duty plain: *You will have to be stronger than he.*

Now Mirabar understood why only she could protect Elelar. Who in all of Sileria but a fire sorceress carrying a water-lord's immensely powerful child in her womb could possibly confront Cheylan now, here, with any hope of surviving to take Elelar away from him?

Fire and water, water and fire . . .

Mirabar placed a hand over her stomach, again wondering how to find Elelar. Cheylan wasn't the only threat. Who knew how long these caverns would withstand the volcano's tantrums? The trickles of lava and the intense heat suggested the tunnels could collapse at any moment.

Why here? she wondered. Of all the places Cheylan could have chosen to conceive his child and imprison its mother, why such an uncomfortable and obviously hazardous one?

Had he chosen it because Mirabar had foreseen it, or had she envisioned it because he was bound to choose it? Was he so convinced of his destiny that he believed nothing could harm his pregnant captive, not even earthquakes and eruptions?

Why here?

Suddenly a terrible, piercing, pain-wracked scream echoed through the cavern, filling her with panic and driving all thoughts but one from her head.

"Elelar!"

61

DAR FAVORS THE BRAVE, THE HONORABLE, AND
THE GENEROUS; BUT SHE FAVORS THE FAITHFUL
MOST OF ALL.

—Guardian Prayer

TANSEN'S BLOOD RAN hot with fury at himself, his heart thundering in rejection of what he knew he must finally admit to Faradar.

"I've lost her trail."

The maid looked exhausted and filthy, but she took his bitter announcement with impressive calm. They had already doubled back twice to the last sign of Mirabar's which he'd been able to find, and Faradar evidently knew there was no point in suggesting they try once more. Instead, she said sensibly, "We must go about this in another way, then."

He shook his empty waterskin, his throat raw with thirst, and tried not to think about the condition Mirabar must be in by now. "There's a Sanctuary farther ahead. On the lower slopes of Darshon. We'll get water there."

She nodded and tried to conceal how thirsty she must surely be. They'd already passed two dry streambeds.

Will the rains never come?

Faradar prodded, "And after we find water at the Sanctuary?"

He frowned. "Mirabar thought Cheylan must be hiding Elelar somewhere around Darshon. Underground or in a cave." Considering the way Mirabar had come last night, this seemed increasingly likely. Her trail, where he'd lost it, seemed to be leading straight to Darshon. He gazed up at the tumultuous mountain which completely filled the sky in the dark gray air of this sunless day. "So we'll ask for help from the people who know Darshon and its surroundings better than anyone else."

"The *zanareen*," Faradar breathed.

"Yes." Many of them were still there, on Darshon, mourning the death of the Firebringer, seeking guidance from Dar, and awaiting Her pleasure. Many others had reputedly died in the explosions and eruptions tormenting the mountain since Josarian's death. Thousands of pilgrims were reportedly there, too, as deliriously enraptured by religious fever as the *zanareen* usually were. "If nothing else," Tansen said, "we can organize them to search. Thousands of them. Surely even Cheylan can't evade that many people for long." Especially since most of them had, by all accounts, already demonstrated a stunning disregard for their own lives just by remaining on Darshon. They wouldn't care how dangerous Cheylan was if they thought it was Dar's will that they find him.

Now Tansen and Faradar shrugged off the weight of their own lives, too, as they pursued their duty and their loved ones, heading straight towards the angry volcano as fast as they could travel over the treacherous landscape.

"ELELAR!" MIRABAR SHOUTED again, realizing that if Cheylan was here, her first instinctive cry had already given away her presence and there was no point in attempting secrecy now.

"Help!" The *torena*'s voice echoed all around her, confusing her. "Help!"

"Stop shouting!" Mirabar ordered. "Stop! Do you understand me?"

"Mirabar?"

"Yes! I've come—"

"Argggh!"

Mirabar recognized the shriek as one of pain. "What's wrong?"

Elelar screamed again.

"Elelar!"

"Something's wrong with the baby!"

Damn Cheylan! How could he keep her in a place like this? "Are you injured?"

"No! Well, not badly."

"Stay where you are! I'm going to come to you. I'll keep talking, and you keep telling me when my voice seems closer or farther away."

"Yes, I underst . . . Aghh!"

Mirabar tried to ignore her panic and, when Elelar's scream of pain faded, she asked in a calm voice, "Am I closer or farther?"

No answer.

She's not dead, you're just farther. Keep your head. Try another tunnel.

"Closer or farther?"

"Closer!"

She ventured down that tunnel, talking the whole while. "Where is Cheylan?"

There was a pause as her echoes died, and then Elelar replied, "I don't know. You're closer."

Mirabar came to yet another split in the tunnels. "He's not here?"

"You're farther." As Mirabar doubled back and tried another tunnel, Elelar continued, "No. He comes and he goes. He's been . . ."

Mirabar couldn't hear her anymore and realized she had again chosen wrong. She doubled back. "He's been what?"

"You're closer. He's been gone a long time, this time."

"Do you have any idea how long?"

"Not really. It seems like days. You're closer."

"Ow!"

"Mirabar?"

"It's nothing," she called through tight lips. A tiny drop of lava had fallen onto her shoulder, and she hadn't invoked her power quickly enough to prevent the searing pain. She followed the sound of running water until she came upon one of the stream's branches again. She stooped to wet her sleeve with its soothing chill, then pressed it to the burn. "Am I closer or farther?"

"Closer," Elelar replied, her voice coming clearly from a tunnel on the other side of this chamber.

Mirabar whispered to her daughter, "I'm counting on you," then gritted her teeth and waded through the knee-deep stream, waiting for some new trap to attack her. However, nothing happened, and she breathed with trembling relief when she reached the other side. "Elelar?" she called down the tunnel which had attracted her attention.

"You're closer!" was the excited reply. "Where are you? You sound very close!"

"Not so loud," Mirabar instructed. "It echoes too much, and then I can't tell where your voice is coming from."

"It's his child," Elelar said more quietly. "Cheylan's."

"I know," Mirabar replied, following her voice.

"Is he crazy?"

"No, but he's very, very dangerous."

"I know. We can't let him have the child."

"That's why I've come."

"I'll kill myself before I'll let him have it."

Elelar's voice was very clear now. Mirabar was nearly there. She was peering down the length of the tunnel, dimly lit by dripping lava, glowing plant life, and bright little scurrying things. Her booted foot touched—

"Yaghhh!"

"What?" Elelar cried.

"Blegh! Oh, *yuck!*"

"What?"

Mirabar wiped her boot on the damp lava stone underfoot, her heart thudding with disgust. "I just stepped on some fat, glowing, slithering thing without legs or eyes." She shuddered with revulsion and added, "It's dead now. Whatever it was."

"You're nearly here. I can tell. You sound very . . ." Elelar moaned loudly. "Oh, what's happening? Why does it hurt so much?"

"I don't know." Mirabar snatched her hand away from the tunnel wall an instant before touching something else disgusting. "What does it feel like?"

"It's like exploding lava inside of me. Do you think I'm losing the baby?"

"You can't lose this baby!" Mirabar insisted.

There was a short silence, and then Elelar asked, "Are you saying he's right? This child is . . . the one you've seen in your visions? The one you've prophesied will rule Sileria?"

"Yes, he's right. So we've got to get you out of here and to a Sister right away."

She turned a sharply curving corner and gasped as she found herself on the threshold of a vast cavern of fire and water, identical in every way to the one she'd seen so often in her visions. With one significant difference: a small river of lava flowed through this one.

"Fires of Dar," she murmured.

"It happened recently," Elelar said. "Yesterday? Today? I'm not really sure. Lava broke through that wall."

Mirabar sought her in the dim, steamy air. She finally made out a form huddled on a ledge of rock along the far wall. *"Elelar?"*

She wouldn't have recognized her had she not been expecting to find her. Elelar was pale, wet, filthy, and haggard. She bore several nasty bruises and cuts, and streaks of dried blood marred her skin and clothing. No one would have ever taken her for a *torena* now.

They stared at each other in mutual astonishment.

"You're pregnant," Elelar said slowly.

"Does it show?" Mirabar asked in surprise. She looked down and saw how wet she was. Ah, that explained it. Her normally modest clothing was damply plastered to her body, now revealing the small but distinct bulge which is usually concealed.

"Is it Baran's?"

She glared at Elelar. "Of course it's Baran's."

"Oh. I didn't mean—" Elelar's face contorted with agony. "Oh, this *pain*, Mirabar," she gasped out after a few tormented moments. "Is this my punishment? For the things I've done?"

"Perhaps," Mirabar said, hoping it would forestall panic. She herself had suffered nausea and dark moods in her pregnancy, but no pain. She had a feeling Elelar's agony was, in fact, a very alarming sign; she just didn't see that it would help matters to say so. "Can you walk? We have to leave before Cheylan returns."

"Yes, I think . . ." The *torena* pushed herself away from the rock and started to ease herself down to the cave floor. The mountain rumbled menacingly, the cave moaning and creaking all around them as the cavern shook and lava roared through the mountain. Elelar screamed, doubled over in pain, fell off her perch, and tumbled down to the hard cave floor.

"Elelar!"

Mirabar gathered her strength, shielded herself with the fiery power she commanded, and then plunged into the lava flow separating her from the *torena*. The melting liquid heat was overwhelming, and the child of water in her womb convulsed painfully in response to it.

Don't be afraid, she urged the child, *I can protect you. We must trust each other.*

Worse than the heat was the strength of the current, moving hard and fast. This must be a tributary of the caldera, flowing with fierce energy towards the very heart of Dar's power.

Mirabar dragged herself through it, resisting the force with which the flow tried to propel her out of the cavern and into another tunnel. She emerged from the river of fire unharmed but briefly exhausted. She paused for a moment, her heart pounding, and then staggered over to the prostrate *torena*. Seeing that she was unconscious, Mirabar dragged her to the river of water also flowing through the chaotic cavern and started splashing it generously onto her face. Elelar coughed and opened her eyes.

"I don't know how I'm going to get you past that lava flow," Mirabar admitted. "Can we find another way out of here?"

"I've tried," Elelar said weakly. "He always prevents me. But now that you're here . . . Maybe we can get past the fires he uses to block the way. Even so . . . We may . . ."

"Get lost?"

"Yes . . ." Elelar laughed weakly.

"What?"

"Well, you have to admit. The irony of this . . ."

"Oh."

"You here. Risking everything . . . to save me, of all people."

"Let's not dwell on the irony right now, *torena*," Mirabar suggested, trying to help her to her feet.

"I know you sent him to kill me."

"No, I sent him to bring you to Belitar where I could prot—"

"I mean Tansen," Elelar rasped. "I know you sent him to Chandar to kill me after Josarian died. I know how much you wanted me dead."

"Well, aren't we lucky Tansen couldn't bring himself to do it?" Mirabar said dryly. "Otherwise, you and I might never have had this heartwarming reunion."

Elelar sputtered with laughter. "You're starting to sound like Baran."

"There's no need to be insult . . ."

She felt it then, like a sharp shock to her system. That blood-tingling mingling of hot-and-cold power she always sensed when he approached. She had just never before realized what it meant. Apparently no one had, not Kiloran, not anyone. Because none of them had ever felt it before, and so they had no way of understanding it. Because the truth about Cheylan was too impossible for anyone to suspect.

Fire and water, water and fire . . .

"Mirabar?" Elelar prodded. "What is it?"

"Cheylan's here," she warned.

Elelar quivered in her supportive grasp. "How do you know?"

"I can feel him. He's here."

"Can we hide?"

"It's too late," Mirabar said, dread and resignation sinking into her. "He knows I'm here." If she felt Cheylan's power nearby, then he felt hers, too.

"What'll we—"

"We make our stand," Mirabar said. "Here. Now. Against him. There is no other way." Elelar was clearly too weak to run, even if they had any idea where to go. The one escape route Mirabar could follow—the one she had marked with her own torches—was on the other side of that lava flow.

"No, you get away," Elelar urged. "Go! You know he won't kill me. He can't. So—"

"He'll just take you away, and I'll have to start searching for you again."

"But—"

"And he won't leave you alone and unguarded again. Not after this. I'll have to face him sooner or later. So I'll do it now."

"Mirabar . . ." Elelar made a helpless gesture and then, as they awaited Cheylan's approach, said the last thing Mirabar would have expected under the circumstances. "Tansen loves you, not me."

"I know." Mirabar pushed Elelar behind her. "But he'll be very unhappy, even so, if you die."

MIRABAR.

Cheylan knew who was here the moment he felt that bright, golden wave of power emanating from her. She was *here*. And if he felt her, then she felt him.

How had she gotten here, through the maze of tunnels it had taken him years to learn? Had her visions led her here to challenge him? How had she gotten past the water warding these caverns? Was her fire magic even more powerful than he'd realized?

Cheylan braced himself. She would be hard to kill. He had always known that; but there were things about him which she didn't know, aspects of his own power which she couldn't fight.

He entered the cavern, prepared for what he must now do.

"Cheylan," Elelar hissed, her voice full of hatred.

He ignored her, momentarily shocked by what he saw: a lava flow had broken through one wall.

Cheylan stared at it, feeling betrayed. Dar should protect the offspring which Her power had blessed at the moment of conception. Instead, She had come close to killing it. Even with one sweeping glance he could see it was very lucky that Elelar had survived.

The *torena* was a filthy blood-streaked heap on the ground behind Mirabar. She had obviously been injured during an earthquake. That sense of Dar's betrayal, Her recklessness, washed through him again with a cold shock.

Standing protectively in front of Elelar, Mirabar gazed at Cheylan with those bright golden eyes so like his own. Her filthy wet clothing clung to her body, revealing more of her than he'd ever seen before . . . Revealing her belly swelling with Baran's child.

The sense of betrayal was hot this time. "It didn't have to be this way," he told her, knowing there was really very little for them to say to each other.

"Didn't it?"

"You chose Baran. You chose Tansen. If only you had—"

"Oh, no," she said. "This isn't about me, Cheylan. If it had been, you wouldn't have told me so many lies."

"If you could have trusted me, then—"

"I trusted you, and you had Verlon kill Semeon. I trusted you again, and you had Kiloran kill Jalilar."

His brows lifted as he realized how much she had guessed.

"I trusted you," she continued, "and you've done this to the *torena*."

"You made it clear you would oppose me if you knew the truth. I had no choice."

"If I had trusted you even more, who else would have died?" She shook her head. "You've betrayed everyone. There is no one who hasn't been hurt by trusting you. No, this was never about *me*, Cheylan. This is just your nature." Her glowing eyes narrowed. "I'm ashamed I let you fool me for so long, even though I know now that you've fooled everyone for a long time and are very good at lies and deceit, at gaining trust from those whom you mean only to use and betray."

He reached out with his senses to caress the flowing water while she spoke, lecturing him as if expecting him to apologize and hand over the *torena* to her. Mirabar stood recklessly close to the stream, ignorant of the power he wielded over it. Unaware that he would momentarily use it to kill her. She expected fire, was braced for the attack of another Guardian. She was no doubt planning her own fiery assault, thinking he would fight back with power she understood and commanded as well as he did.

He would fool her once again. For the very last time.

"I know how hard your life was," Mirabar continued. "The superstition, the rejection, the loneliness. But it's *because* I know that I can never excuse what you became. I lived with the same burdens, and I didn't become like you."

The water bubbled gently in the grasp of his power, flexing boldly as it came to life in the embrace of his sorcery.

Mirabar said, "Semeon lived with those burdens, too, and you helped murder him." She nodded slowly. "You are exactly as Daurion described you, and I know what I have to do."

"So do I, *sirana*," he murmured, launching his attack.

Elelar screamed, *"Mirabar!"*

Mirabar burst into flames as the stream rose and engulfed her from behind. Great writhing tentacles of water came around her, cold enough now to kill her flesh upon contact. Her controlled self-immolation would protect her from the deadly chill. Cheylan was disappointed she'd reflexively chosen such a defense when Elelar screamed. Still, it wouldn't save her; it just meant he had to try a little harder.

Moving forward, he commanded the watery arms fighting their way through Mirabar's fire to embrace her tightly enough to capture her, then drag her into the stream, under its surface, and drown her.

"Mirabar!" Elelar scrambled to her feet and moved towards the frantically writhing mass of fire and water.

"No!" Cheylan leapt forward and grabbed the *torena*, hauling her away from the struggling Guardian whose leaping flames fought wildly with the shifting water seeking her weaknesses.

"Stop it!" Elelar screamed, fighting him as he held her back.

"Do you want to die with her?" he snapped.

She twisted in his arms, and when she aimed a blow at his eye, he lost patience and hit her—the first time in his life he'd ever struck a woman. Elelar fell to the ground, but then immediately began crawling towards Mirabar. Exasperated, Cheylan seized her long hair and yanked on it.

"No!" Elelar screamed.

Cheylan watched with satisfaction—and, if truth be known, some relief—as the whirl of lava and fire protecting Mirabar was slowly, inexorably dragged under the water's surface. It wouldn't take long now. Shooting flames pulsated frantically in the river, but it would quickly exhaust her to keep generating that much fire underwater. Few Guardians could do it at all, and he doubted even Mirabar could do it for long. Especially when she couldn't breathe. Yes, one way or the other, she had only moments left. Drowning her might not be very original, but it was effective, and that's all that—

He gasped as some new intruder suddenly flooded his river with icy fury, fighting back. Wild, undisciplined, immensely talented, it was a power which careened unpredictably against his senses as it sought a relationship with the water in which it had suddenly sprung to life.

What is *that?*

The water started pulling away from his will, ignoring his coaxing, resisting his seduction.

"No."

It wasn't possible!

Cheylan clenched his teeth and fought it, focusing all his strength on keeping the underground river within his control. It didn't matter. Drop by drop, something was challenging him, fighting with such reckless desperation that he could only conclude that it was Mirabar herself.

Or . . .

Fires of Dar . . .

Something *inside* of Mirabar. Something which would die if she died. A power so bound to Mirabar's life that it would commit everything to saving it.

"Baran's child?" he breathed.

Water geysered up around Mirabar, and Cheylan felt his fluid deathgrip pushed away from her with tremendous force. The release was so sudden that her combative fire shot into the air, hissing as it mingled with the water and filling the hot cavern with more steam.

"What's happening?" Elelar cried.

"No!" Cheylan shouted, fighting back.

As was so often the case when two water wizards reached a stalemate, the river went strangely calm, looking as if no one controlled it.

"Mirabar?" Elelar choked out, crawling past Cheylan.

He lifted Elelar to her feet and shoved her out of harm's way, realizing what would happen next. Elelar staggered backwards into a rough stone wall and stayed there, her face stupid with astonishment as she watched Mirabar rise out of the river, soaked, coughing, and already blazing with offensive fury.

Cheylan called spears of fire out of the nearby lava flow and sent a shower of them flying straight at her. Water rose up in a sudden wave to shield her, and the lava spears sizzled as they met it, then fell like dead birds into the stream. Mirabar flung balls of fire at him which he deflected with his palms.

"You knew!" he snarled, stunned by her trick. She'd *let* him drag her into the river, disarming him and giving her child a chance to use the physical immersion to wrest it away from him.

"You think I stood there talking your ears off because it gave me satisfaction?" she snarled back. "I had no idea it would take you so long to gather your power. You're not as strong as I feared."

He recognized her tactics and ignored the insult. "You *did* stumble into my water traps," he guessed, stopping the bolts of fire which she hurled at him. "That's how you found out the truth."

She came closer. "You can't kill me with water, and I think you already knew you couldn't kill me with fire."

"You can't kill me, either," he warned.

Drenched from the river, her skin still shimmering with defensive flame, she stared at him for a long moment, panting breathlessly. Finally, she nodded. "What do we do now?"

"I take the *torena* and leave."

"Cheylan." She staggered forward, her steps weary, her expression wary. "Even if you think you can leave me here to die . . ."

"I didn't say that."

"Do you have to keep lying?" she said irritably. "You'd douse my torches and leave me to wander here, lost until I starved or died in an earthquake or eruption."

"Is there any reason I shouldn't?"

She came closer. "It's over, Cheylan. Surely you can see that?"

"No, Mirabar," he said, "I don't see that at all. *I* see that I've got the two most important women in Sileria captive here, as well as their offspring."

She shook her head. "The Emeldari and all their allies will want you dead because of Jalilar. Kiloran will come after you because you've betrayed him. Tansen will hunt you down. Even if Verlon trusts you now, he won't for long."

A few steps closer, and he might be able to kill her with his bare hands. He'd never done anything like that before, and she'd defend herself—so they might wind up in precisely the same stalemate they'd just experienced. But it was worth a try, since he was running out of options.

"Give this up, Cheylan," she urged. "Let me take the *torena* out of here. It's your child. It will always be your child. He'll rule Sileria."

"And me?" he prodded.

"Leave Sileria. Promise me you'll never come back."

"The stud who has fulfilled his purpose?"

"You'd get to live. It's more than you'll get if you stay in Sileria." She came so close he could have touched her.

"Leave Sileria and live?" he murmured as if starting to seriously consider the suggestion.

"Yes," she urged, taking another step forward.

He seized her throat. Her leg came up, her knee jabbing into him. He thought for a moment that she was trying to land a blow to his groin—and then the *pain* in his belly! Bitter cold, sharp, brutal, deadly. Unlike anything he'd ever known.

He lost his grip on her throat as agony sent him reeling and drove him to his knees. Instead of escaping, she clung to him, sinking to the hot stone floor with him. She roughly yanked sideways with her arm, gutting him, splitting him open, and the horrific pain made him scream. The sound echoed around the cavern, and the mountain rumbled in response.

"No!" he shouted, furious, betrayed, incredulous.

Mirabar pulled the icy blade out of his gut and then scrambled awkwardly away from him. She was already soaked in his blood. Her right arm was especially bright with it, from the elbow all the way down to the small hand which clutched . . .

"A . . . *shir?*" he rasped.

He collapsed completely, falling facedown on the floor.

He dimly heard her rise to her feet. His blood thundered with frantic pain. He felt a hot pool spreading around him . . . the huge wound she had opened in his body now gushing his life out onto the cavern floor.

No . . .

Where was Dar now? Where was Her favor?

He was so talented. So full of promise gone unacknowledged, ability gone unrecognized, merit gone unrewarded. . . .

Dying?

No!

He saw the lava flow glowing dimly in the encroaching darkness. The betrayal was horrible. Cold, so cold. Dar, the only one with whom he had ever kept faith—always, without fail—had now forsaken him.

Why?

Dar, as I have been faithful and true . . .

"Mirabar," he mumbled.

The mountain was rumbling violently now. So loud, so fierce. Or did it just seem that way because his ear was pressed to the cave floor, so rough against his cheek?

The pain wasn't so bad now. But he was terribly cold. And

the lava flow . . . It was gone. Everything was gone. All black now.

"Mira . . ." he called.

Maybe she heard him and understood. Because now she who had killed him began chanting, praying for Dar and the Otherworld to welcome him. It was his right, to die with the proper prayers.

Dying? No! No, please!

It was his right . . . He was a Guardian, and he had always been faithful to Dar.

Yes, the mountain was roaring now. Angry. Hah! Mirabar would regret this work. Dar was enraged. She had not wanted him to die with all his promise unfulfilled.

Yes. Dar would punish Mirabar for this.

It was a pleasing thought to embrace as death reached out for him.

"WHERE DID YOU *get* that?" Elelar asked her faintly.

Mirabar tucked the *shir* back into the boot where she'd kept it hidden. The feel of Cheylan's blood and vulnerable human flesh were still hot on her hands. She wanted to vomit or weep now, but she forced herself to speak evenly.

"We were ambushed at Gamalan last night." She paused and added vaguely, "Well, I *think* it was last night . . . And I killed an assassin." She had kept the *shir* because she knew that her own power might not be enough of an advantage against Cheylan when she finally faced him.

The *torena* stared down at Cheylan's corpse, then took a few steps back as the pool of blood spread towards her feet. "Even if he had left Sileria, he would have come back."

"He never would have left," Mirabar said with certainty, gazing at his body with mingled loathing and sorrow. "Cheylan had gone too far down his road to ever turn back. He never could have admitted he'd chosen badly. Never would have accepted that anything mattered but what *he* wanted, or that his desires weren't the same thing as his destiny."

Elelar glanced at her in surprise. "You *planned* to stab him," she guessed. "That's why you got so close."

Mirabar nodded. "Once I realized that, just as I'd feared, I couldn't beat him with fire, I knew I had to use the blade. But I'm not skilled with the *shir*, not like Najdan. So I couldn't let Cheylan see it in my hand, see the blow coming. He had to be concentrating on something else for me to take my one chance and succeed with it."

"Something else?" Elelar repeated. "Like breaking your neck?"

Mirabar rubbed her throat. "Actually, I was hoping he'd kiss me. It was how he usually tried to influence me in the past."

"Sex or violence. It's how men *always* try to influence a woman," Elelar said, evidently feeling more like her old self.

Mirabar shuddered with delayed reaction. "The sudden attempt to break my neck . . . That scared me."

"Yes," Elelar said dryly, "I can see how that might be alarming."

The roar and rumble of the mountain got louder. "We have to get out of here," Mirabar said, dragging her attention away from the man she had just killed.

Elelar nodded, then gestured to the lava flow. "Can you think of any way . . ." Her dark eyes widened and her voice trailed off as the cavern started shaking. "Oh, *no*."

Oh, no.

Mirabar looked around, trying to guess where they'd be safest as the earthquake began. She felt Elelar clutch her hand, and she returned the grip, as scared as the *torena*.

"Against the wall," Mirabar shouted, hoping she was right. She started to drag Elelar with her.

The cave suddenly rocked hard, throwing them around like feathers on the wind. Mirabar lost her grip on Elelar, who staggered backwards as Mirabar stumbled forwards. Elelar fell down, then screamed and rolled farther away a bare instant before shattering rocks landed where she had fallen. Mirabar sought to protect her unborn child from harm as she was hurled down onto the shuddering ground while the mountain roared and the cavern ceiling groaned.

"Elelar!" she shouted, trying to crawl towards the *torena* as this hidden world of fire and water tore itself apart.

Elelar was trying to shield her head from a shower of falling rock and dust. "Stay back!" she shouted at Mirabar, pointing to the cavern ceiling. "It's coming down!"

Mirabar looked up and froze with horror. The high cavern ceiling moaned hideously, then bulged and writhed as if coming to life. *"No."* She looked at Elelar again. "Run!"

Elelar looked behind her, to where the lava flow blocked her path to any passages on that side of the cavern. She turned her desperate gaze back to Mirabar, then pushed herself to her feet, took three staggering steps towards her, and was again thrown to the ground by the heaving and shaking.

Mirabar crawled forward as she kept her own gaze fixed on the bulging ceiling. "Yes! Come on! It's your only chance!"

"Go!" Elelar shouted at her, hauling herself forward over broken rock. "Go now! Don't wait for me! *Go!*"

"Come *on!*" Mirabar screamed, crawling closer, stretching out her arm. "Faster!" She was thrown sideways as the ground quivered roughly again.

Elelar scrambled to her hands and knees—then collapsed without making a sound when a falling rock plummeted straight into her head. She lifted her bleeding face from the ground and tried again, fumbling clumsily as Mirabar tried to move forward over undulating, shivering rock.

There was a terrible explosion. Blood-chilling. Bone-freezing. Then Mirabar heard the sound of cracking walls, tumbling rock . . . and the fury of lava bursting through solid stone. She looked up and saw the bulging ceiling glow gold, then orange.

"No!"

The ceiling collapsed with a furious wail of protesting rock and explosive fire. Elelar's scream of terror and agony was high-pitched as the enormous river of falling lava engulfed her, sweeping her into its fiery, destructive embrace.

"*Elelar!*" Mirabar screamed as the *torena* disappeared in the torrent of liquid fire.

No! No, it couldn't come to this! No!

In her fury and despair, Mirabar barely remembered to shield herself in time as the river of fire flooded the cave, completely engulfing her, too, and swept her into its raging current.

62

THIS IS DARSHON, WHERE ALL STAND HELPLESS
AND HUSHED BEFORE THE GODDESS.
—Jalan the *Zanar*

THE SEA BECAME even rougher as another grimly black night took the place of the dark gray day. The Lascari boat heaved wildly as the volcano roared and the distant coast rumbled with another earthquake. Wave after wave of seawater washed across the deck. They tried to keep lanterns burning so other boats could see them and avoid collision, but the sea kept dousing them. It probably didn't matter, Zarien knew; no one could really navigate on tonight's vicious sea, anyhow. Some would collide and perhaps die. That was simply the price of being sea-born when the sea was wrathful and cruel.

"No, don't!" Zarien shouted at *Toren* Ronall as he tried to tie himself to the mast. "If the boat goes down, you'll drown."

"I thought I was supposed to stay with the boat?" Ronall shouted back.

"Not if it goes down!"

"Let's not talk about the boat going down! Agreed?"

Zarien looked over at Najdan, noticing that even he looked as if he wanted to be sick tonight.

"So, Zarien," Ronall shouted above the roar of sea and land and sky, "do you indeed feel safer here, farther out at sea?"

Zarien laughed. Ronall shook his head. Najdan looked mean.

"Zarien!"

He turned to Linyan, who ordered him to help haul down the foresail, which had come loose, unrolled, and was now flapping wildly. Zarien, who could scarcely even see it in the intense dark, shouted his acknowledgment. It would be too dangerous to brail the sail back up to the yard again right now, and they couldn't leave it flapping like that.

"No!" Ronall shouted, reaching for him as he moved to go do the work. "Stay here!"

"I'll be fine," Zarien shouted back.

"No!" Najdan said, for once in agreement with the *toren* about something.

Zarien evaded Ronall's grasp. "It has to be—"

"I said no!" Najdan warned him.

"This is no time— *Agh!*"

Zarien blacked out for a moment as something struck him in a blur of motion. Vision dark and head pounding, he suddenly found himself lying on the deck, confused and stunned, with someone's foot planted in his back. He groaned, then he felt hands hauling him to an upright position.

"Are you out of your mind?" Ronall demanded, his voice coming as if from a distance.

I was only going to . . . Zarien's tongue wouldn't obey.

Then Najdan's voice. "He is overconfident and reckless. It's clearly not safe."

"You didn't have to hit him!"

"It's easier than arguing. He is a *very* argumentative boy. Tansen should beat him."

"*Tansen* doesn't approve of people hitting the boy."

"That could explain his bad behavior."

Ronall said something critical about assassins. Zarien started pulling his senses together. Now he heard Linyan shouting at Najdan.

"If he is not one of you," Najdan snapped at Linyan in common Silerian, "then don't expect him to do your bidding on your boat. Your habit of excluding him until it's convenient for you to include him is very distasteful." He added ominously, "Tansen wouldn't like it."

The roar of the sea got louder, and Zarien couldn't hear whatever else they all said. There was another explosion in the distance. This one seemed very noisy, almost teeth-shatteringly loud . . . but maybe that was because *Najdan* had just hit him in the head.

I really hate him.

Feeling indignant and ill-used by everyone, Zarien grabbed a rope tied around the mast and started hauling himself to his feet.

Furious at them all, he began, "If anyone *else* . . ."

But they'd forgotten him. Instead, they were all staring past him with horrified expressions which were clearly visible even in the dim light from the sole remaining lantern. Their faces suddenly looked so alike it would have been comical if it weren't so terrifying. He whirled around to see what held them all frozen with dread even at the same moment that the screams of the other Lascari aboard the boat made his stomach clench.

We're dead.

It was all he had time to think before the enormous wave hit them, sweeping him off the deck and into the furious sea.

TANSEN HAULED FARADAR to her feet. She was breathing hard and looked dizzy, having been thrown hard to the rocky ground when the earthquake hit. Faradar looked up as something exploded in the sky, then she gasped and flinched.

Tansen looked up, too, and saw lava shoot straight up out of the caldera, piercing the colored clouds and shifting lights at Darshon's summit. The fountain of liquid fire glowed brightly against the heavy black sky before falling through the air to paint the mountain with hundreds of fiery rivulets which began flowing down Darshon's slopes.

"How can anyone survive here?" Faradar asked hoarsely.

"But they are surviving," Tansen said. "Some of them, anyhow. Can't you hear them?" Their noise was faint but discernible as the mountain's roar slowly faded.

"Hear . . ." She blinked, then drew a sharp breath through her nostrils. "What *is* that? That . . . wailing, that chanting, that . . . Those *sounds?*"

"The pilgrims." He'd known about this from local gossip, but it was the first time he'd heard it for himself. "Praise singers. Worshippers. Ecstatic devotion."

"They sound insane," Faradar said.

He looked up at the menacing peak of Darshon beneath which the pilgrims lived and said, "They probably are."

MIRABAR STRUGGLED TO survive as the searing river of lava gathered speed, shot her forward like an arrow loosed from a bow, let her fall like a dead bird, and then dumped her on some unyielding surface, the lava's own fluid texture being her only protection against the force of her landing.

She couldn't breathe. She *had* to breathe. She would die if she couldn't get air in another instant.

She lifted her head, praying the insane journey was over, and started trying to break through the fiery lava covering her. She felt weak, exhausted, at the end of her strength. She had to get out of this flow or she'd be dead in moments. She couldn't protect herself from this liquid fire any longer.

Mirabar brushed lava from her face as if it were sticky syrup, then inhaled the hot, fume-thick air as soon as her nostrils were clear. She choked, wiped her mouth, then shook her head and rubbed at her eyes.

Screams assaulted her ears as the lava started melting away from them. She looked around in scared confusion and saw areas of blackness. Darkness. Something which wasn't lava, whatever else it might be. She started crawling towards it, relieved the current was no longer so strong. It was as if the lava were now willing to release her.

I'm not dead. I'm not dead. Dar be praised, I'm not dead.

She reached the rough ground, free of the flow, and started commanding the remaining lava to melt away from her body. Only then did any other thought enter her mind.

Where am I? And what is all that noise?

She looked around.

Darfire!

There were people everywhere, many of them holding torches—spots of golden light amidst the mingled black of the land and the glowing orange rivers of lava flows. Lava everywhere. Some of these people gaped at her in wide-eyed shock, which she supposed was understandable. Others were screaming, though they seemed more exultant than scared.

Lava flows everywhere . . .

Mirabar looked up and saw Darshon's tumultuous summit above her. She was just below the the snow line.

"I'm on the slopes of Darshon," she murmured.

Mirabar studied the lava flow she had just escaped. It was coming from the summit. It had evidently carried her straight up from the underground caverns and through the caldera itself. Tears misted her eyes. She had been in Dar's presence, in Dar's abode, in the very womb of Dar's divine power! She had been where no one else had ever survived going except for Josarian himself. The Firebringer . . .

She gasped as she realized who else Dar might have wanted to survive such an ordeal.

"Have you seen another woman?" Mirabar demanded of the people surrounding her.

"What?"

"Someone like me. Someone else who, uh . . ." She gestured to the lava flow.

"Someone brought here by Dar?"

"Yes!"

"Only you, *sirana*."

"She may still be alive! I've got to find her!"

"Are you . . . are you Dar in the flesh?"

"No!" she replied, startled. "I'm Mirabar."

"Mirabar! Mirabar!"

"Not now!" she shouted. "I've got to find *Torena* Elelar! You've got to help me!"

But they were already chanting louder, lost in a delirium of blind worship and joyful rapture.

"Mirabar! Mirabar! Mirabar!"

"ZARIEN!" RONALL SCREAMED—then choked as water filled his nose and mouth.

No!

Gone. Zarien was gone.

Ronall couldn't see, breathe, or speak. The boat plunged and keeled madly as the enormous wave assaulted it, nearly drowning them all. For a long, horrifying moment, he was absolutely sure the vessel would go under. There seemed no hope, no escape. Then, by some miracle, it righted itself—heaving so hard that he hit the deck headfirst and almost lost his grip on his rope. Then he felt someone move past him and realized it was Najdan, going after the boy.

Ronall tried to grab him, sensing that pursuit was futile. Certain death. Hopeless and pointless.

Then Najdan was gone, too.

Of course, Ronall realized. The assassin had pledged his life to protect Zarien. So he'd rather die than stay with the boat while letting the boy drown.

Zarien . . .

"No!" Ronall howled.

He could hear the frantic screams of the Lascari. There was a hideous shudder and terrible crashing noise as the sea tossed this boat into another one. Then they sprang backwards, rebounding from the blow, only to be slapped around by another wave.

"Dar!" Ronall screamed, choking on the seawater battering him as he flailed around, clinging to the rope and being repeatedly flung against hard surfaces. "Stop, damn you! *Stop!*"

Zarien . . .

That boy, so lost, so young, so confused. And Najdan, such a complete contrast to the boy.

They had been Ronall's friends, in a way. At least, he wanted to think so as he wept for their deaths.

Their deaths . . .

It came to him then, what he must do, why he had come here. He couldn't save the Valdani in Sileria—how could he even have imagined himself meeting such a formidable challenge? Perhaps he couldn't even save the drowning sea-born boy, nor the grim assassin . . . But he would die trying.

He had left Shaljir so long ago, it seemed, fleeing Elelar's hatred and seeking death. Seeking an end to his pointless existence, an escape from his soul-deep hunger for something he could never even define.

"Zarien!" Ronall screamed again.

May the Three have mercy on my soul. May Dar welcome me as I travel to the Otherworld. . . .

Weeping with terror and a terrible elation, Ronall let go of the rope as another wave assaulted the boat. He staggered as the boat heaved, then he flew overboard with sickening speed as the sea attacked, engulfed, and carried him away.

He had avoided death the many times it had come courting him on land after he'd fled Shaljir. He had run, hid, broken his private vow over and over, and so he was still alive.

Now his body plunged below the churning surface. He'd

already lost all sense of direction, had no idea which way Zarien had fallen or where the boy might be now. He fought to reach the surface again.

"Zarien!" he shouted as his head emerged.

Waves covered him, forcing him back under. His body started panicking, fighting for air, burning for breath; but his mind was calm.

He would finally end the long, coy seduction and let death embrace him. The only way Dar and the Three could convince him they didn't want him dead was to let him find and save the boy. If he couldn't even do that, then he was ready for it all to be over.

Something enormous briefly bumped him. He lost control and inhaled involuntarily. Suffocating and choking, he again rose towards the surface, wondering what had hit him. Coughing and heaving as he bobbed up out of the water, he found the swelling waves moving rhythmically enough, for the moment, that he could catch his breath and look around.

"Zarien!"

He thought he heard a voice.

Scarcely daring to believe it, he started swimming towards it, cursing himself for never having learned to swim well.

"Zarien!"

This time he heard it, above the roar of the dark sea and the distant thunder of the volcano: *"Toren!"*

"Zarien!"

"Where are you?"

"Over here! Where are you?"

"Keep talking!" the boy shouted. "I can find you by your voice!"

"Najdan's in the water, too!"

"We'll find him!" Zarien shouted back. "Keep talking! I'm coming!"

Ronall wasn't sure that treading water and shouting to the boy counted as rescuing him, but it did seem rather like an answer to the ultimatum he had given the gods. Perhaps they didn't want him dead, after all. Perhaps he was indeed meant to live. Maybe even *he* counted for something in this chaotic world.

There had been very few moments of real happiness in his life, so he wasn't quite sure if that was what he felt now. It was not an emotion he had much experience recognizing.

Then Zarien's voice came, from much closer than he'd expected, full of panic: *"Ronall! No!"*

He felt the sudden, shocking blow, the immense power and weight and size rushing into him with malicious violence.

Then there was nothing. Only darkness. Only the sea.

"MIRABAR! MIRABAR! MIRABAR!"

"Have you come to show us Dar's chosen one?"

"We have waited for a sign!"

"Quiet!" Mirabar snapped, pushing her way past endless throngs of pilgrims.

The mountain roared again, filling Mirabar's head with its angry tantrum. The terrible noise seemed to penetrate her bones, flooding the night, filling her blood.

Oh, and the *heat* of all these lava flows. Its intensity melted snow from the summit, then turned the water into steam, creating a bewildering veil of fog broken by occasional explosions and sudden bursts of flame. Her skin was hot, like any normal person's skin would be in such oppressive air, and she was sweating as the cool glow in her belly quivered in weary pleading.

She placed her hands over her stomach, trying to comfort her daughter in this strange place, surrounded by people who made her sorry she'd ever once called Baran crazy. Mirabar started pulling her clothing away from her sweat-drenched body, shaking in reaction to her ordeal. She gasped and nearly jumped out of her skin as steam suddenly spewed out of the ground nearby.

"Wait . . ." She looked around. "I've felt this before. Been here before." Yes. In a vision. She closed her eyes and listened.

The chanting . . . Yes, it was familiar, she'd heard it before, but only in her tormented mind. Beyond the shrieking of her name she heard other voices, other songs. Chanting. Trilling. Ululating. A bewildering mixture of voices filled with passion and fervor, ecstatic praise-singing flooding the hot, roaring night with fearsome urgency. Her head was reeling with it!

The ground was shaking again, but it wasn't an earthquake this time. It was power . . . tremendous power. Lava moving through the veins of the mountain, flowing somewhere beneath her feet, making the ground tremble with Dar's blood, Dar's breath, Dar's life . . . Mirabar gasped and leapt back as more lava erupted at her feet, its intense heat making her dizzy, weakened as she already was. The fumes, the sudden flames erupting out of the flowing ooze of the lava spilling forth from the world's womb . . .

Now a woman was screaming. Her panic and pain were distant, nearly drowned out by the fervent wail of the praise singers.

"Quiet!" Mirabar shouted at them all, but they ignored her and continued singing, their bodies writhing in frenzied dances.

Mirabar watched in astonishment as some of them danced upon the lava, apparently impervious to it . . . Or no. Not *all* of them. Lava sucked in one wailing worshipper, whirled around him, and flowed over his body. Flames ignited in his long hair. He died screaming right in front of her, sinking into the lava as she would have expected all of them to do. The others continued dancing atop the lava as if oblivious to the horrible death.

Who were the ones who lived, Mirabar wondered in a daze? Were they Guardians? *Zanareen?* The favored faithful? Their clothes were in such tatters, it was impossible to tell who they had been before they had come to Darshon to be . . . whatever they were now.

She grasped one of the lava dancers, taking her by the shoulders and gazing hard into her wild-eyed face. "Are you a Guardian?"

"No, *sirana!* I am only a humble worshipper of Dar's divine—"

"Why are you here?"

"To praise Dar!" she cried gleefully.

"Dar demands praise!" someone else screeched.

"Praise Dar and welcome Her judgment!"

They started ululating wildly, drowning out whatever other questions Mirabar wanted to ask.

Through their shrill ecstasy, Mirabar heard more screaming. She looked around desperately, unable to tell where it was coming from. "Where is she?"

"Dar is in the—"

"No! That woman who's screaming! Where is she?"

"Screaming?"

Screaming! Screaming for help. For mercy. Screaming in pain, in terror!

"We've got to help her!" Mirabar shouted, turning and wading through the lava upon which they were dancing—the lava in which she had just watched someone die horribly. Whatever power enabled them to dance on its surface, Mirabar didn't possess it; and if their obvious madness was inseparable from that strange talent, then she was quite willing to forego it. She pushed her way through the lava flow as if it were heavy, thigh-deep mud.

Oh, how it burned! She was so tired now, so weak, the searing heat pained her, scared her. The agony was unbearable, but the screams pulled her on.

Someone asked, "Who's she looking for?"

Wild-eyed pilgrims continued reeling in divine rapture on the liquid fire, shrieking and trilling, praising Mirabar's name.

"She emerged from the holy caldera in a river of fire! She is beloved of Dar! Praise her! Sing her name!"

"No, don't!" Mirabar shouted. "Just help me!"

"Mirabar! Mirabar! Mirabar!"

"What help can we offer, *sirana?* Shall we fling ourselves into the caldera to prove our love of Dar?"

"*No!* Help m**e** find Elelar! Can't you hear her screaming?"

Was it Elelar? **Or** was it only more of these mad pilgrims dying farther up t**he** mountain?

"The screaming . . ." A mud-streaked pilgrim's face suddenly focused with alert interest. "Yes. I hear it! I do!"

"I do, too! Yes, I hear it!"

"Move out of my way," Mirabar said, trying to get out of the lava flow and onto solid ground again.

The screams were louder now, beckoning to her over the lava's roar and the intense, hysterical trilling of the worshippers.

"Elelar!" Mirabar shouted, now running across rough ground, choking on fumes and trying to see through the smoke, steam, and ash clouding the air. "Elelar!"

Screams of unthinkable agony, unfathomable pain. Screams unlike anything Mirabar had ever heard even in this tormented, war-torn land.

"Elelar!"

"Sirana?"

She looked around to see who had addressed her. A man stumbled through the ankle-deep volcanic cinders to reach her. He was so filthy it took her a moment to recognize him. "Jalan?"

"Sirana!" Jalan cried. "She who foresaw Josarian! She who—"

"Tell me—"

"Have you come to offer yourself to Dar, too?"

She seized his shoulders. "What's happening here?"

"There is life in the new lava flow!" he cried gleefully. "Divine life! Our prayers and praise, our devoted worship, our—"

"What life? What lava flow? Show me!"

"Just here! See? We praise Dar for bringing you to us! You can tell us what this means! Has the Firebringer returned?"

"Josarian?"

"Who else could it be?"

Jalan dragged her through more huddles of praise singers chanting with relentless fervor, then pointed through the misty, glowing air to another broad lava flow and announced, "He is coming!"

Mirabar drew in a sharp breath. "He is coming . . ."

She walked forward, the screams scraping harshly along her senses now, so awful they brought tears of sympathy to her eyes. But she knew that wasn't Josarian screaming. It was a woman. And her voice was coming from within the river of fire which Mirabar approached.

It was impossible. The *torena* wasn't even a Guardian.

And I couldn't survive in that flow for as long as she's been in there.

Nonetheless, she shouted, "Elelar!"

The lava erupted in sudden motion, as if it were struggling to rise from the ground. Gradually the heaving shape clarified into . . .

"She has come!" someone cried. "It is Dar taking flesh!"

"Sirana?"

"No," she told Jalan as he approached her, his eyes gleaming with religious passion. "That's not Dar."

"The Firebringer?"

"No." Seeing the grotesque, burning form lurching about in pain and confusion, Mirabar gathered her strength and stepped into the lava flow, steeling herself against the melting heat. "Elelar! I'm here!"

"Sirana!" Jalan followed her. "I will consecrate myself—"

"Stay back!" she ordered Jalan. "Make them stay back, too!"

Uncharacteristically, the *zanar* obeyed her. "Yes, *sirana.*"

Mirabar approached the reeling, screaming figure of lava and flame, talking to it the whole time, and placed her hands on it. It went still and silent, shuddering briefly, then accepted her touch. Tugging hard, Mirabar laboriously dragged it out of the lava flow. After it finally lay on the dark, rocky ground, she watched in blank-minded shock as the lava started melting away from it, gradually trickling back into the river of fire from which it had come.

Drop by drop, the lava drizzled away to reveal a large, glowing, apparently human shape. This couldn't be Elelar, though, Mirabar thought in confusion; this person was much too big.

Even when Mirabar saw the long black hair and delicate facial features, she found it hard to believe . . . Only when the *torena*'s pale body was fully revealed, its clothes all burned away, did Mirabar finally understand.

"Dar have mercy . . ."

Elelar lay naked, panting, and barely conscious on the rocky mountainside beneath the thick black sky . . . with a belly so swollen that she looked ready to deliver her child at any instant.

"That's why it looked too big to be you," Mirabar whispered, feeling her knees give way.

Elelar weakly turned her head. "Mirabar . . ." she croaked.

Mirabar sat down hard. "Oh, by all the Fires . . . What do I do? It's going to happen here," she babbled. "Now. Dar has intervened. Brought him forth. Blessed you with Her . . . um . . . She has made him ready to come among us right now. Here."

Elelar was dazed and confused. "What . . ."

"Divine . . ." Mirabar's voice trailed off.

"Divine birth!" Jalan cried.

"Yes," Mirabar whispered, still staring dumbstruck at Elelar's enormous stomach.

Elelar suddenly screamed and clutched her belly. "He's coming!"

"Is there a Sister here?" Mirabar shouted into the crowd. "Is there anyone who has ever helped a woman in childbirth before?"

But they were all swamped in rapture, chanting and singing too loudly to hear her pleas for help as Dar's chosen one scalded his mother's womb with his demands for release.

"*Mirabar!*" Elelar screamed.

"I'm here, I'm here." Mirabar scrambled forward.

"He's coming right now!" Elelar cried.

"It's just childbirth," Mirabar said, trying to sound reassuring.

I can do this.

Elelar looked momentarily furious. "*Just* child—"

"You can do this," Mirabar insisted.

We can do this.

"No, there's fire!" Elelar said through gritted teeth. Then she screamed again. "Oh, the *burning* . . . Mirabar! I can't stand it! I can't!"

"Jalan, help me!" Mirabar ordered.

We have to do this.

He fell to his knees beside Elelar. "How, *sirana?*"

She thought of the only birth she had ever seen, an event within her Guardian circle several years ago. "Um, kneel behind her, brace her shoulders against your legs, hold her hands." A moment later she added, "No, not like that. Place your hands so she can push against them. Yes, that's better."

"The *fire!*" Elelar screamed.

The praise-singing all around them filled Mirabar's head as she knelt between Elelar's legs, raised her knees, and investigated the birth canal.

Dar shield me . . .

This couldn't be normal. She knew that much.

"Look!" a pilgrim cried behind Mirabar. "Lava is pouring from her womb!"

"Stay back!" Mirabar snapped.

"What did he say?" Elelar demanded faintly.

"Pay no attention, they're all crazy," Mirabar assured her, staring at the lava which was dripping out of the birth canal.

"Make them go away," Elelar panted.

"I can't," Mirabar said. "I'm sorry. Even if I could . . . I think they're supposed to be here."

"Why, for the love of— *Argggghhh!*"

"Agh!" Jalan screamed, too, his face contorting as the *torena* squeezed his hands in her agony.

Mirabar tried to feel for the baby. *"Ow!"*

"What?" Elelar gasped.

She'd burned herself on the child's molten head. "Nothing . . . I mean, these people are meant to see this. I understand now. It's why Dar has been Calling pilgrims here. Just as there had to be witnesses to the Firebringer's rebirth in the caldera, now there must be witnesses to the birth of this child, so he can be acknowledged as Dar's chosen ruler without doubt or dispute." She kept talking, hoping to distract Elelar from what she imagined must be excruciating torment. Even ordinary childbirth was, Mirabar knew, usually agonizing. But this . . .

And to think I merely wanted her dead.

Dar's own plan to punish Elelar had been so much harsher, Mirabar now realized.

"By all the gods above and . . . I'm naked!" Elelar was clearly appalled. "In front of all these—"

"It doesn't matter now. Just—" She was interrupted by another of the *torena*'s hideous screams.

"This is why it hurt so much before, isn't it?" Elelar said between gulps of air. "In the cavern, when I was a prisoner. I thought I was miscarrying . . . But this child is . . . made of fire . . ."

"A child of fire, a child of water." *And sorrow?* She didn't know. Had Cheylan been twisted by sorrow, or merely bitterness, hatred, and thwarted ambition?

"A child of fire and water," Elelar breathed. "In that cavern, all the pain while the volcano raged . . . This baby was . . ." She paused, grimacing in brief agony. ". . . was preparing to . . . meet Dar in the caldera? Was preparing for . . . this?"

"That's why it had to be here!" Mirabar exclaimed, finally understanding. "In the cavern I envisioned, the cavern where Cheylan imprisoned you. Where Dar could embrace this child after he was conceived."

"Then why did you—arggggh!—you come there?"

"Cheylan could have survived what happened, and he'd have been here with you now instead of me."

Perhaps Dar had even been unwilling to kill Cheylan Herself. He had been faithful to Her, after all; to Her alone.

"Dar wanted you . . ." Elelar panted, ". . . with me . . . and the baby . . ."

Mirabar's own religious fervor briefly took over. "Do you remember anything about being in the caldera? Anything about how this—" She placed a hand on Elelar's swollen belly. "—came to happen?"

"Just the fire. And the *pain*. Worse than this. So much worse." She added weakly, "It would have been easier if Tansen had just killed me in Chandar."

Tansen . . .

"I don't know if he survived the battle at Gamalan," Mirabar said suddenly. "I left during the fighting, and I—"

"Tansen always survives," Elelar said. "You should know that by now."

Before long, Elelar started shivering. Mirabar demanded someone in the crowd give her a blanket, but covering her with it didn't seem to help. Her shivering turned to shudders which fought for dominance with the hard contractions of imminent childbirth.

"He's gone cold," Elelar said through chattering teeth, running a shaking hand over her stomach. "So cold."

"Fire and water," Mirabar murmured. She searched for the baby's head again, but was careful not to touch it this time; even without contact, she could feel the bitter chill which emanated from it, worse than any *shir*.

Impulsively, Mirabar put a hand on Elelar's leg and squeezed reassuringly. "He's very powerful."

But Elelar was already lost in her screams again and didn't hear her. After a while, the *torena* threw off the cloak and broke into a heavy sweat. Mirabar knew that the baby, so close to life, was again veering towards the other extreme of his nature as he sought entry into the world.

When the contractions starting coming one upon the other, with almost no pause between them, she knew it was time. She didn't even bother trying to talk to Elelar, who couldn't have heard her above her own screams and the noise of the exalted praise-singing. A river of fire poured out of Elelar's womb, turning into a flow of water that chilled and burned all at once. Mirabar asked her own unborn child for protection as the moment came when she could no longer avoid touching this child of fire and water whom Dar had brought her here to protect.

In the end, he came like any baby, born with hardship and pain in a sea of his mother's blood. The warm red flow of Elelar's blood shouldn't have startled Mirabar so much; the normalcy of it was just so unexpected in the film of fire and ice covering this child as he left his mother's body.

"Is he all right?" Elelar asked between harsh gulps of air.

Mirabar cleaned lava and blood away from his face, then rubbed his back hard, coaxing him into taking his first breath. He did so . . . and then wailed loudly. Elelar laughed with exultation and collapsed against Jalan.

"The fire," Jalan said.

"What?" Mirabar said, staring stunned at the baby.

"No, that's not fire. It's his hair," Elelar murmured.

The infant's orange eyes glowed like all the Fires of Dar. His skin was smeared with blood, and he cried like any other baby. The faint fuzz of his red hair gleamed lava-bright on his vulnerable head . . .

"I know who this is," Mirabar said hoarsely.

"It's my son," Elelar replied.

"It's the ruler you foretold in prophecy!" Jalan cried, and the hundreds of pilgrims around them roared with exultation.

But Mirabar knew who this *really* was.

Come to me, he had said upon leading her to Elelar. To her destiny. To this moment. *You are looking for me.*

"It's the Beckoner."

63

DAR DEMANDS WORSHIP, BUT THE SEA DEMANDS RESPECT.

— Proverb of the Sea-Born Folk

TANSEN HAD TRAVELED the world, met extraordinary people, seen unimaginable places, witnessed strange customs and bizarre rites, and encountered truly bewildering events.

But he had never come across anything like *this*.

"They *are* insane," Faradar said with certainty, shouting into his ear to be heard above the hysterical trilling and ululating all around them. "All of them. They will be of no use to us."

Dar had been Calling these people here, to Darshon, from all over Sileria, and no one knew why. Now Tansen understood the confusion: These people were all clearly too incoherent to explain what drew them here. He'd be surprised to find one who could answer a simple question, never mind clarify what was actually happening here.

Most of them were filthy and wearing only tattered rags, as if they'd been here a long time. Others were better groomed, but their behavior was just as strange. Men and women reeled in maniacal dancing, shaking their heads madly, waving their arms, spinning around and around until they fell down—or else entered some kind of fevered state which enabled them to touch the lava flows without being burned. Tansen and his companion stared in disbelief as some of these enraptured praise singers walked on the lava— even danced on it.

Faradar asked, "Have you ever seen—"

"Never."

"Are they Guardians?"

"No." The Firebringer's loyalists relied too much on Guardians to lose them without complaint; Tansen would know if they'd been deserting in such great numbers.

"They're just . . . ordinary people, then?" Faradar asked.

"I think so."

"Favored by Dar."

"Yes . . ."

In addition to the dancing, screeching worshippers who seemed to be *everywhere* on Mount Darshon, there was also— mercifully—water. He and Faradar drank, then filled their waterskins. He'd been to Darshon in the past but had never before seen so much water here. The intense activity of the caldera and the increasing number of lava flows were melting the snow at Darshon's summit and swelling the water supplies lower down on its slopes.

Dar was ensuring that Her most devout worshippers had water in a land tormented by the enduring dry season and the war against the Society.

"Siran!"

Tansen looked at Faradar, then followed the direction of her horrified gaze, hearing the screaming even as his eyes found its source. He took a reflexive step forward, then stopped himself. There was nothing he could do for the pilgrim whose ecstatic dance on the nearby lava flow was ending in agonizing death as Tansen watched.

"These people cannot help us find the *torena,*" Faradar said. "They are beyond helping even themselves."

He looked around, trying to decide what to do. By now, Mirabar could be any—

"*Tansen!*"

Stunned to hear his name called under these circumstances, he peered through the glowing, mist-filled, ash-thick air. "Yes! Who's that?"

"Jalan!"

"Jalan?" Well, yes, if anyone was bound to be part of this religious madness, it was surely Jalan the *zanar*. "Where are you?"

"Here!" An absolutely filthy man jumped up and down, waving at him from the other side of the lava flow.

Tansen scarcely recognized him, he was so ragged and sooty. "Jalan, I need your—"

"She sent me to find you!"

He froze. "Who sent you?"

"The *sirana!*"

"Mirabar?" he shouted in mingled hope and relief.

"Yes! She said you would be looking for her, and I was to go as far as Gamalan if I had to, to find you and lead you to her."

"Is she all right?"

"Yes! She's with the *torena* and her son!"

"Her *son?*" he repeated incredulously.

"She's had a baby boy!"

"Elelar?"

"Yes!"

"The baby's been born *already?*"

"*Siran*," said Faradar, "the *torena* was definitely not—"

"The promised one has come!" Jalan shrieked. "Dar's chosen ruler is among us! The child—"

"And Cheylan?" Tansen prodded, wondering if the women and the baby were in immediate danger.

"The *sirana* said to tell you he is dead!"

"By all the gods above and below," he murmured. "She did it. Mirabar succeeded."

"But *siran*," Faradar said, "how is it possible that the *torena* has already—"

"I don't know." His head was reeling. "I'm sure they'll tell us when we find them." He shouted to Jalan, "Where are they?"

Above the roar of the mountain, Jalan shouted, "Back that way!" He pointed vaguely behind him. Then he gestured to the lava flow separating them. "This flow wasn't here yesterday! What do we do?"

Tansen stared hard at the flow, his mind working. It was too broad to jump, even if he could find a good vantage point. He could scarcely believe what he was thinking of doing. Dar had spared him once before on this mountain, when he had come here to stop Josarian from jumping into the caldera. She could have killed him then—and nearly did—but She had wanted him to live, and so She had shown him mercy.

"Let's hope She still wants me to live," he muttered.

"Siran?"

"Go back down to the Sanctuary we found earlier," he advised Faradar. It had been abandoned and had a dry well, but it was the best place he could think of right now. "I'll bring them there. It may take some time, depending on Elelar's condition, and on . . . these lava flows."

"But *siran,* how will you . . ." She must have seen it in his face. "No! You can't!"

"If they can," he said, nodding to the chanting lava dancers, "maybe I can."

"And if you can't, you'll die—"

"If Mirabar is the shield and I am the sword," Tansen said, watching the river of fire ooze slowly down the mountain, "then Dar will want me to go to that baby now. The Society has already murdered a pregnant woman in Sanctuary to keep this child from finding his place in the world, and right now he's got no protection except Mirabar—who sent Jalan to bring me here, so she must want help."

"You can't . . . What if . . ." She made an awful sound. "I can't watch this."

His heart was pounding with fear, because no matter how clear his reasoning . . . Nonetheless, he went to the edge of the lava flow, stared into its liquid fire for a dizzying moment, then shifted his weight to—

"*No!*"

He paused and turned to find Faradar staring at him in appalled horror.

"You said you weren't going to watch," he reminded her.

"I can't look away."

He shook his head and turned his back on her again. Right in front of him, a lava dancer was suddenly swallowed by the flow and sank screaming into its glowing embrace.

Tansen clenched his teeth and gently placed one boot on the flow. It moved, startling him into momentarily losing his balance—Faradar shrieked behind him—but . . . it didn't burn. He shifted his weight onto that foot and didn't sink. The heat was intense, so overwhelming it blurred his vision, but several more steps carried him into the center of the flow without mishap.

He'd never felt anything like it. He was walking on liquid fire! It gave gently beneath his feet, then sprang back, as if lifting him, urging him to take each new step. The slow downhill movement threatened his balance, and he felt like a child just learning to walk; but he no longer felt afraid. Whatever quarrels existed between him and Dar, She nonetheless welcomed him now as he sought to protect the ruler foretold in prophecy.

When he reached solid ground again, the ash-strewn rocky surface on the far side of the flow, Jalan embraced him and started chanting his name. Tansen looked over his shoulder at Faradar, who stood open-mouthed on the far side of the flow. He made a gesture urging her to go back to the abandoned Sanctuary they'd found earlier and wait there.

"Take me to the *sirana*," he ordered Jalan.

ELELAR WORE SMELLY, filthy clothing that a pilgrim had given her. She felt as if someone had tried to break every bone in her body before setting her on fire and then splitting her in half.

Which, she reflected, was more or less what had happened to her recently. However, the humiliation of lying naked and bearing a child in front of hundreds upon hundreds of strangers was fading in the glow of exultation she now felt as her child—*my child!*—slept in her arms.

Mirabar was sitting nearby, looking haggard, exhausted, and battered. Her fiery red hair was a mass of tangles, her clothes were singed, her skin was streaked with soot and ash, her glowing eyes looked almost eerily yellow, and she seemed to be in a bad mood.

"Did you sleep?" Elelar asked her.

Mirabar lifted her head and frowned, obviously not having heard her clearly.

Elelar raised her voice to be heard above the cacophony of the pilgrims singing her praises, Dar's praises, the baby's praises, Mirabar's praises . . . *"Did you sleep?"*

Mirabar looked around her in disgust. "Who could possibly sleep through this?" she shouted.

"I did. But then, I just gave birth." No matter how many times she repeated this in her mind, it still astounded her.

"What?" Mirabar shouted.

"Never mind."

My child.

She had never known it was possible to feel this way. To love this fiercely. Just looking at him brought tears of protective love and motherly pride to her eyes.

He was not just any child, of course. Although he now seemed mere flesh, rather than fire and water, he possessed extraordinary power which she would have to teach him to use wisely. She'd need help, of course, since she didn't even understand his power.

Fire and water, water and fire . . .

She'd never even suspected it was possible. Nor had Mirabar, it seemed. And as for Cheylan . . . She shuddered and gave thanks that he was dead, even as she silently thanked him for giving her this child as his parting gift.

Because, although this baby was a ruler foretold in prophecy, favored by Dar, and brought into this world through divine forces, he was, above all, *her* child.

My son . . .

She had always wanted a daughter, actually, but now she found that it didn't matter. He was *hers,* and her love for him was already overwhelming and unshakable.

"Are you hungry?" Mirabar shouted.

She glanced up from her red-haired, fire-eyed baby and saw people presenting offerings of food and drink to Mirabar. Under normal circumstances, Elelar would have refused the frankly unappealing fare, but her circumstances hadn't been normal ever since leaving her estate.

"I'm starved!" she suddenly realized.

Mirabar helped her shift her position so she could reach for the food which the pilgrims placed between them. Then the two of them attacked the hard cheese, shriveled fruit, and bitter olives with graceless hunger.

Every so often, Mirabar rubbed her head as if it ached from all the noise.

The plan was to remain here, where they were surrounded by worshippers who would die to defend the child, until Jalan found Tansen and brought him here. Elelar supposed it could take days, and she wondered if she could restrain Mirabar from murdering some of the praise singers before then. The famous *sirana* was starting to look very cranky.

"The volcano has been quiet since . . . since this happened," Elelar commented, leaning close so she didn't have to shout so loudly. "Do you think . . . I mean, could Dar's rages finally be over?"

Mirabar's weary gaze sought the snow line high overhead. "I don't know. The dancing lights, the colored clouds . . ." She met Elelar's gaze. "They're still there. I don't understand it. If She was preparing for the baby's birth . . ."

"Gaborian."

"What?"

"That's his name. Gaborian. After my grandfather."

"Oh." Now Mirabar stared at the baby, her expression unreadable.

"What did you mean, before?" Elelar asked. "When you said he's . . . the Beckoner?"

"He's the one who brought so many of my visions, from the beginning," Mirabar said slowly, still staring at Gaborian.

"My baby?"

"He wasn't your baby then. He looked . . ." She shrugged. "More or less how I suppose he'll look when he's a man."

"Is he . . ." Elelar frowned. "Is he Daurion come back to life? Or . . ." She couldn't even bear to say it: *Josarian.*

"No," Mirabar replied. "He is . . . I think he is only who he is. This child. Gaborian. Someone whose will is so fierce and whose destiny is so strong . . . someone so necessary to all of us that he had the strength to reach out from the Otherworld, after centuries of waiting, when the time was right."

"You mean when men like Tansen and Josarian were living and ready to sacrifice . . . what they've sacrificed, if someone could convince them the time had come."

Mirabar nodded slowly, considering this. "And a time when someone of Cheylan's unique power came before Dar. Cheylan could never be the one to lead Sileria. He was too . . . twisted. But he had tremendous gifts to contribute to the future. As does Baran, though he . . ." Mirabar's pensive expression turned sad.

"Above all, the Beckoner chose you," Elelar said with certainty, wanting to acknowledge the tremendous bravery which accompanied Mirabar's extraordinary gifts. "Someone who could achieve the things you've achieved. Someone with your strength of will, and your courage. If he had to wait for someone who could become the Firebringer, and for Tansen, and for Cheylan . . . He also had to wait for you."

"And perhaps because of me," Mirabar acknowledged, "a time when people would be prepared to accept him."

"Yes," Elelar realized, looking down at her baby's eyes of

fire and hair of flame. For centuries, the Society had convinced Silerians that children like this were demons—when the truth was merely that someone like this was powerful enough, as Mirabar was, to be a threat to the waterlords.

"I wonder . . ."

"What?" Elelar leaned forward.

"I wonder how many times the Beckoner tried before, and failed."

Elelar caught her breath. "Do you really think . . ."

Mirabar shrugged. "It seems likely. There were many times *we* could have failed, after all. So many ways we could have gone wrong. Surely Dar has tried before to find the right time, the right people, to bring about . . . what we have all brought about."

Elelar didn't really know why, but she suddenly started crying. When Mirabar looked startled, she tried to apologize, but it only came out as incoherent sobs. The praise singers became alarmed and started crowding them.

"The *torena* is very tired," Mirabar said to them, patting Elelar's shoulder. "Stay back!"

"Am I supposed to . . . to guide this child now?" Elelar wept. "Is that what Dar wants me to do? Or am I to give him up? Will that be my punishment for . . . for what I did?" She couldn't give up this baby. She *couldn't*. They'd have to kill her to separate her from him.

Mirabar continued patting her back. "Tansen believes you're supposed to raise your son and teach him the things you know. I think he's right."

"I thought . . ." She cried harder. "Mirabar, I swear to you . . . What I did . . . I thought it was the right thing for Sileria."

The patting stopped. Mirabar withdrew her hand. "Don't ever ask me to forgive you, Elelar."

Her voice was so cold that Elelar felt as if she'd been slapped.

"Don't ever even speak his name to me again," Mirabar

added, her expression hard. "I will not destroy my life—let alone Sileria—to take vengeance for what you did, but don't ever expect me to forget it or forgive you. It will always be there between us. I will always know the terrible things you do when you're so blindly certain you're right." She paused. "And unlike Tansen, I have never been fond of you, so I promise you I will kill you if I ever think it necessary."

In a way, Elelar was grateful. The words were a kind of punishment, and she wanted that. The promise was a kind of pact between them. They would need each other in the future, because of this child; so they needed to understand each other, and—strangely—they finally seemed to do so, now, as Mirabar threatened to kill her and she accepted it.

"If you ever find it necessary," Elelar said, her sobbing now finished, "then I know you will."

"Mirabar!"

They both recognized his voice at the same instant.

Mirabar scrambled to her feet with renewed energy. *"Tansen!"* Her dirty face looked suddenly radiant.

He appeared then, a tall, familiar silhouette coming through the murky air, lit from behind by a lava flow farther down the mountain. Mirabar ran to him, and Tansen, normally so stoic and reserved, wrapped his arms around her in a fierce embrace.

Elelar watched them for a moment, then gazed down at her beautiful child. If Cheylan was right and Baran was dying . . . *Well.*

After all, Mirabar's child would need a father, and Tansen had already started practicing on that sea-born boy.

If Elelar felt any regret, she nonetheless knew that, she and Tansen being the people they were, things probably couldn't ever have been any different between them.

Mirabar untangled herself from Tansen's embrace and led him over to Elelar. He stared for a moment, looking exhausted and surprised, then—all *shallah* now—crossed his fists and lowered his head. *"Torena,* I am pleased to find you safe, and I congratulate you on the birth of . . ." He raised his head and suddenly grinned. "The new Yahrdan."

She smiled back. "Mirabar says . . . I am to take my place as the Yahrdan's mother."

Tansen nodded, his gaze flickering between them with evident curiosity. "And Cheylan will disappear from his official bloodline."

She frowned. "It's not that I object to forgetting Cheylan, but won't I need to name a fath—"

"Ronall."

"Ronall?"

"He's waiting in the bay due east of Gamalan, with my son." He looked troubled. "At least . . . If they're safe. But . . . I think they must be safe, because Zarien—"

"Ronall?" she repeated.

"He *is* your husband," he pointed out.

"He's also a Valdan," Elelar said.

"Half-Valdan," he reminded her. "Which will be politically advantageous in dealing with—"

"And he's a drunkard and a fool," Elelar added, feeling renewed loathing flood her. "No! I absolutely refuse—"

"Elelar—"

"Don't even *try* to convince me to put up with that—"

"I told you to kill her," Mirabar said to Tansen. "I want you always to remember that I was the one who told you to kill her when you had the chance."

"Oh, you were *also* the one who trusted Cheylan!" Elelar snapped, thoroughly annoyed with Mirabar now. "Just how naive could you—"

"Don't you *dare*—"

"Enough!" Tansen shouted at them both, provoked into a rare display of temper.

They both fell silent and glared at him.

"We're going to focus on the task at hand," he informed them both, "and quarrel some other time."

"What *is* the task at hand?" Elelar asked with chilly dignity, comforting Gaborian as he fussed.

"Getting you safely back to Shaljir where your son can be acknowledged. Normally, the best way would be to go overland, but it's a hard journey for a woman who's just given birth. Besides, it's not a journey you should make without me, under the circumstances, and I'm going back to sea to find my son before I do anything else. Now, since your husband is also waiting there—"

"If he's still alive," Elelar grumbled.

"Don't talk like that," Mirabar snapped at her. "Zarien is with him. So is Najdan."

"I'm sorry." She took a calming breath. "I shouldn't . . . I'm sorry."

"We'll go down to the bay," Tansen said briskly. "I know an easy path. I used to smuggle along that coast."

"Of course," Elelar said dryly.

"We'll find my son, your husband, and Mirabar's . . . assassin. If the sea seems safe, you and Ronall will take a boat to Shaljir. If, that is, we can find someone willing to leave the bay. The sea-born are all gathered . . ." He looked around and frowned. "Like these pilgrims. I wonder . . ."

"You think they were waiting for the birth, too? These people didn't know what they were awaiting until it happened," Mirabar said.

"All right, the sea," Elelar agreed. "I will . . ." Her temples started throbbing at the very thought. "I will acknowledge Ronall as the father and . . . return to Shaljir with him." *If he's still alive*. Which wasn't a prospect she could pray for with genuine sincerity.

"Can you walk?" Tansen asked.

She was about to reply when a sudden crash, like mountains colliding, made her flinch. She looked up towards Darshon's summit, as did everyone else, tense with fear. Another eruption? Another earthquake?

No, please . . .

Something hit her upturned face. She flinched and brushed it away. Dust? Ash? A falling pebble? More of it hit her face, little drops in quick succession.

Tansen inhaled sharply. "Is that . . ."

"Oh, please, Dar," Mirabar said, "let it be . . ."

Elelar realized what it was. *"Rain?"*

"Rain!"

"It's *RAIN!*"

There was another deafening crash of thunder, and then the skies opened up, pouring down life-giving rain upon them.

Jalan screamed in ecstasy, *"Rain!"*

"The rains!" Tansen shouted, impulsively embracing Mirabar again. "The rains have come!"

The skies had been so thick with smoke and ash in recent days, they'd never even seen the rain clouds gathering.

Elelar laughed and hugged Gaborian, who wailed as water drenched them all.

The long rains had finally begun. The dry season was over.

"Is that really rain?" Baran asked Velikar. "Or am I hallu-cinating again?"

She squealed and embraced him. "The rains! The rains have come!"

"Please, I'm a married man," he reminded her.

He heard a woman's delighted shriek from somewhere else in the household. A moment later, Haydar ran into his study, still shrieking. *"Siran!* Do you hear it? *Rain!* Look out the window!"

"I've already looked, thank you, Haydar. If you hug me, too, I'm going to throw up. I really cannot tolerate all this happiness."

Velikar snorted and stuck her head out the window, laugh-ing maniacally. Haydar pouted and left the room. A moment later, he again heard her shrieking, "Rain!"

Predictably, Vinn appeared shortly thereafter. "It's raining, *siran!*"

"I'm starting to miss the good old days," Baran said crankily, "when we used to mourn the arrival of the rains."

"Those were different days for us, *siran.*" Vinn went to another window and gazed out at the ensorcelled moat. "But I'm sure Kiloran is mourning right now, if that comforts you."

"You always know the right thing to say to me," Baran assured him.

"He's mourning more than the rain, *siran.*"

Baran eyed him. "Let me guess. We've had news from Cavasar?"

"He hasn't precisely lost the city yet," Vinn said, "but Cavasar is consumed in all-out battle between the Society and the loyalists at last report, which arrived while you were resting."

"He's still got the mines of Alizar and the Idalar River, though," Baran muttered. "The Olvara and I tried to surprise him last night—which is why I was then obliged to spend most of the day resting."

Velikar snorted. "You're lucky you didn't spend most of the day *dead.* You can no longer afford to expend that kind of—"

"Velikar, look!" Baran cried. "Rain!"

She scowled at him and turned back to the window.

Vinn asked Baran, "And did your surprise produce results?"

Baran shook his head. "I think he was expecting it. Or at least shrewd enough to be prepared for such an attempt."

"Now what?"

Baran sighed. "In all honesty, I'm running out of ideas, Vinn."

"But now that the rains are here . . ."

"It's heartening, I'll go that far. But it's not an answer to the consuming problem of our happy days together: How do we destroy Kiloran?"

"He is losing too much influence and terri—"

"That's how it looks," Baran agreed.

"You still think he has another plan, a new surprise for us?"

"I know that old man too well to think otherwise."

"But given his situation, *siran*, wouldn't he have employed it by now?"

"Maybe he has," Baran said, "and we just don't know it."

NAJDAN RELIEVED LINYAN at dawn and continued the search. The renewed downpour obscured visibility, yet it had also washed so much smoke and ash out of the air that there actually *was* a dawn today, which was a blessing.

Another sea-born family had found Najdan unconscious in the water, mostly dead, while searching for one of their own. They'd hauled him aboard and forced the water out of his lungs. By the time he finally regained consciousness, even he had to acknowledge that it was too late to dive in after Zarien again. Then the rain had started, initially making the search even harder.

The family who rescued him had helped him search for Zarien until they encountered Linyan's boat, to which they returned him. Although not a laborer, let alone a sailor, he had done all he could to help repair the damaged boat, and then they'd gone in search of Zarien again.

Now, more than three full days after the boy had gone overboard, he knew he would have to face Tansen and tell him he had let Zarien die.

They were only searching for a body at this point.

As for Ronall . . . Najdan was sorry about the *toren*. Ronall was not his responsibility, as Zarien was, but he recalled how much the *toren* had wanted to go ashore, and he regretted that his own decisions had cost the man his life. They looked for Ronall, too, but they had lost hope sooner. Zarien was sea-born and would survive as long as possible in the water. Ronall . . . no, they had lost hope well before now.

The *toren* was certainly dead.

* * *

THE ARMS WHICH held him were cool and soft, pulling him ever deeper into the dark water.

His thoughts returned slowly, coming to him one by one, like lazy waves lapping at the side of a boat. He was underwater. He felt peaceful and serene. He wasn't holding his breath, nor was he drowning. Someone soft, voluptuous, and cool-skinned embraced him. He felt no pain. No more pain. . . .

Three have mercy on me, what happened?

A feminine voice, rich and unfamiliar, filled his head. It seemed to come from within him as much as from all around him.

Don't call on them anymore. I will give you mercy. All the mercy you will ever need.

Ronall went rigidly still, startled and confused. He tried to speak, but water filled his mouth. So he asked the obvious question in silence: *Am I dreaming?*

No, you are finally awake. For the first time.

He didn't understand. He'd been in the water, and something had hit him . . .

A boat, she said, silent and yet echoing all through him. *The boy didn't understand. He would have taken you from the water. From me. So I swept the water to bring you into my arms.*

Ronall felt a dark suspicion. *Are you Death?*

The gentle laughter which greeted this question seemed so incongruous that his eyes snapped open—which was when he finally realized they'd been closed.

For you, I am a new life.

She was as beautiful as she was strange, with veil-like fins flaring around her translucent body, alternately revealing and concealing her voluptuous form as they flowed back and forth. Her diaphanous skin glowed silvery-pale, like the moons on a misty night. Her full hips flowed down to a sleek tail whose undulations kept propelling both of them away from all that Ronall had ever known. Heat crept through him as he became aware of the soft globes of her breasts pressed against him. Instead of hair, something like spun pearls grew from her scalp, flowing around her in pellucid strands. Her incandescent glow illuminated the darkness all around them.

I'm not . . . dying?

She assured him, *You are safe. I will always keep you safe when you come to me.*

Always . . . He still didn't understand. *Why . . .*

Dar has chosen you for me, as She has chosen me for you.

He flinched with shock, and her body undulated in response to his impulsive movement.

This can't . . . I can't . . .

The world is changing, she told him, *and you have changed with it.*

He felt the cold and the texture of the water, and he concentrated on it, trying to understand if it was real. If *he* was still real. Her strong strokes propelled them ever deeper, and the currents which touched him were as real as anything he'd ever felt. The arms which embraced him, protected him, and kept him safe felt even more real.

You're the sea goddess Zarien told me about, he realized.

I am Sharifar.

Looking for your consort.

Zarien has brought you to me, as was his duty.

No, he protested, *Zarien thinks it's Tansen.*

What he thinks doesn't matter. He has done what he had to do.

And what do I have to do? he asked, aware of her translucent flesh, her glowing beauty, the rich feel of her body against his.

Belong to me, she coaxed. *Make me belong to you.*

He was quivering with longing, yet bewilderingly close to shedding tears in mourning.

You lose only the pain, she promised. *Only the loneliness, the sorrow, the shame.*

It's . . . He felt her encompassing him, healing him, engulfing him in an embrace which sank through his own flesh and into his soul. *I didn't think it would be hard to give up those things, but it is.*

You gave up your life to save Zarien. Clear-headed when you did it, cleansed of all your poisons . . .

He felt as if he were inside of her now, and she inside of him. He felt half water god, and now she felt half human to him.

Cleansed of my poisons . . . He learned from her, letting her teach him how sea spirits made love, how he could share himself with a creature whose miraculous and exquisite body was so different from anything which walked the dryland.

Poisons of the soul, she said, *poisons of the body . . .*

All that seasickness, he suddenly realized. It had emptied his stomach every time he drank. Sharifar had inflicted it, not wanting him to come to her so numbed by liquor that he felt only half alive.

That was no dragonfish I kept seeing in the water, he realized, *it was you.* Not a monster stalking its next meal, but a lover preparing to welcome him into her watery domain.

I waited until you were ready.

The first time Zarien went in the water . . . he realized.

Yes.

You did that to him?

And fear still poisoned you.

I didn't go in after him. I failed.

You weren't ready, she said. *So I waited . . .*

Until I was ready to die to save him?

Until your fear was gone, and only your hunger remained, she told him.

That consuming hunger for something he could never name, that endless craving which had ruled his life . . . She was feeding it now, satisfying it at last, nourishing that long-starved void within him.

Sharifar . . .

Contentment flowed through him in soft waves, filling that ravenous ache inside of him.

Why? he wondered, truly coming to life for the first time in his whole miserable existence. *Why me?*

Because you need what I can give, she said inside his heart, *and I need what you can give.*

And what was she describing if not . . .

Love?

64

SECRETS ARE LIKE CHILDREN. NO ONE CAN
GUARD THEM NIGHT AND DAY FOREVER, AND NO
ONE CAN PREDICT WHAT THEY WILL BECOME.
— Kiloran

DESPITE TANSEN'S EAGERNESS to get to sea, he nonetheless took time to meet with Jagodan's son-in-law, the new leader of the Lironi, to plan a complex counterattack on their enemies.

"Then, while you've all got Verlon's remaining allies fully engaged in half a dozen skirmishes," Tansen explained, going over the plan he had formulated on the way here, "I'll lead the assault on his stronghold." He paused, allowing himself to hope. "If our timing is good, I think we can finally break the Society in the east. Forever."

"Surely the *torena* is traveling slowly. Does your plan allow enough time for you to accomplish what you must when you reach the coast, then rally with the Moynari to attack Verlon in his lair while we're conducting our battles elsewhere?"

"It does. Don't worry. I'll be there," he promised.

"You'd better be. We're all likely to die if you fail to engage Verlon when you're supposed to."

It was a bold plan—even risky. Tansen suspected it would also seem restful after so much time spent with *both* of the women who had obsessed him during his life. Mirabar and Elelar incited such regular and uncontrollable bad temper in each other that he couldn't imagine how they expected to co-operate in the education of Elelar's remarkable child. In a moment of exasperation with them both, he had foolishly said so—and then they had united in turning on *him*.

Women.

He loved Mirabar and cared about Elelar, but he didn't really regret that his duties here would prevent him from going all the way to Shaljir with the two of them. Even Faradar's sturdy temperament was starting to show signs of the strain.

Nor was Jalan, also traveling in their entourage, the most enjoyable companion. If Tansen had to hear one more long-winded, convoluted, effusive recounting of Gaborian's birth, no matter how extraordinary . . .

Then there were the praise singers who made up the greater part of their entourage. Tansen permitted them to come along because he knew they'd die to protect Gaborian if anyone tried to attack. Moreover, now that the child had been born, Dar seemed willing to let most of the pilgrims return to their own lives. Many of them were already drifting back to their native villages and cities, spreading the news of Gaborian's arrival across Sileria as they abandoned the tormented slopes of Darshon. Witnesses to the baby's Dar-blessed birth, they would convince the rest of Sileria that he was indeed the prophesied ruler.

Tansen only wondered if those pilgrims were all as *noisy* as the ones now traveling with him. The constant chanting and singing, the praises and prayers, the elaborate vocal celebrations of Gaborian's birth and Dar's merciful favor were . . . getting on his nerves. He'd always been the quiet type.

He sighed, cleared his thoughts, and returned to discussing with the Lironi leader what he hoped would be the decisive battle in eastern Sileria.

* * *

NAJDAN FELT THE boat shudder violently, yet when he looked around, they were a safe distance from the many other vessels and the water was calm. The rain had ceased for the time being, and there had been no eruptions or earthquakes for several days. Even the smoke-filled sky was clearing rapidly, though the summit of Darshon itself still looked ominous.

"What was that?" he asked Linyan. "Did we hit something under the surface?"

The old man shook his head, his tattooed face frowning in perplexity. "The water is very deep here. And it's not coral or—"

"Dragonfish?"

"It would have to be an unusually big one to hit us *that* hard."

They were heading back into the bay, the Lascari having agreed to escort Najdan as close to shore as they themselves were willing to go. They had reluctantly given up the seemingly futile search for Zarien's body, and there was nothing left for Najdan to do now but find Tansen and tell him what had happened. He was ashamed he had failed to protect the boy, but it would only compound his failure now if he postponed informing Tansen of the boy's death.

Suddenly the boat rocked so hard that Linyan and Najdan both had to seize the railing to keep their balance.

"*Whatever* that is," Linyan said, wide-eyed with alarm, "it's not a dragonfish. There's no—"

The boat rocked again, and now the sea started roaring.

"What's that noise?" Najdan demanded.

"I don't know!"

He looked around. "Where is it coming from?"

"I don't know!"

The women and children were screaming. People on nearby boats were shrieking. The roar turned to a threatening rumble, and the sea around them started churning.

Nothing about this seemed familiar. Najdan asked the old man, "Is this an earthquake?"

They both looked landward at the same time, then looked at each other. Najdan looked back down at the water, even more confused . . . Then his blood froze. "It's . . . *glowing*."

Linyan stared open-mouthed, then shouted to the rest of his family. They all abandoned their posts on the boat and joined him at the railing to stare down at the water with him.

Bewildered and alarmed, Najdan looked out across the sea. The glow which had started near their boat was now spreading like fire, shimmering across the surface, engulfing other boats as far as the eye could see. Even through the liquid rumbling that was filling his head and shaking the boat, he could hear cries of wonder and alarm on other boats.

Had lava traveled from the mainland through underwater channels? Were they about to be engulfed in an eruption at sea?

He clung to the railing of the shuddering boat as he discarded this theory. The glow spreading across the sea was silvery-blue, not the rich orange he would expect of lava spilling into the sea. And wouldn't the sea become wild and vicious if there was an eruption right underneath them? Wouldn't the water boil and send dead, blistered fish bobbing to the surface?

Although the water was churning and the boat was shuddering, they held their position and seemed to be in no imminent danger of capsizing or sinking. And instead of boiling heat, a cool silvery mist was now rising off the water, glimmering gently in the hazy sunshine.

Suddenly Linyan grasped Najdan's arm. "Could it be Zarien?"

"I have no idea what it could be," Najdan said.

"He came back to life once before. Perhaps . . . But when he told us about it, he never mentioned . . . *this*."

Hope awoke inside of Najdan. If there was even a faint possibility that Tansen's son might be alive . . .

There was a tremendous roaring sound, so loud it drowned out the screams of people within arm's reach. The boat suddenly dropped, making Najdan's stomach lurch sickeningly, then it sprang back, as if tossed by a giant hand. He fell down, momentarily stunned. By the time he regained his feet, a vast, foaming pillar of water was rising out of the sea.

Najdan said, "What *is* th—"

"I don't know!"

The women starting wailing rhythmically, and he supposed they were praying. He watched as the pillar rose higher and higher, as if reaching for the sky, until it was so tall it must surely be visible from very far away. His heart quivered in response when the pillar stopped growing and just held itself there, towering over all of them, over the sea and the eastern coast, for long, tense moments.

Was this the work of a waterlord? At *sea?* He had never heard of such a thing, but . . . If it was, he had a feeling they'd all be dead within moments.

Then the pillar collapsed, as if a spell had been broken, and the immense tower of water fell back into the sea. The boats were thrown around, rocking wildly, as enormous waves drenched them and washed into their holds. Najdan wiped stinging saltwater out of his eyes and peered at the foaming whirlpool from which the pillar of water had risen.

"Look! There's something there!"

It seemed to shape itself out of the silvery-blue fire still shimmering through the water, emerging from the roiling foam of the tumultuous sea like an enormous bubble of glimmering air. As the glow started to melt away from it, like water pouring off a rock, Najdan realized there was something solid under there. Something shaped like . . .

"A *man.*"

He nearly flinched when Linyan let out a piercing wail. The rest of the family joined in and, to Najdan's astonishment, the same wail—now turning to a shrill chant—started coming from all of the nearby boats, too.

"What's happening?" Najdan shouted.

They ignored him. Or, rather, didn't even notice him. They were all singing, swaying, shrieking. Tears streamed down

Linyan's face. Women raised their arms as if in worship. Children screamed ecstatically and pointed to the man—now clearly just made of flesh—floating in the glowing sea.

The churning of the water gradually subsided, and the boat stopped shuddering. The glow remained upon the sea, but Najdan looked into the distance and could see it slowly fading, retreating to the place from which it had begun. Soon, he guessed, it would be gone altogether.

The man in the water started swimming towards them.

Since no one else seemed capable of rational thought or practical actions at the moment, Najdan threw him a line. The man waved, and Najdan suddenly recognized him.

"Ronall?"

The *toren* hauled himself aboard, soaking wet, stark naked, and looking dazed.

Najdan stared at him in uncomprehending wonder. "We thought you were dead."

Ronall shook his head, panting, and shivered a little. "No. I'm . . . It's me, Najdan! I'm the sea king!"

"Zarien brought him to us!" Linyan cried. "Zarien has delivered the sea king! It's why the sea-born from every coast felt compelled to come to this bay! We were brought here to await the sea king! To witness *Toren* Ronall's divine rebirth!"

The women were still singing, now rocking rhythmically and waving their arms at Ronall, clearly sharing Linyan's view of events.

"You," Najdan said to Linyan, "who would not even accept your own grandson any longer because he had walked on land . . . *You* accept this man, a drylander, as the sea king?"

Linyan was weeping, though he looked more ecstatic than sad. "Who could deny him? You saw what we saw! What we were brought here to see! Zarien promised him to us! And Zarien brought him here. He is the one!"

Najdan disliked inconsistency, but he had learned by now that there was no point in arguing with people in the grip of religious fervor. "Get the *toren* a blanket," he snapped.

Shuddering with cold now, Ronall murmured, "Thank you."

"What happened?" Najdan demanded.

"I'm afraid it's true." Ronall started laughing. "I'm . . ." He laughed again, and it was a surprisingly happy, wholesome sound. "I'm consort to a goddess."

"This is unexpected," Najdan commented, which made Ronall laugh harder.

The *toren* wrapped himself in a blanket, returned Linyan's enthusiastic embrace, and then asked, "Where's Zarien?"

Najdan went still. "You don't know?"

Ronall frowned. "No, I . . ." His expression changed. "He's not here?"

Najdan shook his head. "He never came out of the water."

Ronall sat down suddenly, looking shocked. "He can't be dead!"

"He must be, by now. He couldn't survive this long—"

"No," Ronall said. "She didn't say he was dead. I'm sure she wouldn't have let him die."

"Who?"

"Sharifar!"

"A goddess might not—"

"No!" Ronall insisted. "She wouldn't inflict that kind of guilt on me. Zarien brought me here. He was taken by that wave to test *me*. He was trying to save me the last time I saw him. She knows how I would suffer if he died looking for me."

"Nonetheless—"

"He's alive," Ronall told Najdan. "I know he is."

The *toren* didn't sound desperate or afraid. He sounded convinced. Completely sure. Even confident. More so, in fact, than he had ever sounded about anything before.

"She would have saved him," Ronall said. "She would have done that for me. I know."

"The sea is notoriously cruel," Najdan pointed out, wondering exactly what had happened to Ronall in the days and nights he had spent underwater.

"But Sharifar can't be cruel to *me,* and I need that boy to be alive."

Linyan had stopped singing, and now he chose to venture into the conversation. "Zarien said that when Sharifar spared him after the dragonfish attack . . ."

"Yes?" Ronall prodded.

"She sent him ashore. If she has saved him now, perhaps she has sent him ashore again. He is no longer, you know, one of us."

Najdan and Ronall looked at each other.

"We're going ashore," Ronall said decisively.

Linyan flinched. "What?"

"We're *all* going ashore," he added.

"But we're sea-bound!"

"The time for living completely separate from the landfolk has passed," Ronall told him. "The sea-born must learn to care about what happens on land in this country. You can't contribute to Sileria's future if you continue to live as you have lived until now." He paused. "The world is changing, and you must change with it."

The Lascari looked shocked. Najdan was impressed by the air of conviction and command which the *toren,* previously so confused and ineffectual, now assumed with surprising ease; but Najdan had lived long enough in the Society to understand what best motivated a doubtful and recalcitrant people when faced with new challenges.

He took his *shir* in hand and held it to Linyan's throat. "We are going ashore as the sea king orders," he explained, "or else feeding your remains to a dragonfish. Which would you prefer?"

As Nadjan expected, the old man made the choice with alacrity.

"WHAT *IS* THAT?"

Tansen, who carried the baby on his back, looked to where

Elelar was pointing. From their vantage point on the cliffs, as they descended to the bay, they had a magnificent view of the sea. When he saw what she saw—the sea on fire with a silvery-blue light, and an immense tower of water rising out of the bay—he felt his stomach give a sickening lurch.

"Mirabar," he said, hearing the fear in his voice.

"I don't know," she replied instantly.

"Could a waterlord do that?" Faradar asked.

Tansen wondered, "Could it be . . ." *Zarien . . . So soon?* ". . . the work of a sea goddess?"

As they watched, the pillar collapsed. The sea was chaotic for a few long, awful moments, with boats rocking and bouncing on the water's surface. Then relative calm descended, and the silvery glow started to fade gradually from the sea.

"Whatever it was," Mirabar said, placing a hand on his shoulder, "it doesn't look like anyone died from it."

One of the many people traveling with them, though, pointed to the coastal beach directly below them. "People *have* died here, though. Look at that mess."

Tansen thought he would be sick. The shore was a wasteland of smashed and shattered boats, stranded people . . . and corpses.

"Let's hurry." His voice sounded far away and expressionless. "I want to find him before dark."

Nobody needed to ask whom he meant by "him."

THERE WAS NOTHING. And then—quite suddenly—there was *pain*. The contrast, the stunning instant journey from a dark empty void to such vivid sensation, was as startling as the pain itself.

"*Argh!*"

Water flooded his throat. He choked on it, then got slammed against a rock again—which made him inhale again, which made him start strangling again.

What in the Fires . . .

Dazed, confused, and probably about to drown, he had sense enough to cling desperately to the next rock he was smashed against, rather than letting the sea continue to toss him around like flotsam.

It dawned on him that there shouldn't be any rocks here. They were well out to sea . . .

"Agh!"

Nonetheless, he realized, these were definitely rocks he was being flung against. And he was pretty sure he was bleeding now.

Zarien hung there for a few moments, trying to catch his breath and gather his senses. He remembered seeing a boat, slapped around by a huge wave, careen into Ronall and send him under, unconscious and perhaps already dead. Zarien remembered diving repeatedly, searching for him, unwilling to accept that Ronall had finally found the death which, in a way, it had always seemed he was half seeking—might even consider a release, a relief. But the sea-born did not easily give up their dead to the merciless waters on which they lived; and besides, Zarien liked Ronall and was sorry he hadn't shown it more. So he kept diving beneath the roaring, tumbling surface of the furious sea. Until . . .

I got . . . caught in a wave.

He remembered now. Vaguely. The waves had been so enormous, unlike anything he'd ever seen before, even in the worst of storms. One had simply swept him up, denying him air, oblivious to his attempts to escape its immense power. He remembered the burning in his lungs, the weakening of his limbs, the terrible fear as he realized . . .

I was dying.

Had the wave carried him this far? All the way to shore? Even if it had, how had he survived? It didn't seem possible. He couldn't remember anything that had happened after the burning in his lungs led to be a blackness in his head which finally engulfed him completely.

Now he became aware of something bumping gently but insistently against his back. One of his hands let go of the rock and fumbled behind him. His blood ran cold when he touched it and instantly recognized what it was.

Zarien took a few harsh breaths, then willed himself to grasp the oar. He flung it up onto the shore, then laboriously hauled himself out of the water, climbing up after it. He rested on his hands and knees, panting hard, and stared at it.

It was the *stahra* which Sharifar had given him when she sent him ashore for the first time ever, in search of the sea king.

He suspected he had died again. And she had spared him a second time. Why? So he would bring Tansen to her? Well, he never would! *Never.*

Zarien's head was pounding and he couldn't think clearly. He was also dying of thirst. How long had he been in the water?

How long have I been dead?

He rose to his feet, shaking in reaction, and looked down at the *stahra.*

"No, Sharifar. I won't do it."

She should have killed him when she had the chance. He turned his back on the *stahra* and walked away from it, turning his back on Sharifar, too.

He supposed that was foolish. He'd probably have to go right back to sea to find out what had happened to Najdan and the Lascari, and then Sharifar would finally take her revenge on him. He tried not to think about it, though, because he would not pick up that *stahra* and renew his pact with her. He would *not.*

As Tansen would say, focus on the task at hand.

Which, for now, meant finding water. He felt very disoriented, but he could tell he'd washed ashore at the southern end of the bay, well beyond where people were counting the dead and gathering to mourn their losses. He wasn't familiar with this coast, but he let his senses lead him, and soon he found what he sought—a small pool of sweetwater gathered in the rocks well beyond the shore.

He drank his fill, then realized he'd need to find someone with an intact boat who could take him back out into the bay in search of the Lascari. Tired and depressed, he started wandering among the sea-born stragglers, making his way along the shore, asking for news about the Lascari and for a boat to take him to them. It seemed he did this for a very long time, wearing himself out, before someone finally encouraged him.

"You're looking for the Lascari?" said a deep voice behind him.

"Yes!" he whirled to face the man. "Do you know what's happened to them? Or can you take me . . ."

His voice trailed off and his head felt light as he took in the man's appearance. Tall, short-haired, powerful looking. His clothes were well made, and he was handsome despite the long scar running down one cheek.

Zarien choked on his shock and started stumbling backwards. *"Searlon."*

"Ah. Zarien, I presume? I've been looking for you for a long time."

"Stay away from me!"

Someone asked them, "Is there a problem here?"

"Yes!" Zarien said.

"The boy is upset," Searlon said smoothly, gesturing to the sea. "His family, you know."

"Of course," said the sea-born stranger, moving on.

"Wait!" Zarien wanted to run after him, but he was afraid to turn his back on Searlon.

"I won't hurt you." The assassin stood still.

No one else came close to them. Perhaps they sensed how dangerous Searlon was? "I saw what you did to my family!"

"They aren't your family," Searlon said calmly. "Not anymore. They told me you were dead. Zarien, they *wanted* you to be dead."

"No, they—"

"Tansen will want you dead, too, when he knows the truth."

"He won't!"

Searlon's dark gaze sharpened. "Then you know?"

"No!" Zarien shouted, feeling naked before this stranger. "No! I don't know anything!"

"You do know," Searlon said with certainty, still not moving. "Does Tansen know yet? Has he already tried to kill you? Is that why you're wandering alone and unprotec—"

"*Kill me?* No!"

"He doesn't know, does he? But he'll find out, you know. In the end, he *will* find out."

"No," Zarien said, and then was sorry he'd spoken. "I mean . . ."

"There's still time for you to escape him. I can help."

"No, you've come to kill me! He's been protecting me from you!"

"That's what he thinks, but only because he doesn't yet know who you are. I know, and I want to help."

"No, you don't!" He should run away, not stand here rooted to the ground and talking to this assassin. But he couldn't. He was too terrified to move. "I've heard how clever you are. You'll trick me, and then when I don't expect—"

"You're still a boy, and I am very good at what I do," Searlon said gently. "I don't need to trick you to kill you. I haven't come for that. I've come to protect you from Tansen."

"I don't need protection from Tan—"

"Do you know he killed his own bloodfather?"

"—sen, I need . . ." Zarien felt like he was falling, but he was still standing. As if the inaccuracy mattered, as if it were reasonable to discuss this now, he said, "Tansen never had a bloodfather."

"Oh, yes, he did. And he killed him."

"No, he . . ." Zarien frowned. "No."

"Has he never told you why he left Sileria for nine years? The exact length of a Society bloodvow?"

"What does that matter? It's not . . . I don't care . . ."

"Kiloran swore a bloodvow against him because Tansen murdered someone Kiloran cared about."

"He . . ." Zarien didn't want to listen. *Shouldn't* listen. "He did?"

Searlon nodded. "His own bloodfather."

"No." Zarien shook his head. "He wouldn't do something like that. He believes in . . . He wouldn't!"

"He never told you he had a bloodfather, did he?"

"I . . . No, but, I don't believe you!"

"Yes, you do," Searlon said, and, by saying it, somehow made it true. "Don't you wonder why he never told you, his own bloodson, that he himself had a bloodfather?"

"I . . . You're . . . Why should I believe—"

"And do you know *why* Tansen killed the man who loved him enough to become his father?"

"You're lying!"

"Because that man was a waterlord's son, Zarien."

His heart was pounding, his blood roaring in his ears. He felt dizzy and sick. He wanted to throw up. Wanted to run away. "You're making this up. Just to make it easy to kill me. So I won't run away or . . ." He was breathing hard, his head throbbing. Tears misted his eyes, and he fought them.

He knew Searlon didn't need to catch him off guard. If Searlon was as good as Najdan, he could easily have killed Zarien by now, and just as easily killed or evaded anyone in their vicinity who objected.

"Zarien, I know what Tansen will do to you when he finds out."

"No." Zarien felt his lips tremble, heard his voice crack.

"His father loved him, too, just as you do," Searlon said sympathetically. "His father believed in him, too. Trusted him, too. And Tansen beat him to death with a *yahr*."

Zarien felt like he was choking on his own breath.

Did your father die terribly? he had asked Tansen.

Zarien said insistently to Searlon, "Outlookers killed Tansen's father."

The assassin nodded. "His sire. When he was very young."

Tansen's nights were tormented by terrible dreams of his past. Sometimes he cried for his father . . . His bloodfather?

No, no, no!

The silence was awful. Within it, Zarien again heard everything Searlon had just told him.

I know what Tansen will do to you when he finds out.

"Come with me before it's too late," Searlon urged quietly. "Let us protect you. It's what my master wants more than anything."

"Zarien!"

He flinched at the sound of his name, having briefly forgotten about the world surrounding them. He turned and saw a man in dark, tattered clothing running towards them.

"Najdan?" he murmured incredulously.

"Najdan." Searlon's voice was like ice.

Najdan slowed to a walk as he approached them, his eyes hard as he watched Searlon. To Zarien he said, "Ronall said you would still be alive."

"Ronall's not dead?" Zarien blurted.

Najdan moved to stand between him and Searlon. "A moment later, and the *toren* would have been wrong."

"This is a pleasant surprise, Najdan," Searlon said. "I've looked forward to killing you ever since you betrayed our master, but you've been very elusive."

"You've searched harder for this helpless boy than you've searched for me," Najdan replied coldly.

"I doubt he's helpless," Searlon said, "though I suppose only time will tell. Najdan, have you never noticed anything unusual about him? I would have thought that you, of all people—"

"You talk too much." Najdan's *shir* appeared in his hand, glittering with the unnatural brilliance of an assassin's unique weapon. "Let's finish this work now."

"By all means."

"No!" Zarien cried as Searlon suddenly dropped to the ground to kick Najdan's legs out from under him.

Incredibly, Najdan evaded the move, then did a diving roll and nearly gutted Searlon—who hit Najdan with his elbow, then rolled on top of him with his *shir* raised. Zarien didn't even know where Searlon's *shir* had come from or when he'd reached for it.

Najdan punched Searlon with the hilt of his *shir,* then the two of them rolled over and over on the ground, struggling in silence. Zarien became aware of people screaming all around them, gathering to watch. No one interfered, though. It would be deadly to intervene. Besides, these two men were assassins. This was their way. This had always been their way.

Searlon and Najdan were both like Tansen when they fought, their faces revealing no emotion, their concentration fierce, their moves fast and effective. Zarien tried to think of a way to make them stop, since he didn't want either of them to die because of him. He was afraid to shout or plead, let alone come between them, lest it distract one of them and give the other a deadly advantage.

For a terrible moment, it seemed Searlon would win as he pinned Najdan to the ground and moved his blade to the other man's throat. Then Najdan's legs rose to grasp Searlon's neck between his ankles while he heaved his body, and Searlon flew backwards. Both men rose to their feet and started circling each other.

"You've made bad choices, *sriliah,*" Searlon said with open contempt.

"Not as bad as murdering Josarian's sister in Sanctuary," Najdan said with equal disdain.

"It was distasteful," Searlon replied, "but less so than betraying Kiloran must have been."

"It was also foolish. Sileria will never forgive what you did."

"What we gained—"

"Was nothing," Najdan said.

"I see Mirabar doesn't confide—"

"I see you don't know the truth." Najdan suddenly smiled. "You killed the wrong woman."

Searlon was briefly disconcerted enough for Najdan to surprise him with a sudden attack, but the advantage was only momentary. Najdan retreated again, and the two of them fell silent as they engaged in a deadly dance of feints, counters, stabs, and passes. Zarien felt dizzy and realized he was forgetting to breathe.

Oh, please, Dar, please, make them stop.

Najdan was older, and he was the one who started tiring first. If Zarien could see it, then surely Searlon could see it. Indeed, his increasingly confident expression suggested that he knew time was now on his side.

"I will not . . ." Najdan was panting now. ". . . let you kill . . . Tansen's son."

"He's not Tansen's son." Searlon smiled briefly. "You don't know the truth either, do you?"

Najdan looked distracted. "What truth?"

But Searlon had seen that brief moment of distraction and made his move. Najdan stiffened and made an awful sound when Searlon's *shir* slid past his guard and plunged into his belly. His hands flailed limply behind his back for a blurry moment. Zarien tried to shout, but only choking sounds came out of his mouth.

"The boy," Searlon murmured to Najdan, "is—"

Najdan's left hand moved suddenly, and before Zarien realized what had happened, Searlon staggered backwards, eyes wide with shock, his hand clasped to his throat. Blood seeped out between his fingers.

Najdan fell to his knees. "You always were," he said weakly to Searlon, "too confident once you had made your killing blow."

"Najdan!" Zarien ran to him and—stupidly—tried to haul him to his feet.

"Stay back, boy!" Najdan snapped. "He's not dead yet."

That was true, but Searlon's death didn't take very long. Zarien clung to Najdan as Searlon collapsed and a river of blood poured from the broad slit in his neck. His eyes remained open, turning dull and blank as his life ended.

"When your hands flailed like that," Zarien said hoarsely to Najdan, now understanding what had happened too quickly for him to see clearly, "you were shifting your *shir* to the hand he thought was harmless once he'd stabbed you."

Najdan sank lower, starting to double over. "I was getting too tired. He'd have succeeded if I hadn't . . . done something . . . extreme."

"You let him stab you *on purpose?*"

"It . . . distracted him . . ." Najdan fell slowly onto his side, curled around the wound in his belly. "I swore to Tansen . . . wouldn't let Searlon kill you."

Zarien started crying. "He didn't want to kill me! You didn't have to do this! Najdan! *Najdan!*"

Blood was spreading out from Najdan's body, too, soaking the ground around him.

"Get help!" Zarien shouted to no one in particular as he tried to get a look at the wound. "Get a Sister!"

"A Sister . . . no good . . . ," Najdan muttered, his eyes looking dull and unfocused. *"Shir . . ."*

"Najdan, no!" Zarien howled.

"Zarien! Is that you?"

He looked up, numbly recognizing Tansen's voice. "Father! I'm here! Help! Father!"

A moment later, Tansen shoved his way through the now-vast crowd of people. "Zarien!"

"They fought! I didn't know how to stop them!" Zarien babbled as Tansen took him by the shoulders and stared in shock at Najdan. "And then Najdan let him . . . let him . . . What do we do? Father, what do we—"

"Najdan!" a woman screamed.

She rushed forward and bent over the assassin, her red hair somehow almost blinding in this hazy light. "No! Noooo!"

"*Sir . . . ana . . .*" Najdan's blood-drenched hand grasped hers as she kept wailing in denial of his death.

"I didn't want them to fight!" Zarien cried. "Get a Sister! Someone get a—"

Those fierce golden eyes suddenly turned upon him. "*No. Not a Sister.*" Mirabar rose to her feet, staring at him and Tansen as she panted with agitation. "It's a *shir* wound."

"But—"

"Like the one Tansen had. The one that healed, as if by magic." Her gaze fixed on Tansen. "Najdan thought it was water magic."

Tansen said, "But we don't know what—"

"What was different in your life that day?" Mirabar demanded, her voice deep and harsh. "What can't we explain?"

"Mira—"

"This boy!" She seized Zarien's arm, pulled him to the ground, and placed his hand over Najdan's wound. "What happened when Tansen's wound healed?"

"I don't know," he said, his mind whirling with panic. "It just—"

"*What did you do?*" she screamed

"Um . . ."

"*Exactly* what did you do?" she said more coherently.

"I was . . . washing the wound. Yes, that's right, washing the wound with water and a cloth."

Mirabar sank her teeth into her sleeve, yanked hard, and tore off a long strip of dirty material.

Tansen said, "Mirabar . . ."

"Water," she snapped at him.

Tansen handed her his waterskin. She gave the cloth and the waterskin to Zarien, who soaked the cloth and started cleaning the wound. Najdan groaned slightly.

"Then what?" Mirabar prodded.

"I remember that the blood wouldn't stop flowing."

So he pressed down on Najdan's wound now, as he had pressed down on Tansen's wound then, willing it to stop bleeding. But the assassin's blood wouldn't stop flowing, just as Tansen's hadn't.

"And?" Mirabar's voice was dark with desperation.

"I . . ." *What did I do then?* "I prayed!"

"Pray now," she ordered.

"Yes." *Pray.*

His heart pounding with fear and confusion, Zarien begged Dar to make the wound stop bleeding. He prayed to all the gods of the wind and sea to save Najdan. He admonished the assassin to heal.

"*Sirana,*" Najdan rasped weakly.

Heal, please, heal, Zarien begged in silence.

A chilling heat passed through him, a cold fire that made him shiver even as it burned him. He inhaled sharply, remembering this sensation from the moment Tansen had healed. He slowly drew his hand away as an icy mist rose from the wound, a crystalline glow that shimmered in the hazy air.

Zarien watched with a mingled sense of relief and dread as it faded away, leaving only Najdan's flesh in its wake. He saw Mirabar's stunned expression as she stared at the result. The life-stealing *shir* wound was gone. Only a silvery scar was left in its place.

65

KNOWLEDGE IS HOLLOW.

— Kintish Proverb

TANSEN GAPED IN stunned silence at Zarien, who knelt in the blood-drenched sand next to Mirabar and Najdan.

Najdan thought it was water magic . . .

All around them, the sea-born started chattering excitedly.

Water magic . . .

"No," Tansen said, even though it was clearly a stupid thing to say now.

Zarien looked up at him, that young, tattooed face confused and afraid. "Father . . ."

Tansen heard the pleading in the boy's voice, but he was too shocked to respond.

Mirabar said hoarsely, "Najdan? How do you feel?"

"Better," was the weak response. "Just . . ."

"You've lost a lot of blood." Mirabar clutched his hand in both of hers and raised it to her cheek, inadvertently smearing her face with his blood. "You'll need rest now."

"Thank . . ." Najdan tried to lift his head, but gave up the effort after a moment. "What . . . happened?"

"Zarien healed you," Mirabar said, brushing Najdan's hair away from his face.

Najdan frowned vaguely. "*Shir* . . . wound."

"Can anything heal a *shir* wound besides water magic?" she asked him.

"Only . . . time," he replied.

And time, they all knew, wouldn't have healed the deadly wound Searlon had given Najdan. Only . . .

"Water magic," Mirabar said with certainty, now looking at Zarien in wonder. "It was you. And it was you who saved Tansen's life that day."

"No!" Zarien cried as if accused of a terrible deed. "It's because Tansen is the sea king! That's why—"

"No, it's not . . . Tansen," Najdan said, sounding weary but more clear-headed. "It's Ronall."

"Ronall?" Zarien bleated.

Ronall? Tansen thought.

Najdan said, "I saw . . . it happen. Lascari . . . all saw. We were there. He is . . . the one."

Mirabar gasped and looked up at Tansen, who felt as if he were at the other end of a long, dark tunnel. "That's what we saw!" she exclaimed. "That's what was happening in the sea. The birth—rebirth?—of the sea king!"

"Made me feel . . ." Najdan muttered, ". . . sick to my stomach."

"The sea king . . ." Zarien murmured, looking out to sea with a shocked expression. *"Ronall."*

"So you see, Zarien," Mirabar said, putting a bloody hand on the boy's arm, "it *was* you who healed Tansen." She gestured to Najdan and added, "Just like this. You're gifted . . . with water magic."

"No." Zarien sounded panicky.

"That's why . . ." Tansen's voice sounded hollow and his tongue felt clumsy. ". . . why you always know where there's water . . ."

"Father, please . . ."

"You can always find it," Tansen said, remembering. "No matter how dry the season or how unfamiliar the surroundings."

"You just can't smell it because you're a drylander!" Zarien insisted. "I don't have any special power!"

"Yes." Tansen rubbed a hand over the place where Zarien

had healed his own *shir* wound. "You do. And the Olvar . . . Fires of Dar! The Olvar knew it!"

Zarien rose to his feet, looking increasingly distressed. "He was just a crazy old—"

"You felt strange down in the tunnels. So close to all their water magic," Tansen said with growing conviction. "Because you felt things there that an ordinary person can't sense. That *I* can't sense."

Tears gathered in Zarien's eyes. "It's not my fault!"

Mirabar quickly said, "No one is blaming you for anything, Zarien. This is a gift. This is—"

"*He* doesn't think so," Zarien told her, gesturing to Tansen.

"I'm . . . very surprised." Tansen congratulated himself on such restrained understatement. "This isn't what I, uh . . ."

"Zarien," Mirabar said, giving Tansen a threatening look as she rose to her feet, "have there ever been any waterlords . . . er, I mean, water magic among the sea-born? It's a gift which can skip so many generations that someone like Baran can inherit it without even having known it was in his bloodline, but—"

"How do you know that?" Tansen asked.

"I've been living with a waterlord for a while now," she reminded him. "I already know many things about water magic which I didn't know before." She rubbed a hand cross her gently swelling belly. "And I'm learning more every day."

"I've never heard of water magic among the sea-born," Zarien said, sounding tragic.

Najdan spoke from his prostrate position. "Your grandfather . . . might know. He's very—"

"No!" Zarien said emphatically.

"Your grandfather," Tansen breathed. "We should talk to him."

"No!" Zarien repeated.

Najdan said, "Linyan should be nearby, with Ronall. They—"

"*No!*"

They all looked at Zarien.

"I'll talk to him alone," Tansen offered. "You don't have to see him or sp—"

"I've seen him," Zarien ground out. "We've been living on his boat for days."

That surprised Tansen. "Have you talked to him, then?"

The boy's complexion darkened under his tattoos. "Yes."

Tansen frowned. "You've found out the truth?"

"Let's go," Zarien said suddenly.

"The truth . . ." Najdan repeated.

"Stay out of this!" Zarien warned the assassin.

Mirabar asked, "Out of what?"

Najdan raised a hand to Mirabar, who helped him rise to a sitting position and then knelt on the ground to support him. "Why didn't Searlon . . . want to kill you?" he asked Zarien.

Tansen glanced in confusion at the dead assassin. "What?"

"He had plenty of time," Najdan said to Zarien. "But he didn't do it. And you told me he didn't intend to do it."

Zarien just stared mutely at the ground.

"Searlon said . . ."

"What?" Tansen prodded, feeling bewildered and slow-witted.

Najdan finished, "That he knew the truth about Zarien."

It was like being slapped without provocation. "What does Searlon know about my son that I don't? *What* truth?" His gaze sharpened as he looked at Zarien, who continued avoiding his eyes. "The truth about your parents?"

Mirabar asked, "Zarien, is it that you're not really sea-born?"

"I am!" Zarien said defensively, suddenly coming to life. "My mother was sea-born. But she went ashore, and so the Lascari shunned her. When they found out I went ashore, too, Linyan said it was in my blood, because my mother had left them to marry a drylander . . . The rest doesn't matter."

"A drylander? And your mother . . ." Mirabar suddenly gasped, her brilliant eyes going wide as she gazed at Zarien. "A

sea-born woman ... fifteen years ago ... water magic ..."
She forgot about Najdan, who sagged a little as she abandoned
him to rise to her feet, her gaze fixed on the boy. "She made
choices which brought her ashore ..." Mirabar made a funny
sound. "It was her, wasn't it, Zarien? Your mother was Alcinar."

Zarien flinched violently. "How do you know that?"

"Who's Alcinar?" Tansen demanded.

"A sea-born woman," Mirabar said slowly, "who went to
live in the mountains, where she was loved obsessively ... by
two waterlords."

"Two waterlords?" Tansen suddenly remembered what
Mirabar had told him about Baran and Kiloran, about the origin of their mutual enmity. "Are you saying Zarien's mother
was Baran's wife?"

"Yes."

"But you said Kiloran killed her."

"After I married Baran, Kiloran sent a letter to Belitar
telling Baran that Alcinar had not died, that she had, in fact,
escaped Kandahar and eluded pursuit. He promised to tell
Baran everything ... in exchange for my corpse."

Tansen felt his temples throbbing.

"I thought Kiloran was lying," Mirabar said, "but I was
wrong. Alcinar must have run away after she realized she was
pregnant." She placed her hand over her stomach again. "She
may even have had the help of the child in her womb. That's
probably what enabled her to escape Kandahar."

"And then she returned to sea," Tansen murmured in a daze.

Mirabar nodded slowly. "The best place for a tattooed sea-
born woman to hide from a waterlord."

"And the Lascari protected her," Najdan guessed, "which
no one would have expected—"

"Because," Tansen said hoarsely, "the Lascari shunned her
when she chose Baran."

"But when she returned to them, pregnant," Mirabar said,
"believing that Baran was dead ..."

"They cared for her and then took the baby as their own when she . . ." Tansen looked at Zarien and guessed, "Died in childbirth?"

He shook his head. "Drowned herself after I was born," he muttered. "Linyan says she was . . . not right in the head when she returned to them. Sorin and Palomar had just lost a baby, so they became my parents then."

"I don't understand," Mirabar said, "why they never contacted Baran to tell him about her or you. He had a right to know, as her husband. And even the sea-bound must have heard of him as time passed and he grew so famous. Is it because he's a drylander? Or because he's a water—"

"They just didn't know it was the same man," Zarien said quietly. "*I* didn't know until you told me just now. They thought her husband was a merchant who died before I was born."

"Of course," Mirabar said. "Alcinar told them the Baran she had married was dead."

"I'm so sorry, Zarien," Tansen said, placing a hand on the boy's rigid back.

"A child of water, a child of sorrow," Mirabar murmured. "You've been right here all along."

The true implication of this story, in light of Zarien's newly discovered gift, suddenly struck Tansen like the blow of a *yahr*. "Which one of them is your father?" he demanded.

Zarien flinched again. "It doesn't matter."

A terrible dread settled into Tansen's belly. "Which one?" he insisted.

Zarien started backing away from him.

Tansen's heart pounded so hard he felt dizzy.

No, it can't be. I won't let it be. Not this. I can't bear this.

Mirabar said, "Tansen, maybe we should—"

"You know, don't you?" he said, stalking Zarien as the boy continued backing away from him. "Your mother might have been unbalanced, but if she still knew enough to find the Lascari, then she surely knew which man's child she was carrying."

"Why does it matter which one of them it was?" Zarien said hoarsely.

Tansen's blood was roaring in his ears. "If Searlon didn't come to kill you, then he came to take you back to Kiloran."

Zarien licked his lips. "Searlon's dead. Let's just—"

"*Didn't* he, Zarien?"

Zarien stumbled in his retreat as his feet encountered Searlon's corpse. "Stop!"

Tansen caught him, then seized his shoulders. "Did Kiloran mean to capture you to torment Baran? Is that why Searlon didn't kill you?"

"Let go!" Zarien shouted.

"Or did Kiloran want you for himself?"

"Tansen!" Mirabar said. "You're frightening him!"

"*Sirana,* help me up," Najdan insisted.

"No, you're too weak."

"Help me up!" Najdan ordered.

Tansen shook Zarien. "*Answer me!*"

"Stop! Let me go! No!"

Something hit Tansen from behind. He reacted instantly, releasing Zarien to defend himself. Zarien fell down, sprawling across Searlon's body, and howled in revulsion. Tansen glared at Najdan, groggy and swaying, who had interfered.

"Stay out of this!" Tansen warned.

"Control yourself," Najdan chided wearily.

Tansen looked at Zarien, now making horrified noises as he rolled away from Searlon's corpse only to land in a pool of Searlon's blood, which made him howl again.

Tansen was suddenly, bitterly ashamed of himself.

He moved to extend a hand to his son. "Zarien—"

"*Kiloran!*" Zarien screamed at him, tears streaming down his tattooed face. Blood splattered him as he drummed a fist against the ground. "I'm Kiloran's son!"

Tansen froze. Shame was replaced by blank shock. A long moment of sheer empty idiocy.

Kiloran's son.

All this time he had thought Kiloran wanted to kill Zarien. All this time . . . Kiloran had just wanted to bring him home.

Tansen thought he was going to vomit. Overwhelming denial flooded him.

No.

He felt revulsion. Fury. Nausea. Fear. He utterly and completely rejected . . . *this.*

Water magic. A waterlord. Kiloran's heir.

"No." He only knew he'd spoken aloud because of the reaction on Zarien's face.

Mirabar said, *"Tansen."* But she seemed so far away, so faint and distant.

"He will be," said the Olvar, looking at Tansen, *"more than you imagine. Perhaps more than you can accept."*

Zarien rose to a kneeling position, covered in blood now. Red with it. Streaked and painted in it. Drenched in blood.

Kiloran's heir.

Tansen remembered strange dreams, voices warning him, a suspicion in his nightmares that the boy was more than he seemed . . . Perhaps he had clung to believing Zarien was the sea king because it shielded him from fears he'd been unable to face or acknowledge.

A waterlord.

My own son with their power in his veins.

Yes, the very thought, even the faintest flicker of suspicion had been too awful for him even to consider. He knew that now.

But *Kiloran's* child? No, he had never imagined that, not even in the torment of his dreams.

"Are you going to kill me, too, now?" Zarien asked harshly.

Tansen's mind was working slowly. "What?"

"The way . . ." A terrible expression crossed Zarien's face. "The way you killed your father?"

The ground seemed to give way beneath him. *"What?"*

"Searlon told me, before he died." Zarien kept a hard, wary gaze fixed on Tansen. "You murdered your own bloodfather."

He heard harsh breathing. Someone panting in sudden panic. The pounding of an appalled heart.

"You killed him because he was a waterlord's son." There was betrayal in the boy's voice. Awful suspicion in his expression.

Tansen tried to think. "Zarien, no. It wasn't—"

"Who was Armian?"

His blood froze.

"Armian?" Najdan repeated in surprise.

"Najdan," Mirabar admonished.

There was a terrible silence.

"*Dar . . .*" Tansen said, hating Her.

He understood now. This was his punishment for what he had done. To love Kiloran's son as his own, and to lose the boy's love because of Armian.

She was truly the destroyer goddess.

"That's the name you cry in your sleep that I don't recognize," Zarien said in a low, hate-filled voice. "It's him, isn't it? He's the one you beat to death with a *yahr.*"

He heard Najdan draw in a shocked breath.

"I can explain," Tansen said, willing his son to believe in him.

"He was your father! And you killed him!" Zarien shouted.

"Yes, I did," he confessed, trying to keep his voice even. "But—"

"No wonder you never told me about him!"

"I didn't know how to tell you. Please, listen—"

"You had no right to make me your son without telling me what you had done to the man who made you his!"

It was true. He couldn't deny it. "You're so young, I didn't want to—"

"But you didn't know the truth about me. And now that you do?"

Tansen's vision was blurry. "We'll work it out. I pro—"

"Stay away from me," Zarien ground out.

"*Zarien.*"

"You are not who I thought you were."

"And you're not who I thought you were, but that—"

"You are not who you told me you were."

"I'm sorry. I—"

"Armian didn't know the truth about you," Zarien said, "but I do. It's too late for him." That young, innocent face looked as cold as Kiloran's had ever looked when he said, "What about me, Tansen? Am I next?"

He was horrified. "No! Zarien!"

"Searlon said that when you knew the truth—"

"I don't give a damn what Searlon—"

They both leapt back as a ball of fire appeared out of nowhere and exploded between them.

"That's enough!" Mirabar announced.

Tansen ordered, "Don't inter—"

"You've both said quite enough for now," she snapped, giving Tansen a hard look. "Zarien, come with me. We'll go find Elelar and tell her the *toren* is alive. If she has questions, you can explain to her what the sea king is."

"But I—"

"We will all take time to calm down before returning to this discussion," she added. "Tansen, Najdan will take you to the Lascari—*slowly*—and you will inform them how many of us need to leave for Shaljir tomorrow."

"Shaljir?" Zarien repeated blankly, resisting her tugging on his arm.

She said, "I am sure your father . . . I mean, I am sure Tansen would like you to remain in the east with him—"

"Yes," Tansen said.

"—but that may not be wise, since he has a battle to fight."

"More waterlords to kill?" Zarien muttered.

Tansen clenched his teeth rather than offer yet another unwise comment.

"Baran will certainly want to meet Alcinar's son," Mirabar continued, "so I suggest you come to Shaljir with us, Zarien, and then you will go on to Belitar with me and Najdan. Tansen can come there for you after his work here in the east is done."

Tansen wanted to protest, but another warning look from Mirabar silenced him. Realizing how badly he was reacting to these successive shocks, he forced himself to say calmly to Zarien, "What would you prefer to do?"

"I'll go with the *sirana*," Zarien said sulkily.

It felt wrong in his bones to be separated from the boy now, but he didn't know what to do or say. He couldn't take back his initial reaction to discovering Zarien was Kiloran's son, and he certainly couldn't take back what he had done to Armian all those years ago.

"A little time apart to calm down and accept things," Mirabar suggested, "might be best for both of you."

"Yes," Tansen replied vaguely, hoping she was right. He only knew that his own judgment was terrible at the moment.

"Besides," Mirabar added, "you're going into battle, so you'd have to leave Zarien somewhere, anyhow."

Tansen sighed and nodded. "I'll, uh . . ." He looked at his son, dirty and blood-drenched, who wouldn't meet his eyes. "I'll come to Belitar for you, Zarien. After I'm done here."

Zarien shrugged.

He knows about Armian. He knows.

How could Tansen ever explain it to him?

Kiloran knew what would be even worse than taking him from me. Kiloran knew what would hurt me the most.

Tansen should have told Zarien before now. Searlon should not have been the one to break it to him. Tansen's blood ran cold when he imagined how Searlon must have explained it to him.

"Zarien," he said, "do you remember what I told you about bloodpact relations?"

Zarien shrugged again.

"It's as binding as a birth relationship. You're my son. It doesn't matter who your sire was."

"Even if he's still alive?" the boy asked icily.

Tansen glanced at Najdan, who shrugged. Mirabar looked

uncertain, too. It was such an unusual circumstance that none of them knew what it meant, in traditional terms.

Tansen knew what it meant to *him*, though. "You're my son, and nothing can change that. *Nothing*."

"Is that why you killed your father?" Zarien asked. "Because nothing could change that, either?"

"No. I did that because . . ." He closed his eyes and tried to form coherent statements which could possibly make his son understand what he had done to his father. "He was—"

"The *torena* will want to know her husband is alive," Zarien said gruffly. *"Sirana?"*

Mirabar gave Tansen a worried look, but agreed, "Yes. Let's go find her, Zarien."

She turned and led the boy away. Najdan swayed on his feet as he and Tansen watched them for some time.

"He's a very willful boy," Najdan said, "and keeping him alive was harder than I expected."

"I don't know what to do," Tansen muttered.

"Kiloran's son," Najdan said. "I never knew . . . It would seem that even Kiloran never knew."

"Or he'd have gone after Zarien years ago."

"He has always wanted an heir."

Fear flooded him. "And if he finds out what we know now . . ."

"That Zarien has the gift?" Najdan nodded. "That would be very dangerous indeed. However, we have protected the boy this long, and now Searlon is dead. Belitar is extremely safe . . . as long as one doesn't annoy Baran, that is."

"Then keep him safe until I come for him."

"Of course." Najdan rubbed his brand-new scar. "And it's not a promise I make lightly. A *very* willful boy."

ELELAR STARED AT Ronall in stunned, disbelieving silence as he approached her on the beach. She was surrounded by an entourage of praise singers who now lived to protect the baby in her arms. Ronall—*Ronall!*—was surrounded by sea-born folk who revered him as the sea king, consort to a goddess and chosen to lead them as a people.

"You look . . ." Elclar paused, trying to determine what was so different about Ronall, apart from the ragged sea-born clothes and the healthy glow of his sun-darkened skin. "Sober?"

He nodded and smiled. "Sober. You look . . ." He glanced at Gaborian and laughed, a surprisingly light and happy sound. "Like a mother!"

"Where's my horse?" she asked suddenly.

He shook his head and looked amused. "I always suspected that would be your first question if we ever met again."

"Well?"

"I'm sorry, Elelar. It was stolen from me some time ago. In the mountains."

"That was my favorite horse," she said irritably.

"I know. I'm sorry."

"And as for leaving that chattery fool Chasimar at my estate . . ."

"She had nowhere else to go, Elelar." After a moment, he added wryly, "All right, I also did it to annoy you. I'm sorry about that, too."

She realized that these subjects were far from the most important things they needed to discuss, so she resisted the undeniable urge to utter recriminations. Instead, she said, "We should talk."

"Of course."

He led her to some wreckage upon which they could both sit, then politely suggested everyone else remain at a respectful distance while he got reacquainted with his wife. Elelar explained what had happened to her, amazed at how calmly he accepted the whole story.

"I am to . . ." She took a deep breath and concluded, "Acknowledge you as Gaborian's father."

"I won't deny it," he promised her. "Though it does seem as if the gods are enjoying a good joke, doesn't it?"

"Did you and a sea goddess really—"

"Yes." He sounded as if it were a perfectly normal circumstance.

"But how did you and she actually—"

"That's none of your concern, Elelar." When she sat back in surprise, he added, "I haven't asked for details about you and Cheylan, have I?"

She realized that a number of subjects were indeed best left closed. Instead, she asked cautiously, "Will you live at sea from now on?"

His smile was bittersweet. "You mean, you want to make sure that I won't be living with *you* from now on."

"Yes," she admitted. "That's what I mean. I suppose we'll have to see each other from time to time, if you are to be Gaborian's father, but—"

"I will live at sea," he replied. "I will come ashore often, though. As the sea king and as Gaborian's father, I hope to have enough influence with the people to prevent any more Valdani in Sileria from being murdered. Starting today."

It was such a calmly selfless answer, it momentarily surprised her. Nonetheless, she said firmly, "And *when* you come ashore—"

"Don't worry," he assured her without resentment. "I will never disturb your bed again. I belong to her now, and . . ." He shrugged. "It wouldn't be right to go to another woman—least of all to one who doesn't love me."

"You're . . ." She thought she'd misunderstood. "You're going to be faithful to her?"

He grinned. "Yes, Elelar. I am."

"I don't believe you."

"I know." He shrugged. "It doesn't matter."

"No, I suppose not."

"But I would indeed like to be Gaborian's father," he added, "and to see him often. I imagine he's the only child I'll ever have."

She nodded in acceptance of that. "Now the sea-born will have a stake in what happens on land, since the sea king is father of the Yahrdan."

"I think it's why a drylander was chosen," he admitted. "Well, one of the reasons, anyhow. To unite the sea-born and the landfolk of Sileria."

"Your Valdani blood will also help convince the Valdani—"

"That they have an ally ruling Sileria, instead of an enemy."

They sat in silence for a long moment.

"You and I . . ." he said at last.

"Yes?" she asked warily.

"I suppose we will never be close," he said, "but I hope we can learn to be at ease with each other."

"Perhaps, Ronall," she said. "In time."

He smiled serenely and agreed, "In time."

MIRABAR AWOKE FROM the nightmare with a pounding heart. She lay there panting in reaction, hoping she hadn't cried out and disturbed anyone else. She listened to rain drumming against the simple shelter which the pilgrims had constructed out of flotsam, and tried to bring her frantic breathing under control.

Even after she calmed down, though, sleep was impossible. So, when the rain stopped, she finally rose and escaped into the open air. It was nearly dawn, anyhow, she noted; too late to bother going back to sleep. Tansen was out here, practicing in the dark with his swords. She supposed she should have expected him to be awake tonight.

When he realized she was present, he paused, and asked breathlessly, "What are you doing awake?"

"Nightmare," she said briefly.

He sheathed his swords. "About?"

"Cheylan."

He came to her and put his arms around her.

She sighed wearily and rested against him, not caring that he was damp. "I'll . . . I'll dream about killing him for a long time, won't I?"

"Probably," he admitted.

"It wasn't just . . . stabbing him, which was bad enough. It was . . ."

He kissed her hair. "You cared about him. Trusted him."

"It makes killing him . . . the stuff of nightmares."

"I know."

Of course. If anyone would know, it was Tansen.

"Would you like me to try to explain to Zarien?" she asked. "We'll be together for a while, and he may listen to someone who . . . who isn't you."

He thought about it, resting his cheek on her hair. "If you think he wants to talk about it," he decided. "If he seems willing to listen. It may be easier for him to talk about all this with you than with me." He moved away from her as he added, "And so far, he's only heard Searlon's version of what happened."

"Then someone *must* speak to him," she said with certainty.

"And I have to leave tomorrow if I'm to attack Verlon, as planned. I can't delay. The whole plan will collapse if I delay. I can't . . ." He rubbed his forehead. "I can't stay and try to show Zarien that I don't care who his father was. I can't . . . I have to go tomorrow, Mirabar. I *have* to."

"I know."

"I handled it so badly today . . . Yesterday? Finding out about the water magic. About Kiloran." He spread his hands. "I was just so . . ."

"It was a shock," she agreed.

"Yes, but that's no excuse for what I . . . for how I responded."

"You don't need an excuse," Mirabar said. "You're human and you make mistakes."

"I *frightened* him, Mira."

"Yes. And if you learn from this mistake, perhaps you won't frighten him again."

"I lost my head. I know better, but I—"

"You know better as a *warrior*. You're not so highly trained as a father." She smiled and added, "Or as a lover."

"No," he said wryly. "Maybe if I went and trained for another five years . . ."

"I think we would miss you."

"And I might not learn to keep my head, anyhow. Being a father and being in love are both a lot more difficult than being a *shatai*. No wonder there are no schools. Who could possibly master love well enough to teach others?"

She smiled and took his hand. "Apart from how you reacted, keep in mind that Zarien had also been through a great deal by the time this happened. And he was already terrified of how you would react even before you said or did anything." She squeezed Tansen's hand. "He's young, and he'd been through too many ordeals to do anything but panic and lash out. You didn't handle things well, I admit, but he would have been afraid and angry no matter how you had behaved."

"Not *that* angry," Tansen said with self-condemnation. "Not *that* afraid."

"The water magic was a shock to him, too."

"Did you suspect from the beginning?" he asked.

"No. I suppose I should have, but I knew so little about water magic before I married Baran. Zarien himself seemed so sure that the healing of your *shir* wound had something to do with your destiny, while you thought it might be some power he possessed because *he* was destined to be the sea king." She shrugged. "But when Najdan lay dying of a *shir* wound like yours . . . You had survived, and so I reached for the only thing that might make him survive, too. I don't know how I thought of it. It was just . . . instinct. Desperation." She smiled wryly and added, "If it hadn't worked, I suppose I might have made *you* try, next."

"Zarien didn't suspect, either," Tansen murmured. "He had

no idea about his gift. The surprise on his face when Najdan's wound healed . . ."

"It must have been an overwhelming moment for him," Mirabar said. "Especially knowing how you feel about water-lords. And can you imagine how he felt about admitting he's the son of your most hated enemy?"

"Can you imagine how he felt about finding out I killed my bloodfather?"

She rested her cheek against his shoulder. "I'll talk with him. And when you come to Belitar, you'll talk with him, too. When he understands, he'll be able to forgive you."

"I hope so," he whispered.

"He has to," she said. "What else can he do? You're his fa-ther."

ZARIEN WATCHED WARILY as Tansen approached him in the hazy morning light.

"I would take you with me," Tansen said, "but it's danger-ous. You really . . . can't come."

Zarien shrugged. "Fine."

Tansen added with a strained attempt at humor, "And don't try to follow me, either, the way you did that time I left you at Dalishar."

He didn't have the *stahra* anymore. "I can't follow . . ." A cold memory swept through him.

Follow him until you cannot, Sharifar had said, glowing in the strange light of the Guardian Calling in the sacred caves of Mount Dalishar.

"I can't follow you," Zarien murmured to himself.

Sharifar had told him to let the current carry him, and it had brought him here. To this moment. To the things he now knew and had spent the night wishing he didn't know.

"I'll come to Belitar when I'm done." Tansen placed a hand on his shoulder.

Lost in thought, Zarien flinched.

Tansen frowned and removed his hand. "We'll talk then."

"Fine."

Follow him until you cannot, Sharifar had said.

"When will that be?"

You will know.

Now he knew. Now he understood. It had always been his destiny to part with Tansen. This day had to come.

Now it was finally here.

"I have to go now, Zarien," Tansen said.

Zarien nodded. "Well. Go."

Tansen hesitated, as if wanting to say more, but then he finally turned and walked away.

"Tansen!" Zarien said, a sudden panic flooding him.

Tansen turned back instantly. "Yes?"

"I, uh . . ." Zarien shrugged. "Good luck."

Tansen smiled. "Thanks."

Only when Zarien was sure that Tansen was too far away for anyone to catch up with him did Zarien say casually to Mirabar, "I have to go get something I dropped yesterday. When Searlon . . . you know."

"You shouldn't go alone," she said instantly.

"*Sirana,* Searlon is dead, and there are sea-born and pilgrims everywhere. I'll be safe."

"All the same—"

"I'd rather do this alone. I . . . need a little time to myself."

She hesitated a moment, then nodded. "Of course. Just don't be long. We need to leave very soon."

Zarien nodded and left her side, walking south along the shore. He felt bad that he would cause a delay in their departure, but that couldn't be helped. They would search the shore and the beach for him, then probably search the coastal cliffs. They wouldn't find him, though, and sooner or later they would have to give up and take the *torena* and the baby to Shaljir.

It was a while before he reached the extreme southern end of the bay and found the rocks upon which he had washed ashore yesterday.

It was still there. Right where he'd left it.

He picked up the oar which was Sharifar's gift to him. She had already claimed the sea king, so there must be another reason she had returned this *stahra* to him now.

As Sharifar floated in the enchanted Guardian fire on Dalishar, she had said to Mirabar, *His gifts will lead him home.*

Water magic. The gift inherited from his father. The gift which Tansen hated. Zarien would not go thirsty on his journey, even if the longed-for arrival of the rains had yet to swell the rivers and ponds inland. He knew he would find whatever he needed along the way. It was one of his gifts.

It's time for you to seek your true father, Sharifar had told him when she first sent him ashore. He later grew to believe she meant Tansen, to whom this *stahra,* a gift from the goddess, had led him before. But now he knew it had led him to Tansen as the man who would search for Ronall, when he disappeared from Shaljir on his strange quest for death, and eventually help Zarien bring him to Sharifar.

No, Tansen was not his true father. Now Zarien understood. And now he knew why Sharifar had given the *stahra* back to him. She was fulfilling her part of the bargain. He had brought her the sea king. Now she would send him to his father.

He picked the *stahra* up off the rocky shore and held it in his hands, feeling its familiar weight, reacquainting himself with its texture.

If Tansen had killed his bloodfather, why wouldn't he kill his bloodson? Zarien shivered when he remembered the shock and revulsion on Tansen's face after he saw Zarien heal Najdan and realized what it meant. Zarien remembered Tansen advancing menacingly on him, his expression full of anger and hostility, then shaking him and shouting into his face when he suspected the truth about Zarien's parentage.

Zarien remembered thinking in that instant that Tansen was going to kill him, and that only Najdan's interference and Mirabar's presence stopped him from doing it.

He killed Armian, so why wouldn't he kill me?

Zarien hadn't wanted to believe Searlon, but Tansen himself admitted it was true. He'd done it. Murdered his own bloodfather.

By all the winds . . .

Armian's father was a waterlord. How much more would it gall Tansen that Zarien's father was Kiloran?

And he knows I have inherited Kiloran's power. He saw.

Armian had trusted Tansen, and that was why he was dead. Zarien wanted to live, so he mustn't make the same mistake.

He turned the *stahra* over slowly in his hands, knowing his bonds with the sea were finally being dissolved. He must live on land, and he only knew of one person who would protect him from Tansen.

"I want to meet my father," he whispered.

The *stahra* quivered slightly, and then began leading him west.

He was finally going home.

66

UNITY AMONG THE HERD MAKES THE LION LIE
DOWN HUNGRY.

— Moorlander Proverb

KILORAN FOUGHT DESPAIR as he had fought every other enemy in his life; but it was the most ruthless foe he'd ever known, and unlike other enemies, it did not bleed when he fought back.

He had lost Cavasar. The defeat was now conclusive. Hundreds and hundreds of those who'd been loyal to him were dead. Many of his assassins were lost. Guardian magic now shielded the city's water supplies, thwarting every effort he made to push it away.

Meriten was dead, too, and so the Shaljir River, as well as all its surrounding territory, now belonged to the loyalists. Even Kiloran's own traditional territory was threatened. So far, he defended it; but with so many of his allies dead, the loyalists now had far more people and power to direct specifically against *him*.

He was losing men nightly to ambushes and skirmishes. And he was—yes, he must admit it to himself privately—growing tired. The constant struggle to ward off the Guardians pushing at his power was exhausting. Moreover, whoever was helping Baran try to take the mines of Alizar and the Idalar River from him, they were getting stronger. They were wearing him down.

And now the long rains had come, ending the season when Sileria could not survive without Kiloran's mercy.

Even worse, he'd heard the rumors spread by pilgrims returning from their sojourn on Mount Darshon: The new Yahrdan had been born and was already being acknowledged as Dar's chosen ruler, the number of his followers increasing every single day. Meanwhile, the people of Sileria now turned on Kiloran for violating Sanctuary and killing a woman.

And she was the wrong *woman.*

Here in the depths of Kandahar, where he had launched the various schemes which had made him the most powerful waterlord in the Society and which had ensured that he had maintained that stature for many years, he was starting to feel trapped, even desperate.

Had he been wrong about his destiny? Even he, who had wrested victory out of so many discouraging situations over the years, was losing heart and felt unable to measure what could now be gained by persisting.

Could he, alone against so many enemies and with so few allies left, still triumph?

Kiloran suddenly felt old. Old and alone.

A young assassin entered the hall to disturb his brooding. The lad crossed his fists and bowed his head. "*Siran,* someone is approaching."

Kiloran lifted his brows in silent inquiry.

"A boy." The assassin looked puzzled. "Sea-born, it's reported. Tattooed. Carrying an oar."

His heart stopped for a moment, and then began thudding loudly. "Is Searlon with him?"

"No, *siran.* He's alone."

Kiloran was briefly distracted by that news. Where was Searlon? What was the boy doing here unescorted?

He brushed aside these thoughts. What mattered was that the boy was here. Renewed optimism flooded Kiloran. How could he have sat here moping so pathetically when he knew Searlon was busy accomplishing his most important, most secret plan? Yes, the plan which could still change his fate. The alternative which no one even suspected.

"No one is to interfere," Kiloran instructed the assassin. "Let the boy come to the lake. I will admit him."

When he felt someone approach the water he commanded, he began whirling it around with his power, spinning it and then hardening it to create a crystalline staircase which led into this very room. He sensed the moment the boy set his foot on the first step.

He also sensed what he had hoped to feel ever since learning of Zarien's existence: the cold, clear gift of another water wizard. Yes, when Zarien's foot touched the ensorcelled stair, Kiloran immediately sensed the water's response to the boy's inherent, ungoverned power.

He has it!

Kiloran had more than a son. He had an heir.

There would be no more morbid brooding. No more time wasted in regretting what was lost. He and his son had so much work to do together. So much to accomplish and achieve.

This turn of events would come as a terrible blow to

Tansen. Perhaps hurt his judgment and damage his effectiveness. As for Baran . . . Ah, what mistakes *wouldn't* that emotional madman make once he learned that Alcinar's son was here, in Kandahar, with Kiloran?

Yes, I can still win. I can turn this around. Anything is possible now.

He would teach his son everything he knew, so that even if he died before achieving unchallenged rule of Sileria, he would die knowing that his heir would achieve it.

The boy came into his presence now, descending the stairs. First one foot appeared, then the other. He was indeed carrying an oar. Kiloran smiled in puzzled amusement. Then he saw the rest of his son. A good-looking boy. Dark, dark-eyed, slim, and wiry. He wouldn't be a tall man, but he would be a memorable one. His face was intelligent and sensitive beneath those sea-bound tattoos. His eyes were curious, quick, and momentarily filled with awe as he entered Kiloran's underwater palace and looked around.

Their eyes met, and Kiloran liked the courage he saw there.

"You have the look of your mother," Kiloran said without thinking. Yes, the boy was very like Alcinar.

Zarien held his gaze. "Hello, father."

Kiloran smiled. Oh, yes, he had everything to fight for now. "Welcome home," he said to his son.

MIRABAR STOOD ON the balcony of Santorell Palace next to Elelar, acknowledging the cheering crowds in Santorell Square while her mind dwelled yet again on Zarien.

How could she face Tansen? What could she tell him?

After Zarien disappeared, she made pilgrims, praise singers, and sea-born folk spend four full days searching for him. No one had seen anything, and no one could find any trace of him.

What will I tell Tansen?

Had Zarien thrown himself into the sea and drowned? Why couldn't they find a body? Had he run away? Had another of Kiloran's assassins found him?

After four days, she knew they wouldn't find Zarien. More-over, word had spread that Gaborian was there, and she knew it might be only a matter of time before someone from the dwindling Society launched an attack on them. She didn't re-ally know where Tansen was, nor how to get word to him. All she could do was get Elelar safely to Shaljir, and then go to Belitar to await Tansen's arrival.

How can I face him? I've lost his son!

"You're scowling at them," Elelar said to her. "Smile and wave."

"Huh? Oh!" Mirabar stopped scowling at the cheering crowd and did as advised.

The people of Shaljir were gathered here to celebrate the birth of the prophesied ruler, whom Mirabar—backed up by Jalan and other witnesses to Gaborian's birth—proclaimed as the child foreseen in her visions and chosen by Dar to lead Si-leria.

"I think that's enough," Elelar said, turning away from the adoring crowd at last.

Mirabar followed her inside with relief. Elelar handed the baby in her arms over to Faradar. Radyan was nearby, as he always seemed to be ever since their arrival in Shaljir. Mirabar could tell by the way he looked at Faradar—and she at him— that protecting Gaborian was only his *other* reason for being underfoot all of the time. Still, Mirabar liked him, and she was glad that Faradar was finding happiness.

Later today, the members of the Alliance who had set up a temporary government here would meet with a large group of Guardians, as well as with Radyan and other available leaders of the loyalists, to start determining who would govern the country while Gaborian was clearly too young to do so.

Mirabar would stay for the first few meetings, but then she

and Najdan would have to leave for Belitar. She didn't know when Tansen would arrive there, and she didn't want him to have to wait for her.

RONALL WALKED ALONG the shore of the Bay of Shaljir, accepting the prayers, blessings, and praise of the sea-born folk. Some of these people had seen his rebirth and had sailed here alongside the Lascari. Others were only just now learning that he was the sea king.

He had been acknowledged at Santorell Palace as the new Yahrdan's father, and he had commenced the work of convincing Silerians here, as well as in the east, to start living in peace with the Valdani among them. However, he had no interest in remaining at Santorell Palace now to watch the Alliance, the loyalists, and the Guardians all haggle over who would rule—and how—until Gaborian came of age. Yes, Ronall cared about what happened on land, and he would teach the sea-born to care, too, to become part of Sileria so they could serve her—and serve Gaborian. But the details of how the landfolk allotted power hadn't interested him even when he'd been one of them.

He was eager to go back to sea now. Tonight. Where he would again slip overboard and embrace *her*.

The sea breeze ruffled his hair, and he tasted salt on his tongue. The square-sailed boats of the sea-born folk rippled in the changing wind as another rainstorm blew down from the mountains. Water lapped at the shore, and he listened to the sea-born dialect being spoken all around him, realizing that he'd need to learn it.

"Will you be tattooed, *siran?*" Linyan asked him hopefully, walking awkwardly by his side on the dryland. "We would like to mark you as the sea king."

Ronall considered this. "Does it hurt?"

Linyan laughed, as if Ronall were joking. Ah, well.

This was his life now. And it was a good one.

* * *

BARAN FOUND IT amusing that Tansen clearly felt awkward about arriving at Belitar before Mirabar did. Enjoying himself, Baran did his best to make the *shatai* as uncomfortable as possible. Starting with nearly drowning him in the moat.

"I'm so sorry about that," Baran apologized as Tansen, drenched and dripping, was escorted into his study. "I haven't been feeling my best lately, you know."

Scowling, Tansen replied in an unusually surly tone, "I hear you're dying. My condolences."

"Oh, dear, you're just *soaked,* aren't you?"

"Where's Mirabar?" Tansen demanded.

"In Shaljir. I've had a letter from her. She mentioned you might be arriving, though I had no idea you'd impose on us quite so soon."

Haydar entered the damp study with a blanket for Tansen, which Baran found disappointing. Then she returned with refreshments for Tansen and stayed to ask questions about Najdan, whom Mirabar had neglected to mention in the letter which Derlen the Guardian wrote to Baran at her request.

"That will be all, Haydar," Baran said after a while, growing bored with the subject of Najdan's health.

She protested, "But I also wanted to ask about—"

"Leave the room, Haydar," Baran said pleasantly, "or I'll kill you."

She left the room.

"I occasionally," Baran confided to Tansen, "find her a little annoying."

Tansen dripped on the furniture and maintained a stoically blank expression.

"So I take it Verlon is dead?" Baran mused.

Tansen briefly looked as if he thought this might be a trick question, then he nodded. "While we attacked Verlon, the Lironi and their allies engaged Verlon's remaining friends elsewhere, in a number of decisive battles. The Guardians with me managed to occupy Verlon completely with an attack on the streams crisscrossing his land," he said. "Then we invaded his estate, and more Guardians set the house on fire while we fought his men. He couldn't douse the fire, and so he came outside."

"Where you killed him," Baran surmised.

"And when I left the east a few days ago, the remaining waterlords and assassins there were being hunted down and killed, or else fleeing Sileria."

"So the Society in the east is shattered," Baran murmured.

"Yes. They're finished. Now we just have to finish our work here."

"Have you heard the latest news about Gulstan and Kariman?" When Tansen shook his head, Baran told him what had happened while he'd been in the east. "Then, with Gulstan depleted after having finally destroyed Kariman, your friends overran Gulstan's remaining territory and killed him." He paused. "So your plan worked. Er, I assume it *was* your plan, from the start?"

"Yes," Tansen admitted, his face remarkably inexpressive.

"I thought so. It had your touch. I could never understand why neither Gulstan nor Kariman realized that. Well, no, I'm lying," he confessed. "I always thought they were fools, and I'd have been astonished if they were shrewd enough to realize that you murdered Geriden and planted gossip, all in an effort to get them to destroy each other. Oh, Kiloran probably suspected. But those two? No. They just did what you wanted them to do." He clucked his tongue. "It's really rather sad, if considered from a certain point of view."

Tansen drank the tisane Haydar had given him and said nothing. What a dull fellow. What in the world did he and Mirabar find to talk about when they weren't plotting the deaths of their enemies?

"The letter which my wife sent from Shaljir," Baran said, choosing the marital phrase deliberately, "also mentioned the extraordinary birth of *Torena* Elelar's baby. We live in such interesting times." When Tansen didn't respond, he added, "Pilgrims have been passing through here with the same story, too. Returning from their sojourn on Mount Darshon. Their accounts are a trifle incoherent, but very enlivening."

"Has Mirabar told you anything else?"

"Should she have?"

After the slightest hesitation, Tansen said, "She's bringing my son here with her."

"Ah, the sea-born boy."

"She told you?"

"That she was bringing him here? No. As your increasingly burdened host, may I ask why?"

Tansen was silent for a long moment, and Baran found himself wondering what was going on behind that habitually controlled face. Tremendous tension entered the room, without any obvious source. To Baran's surprise, he suddenly felt anxious. No, this was no ordinary man, he noted. Despite Tansen's lack of sorcery, no one should ever make the mistake of assuming he was without power of his own.

Finally the *shatai* spoke. "My sea-born bloodson, Zarien, is Alcinar's child."

Baran fell back against his chair as if he'd been kicked in the chest. His mind jumped wildly from one thought to the next, then settled on protesting, "She wasn't pregnant."

"The last time you saw her? No. She wasn't."

Baran felt his mouth hanging open stupidly as he stared at Tansen. His blood roared in his ears as he realized what the other man was saying. "You're telling me . . . *No.*"

"Kiloran sired a child on her. Zarien. We only learned this . . . very recently."

"Alcinar." Kiloran raping her, forcing her, doing whatever he wanted to her . . . And then . . . "She got pregnant?" he whispered weakly, feeling tears gather in his eyes.

"And she escaped," Tansen said. "Mirabar thinks it was the child in her womb that enabled her to leave Kandahar. Alcinar thought you were dead, so she went to the Lascari for help."

"It was true, then," Baran muttered. "What Kiloran wrote to me after I married Mirabar."

"Yes. Alcinar ran away. Alive."

A terrible, cruel hope washed through him. "Is she still alive?" he pleaded.

"No. I'm sorry."

It took a moment for Baran to find his voice again. "How did she die?" When Tansen hesitated, he snapped, "Tell me or I'll kill you."

Tansen sighed. "She drowned herself after the baby was born."

"Alcinar . . . *No* . . ." Baran groaned, grief-stricken, and slowly bent over in his chair, weeping now. "I would have cared for her . . . I was still trying to free her . . . Noooo . . ."

He was shaking, horrified anew, as if it had happened yesterday rather than fifteen years ago. Hatred and the thirst for revenge burned icily inside him. Sorrow and despair made him weak and wild.

He only faintly heard Vinn shout, *"Siran!"* There was a scuffle and the sound of something clattering to the ground. Then Vinn demanded breathlessly, "What have you done to Baran?"

"I've brought news," Tansen said quietly.

There was a pause before Vinn asked, "Has something happened to the *sirana?* To the child she carries?"

"No," Tansen replied.

Baran finally lifted his head and looked at them. Tansen, without unsheathing his swords, had disarmed Vinn and now held him in what must be a very painful position, judging by the grimace on Vinn's face.

"Siran, what's wrong?"

"My wife . . . My first wife . . ." Baran sighed and wiped his eyes. "Had a child before she died." Vinn's face brightened momentarily. "No," Baran said, forestalling the question. "Kiloran's child."

Vinn's expression changed to one of dark understanding. "Where is the child now?"

"On his way here, by now, I think," Tansen said, releasing Vinn.

"He's Tansen's sea-born bloodson. A Lascari. As Alcinar was." Baran sighed. "Lascari . . . It was a name we never even said aloud again after she chose me and they shunned her. We married and came to the mountains, where she'd never see or hear the sea again, never be reminded . . ." He was still shaking. "Kiloran's son."

"He's *my* son now," Tansen said firmly. "But Kiloran has learned the truth."

"How?"

"He wanted to know more about Zarien. Maybe because he's my son. Maybe because it bothered Kiloran that there was another Lascari on land. So Searlon interrogated Zarien's grandfather—"

"Linyan."

Tansen nodded. "Yes."

"I knew him. I sailed as his passenger when I was a merchant. That's how I met Alcinar. She was his daughter. Linyan didn't like transporting landfolk, but he liked the profits." Baran paused. "I can't say I'm sorry to hear Searlon got a hold of him. Intolerant, bigoted old—"

"The point is, as a result of Searlon's interrogation, Kiloran knows who Zarien really is and wants him back."

No one but Kiloran could inspire the mindless panic which momentarily seized Baran. "I won't let him have Alcinar's child!"

"And I won't let him have my son." Tansen paused. "So you and I finally have something in common."

"Mirabar should have brought him straight to Belitar," Baran said frantically. "She shouldn't stall in Shaljir."

"Searlon was the one looking for him, and Najdan has killed Searlon. Kiloran has no way of knowing Zarien is in Shaljir now, and I don't believe he'd expect it. We have time."

He met Baran's eyes and added, "But I will feel much better once he's here."

"He'll be safe here," Baran promised. "I swear I will keep him safe . . . as I could not keep *her* safe."

"So that's something else we have in common," Tansen said without sympathy. "We each lost the woman we loved to a waterlord."

"But you'll get yours back," Baran said bitterly. "I'll be dead before my own daughter is born."

"At least you will see Alcinar's son." After a moment, Tansen added, "He's a fine boy. And . . . he has the gift." When Baran stared at him, he elaborated, "Water magic."

"We must never let Kiloran have him," Baran said, feeling sick and not sure if it was raw emotion or just his illness. "Kiloran will corrupt him. I know. He corrupted me."

"Zarien," Tansen said, "is not corruptible."

Baran snorted. "You don't understand what water magic can do to a person. You don't know what Kiloran can do to the mind."

"Oh, yes, I do," Tansen replied grimly.

"LET THE WATER be in you, that you may be in the water," Kiloran said to Zarien. "Answer when it whispers, so it will answer when *you* whisper."

Concentrating fiercely, the boy closed his eyes and spread his tattooed hands towards the deep pool of water which currently sat in the center of the floor of Kiloran's great hall.

"Let it seduce you," Kiloran said, "that it will be seduced by you, too."

The boy had tremendous natural talent, and he had come here at an age when he was ripe to develop it. With the arrival of this lone young man, Kiloran felt the burden of age melt away from his spirit as renewed ambition and vigor flooded him. Even the sorrow of Searlon's death—a terrible loss which Zarien had reported to him—couldn't discourage Kilo-

ran now that his heir was here with him. And *Najdan* . . . Yes,
taking revenge on Najdan was yet one more reason to survive
and triumph, whether he did it himself or through his son.
Meanwhile, based on Zarien's vague explanations of what
had happened in the cast, he also knew that Cheylan was dead.
That was one more enemy eliminated, and Kiloran was glad.

"Love the water," Kiloran taught Zarien, "so that it can love
you in return."

This was where a waterlord gave his heart of stone. To *this*.
To the pure chill of power which rewarded his talent beyond
anything Dar could ever offer. This great gift drank a man's
heart like wine, and he never missed what lesser men thought
of as love.

"And when the water loves you," Kiloran told his son, "then
you will own it and do with it as you will."

They had been working on this lesson for a long time, and
the boy's skin gleamed with the sweat of exertion. He was
breathing hard, his arms trembling . . . and then suddenly the
pool of water bubbled.

"Yes," Kiloran encouraged. "Don't lose focus now."

"Focus on the tas . . ." Zarien murmured, blinking as his
concentration suddenly broke.

"What?" Kiloran snapped.

"Nothing," Zarien said, resuming his work. "Nothing."

The bubbling water started to churn, turning itself over and
over in response to the boy's will. Cold steam rose from it,
dancing uncertainly in response to Zarien's inexperienced
and ungainly power.

"Yes." Kiloran inhaled. "Now bring it under your will. Can
you feel it responding? Can you grasp it in your senses and do
with it as you please?"

Breathing hard, Zarien stared unwaveringly at the
water . . . which finally began to grow still, solidify, and resolve itself into the crystal-hard floor of the room.

"Excellent!" Kiloran said, very pleased. Dyshon had ap-
prenticed for more than a year without demonstrating the abil-

ity Zarien was revealing after only a few days. "This is very promising!"

"I'm glad you're pleased, father."

"And are *you* pleased?"

"Of course."

Kiloran examined the floor. It was bumpy, and some of it was not as solid as it should be, but this was nonetheless a very good first effort. He turned to Zarien and saw how tired the boy now looked. Yes, that was natural. Kiloran thought back to the distant past when he had begun learning to command his power and remembered how draining and exhausting the work had been at first.

"That's enough for today," he announced.

Zarien looked relieved. "I am . . . a little tired."

Kiloran went to sit in the gold-encrusted chair of shells where he normally received visitors. Zarien now wandered idly around the room, looking at the collection of beautiful objects which came from all over the three corners of the world, as well as the mementos Kiloran kept here of victories won, allies lost, and lessons learned. He would give the boy Alcinar's bracelet, which he had kept here for so long, but he no longer had it, having used it as bait to enable Dyshon to kill Wyldon.

"You did not make all of these *shir*," Zarien guessed, studying the vast display of wavy-edged daggers on one watery wall.

"No," Kiloran agreed. "I took them from the bodies of my enemies."

"But there are also *shir* here which look like yours."

"They are. I keep them to honor valuable men I've lost. And to remind me of past mistakes." He paused before pointing to a particularly beautiful *shir* and saying, "That one was Armian's."

Suddenly transfixed, Zarien impulsively reached out to it. Perhaps he felt the vicious cold emanating from it, because he stopped himself just before touching it. "What's it doing here?"

"Tansen returned it to me when I rescinded the bloodvow and joined the rebellion."

"Tansen kept it for a long time, then?" Zarien's voice was very soft.

"Nine years."

"He never keeps them," Zarien murmured, frowning vaguely at the *shir*. "Well, maybe just for a little while, if he needs them for a plan. But he doesn't ever . . ." He stopped speaking for a moment. "Why do you think he kept it?"

"Guilt? Safety? A trophy?" Kiloran shrugged. "One rarely knows, with Tansen." He watched the pensive boy, wondering what he was thinking. "Armian was Harlon's son—a great waterlord who died many years ago—and Armian had the same gifts which you possess. Tansen, as you must know, hates water magic and wants every waterlord in Sileria dead." Kiloran knew that the young could be very sentimental, so he added for good measure, "He would have killed you, Zarien. Surely you know that?"

"Yes, father," Zarien replied absently.

"There can be no other way, not for Tansen. He murdered his own father, and he'd have murdered his son. You must never doubt that."

"No, father."

"I imagine you were fond of him, but you must never trust him. As long as he lives, he is a terrible danger to you."

Zarien turned his back, ostensibly studying more of the displays along the walls. But Kiloran felt his tension as he turned to a new subject and asked, "After you joined the rebellion . . . Why did you kill Josarian? He was the Firebringer."

Fire, the old Guardian woman had promised him.

Kiloran ignored the intrusive memory. "Josarian killed my son, Srijan."

"But you had already tried to kill Josarian, hadn't you?"

The boy was bold. It was an important quality, so Kiloran didn't try to discourage it. "Josarian challenged me. Publicly as well as privately. Tried to give *me* orders. Told *me* how to run the Society. He interfered in our business and opposed our plans. He became my enemy, and so I had to treat him as an enemy." His son turned to face him as he said, "This is an important lesson, Zarien, so remember it well: Pardon one offense, and you encourage the commission of many."

"I . . ." Zarien again looked at Armian's *shir,* his brow furrowed.

"Permit rudeness, and you're offered insolence next. Permit insolence, and opposition follows. And opposition . . ." Kiloran waited for Zarien to meet his gaze again. "That we cannot allow."

"Never?" Zarien asked.

"Never," Kiloran confirmed.

"But is it right to make people go thirsty just because—"

"If you want to be one of us," Kiloran told him, "you cannot be one of them. And you, Zarien, are one of us. Your gifts have determined your choice for you."

"My gifts," the boy murmured.

"Our destiny," Kiloran taught him, "is to be obeyed. Demanding obedience is the source of the Society's power."

"But the Society is all but finish—"

"You and I are just beginning," Kiloran informed him.

"Why must it be this w—"

"What do the waterlords seek when they withhold water?" Kiloran prodded.

Zarien hesitated before replying, "They seek obedience."

Kiloran nodded, pleased. "Now do you understand?"

"Yes, father, now I understand."

MIRABAR AND NAJDAN traveled through territory which was increasingly coming under the loyalists' complete control. They pushed themselves hard to return to Belitar in haste now that they'd left Shaljir.

When they encountered some Guardians traveling from the

sacred caves of Mount Dalishar to Shaljir, where they would join in celebrating the birth of the Yahrdan, Mirabar was shocked by what they told her.

"The visions are continuing at Mount Dalishar?" Mirabar asked in astonishment, certain she must have misunderstood.

"Golden eyes in the sky at night," one of them confirmed.

"Or sometimes a fist," another added.

"And a voice. 'He is coming.' "

"But he is already here," Mirabar protested. "I don't understand."

"We saw this again just three nights ago, *sirana*."

By then, Gaborian had already arrived in Shaljir.

"Perhaps, *sirana*," another of the Guardians said, "it's Dar's way of assuring the people that Gaborian is indeed the one? The pilgrims at Darshon witnessed the birth, but the pilgrims at Mount Dalishar did not. So Dar may feel they need encouragement."

"Perhaps," Mirabar said, frowning in puzzlement.

"Sirana," Najdan called from his position on a rocky ledge, where he kept watch for the approach of strangers. "If we want to reach Belitar by sundown, we must press on."

She agreed, took her leave of the Guardians bound for Shaljir, and waited for Najdan to help her mount her horse.

"What do you think?" he asked.

"I don't know," she admitted.

It soon began raining again, which made their progress slower than they would have liked. It was nearly dark by the time they reached Belitar. Baran must have been advised of their arrival, since the moat hardened for their crossing as soon as they reached it. As they entered the main hall of their damp, crumbling home, Haydar flung herself at Najdan.

Mirabar assumed Baran was, as usual, in his study, so she immediately headed in that direction. She stopped in surprise, though, when Tansen emerged from that room.

How can I tell him? What do I say?

She was so distressed that it took her a moment to realize that he looked tense, furious, and . . . *scared*. Yes, *Tansen* looked scared.

"Baran's just received a letter from Kiloran," he said without greeting her or acknowledging Najdan.

Somehow, she already new what he would say next.

"He's got Zarien."

THEY BEGAN FORMING their plan that very night, then explored possible problems and new solutions the next day as they prepared for battle.

"*This* was his contingency plan. And it's a good one, you must admit," Baran said to Tansen. "A son, an heir, someone to carry on Kiloran's plans for years to come. Even better, a weapon, one exquisitely crafted to hurt *you* and affect your judgment. And as for me . . ." They were in the waterlord's study, examining a detailed map which Najdan had made of Kiloran's territory and of Kandahar itself. "Kiloran thinks I'd never attack, now that I know he's got Alcinar's child. He thinks I'd be too afraid of the boy getting killed. Maybe he even thinks this news will crush me. Distract me. Make me too irrational to do anything to interfere with his plans."

"Will it?" Tansen asked grimly, studying Baran's haggard, thin, pain-lined face and the wild glitter in his feverish eyes.

"I would rather Alcinar's son died," Baran said coldly, "than become what Kiloran will turn him into. What Kiloran turned *me* into."

Tansen seized Baran by the front of his expensive tunic and flung him hard enough against a damp wall to get his full attention. He ignored Mirabar's cry of protest and took Baran's throat in his hand.

"Zarien is my son," he reminded Baran, "and if he dies, I will kill you and every single one of your assassins. Do I make myself clear?"

"Tansen," Mirabar admonished.

Baran wheezed with laughter. "The amusing thing," he choked out, "is that Kiloran undoubtedly thinks *you're* the one who'll be willing to kill the boy. Perhaps even passionately determined to kill him. Kiloran has never understood love, after all, and everyone knows how much you hate waterlords."

"Zarien's not a waterlord," Tansen growled. "He will never be one of *you*. If I thought for a moment that he would be . . . yes, I'd kill him. But he's better than you! He's strong enough to have this gift without letting it twist him into what the rest of you became."

"Oh, and is *that* why he ran away and sought out Kiloran the moment he knew what he was, what he could become if guided by a master?" Baran prodded nastily.

"He ran away because he was scared and confused," Tansen insisted, pressing harder on Baran's throat in his anger at himself, in his knowledge of what his instinctive rejection had driven Zarien to do. "He went to Kiloran because he believed he had to. And because . . ."

"Because," Najdan said quietly from across the room, "he is a *very* willful boy."

"Yes," Tansen admitted, "he is."

Baran sighed. "Tansen, this physical violence is unnecessary, ill-mannered, and—dare I mention?—extremely unwise." The fountain started bubbling menacingly behind Tansen.

"Stop this right now or I'll set you *both* on fire," Mirabar warned them.

Realizing he was wasting time and losing focus, Tansen released Baran, who sank weakly into a nearby chair.

"You're lucky Vinn didn't see that," Baran said. "He'd kill you for such disrespect. Well, he'd *try,* anyhow—and then just think of what a mess we'd have on the carpet."

The assassin was busy preparing Baran's men for an assault on Kandahar. Tansen had already sent messages to Lann in Zilar and to Pyron at Dalishar with detailed instructions to organize as many people as possible for an invasion of Kiloran's territory which must work in coordination with the attack on Kandahar itself. The rest of the Society was dead, fleeing, or in shambles. Most of Sileria was coming under the loyalists' control. Now, Tansen knew, the time was right to make a direct, all-out attack on Kiloran. Their losses might be terrible, but if they defeated him, then the war would, at last, effectively be over.

The complication was that there was one person inside of Kandahar who mustn't be harmed under any circumstances. One person who absolutely must be taken away from Kiloran, by any means available, and the sooner the better.

"I will go into Kiloran's palace," Tansen told Baran. "Alone. I will not have one of your men panic and gut my son."

Baran replied, "I feel compelled to point out that Kiloran will certainly kill anyone who enters his—"

"And you," Tansen ordered, "will distract Kiloran so I can get the boy out safely."

"I'm not as strong as I was," Baran said. "I may not be able to fight Kiloran long enough to—"

"Would you really sacrifice Alcinar's son?" Tansen snapped, loathing this mercurial wizard. "Is that what you want for her bloodline?"

Baran slumped in his chair and looked suddenly older. "I should have been his father."

"If you were," Tansen said coldly, "Searlon probably would have killed him and sent you his corpse."

"I have always," Baran said, "found your company unpleasant."

"Give me time to get Zarien out of Kandahar." The waterlords had taught Tansen to be ruthless, so he added, "Since you didn't save Alcinar from Kiloran, saving her son's life does seem to me to be the very least you might do for her now."

"Damn you," Baran growled.

"If we're leaving tomorrow," Mirabar said to Baran, obviously trying to end their argument, "you will need to rest now."

"First," he said, "I would like to take my leave of the Olvara. I daresay she will miss me when I'm gone."

Mirabar looked stricken as she stared at him.

She cares, Tansen thought. *She actually cares about him.*

It hurt. He once again understood how much his feelings for Elelar must have hurt *her*. And she was upset now, as she escorted Baran out of the study, because . . .

Baran thinks he won't be coming back to Belitar.

While Tansen wouldn't miss him, he did find this pessimism disturbing. If a waterlord of Baran's experience and still-formidable power didn't expect to survive a direct assault on Kiloran . . .

What chance does a shatai *have?*

And how likely was it that he could last long enough to get Zarien away from Kiloran?

Focus on the task at hand.

"Najdan," he said to the assassin, "I have more questions about Kandahar itself."

"Of course." Najdan came over to the table upon which lay the map he'd drawn and began discussing details of the attack with him. They were surprised by Mirabar's return.

"Velikar is accompanying Baran down to the caverns," she said. "I wanted to talk with you while there's time."

Tansen nodded and gave her his attention.

"Have you thought . . ." She folded her hands. Cleared her throat. Unfolded her hands.

"What?" he prodded.

"What will you do if Zarien doesn't want to come with you?"

"I'll bring him out anyhow."

"I mean . . . if he resists." She sighed. "Tansen, what will you do if he tries to kill you?"

"He won't."

"What makes you so sure? He has already run away and gone to Kiloran. Who knows—"

"*I* know. I know Zarien. I know his heart. He is not a killer."

"Since the moment he arrived at Kandahar," she persisted, "Kiloran has been turning him against you."

"Kiloran has been trying to make him afraid of me. But he can't convince him to kill me."

"Zarien is powerful, and probably already learning how to use his p—"

"He won't use it to kill." Tansen shook his head. "He doesn't have that in him."

"Is that what Armian thought, before you killed him?"

The silence was tense and cold.

"I always had it in me," Tansen said at last. "Zarien doesn't—"

"Isn't that what Armian thought? I *know,* Tansen. I've Called him. I've felt the surprise he felt. Not just that you could kill *him,* but that you could kill at all!"

"Zarien's a better person than I was, Mirabar. He's never dreamed of becoming an assassin. He's never admired killing or wanted to be in the Society. He hates violence."

"Tansen," she pleaded, "what if he's changing? You changed. What if you don't know him as well as you think you do? What if you've seen only what you want to see?"

"I'm not that—"

"Aren't you? You've been with him all this time and never suspected he had water magic, even though you now realize there were many signs, right from the start."

"Even you didn't sus—"

"I hardly know him! You lived with him as his father. You didn't see it because you didn't want to see it!"

"That doesn't—"

"Now you don't want to see this!"

"There's nothing to see!" he shouted.

They stared at each other, their fast, angry breathing competing with the sound of the tinkling fountain.

"This bickering," Najdan said, "is pointless."

"This bickering," Mirabar snapped, "may mean the difference between life and death for Tansen."

"You're wrong," Tansen told her.

"I hope so. But what if I'm not?"

"The *sirana* may or may not be wrong," Najdan said to Tansen. "We cannot learn the truth in advance. Therefore, I would suggest that you be very careful when you approach Zarien. It's undeniable that you have not yet learned everything about him which there is to know."

"I know *this*," Tansen said firmly. "He won't hurt me."

Najdan and Mirabar looked at each other. Both of them looked worried.

"FATHER!"

Armian didn't respond. They were on the dark cliffs east of Adalian. The long rains had finally come.

Tansen knew he should do it now.

"Father," he said again.

Fast, please Dar, let it be fast. Let him not suffer. I can't bear to make him suffer . . .

It was Tansen's weakness, Armian said, this distaste for suffering.

Father!

"Do you know what you're doing?" Josarian asked.

Tansen insisted. "It's not in him to hurt me. It's not!"

"You wouldn't believe this *was in him either, would you?" Josarian lifted his tunic and revealed the silvery scar of a* shir *would healed by water magic. "You refused to see it. What else are you refusing to see?"*

"No! You're wrong!"

He saw Armian's silhouette faintly outlined against the tormented coastal sky . . . then realized it was himself.

"Be careful!" he warned the man as the boy prepared to betray him.

"It's too late," Josarian said sadly. "He won't listen. You know he won't."

"Father!"

Tansen looked over his shoulder in response to Zarien's cry.

The boy struck out. The blow connected, reverberating through Tansen's soul. He fell to his knees.

Tansen froze, like a statue, when he saw his son standing above him on that windswept cliff.

"Zarien?" he said incredulously.

No! No! No!

"Tansen?" Armian said.

"Forgive me, father," Tansen whispered.

"How could you do it?" Zarien asked him angrily. "Am I next?"

"I can't hurt you," Tansen told him. "I could never hurt you."

"Does he know?" Josarian asked.

"I don't know," Tansen admitted. "I thought so, but . . . I've made mistakes."

"You always do."

"I want him to know."

"Then you have no choice, do you?"

"I have no choice," Tansen agreed, as the rain fell all around them.

"Tansen?" Armian repeated in that shocked, disbelieving voice, that voice so rich with betrayal, so wounded by treachery . . .

"Father . . ."

"Father!"

Tansen awoke with a pounding heart and quivering limbs. Breathing fast, he sat up and held his pounding head in his hands. Rain drummed hard on the crumbling roof of Belitar and pattered noisily on the moat outside his window.

"Zarien . . ."

The damp bedchamber seemed to close in on him as he took harsh gulps of air.

Did Zarien have nightmares about *him* now, he wondered?

Oh, Dar, how did we come to this?

Step by step, he realized wearily, as all journeys were made.

Had he been a bad father? He had tried so hard . . . and he had been one so briefly . . .

No. He would not accept the ache of unbearable loss which threatened to eat his heart. He was *still* a father. He would show Zarien he loved him and would never hurt him. And he would get his son back, or die trying.

In the end, it was the only choice he could make.

67

MAY THERE BE ONE THING IN YOUR LIFE FOR
WHICH IT IS WORTH GIVING UP EVERYTHING ELSE.
                                        —Kintish Proverb

MIRABAR WAITED IN the dark with other Guardians. Two full moons glowed orange-red in the starless night sky. Blood moons hovering over a nation which had torn itself apart in pursuit of this moment.

Tonight the past and the future came together in the present. The tragedy of wasted lives, the waste of squandered talents, the enmity which ran stronger in their blood than love, the love which they had twisted into something too destructive to survive.

Fire and water, water and fire . . .

The bloodlust of a people which they must learn to stop quenching. The vengeance which could no longer be their whole way of life. The passion for betrayal which they must stop indulging.

Tansen had promised the loyalists they would end the war here. Now. With this battle. He had brought them to the edge of Kiloran's territory from all over western Sileria; quietly, so as not to alert Kiloran; quickly, because every day that Zarien remained at Kandahar tormented him; and in great numbers, because Kiloran was cornered and desperate, and therefore more deadly than ever.

Next to Mirabar, Baran was spitting up blood in the dark while Velikar held his shoulders.

"Can you do this?" Mirabar asked Baran, frowning with grim concern. The journey from Belitar had already nearly finished him. She didn't see how he could possibly confront Kiloran now.

"I suppose I have lived *only* to do this," he assured her weakly. "Stop fussing, Velikar."

"Drink this," the Sister growled at him as he sat back, breathing hard. She handed him a waterskin filled with one of her tisanes.

Right after dusk, Tansen's advance scouts had invaded the territory from all directions and started killing Kiloran's sentries. Now the Guardians were waiting for him to order them to commence the next part of the plan.

"Baran," Mirabar said, feeling her eyes mist as she tried to say goodbye to him. "If you and I don't meet again—"

"Oh, don't get sentimental now," he grumbled. "I was just starting to get used to you disapproving of everything I say and do."

"You *enjoy* my disapproval," she said as a tear rolled down her cheek.

He changed the subject. "You will stay back here, surrounded by your friends?"

"She will," Najdan said from his lookout position nearby.

"Mirabar?" Baran prodded.

"Yes," she promised.

"You have a child to think about." Baran was thin-voiced and breathless. "Remember that she takes whatever risks *you* take . . . and she's taken enough of them lately. A father mustn't be too lenient about that kind of thing, after all."

"I . . ." She impulsively reached out, took his hand, and

placed it on her swelling belly. "What do you want me to tell her?"

"The truth," he said. "All of it." He shrugged. "She'd find out anyhow, I imagine." After a pause, he added, "Tell her I only regret the things which weren't my choice—and that includes never meeting her." When he heard Mirabar sniffle, he pulled his hand away and wondered irritably, "Where in the Fires is Tansen? I'd have stayed home in bed if I knew he was going to wait until this illness kills me before starting the attack."

Tansen said from somewhere in the dark, "Keep your voice down. People in *Cavasar* probably heard that."

"Finally," Baran murmured. "We were afraid you'd changed your mind and joined the enemy."

Mirabar heard Tansen's stealthy footsteps before she saw him, and she could only recognize him once he was very close. They wouldn't normally launch an attack like this on a twin-moon night, but the lingering smoke and ash in the sky ensured that the light from the moons was rather dim. Now, even as she greeted Tansen, one of the moons disappeared completely behind another rain cloud.

Tansen squatted down beside them. "I don't think Kiloran knows anything's amiss yet, but we need to move right away. He probably has a relay system set up for regular reports from his sentries, and he'll be suspicious the moment the pattern is disrupted."

"Everyone's in position, then?" Najdan asked.

"Yes," Tansen replied. "Lann sent a runner asking how soon his men can start killing assassins. Pyron sent a runner complaining that his men have got the worst terrain and greatest number of obstacles. Vinn sent a runner saying he's getting bored."

Najdan replied dryly, "They sound ready."

"They are." Tansen asked Baran, "Are you?"

"I'm aflutter with girlish excitement," Baran assured him. "Velikar?"

As the Sister helped Baran to his feet, Tansen helped Mirabar to hers and said, "Use your judgment. When you think we're about halfway to the lake, start the attack. The men will go into action when they see your signal."

"Please come back," she said helplessly, clinging to his hands.

"If we don't succeed," he said, returning her grip, "go straight back to Belitar. Immediately."

"Tansen—"

"You understand how important it is that you live," he persisted, freeing one hand to touch her stomach gently. "Not just to me, *kadriah*, but to her. To Gaborian. To the future."

"I do wish," Baran said, "you'd remember that's my wife you're handling so casually."

Tansen froze for a moment. Then, very deliberately, he leaned forward and kissed Mirabar on the mouth.

Baran, rather predictably, laughed.

"Let's go," Tansen said to Baran.

"I do feel," Baran said, "that we've grown closer through these hardships, don't you?"

"And," Tansen added, "try not to talk. I'm feeling irritable."

"Before we part," Baran said to Mirabar, "I would like to ask one burning question—what in the world do you see in him?"

She touched Baran's cheek. "I suspect you'll survive this and live long enough to torment me while I'm in labor."

He grinned and, to her surprise, kissed her hand before turning to go. A moment later, he disappeared into the dark with Tansen.

"One really cannot blame Kiloran," Najdan said, "for having spent the past fifteen years trying to kill him."

THE FIRST SENTRY report of the night had failed to arrive.

"You seem worried," his son said.

Kiloran replied, "A waterlord can never afford to be lazy, complacent, or careless. Especially not in times like these."

He looked at Zarien. "Rather than send men in search of my missing sentries, to suffer an ambush in their turn, we will prepare for attack."

Zarien's eyes widened. "You really think we're about to be attacked. *Here?* This place seems as if no one could—"

"They can't, but I will be surprised if they're not about to try." He placed a hand on Zarien's shoulder, sensing the boy stiffen slightly as he did so. "You're frightened."

"Yes," Zarien said slowly. "I am."

Kiloran sighed. "I had hoped that some lingering sentiment for you, some remnant of fatherly feeling, might have prevented Tansen from doing this."

"He doesn't know I'm here," Zarien protested.

"Oh, I imagine he does." He shook his head. "I had also hoped that even if proper feeling didn't prevent him from attacking, then Baran would stop him. But Baran is weakening rapidly, perhaps too weak even to interfere with Tansen now. That power which I told you is cooperating with Baran to fight me for the Idalar River and the mines of Alizar . . . It's ascendant now. There's been a shift in the past few days. I can feel it. It's as if Baran can no longer hold on."

"Baran?" Zarien was momentarily surprised, then he drew in a sharp breath through his nostrils. "You *told* him I'm here."

"Yes, in a letter," Kiloran replied. "And unlike Tansen, Baran is sentimental."

"So you thought he'd interfere with any plans to attack Kandahar—"

"Plans which Tansen was bound to make very soon."

"—because I'm Alcinar's son."

"It seemed a wise precaution. Unfortunately, it appears to have been a wasted effort."

"And since Tansen expected to find me at Belitar—"

"He'll know by now that you're here." Kiloran paused to make his next point crystal clear. "And Tansen is probably attacking us tonight."

Zarien looked horrified and turned quickly away. Kiloran

watched sympathetically. Betrayal was indeed a terrible wound, and Tansen had the habit of inflicting it on those who'd loved him.

BARAN'S INSIDES CHURNED like liquid fire. His legs trembled with weakness. His vision blurred. He felt Tansen's hand on his arm, partially supporting him, partially dragging him. He wanted to say caustic things, but he didn't have the strength.

Then he felt a sudden explosion of power all around him and drew in breath through his teeth in revolted surprise.

Tansen whispered, "What's wrong?"

He didn't need to answer. Tansen saw, as he did, pillars of fire start shooting up from a dozen different places in the dark. Then more. Then still more. The Guardians had commenced the attack and would now try to overrun Kandahar with their power. The flames shot so high up that loyalists positioned all around Kiloran's vast territory would see it, even if they were a day's journey away, and begin their attacks, too. Now Baran perceived more sky-reaching fire in the distance, as other hidden groups of Guardians saw the initial signal, passed it on, and commenced their own skirmishes.

"I hope," Baran said weakly, "that Kiloran finds this much fire magic as nauseating as I do."

"We've got to keep going," Tansen said, pulling Baran's arm over his shoulder. "You've got to approach the lake while he's distracted, before he realizes you're here."

Baran staggered along at the *shatai*'s punishing pace, letting Tansen carry half his weight, concentrating hard on moving his feet in some semblance of walking.

He felt the power emanating from Kandahar already, and it got stronger as he approached it. It couldn't obliterate the appalling feel of fire magic closing in from every direction— honestly, he'd vomit again if this kept up—but it was nonetheless monumental, extraordinary, and wonderfully cold. It invigorated him, even cleared his head.

This icy, pure power which he and Kiloran commanded began seducing him all over again as he approached the place where he had first learned to master it. And the thought of finally confronting that vicious old reptile in all-out, unrestrained, mortal combat . . . Yes, it almost made him feel renewed.

I should have done this years ago, he realized.

"I feel him," Baran murmured to Tansen. "Oh, I feel the old man now. All of his strength. Right here."

Tansen released him and he sank to his knees. Smelling the water. Feeling it warn him away, so well protected by its master. Hearing it lapping at the shore.

Lake Kandahar, where Alcinar had been held prisoner.

"I couldn't do it then," he said grimly, "but I can do it now. I have learned so much since then."

"I hope you're right," Tansen said. "Zarien's life depends on it."

"Yours, too," Baran said with a nasty smile. "Now aren't you sorry you tried to seduce my wife right in front of me?"

"I've already seduced your wife," Tansen replied. "Now wouldn't you like me to survive long enough for you to punish me as I deserve?"

"*Mirabar* was unfaithful?" Baran shook his head. "No one has any standards anymore."

"What do we do?" Tansen prodded impatiently.

Baran rose slowly to his feet, then moved towards the water. He felt the deadly chill and said, "Don't touch it. Not yet."

"Baran, wait, what are you—"

Baran ignored him, wading into the dark lake which Kiloran had ruled, unchallenged, for so many years.

"He knows you're attacking," Baran said over his shoulder to Tansen. "He knows you're here."

"How do you know?"

"Remember the mines of Alizar? He's doing the same thing here."

"Making the water so cold it'll kill anyone who touches it?"

"He's protecting his home from the attack. Protecting Zarien. However, if I can reverse what he's done . . ." He smiled sweetly at the *shatai*. "I hope you can swim?"

"*GUARDIANS.*"

"Where?" Zarien asked, his heart pounding.

Kiloran looked even paler than usual. "Everywhere. All around us. Pushing into my territory. A huge number of them."

"*Siran,*" one of the assassins said, "I want to join the battle!"

"Yes, take everyone with you except those four." Kiloran gestured to the men he meant. "They will stay here to guard my son."

"Surely no one can get inside the palace?" Zarien asked.

"No, but I do not intend to leave you unguarded, even so."

As Kiloran turned to leave him, Zarien said, "Where are you going?"

"Up to the surface. This is a battle. I need to see what's happening in order to fight our enemies most effectively."

"I want to come, too," Zarien said quickly.

"No, you'll be safer here."

"But I—"

"No," Kiloran said. "Stay here, with these four men."

Zarien nearly protested again, but he saw the look in Kiloran's eyes and held his silence.

TANSEN WAITED UNTIL Baran told him it was safe, and then he waded into Lake Kandahar, his flesh crawling as he did so.

"Faster," Baran chided. "I don't think he's noticed me amidst all the fire magic yet, but he will any moment."

This is even worse than jumping into the gorge below Geriden's house was.

But Zarien was down there, so Tansen took a deep breath and dived for the center of the lake. Once again, he wished he'd asked his son for swimming lessons. Fortunately, there were no strong currents here. Nonetheless, the lake was deep, dark, cold, and terrifying—he'd have been scared even if there *weren't* a waterlord somewhere in this lake eager to kill him. However, he'd survived this journey once before, albeit as a captive—when he'd returned Armian's *shir* to Kiloran— so he didn't turn back, not even when his lungs felt close to bursting.

And then he saw it—the glow of light from the underwater palace. By now, his whole body ached with the need to breathe and he feared his lungs would reflexively gulp for air at any moment. Desperate to inhale, he headed for the glowing dome directly beneath him, letting the weight of his swords and his boots help carry him there as his arms pushed water behind him.

He hesitated briefly when he reached the palace ceiling. There were figures below him. People moving around.

They've seen me.

He couldn't hesitate. Surprise was his only weapon against Kiloran now. He unsheathed his swords and tumbled through the domed ceiling as if it were made of . . . water.

The *floor,* however, felt as if it were made of crystal, and hitting it knocked the wind out of him.

Tansen heard Zarien scream, "*No!*" and rolled to defend himself just as two assassins jumped him. He killed one of them instantly, but the fall had disoriented him enough that the other made a deep slash in his shoulder before Tansen parried the blow and slit his throat.

"Stop!" Zarien shouted.

He was on his feet as two more men circled him. *Only* two, he saw to his relief. He made them retreat with a flurry of thrusts, and used the moment to look around. They were in the main hall, where Kiloran had once nearly killed him; and Kiloran was nowhere in sight.

"Don't! No!" Zarien cried.

Make it fast, he advised himself, *and get out of here.*

He attacked, making one of the assassins fall over Kiloran's gaudy chair, which gave him time to kill the other one. Then he beheaded the assassin who was recovering his balance.

Only when they were all four dead did he feel the intense pain of the *shir* wound one of them had just inflicted. He turned to Zarien, his heart racing, his lungs still aching, and his body protesting that hard fall.

KILORAN, WHO WAS too old for steep climbs, let a large bubble of water carry him to the surface. He was only halfway there when he realized what else was invading his territory besides fire magic.

Baran.

He knew the flavor of Baran's reckless talent too well to mistake it now.

So *that's* why Baran had let his ally, whoever it was, completely take over their battle for Alizar and the Idalar. Not because he was dead or very nearly so, but because he was consecrating his remaining strength to violating Kandahar tonight.

Kiloran felt a moment of elation as he realized he would finally get to kill Baran, who'd been fool enough to return to Kandahar after all these years.

The moment was short-lived, though. All that Guardian magic! The sudden assault, on such a huge scale. He should have realized it was Tansen's plan, designed to confuse Kiloran's senses long enough to keep him from sensing that Baran was here . . . until Baran had had time to remove the deadly, flesh-killing chill from the lake.

Zarien.

The boy was no longer protected. The lake was vulnerable, and so was the palace.

Was Tansen already in the lake? In the palace? He couldn't

tell. Baran's power was now assaulting his domain, trying to pull Kandahar away from his command, and the fire magic everywhere was corrupting his senses.

The one thing Kiloran couldn't afford to lose was his son, his heir, his future. Zarien might be able to protect himself with his power, but they hadn't actually practiced any such skills yet. Therefore, saving the boy from Tansen must be Kiloran's first priority, even above the battle raging for control of his entire territory.

As for Baran . . . Did that madman really think he could invade Kiloran's domain and survive? Did he think Kiloran had never prepared for the assault of another waterlord?

As Kiloran commanded the water to take him back down to his palace to protect his son, he closed his eyes, ignored the clamoring of fire magic spreading rapidly throughout his territory, and called upon the darkest, strongest power of a waterlord: the White Dragon which guarded Kandahar against the attack of another waterlord.

Kill Baran, he commanded his watery offspring in silence. *He has finally come home, so we can kill him, at last.*

TANSEN'S EYES MET Zarien's. The boy looked shocked and horrified. He was also, Tansen realized with a sick feeling, backing away from him.

Tansen said, "Let's go."

Zarien's gaze dropped to the swords in his hands. Tansen looked down and saw they were drenched in blood. He didn't even bother to flip it off, simply resheathed them as they were, though he supposed he'd regret that later.

"Zarien," he said calmly, trying to break through the boy's evident shock. "We're leaving."

Zarien froze. He looked confused. "We . . . You . . . you came . . ."

Tansen prodded. "*Now,* Zarien."

"Are you . . . Why are . . ."

Suddenly, he just snapped. Simply couldn't focus anymore. Whether it was the way Zarien had backed away, or the shocked expression on the boy's face, or his own fear, he didn't know; but Tansen completely lost control of himself. He forgot how much danger they were in, forgot about the battle. He suddenly couldn't think of anything but how incredibly, blood-boilingly furious he was with his son.

"And *you*," he informed Zarien in harsh tones, "are in so much trouble! What did you think you were *doing*? Running away like that! And coming *here*, of all places!"

"I . . . I'm . . ."

"Najdan is right!" Tansen shouted, heedless of who might hear. "I should beat you! And don't think I won't!"

"I didn't . . . I couldn't . . ."

"I don't want to hear your excuses!" he raged. "When will you learn to think before you act? Anything could have happened to you! Anything could *still* happen to you! Do you *ever* think?"

"I'm . . . I'm . . ."

"What?" he snarled.

"I'm *sorry!*"

"That's hardly helpful right now, is it?" Tansen snapped.

Tears welled up in those dark eyes and started to slide down that young, tattooed face. Zarien brushed them aside. "I didn't know what to do," he choked out. "I was afraid . . . I thought you'd hate me . . ."

Tansen closed his eyes and tried to control the torrent of anger. "And you thought I'd kill you? Zarien, is that really what you thought?"

"I don't know. At the time, you seemed so . . . I don't know!"

"But no doubt *he's* been telling you I'd kill you."

The boy suddenly stumbled towards him, panic replacing the confusion, sorrow, and guilt. "He'll kill you if he finds out you're here! You've got to go!"

"We've got to go," Tansen corrected. "I'm not leaving without you."

Zarien looked at him darkly. "Do you just want to take me from him?"

"Is that what he says? If that's what I wanted, I *would* just kill you." Tansen took him by the shoulders. "I don't want him—or anything else—to take you from *me*."

Zarien's face crumpled. "I'm sorry. I didn't mean to . . ."

"I'm sorry, too," Tansen said more calmly. "I know I said and did things I shouldn't have. We have a lot to talk about. But no matter what happens, I'm your father and nothing can change that." More in command of himself now, he looked around, "Where is he?"

"He went up to the surface."

"Let's go before he realizes I'm here and comes back."

"How?"

"We'll have to swim for it."

Even as the words died in the air, the walls of Kandahar suddenly started roiling like wildly boiling water.

Zarien gasped. "He knows."

Tansen seized his arm and dragged him towards the nearest wall. By the time he reached it, only an instant later, it was impenetrable, as hard and unyielding as the floor beneath their feet.

They were trapped.

BARAN STOOD THIGH-DEEP in the chilly water and felt it change, felt something raging and powerful come to life in it. *Ah* . . .

It was disappointing to see Kiloran do something so predictable. A White Dragon had killed Josarian in the Zilar River, after all. One would really like to think a waterlord would be more creative about guarding his own home than he was about murdering some upstart peasant in a minor tributary of a secondary river. But, *no*, Kiloran was repeating himself now.

"As I said before," Baran murmured to himself, "no one has any standards anymore."

The power of hundreds of Guardians assaulted him, burdening his senses. He could see enchanted wildfire approaching the lake from several directions now. His insides felt as if they were dissolving in the relentless flow of his illness. Velikar's tisane had made him more lightheaded than he'd expected—or perhaps this feeling was just exhaustion.

He watched the White Dragon rise out of the lake, an enormous, glittering, brilliantly grotesque monster born of Kiloran's union with the water. The creature's long, curved claws looked terrifyingly deadly, and its teeth were like a cluster of *shir*. Though it had no discernible eyes, it turned unerringly towards him, moving like a giant lizard.

"I'm disappointed with the aesthetics," Baran said to it. "I hope you won't be hurt if I admit I expected something a little more attractive."

As it moved towards him, he crystallized the water around it. The creature looked almost comically startled as it came to a sudden, involuntary halt—well, *Baran* thought it was comical, though he supposed few people shared his sense of humor.

The White Dragon roared with rage and struck out at the hardened water. A few shards chipped off and flew around randomly in response to the immense power of these blows, but the solid substance withstood the attack.

Next, the creature started foaming. Baran briefly wondered if this was a sign of rage, but then he realized it was another attempt to challenge his power. The entire body of the White Dragon dissolved as it roiled and foamed. It melted and sank into the crystal-hard water . . . which also began roiling and foaming. Baran resisted it, trying to keep it solid, but the creature was too strong. It would, he realized, succeed within moments.

He himself couldn't create a White Dragon of his own. Not here and now. The process required time, strength, and water that wasn't already in another waterlord's grip.

As the White Dragon dissolved the water imprisoning it

and slowly began reemerging, to attack again, Baran wondered what to do next.

TANSEN TURNED AWAY from the solid wall and looked around the room, trying to form a plan. Kiloran entered a moment later, looking as he always looked—fat, old, shrewd, and formidable.

Tansen reflexively reached for his swords. The moment they were in his hands, enormous tendrils of water shot out of the ceiling and seized them from him. Startled, he looked up and saw his swords dangling from watery coils high overhead. Out of reach.

Then, before Tansen could stop him, Zarien raced forward. "No! Don't!"

"Stay away from him!" Tansen ordered, following the boy. A pillar of water crashed down upon him from the ceiling, then turned hard as rock and pinned him to the floor.

"No!" Zarien cried. "Don't hurt him!"

Barely able to breathe, Tansen turned his head to look at them. The floor beneath his cheek was glassy, smooth, and cold.

Kiloran stared at Zarien. "You're *protecting* him?" The tone was so ominous, Tansen suddenly feared for Zarien's safety.

"Let him go," Zarien said firmly.

"This will happen again," Kiloran warned the boy. "You will never be safe while he lives."

"He didn't come here to kill me."

Kiloran sighed heavily and shook his head. "Do you think Armian was willing to believe it, either? And look what happened to him."

Tansen snarled, "Leave Armian out of this!"

Kiloran made a fist, and the pillar of crystallized water suddenly pushed down harder on Tansen. He made an involuntary sound and thought he felt a rib crack.

"Stop!" Zarien shouted.

"It's him or us!" Kiloran gestured to the corpses of the four assassins on the blood-drenched floor. "He's already murdered the four men I left here to protect you! What else to do you need to see to accept the truth, Zarien?"

"No, he only—"

"Damn, Baran!" Kiloran looked distracted and seemed, momentarily, to forget Zarien and Tansen existed.

Zarien ran over to Tansen and started pushing at the pillar coming down from the ceiling. Nothing happened, of course.

"Water magic," Tansen said between gritted teeth.

"Tansen killed his own father," Kiloran warned Zarien, now focused on them again. "Armian was a shrewd man, and he never saw it coming. If Tansen has made you believe he won't hurt you, then you must believe *me* when I tell you he's lying!"

"*Please,* let him go," Zarien pleaded.

"No. I'm sorry. He has to die."

BARAN CALLED ENORMOUS tendrils out of the lake to twine around the White Dragon, capturing it. Once it was indisputably his prisoner, he tightened the tendrils, commanding them to cut through the White Dragon's body like blades, dismembering the creature. When it was sinking into the water in three separate pieces, he let go, exhausted, sensing the end of his strength was approaching.

Where in the Fires were Tansen and the boy? He couldn't hold out forever, and who knew what else Kiloran had in store for . . .

"Dar have mercy," he suddenly breathed, staring in stunned surprise as the water heaved where the remains of the White Dragon had dissolved. Then he laughed. What an absurd thing to say. Of course She wouldn't have mercy! When had She ever?

Now *three* creatures rose out of the water, each forming itself from the remains of the one he'd destroyed by sundering it into thirds.

"I admit, I'm impressed." It would be petty to pretend otherwise.

He lifted a high, roaring wall of water between himself and his attackers, and used it to force them back. They were strong, though, and he was indeed getting weaker. One of them finally broke through and seized him in its claws.

The agony was appalling, but Baran had been living with pain too long to be distracted by it. He formed a *shir* blade out of the water and used it to slit the creature's throat. This only seemed to slow it down, so he cut off its head. It dropped him, and he sank under the surface for a moment, realizing that the White Dragon he had just beheaded would probably become *two* new opponents in a few moments. A little discouraging, all things considered.

When he lifted himself out of the water, supported by a swelling wave meant to carry him away from the next attacker, he discovered his reflexes were getting too slow. One of the creatures knocked him sideways, back into the water. Disoriented, he didn't have time to form a shield around himself before it grabbed him. Fortunately, he hadn't let go of the *shir* blade, which he used to slice its gut open. Rather than killing it, this just distracted it long enough for the other White Dragon to seize Baran, stealing him as if he were a juicy meal. Which, he realized, he was.

Baran screamed in agony as the creature's enormous fangs sank into him. He tried to retain enough control to keep fighting the thing in the few moments he had left to live.

"I WON'T . . ." ZARIEN took a step forward and said to Kiloran, "I won't let you do this."

Kiloran's eyes narrowed as Tansen watched, but rather than reprimand or punish the boy, he chose another tactic. "Why not ask him about Armian? Then see if you're still determined to protect him."

"All right."

"Well?"

"Let him up first." When Kiloran hesitated, Zarien added, "How can he talk with you crushing him like this?"

Kiloran shrugged—and the pillar of water dissolved, drenching Tansen. Startled by the cold, bleeding from the *shir* wound in his shoulder, and now positive that a rib was cracked, Tansen rose slowly to his feet and met Zarien's eyes.

"Armian made me his son after the Valdani slaughtered my family. When he met Kiloran, they made plans together for the Society to rule all of Sileria," he said, moving slowly towards the two of them. "Armian wanted to be like Kiloran." Tansen paused, remembering. "They'd have ruled the mountains together through bloodshed and terror."

Kiloran sneered. "We were going to *free* Sileria—"

"Zarien wants my story," Tansen said. "Your version can wait until after I'm dead, old man."

Zarien, looking hollow-eyed, said to Kiloran, "Let him tell me why he did it."

It was the most important thing he would ever say, and quite possibly the *last* thing he'd ever say, so Tansen spoke honestly, keeping it simple and clear. "He was my father, Zarien, and he tried hard to be a good one, as I've tried. And he made mistakes, as I've made them. But I believed that killing Armian was the only way to stop him. To keep the Society from unchallenged rule of Sileria. To save this country from another thousand years of slavery—under the waterlords, rather than under foreign conquerors."

"Couldn't you have talked to him?" Zarien pleaded, sounding as if he thought that long ago murder could now be undone, taken back.

"I tried. Many times. He wouldn't listen."

"Couldn't you have done something besides *kill* him?" Zarien begged.

He must be truthful, since he knew this might be the last time he ever spoke to Zarien. "Maybe I could have," he admitted. "At the time, I didn't think so. Even now, I don't really know. I came from a people who viewed killing as the solution to over-whelming problems, and when I couldn't solve mine by talking to Armian . . . When the rains came and I ran out of time . . . I killed him, so I could stop his plan." He again felt the weight of what he'd done as he gazed into Zarien's sad eyes. "I loved my father, Zarien, despite his faults. And I have dreamed of that night more times than I can count. But even now, in the same circumstances . . . I think I would do it again. I'm not sure, but I think . . ." He wished he could say he'd been absolutely right, but he knew better. "Since then, the only thing I've done that I'm as ashamed of is keeping this secret from you, when you had a right to know. I just . . ." He started to sigh, but stopped when his rib protested. "I didn't know how to tell you. I didn't want . . . I didn't want you to know this about me. I'm sorry."

Zarien bit his lip and looked down.

"He will only try again, Zarien," Kiloran said calmly. "Even if you believe he won't kill you, you must surely know his desire to kill *me?*"

Zarien lifted his head and met Tansen's gaze again.

"You might prefer," Kiloran advised Zarien, "not to watch this."

Zarien's eyes widened. "No!"

"It must be this way, Zarien." Kiloran's expression was cold, his tone inflexible.

The floor suddenly curled up to seize Tansen in a dozen icy, twining arms. He felt himself sinking into it and realized Kiloran meant to push him beneath the palace to drown him there.

"No!" Zarien cried. "Stop!"

Tansen struggled against the water capturing him and drag-ging him down. He saw Zarien drop to his knees and frown fiercely at him. Then, even as he fought . . . the tendrils melted away.

"What are you doing?" Kiloran shouted.

Zarien turned to the old waterlord as Tansen hauled himself out of the hole he'd been sinking into.

"Don't do this!" Zarien insisted.

Tansen's swords were still hanging from the ceiling; but there was another weapon here which belonged to him, too. Instinct warned him to move, and he made a rolling dive the very moment Kiloran opened up the floor beneath him.

"Stop!" Zarien said, and a geyser erupted in the same spot as the boy rebelled against his teacher.

Tansen recognized Armian's *shir* even among so many. It had lived with him too long for him ever to mistake it for any other. He seized it, turned, and leapt on Kiloran, sliding the enchanted blade into the old man's body.

Kiloran cried out in pain and sank to his knees, dragging Tansen with him.

"Father!" Zarien cried.

It wasn't a mortal wound. Tansen could tell. He twisted the blade and tried to open Kiloran's gut, but the old man's surprisingly strong grip on his hand opposed him.

"Father!"

As Tansen looked over his shoulder in response to Zarien's cry, a chill swept through him.

Zarien's arms were raised for a blow. Tansen froze and stared at him, stunned, disbelieving.

The boy leapt at him and forcibly knocked him away from Kiloran. Well trained, Tansen kept his grip on the hilt of the *shir,* taking it with him—as part of the watery ceiling collapsed upon Zarien and Kiloran. Even the few drops which landed on Tansen's leg were so cold they burned painfully.

Kiloran had tried to kill him with that move.

Zarien had saved him.

"Get away from him, Zarien!" Tansen shouted.

The icy water rose around the two of them, a barrier which Tansen couldn't pass. Zarien was crying as Kiloran clutched at him.

"I'm sorry," the boy rasped. "I am sorry."

Blood from Kiloran's *shir* wound spilled onto the floor, mixing with the water as it started to twist and heave. Kiloran was panting, his eyes shocked, his grasp on Zarien weakening.

"Noooo!" Kiloran said in the most awful voice Tansen had ever heard. *"No."*

Tansen realized what was happening. *"No!"*

"I'm sorry," Zarien said as he made tendrils of water twine around his father's throat to murder him. "I didn't want to . . ."

"No!" Tansen shouted.

Hoping he wouldn't lose a foot in the flesh-killing water surrounding the two wizards, Tansen lashed out at Zarien with a swift kick, sending the boy sprawling and distracting him enough to stop him. The water collapsed away from Kiloran and spread around him. Just in case it was still ensorcelled with deadly cold, Tansen didn't risk stepping into it. Instead, he threw the *shir*. His aim was true and it landed in Kiloran's chest, lodging solidly there. Kiloran fell backwards and lay in the mingling water and blood.

BARAN FELT THE White Dragon suddenly dissolve and drop him into the water. Bleeding from a dozen places and barely alive, he vaguely realized what that meant. Only one thing could stop a White Dragon.

Kiloran must be dead.

It was done. The old man was gone.

I've finally won.

It was why Baran had broken his vows and chosen new allies, knowing it was his only possible chance of outliving Kiloran. Working together, they had now destroyed him.

And Baran could finally let go. . . .

Or life will let me go, he thought, as he willed the water to carry him to the lake's shore.

He lay there for a while before he heard a familiar voice shout, *"Siran!"*

Then rough hands hauled him out of the water and turned

him over. It hurt monstrously, but he was too weak to protest, even to open his eyes. He heard pleading and felt someone trying to shake him into consciousness.

Now, really, is that considerate?

"What *happened* to him?" someone asked with obvious horror.

"*Kiloran* happened to him," Vinn snarled, sounding extremely upset.

Yes, in the end, it was the answer to Baran's whole miserable life.

Kiloran happened to me.

Baran was ready to go, so he didn't fight death when it embraced him. And if he happened to meet Dar during his sojourn, he fully intended to spit in the old bitch's face.

ZARIEN GAPED AT Kiloran in wide-eyed shock for a long moment, then turned his gaze on Tansen.

"I live every day with knowing I killed my father," Tansen told him. "I don't want you to live with that, too."

Zarien rose slowly to his feet and looked down at Kiloran as he lay dying. Tears rolled down the boy's cheeks.

"He's not my father," Zarien said at last in a broken voice. "He's just the man who raped my mother."

"Fire," Kiloran rasped.

"What's he saying?" Zarien asked.

"I don't care," Tansen said.

"*Fire,*" said the old man.

Something clattered to the floor behind them, startling them. Tansen whirled around and was relieved to see that his swords had fallen down. Kiloran's power was dying with him. Tansen retrieved them, sheathed them, and said, "Let's get out of here before the palace collapses and we drown."

Zarien said, "It sounds like—"

"Zarien, we're leaving," Tansen insisted.

The boy went closer to Kiloran. "Fire?"

Tansen went to his side, meaning to pull him away. However, the expression on the dying man's face made him pause. Kiloran looked utterly astonished . . . No, he looked . . . *frightened.*

As Kiloran's eyes closed, he murmured one last time, "Fire." His body shuddered briefly, and then he was still.

"What does it mean?" Zarien asked.

"He probably felt the Guardians encroaching on his territory." Tansen bent over to retrieve the *shir.*

"What are you *doing?*"

Tansen yanked hard to pull it out of Kiloran's chest. "I want it. It was my father's."

The palace suddenly heaved, as if caught in an earthquake, and then the solid walls started slowly dissolving.

"Let's go," Tansen said.

"Something's wrong." Zarien looked around with a strange expression.

"*Yes,* something's wrong. The wizard who made this palace is dead and we'll die, too, if we don't—"

"No, something *else,*" Zarien insisted. "Something . . ." He started breathing hard, as if scared. "Something's *here.*"

Tansen felt a chill sweep through him. Had Kiloran created something which would avenge his death? Something which this powerful boy could sense? A White Dragon? Something worse? He tucked Armian's *shir* inside his boot and grabbed his son's arm, determined to escape. When they turned around, though—

The floor was *glowing.* Not the silvery glow of water which he'd seen the day the sea king was reborn, but a fierce orange glow like the caldera at Darshon. It spread across the floor, ran under their feet, crept up the walls, and flowed across the ceiling. There was a terrifying rumbling all around them, and the palace started shaking hard even as it continued dissolving.

Then the floor beneath Kiloran abruptly caved in. Rather

than swallow him, lava flowed up, engulfed him, and set him on fire. Tansen fell back, as astonished as he was afraid—especially when the dead wizard started screaming. Horrible, fierce, agonized screams . . . Screams he'd heard in his nightmares. Screams he recognized.

"That's not Kiloran," he said slowly, watching the lava heave and bubble after Kiloran's body had been consumed.

"What?" Zarien bleated, staring fixedly at the transformation.

These were the screams he'd heard the night Josarian died. The night the White Dragon, born of Kiloran in a mystical union with water, had devoured the Firebringer whole before sinking back into the river which Kiloran commanded.

"It's . . ."

"What?" Zarien asked weakly.

He knew, even as the lava turned to fire, and an insubstantial form began to take shape in the flames, who it was. *"Josarian."*

"Where?"

Tansen.

"Josarian!" He started forward.

"Father, don't!" Zarien held him back. "It's fire!"

"It's Josarian!"

"Let's get out of here!"

"Josarian!"

His brother looked pleased for a moment, but then worried. *He's right,* Josarian told him. *You have to go.*

"What are you . . ."

Tashinar is here to help me, but I still can't control it.

"Control what?"

It's happening very fast, Tan.

"What's happening?"

You've got to go now! Get away!

"No, I—"

I will always be here, Josarian promised him. *Right here. It's what Dar wanted.*

"What Dar wanted?"

Why did he die, Dar? Why did You let him die?

For this, Josarian answered. *For this.*

"For *what?*"

Go now.

"Father!" Zarien pulled him so hard he staggered.

Tansen went with his son, who clutched his arm with one hand as he explored a dissolving wall with the other.

"The lake's not ensorcelled anymore," Zarien said with certainty. "All you have to do is hold your breath and kick your legs. I'll get us to the surface. Don't let go of me."

Tansen glanced over his shoulder for one last look at his dead brother, but Josarian was already gone. In his place there was a small volcanic eruption occurring. If the water didn't kill them both, then the lava surely would.

The ceiling collapsed, showering water into the lava-flooded room, raising skin-searing steam which spread out and rolled toward them.

Tansen took a deep breath and held on to his son as they dived through the wall and into the cold waters of Lake Kandahar to swim to its surface.

68

WHATEVER DOESN'T KILL US SETS US FREE.
— Kintish Proverb

NOW THAT HE wasn't distracted by imminent death, Tansen's *shir* wound hurt like all the Fires, his cracked rib was hideously uncomfortable, and every bone in his body ached from falling through Kiloran's ceiling to land on Kiloran's floor.

"I don't want to do anything like this again for a very, very long time," he said, sitting on a high hillside with Mirabar, overlooking Kandahar in the distance.

Her responding smile was distracted.

He hesitated, then said, "I'm sorry for your loss. I know you . . . were fond of Baran."

She nodded and looked very sad for a moment. "I will mourn him."

"Of course."

"For a year."

"A *year?*" he blurted.

Her expression was uncompromising. "It's customary."

"But *he* was hardly customary!"

"I suppose he'd find it amusing if he knew—"

"Oh, wherever he is right now, he's laughing, I'm sure." When she didn't reply, he added, "I have to wait a whole year?"

"Yes," she said serenely, gazing from this quiet hillside to the violent eruption still occurring in what had been Lake Kandahar only yesterday.

The dramatic light of the setting sun, streaked with the volcanic ash and smoke which were only slowly fading from their skies, touched her fiery hair and cast a shadow along her cheek. Oh, well, Tansen thought. She was worth a year's wait, if that's the way she wanted it.

By dawn, the loyalists had won the battle decisively. There were still assassins somewhere out there, as well as a few surviving waterlords, but they were being hunted down and killed, or else fleeing Sileria. The Honored Society was crushed and shattered. Kiloran was dead, as were almost all of his allies. After a thousand years, the waterlords' era was now passing into legend, their way of life vanishing with today's sunlight.

"The world is changing," Tansen murmured, "and we must change with it."

Zarien returned from the stream where he'd been fetching

water. "Sister Velikar is a nasty woman," he said. "Don't make me go anywhere with her again."

"She's grieving for Baran," Mirabar said. "She adored him." Her face suddenly crumpled and she turned away.

Zarien gave Tansen a panicked look, as if expecting to be accused of having made her cry.

"Baran never got to see you," Tansen said gently. "Mirabar knows . . . how much he wanted to."

"Oh. I'm sorry I didn't get to meet him, *sirana*." Zarien looked polite as Mirabar made a watery reply, but Tansen knew he didn't really understand. The man who had wanted to be his father, like the woman who had been his mother, probably didn't even seem real to the boy.

Kiloran had been real to him, though. And Zarien, who hated violence and loathed killing, had nonetheless been willing to kill to save Tansen from the old waterlord.

Without asking, Zarien peeled away the dressing on Tansen's *shir* wound—ignoring his protest—and examined it. "I can heal this for you, you know."

"Oh . . . let's just leave it."

"No, I can—"

"No, I really don't want—"

"Why not?" Zarien demanded impatiently.

"It's not that bad."

"You don't trust me?"

"I trust you. Water magic just makes me queasy."

"You'll be sick a lot then," Zarien informed him. "Especially if we're going to live at Belitar."

"We're not going to live at . . ." He saw the look Zarien exchanged with Mirabar. "We're going to live at Belitar?"

"Well, not while I'm mourning Baran, obviously," Mirabar said virtuously. "But eventually . . ."

"I hate Belitar!" he said. "It's damp! And depressing. Everything's moldy. And it's haunted."

"Nonetheless," Mirabar said with a distinct lack of sympathy for his views, "the ones who can teach Zarien to use his water magic wisely live there. Since your son and your wife will live there, I naturally assumed . . ."

He sighed, then winced as his rib protested. *"Belitar."*

"I was thinking of having some repairs done," she offered.

"It won't help," he said gloomily.

"Do the Beyah-Olvari still have to remain a secret?" Zarien asked.

"No," Tansen said. "The waterlords will no longer be a danger to them, and they deserve to be acknowledged for helping the Firebringer, and helping Baran fight Kiloran. I don't know exactly how we'll introduce them to Sileria . . . It's the sort of thing Elelar can probably do well."

"So the Idalar River and the mines of Alizar are finally safe," Mirabar murmured.

"Elelar said the country needed money. Now the Yahrdan—or whoever becomes the regent, I suppose—can hire people to work the mines." Alizar had been rich enough to please the voracious Valdani, so it would surely provide well for Sileria now. "It'll help us recover from two years of war."

"Elelar will probably become the regent, won't she?" Mirabar said sourly.

"It seems likely," Tansen agreed.

"And perhaps you'll live in Shaljir for the next year," she added, her tone growing cool.

"There are Beyah-Olvari in Shaljir I could learn from." Zarien frowned and added, "But I didn't really like the Olvar, to be honest."

"I'm sure the *torena* could smooth things over." Mirabar's tone was almost icy now.

"Or we could settle in Emeldar for a while," Tansen suggested, thinking fast. "Since Baran cleansed the water supply, it's safe."

"Is Lann going back?" Mirabar asked.

Tansen shook his head. Lann had survived the battle, as had

Pyron, and Tansen had talked to them both earlier today. "Too many sad memories, Lann says. He and his family want to remain in Zilar. Which is just as well. He'll be needed there." Lann had become a very important man there during the struggle against Mentcn.

Pyron, on the other, said he was sick to death of Dalishar, visions, war, and risking his life. *He,* he had informed Tansen, was going back home as soon as possible.

Vinn, who had also survived and would return to Belitar with Mirabar, had told them about Baran's death. The waterlord may have been a madman capable of any treachery, but he had fought a White Dragon in Kandahar to save Zarien and destroy Kiloran.

So Tansen supposed he couldn't reasonably object if Mirabar wanted to observe the traditional mourning period for her husband.

Now, gazing out at the growing mountain of lava which had once been Kandahar, Mirabar mused, "So this is why Josarian died."

"I still don't understand," Tansen said. "Why? What did Dar want?"

"The Firebringer wasn't just a leader," she replied. "Don't you see now? Dar also chose him as a consort."

"As a . . ." His gaze flashed to the mountain which was growing even as they spoke. "Do you mean . . ."

She nodded. "A lover. A partner. A companion."

"So you're saying *that*—" He gestured to the active lava at Kandahar. "—is Josarian now?"

" 'He is coming.' That's what the continuing visions at Dalishar meant. Josarian was coming. Dar's consort. It's what some of my visions told me, too, I think, only I didn't understand. And perhaps why there were so many earthquakes. Dar was trying to reach out to Kandahar to help the Firebringer emerge, if Kiloran could be defeated to free him."

"And Tashinar remained to help Josarian, too," Tansen guessed, "when she died there."

"Yes." Mirabar looked sad again. "I believe her torment is now ended, too."

She tilted her head, gazing at the eruption, which was fairly calm and steady. It didn't seem to threaten anything except Lake Kandahar itself, which it was gradually destroying as it rose higher and higher. It produced no ash and very little smoke. "Fire and water, water and fire . . . And when the mountain is formed, Josarian will inhabit it the way Dar inhabits Darshon."

"So that's what he meant," Tansen asked, "when he said he would always be here?"

"I didn't hear anything," Zarien said. Again. He still seemed to think Tansen had imagined seeing Josarian. But Tansen knew his brother had been real and, for a moment, had spoken to him from beyond the barrier of death.

Mirabar said, "He's immortal now. A kind of god."

"Then those vague stories Guardians and *zanareen* tell are true?" Tansen asked. "About a consort of Dar's who once lived in Mount Shaljir, long ago . . ."

"And before that," Mirabar replied, "there was a consort who lived in a mountain which exploded and fell into the sea. Where the sacred rainbow-chalk cliffs of Liron are now."

"Dar uses them up and burns them out," Tansen observed.

"She *is* the destroyer goddess," Mirabar said.

"So Josarian's not immortal now, after all."

"No, I suppose not," she conceded. "But he will be here for centuries after you and I are gone."

"And Dar wanted him to rise out of Kandahar," he mused.

"What better place?" she said. "The most powerful waterlord in Sileria—perhaps in all Sileria's history—has been replaced by the Firebringer."

"I'd rather Josarian had lived," Tansen said.

"I know." Her voice was gentle. "But would Josarian rather have lived?"

He met her eyes and nodded in acknowledgment of her

point. Josarian had always been prepared to die. He consecrated his life to Dar and to Sileria, and was never again the
same. Perhaps this was the way he'd have wanted things to
end. In any event, it was the way things *had* ended, and
Tansen had little choice but to accept that.

He could bear it. Josarian would always be here now, in a
way. Always watching over them.

"Sirana?"

Tansen looked up from his seated position on the ground to
see Najdan approaching them, looking a little drawn and tired
after a wakeful night of guarding Mirabar while she partici-
pated in the Guardian assault on Kiloran's territory.

Najdan said, "We will be ready to leave for Belitar at first
light."

"So soon?" Tansen asked.

"The *sirana*," Najdan said, "should return home and rest."

Aware of the stern gaze her protector cast upon them,
Tansen nonetheless tried, "Perhaps I should accompany—"

"That will not be necessary," Najdan said.

"But—"

"The *sirana* is a widow," Najdan pointed out, "and therefore in a delicate position. The war is essentially over, and she
will now retire to her estate and respectfully observe the customs of her new situation."

"Mourning," Tansen said.

"Yes." After a brief hesitation, Najdan added, "However, it
is not too soon for you to begin thinking about sheep."

"Sheep?" he repeated blankly.

"Yes. The bride price will be high."

Najdan turned and left them. Tansen stared after him, not
realizing for a few moments that his jaw was hanging open.

"He's very annoying sometimes," he said to Mirabar.

"And you," Zarien said, "have never even been stuck on a
boat with him."

"I suppose I owe you an apology," Tansen conceded.

"Many apologies," Zarien said.

"I know." Tansen regarded him seriously. "We have a lot to talk about."

"Yes. But I understand now."

"Understand?"

"About Armian," Zarien clarified. "I understand that he was . . . like Kiloran. And I didn't have to be at Kandahar long to understand what Kiloran was like."

"I'm sorry. I should never have—"

"Maybe it was meant to be this way," Zarien said. "Sharifar told me, the night she first sent me ashore, that someday I would have to decide what to do about my father. I was meant to . . ." The boy shrugged. "To *choose*. And I did. You were right: You're my father." He was silent for a moment before adding, "I was afraid of Kiloran, and afraid for everyone else because of him. He was . . . I didn't want to kill him, and I didn't really want you to kill him. But I know that he had to die. Sharifar said the world was changing, and I saw that he could never change with it."

"No," Tansen agreed, "he couldn't."

"Maybe . . . maybe Armian couldn't have changed, either."

"No, I don't think he could have."

Zarien nodded and fell into a pensive silence. After a while, he said, "I'm going to go back down to the stream—if you don't mind?"

"Don't stay long," Tansen said. "It'll be dark soon."

"Don't worry, I'll be back by then."

Tansen watched the boy go back downhill.

"If Zarien would like," Mirabar said quietly, "I can try to Call his mother for him."

Tansen was startled. "Alcinar? How?"

"I have something of hers, back at Belitar. A necklace of silver and jade."

"Silver and ja— That necklace Baran always used to wear?" Tansen asked. "It once belonged to Zarien's mother?"

"Yes. Baran let me have it, so I might try to Call her and

learn her true fate. She's never answered me in the flames, but—"

"How do you know that necklace won't Call *Baran?*" Tansen said grimly. "If he wore it ever since losing Alcinar . . ."

Mirabar looked stunned for a moment, then gave a rueful laugh. "Of course! It never even occurred to me, because *he* thought of the necklace as hers. But it hung around Baran's neck all those years, absorbing his bitterness and grief, his hatred—"

"His madness and his cruelty." Tansen shook his head. "Promise me you'll never Call him."

"I can't promise you that. Someday his daughter may want—"

"We'll deal with that when the time comes," he said. "But—"

"Baran's talent and skill were extraordinary," Mirabar pointed out, "and Zarien may occasionally need advice that the Beyah-Olvari can't provide."

"I don't want my son learning anything from Baran," he said firmly.

"Oh, but Baran could have been . . ." For a moment, the look on her face as she remembered the waterlord made Tansen darkly jealous. Then she sighed and shook her head. "No, that's the past, and we must look forward."

"Zarien will find his way without help from a waterlord. Living or dead." He relaxed a little when he saw her nod in agreement.

"Now that he knows he has this gift, it calls to him," Mirabar observed, her gaze following the path Zarien had taken to the stream.

"It called to him even before he knew," Tansen admitted, remembering.

"Baran always said it was seductive."

"Zarien will be fine, though," Tansen said with certainty. "He doesn't have it in him to become like them."

"And you and I will teach him." She put a hand on her swelling stomach and added, "We'll teach them both."

He covered her hand with his. "Yes. We will."

Their eyes met and held for a long moment, full of promises and silent vows. Then, fearing Najdan might suddenly come upon them again, Tansen pulled his hand away.

"Before you leave . . ." he said after a while, coming to a decision.

"Yes?"

"There's something I'd like to ask of you."

"Anything."

He reached into his boot and pulled out Armian's *shir*. Her eyes widened in surprise, and he saw that she immediately guessed whose it was. Tansen said hesitantly, "He died . . . I killed him at the start of the long rains. So the season should be about right."

"You want me to Call him for you," she murmured, staring at the *shir*.

"It's time to confront my nightmares."

Mirabar met his eyes again, then nodded and rose to her knees. She blew a fire into being, the enchanted flames curling magically to life out of the Dar-blessed miracle of her breath.

"I can't touch the *shir*," she said. "You'll have to put it in the fire."

He did so, and watched it dance as if it were alive while Mirabar started chanting. His heart pounded with mingled eagerness and dread as he prepared to again face the father he had loved, betrayed, and murdered.

"He is coming," Mirabar whispered, her voice tense with anticipation.

He grew out of the flames, and Tansen caught his breath as he gazed at him. This was exactly how Armian had looked the night he died. Exactly how he appeared again and again in Tansen's dreams.

"Father," he said hoarsely.

"Tansen," Mirabar said, startling him—then he remembered that shades of the dead normally spoke through a Guardian rather than directly to the supplicant.

He just stared at Armian for a long moment. Then he said, "I've thought of you almost every day since I killed you."

"It's right to think of me often."

"I wish . . . I wish things could have been different."

"If you're content now," Mirabar said, her voice eerily like the one he heard in his dreams, "then things are as I would have wished them to be."

Tansen felt his eyes mist and, for a moment, he couldn't speak. Finally, he was able to say, "I'm sorry for what I did to you, father. I'm so sorry."

"I know," Armian said. "I know."

"I think . . . I've asked her to Call you so I can beg for your forgiveness."

"I am your father," Armian told him, Mirabar's voice rich with love. "I will always be your father."

"I'm a father, too, now," Tansen said. "I want to be a better father than I was a son."

"You were a good son," Armian assured him. "I tried to be a good father."

"You were!" Tansen insisted.

"And if we were the wrong father and son for each other . . ."

"Were we?"

"We nonetheless made our choice."

"When you made yours, you didn't know I would kill you," said Tansen, his chest aching.

"Neither did you. But having made the choice and knowing the consequences now . . . I would make the same choice again. This was our destiny, yours and mine. If I can accept it, so can you."

Tansen closed his eyes and lowered his head. "Thank you, father. Thank you."

He heard Mirabar breathing harder and knew she was getting tired. She hadn't slept in more than a day, and she'd had an exhausting night, as had he. He didn't protest as she let Armian slip away, just watched silently as his father faded from the woodless fire and finally disappeared altogether.

A soft drizzle started falling as Tansen stared thoughtfully into the empty flames where the *shir* still floated, its frantic dance slowly dying along with Mirabar's energy.

After a while, he felt her hand fumble for his. He clasped it and squeezed. "Thank you."

"How do you feel?"

"I feel . . ." He smiled and lifted his gaze to the new mountain emerging before their eyes as the gentle rain washed their faces and soaked the soil. "I feel *free*."

There would no more nightmares. From now on, only dreams.

Epilogue

THE RAINS COME AND THE RAINS GO; BUT DAR
REMAINS STEADFAST. AND SO DO WE.

—Silerian Proverb

AT THE SUMMIT of Mount Darshon, whose snow-capped, cloud-piercing peak dwarfed the rest of this rugged, mountainous land, the colored lights and dancing clouds which had so alarmed Dar's people slowly began to fade, spreading themselves thinly on the wind, until only the wind remained.

She had worn Her plumage to welcome the arrival of Her consort, the Firebringer, and to alert Her people to his imminent rebirth, if only they would have the strength to conquer Her enemies. For their sake, She had undergone terrible labor which repeatedly shook this land and made Her bleed long and hard. She had demanded a great deal of them in exchange for Her blessings; but She was the destroyer goddess, and that was Her right.

For a thousand years, Silerians had looked to Dar, the most powerful goddess in a nation of many sects and cults, to liberate them from the yoke of slavery. Now, finally, they had offered Her the courage, strength, and devotion which had always been needed, and which they had never before been able to give.

Deep in the heart of Darshon's raging, fire-spewing sea of lava, Dar rumbled with contentment as She considered the nation She had forged with Her fiery will.

Glossary

Bharata Ma-al: the Time of Slaughter, an annual sea-born festival for killing dragonfish

jashar: elaborately knotted and woven cords dotted with beads, used in place of writing to convey information; often worn as a belt or headdress

kadriah: an endearment, used between lovers or spouses

lirtahar: the code of silence

roshah: stranger, outsider, foreigner

shallah: mountain peasant

shatai: a Kintish swordmaster

shatai-kaj: one who trains *shatai*

shir: the wavy-edged dagger of an assassin, made from water

siran/sirana: a form of address used to show respect

sriliah: traitor

stahra: a weapon of the sea-born folk which resembles an oar

the Three: a trinity worshipped in Valdani religion

tirshah: a public house

toren/torena: a male/female aristocrat

yahr: a flailing weapon, made of two pieces of hard wood joined by a short cord

zanar: member of a fanatic religious sect

Author's Note

Just in case you haven't figured it out yet, this book is the second half of *In Fire Forged*; the story begins with *The White Dragon: In Fire Forged, Part One*. (I'm not making fun of you; I once sat through the entire second half of an Oliver Stone film before realizing it was the second half.) Both volumes together comprise the sequel to *In Legend Born*.

In Fire Forged has been published as two volumes because the only other alternative was to eliminate so many pages that the remaining story wouldn't have made any sense. When presented with this choice by my long-suffering publisher, I decided it was better to release a good book in two parts than to release a bad book in one sole volume.

As you've probably gathered (unless you're peeking ahead to this note), Sileria's struggles end here. I may come back to these characters with a new story someday; but for now, they're enjoying a well-deserved rest while I move on to new tales set elsewhere in the same world. My next two novels for Tor Books are *Arena*, set in the Moorlands, and *The Palace of Heaven* (go on, take a wild guess about where it's set).

I want to thank Mary Jo Putney, Valerie Taylor, and Cindy Person, who all read and commented on the original manuscript of *In Fire Forged* for me—the whole thing! Many thanks to my agent, Russell Galen, for heroics above and beyond the call of duty, and to my energetic foreign agent, Danny Baror. And a special thanks to Elizabeth Haydon.

Other friends and colleagues who also helped me through the marathon of writing this story include: Julie Pahutski, Lee

Ann Thomas, Karen Luken, Toni Herzog, Kathy Chwedyk, Jerry Spradlin, my parents, Scott Street, the Sisters Foundation, Marty Greenberg, Denise Little, John Helfers, Larry Segriff, and Grandpa Bill (1912–2001). Someone else who helped long ago, though neither of us realized it at the time, was Elf the collie.

I read (and tried to respond to) every letter asking when *In Fire Forged* would finally be written and published. Knowing readers were waiting for it kept me in my chair at times when nothing else could have done so. Now I can only hope that you've found it worth the wait.

If you enjoyed this book, you won't want to miss. . .

NEW YORK TIMES BESTSELLING AUTHOR
CONSTANCE O'DAY-FLANNERY

0-765-34889-6 • $6.99/$9.99 Can.

Shifting Love

SHIFTING LOVE
CONSTANCE O'DAY-FLANNERY
IN PAPERBACK NOVEMBER 2004

Tor is proud to launch its Paranormal Romance
line with a passionate tale of magic and love
from *New York Times* bestselling author
Contstance O'Day-Flannery.

**"An author of incredible talent and
imagination. She has the magic."**
—*Romantic Times Bookclub*